THE BLOODDAUGHTER TRILOGY

All Three Books in One Volume

Second Blood - - Blood Huntress - - Blood Reprisal

Wil Ogden

The Blooddaughter Trilogy

Copyright © 2013-2015 William Ogden

Cover Art:

Shauna Elsa Moon by Wil Ogden

**ISBN-13:
978-1514888575**

**ISBN-10:
1514888572**

DEDICATION

Dedicated to those who, like me, prefer moonlight to sunlight.

CONTENTS

THE BLOODDAUGHTER TRILOGY BOOK I: SECOND BLOOD 4

- CHAPTER 1..1
- CHAPTER 2..11
- CHAPTER 3..29
- CHAPTER 4..42
- CHAPTER 5..57
- CHAPTER 6..71
- CHAPTER 7..87
- CHAPTER 8..96
- CHAPTER 9..107
- CHAPTER 10..113
- CHAPTER 11..126
- CHAPTER 12..134
- CHAPTER 13..155
- CHAPTER 14..174

THE BLOODDAUGHTER TRILOGY BOOK II: BLOOD HUNTRESS 187

- CHAPTER 1..1
- CHAPTER 2..12
- CHAPTER 3..29
- CHAPTER 4..39
- CHAPTER 5..53
- CHAPTER 6..66
- CHAPTER 7..73
- CHAPTER 8..83
- CHAPTER 9..91
- CHAPTER 10..113
- CHAPTER 11..132
- CHAPTER 12..143

CHAPTER 13	155
CHAPTER 14	171
CHAPTER 15	187

THE BLOODDAUGHTER TRILOGY BOOK III: BLOOD REPRISAL 190

CHAPTER 1	1
CHAPTER 2	10
CHAPTER 3	23
CHAPTER 4	36
CHAPTER 5	47
CHAPTER 6	64
CHAPTER 7	72
CHAPTER 8	88
CHAPTER 9	94
CHAPTER 10	106
CHAPTER 11	117
CHAPTER 12	123
CHAPTER 13	134
CHAPTER 14	147
CHAPTER 15	166
CHAPTER 16	173
EPILOGUE	183
ABOUT THE AUTHOR	187

ACKNOWLEDGEMENTS

Thanks to my wife and the editing assistance from Lea and the Notebored crowd..

THE BLOODDAUGHTER TRILOGY
BOOK I: SECOND BLOOD

CHAPTER 1

"It's Six-Thirty, Shauna," Lawrence, the cashier standing beside her, said. "Break Time, right?" There was no line for the first time that day. Tuesdays at the bookstore were always busier than the other days of the week. Even in the age of the internet, people wanted their new books as soon as they were released.

Shauna looked at the clock. How could the time have snuck up on her? She had been waiting all day for the chance to sit down with a new book from her favorite author. She headed for the door, grabbing a copy of A. A. Aaronson's newest release, "Dying by Daylight", from the display on her way out.

Outside the door she found her favorite corner and sat with her back to the store's wall. A store window provided enough light to read by and the corner protected her from November's chilly breezes. Opening the book, she gave the title page little more than a glance. Inside the cover was the same picture A. A. Aaronson had used for the prior nine books in the series. It wasn't actually a picture of anyone, just a black and white image of feathered plume quill pen and a pair of wire rimmed sunglasses. Miss Aaronson kept her privacy well; Shauna wasn't even sure if the author was a 'Miss'. By the way she wrote her sex scenes, Shauna was fairly certain the author was a woman.

Shauna hadn't finished reading the dedication page when she noticed that someone had stopped to stand just in front of her. Looking up, she noticed one of her regular Tuesday customers watching. The older man wore a dark grey wool trench coat over a darker grey suit. Even the tie was charcoal and matched perfectly to his shoes.

"Good evening, Miss McAllister," the man said. Her nametag had only her first name, but when she'd first met him at the special orders counter a few years earlier, he'd introduced himself with his full name, James Alden, so she'd responded in kind. Though they often made small talk about his purchases, he'd never used her first name.

"Good evening, James Alden," She said. She hadn't called anyone mister, miss or misses since her high-school teachers. She used his full name because that was how he'd introduced himself. "How can I help you?" She didn't want to discourage the customer by telling him she was on break, though she felt a bit peeved that he hadn't taken the fact that her face had been buried in a book as a hint.

"James is fine. I was just noticing we had similar tastes in fiction," he said. That he finally asked her to use just his first name stunned Shauna a little. He always spoke in very proper English, though he didn't have an accent that she could discern. He reached in a bookstore bag and pulled out a copy of "Dying by Daylight".

"I wouldn't have guessed," Shauna said. "Haven't you been on a nineteenth century historical fiction kick for a year or so?"

James looked down at his bag. "I have been reading about the Cossacks, but even great history can get dry and I find nothing relaxes the mind like good shallow fiction."

Even Shauna, despite being a fan, had trouble labeling Aaronson's work as 'good'. Fun? Yes. Good? Not so much. "Does your wife know you read this stuff?"

James laughed. "You mean trashy vampire sex fiction? If I were married, I don't think I could keep it a secret. There is no Mrs. Alden."

"If you're hitting on me, you should know I'm probably half your age." He looked fifty, she thought, maybe almost fifty. There wasn't much grey in his dark hair. The longer she looked, the less sure she was. His tanned skin made him look rather Mediterranean, but she didn't see any sag or wrinkles in his skin as she'd expect from a man in his fifties. Maybe forty with experience?

"I'm just making polite small talk while I wait for my ride. I am certainly too old for you." James held the book up. "What do you think so far?"

"Um," Shauna mumbled. She shrugged. "I like the shade of purple they used for the cover. I've only read the chapter that's been posted online. A steamy sex scene right in the first chapter; it seems less and less like the author's even pretending to be writing about vampires."

The door to the store opened and Stuart, her boss, popped his head out. "Shauna," he said, "could you come into my office?"

"On my way," Shauna called back. Since her conversation with James had mentioned sex more than once, she began to feel a little uncomfortable. She stood up and nodded to James. "Good chatting with you," she said.

"Anytime." He turned and stepped closer to the curb and looked up the street. He then checked his watch.

"Is your ride late?" Shauna asked.

"No," James said. "She'll be on time. I just took less time in the store than I expected."

With a polite smile and slight nod, Shauna left him standing alone while she went to see what Stuart wanted. When it struck her that James' ride was a she, she stopped flirting with the idea of convincing James to ask her out. She caught a glimpse of her blood-red dyed hair in the security mirror and realized how silly the idea had been. She was, without question, not his type.

"Stuart is looking for you," Lawrence called over from behind the counter.

"He found me," Shauna said. She took the most direct route to the storeroom and went up the stairs. She stopped in her own office to grab a wool lace shawl. Stuart always kept his too air conditioned. She noticed a stack of boxes of paper sitting inside her door and wondered briefly why anyone would put those by her desk, before heading to see her boss.

She stepped into his office and asked, "This is bad news isn't it?"

Stuart tightened his lips. He didn't nod, but didn't shake his head or say no either.

"If this is about Lawrence," she said, "I talked to him last Monday and he hasn't been late at all since."

"Lawrence is fine, Shauna." Stuart gestured to a chair by his desk. "Have a seat."

"I'll be buying this after my shift," she said pointing to the book in her hand. She'd always read on her dinner break and always bought whatever she read.

"You can have the book," Stuart said. "But, I need to let you go." He handed her an envelope. "That's two months in severance and a sparkling letter of reference."

Shauna pulled a lock of hair in front of her face and wondered if dying it blood red to fit in better at the clubs had been a poor idea. "Is it because of my hair?" she asked.

"I can't say that didn't factor in," Stuart said. "But it's really just about the bottom line. I just can't afford to have an assistant manager. I have to either let two cashiers go or let you go to balance the books. I have a plan that should give me something the big chains don't offer, but I don't know if it will be enough to compete with online stores."

Stuart had mentioned his plan to start selling independent authors and even hoped to start an indie eBook publishing shop that could be accessed from within the store for a discount. Offering indie authors had been her idea. She wasn't sure that anything about the eBook market would do anything to keep the store solvent. "You could demote me?" Shauna winced as she suggested the idea.

"I wouldn't be doing you a favor," Stuart said. "Your odd choice in hair dye doesn't take away from the fact that you understand both people and business. You belong in management. You'll find a job, somewhere. It will probably be even better than the one you had here."

Shauna took the envelope from Stuart's hand. "Thanks," she said. She couldn't make it sound enthusiastic, though she considered that Stuart might be right. She felt fear well up in her stomach as she wondered what she could do next. As she stood and walked away, she took a long slow breath to hold the uncertainty at bay and to keep the tears back.

She went to her office and found the paper boxes were empty; Stuart had left them for her to pack up her stuff. It only took one box to hold her collection of author signed books. She hadn't read any of those. Her favorite authors never seemed to have their book signings in the bookstore. She hadn't even heard of A. A. Aaronson going on tour. Nothing else in the office was anything she needed to keep. She put her newest book in the box then grabbed the framed picture of her parents and sat it on top of the box.

Her parents were probably still sitting on the patio of their RV in the same plot down in Florida. As soon as Shauna and her sister graduated, they went south. They had figured out how to retire very early by cutting costs, such as travelling. If worse came to worse, she could always go down there, but that much sun didn't appeal to her. She tucked the framed picture between two books and sat down at the computer. She had one last thing to do before she could leave.

Without a computer at home, she was about to lose her only access to the A. A. Aaronson fan boards. She logged onto the one with the most other members and left a message saying she'd be away for a while. If she found another job quickly enough, she could use the severance to get her own computer. She didn't have a plan yet on how to go about finding a new job. She shut off the computer then picked up the box of books and carried it down the stairs and out the back door. She didn't feel like saying goodbye to anyone. Stuart could explain her absence to the crew.

The box seemed heavier than the books inside as she stepped to the end of the alley and headed towards the bus stop. The tears on her cheek weren't of sadness, she tried to believe. It had been a warm day for autumn and the stench of the air coming up from the Italian Market was making her eyes water. The fresh aromas never seemed to make it as far as the smell of decay. She had the opportunity to find a better job, maybe one that wouldn't mind her lacy clothes and dyed hair. Where did all the people with pierced faces and more tattoos than skin work?

"That box looks a bit heavy." The voice was familiar, fresh in her memory. She stopped and looked at where James was pushing a hand truck of crates towards a car with an open trunk. The store behind James was a wine store. He stopped beside her. "I might have room in my trunk, if you'd like a ride somewhere."

Shauna glanced at the car; it was a huge sedan with dark windows. Her expression must have betrayed her uncertainty. James hastily said, "There's room for the box in the trunk, you'd ride in a seat."

Still hesitating to answer, she didn't object when James lifted the box of books from her arms and set it in his trunk. He added three cases of wine to the trunk then folded up the hand truck and slipped it in as well. "This has got to be better than the bus," James said as he opened the back door for her. She stepped into the car but not before making sure it had a handle inside and that the switch that keeps kids from opening the door wasn't activated.

Sitting, Shauna realized it wasn't just a large sedan; it was a limousine and the driver's seat was hidden behind a dark window. The silhouette of the driver was barely visible. James closed the door and walked around the car and entered from the driver's side, taking the seat beside her. "I'm all out of mustard," James said. When Shauna didn't react, he sighed. "No one gets that joke anymore."

"Oh," Shauna said. "This is a nice car. I've never been in an actual person's limousine. It's not at all the same as the rental I rode to prom in." James' car only had two seats in the back, but with plenty of leg room. There was a bar behind the driver's seat with a selection of wine bottles and a pair of glasses.

"If you'd like a drink, just ask," James said. "I was really just offering you a ride, but it would be rude of me not to offer refreshment when it's so readily available."

"No thanks," Shauna said. "I live across the river, if that's not too much trouble."

"A Jersey girl," James said. "You don't have the accent."

Rather than give her exact address, she gave an intersection that was just a couple blocks away from her apartment. "7th and Cherry," she said towards the silhouette on the other side of the glass. "Should I be asking nicer? Does the driver have a name?"

"In fact, she does," James said. "But she's fine with simple directions. That's not a great neighborhood, if I recall." The car moved out into traffic slowly. It felt like it was gliding on clouds.

Shauna didn't think her neighborhood was so bad. It was affordable, which was most important to her. "I grew up down on 19th." She nodded back towards her old neighborhood. She hadn't really travelled very far in her lifetime. "Are you local too?"

"Actually, I'm from out west. Ever heard of Lionville?"

She shook her head, she hadn't.

"It's less than an hour down 76, but no one here seems to be aware of anything beyond West Chester."

"I've heard of West Chester." Shauna said.

James chuckled, "You prove my..." He was interrupted by Shauna's phone.

Shauna panicked, suddenly embarrassed as she dug for her phone in her pocket. She didn't recognize the number. With a sigh and an apologetic look to James, she answered the call, "Shauna here."

"Sis, can you come down to the courthouse?" Her sister, Laura, sounded penitent. It wasn't the first time Laura had called her from the courthouse. The last time had been over a year earlier. Before Laura's last stay in rehab.

"Do I need to bring bail this time?" Shauna asked. She kept a minimum balance in her savings account equal to Laura's last bail.

"Nah," Laura said. "They just want me to pay for a speeding ticket I got last winter before they'll let me go. It's just a hundred and twenty. I can pay you back at home."

"They arrested you for an unpaid ticket?" Shauna asked. Her sister started to say 'no', but Shauna cut her off. "I don't think I want to know. I'll be there." She hung up and pocketed the phone after turning off the ringer.

"I guess we're going to the courthouse," James said to the silhouette driving the car.

Shauna nodded. "My sister is trying to straighten out her life. She just has certain weaknesses."

"Drugs?" James asked.

"It's not really the drugs, but she likes 'bad boys' and is very compliant to go along with whatever they're doing and it led to an addiction. She's been clean over a year. I was proud of her." Shauna said. "I'm talking too much, aren't I?"

James smiled sympathetically and shook his head. "I don't mind learning about the people you care about. I do hope your sister is not in too much trouble. It'll be a tight fit, but I'm sure we can fit her in here as well."

"I don't think there's enough room in here for her exuberance. I think we'll take a cab," Shauna said. "I'm not convinced meeting her would help your impression of me and I'm sure her meeting you would lead to days of questions about you that I won't have answers for. Thanks for the offer, but a cab would be best."

James didn't press the offer. He gestured to the wine rack. "Are you sure you couldn't use a little something to relax?"

"I'll be okay," Shauna said, though the wine did sound tempting.

"Be sure you don't try to walk tonight," James said. "It's a bad night to be a woman out on the streets."

Shauna was a little taken aback by the sudden turn in the conversation. She asked, "Why?"

"There'll be a murder tonight. The A. A. Aaronson copycat killer has replicated the first killing in each of the books on their release dates. The first death is a girl pulled randomly off the street."

She'd been hearing about the copycat killer all day, but never considered herself a potential victim; she was too unimportant, too boring and knew the streets too well. "You think it was random?" Shauna asked about the plot of the book. She hadn't gotten far enough in the book to find anything to indicate that it wasn't a planned murder.

James pulled his copy of the book from a pouch beside the bar. A bookmark indicated he had already read about a fifth of the book, far more than Shauna. He opened to an early chapter and pointed at the page. "The only character they've introduced with any relationship to the victim, her boyfriend, had an airtight alibi. If the story follows along the usual Aaronson construction, we met the killer somewhere in chapters two, three, or four and no one else we've met knew the victim at all. We just don't have the information yet to connect the killer to the crime."

"Her books are that predictable?" Shauna asked.

"The main plotline is," James said. "I read them for other parts of the stories."

"The sex scenes?" Shauna asked, regretting it as soon as she did. Aaronson wrote graphic sex scenes, which was part of what drew Shauna to the stories. It made them a very guilty pleasure, especially when she read those parts at work.

"Aaronson does have a talent for creativity in that area, but my focus will always be the characters and the setting itself." James said.

"A world where vampires can exist is an interesting enough setting to put up with a book you can predict the outcome of?" Shauna asked.

"It is a fascinating myth," James said. "Her particular flavor of vampire is among my favorite of the various romantic vampire mythos. Completely unrealistic. If such parasites could exist, people couldn't know about them and not hunt them to extinction. Vampires would have to be terribly easy to hunt with their being asleep anytime the sun is up."

Shauna didn't really agree that the vampires were impossible to be real. Her own research, which used Aaronson as a source of a version of the truth, seemed to indicate they were more than just a remote possibility. She'd also stumbled across a manuscript that claimed to be copied from a hand written journal from a vampire hunter in the days of the American Revolution. It had been mailed to her store decades ago, probably thinking the store had an inside track to a publisher. It was poorly written if it was meant to be fiction, as Stuart had suspected it was. Shauna took it so seriously, she'd stowed it at her apartment, under her bed.

"What if Aaronson is almost right?" Shauna asked. She then added, "What if she knows something and tells just enough truth to make it believable and just enough lies to hide that she's telling a truth?"

James didn't answer. He just looked at her in a way that made her slightly uncomfortable. It was as if he were measuring something about her. She felt suddenly exposed and resisted the urge to cover her breasts.

"We're here," he said.

Shauna blinked and looked out the window. The car had stopped in front of the courthouse. "Great, thanks for the lift." She let herself out of the car and rushed to the doors of the courthouse. She glanced back to see James' limo drive off when she realized her books were still in the trunk. She started to jog after it, but a few steps later, the limo was several blocks away. Maybe the whole ride had been an elaborate plan to get her signed first editions, she thought, but quickly dismissed the idea. As she walked back to the courthouse doors she wondered if maybe something she'd said had made him as uncomfortable as she felt in the last moments in the limousine.

CHAPTER 2

After Shauna paid the fine at the counter, her sister emerged from a door nearby. A year clean and to Shauna, Laura still looked like a skeletal heroin addict. Despite being identical twins, Laura always seemed to find a way to be prettier. By the rest of the world's standards, with her pixie-cut blonde flecked chestnut hair and lightly tanned skin, Laura looked like a supermodel. The outfit she was wearing, a plaid skirt and a dress shirt with a loosely tied tie made her look like a man's schoolgirl fantasy.

Shauna sighed. She figured out what Laura was arrested for. "Prostitution, really?"

"Not really," Laura mimicked Shauna's tone. "I was just offering erotic massage on a classifieds webpage. I wasn't going to actually do anything illegal. The undercover cop who hired me didn't believe me though. I was thinking a nice baby oil backrub with some teasing fingernail runs, all on the back and maybe the thighs, and the cop was thinking it would include a happy ending."

"Laura," Shauna said, trying unsuccessfully to keep the pity she felt from her voice.

"The A.D.A. believes me. There nothing technically wrong with offering backrubs for money, though," Laura said. "Well, except that you're supposed to have a license or something."

"So, that was the ticket?" Shauna asked. "I suspected it wasn't a traffic ticket. You haven't driven a car, ever."

"Maybe I pled down to civil indecent exposure, barely a misdemeanor," Laura said. "Apparently taking my shirt off is problematic even if it wasn't part of the deal for money."

The biggest problem holding her sister back from a good job was a lack of experience. She'd never actually had a job. She'd let men take care of her and had a few entrepreneurial experiences, mostly borderline illegal, but never taken a job where she'd worked for anyone else. Laura refused to settle for entry level food service or retail work, and wouldn't put in the time to train for anything better because she always had a plan for her next venture. "You need to find a job. Any real job is better than demeaning yourself," Shauna said.

"That's exactly what the A.D.A. said." Laura waved to a guy standing in a line of men chained at the ankle and at the wrists that marched down the hall escorted by several uniformed police.

Shauna assumed the men were heading to a prison bus. "Could you seriously pick a better class of people to flirt with?"

"They're not bad people," Laura said.

"Yes, they are." Shauna took her sisters shoulders in her hands. "They're in prison because they did something criminal, something bad. That makes them bad people."

"Robert is cute," Laura said. "He's only in for dealing pot."

"Which is illegal." Shauna released her grip on her sister and headed out the front doors. "That guy wasn't even that cute. You have some weird perspective where being a rogue is romantic."

"Don't get me started on weird perspectives," Laura said. "You're the one who not only thinks vampires may be real, but you're actually looking to find them."

"That's just a hobby," Shauna said, trying to play it down. She'd told Laura she wanted to write about vampires and thought it would be cool if they were real so she could observe one to add realism to her book. It was a lie. Shauna never planned really to write a book. Her true intentions, to become a vampire, were too far out there for her sister to accept.

"So if it's just a hobby, you won't want to go to this new club I found out about?" Laura asked. "There's supposed to be a VIP room with a blood fountain for their vampire clientele."

"You're pulling my leg. Stop teasing." Shauna looked to the street, hoping to see a cab. She saw James standing by his car, holding her box of books. She walked over and let him hand the box to her.

"I've been thinking," James said. His voice was calm and conversational, like they hadn't had a weird moment when they'd last parted. "You and your sister probably need jobs and I happen to have a couple openings in one or two of the companies I own."

If he could pretend there was nothing weird between them, so could she. "Oh?"

Laura said. "But Shauna has a job." Laura then looked at the box in Shauna's arms and said, "Shauna, please tell me you're just cleaning out your office. Tell me you still have a job," Laura implored.

"Not anymore," Shauna said. "Bookstores aren't exactly a growing business these days."

"That sucks." Laura peered into the box. "Did you steal these as some kind of revenge?"

Shauna didn't bother to acknowledge her sister. It was typical of her to assume everyone was a little bit criminal.

James extended a hand toward Laura and said, "We haven't met." When Laura took his hand, he gave it a gentle shake then said, "James Alden at your service."

"Laura McAllister. Charmed."

After releasing her hand, James said to Laura, "The one job I have in mind for you is nothing special. Your sister tells me you can be a bit of an extrovert and I happen to have an opening for that kind of person. It's honest work for honest pay. I'll make a call later and set it up." He turned to Shauna and said, "Miss McAllister, I'll need a couple days to get the arrangements together for your job. I would prefer not to discuss it until I'm more certain of the details."

James handed Shauna and Laura each a business card. It was the simplest card Shauna had ever seen. On the vellum card, in black ink it said, 'James' and had a phone number beneath the name.

"I believe your earlier assessment of the travel arrangements is correct; my car is too cramped for the three of us," James said. He gestured to a taxi behind his car. "I got that cab's attention for you. Call me Thursday." He gave Shauna a nod, which she wasn't sure wasn't actually a subtle bow, and then went to his car. As soon as he closed the door, it drove away.

Shauna and her sister took the cab back to her apartment. The cabbie never turned the meter on and refused to even accept a tip from them. It irked Shauna that she'd not had the chance to refuse to allow James to pay for her cab. She would have protested once and then let him insist, but she wanted the chance to do so.

Laura flopped onto Shauna's couch. For the first time ever, she kicked off her shoes first without being asked. "You're new boyfriend seems to have enough money to make up for the fact that he was kind of weird or maybe he was just kind of old."

"I'm not seeing James." Shauna set the box of books on her counter. She pulled out Death by Daylight and set it beside the box. "I haven't eaten yet. If I make myself a sandwich, will you want one?"

"No way," Laura said. "I still have a figure to watch and until they manage to make diet rum to go with my diet cola, tonight's drinking is going to overrun my daily limit as it is."

Shauna shrugged and threw together a peanut butter sandwich. Before taking a bite, she asked her sister to tell her about the new club she'd heard of.

"It's not new; it's supposed to have been there for years. It's not even off the beaten path by much; just a block off of South Street. It's not advertised in any of the hotspot rags. It's called Grue's Home."

"Gruesome?" Shauna asked.

"No, Grue's Home; like the place where Grue lives." Laura scrunched her face in thought. "I don't know who Grue is."

"Me either." Shauna finished her sandwich then headed for the bathroom to get ready for the club.

§

A few hours later, Shauna and her sister emerged from a cab on Lambert Street at the end of an alley leading to South. Shauna wore a simple black dress with an ivory lace shawl. Her sister wore black jeans and a black tee, both skin tight, and a pair of fingerless black lace gloves. Both had masked their eyes with plenty of dramatic shading. While Shauna had chosen a blood-red lipstick to match her hair, her sister went with a bright orange.

The club was exactly where Laura had said it would be. The alley was well travelled and was lined by half a dozen boutiques and a spa. A descending flight of stairs with a small sign on the wall in black iron lettering that read "Grue's Home" marked the entrance. Shauna had been down the alley to patronize the other stores but had never looked twice at the stairwell. There were even a handful of people waiting in line to get in.

Laura took Shauna's hand and pulled her past the line and past the door man. "I'm on the list," was all she said to the large man in the black on black suit. He glanced at her and at Shauna and nodded.

"There's a list?" Shauna asked as Laura continued to drag her through the club. Grue's Home took up a full quarter of the block. It was much larger inside and, though the entrance had been at basement level, the club had multiple levels inside. It was full but not packed. The band was on stage, but just running sound checks, so maybe it was still early yet.

"I have no idea," Laura said. She pointed up to a ground floor booth. "I'm going to go grab that, you get the drinks."

The bar was down on the basement level and had a crowd of people packed around it. Shauna squeezed into a gap and waved to one of the two bartenders. He pointed to the other bartender then leaned over to take an order from someone else.

The other bartender was deep into a conversation at the far end of the bar with a man wearing black lipstick and heavy eyeliner. It almost seemed as if they were arguing, but Shauna couldn't hear them over the din of the crowd.

The bar itself was old and made of a dark carved wood. For a moment Shauna thought it was unusual for a modern club, but then looked around and noticed all of the décor was over a century old. Even what little lighting there was wore disguises so to appear as flickering candles. An occasional recessed black light only added to the dark feel of the club.

It was all familiar. Knowing she'd see crystal chandeliers, she let her gaze roam to the ceiling. The chandeliers were there. Had she been there before? No, the sights were new to her. She'd only imagined what they'd look like while reading the last Aaronson novel. Only, in the novel, the crystals of the chandeliers had been illuminated with dark red lasers to give them the appearance of dripping blood. That club had been called "Nibbles" and was a vampire friendly bar with a vampires-only VIP room.

The bartender that had been arguing at the end of the bar interrupted her, "What can I get you?"

"I need a rum and diet, and do you have wine?" Shauna asked. The bartender started to hand her a wine list, but she brushed it aside. "I really don't know wine well enough. Can you give me a good bottle in the twenty dollar range, red?"

The bartender began to tuck the list back into a stand when a lithe and pale hand snatched it away. The woman who had grabbed the list said, "Allow me to make a suggestion." The woman looked as goth as anyone Shauna had ever seen. She wore a tattered lace wedding gown and had skin almost as pale as the fabric. Her hair was pure black and hung straight past her waist. She pressed her finger to the list and showed the bartender. "Grigor, give her this one."

"Thanks, I hope," Shauna said. "I really should take the time to figure out exactly what I like in wine." She held out her hand to the woman. "My name is Shauna."

"Elsa." The woman glared at Shauna's hand but didn't touch it. "Wine appreciation is more art than science. You either have to taste every vintage ever made, or accept that even if you know where, when and how the wine was made, the results can vary from pure bliss to undrinkable piss."

"I just try to find a brand I like and can afford." Shauna said. In truth, her only requirement for wine was the absence of a screw cap.

"First time at the Grue's Home?" Elsa asked.

"It's not my usual club," Shauna said. "You?"

"I like the vibe here." Elsa glanced quickly around the club. "Usually. It's better when there isn't a band."

The bartender passed Shauna an opened bottle of wine and two glasses beside a tall thin cocktail. She slid one of the wine glasses towards Elsa. "I'm here with my sister, but you're welcome to join us."

"You're cute, but not my type," Elsa said. "See you around." She wandered into the crowd, leaving the wine glass. Shauna couldn't manage to carry it either, so she took the wine bottle and one glass in one hand and Laura's cocktail in the other and squeezed through the gathering audience to the booth where her sister waited.

The band began to play. Shauna had expected a goth or emo band, but the 'Skeledudes' seemed to be a Grateful Dead cover band. By the way Laura was getting into the music, this was something she'd been aware of. Shauna didn't mind the music, but had more important things to pay attention to. If the club had been a setting for Aaronson's book, then maybe she could spy a real vampire.

It didn't take long for her to locate the entrance to the VIP room. A stairway leading to a top floor balcony was guarded by two large men in black on black suits. The few people she'd seen walk past the guards had been dressed even more dark and vampish than she was.

Halfway through the second set, a group of Laura's friends found them. Shauna was squished into the back of the booth by a large woman in a tie-dyed muumuu and reeking of patchouli. Unable to see much of the club, Shauna resorted to focusing on her wine and trying to just enjoy the music.

When the music stopped, she pointed out the VIP room to her sister. "Think you can charm your way past those guys?"

"I'm kind of tired," the patchouli wearing girl said. "I don't think I want to stay here much longer. This place is creepy."

"We'll be back in a minute," Laura said. "Shauna just has to peek inside, then we can all go back to your place for a," she looked at Shauna and shrugged, "uh, nightcap."

Shauna rolled her eyes as she extricated herself from the booth. Laura led them up to the men, but instead of just waving her by, they closed together, blocking the stairway.

"You don't want to go up there, ladies." One of the bouncers said. "It's a private party and things get a little weird if you don't know the deal."

"We know the deal," Laura said. "We're here all the time."

The guard's face said that he didn't believe her. "You two really want to go up to The Chrystal Room? Tell me the password then," he said.

"Um," Laura said. She turned to Shauna, "What's a good vampire password?"

"Mina," Shauna said.

"Good guess," the bouncer said. "But you're wrong. You need to leave, now." He pointed a finger at the club's entrance.

"This is bullshit," Laura said and headed back to the table.

Shauna walked with her, then noticed the rear exit sign over the entrance to a hall in the back of the club. In the book, 'Nibbles' had a secret entrance to the VIP room by the back door. That entrance hadn't been guarded. She tapped her sister's shoulder. "You go ahead, just be good. No needles or anything."

"I'm just getting a ride home from them. They live a block from me," Laura said. "I don't like the same kind of high that they do."

Shauna knew her sister was mostly telling the truth. Laura would go back and party with her friends before going home, but she didn't really get into any drugs besides heroin. Being in recovery, Laura wouldn't be hanging with anyone from the injection drug scene. If she's stuck to her support group's plan she wouldn't be socializing anywhere drugs or alcohol would be present, but, to Laura, that would remove all purpose from her existence.

The bar had gone from packed to almost empty in minutes since the music stopped. Not one person had left the VIP area, though. Shauna walked back towards the exit, passing the bathrooms and where the band was signing autographs and selling CDs. A dark passage, several paces deep, led to the rear exit. A huge sticker warned her not to open the door or an alarm would sound. A smaller sticker warned of a dog outside the door. She had no intention of opening that door. Instead, she felt back along the dark walls and pressed the wall every foot or so.

She jumped a little when the wall popped open revealing a room with a spiral staircase leading up. She jumped, startled, when a hand grabbed her by the shoulder. "I guess you wouldn't believe I was looking for the bathroom?" Shauna said before she turned around to see it was James who had grabbed her.

"You won't find what you're looking for up those stairs, Miss McAllister," he said.

"Are you stalking me?" Shauna asked. "I mean this is like four times we've bumped into each other today."

"Only that last time was contrived, but I had to return your books to you," James said. He closed the door to the stairway and gestured for Shauna to return to the main room of the club. "I'm actually here on business. I sell wine to the club and the proprietor of this establishment and I usually do our business after closing, which will be a short while yet."

Shauna returned to the booth she'd shared with her sister earlier, though it and most of the other tables in the club were now empty. Several songs worth of empty bottles and glasses still sat on the table.

James waited for her to sit before sitting across from her. He grabbed one of the wine bottles and held it up towards the bar. "A Chilean Merlot would not have been my first guess for you," James said. "You seem more a French or German white."

"I don't like my wine chilled," Shauna said. "Other than that, all I usually care about is that the cork doesn't screw off."

"So, no opinion on the oh-five Napas?"

Shauna had no idea what he was talking about. "You mentioned something about me not finding what I'm looking for here."

"There are no vampires in the VIP room," James said. "Before you ask why I think you were looking for vampires, let me remind you that I read Aaronson too." A bartender sat a new bottle of wine on the table with two clean glasses. He cleared the empties from the table before returning to the bar.

"So you know this place is a dead-ringer for 'Nibbles'," Shauna asked.

James nodded as he poured a small amount of wine into a glass. "But unlike you, I knew the club before I read the book. Still, I can guess the impression it might have on someone as alert as you. But you are a much more impressive individual than anyone you'll find in the VIP room. They would just waste your time." He sipped the wine and smiled. He then filled both glasses almost to the top.

"Why would I want to find a real vampire? I'd just be food for them." Shauna said. "If vampires were real," she added. After a moment she also added, "And I don't believe in them."

"You want to," James said. "But if they were real, you would just be food."

Shauna had to be careful with the overly full wine glass, but managed to take a sip without spilling. "So what's the deal with the VIP room? If it's not vampires, why should I be afraid?"

"It's people somewhat like you," James said. "It's people who want to be vampires. They want it so much they pretend they are." He drank heavily from his glass, downing almost half in one draught.

"What makes you think I want to be a vampire?" Shauna said.

"You are what is currently labeled as 'goth', are you not?" James said. When she nodded, he went on, "Doesn't every goth aspire to become a vampire?"

"I suppose it's something many Goths have in common." Shauna took a light sip from her glass. She was sure she couldn't drink it all. "Maybe I'm just morbid and suicidal?"

"Chasing vampires, if they were real, would be quite suicidal," James said then threw back the rest of his wine glass like it was a shot.

A man came by the table and set down another wine bottle with the cork only loosely in place.

"Rick," James said, "Thank you, but I am not quite ready for another bottle yet."

"You will be soon enough," Rick said. He looked younger than Shauna with long sandy brown hair trying to escape from a hasty ponytail. He wore a black turtleneck under a black sports coat and tight black jeans. "I have to go settle with the band and they seem to have the usual misunderstanding about how we agreed to handle the bar tab, so it may take me a while. In the meantime, try this one. It's a favorite of one of my regulars and I cannot seem to find it anywhere. I can sell it for two fifty a bottle, so I can pay well for it."

"Ninety Seven may be a bit past its prime for this particular Bordeaux," James said.

"Does it matter if I have a customer who will pay for it?" Rick asked.

"It makes it hard to find, but also less expensive when I do find it," James said. "We'll discuss it later."

"Right," Rick said. He turned to walk away then spun back. "Where are my manners?" He extended a hand to Shauna, "Rick Buonarroti, owner of the Grue's Home."

Shauna took it and replied, "Shauna. This is my first time here."

Rick stood back and spread his hands wide. "So, what do you think of my place?"

"Very classic. I like the dark Victorian vibe." Shauna ventured.

"Hah, that's funny. It's what happens when I'm too cheap to renovate, just like the previous two owners," Rick said and then walked away. Shauna watched as he meandered by a pool table where the bartender, another man and three women were playing some game on a table with only three balls and no pockets. There was something wrong with the way they all moved. To be more precise, there was absolutely nothing wrong with the way they moved. They all had extraordinary grace.

"That is not a bad wine," James said. He held the bottle Rick had brought and studied the label. "I mean, it is a little past its peak, but still a great wine. Shall I pour you a glass?"

"I'm good with what I have." She held up her still more than half full glass.

As her gaze wandered back to the group of people at the pool table, James put a hand on her forearm. "So, if you're up for a good laugh, what say I show you The Chrystal Room?"

"You mean all the vamp wannabes?" Shauna asked. She wanted to see the people who pretended to be vampires, if only to understand where not to go with her obsession. "Sure."

James took her hand and led her out of the booth and up to the men guarding the stairway. They didn't bother to step in front of James and just smiled at her as she walked by in tow.

At the top of the stairs, maroon velvet curtains parted to reveal about twenty people in various stages of undress. A three tiered fountain of what Shauna could only believe to be blood sat in the middle of the room. A man walked over and dipped a goblet into the thick liquid and returned to pour it over the chest of a woman and then he began to lick it off of her.

The walls of the room were black with dark red curtain panels interspersed with bare walls. Dim blue light barely escaped from behind the curtains, making the colors of the room shift to mostly variants of gray. The only thing well lit in the room was a painted portrait of a man on the wall. Shauna recognized him as Lord William Chrystal, the hero of A. A. Aaronson's novels. In the stories, the Scottish expatriate somehow would find himself accused of a crime and then sleep with everyone to get off the hook and usually, but not always, identify the actual culprit. More often than not, Lord Chrystal was the only human in a story full of vampires and werewolves. At least she knew why they called the room The Chrystal Room.

On a small dance floor, people were slow dancing to trance music. To call it dancing was using the term liberally. They were generally still wearing more than the people lounging on the couches or in the piles of cushions, but they weren't letting the clothing get in the way of activities more intimate than Shauna was comfortable watching.

One woman stood out from the rest in that she sat on a gilded throne and was surrounded by three naked women and one naked man, each with a collar that was chained to the throne. The woman sitting in the fancy chair smiled at Shauna and James, showing a pair of fangs. She had long curling naturally red hair and the pale skin that accompanies true redheads, but not a single freckle. She wore layers of black and red gauzy scarves and somehow still managed to show more skin than not. James walked over to the woman and bowed low. "Queen Lorna," he said.

"Mr. Alden," the woman on the throne replied. "Is this tasty morsel a gift? Or are you both merely taking in the sights?"

"This is Miss McAllister," James said. "We're just sightseeing, if you wouldn't mind."

"She looks pretty darned real to me," Shauna whispered, leaning close to James' ear.

"Do as you will, Mr. Alden. You know I don't mind as long as you maintain your composure and are not disruptive. Do let me know if you change your mind concerning leaving Miss McAllister with me."

"Thank you," James said. He then leaned close to Shauna. "If she were real, don't you think she might have heard your whisper?"

"So if this isn't real, what's with the blood and the teeth?" Shauna asked. She noticed she was unconsciously hiding behind James, but decided it was probably a good instinct to go with.

James led her to the fountain and dipped a finger in. Shauna expected him to lick it clean or to offer it to her but he only sniffed at it. "Pear Nectar," he said. "With coloring." He took a black napkin from a table and wiped his finger clean on one of them. The table was arranged like a catering table with wine glasses, napkins and four bottles of varied wines.

Shauna found the courage to dip her own finger in and, after a quick sniff to make sure it didn't smell coppery or like rotten eggs, she licked it. It was definitely pear nectar.

James waved a shirtless man over to them. It was the same man with the black lipstick she'd seen arguing with Grigor the bartender. "Sir, could I trouble you to remove your teeth?" James asked.

The man shrugged and pulled out his fangs. They had been nothing more than a fancy overlay. James thanked him and the man snapped his teeth back in and returned to his role-playing.

"Lorna's aren't just an overlay," Shauna said. She'd seen slight gaps between her front teeth, something an overlay wouldn't have.

"Lorna has had permanent implants," James said. "If you're interested I know a dentist willing to do that kind of custom work."

Shauna had no idea such things were done in the real world. "No, I don't think I'm there yet." She couldn't help but watch the profane things people were doing in the name of role playing. It struck her that they were in a private sex club with a vampire theme rather than in a vampire role playing club. When she noticed James wasn't paying any attention to the other people in the room, she asked, "You come here often?"

"I've done a bit of research on this role-playing society," James said, maintaining his prim composure. Had he winked or cracked a wry smile, she'd know he'd played with these people, but with his stoic demeanor, it was hard to tell one way or another if there was anything to read between the lines. Maybe he'd just sat and watched and took notes. She wasn't sure if that would make him seem more appealing or weirder.

"Are you A. A. Aaronson?" Shauna asked sounding more accusing than she'd intended. It made sense. James wasn't really the kind of person to read that sleazy material. It would explain his presence here and why the story's club matched so perfectly with the real one.

"I am not she," James said. "You are correct to assume she is connected to this place. I believe the little brass plaque under the portrait will tell you that she donated the funds to create the space and maintain it. Are we done with the tour?"

"I've seen enough," Shauna said. While she could certainly get into some of what she saw, the idea of pretending to be a vampire seemed over the top. She had, in watching the role-players at play, discovered a couple new things to try the next time she had a boyfriend.

James let her exit the room first. He bowed to the queen on his way out and blew her a kiss.

"This research," Shauna asked. "Just how in depth did it go?"

"That question is too personal for where our friendship is at this time," James said.

As they walked past the guards, one of the people who'd been playing pool earlier intercepted them.

"Charlie," James said. "How can I help you?"

"Rick says he's not in the mood to talk business tonight. The Skeledudes trashed the stage when he deducted their forty dollar bar tab from their several hundred dollar gig fee." Charlie said. He then turned to Shauna, "And Allison told me to tell you to stop staring at me."

Had she been staring? If she had it wasn't at Charlie. Of all the people at the pool table, he was the least attractive. He looked like a cross between an ape and a drill sergeant without the uniform, which pretty much meant he looked like an ape.

"That's unfortunate," James said. "I'll call again another night." He grasped Shauna's arm at the elbow and led her towards the door. "I am not driving at the moment, but I'll walk with you to the street to catch a cab."

"It's half a block, James," Shauna said as they climbed the stairs leaving the club. "And besides, the victim in the book was grabbed from a bus stop. I promise to avoid the bus stops and I won't have to worry about the A. A. Aaronson copycat murderer."

When they arrived at South Street, James headed west, deeper into Philly. Shauna headed east, toward the river, towards Jersey. South Street was still closed to vehicle traffic. She got to Front Street, where she expected to find a row of cabs waiting to pick up the late night clubbers, but the street side was devoid of taxis. Several other people were waiting for cabs already. Deciding not to make herself an easy target, Shauna waited as well.

After twenty minutes she gave up on waiting and started walking towards the bridge. Normally she would take a bus, but not with James constantly warning her of the A. A. Aaronson copycat. In all likelihood, the murder had already happened, but no one knew. It was almost two in the morning, after all.

A red convertible pulled up to the curb beside her. A blonde woman in a dress that matched the car, called out to her. "You don't look like you could actually walk very far in those shoes."

Shauna looked down at her shoes and agreed. They were not comfortable and would probably be ruined by walking the miles to and from the bridge. "Do I know you?" Shauna asked.

"I was just driving by and noticed a woman walking alone. It's not the time of night for that kind of thing. This is a pretty safe area, but you're heading towards the Ben Franklin Bridge, and the areas around there are less safe."

The thought the woman might be the A. A. Aaronson copycat crossed her mind, but everything she knew about serial killers was the opposite of the blonde in the sports car. "Please tell me you're not hitting on me," Shauna said.

"Maybe I am," the woman in the car said. "You'd make it easier if you'd get in the car."

"If I get in, all I'm going to want is a ride home," Shauna said. "It's been a really long day."

"All I'm promising is a safe ride to your home," the woman said. "The truth is I don't get to drive this baby much and I'm looking for any excuse to drive it around for a while."

"Fine," Shauna said, climbing into the car. The seat was lower than she was used to but very comfortable. "I live at 7th and Cherry."

"No problem. Buckle up," the driver said. No sooner had Shauna snapped the lap belt into place than the car was spinning in a u-turn then heading north towards the bridge. Tapping Shauna's arm, the driver yelled, "Let me know if I go too fast for you."

Shauna looked at the speedometer and couldn't help but gasp. She'd never imagined going three times the speed limit. "I'm fine," she lied.

It was only a few minutes before Shauna was climbing out of the car near her apartment. "Thanks, I didn't get a chance to ask your name. Mine is…" The woman reached over and placed a finger on Shauna's lips.

"No need for names. If you tell me yours, I'll feel pressured to tell you mine and I don't need to share my name with you tonight."

Shauna shrugged and walked away. Just another weird experience for a day she planned to note in her journal as the oddest one she'd ever had.

CHAPTER 3

Shauna closed the apartment door behind her and turned on the light. She started to scream when she realized her living room was full of people. A man she'd swore had been sitting on her couch across the room intercepted the scream with a hand over her mouth. His other arm wrapped around her chest, pinning her own arms at her sides.

Recognition set in. She'd seen all of these people just minutes earlier. Rick, the owner of Grue's Home was sitting in her easy chair. One of the women from the pool table crowd stood behind him. Charlie was the man holding her. Another man stood by the door to the kitchen. He embraced a woman who hid her head in his chest. Two women still sat on the couch. One, with a bored look on her face, wore a pair of copper wire-rimmed sunglasses with pink lenses and the other had a twisted grin, almost a giggle consuming her face.

It was Rick that spoke first. "I'd expected something more dark and broody. All these country crafts don't really mesh with your wardrobe." He gestured around at Shauna's décor. The crafts were a phase she went through when she'd first moved into her own place. "Now Shauna, if Charlie lets you go, do you promise not to scream?"

Shauna tried to scream again, but her voice was muffled in Charlie's huge hand.

"I see." Rick stood up from the chair and moved to stand in front of Shauna. His movement was a blur. One instant he was sitting, the next he stood calmly before her. His long hair still flowed from the wind of his movement when he said, "No need to hide who we are, since you've already deduced that we're the real deal. Well, most of us are exactly what you think we are: vampires. Allison, Lily and Teresa are just pets."

Shauna realized at that moment that Rick spoke the truth. Not only were vampires real, as she'd suspected, but there were four of them in her apartment. Something of her realization must have shown on her face.

Rick said, "You didn't know?"

Shauna shook her head. His tone was almost sympathetic. She no longer felt the need to scream.

"That is sadly ironic," Rick said. "Under our laws we have to protect our secret, which meant we had to kill you because you knew. But you didn't know. But now that you do, you have to die."

Die? Again her screams were muffled by Charlie's hand.

"I used that right, Rhiannon?" Rick turned to the couch. "That is ironic?"

In a nonchalant monotone, the woman in the sunglasses replied. "Correct in usage, this time."

"Shall we drain her or go with a more conventional method?" Rick asked.

The woman hiding her face in the man's chest by her kitchen pushed away from him. "Grigor, I don't want to watch this," she said then left the apartment.

"I could use some fresh blood," Charlie said. Shauna felt his lips on her neck. The lips parted and she felt his fangs brush her skin. She tried to bite his hand but he held her carefully, not giving her teeth the chance to find purchase.

"Wait," The woman behind Rick's chair said.

"Yes, Teresa?" Rick held a finger towards Shauna and Charlie pulled his mouth away from Shauna's neck.

The woman continued, "No one needs to die. We were thinking she had to die because she's been aware of us for hours, but she just found out. We can still coerce her and make her forget. If you use a drop of blood, there's no chance she'll remember."

"Lucky you," Rick said. He opened his mouth to reveal his fangs and placed one of his fingertips against the point of a fang. A tiny droplet of blood appeared. He gestured and Charlie removed his hand. As soon as Charlie's hand was

SECOND BLOOD

clear, Rich thrust his finger into Shauna mouth, smearing the blood on her tongue. He then grabbed her face in both hands and forced eye contact. "We were never here. You don't want to go back to Grue's Home. Vampires are still only something you wish were true, but they're just a myth. Go take a shower and get some sleep."

Shauna felt serene. She headed for her bathroom, dropping her clothes on the hall floor outside the door. She glanced back at her living room, not knowing what she expected to see, but it was just as she remembered it, her lonely, empty living room. The box of books from work still sat on the floor by the door, except her new Aaronson novel, which was on her coffee table, just where she'd left it before going out to that club.

The warm water of the shower relaxed her muscles, which seemed oddly tense. She didn't think that woman in the sports car had made her that stressed. She stood under the showerhead letting the water run over her muscles. All of her efforts to relax them were thwarted when she heard her front door close.

"Laura?" Shauna called out. No one replied. Not bothering to dry off, she tied a towel around herself and grabbed her plunger and held it with both hands like a softball bat.

She peered out of her bathroom and a large hand grabbed her by the neck and yanked her into the hallway. The man who grabbed her was large and apelike. As he dragged her to the living room she recognized him as Charlie from the club she'd been to earlier that night. A woman she'd seen at the club was with him. She held one of her kitchen knives

Shauna screamed and swung the plunger as best she could at the man holding her, but she couldn't get any force into her strikes. Charlie changed his grip to hold her around the waist, gripping one of her wrists and pinning the other to her side. She dropped the plunger, but continued to scream.

"Don't worry," Charlie said. "We'll be quick. Won't we Allison?"

The woman pouted, "I was hoping to get to enjoy it a little."

Shauna wanted to form words to tell the people to leave, to ask what they wanted, but her voice would only scream using all the volume it could.

"Take off the towel, Charlie," Allison said. When the towel was ripped away, Allison stepped up and ran the back of the knife over her exposed skin. "It's a shame that Miss Aaronson hadn't been more creative this time. You've got a nice body. I'd so love to ruin it first."

"People are coming," Charlie said. "Just do it."

"Fine," Allison said. She flipped the knife in her hand once then slashed out, cutting through Shauna's throat.

For a brief instant Shauna felt pain, but then nothing.

Then warmth. She was drinking something thick and metallic and tasted like salted egg yolks. The blackness came again for what seemed like days. When her awareness returned, she was with someone else, someone who wasn't Charlie or Allison.

James was holding Shauna, cradling her in his arms. He held the palm of his hand to her mouth and she was suckling it. No, she was drinking blood from two holes in his hand.

"You're conscious," James said. He pulled his hand away and Shauna saw the holes close, healing instantly. Her hands went instantly to her neck. She was covered in blood--too much blood. But she could find no wound on her neck.

"You healed me?" Shauna asked.

"If only that were all I did," James said. "You won't be able to think clearly for long. The blood will fog your mind. When it clears you'll be fine. "

Her vision was already blurry. She tried to ask him to clarify but she couldn't think how to use the words. She had the feeling of motion and, for a moment, thought she could see the stars above her and the clouds below her.

Then she was sitting on a concrete floor with her back to a concrete wall. Even the ceiling was concrete. James put something in each hand. "Drink these both; they'll help with the pain. I have to leave you for a few hours while you undergo the transformation. I'll be here when you wake up." The last thing Shauna remembered was being naked. When she moved to cover herself, she realized she was wearing the black dress she'd left on her hall floor.

He disappeared. She heard a door close somewhere and a thick sounding lock mechanism. She looked at her hands. She held a bottle of wine in each. Both bottles were already open, their corks only barely set. It was only a second before the thirst hit and a wave of pain started at her toes and rode all the way to her chest. A burning sensation followed. Another wave started and carried all the way through her. She fell to the concrete floor, spilling wine across her lap. When the pain subsided she drained the half full bottle and set it down, fearing to break it should she fall on it.

It was then that she noticed the two sarcophagi in the center of the room. She peered more closely at the sarcophagi and realized there were no slabs to cover the top and no coffins, as she had expected, inside. In fact, aside from the two concrete boxes and faux stone walls, the room stood plain and empty. The only illumination came from recessed lighting along the edges of concrete ceilings with heavy Plexiglas protecting it.

The clearly solid construction of the room made Shauna feel imprisoned. What if James put her down here to die? Another wave of pain flooded her, dropping her to the floor. This time the pain racked her body for several minutes leaving a sensation that her flesh was on fire. She gulped down the remaining bottle of wine in an effort to stave off the flames. It seemed to work for a moment but the next wave of pain tore through her. She slammed her fist against the floor at her side and the concrete cracked where she hit. This wave brought a sensation of cold. To her touch, the floor now felt warm. For the next hour she caught her breath and waited for the next wave of pain. Just as she began to suspect the wave would not come, it hit. Instead of falling to the floor again, her muscles jerked in spasms, throwing her across the room into a sarcophagus. The concrete shattered, leaving three sides of the box standing and her sprawled inside, surrounded by chunks of debris.

Time moved slowly and the painful seizures got worse and lasted longer. She tried banging on the door at the top of the stairs. The heavy steel didn't budge, but the concrete around the door cracked. When she made the effort to hit the door harder, perhaps to break it free from the wall, another wave of pain and muscle spasms threw her back down the stairs. Confusion overcame her, giving her only moments of awareness as hours passed where her body felt like it was tearing itself apart.

After a pain attack that seemed milder than the previous, Shauna checked her watch, a plastic model with hands instead of being digital, and realized she had been down in the basement for over twenty four hours before she'd broken the now functionless piece of plastic. Digging into her pocket for her phone, she found only shards of plastic, metal and glass. Still the terrible aches came. Both concrete sarcophagi were spread across the floor as tiny chunks and white dust.

Panic welled up. What had she become? She was certain she was a vampire, but didn't know exactly what that meant. Her hands again found her throat, relieved to still find it healed. She wouldn't have wanted to exist as an immortal with a perpetual gaping wound. From what she could see of her body through the blood and dust, little had changed physically. Emotionally she'd expected to feel stronger, but the only thought that entered her mind was worry for her sister. Would she be able to see her again? Could Laura go on without her?

When no pains came for long enough that she believed they had passed, she walked up the steps and knocked on the door. She had feared no one would answer and that she would be stuck in the basement forever. The door swung open at her gentlest knock. She suspected she had gained strength but didn't attribute the door opening so easily to that. The door had been left slightly ajar. She didn't know when that had changed.

"James!" She called out. The curtains on the windows were open and starlight lit the room brightly enough for her to see clearly. An envelope lay at her feet with her name scrawled across the front in thick marker. Her first name nearly covered the entire front of the envelope. She chuckled at James' manners. Now that they were close by blood, he allowed himself to use her name. After picking it up, she pulled a letter from inside.

"Shauna," The letter read, "My Apologies, I have been called away for something far more important than I would like to deal with. I wish I could stay with you to show you the ropes of your new life. 'Be careful' is truly the best advice I can offer. Be gentle in everything you do. Match the pace of the world around you; it will seem very slow to you at times. We all have secrets to keep and one you must keep is my identity. Others of our kind do not know I am of their ilk. Please maintain that secret. Trust Amber. Good luck. I will return.

"Your father, James.

"P.S. You must find a full meal within forty eight hours or you will perish. This is the one and only time a full meal is required. I probably don't have to mention that discretion is everything."

It occurred to her that by secrets he meant that Rick and his friends didn't know he was a vampire. His tanned skin had certainly kept her from suspecting. Her memories of Rick and his friends at her apartment returned and she understood the value of the secrets she had to keep.

Who was Amber, she wondered. Perhaps it was his driver, whom James had referred to as a woman. It would have been nice if he'd left some contact information. His card was back at her apartment stuck to her refrigerator.

Wondering what time it was, Shauna found the clock on the oven.

She wondered briefly why a vampire would have an oven but realized it would be suspiciously unusual to have a house without one. The clock read five-thirty in the morning, which meant she had to find somewhere dark and wouldn't have time to hunt until evening. She didn't want to return to the basement. Clearly James didn't need to, so he must have somewhere else. She looked around the house and found the bedrooms all had black velvet curtains. She found James' room and its rich red velvet and mahogany furnishings and laughed at how stereotypically vampire his room was.

When she caught her own gaze in the dressing mirror that stood in James' room, it startled her. She hadn't expected to see her reflection. Stepping closer, she looked to see how she'd changed. Nothing seemed terribly different. Her hair was still blood red and her chestnut roots were showing. Her eyes were the same shade of brown. She'd have to find a hairbrush after she found a shower. When she opened her lips, she saw the first difference. Her upper canines were noticeably longer than the rest of her front teeth. She also noticed that none of her teeth were as she remembered. All of them were bright white without any fillings or chips. She closed her mouth and looked closer at the mirror. Her skin was completely perfect, without any scars or blemishes. The shade didn't seem to have paled, just evened out. She smiled, admiring her fangs. She touched her finger to the tip of one. It was as sharp as she expected from a tooth, but not as sharp as she'd expected from a fang.

Realizing she'd have to pass as human, she smiled again, keeping her lips closed. She didn't think she looked too different than she had the day before.

The bathroom wasn't hard to find. She went to turn the shower on, but as she reached for the handle, she remembered that there were legends about the harmful effects of running water on vampires. It paralyzed them or kept them from crossing somehow. The shower had a caddy with a razor and a half used bar of soap, but they could be there for the same reason the oven was, to throw off suspicion.

Unsure if water would be safe, she instead took a washcloth and dropped it in the sink. She stepped back as far as she could and still reach the knob and turned on the water for a couple seconds, soaking the washcloth. She then wiped the dried blood off of her neck, shoulder and chest. She had difficulty washing her hair and gave up on getting it clean. She just ran a comb through it enough to separate the clumps and tangles.

She hadn't seen a coffin in his room or any of the others so she hoped that the rumor that vampires were required to sleep in coffins was false. She picked a room with a lavender motif and closed the curtains tight then undressed. Her poor little black dress was ruined, nearly shredded. She climbed into the bed and fell asleep nearly instantly.

When she woke, the sunlight glowed dimly around the edges of the curtains. She waited under the covers for the light to fade to the blues after sunset then went to explore the house for a car or another way to get home so she could change clothes. She couldn't find any clothing in the house other than in James' closet. His wardrobe was sparse, just a dozen or so suits and twice that many ties. He had a single pair of jeans that looked like they'd never been worn. Three pairs of dress shoes and one pair of boots sat on the floor of the closet. She borrowed one of his dress shirts. It did the job of covering her, hanging lower on her thighs than her black dress had.

All she knew was that she had to find someone to consume their blood and she'd have to do it soon. She'd be better returning to the city, she decided. There would be more people there, a better selection of prey. When the thought of hunting a person hit her, she wondered if she could do it. Months of wanting to be a vampire and she'd never prepared for the reality of having to kill. Then she wondered if she could find a person whose death would be more insignificant than that of other people.

Maybe she could play the part of a vigilante, she thought. She envisioned herself scouring alleyways until she found a violent criminal. When the vision included her prowling wearing only James' shirt, she decided her first stop would be home to get a change of clothes.

Shauna couldn't find a garage anywhere in the house, but she noticed the keys to a Mercedes on a table by the front door and found the car sitting in the driveway. A note under the keys read, "Take the car. Drive Slow."

When she sat in the car, her first thought was to worry that she was still too dusty and bloody and might mess up James' leather seats. She reminded herself she had things to do and limited time. As she drove off, she wasn't sure where she was, but assumed James hadn't been lying when he'd said Lionville. All she knew was that it was farther west than West Chester. She picked a direction at random and followed it until she saw signs for the Pennsylvania Turnpike. That would take her straight into Philly.

As soon as she encountered traffic, she understood what the letter had meant about the world seeming very slow. The car had seemed to cruise along slow enough but when she realized that, even at her excruciating slow speed, she was passing other cars on the street like they were standing still. Looking at the speedometer she gasped when she realized she had been going over a hundred miles per hour. The gasp made her throat burn and she noticed that she didn't remember breathing at all since the previous night. Slowing to a safer twenty-five, she felt the world pass agonizingly slowly. It took her several minutes to adjust, but she managed to get the slow world to seem normal again. She pulled into the parking lot for her apartment building and hopped out of the car, taking the keys with her. Her hatchback sat parked exactly where she had left it, rusting away. She didn't drive it much, opting instead to use public transportation. Parking in the city simply cost more than she felt willing to pay.

As she approached the door, she heard the voices of two women. She recognized Allison and Teresa's voices. Memories of the whole night, from visiting Grue's Home to finding Rick and his cohorts in her apartment to Allison slitting her throat, flooded through Shauna. Her hunt for prey would be easier than she anticipated.

"Rick's going to be pissed if she didn't die. He's already pissed enough that you killed her, but if you tried and failed it will be worse." Teresa said.

"I saw her bleed out." Allison replied. "She might not have been dead but there was no coming back from that. That stupid bitch is probably already on ice down in the morgue."

"I don't think so." Teresa said. "There would be police tape. Rick wouldn't have sent us to clean up the place if the cops knew. Edmund must have disposed of the body. She left too much blood on the carpet to have made it to a hospital. Let's finish taking what we want from this place and get out."

Shauna could hear the abrupt jump in the women's heartbeats as they realized they were not alone in the apartment. They jumped, startled, and then turned slowly to look at her.

"Shit!" Teresa screamed then ran for the door. "She's a fucking vamp!"

Shauna instantly let her perceptions slip back to their natural accelerated state and leapt to intercept Teresa. She grabbed Rick's pet by the head with both of her hands, cradling Teresa's face with a very tight grip.

"Don't kill me, please." Teresa muttered with her jaw nearly locked in place with Shauna's grasp.

She was angry at Teresa, but not enough to kill. "You get to live, tonight." Shauna sneered. "I need you to pass a message to Rick and Charlie." Shauna drug her nails down Teresa's face digging eight deep tracks that bled instantly.

Suddenly thirsting, Shauna threw Teresa through the doorway and turned to Allison.

"Don't scar me like that, please." Allison fell to her knees and sobbed. The scent of fear nearly overwhelmed Shauna. It smelled sweet and salty.

The anger Shauna felt for Allison seemed boundless. How perfect was it that she could cement her eternal life and exact vengeance on the woman that killed her in the same act. Shauna sighed. If she had to kill someone, at least it was someone who'd already accepted the danger of playing with vampires. "Oh, no, I have no intention of leaving marks on you. Well, maybe just two. What I need from you doesn't require you to live. It requires you to die." She briefly noticed Allison's eyes go wide with realization as Shauna swept forward embracing Charlie's pet. A whimper escaped Allison's lips as Shauna bit into her prey's neck. As her canine pierced her victim's carotid, she felt the warm gush of blood flood her mouth. She drank as fast as she could, not letting a single drop escape. When the pressure within Allison's veins no longer pushed the blood out fast enough, Shauna began to suck. Allison stopped breathing but death would still be a moment away. Shauna squeezed, using pressure to help push the blood into her mouth. A wave of intense pleasure overcame her, filling her. Shauna knew she had just consumed Allison's death. She dropped the corpse and fell to the couch, soaking in the afterglow.

"No!" Charlie screamed from the doorway. "Allison! No!" He fell to his knees over the crumpled form of his pet. He turned his head up and looked Shauna in the eyes. "Bitch," he said, and then collapsed on top of Allison. Though he was beyond her reach, Shauna felt him die too; it was as if the room dropped in temperature for a second before returning to normal. She hadn't expected a vampire to just die like that. There must have been a connection between the vampire and his pet; something joining their lives in a way she could not perceive.

Shauna just smiled; she felt as if justice had been done. Moving as quickly as she could, she grabbed a pair of jeans and a sweatshirt from her closet. She pulled James' card from her fridge and grabbed the phone on the kitchen wall.

When she tried to call James, a woman answered and Shauna panicked and hung up.

Looking at the bodies on the floor, she noticed Charlie was deteriorating rapidly, his extremities turning to dust. She'd have to come back later and deal with Allison, though. She locked both deadbolts on her way out. No one other than her, not even Laura or her landlord, had the keys to the second deadbolt. She pulled out of the parking lot in James' car less than a minute later and drove back towards his house.

She felt full of energy. Maybe it was the feeding that invigorated her. Maybe it was just because she'd killed. She wondered if she'd kill again.

Killing Allison had been a necessity, a simple trade of one life for another. Was it being selfish to choose her own life as the more important one? Certainly her life was worth more than that of a killer and Allison had been the A. A. Aaronson serial killer, hadn't she? Had she admitted it? A feeling of dread came over Shauna as she realized that now that she was a vampire, she was a killer as well. James' letter had said she only needed to kill once. She hoped that was true.

CHAPTER 4

As Shauna pulled into James' driveway, she noticed his home was little different from the one on either side. It looked like a typical large suburban house from outdoors. Other than the heavy curtains, the inside hadn't been atypical either. She left the car where she'd found it and went in. Surely there would be more information somewhere inside that would tell her who James was, and more importantly, who she was.

The first thing she did was clean up and change clothes. She dumped her ruined black dress into the kitchen trashcan, which hadn't looked like it had ever been used before. A shower is what she really needed, but she had to know more before she was going to risk anything. Again, she did the best she could with a damp washcloth.

Seeing pink on the washcloth and recognizing it was blood made her pause. The blood wasn't hers; she'd cleaned that off earlier. She'd stolen a life just to have one for herself. Was it a monster staring back at her from the mirror or was it just a survivor with blood on her chin? She continued to wash, staring herself in the eyes, hoping to understand who she had become.

Once clean, Shauna decided to search the house for some answers. She dressed in the jeans and sweatshirt and took a less hectic tour of the house than the one immediately after she'd turned.

Aside from the basement, the only room in the house without windows was a two story library in the back. There were thousands of books; many of them looked centuries old. A computer sat on a desk in the center of the room. It had a tripod beside it. Atop the tripod was a camera aimed straight down at an ancient looking tome laying open on a table. The book was printed, not hand written, and it was in modern English -- something to do with Victorian era Russia. It looked fragile so Shauna didn't touch it.

Though she'd hoped the computer had a catalog of the library, turning it on brought up a password screen and Shauna didn't know where to start in guessing James' password. Maybe, if she knew more about wine or vampires, she could venture a few guesses.

A ladder rolled along a rail that followed the shelves. She started by the door and perused the spine of each book. Every book in the library was fiction. They were sorted by language then by author. Shauna skipped right past the languages she didn't know. She'd studied French, Spanish, Latin and Italian in high school and college, but there were books in James' library in every language she could think of.

She looked for a common theme, but apart from the section devoted to modern vampire fiction, she couldn't identify one--at least, not by their titles.

After she'd read several other books, somewhere in the house a long series of bells chimed. Shauna recognized the pattern as meaning midnight and realized she'd heard it for the second time since starting her perusal of the library. She'd spent almost two days riffling the library. She rushed back to her apartment, intent to clean the crime scene. The drive back was quick and Shauna decided she could get used to late night driving with such light traffic.

When she got to her apartment, she felt relieved to have to undo all of her locks. Upon opening her door she realized her relief had been premature. The bodies were gone, but so was everything else she'd owned. For a moment she felt homeless.

The bland off-white carpet had been replaced with plush, new, deep burgundy carpet that now covered the floor of her living room. The curtains had been changed to thick velvet that matched the color of the carpet. Instead of her old couch and recliner she had a Victorian couch and matching settee. Where her old wicker coffee table had been, was one that matched the woodwork on the couches. The corner had a dozen candles in wrought iron candle holders. Someone had replaced her carved wood crafts with bronze and black iron sculptures. The single thing that stayed the same was her copy of A. A. Aaronson's latest novel which sat on the coffee table.

When she saw the framed photos on the wall, she felt a little more assured it was her home. The frames were black wood, carved into roses complete with thorny stems. The pictures were of her and her parents and sister the last time they were together when her parents moved to Florida. Even the picture from her desk at work was on the wall.

A folded card on the kitchen counter read, "Anything that looked personal is in your storage locker in the basement." She couldn't think of who would have done this. She wondered if it had been James, but surely he would have found her first upon returning from wherever he went. She didn't know him that well, but he seemed too respectful of boundaries to invade her home and change it without her input. Maybe either Rick or Teresa was trying to apologize. Whoever did it, she had a bit of trouble appreciating the changes.

The country crafts décor that disappeared, Shauna wasn't concerned with, but there had been several things that had significant sentimental importance. Would whoever had redecorated have known that the three half burnt candles tucked behind her pink cat were a reminder of her first real boyfriend? Fear of having lost so much of her past overwhelmed her. While she'd long prepared for the idea of having to leave her past behind, when faced with having it stolen from her, she couldn't help but sob. Tears welled up and ran down her cheeks. She quickly wiped them away, fearing they would be blood, but they were clear. Tears were still tears.

The phone hanging on her kitchen wall rang and she rushed to pick it up, hoping for answers. "Hello?"

"Hey sis, I finally caught you," Laura's voice came through the receiver. "I got a new club for you to try."

"I'm not sure I'm up for it," Shauna said.

"You always say that," Laura said.

"You bailed on me at the Grue's Home." Shauna wasn't really angry but she was looking for any excuse not to expose her new self to her sister. She'd seen herself; she could see the differences, though they were minute. Her sister might be just too familiar with her to not notice.

"Yeah, sorry about that," Laura said. "My friends were creeped-out by that place's vibe. I don't know about you, but after being there, I'm a little more open to your crazy idea that vampires might be real."

"Um," Shauna said. Surely James' mention of discretion in his note implied that vampires guarded the secret of their existence. How long could she keep the secret from her sister? Was Rick lying just to scare her when he said that people who found out had to be killed?

A man's voice behind her startled her. "Shauna McAllister, I presume?" the unfamiliar voice said.

Shauna turned to see three people standing in her doorway. She didn't recognize any of them. One was a woman with short auburn hair dressed in a business suit and long skirt. The men both wore suits and ties as well. When she blinked, for a brief instant all three had a pinkish mist of light around them. Shauna sensed all three were vampires.

"Sis, I gotta run," Shauna said then hung up the phone. Setting it on the counter she asked the group that stood before her, "Did you do this for me?"

"Miss McAllister," the man said. "I am Edmund, Seneschal of County Chester. This is Natalia, First Minister to Countess Portia, and this is my assistant, Dean. We're going to have to ask you to come with us."

"Where to?" Shauna asked. Edmund's tone seemed more serious than polite.

"The countess would like to meet you," Natalia said.

Edmund gave Natalia a glance that told Shauna there was more to it, but she didn't want to argue with three vampires. With her new strength and speed, she was sure she could fight any three humans, but she didn't know how strong she was compared to even one other vampire, let alone three.

Shauna gestured to her door. "I guess I'm coming with you."

§

Edmund insisted she ride with them. The drive was short; they didn't leave the city. The car pulled up to the front door of an art museum Shauna hadn't visited since college. On her way up the stairs Shauna noticed the building didn't have a single window. She knew that art museums either had no windows or used special glass that filtered the light to protect the paintings. She'd never guessed the same concept could also be used to protect vampires. Natalia and Edmund led her to a central room.

In the middle of the room, a woman sat on a plush settee. The woman was clearly the countess. She had golden blonde hair spun into ringlets that draped down across a porcelain white body that was barely covered in a dress of layered white gauze. For a moment the countess caught Shauna's gaze then looked upward.

Following the countess' lead, Shauna glanced upward to a vaulted ceiling. The panels were very reminiscent of Michelangelo's Sistine Chapel, except that rather than tell of the creation of man, it showed scenes from history starting with the crusades. Between the beauty of the countess and the history overhead, Shauna not only felt small, but insignificant as well.

"Kneel," Edmund said. She noticed that he had dropped to one knee to her left. To her right, Natalia knelt on both knees. Shauna climbed down to emulate Natalia's posture.

The woman on the settee stood. She walked over and pulled Natalia to her feet. In a very soft, but almost musical voice, the countess said, "Please, leave us. I expect my uncle to arrive as the accuser. When he arrives, delay him."

Natalia stood and walked out of the chamber, closing the doors behind her.

"Edmund, you and Dean guard the back door. Rick is likely to try other means once Natalia tells him to wait," the countess said.

The countess watched the others leave before putting her hand out towards Shauna, "You may stand."

When Shauna took the offered hand, the woman tugged ever so gently. Shauna climbed to her feet without pulling at the countess. The aura she'd seen after her blinks glowed more brightly around the other vampire when their skin touched.

"Thank you," Shauna said. Being in the presence of a royal intimidated her. She didn't know whether the countess would have earned the position through some kind of battle or inherited it or if she'd been elected. All she knew was that at least two other vampires recognized the woman's authority. If nothing else, the countess would know more about being a vampire than Shauna did. "Is there some form of address I should be using, like 'Your Highness'?"

"There is," the countess said. "Let's not get too concerned with propriety. I am Portia Medici, Countess of County Chester."

"Isn't Chester County west of here?" Shauna asked.

"The mortal political boundaries are not the same as ours," Portia said. "County Chester is the territory between New Amsterdam and Columbia along the coast and extends west a hundred or so miles from here. We center our kingdoms in the population centers and extend as far as vampires chose to reside until we meet the borders of another kingdom. We call our kingdom a county because I prefer the title countess to queen, but I am a queen. The proper address is 'Your Majesty', but for you, call me Portia."

"Why treat me differently?" Shauna asked.

"For either of two reasons," Portia said. "A vampire died a couple nights ago. It is a heinous crime to kill another of our kind and the punishment is a day chained to the roof. I shouldn't have to tell you that no one survives that."

Shauna felt suddenly confused. She was being accused of some kind of crime? "So, you plan to kill me, so you're being nice." She began to wonder if the vampires at the doors were meant to keep her in rather than keep Rick out.

"That is one of the reasons," the countess said. "The other is that I hope it does not come to that, and in that case, I would call you friend."

It was an odd threat. Shauna couldn't fathom the two extremes or how Countess Portia conversed as if she were choosing a salad dressing and willing to accept whichever the restaurant had.

"Is there a way I can sway the result?" Shauna said. "I'd like to live, well, if that's what we do. Do we live?"

"You don't have to be alive to live, Shauna." The countess said. It was the first indication that Portia knew who she was. "But you are not dead, yet. If things go as I'd like, you won't be dead for quite some time."

Something about Portia's demeanor kept Shauna calm when all her thoughts told her she should be panicking. The words Portia spoke told of a life or death matter, but the tone of the conversation was welcoming. "You are a queen," Shauna said. "If you want something, can't you just have it? If you want me alive, why would you let me die?"

"Rules must be followed," Portia said. "If I make exceptions without clear reason, others will expect the same exceptions, which would nullify the existence of the rules. Without rules, there is chaos and I have no role in the world."

"Tell me what I must do," Shauna said.

"Tell the truth," Portia said. "If I understand what happened, I can know how your actions might have fit within our rules. Rick is out with Natalia, I'll tell her to let him in."

"You can speak to her from here?" Shauna asked.

"All of us can speak with our immediate blood kin," Portia said. "Surely you can speak with the vampire who made you."

Shauna hadn't heard any voices in her mind. She shook her head.

The doors opened and Rick and Teresa walked past Natalia into the room. Natalia followed with another woman at her side. "You?" Shauna said, recognizing the new woman as the driver of the sports car that had given her a ride the night Allison had killed her. "You were part of this?"

The blonde woman, who looked almost like a lawyer wearing a suit jacket with a long skirt, held up a hand and said, "Not in any way you might think."

Shauna blinked, checking the auras and the other woman didn't have the same pinkish aura as the rest of the people present. "You're not a vampire."

"I am not," the woman said. "I am Amber, the pet of the vampire who made you and he would prefer to not have his name mentioned if you haven't divulged it already."

"She has not," Portia said.

"Who made her?" Rick asked. He turned to Portia and said, "Nipote, justice requires her to share her bloodline."

"I know of no such rule, nipote," Portia said, keeping her tone light and friendly as she had all night.

"Nipote?" Shauna asked. "Is that a vampire word for something?"

"It's Italian," Portia said. "It means niece or nephew. Rick and I were related as mortals. He is my father's brother. The vampire that made me, also made the vampire that made Rick, making me his niece as a mortal and his aunt as a vampire. Speaking of my blood brother: how is Francesco?"

Rick grimaced. "You know my father and I have not been close in centuries. Last I heard, Frank was banished from New Amsterdam and looking for a new place to put down roots. Could we focus on the crime at hand? This shouldn't be difficult. She killed Charlie. My pet will bear witness."

Teresa glanced at Shauna and touched the lines on her face. They weren't as clear as Shauna had hoped, but they were still there. When her eyes met Shauna's, Teresa's gaze fell to the floor.

"Shauna," Portia asked, "Is this true?"

"I killed Allison because I needed to feed and she'd tried to kill me," Shauna said. It was the simple truth. Wasn't that what the countess asked for?

"And Charles Grimsworth died when his pet died," Portia said, nodding, her voice somber. "This will require an exceptional reason. Revenge is not going to be enough to make exception to our laws."

"I represent Shauna," Amber said. "I act as proxy for my master."

"So permitted," Portia said. "What have you to add, Pet Amber?"

"Shauna, how did Allison kill you?" Amber asked.

"With a knife, a cut to my throat," Shauna said. So much was happening she didn't know who she should be talking to. She kept her focus on the countess and, speaking to royalty, kept herself from mimicking a knife across her throat.

"And what does this tell you?" Amber asked as if there were some obvious answer.

To Shauna, there wasn't. "She was a mean bitch?" she ventured.

"I'm going to try this from a different direction," Amber said. "What book are you now reading?"

"A.A. Aaronson's 'Death by Daylight'," Shauna said. Then she saw the connection "Ah, I see. Allison was the Aaronson copycat killer. The first murder in that book was the same as Allison did to me. She even admitted that was the reason for killing me the way she did or tried to do."

"And Charlie was involved in this attempt to murder you?" Amber asked.

"He was holding me," Shauna said.

"You have no proof," Rick said. "Just the word of a scared new vampire and a pet of unknown origin."

Amber said, in a loud voice as if she knew she had the last word, "If Allison was the Aaronson copycat killer, Shauna was not just enacting revenge, she was upholding our laws against risking revelation to the mortal world."

Portia smiled and returned to her friendly voice. "If Allison was a serial killer, creating a trail for mortal authorities that could have led to us, it would be every vampire's duty to stop her by any means, including killing her. Charlie, as a knowing accomplice, would face the same fate."

"I require proof," Rick said. "I don't believe they were serial killers. We all kill, sometimes."

"But," Portia said. "To do so in a pattern, creating a trail, would be a crime in our eyes."

"And to that end, I require proof," Rick said.

"I do as well," Portia agreed. She stepped close to Shauna and grasped her by the shoulders. "You have ten days to bring me something to show Allison's guilt."

"Ten days?" Rick asked, incredulous. "She should be sent to the roof before the next sunrise."

"Begone, nipote," Portia said. "I am the countess here. I enforce our laws without need for your opinion."

Rick bowed and then stormed from the room. Teresa, who'd spent the night in silence, chased after.

Caught between being grateful for having time, and fear for maybe only having ten days to live, Shauna's first instinct was to run. She wondered how far would be far enough to be safe. But her sister was still in Philly and Shauna didn't have the money to travel. She'd at least try to do what she had to so that she could stay and keep Laura out of too much trouble. She asked aloud, to no one in particular, "Could someone maybe enlighten me as to what laws I am supposed to abide by?" The vampire society in the Aaronson books had a king and queen that reigned over the whole continent and the only law was to not anger the monarch.

Portia took Shauna by the hand and walked her around the room. She stopped by one of five pillars that supported the vaults of the ceiling. A large parchment hanging on the pillar had script written in blood, using a language Shauna had never seen. Somehow, she could read it and she did so as Portia read the words in her solemn voice. "First: Choose your royals and obey them unto their end."

She leaned close to Shauna and said, "That's me. In case you were curious my first edict is 'Don't kill me', which is redundant because…" Portia pulled Shauna to stand before another parchment on another pillar. "Second: Kill not those of our family," Portia read. She again spoke quietly to Shauna, "All vampires, collectively, are our family. This is the one you violated. I know you didn't know, but there is no clause to allow lenience for ignorance."

Portia continued around the room, barely pausing to read, "Third: Pets are family."

The fourth parchment said, "Fourth: Do not allow the food source to become aware of us."

When they reached the last column, Portia patted Shauna on the back and said, "And this is where it's going to hurt." She seemed sad and Shauna noticed the countess had very watery eyes. "Five: Those that violate these laws must spend a day in the sunlight."

"But," Shauna said. Wouldn't that kill her? "What if I flee the city, exile myself?"

"That would be worse for you," Portia said. "I like you. You were born in my county. Other kings won't look kindly on new blood in their lands. It is a careful balance we maintain in our numbers. We cannot have more vampires than a population can support. You inadvertently created an opening for a new vampire when you killed Charlie. I have three hundred vampires in my county, more than half in Philadelphia proper. If there comes a three hundred and first, that vampire will be sent immediately to spend a day on the roof."

"Vampire laws seem harsh," Shauna said. "Everything is a life or death decision."

"It's a precarious existence, having to feed on the human race," Portia said. "If they learn of us, we all die. For that reason, we have strict laws." Portia took both of Shauna's hands into her own then added, "I haven't executed anyone in a hundred and fifty years. I have no intention of ending that streak."

Amber approached and asked, "Majesty, may I get my master's newest child started on finding that proof?"

"I do still have questions about your master," Portia said then looked at Shauna. "Now, more than ever."

"I am a mystery?" Shauna asked. So much of what she'd become was still a mystery to herself.

"No," Amber said in a very sassy tone. "You are answers to a mystery your blood father would rather have left unsolved, such as his name. Do you understand?"

"But Portia is the queen, I mean countess," Shauna said. "Can't she just command our answers?"

"I could," Portia said, her voice back to charming tones. "But, that's not how we build trust in people we'd like to be friends with."

"And she's told you far more than you've known before now," Amber said evenly as if she were straining to remain polite.

Portia said, "I did learn a few things from James' new blood-daughter."

"You told her his name?" Amber asked Shauna.

Shauna thought back. It hadn't come up. She shook her head. "No," she said.

Portia sat back on her settee. "I don't think a vampire could live in my county for three centuries and have me remain unaware. I've known James' name since the days when he sat on Ben Franklin's Junto. I even know his face. He's particularly crafty and I've never been able to get within ten feet of him. I didn't know how pure he was, and I still know little about that except he's pure enough that his daughter is much purer of Venae than I am."

"Purer of Venae?" Shauna asked Portia.

Portia looked at Amber and said, "She will fill you in on the finer details, as will James. I am satisfied that you know our laws and I do hope you see my efforts towards friendship as sincere."

"I don't know who I can trust," Shauna said. She'd already decided to at least play along with Portia, but she didn't know if the feelings of trust she had were natural or caused by some enchantment of the countess's. Amber, on the other hand had done nothing to prove she was anything but a helpful aide. James' note mentioned her, but she wasn't sure she trusted James since he disappeared at a time she needed answers.

"You can rely on us both," Portia said.

"Yes," Amber said. "We both have your well being as a priority."

"Then tell me of Venae." Shauna said.

"As we walk to my car," Amber said. "Bow to Countess Portia and let's go." Amber bowed low then started walking to the door and Shauna followed suit.

"Venae is the essence in your blood that makes you a vampire," Amber said. "I have it in my blood as well, since I feed regularly on James' blood. It dilutes with each passing from sire to child."

"Like generations of vampires," Shauna said.

"Like that, but we just call it purity of Venae," Amber said. "Vampires of purer Venae are stronger and can lay claim to political power because of that. The aura you see when you touch a vampire…"

"The pink one?" Shauna interrupted with her question. With everyone being so secretive, she wasn't sure she should tell Amber that she could see the aura just by blinking.

Amber just nodded and continued, "The aura tells you how that vampire compares to you in Venae. Pink means they are not as pure. A white aura will tell you that the other vamp is close to your purity. A dark, blood red aura will tell you that a vampire is purer than you. Portia saw you as blood red, I'd bet. She'll want you as a friend because you are too strong to have as an enemy."

"You can see Venae as well?" Shauna asked as they left the building and headed to the street. Amber's red convertible sat by the curb.

"I'm just a pet," Amber said. "I get to be a little stronger, a little faster and won't age, but I am dependant on James' blood. In return, I protect him during the day and handle any business that can't wait until the sun sets."

As they got into the car, Shauna asked, "So I'm stronger than Portia?" She then remembered she could see the aura when she blinked and all the auras looked the same pale pink. "I'm stronger than all these Vampires."

"Your Venae may be purer and that will count for a lot, but these other vampires have something you don't: they've been vampires for decades or centuries. Age and wisdom matter as well. I know of a few others, but I don't keep tabs on the other vampires in town any more than I let them keep tabs on James. I'd bet Portia is five hundred years old." Amber started the car and made the wheels scream and smoke as she drove off into the city, towards the Delaware River Bridge.

"I can't go home, yet," Shauna said loudly, trying to make more noise than the wind rushing past.

Amber didn't respond. She just kept driving, looking at Shauna occasionally and smiling. When the car stopped in the parking lot at Shauna's, Amber said, "Conversation and convertibles just don't go well together. " Amber hopped out over the driver's side door. Shauna just opened her door and stepped out. Heading to the apartment building, Amber rushed ahead.

When Shauna caught up to Amber at the door to her building, she asked, "Is this you being impatient or protective?"

"I'm never impatient," Amber said.

"Then, protective much?" Shauna asked.

"It's what I do," Amber said. "Habit, really."

"I understand that, as a pet, you're James' bodyguard." Shauna said. "I'm not used to being escorted places. I did have plans other than staying home, you know."

"I know," Amber said. "We're just here to change then on to see your sister at The Mists."

"You tap my phone too?" Shauna asked. She'd believe anything at that moment. So much of what she'd thought she'd known turned out to be so different than her expectations.

"No, I'm not very high tech. I got Laura that job that James promised," Amber said. She gestured toward the apartment building. "I'd really rather talk behind closed doors. There are still secrets to keep and plenty of ears trying to make that hard on us."

CHAPTER 5

Amber insisted on being the first into the apartment. She checked the rooms before flopping onto the couch and picking up Shauna's copy of 'Dying by Daylight'. After opening the book, she said, "I'm not much of a reader, so please be quick in getting ready. The Mists is just a bar, not a club, so no need to go all out."

"Was it you that redecorated for me?" Shauna asked.

"Someone redecorated?" Amber asked. "I was wondering why there weren't any blood stains. Edmund usually does a good job of cleaning up messy situations. You should put his number in your phone."

"If I had a phone," Shauna said. "I'm in the stone age since my phone didn't survive my change. I just have the land line in the kitchen. Edmund says he didn't clean up here."

"Was it A. A. Aaronson?" Amber asked.

"Why would you suggest that?" Shauna replied.

"She was here," Amber said, holding up the cover page of the book. "It says, 'This is my first ever signing one of my books, so I don't know what to say…A. A. Aaronson.' At least this wasn't signed when I saw it in the trunk of the car and I doubt you ran into her at the courthouse."

"I've never seen that," Shauna said. She thought back; it had certainly not been signed the last time she'd read it. It could be shelved with her signed first editions, except whomever redecorated had removed Shauna's bookshelves and all of her other books. She had James' library if she needed to read, so the books weren't important. She still felt a little odd, almost violated that someone she didn't know had been in her house and made such sweeping changes. She liked the new décor, but it still felt like it wasn't quite her own.

"Go," Amber said. "Shower. Vamps don't sweat, but you still get dirty, especially your hair. And you'll probably want to redo your make-up. The Mists is not a club, but it's not fast-food either."

Afraid of running water, Shauna hadn't fully washed or changed her make-up since she'd awakened in James' basement. If Amber told her to shower, surely the water wasn't going to harm her. "I guess I'll be back soon," she said.

After spending just long enough in the water to wash her hair twice, Shauna took a moment to look at herself in the full length mirror behind her bathroom door. She'd lost weight. She hadn't been overweight before and she hadn't become as skinny as her sister, but she was trimmer or perhaps fitter. Her skin hadn't turned any paler and she still liked how it was completely free of blemishes or bumps across her whole body. That was one step of applying her make-up she could skip. After putting on her mascara, eyeliner and her favorite blood-red lipstick, she felt good to go for the night.

When she opened her closet, she discovered that most of her clothes were gone. She hadn't previously discarded any of her pre-goth era clothing, but someone had. In its place were two dozen lacy gowns and a few other outfits that epitomized the style. She picked a black and purple lace-frilled skirt and a black loose fitting, low-cut shirt. Once she added a leather corset that matched the skirt and calf high combat boots, she realized she'd probably over dressed for what Amber had called 'just a bar'.

Stepping back into her main room, she found Amber had changed into a tight black v-neck t-shirt and red leather pants with matching stiletto boots. She must have noticed Shauna staring; she said, "I keep a few changes of clothes in my trunk. James' activities often require several different styles in one night. It's not fair, really. He can get by in the same suit, but I can't wear this to deliver wine to high-end restaurants and I can't pull off a suit at a bar or club." After giving Shauna a once over, from hair to toes, Amber said, "This is a bit over-the-top."

"I seem to have gotten a new wardrobe from my unknown benefactor," Shauna said. "I may have gotten carried away."

"It's getting late," Amber said. "Almost eleven. We need to go, so no time to change again." Amber went to the door and opened it, gesturing out the door.

"Are we going to talk about what I need to know to be a vampire?" Shauna asked.

Amber closed the door. "James really couldn't have timed his emergency trip worse. James and I tend to not associate with other vamps. I've never seen him hold a conversation with another vamp on the subject and he's never made a child in the time I've been his pet. We've always stayed close to vamps, just anonymously. I'm older than I look so I've had time to learn some things."

"Can I ask how old you are?" Shauna said. "Could you be a hundred? How does being a pet work?"

"I was born at the tail end of the seventh century in what is now France," Amber said. "As long as I get a few ounces of James' blood once a month, I get to stay young, stay strong and stay fast. Vamp society is not as highly structured as Portia would have you believe. Everyone will respect her edicts, but only because she makes very few and they are not terribly inconvenient. Only two things can kill you, sunlight and decapitation."

"Wooden Stakes?" Shauna asked. "Silver?"

"Silver only matters in mirrors," Amber said. "You won't show up in an antique mirror where they used silver to make it reflective. I'm not sure why. A stake to the heart would probably hurt, but it won't kill you. I think it could make you go unconscious though by stopping your blood flow."

"My blood flows?" Shauna asked. None of the vampire myths had mentioned that.

"You have a pulse," Amber said. "It's just far slower than what you had as a human. Your heart beats slowly, contracting three or four times a minute."

"And food?" Shauna asked.

"People blood is all you can ingest other than liquids." Amber said. "All I really know is that you can't feed on kids or virgins."

"Virgins?" Shauna asked. The stories usually had virgin blood as being the sweetest.

"No idea why," Amber said. "I've procured food for James on occasion; he's very specific that virgin blood just doesn't cut it as food. As a new vamp, you'll probably need to eat every few days. You'll know when you get hungry. Just don't put off eating long enough to get too hungry." Amber opened the door again. "That's all I know. Let's get going."

"Um, okay," Shauna said. She was hoping for more, but Amber didn't think she needed it or didn't want to delay any longer so Shauna went out with Amber close behind. Again when they reached the outside, Amber went ahead, looking around.

§

The Mists was a bar in the basement of a liquor store just around the block from the bookstore where Shauna had recently worked. Most patrons sat at tables spread far enough apart to move between without having to bump on anyone's chair. A handful sat at a bar. There were several dozen tables, but only a few were empty. Classic rock music emitting from ceiling mounted speakers created just enough background noise to muddle the conversations at neighboring tables. All of the furniture, walls and ceiling were painted shades of pale grayish blue and the dim lighting seemed to also be filtered to a light blue. It had the effect of making most people appear almost ghastly white.

Curious, Shauna blinked and more than half the people in the bar showed the pinkish aura that marked them as vampires. She'd spent so many months fantasizing about finding them and here they were, only a few dozen yards from where she'd worked. Even one of the bartenders, a man who appeared to be in his late twenties with short brown hair and a blue shirt and tie, was a vampire. Laura worked side by side with him, also wearing a blue shirt and tie.

"I have to wonder if a bar is the best place for a girl like Laura," Shauna said.

"Mort, the other bartender and the manager, is a recovering heroin addict," Amber said. "He was clean for nineteen years before he was made and no, he wasn't made by the same one who made you. My master figured Mort would help guide your sister. The clientele here are generally of a more mature nature than the Grue's Home. Shall we sit at the bar?"

"It seems the best place to get a word in with my sister," Shauna said. She started walking toward the bar and Amber stepped in ahead of her. "I guess a thousand years of habit is pretty ingrained by now."

"My age is one of those secrets we can't talk about in the open," Amber said without looking back. "Your blood-father has reasons for his secrets. You've revealed several simply by your existence, but he knew what he was doing so don't worry about that. Let's try to keep the damage to a minimum, if we could."

"Another new friend?" Laura asked as they sat at the bar. "This one looks kind of vanilla compared to your new crowd."

"Looks can be deceiving," Amber said then turned to Shauna and asked "And which new crowd?"

"I wasn't always this goth," Shauna said.

"I remember when James commented on your dying your hair," Amber said. "What was that, four months back?"

That sounded right, Shauna nodded. She wanted to ask if her hair would keep growing and if it would grow back if she cut it, but those weren't questions she could ask where her sister might overhear.

"So, sis, what'll you have? We have these bottles open if you want wine." Laura pulled a small computer tablet from her apron and opened a page showing a dozen bottles of wine. There were no prices on the screen.

Shauna just put her finger down on the pad, accepting whatever bottle it landed on.

"That's fifteen bucks a glass," Laura said. "But, they're all fifteen bucks a glass. We do sell bottles too, but those have crazy insane prices."

The other bartender stepped up to Laura and said, "These two don't have to worry about the price. Whatever they want, it's on the house. Just put it in the computer under James Alden."

"Even I don't get free wine," Laura said. "I only get to drink it for free if it squirts from a machine."

"I'll just have the Amber's Ale," Amber said. "Tall." When Laura stepped away, Amber leaned to Shauna and whispered, "It's my own recipe. I took an interest in brewing back in the nineteenth century. I think I still own the brewery."

"Think?" Shauna asked. "How wealthy does an immortal get?"

"I don't know," Amber said. "James deals with the accountants and lawyers for both of us. We have vast and diverse holdings. You know that hypothetical model of compound interest about a dollar after a hundred years? After a thousand years, the result has something like fifty zeros before the decimal point. I'm fairly certain we're not that wealthy, but I don't think we need money. James' business is more of a hobby for him. A guy's gotta stay busy."

"I can imagine," Shauna said.

"You can't," Amber said. "You think you can, but you really can't. I hope that you live long enough to at least be able to imagine what it's like."

"What do you mean? Am I in danger?" Shauna asked.

Laura set their drinks in front of them and said, "I'd love to chat, but this place is kind of busy." Shauna didn't have time to respond before her sister went to deal with other customers.

"You're lucky to still be alive," Amber said.

"I know," Shauna said. "It's good James was following me."

"I called him when I saw Rick peer out your window," Amber said. "Whatever they planned could only have been trouble. But that's not where you were lucky. Odds are against even a healthy person making the transition."

"Oh?" Shauna asked. She remembered all the pains and could easily comprehend how they would often prove fatal. Before she could ask more, someone tapped her shoulder.

She turned to see the young man from the VIP room of the Grue's Home. He'd been the one to show her his fang insert. He looked different, more mature, with his shirt on.

"Peter," The man said, holding out his hand. "I'm Peter. You're Miss McAllister?"

Shauna took Peter's hand, gave it a single, gentle shake and then released it. "Peter," Shauna repeated, mostly so she would remember. She then asked, "Are you following me?"

"No, it's not like that," Peter said. He nodded to a table against the wall. "A group of us from the Grue's Home come here once a week or so. Josh, over there, claims he once saw a real vampire here, so we come to see what we can see. I just figured someone invited you and you didn't see our table."

Shauna looked to a table where Peter pointed but none of the others were familiar to her. "That seems..." Shauna tried to think of a non-insulting word.

"It's silly," Peter said. "Everyone knows vampires are a myth, but we of the Secret Society of Sanguinus have our dreams."

"No Lorna tonight?" Shauna asked, noticing their queen wasn't among them.

Peter shrugged. "She never leaves Grue's Home. She even lives in the apartments above. Several of them do. The bar owner, Rick, owns the whole building and likes to rent to his regulars. I think he's just afraid to be sued by someone who drives after drinking there."

Amber pulled at Shauna's sleeve, "We need to go."

"We do?" Shauna asked. "I haven't had time to even talk to my sister."

Amber tapped at her watch and said, "Trust me, we have somewhere to be, and it can't wait."

"Okay," Shauna said. She didn't see any reason not to trust Amber and she seemed very panicked by the time of night. She turned to Peter and said, "We'll meet again?"

"I'll see to it," Peter said. "Can I get your number?"

"No time," Amber said. "Perhaps another day."

"At least your first name?" Peter asked.

"It's Shauna," she said as she let Amber pull her away. When they reached the street, Shauna said, "I wasn't going to tell him anything."

"That's not why I yanked you out here," Amber said. "It's just past midnight and if you heard what I heard we have a place to start looking for evidence."

Thinking briefly about what Peter had said before James' pet became anxious, Shauna asked, "You think Charlie and Allison live in the building above Grue's Home? We should go check it out before the bar closes?"

"We've got to walk from here," Amber said. "Parking down there is difficult."

"I'm not running," Shauna said. "I would draw too much attention and I'd probably go too fast."

"We have time to walk," Amber said then added, "Briskly."

§

Staring up at the fire escape of Rick's building, Amber sighed and gestured to the iron ladder lying on the ground alongside the building. "That's not up to code."

"We could try the front door again." Shauna said.

"We got the apartment number for Grimfell," Amber said. "That's what we needed from the front door. Busting in would draw too much attention. We're going to have to break a window. From then we'll have only a few minutes to search for something to prove they were guiltier than you."

"But how do we get up there," Shauna asked.

"You could fly," Amber said.

"Are you being serious?" Shauna said. Flying vampires always seemed unreal to Shauna. She could never rationalize how such a feat would work and magic never entered into it. Whatever vampires were, she always considered them a scientific possibility rather than a mystical creature. Magic, as far as Shauna was concerned, was still a myth.

"Yes and no," Amber said. "You can probably fly, but it's not something you should try without training. I'm not one hundred percent sure you'd survive being splattered on the pavement."

The thought disturbed Shauna. "So, we climb?" The brick wall probably gave enough for her to pull herself with her new strength.

"Too slow," Amber said. "Throw me up."

"That's thirty feet," Shauna said.

"Yeah," Amber said. "If it were ten feet lower, I'd jump." She walked over and placed Shauna's hands on her hips. "Whenever you're ready."

"Okay," Shauna lifted Amber. She felt lighter than a volleyball to Shauna. "Am I really strong or are you filled with helium?"

Amber chuckled, "You are amusing. Now throw."

Shauna did, and immediately realized she'd overdone it. Amber careened upward fast enough that she would go over the ten-story building if she wasn't aiming right for the fire escape. When the pet closed with the iron grating, she grabbed the rail of the fire escape and flipped herself up and over to land on the platform. "Nice," she called down. "Now jump up."

More careful, Shauna's first hop was a few feet short. Her second brought her close enough that Amber grabbed her and pulled her onto the platform. Before Shauna could think about what they'd just done, Amber was running up the stairs. Shauna followed. Six stories up, Amber stopped. She pointed in the window and said, "Velvet curtains." She was about to punch the window with her elbow when Shauna grabbed her by the shoulder.

"At least check to see if it's locked first," she said. Lifting at the window, it slid up, tearing through a dozen layers of paint. It hadn't been opened in decades.

Amber stepped inside first. "Clear," she said.

Shauna climbed through.

The apartment was larger than Shauna's but not as well maintained. The paint on the walls was cracked and peeling in places. The furniture was mostly modern and arranged around a large television with several gaming consoles. Empty, cheap wine bottles were scattered about the room.

"Why would someone waste immortality playing video games?" Shauna asked.

"I think you haven't had time yet to understand just how much free time you are going to have," Amber said. "There are twelve or so hours each day that a vamp can't go outside because of that silly killer sunlight. James reads; I play video games. Half a century ago, I was bored senseless much of the time. You're going to need a hobby. I've gone through several: Blacksmithing, crocheting, raising hamsters, and hundreds of others. Eventually they get boring. Even James indulges me on occasion and picks up a controller. He's pretty good at the war games and you'd be shocked to hear him talk smack to the twelve year olds."

Shauna couldn't imagine. Her experience with video games ended after three failed games of solitaire. "So who lives here?" Shauna asked.

"You're lucky. Since James is Rick's wine supplier, I happen to know his clique. I'm guessing Edge," Amber said. "He's the newest of Rick's progeny with not even twenty years as a vamp. There's no sign of a woman ever setting foot in here. Rick and Grigor both have women as pets. Edge's pet is his buddy from college."

"He wasn't one of the vamps that ambushed me in my apartment," Shauna said. "That was just Rick and Charlie and another vamp with a woman pet and a woman vamp without a pet."

"Grigor and his pet Lily would have been there," Amber said. "Grigor is Rick's closest friend. The girl vamp would be Rhiannon. She doesn't have a pet that I know of." Once Amber mentioned the names, they sounded familiar.

"We should go find Charlie's apartment," Shauna said. "There's nothing of use here." She didn't like being in a stranger's place without permission. Her standing in the apartment killed the myth that vampires had to be invited in.

Amber opened the front door. The brass number on the door was a sixteen. Amber said, "Charlie's is close. His apartment number was eighteen."

The next apartment down the hall had the number seventeen on the door. Eighteen was the apartment after. "Knocking seems silly since we know no one is home," Amber said. She wiggled the door knob but it wouldn't turn.

"Do we just knock the door in?" Shauna said.

"That would be the easy way," Amber replied. "But it's loud." She produced two small metal tools from her pocket and knelt by the lock. She worked at it for three or four minutes before standing up and putting the tools in her pocket. "I'm better with padlocks, really." Then she punched the door just above the lock. Her arm passed completely through the door past her elbow. Shauna heard the click as Amber unlocked the door from the inside. The pet then said, "Subtlety and me, we're not always in the same place."

"I thought loud was bad," Shauna said.

"Shush!" Amber said, cupping her ear. "I don't hear anyone reacting. Still, a vampire might have heard that two floors above or below us. We won't have more than a couple minutes."

Inside the apartment, Amber ran off to check the other rooms. Shauna closed the door behind her, turned on the lights and looked around. She didn't know what she was looking for, but hoped she'd recognize it when she saw it. The apartment was spotless. The furniture was all black leather, but gleamed; it had clearly just been oiled or waxed. The whole apartment smelled like damp carpet.

"Rick is covering Charlie's tracks," Shauna said, assuming Amber could hear her.

Amber came back down a hallway into the living room and said, "Yeah, the place has been sanitized."

"So, this is a bust?" Shauna asked.

"If I were a serial killer, I wouldn't be stupid about it," Amber said. "Granted, in my time I've had situations where I had to hide a body or cover tracks. That's all simple stuff and I'm sure Charlie and Allison had a method for that. We're not looking for blood or a body or even a weapon. We're looking for mementos. They wouldn't be somewhere that cleaning would uncover."

"Mementos?" Shauna asked. "Like jewelry from their victims."

"Exactly," Amber said. "People, vamp or human, who kill for the experience, will want something to help recall that experience. I checked the jewelry box and either Allison didn't wear jewelry and just kept a box, or Teresa and Lily have expanded their collections. I suspect the latter."

"Something like photographs?" Shauna asked, pointing to a bookshelf of albums and scrapbooks.

"Not usually so obvious," Amber said before she looked at where Shauna was pointing. "I suppose Allison might have been a hobbyist photographer."

Shauna looked at the spines of the books. Most were dated with a season and a year. Those were filled with landscapes. One was labeled 'Mom and Dad's Wedding.'

"That one," Amber said.

"You're sure?" Shauna asked, pulling the book from the shelf. Opening it, she realized Amber was right. The first page had a page ripped from A. A. Aaronson's first book that described a murder with an ice pick to the heart. An instant photograph of a girl with an ice pick stuck into her chest was taped to the page. Shauna had to close the book. Though she'd killed and seen Allison die, it had been different, less disturbing, than seeing images of an innocent person brutally slaughtered.

"Vamps and those who want to be vamps don't usually come from close families," Amber said and took the book from Shauna's hands. She opened to a page in the middle. "And as a bonus, Allison and Charlie liked to pose with the bodies afterwards. I think this is all the evidence you'll need." After flitting through a few pages, she stopped and added, "You don't have such a pretty smile when you're dying. They even took a picture of you in Charlie's arms."

"I don't want to see that," Shauna said, turning away from Amber just in time to see Rick burst through the door with a shotgun in his hands. Having never seen a gun in person, let alone having one aimed at her, Shauna panicked and froze. Rhiannon came into the room behind Rick and stepped up to stand at his side.

Rick turned the gun to Amber. "I figured out who you are," he said. "You're my wine dealer's driver. Does James know you're a leech?"

"That's between me and my employer and my master," Amber said. "Call me a leech again and we'll find out how fast you can pull that trigger."

"I'd shoot you if I didn't think it might kill you," Rick said. "If you die, your master dies and Portia has to start looking for excuses not to kill me." He turned the gun back toward Shauna. "I'd like to see that book. Give it to me or your master's new baby will have a nasty case of lead acne."

"You're not getting the book," Amber said.

"I'm not sure I want to be shot," Shauna managed to squeak. Maybe a shotgun couldn't kill her, but she wasn't looking forward to feeling that kind of pain. "Do you have a plan?"

"Not one that doesn't involve getting shot," Amber said. "We can take it, though. It won't kill us, anyway."

"I'm okay with just hurting you, for now," Rick said. He pulled the hammers back on both barrels of the shotgun.

"Rick," Rhiannon said. "We live here. We can't have gunshots here or the police will have to come."

"Let them come," Rick said. "She killed Charlie."

"She's young and stupid to our ways," Rhiannon said, pulling her sunglasses down her nose and glaring over them at Shauna. "She's bound to mess up in a place less personal. Save your vengeance for a time and place with fewer repercussions. Best case scenario, if the police come, has you just causing the new girl some pain and the city yanking your liquor license."

Rick lowered the shotgun and turned to Shauna, "Take your evidence to your Countess. She may exonerate you, but I never will. They say vengeance is best served cold; I don't plan to wait long enough to find out if they're right."

"Come," Amber said, tucking the book under her arm and grabbing Shauna by the arm with the other. She walked around Rhiannon and out the door with Shauna in tow.

CHAPTER 6

"Where are we going?" Shauna asked when she realized they were driving out of the city to the west. She'd expected to go home. Amber had put the top up as soon as she'd put the book in the back seat. Maybe it could blow out with the top down; Shauna didn't question why. "We're not going to my apartment?"

"No," Amber said. "I doubt they'd go to your place, but I know they won't come to mine."

Glancing back at the album on the back seat, Shauna asked, "Shouldn't we get that to Portia?"

"Probably," Amber replied, but she kept going west.

"Should we drive the speed limit?" Shauna asked, noticing that even with her rapid perception, Amber was making her uncomfortable with the speed. The speedometer was pinned at a hundred and forty.

"Probably," Amber replied, but she didn't slow down. "At this speed they don't even try to chase you. By the time they get a helicopter out here, we'll be home."

"Why are you mad?" Shauna said. "We knew Rick was going to be a problem, but we got what we wanted."

"You got what you wanted," Amber said. "A part of me was hoping for a fight. A really big part. But no, Rick wouldn't pull the trigger. Do you know how long it's been since I got in even a little brawl? I trained for centuries, but I haven't even punched someone since 1896."

Shauna observed, "You're a little crazy, you know?" Agelessness would probably cause everyone to have eccentricities, and probably a bit of insanity in some way or another. She tried to accept Amber for who she was, but was having trouble not gripping the dashboard tight enough to crumple it.

Amber didn't reply. The rest of the ride passed in silence.

They pulled into the driveway of a modest family home in a development populated by similar houses. "This isn't James' place."

"I don't live with him," Amber said as the garage door opened. The garage was two cars wide and two deep. Amber parked behind another sports car, that one black. The limo was parked to the left. "We're great friends, but we need our own spaces. We discovered that in the first century together. His house is just past a line of trees out back. I can be at his house in less than fifteen seconds if there's something he needs me for."

Shauna grabbed the album from the back seat and got out of the car. As they walked from the car to the house, Amber seemed just as alert as she had in Charlie's apartment, scanning every shadow on the way to the side door.

"Are you always this paranoid?" Shauna asked.

"No," Amber said. "There could be some pretty vengeful people after you. Experience has taught me that it's better to err on the side of caution." As Amber reached for the door, it opened before she touched the handle. Immediately, her gun was in one hand and her other pulled Shauna by the wrist behind her back.

The black haired woman from Rick's club, Elsa, was standing in the doorway, looking very bemused at the barrel of the pistol aimed at her chest. "Experience?" Elsa asked. "Is that what you're calling me these days?"

Amber holstered her gun but kept her grip on Shauna's wrist. "I thought, when you called me yesterday, that I told you this is not a good time for a visit, Elsa," Amber said.

"When I'm out of wine, it's always a good time for a visit," Elsa said, stepping aside and gesturing for Amber to enter. "James' new daughter is of no concern to me. I have no plans to participate in Portia and Rick's family spat."

"Don't trust her. She's been here maybe once a year since she moved to Philly during The Great War. She's only here right now because you are," Amber said and looked back at Shauna as she released her wrist. Shauna took it to mean it was safe to go inside and followed when Amber walked in.

"Interesting," Elsa said after brushing against Shauna as she walked past. "One more of James' secrets revealed to me. Amber you really should just tell me everything. I'm going to find out eventually. That James was purer of Venae than I has never surprised me. That this one is purer than me should not be possible. There shouldn't be any vampires purer than the one that made me. He was of the Council and they purged all of their predecessors, which I now know to be a false claim."

"Close the door, Elsa," Amber said gruffly, leading Shauna into a room with two plush couches set across a coffee table. To Shauna she said, "Go ahead and sit down. This is going to take a while." After setting the album on the coffee table, Shauna sat on one of the couches and Amber sat beside her. "We're going to talk about this, I assume," Amber said to Elsa.

"I'll get the wine and glasses," Elsa said. She looked at Shauna and smirked, "I take it the twenty dollar limit doesn't apply tonight." She chuckled to herself as she raced off deeper into the house. She appeared within a few seconds holding two bottles and three glasses and then set them on the table. "I opened the cab almost half an hour ago, it should be drinkable; the other I just opened, so we should let it sit a bit."

"I should have guessed it was you," Amber said. "You redid Shauna's apartment, didn't you?"

Elsa feigned affront. "Country crafts? I couldn't let our newest vamp live among flat wooden cats and pigs. And so much plaid." Elsa shivered.

"How did you know where she lived?" Amber asked. "Or even that she existed?"

"Did you follow me home?" Shauna asked.

"No," Elsa said. When she talked, Elsa spoke with a peculiar aloofness paired with intensity as if she didn't care what anyone thought about what she said, as long as they heard it. "As I mentioned, you were not my type. I was following Amber. Let's go with: When she took an interest in you, you became interesting to me. I was seconds away from saving you myself when James swooped in and carried you off. But, I like it better this way."

"Why?" Shauna asked.

Elsa sat across from Amber and shrugged, "James and I first met when I first came to America in the seventeenth century. I've been after James' secrets for three centuries. I've only learned one or two in that time. Really, all I know is that he's purer of Venae than anyone else I've met and that he does not radiate the aura, so we can't tell just by looking or even touching that he's a vamp, let alone tell how old he really is." She looked at Shauna and said, "Did you know Amber is thirteen hundred and twenty nine?"

Shauna nodded. "She's mentioned it. I usually thought of vampires' ages as a century or two with the really old ones being five or six hundred years old. I'd never considered they could be that old. I had always been of the belief that Vlad had been the first."

"Not by a long ways, though to listen to him, Vlad believed he was." Elsa took a sip of her wine. "When he made me, he was convinced he got his powers by having killed so many people. Sometimes he remembered the truth, but as the centuries passed, he forgot the stories of the woman who made him and simply recalled becoming a god among men."

"He'd mellowed out by the time I was born," Elsa went on. "He was, by the history books, dead, but he still pulled the strings on the politics of the Voivods. I was nineteen when he made me his pet. For the next three decades or so, he lived in our catacombs, running the country, using me as his envoy to the current Voivods. When my husband died, Vlad turned me."

"Elsa?" Shauna said, "As in Elizabeth? As in Elizabeth Bathory?"

"The Blood Queen of Transylvania." Elsa nodded. "The numbers are exaggerated, and I only bathed in blood once, and it was lambs' blood. I'd forgotten to close my curtains one morning and the sunlight hit me for a few seconds. I needed to heal my skin more quickly and thought it might help. It didn't. Of course, the Hapsburgs exaggerated the story and added a few missing girls to my list of crimes. In truth, some people went missing due to my maker's feeding over the course of thirty some years. None of them were maidens. Didn't Amber tell you? Virgin blood is useless to us."

"I've been over the basics," Amber said.

"And I do know the five laws," Shauna said.

"Right." Elsa sighed deeply. "Vampires are creatures of impurity. We are neither alive nor dead, but something else. That which is completely pure abhors our being. Virgins, for example, naturally avoid us and their blood provides no nutrients for us. Some vampires are actually allergic, some very."

By the way Elsa spoke, Shauna got the impression that Elsa knew more about vampires than Amber, or at least she knew more than Amber would share. The other vampire also seemed to enjoy talking. "So, what else do I need to know?" Shauna asked. "What can I do as a vampire?"

"I don't know," Elsa said.

"Every vampire is different," Amber said. "They inherit their abilities from the vampire who made them."

"Every vampire tends to have a little less power than their parent. The Venae in their blood is less pure," Elsa said as she poured the wine. "Some vamps are so impure they are barely unaging."

Shauna took the glass in front of her and sipped. She'd never tasted so many flavors in wine. Before she'd turned, wine was simply a more acrid grape juice. The wine Elsa had poured her had cherry juice and a few spices added.

"Wine thins your blood and preserves the Venae," Elsa said. "It lets you go longer between feedings."

"Wouldn't any alcohol work?" Shauna asked.

"The stronger stuff is more destructive to the blood than thinning," Elsa said. "Beer works, but you don't need so much water and it doesn't taste good. Avoid the mixed drinks. Vodka, for example, will make you very drunk and very hungry."

"So you're saying that wine is the reason that vampires are mostly European?" Shauna said. She couldn't recall any non-Mediterranean sources for anything but alcohol derived from grains.

"I'd never made that connection," Elsa said. "It actually makes sense."

Amber hadn't touched her wine. She'd been glaring at Elsa for several minutes. "Fine," she finally said. "I'll let you tutor Shauna. Only because she needs a vampire mentor and you already know more about James than anyone else. But anything you learn stays in your own dysfunctional brain."

"That's fantastic," Elsa said. "Where shall we start? Should we see if she can fly?"

"Douglas Adams wrote that flying was the art of throwing yourself at the ground and missing," Shauna said.

"Not quite," Elsa said. She set her empty glass on the table in front of Shauna. "Let's start with apportation. Without using your hands, pour me another glass of wine."

"You want me to use my teeth?" Shauna asked. She had never heard the word 'apportation'.

"No, I want you to use your mind." Elsa looked at the table. The glass on the table lifted an inch off the table and hovered its way around the wine bottle before settling back where it had started. "I can lift a couple hundred pounds when fully fed."

Shauna thought about the bottle lifting off the table. It didn't even wobble. Remembering dozens of movies and books where the hero was trying to do something new, she tried boosting her confidence, muttering, "I can do this."

Elsa leaned forward and said in a soothing tone, "Don't just try to make it move, imagine reaching out with an imaginary hand and manipulating it."

Shauna closed her eyes and imagined reaching out and grabbing the wine bottle. When she did, she felt as if she had another hand. She felt something jar against her imaginary fingers and opened her eyes to see Amber holding the wine bottle.

The pet said, "Keep your eyes open, spilled wine is hellish to get out of the carpet."

"I did something?" Shauna asked.

"Yes," Elsa said. "Now this time, watch as you do it."

Shauna again imagined the hand reaching out and grabbing the wine bottle. She could feel her fingers grasp the smooth glass. With little effort, she was able to lift it up and pour half a cup for Elsa.

"That's apportation; it's a rare gift, usually only associated with people in the lineages of Dracul or Artemis. I know James is neither because Dracul is my line and Artemis is an all female line." Elsa said.

Amber said, "Learn what you will, Elsa, but you agreed to keep the secrets."

"I promise this is only to sate my own curiosity," Elsa said. Then looking at Shauna added, "And to help a fellow vampire out. Now, imagine using apportation against the ground."

"I don't know how strong I am, what if I push the Earth out of orbit?" Shauna asked.

"Apportation uses a mystical arm that has a very physical connection to you," Elsa said. "Newton's laws apply. If your hundred and twenty pound self pushes against the billions and billions of tons of a planet that we live on, it's not the planet that's going to move."

"So that's how we fly," Shauna said. She reached out with her mystical hand and pushed against the floor. Her body lifted off the couch.

"James picked a smart one," Elsa said. She picked up her glass and drank the whole thing. "Portia is coming," she said. She then got up and ran into the wall, passing through it like a ghost.

"Phasing," Amber said. "Yes, you can probably do that too. No, we are not going to try it tonight. Let's see what the countess wants." She walked out of the room. Shauna followed.

Amber opened the front door as the doorbell rang. Portia stood outside with two people behind her. Shauna recognized Natalia, but not the woman behind Portia. That woman was not a vampire.

"Your Majesty, you know where I live?" Amber asked the countess.

"Over the course of the years, I learn things," Portia said. "One of the things I learned was to stop trying to follow you to your master. Nine vampires just vanished off the planet after I assigned them that task. One of them managed to get as far as this house before disappearing. That was fifteen years ago. I decided not to try again after that."

"My master wouldn't appreciate those accusations," Amber said. "My understanding is that eight of those nine hastily relocated to New Zealand."

"I accuse no one of anything," Portia said. "There is no evidence of any crime. I am here to beg assistance from our newest sister and to see the book Rick called me about."

Using her apportation hand, Shauna picked the book up and placed it in Portia's hands.

Portia handed the book to the human woman then said to Shauna, "Rachel is nothing to worry about. She's a lawyer, one of the first women to graduate from Cambridge Law. Natalia already knows my plans for you." She sat on the couch and then patted her hand on the couch cushion to her left. "Come, sit."

Shauna obeyed the order and sat beside the countess.

Portia dropped her voice to a nearly silent whisper. "Charlie was not the only vampire to die this week."

Amber said, "Elsa mentioned Katrina and Benjamin. She assumed Katrina was a suicide by sunlight and Benjamin's pet finally turned on him."

"Natalia," Portia said. "Tell Amber of Edmund's report."

Portia's assistant said, "Our rapid and thorough desiccation upon death has helped conceal our existence over the centuries, but it also leaves little evidence when we need to investigate a death. Edmund found hemp strands at Katrina's. Basically, unless Katrina was wearing a dress of rough hemp, she was dragged from her house by a rope. Coincidentally, and I'm being sarcastic, the same hemp dress had also been rubbed forcibly around a tree trunk in her front yard."

Amber said, "So they ran a rope from a truck bumper, around a tree and around Katrina and drove her out to the sunlight."

"That's the theory," Portia said, her voice low and even, not at all the sweet voice she'd used at the museum.

"That's a hunter tactic," Amber said. "We have a genuine vampire hunter in Philly."

"Yes, but that's only part of the problem," Natalia said. "Benjamin was killed when his pet leapt off his balcony and expired on the sidewalk, only Benjamin's pet was so drained of blood, he didn't leave much of a splatter."

"That's not a hunter tactic," Shauna ventured. "Unless there are vampire hunters who are vampires themselves."

"Unlikely," Natasha said.

"A hunter is not a problem," Amber said. "They rarely succeed more than once. I think I've only heard of one hunter living long enough to make a name for himself."

"Henry the Inquisitor," Portia said. "Yes, we have reason to believe he is in town. And two unrelated deaths is nothing to gain too much attention, but earlier tonight, Lord Jon, our emissary to the Council, was visiting some old friends at Valley Forge when he was beheaded by a man fitting the description of Henry the Inquisitor. Through some miracle, his pet Anna, who witnessed the attack, survived her master's passing. She tells of Henry having assistants, one of whom Jon killed and the other wounded before he fell."

"That's twice this council was mentioned tonight. What is it?" Shauna asked.

Portia said to Amber, "Allow me." She then turned to Shauna and said, "Over a thousand years ago, a group of vampires decided they were going to conquer the world. These disagreed with the traditions and the five laws and rose up against the even older and purer vampires who'd established the laws. So the younger vamps—and these were very pure by today's standards, far purer than any alive today—started systematically killing the vampires purer than they so they could take the power over all vamps unto themselves. Let's just say the war was long and bloody and went poorly for everyone. At the end of the war in the fourteenth century, the eldest vampires left were ten generations removed from the ones that started the war. About a dozen of these, all of similar purity of Venae, established themselves as the Council of Elders."

Portia took a glass from the table and filled it with wine. She drank half of it then continued, "All vampires alive today are descended from one of six of the vampires of the Council of Elders. The other bloodlines died out. I am significantly diluted of Venae from the vampires of the council, but not all of the vampires in the city are so impure."

"Elsa," Shauna said, remembering her relationship to Vlad. "She's a child of one of the Council."

Portia nodded. "Most of the current council members are not the same that founded it. Elsa is the daughter of one who did. She is one of eight vampires in Country Chester who could make an arguable claim to my crown if they so chose. The three vamps who died this week were among those eight. That is no coincidence and hunters do not start with the potent vampires, not even Henry the Inquisitor. His usual modus operandi is to arrive in a town, take out half a dozen newer and weaker vamps, then move across the country to another town and do the same thing again."

"I get it," Amber said. "Someone is making an active play for your throne, but eliminating the competition before they go after you. This way their prey is more easily caught off guard. Ideally, when they do come after you, there won't be any other claimants to deal with after you fall."

"That's my assumption," Portia said.

"How could I help with that?" Shauna asked.

"Our kind are very tight lipped around me, very polite and proper, but mostly silent. There are six major houses and several minor houses. I am a Medici. We are of the Mascare bloodline. Rick and his friends are among the few others of my bloodline in this city. I rule here because the other five bloodlines cannot agree on who should attempt to overthrow me. I'm not the oldest vampire in Philadelphia, nor am I the purest of Venae. I am tolerated because I don't have a strong family presence to influence me. No one knows which bloodline you belong to, so no one is ready to completely alienate you."

"But you'll trust me?" Shauna asked. "We've met twice and the first time was to sentence me to die, well almost."

"I distrust anyone else," Portia said. Her sweet, charming voice had returned. "So, by default, I trust you the most. You solved the A. A. Aaronson copycat murders, so you make an adept sleuth."

"I only solved those by having a massive strike of bad luck," Shauna said.

"Your methods are less important than your potential," Portia said. "There are six vampires of sufficient Venae to challenge my position."

"I know of James and Elsa," Shauna said.

"And you," Portia said, "though your age would make you an unlikely candidate. The others are a fellow Mascare, Tureq, then Zahaira and Serath, who are both Zylphite. Rachel will text you the details of where to find them."

"You don't suspect James?" Shauna said.

"He's missing, is he not?" Portia asked. "For all I know Amber might just be another miracle survivor of her master's death. It's rare but not unheard of. Have you heard anything from James?"

"No," Amber said, looking very concerned. She pulled out a cell phone and flashed through several screens. "He hasn't responded to my texts. I've had no communication with him since the night after he made Shauna. But, I truly doubt he's come to harm. He often travels to obtain the best wines in the world."

"He usually takes you with him," Portia asked, "No?"

"Shauna needed a guide and he had to go," Amber said. "It's that simple."

"I do hope so," Portia said, sounding sincere. "I know very little of James, but he is a good citizen of my county even if he is off the records."

"Okay," Shauna said. "If I do this for you, what's in it for me?"

"I'll go along with Elsa claiming that you are her child," Portia said.

"Deal!" Amber shouted, slapping the coffee table hard enough to evoke a cracking sound from the wood.

Portia glanced at Amber then returned her gaze to Shauna. The countess' eyes were pleading. Shauna looked to Amber, "Why is this a good deal for me?"

"As James' child you are a curiosity, an oddity or a threat," Amber said. "As Elsa's you're just a new vampire of old blood. The vast majority of vamps will never notice just how pure your Venae is."

"She is purer than Elsa, isn't she?" Portia asked, but her tone said she'd just learned the answer.

"Fuck." Amber said.

The countess hadn't known anything other than Shauna was purer than she. Amber's being so eager to hide Shauna's purity, and therefore James', had given away the secret to someone who hadn't yet known.

"You realize that you are rewriting vampire history as I know it?" Portia said.

"And I wish you'd stop," Amber added. She turned to Portia and said, "We'll help you, but you have to agree to stop prying. James likes to keep his secrets."

"If Shauna agrees, you have a deal," Portia said. "She becomes officially the child of Elisabet Davlos and James is still just a wine merchant."

"I agree," Shauna said. She owed James something for saving her life and she felt guilt for the secrets she'd already exposed. "But, I need Rick off my back. He came within a hair's breadth of unloading his shotgun my way. I think he's still looking for ways to get me back for Charlie."

"I'll talk to my uncle," Portia said. "I can't make him accept you, but I can forbid him from threatening or harming you. He'll respect my wishes." She looked back at Rachel and asked, "We have what we need?"

Rachel patted the book, "Yes, we do. With what's in this book, I believe Shauna's vengeance was in the best interest of our society."

"Then we can go," Portia said, standing. Shauna stood as well. So did Amber.

"You know about us," Amber said, her words snappy and short. "No need to hide our existence from you, but James would be most appreciative if you didn't share. But, yes, you're welcome in my home any time, Your Majesty."

Rachel handed Amber a business card. Shauna read it while Amber examined it. It listed Pia Rosalina as the curator of the museum and Rachel as her assistant. "Call when you can so we can have your numbers."

"I'll do that," Amber said.

Portia thanked her and as she left insisted on giving Shauna a hug, during which she whispered, "I am giddy to think we will be friends." She then went to the front door. "Amber, I am glad we've had a chance to be more open with each other. I hope we can continue to do so."

When the door closed, Shauna asked Amber, "Is it just me or are all vampires a little gay?"

"That's a tricky thing," Amber said. "You don't have hormones like you had as a mortal. Your body is the shape it wanted to be by your human genes, such is one of the blessings of vampirism. It goes with the curse that you cannot breed. But you'll still experience pleasure in carnal physical contact. Vampires tend to lose the stringent sexual roles of human society. Pleasure is pleasure, intimacy is intimacy. Enjoy what you enjoy and be happy."

"I'm a mom!" Elsa's voice echoed through the house before she hopped back through the wall.

"I guess so," Shauna said.

Elsa hugged Shauna tight. "You have no idea how happy I am. I tried and tried and tried, but everyone I've ever tried to pass my lineage to, died. The change is not guaranteed to succeed, you know. And my bloodline is particularly harsh. I don't think there are more than a dozen of us throughout the world."

"You said you didn't kill all those girls," Shauna said, trying to sound non-judgmental. Was it murder if the goal was to give them eternal life? Maybe it was if Elsa was cogent of the likely outcome, but Shauna promised herself she would not judge.

"No, no, not all of them," Elsa said. "The numbers in the trials and pseudo history were grossly exaggerated, that is true. But, there might have been a handful over the years I was Elizabeth Bathory. And maybe another dozen in the centuries since."

"Don't you have vampire geneticists or something?" Shauna asked. "I mean, we have all this time and it seems money is not in short supply either. I'd think someone has done some kind of study on how stuff works."

"Vamps have tried," Elsa said. "I'm sure some are still trying. It's difficult because the laws forbid us from documenting our existence so all of our notes have to be kept in our minds and shared only verbally. What is known of our history is purely oral. It's probably reliable since most vampires live for centuries. Whatever it is that makes Vampirism work, what we call Venae, is not something anyone's been able to build a machine to detect. I'm a hobbyist when it comes to the history and the science of vampirism, but I can't tell you anything special. The Venae connects us to another layer of energy that's always there in reality, but no one can perceive it, just like a colorblind person can't perceive everything about color. No one can perceive everything about reality. We have control over some of these energies, such as that invisible hand you use for apportation. There is a science to it, but we have to just call it magic until we can find ways to observe and measure it."

"So, you can't even explain why we can perceive if one of us is purer or not?" Shauna asked.

"We can, and I can tell you there are about twenty gradations directly related to generational distance from the Council of Elders," Elsa said. "I can also tell you that the least pure of those gradations is as impure as Venae can get and still be a viable vampire. Our bodies are both decaying and regenerating constantly. The pureness of the Venae affects how quickly we regenerate. At some point of impurity it is no longer capable of keeping up with the decay."

"You know quite a bit about vampires and their history then?" Shauna asked.

"Not as much as I thought I did," Elsa said. "I was a hundred and fifty when I realized Vlad wasn't the first and that there were other vampires besides the two of us in existence. Realizing I had been so ignorant piqued my curiosity something fierce." She glanced at the window then at a clock over on the mantle. "Now, I'm going home for the day. Tonight, when I return, will you want a lesson on our history or one on how to enjoy your new existence?"

"Assuming Rick doesn't find a way to kill me, I have centuries to learn about the past," Shauna said. "I need to know how to live in the present. I am still having trouble calling it living." Undead seemed less and less of a term to apply to vampires as she came to understand them.

"We're alive," Elsa said. "It may not be alive in any traditional sense, but this is a kind of life." She walked to the door and, after opening it, said, "I'll be here tomorrow at nine. I'll send you a change of clothes." She leapt into the air, leaving the door open as she flew away.

Amber closed the front door and shook her keys at Shauna, "Do you want to go home? We only have an hour or so before sunrise."

"Rick still knows where I live," Shauna said. "I'm not up for another ambush." She planned to return to her apartment the next night just to change clothes, but she didn't foresee sleeping there anytime soon.

"I have a guest room in the basement," Amber said. "There is a tunnel there to James' place. I said we lived in separate homes. We don't live far apart. The tunnel is a little dark and wet, but it works. The spiders won't bite a vampire."

Spiders still seemed creepy. "Can you show me how to get there from the backyard?"

"Sure," Amber said. "Are you sure you don't want my guest room? If you're not tired, there's a home theatre down there. I have a ton of DVDs and every game console ever made."

"I bet you have more action movies than romances," Shauna said.

CHAPTER 7

Shauna woke in the lavender room in James' house. She found a change of clothes on the dresser as well as a phone. A note from Amber said she'd recovered the card from Shauna's old phone and that Elsa had sent the clothing. The outfit was a water-stained, lacy wedding gown with the skirt shredded to knee length, and a pair of white leather thigh high boots with ridiculously high heels. The gown was shoulderless, but there was also a pair of arm length white laced gloves.

Amber met her in James' kitchen. Because she still had work to do to fix the basement, she sent Shauna back to her house alone.

When Shauna got there, the doorbell was already ringing.

"Ready for a real lesson?" Elsa asked as Shauna opened the door. Elsa wore a black lace leotard that covered her from her ankles to her wrists and a cream gauze skirt that hung down to the ground.

"I haven't fed in days," Shauna said. "Not since my first. Should we start with that?"

"You don't need to feed yet, I'm sure," Elsa said. "Vampires of purer Venae need less. For example, I feed twice a month, but I probably don't need to do it that often."

"Aside from feeding, what else is there to learn?" Shauna asked.

"How to have fun," Elsa said. "And from what I've seen, you needed lessons since long before you turned."

"What's fun?" Shauna asked. Images of the tales of torture by Elizabeth Bathory ran through her head. She felt a little nauseous.

"I'm a traditionalist," Elsa said. "Drinking and dancing."

"That's it?" Shauna asked.

"Until you've done it as a vamp, you've never really done it." Elsa walked over and took Shauna's hand. "Come," she said and pulled Shauna upward.

Flying wasn't as easy as Elsa made it look. Mostly it involved lifting herself high into the sky then falling, giving the ground nudges to help her go the right direction. Elsa made her stay up for hours, teaching her to control the flight to make it smoother.

They spent much of the night exploring the sky above the countryside as Shauna learned to keep herself airborne and to move quickly across the sky. Staying up was easy. Adjusting her speed to stop in the right places took work. She could move fast enough to cause the already distressed fabric of her skirt to tatter further. She found that speed uncomfortable with all the fighting against the wind it required. She preferred to coast along just a little faster than a car.

They landed on the roof of a building somewhere in Philly. "That was easier when capes were fashionable. You could hold the cape out with your hands and control the glide better, but capes stand out too much these days." Elsa said then opened a door. The thumping bass of club music flowed out into the night. Shauna let her lead the way down into what looked like a large old home barely converted to a club. "This place is open all night," Elsa said. "They have bars but they don't serve liquor. You can bring your own, though."

Most of the people in the club were Shauna's age or a few years younger. The styles of dress were not all similar. There were kids dressed in punk regalia and a clear clique of goths, but most of the people were wearing jeans and t-shirts.

"Let's start small," Elsa said and took Shauna into a small room where only a handful of people were dancing. Several others were sitting on worn out couches along the walls. Elsa took her straight to the middle of the room and started bouncing along with the rest of the dancers. Shauna bobbed her head a couple times and then mimicked the elder vampire's style.

After three or four songs, Elsa changed her style from the bouncing to a writhing. "Watch and learn," Elsa whispered from an arm's length away. Even with the thumping music, Shauna could hear the words as if she'd spoken right up against her ear. That was a trick she'd have to get Elsa to teach her.

The elder vampire stared a young man in the eye and the young man danced closer to Elsa, attempting to match her movements. As soon as he was close enough that their bodies were bumping against each other, Elsa's gaze caught another man and he responded the same way. The third to be reeled in was a woman with long blonde hair. The three people danced as close as they could to Elsa, rubbing against her at any opportunity. "Now you," Elsa whispered.

Shauna chose a long-haired man who looked about her age and caught his eye as she changed her dancing to a seductive writhe. The man came over and tried to entwine himself with Shauna, but she pushed him back to arm's length and kept his gaze long enough to be sure he was snared. She then looked to a man who'd already been staring at Elsa and her from the corner of the room. He set a plastic cup on the nearest table and joined Shauna. Like Elsa, Shauna went with a woman as her third choice and selected a girl sitting on a couch who looked like a European model who'd been surrounded by boys and men. The girl pushed past her admirers to dance with Shauna.

The rush of having all the attention of three beautiful people elated Shauna. Someone handed Shauna an oversized wine glass filled with a bright red wine. It was a girl with blonde hair so pale it was almost white, and skin that was even lighter, who then stepped toward the wall with a wine bottle in her hand. An identical girl was handing Elsa an identical glass. She then went over and stood by the other girl, clearly her twin. The two girls bobbed their heads slowly to the beat of the music.

"Those are Jackie and Jonnie, my pets," Elsa said. "This is their house. Are you ready to go all out with this?"

"Dancing?" Shauna asked.

Elsa nodded then gestured for the door.

When Shauna stopped dancing the three people with her smiled at her then returned to what they'd been doing. Before leaving, one of the men leaned in and asked for her phone number. "Later," was the only answer she felt she could give. He seemed happy and returned to stand in the corner.

An eighteenth century style ballroom took up most of the first floor. A deejay was set up on a small stage at one end and several of the skimpiest dressed women in the club were dancing on a platform in the middle of the room. Elsa pulled Shauna straight to the platform and gestured to a very muscular man in a tight black shirt standing by its base.

The large man climbed up and tapped each girl on the shoulder, shooing them off. When the last of the dancers climbed off the pedestal, Elsa nudged Shauna to climb up.

Shauna did and waited for Elsa to join her, but the elder vampire just motioned for Elsa to dance. Suddenly, Shauna felt very self-conscious about being the center of attention. The other dancers had been beautiful and enticing.

"Dance, vamp," Elsa whispered.

The eyes of so many people in the room watching her unnerved Shauna. Her goth style didn't fit with what she normally considered a platform dancer.

"You're beautiful," Elsa said. "Everyone sees you that way. Dance and make them feel it."

Shauna let her body move as it had in the room upstairs, twisting slowly to the base rhythm of the dance music.

"Now make eye contact and pull people in," Elsa said.

It didn't take more than a glance at the men and women who were already watching her to make them move toward her, writhing to her rhythm at the base of the pedestal. She went around the room, meeting anyone's gaze that fell on her. By the end of two songs, the whole room danced with her, watching her, swaying with her.

The adoration was palpable and it felt great. For two more songs she rode the waves of desire her audience sent her way. Elsa pulled her down after that and walked her out the front door.

"Fun, no?" Elsa said.

As incredible as it was, more stimulating than Shauna could imagine any drug being, it had exhausted her. "Fun, yes," she said. "But I'm tired now."

"Tired or hungry?" Elsa asked.

Shauna thought about it and said, "I guess its hunger, it doesn't feel the same as when I was human. My stomach is not growling."

"You don't have a stomach," Elsa said. "Your organs are simpler now; I could show you, but it would hurt. It would heal, but it would hurt. You've got a heart, lungs, kidneys, a bladder and an organ resembling an intestinal tract, but it doesn't reach the usual exit.

"You won't tire like a person. You may have to train yourself to nap or sleep to rest your brain, but what you are feeling now is hunger. You've used a lot of energy. That charm we were using is not just because we're pretty."

"You're tired?" Shauna asked. "You only danced with those three."

"Three is all I can do," Elsa said. "You had two hundred charmed."

Shauna remembered what Amber had warned her about Elsa. "You bitch," her tone was teasing, but the sentiment was not absent. "You got me to reveal something of James." Shauna covered her mouth. "Oh crap, I just said his name."

"I knew his name, remember? I suspect you're also a little drunk," Elsa said. "But yes, you just revealed how potent James is, by showing me how potent you are. Amber is allowing me to learn what I can, that's my bonus for taking you under my wing. Perhaps charming is one of your particular gifts and you can do it with less effort than me. But I think it's a show of your Venae."

"How do we eat this time of night?" Shauna asked. "Or is your club a means to feed?"

"No, my club is off limits for vampires," Elsa said. "You'll find that most vampires prefer to keep their business and personal relationships as far from anything to do with vampirism as possible. Rick is the only exception I know of, but his blatantly false vampires are actually a pretty ingenious cover."

"Are there other clubs like this?" Shauna asked. She'd read of several all night clubs, but none closer than New York. "Or do we go looking for kids having a party?"

"Dawn is coming soon," Elsa said, pointing to where the sky was only beginning to lighten. "We're going to use my pets; it's part of their duties. Come back to my place."

Elsa hailed a cab. They rode to one of the few high rise condos in downtown Philly. During the ride, Elsa used her phone to send a text. "They'll be home shortly after us," she said after reading the reply.

The doorman at the building opened the door and said, "Good morning, Miss Davlos."

"Good morning, Bill," Elsa said as she entered with Shauna close behind. She bypassed the first set of elevators and continued to the back of the lobby where a single elevator door opened as they approached.

"Fancy," Shauna said.

"Enjoy the little pleasures," Elsa said. "Opulence is one of the little pleasures I choose to enjoy. Consider it highly recommended."

The elevator had white marble walls and a settee upholstered with dark red velvet. There were no buttons or displays inside. Elsa didn't sit, so neither did Shauna. The ride upward took a couple minutes. When the doors opened, they revealed a large open room surrounded by dark tinted glass.

"No walls?" Shauna asked, nodding her head towards the corner where a huge bed sat atop a raised step in the floor.

"I sometimes get claustrophobic," Elsa said. "Spend a few years holed up in a single room with only a hole the size of a brick to see the outside world through and you might find yourself feeling the same."

"Is that your shower?" Shauna stared at what appeared to be half a dozen shower heads hanging from the ceiling. An additional showerhead hung on a hose by a pedestal with a set of levers. There wasn't a shower curtain.

"I designed it myself," Elsa said. "There's a powder room behind the elevator and a galley kitchen back there too, but I don't go there.

The rest of the space was filled with arrangements of couches as if the entire purpose was to entertain. As if to reinforce Shauna's conception, her eyes fell on a round bar with enough room for a pair of bartenders in the middle.

Elsa walked over to the windows and stared out through the dark glass to where the sky was bright. "The windows won't let in enough light to be problematic for any but the weakest vampires. They're made of the same stuff astronomers use to look directly at the sun, only these windows are shatterproof and bulletproof."

"Paranoid?" Shauna jested.

"A healthy level of precautions," Elsa said. "That novel by Bram Stoker got several things right, including the existence of vampire hunters; they're out there and I am one of the people that is rumored to be a vampire. Occasionally someone manages to deduce that Miss Elisabet Davlos, or whatever name I use at the time, is actually Elizabeth Bathory."

"But the vamps all know," Shauna said.

"No, not really," Elsa said. "Portia knows and you know. I assume James knows. There are a few Elizabeths or variants thereof among the vampires of our county. There's no reason anyone would assume any of us are such a legendary monster, and James isn't the only one among us protective of his age. To the vast majority of vamps, I am just a purer vamp than they are. It's rare that another vamp takes particular note of when they are pure enough to pin down just how pure I am, which is all of about one in County Chester, and everyone at our level of purity has identities from their past they'd rather not make public, so we keep each other's secrets."

"So you're letting me know is in the hopes that I'd reciprocate?" Shauna asked.

"Exactly."

The elevator doors opened and the blonde twins stepped out. They immediately went to Elsa and hugged her. Each kissed her before backing away.

"Jackie and Jonnie, this is Shauna," Elsa said. "She's hungry after the performance tonight."

One stepped up to Shauna, so close their chests almost brushed against each other's, and briefly made eye contact before dropping her gaze and smiling. She said, "I'm Jackie, and glad to finally meet you in person. Which vein would you like?"

"Where is best?" Shauna said, wondering how much Elsa had been talking about her that her pet seemed so eager to be close to her.

"For efficiency and safety, go with the arm," Elsa said. "Necks should be reserved for people you don't want to survive the feeding. Your saliva can heal a minor wound, which is sometimes impossible to achieve when biting a neck. There are other places to bite if you want to have some fun with it."

"Will it hurt her?" Shauna asked.

Elsa nodded and said, "Yes, the bite hurts. Jackie and Jonnie have been mesmerized to always experience the pain from the bite of a vampire as pleasure. It is something you should do to anyone you plan to feed from. Has anyone shown you how to mesmerize or coerce?"

Shauna had assumed she could, remembering Rick forcing his blood smeared finger into her mouth. "It's been done to me when I was human," she said. "Do I need to force feed them my blood first?"

"Only if you want your suggestions to be permanent," Elsa said. "It's just like what we did when we were dancing. People in that hypnotic state are very suggestible. Now eat." She pulled Jonnie's forearm to her lips and said, "I wouldn't want to be rude by being the only one eating." She then bit into her pet's forearm. A small trickle of blood ran out from Elsa's lips, down her chin.

Shauna looked at Jackie's face. The pet nodded to her and held her finger on her arm causing her veins to pulse outward. The sight overcame Shauna and she did as Elsa had done. Jackie sighed in near orgasmic pleasure as Shauna drank in her blood. Shauna felt pleasure as well and her exhaustion faded quickly. After a few seconds, she released Jackie's arm. The wounds closed without her having to lick them as she expected she'd have to do.

"Good to see you are in control of your feeding," Elsa said. "I would have stopped you before it got dangerous for Jackie. I am very attached to these two. She reached out with both arms and stroked each of her pet's necks as if they were kittens. The pets reached out and embraced Elsa's arms and began kissing the inside of the vampire's forearms.

The three left Shauna and went to the bed. Elsa gave her a last glance that told her she'd be welcome to join them, but Shauna couldn't bring herself to accompany them. She was curious but lacked the desire. A couch with a view of Penn's Landing and the river seemed as good a place as any to sleep. As she lay on the couch, unable to sleep, she made a mental note to always bring earphones with her if she went to Elsa's for the day. It wasn't until long after the moans stopped coming from the bed area that Shauna managed to fall asleep.

CHAPTER 8

Shauna woke after sunset the next night to the hum of her phone vibrating. Realizing that she was lying on the bed with one of the twins cuddling her from behind brought a vague memory of Elsa carrying her to the bed. Reaching down to pull her phone from her pocket, Shauna felt a little relieved to discover she was still dressed. Elsa and the twins didn't stir as Shauna extracted herself from the one twin's embrace as she climbed out of the bed.

There was a text from Countess Portia. "Tureq is at Guisseppi's meeting with a human. Find out why."

"Received," was the best response Shauna could think to say. Guisseppi's was only a couple blocks away; she had time to touch up her make-up at Elsa's vanity. The elder vampire had drawers filled with hundreds of shades of lip gloss and eye shadow. The jewelry tree on the vanity had several pieces where the gems were larger than Shauna had ever seen outside of a museum. Perhaps they were costume pieces, but Shauna doubted it.

"Up so early?" Elsa said. "Do you have time for breakfast in bed?"

When Shauna looked back at the bed, she saw Elsa sprawled on her back with her head over the edge of the bed. The pets seemed to be still asleep, though they were cuddled together. Shauna said, "I didn't think I needed more blood yet."

"Who's talking about blood?" Elsa said. "I'm talking about your continued tuition in ways to enjoy your new life."

"I'm not that easy," Shauna said. She wanted to be polite so she added. "It is tempting, but I am working for Portia and she's sending me on an errand."

"She's throwing you in the deep end, you know," Elsa said. "Her excuse about the cliques was valid, so I can see why she's using you."

"I'm just talking to people," Shauna said.

"You mean vampires, and not just any, but the most powerful in the city--who might also be killers," Elsa said.

Since Amber had agreed to Portia's plan, Shauna hadn't thought twice about whether she'd be in danger. At that moment, she tried to come up with a way to back out of the deal.

"Who are you off to investigate first?" Elsa said. "I'd put my money on Zahaira--not a lot of money, mind you. I've never really trusted Serath either. There's something shady going on with him."

"I'm checking on Tureq," Shauna said. "Are you coming along?"

"Tureq?" Elsa said. "You're wasting your time. He's a pansy. Do tell me about his basement if you get to see it. He's never let me down there."

"I should go," Shauna said. "He's at Guisseppi's, which I think is about two blocks from here."

"Just to the east." Elsa pointed to one side of her apartment. "Go ahead and fly down. It's dark enough. Call if you need anything." She started rubbing the calves of one of the twins. "Just don't call too soon. Breakfast might take an hour."

Shauna opened a sliding glass door to a terrace. The sunset had passed but the horizon still had a few low bands of orange and pink. Spreading her arms, Shauna dove from the roof, imagining herself doing a swan dive. For a moment she enjoyed the sensation of falling before she took control and glided gently to the ground in the alley behind Guisseppi's.

Seeing the kitchen door open, she considered coercing her way through the back, but decided such an entrance had the potential to seem out of place and might draw attention to her. Her goal was to gain information without being noticed.

She walked around to the front of the restaurant and stepped inside.

"What's the name for the reservation?" A woman a few years younger than Shauna asked. The woman had a red shirt and long black skirt and matching tie; a tablet computer nestled in her arm.

"McAllister," Shauna responded.

After dancing her fingers around the screen of her tablet, the girl shook her head. "I'm sorry, I don't see the name. If you'd like to wait, we can give you a table if anyone cancels."

A glance at a crowded bench by the door told Shauna that any wait would take too long. She looked back at the hostess and read her name tag. "Amy," she said. Once their eyes met, Shauna added, "I spoke with you just a bit ago. You said you'd have a table for me. I'm sure it's just an error in the computer. Surely my table is still there." Shauna hoped she'd made enough of a connection for the suggestion to take.

Amy looked again at the tablet and nodded, "If we squeeze back a few reservations, I can give you a table. Come with me."

Following the hostess to a table near a wall at the center of the dining room, Shauna tried to study everyone who was eating. Though she hadn't met Tureq, he wasn't hard to spot. There was only one pair of men sitting together at a table that weren't leaning over the table toward each other. He was also the only one in the restaurant to show a pink aura when she blinked.

"Can I get you a drink?" The hostess asked.

"I'll need to peruse the wine list," Shauna said as she sat facing the men, though they were several tables away.

Setting a menu and wine list on the table, Amy said, "Your waitress will be here shortly." She then walked back to the front of the restaurant.

Tureq was the darker of the two men, maybe Egyptian, Shauna assumed. The other man looked like a typical American businessman. Both men wore suits, but Tureq had a black turtleneck rather than a shirt and tie under his jacket.

Shauna could hear them speak, but she could hear everyone else in the restaurant as well and had some trouble separating their conversation from the others. What little she could gather was that they were certainly doing something they didn't want to talk directly about. They only referred to "The service" and "The product".

When the waitress arrived, Shauna hadn't yet looked at the wine list. The only thing she could think to ask for was based on the amount of cash she had in her pocket. "Just bring me something dry and red and about forty dollars a bottle."

The waitress's eyes scrunched a little at the request, but she smiled and replied, "Would you like an appetizer until you're ready to order your meal?"

"Just the wine," Shauna said.

"I'll need to see your identification," the waitress said.

Shauna dug her license out and handed it over. Her hair was still brown in the picture. She realized that she'd look young enough to get carded forever which meant she only had a few years before she'd need a good source of false identification. Surely the vampires had a system. She'd have to ask Portia or Elsa about it later. Amber and James, being on the fringes of vampire society, might not be the most connected.

The waitress handed her driver's license back and said, "I'll have that right out."

Tureq had produced several photographs to his dining companion. Shauna couldn't get a good look at them from her position. She considered walking past them to the restroom, but though she didn't know Tureq and he probably didn't know her, she decided it was better to err on the side of caution and do nothing to draw his attention.

Shauna listened as best she could, getting better at picking out their conversation as she got used to the voices. Nothing they said gave her any hints as to the subject of their conversation. As she finished the third glass of wine,

Tureq invited the other man back to see his work in the basement of his shop. The two men then left the restaurant.

By the way they handled their conversation, they were far too paranoid or cautious for Shauna to even attempt to follow. Portia's pet had sent her a dozen long messages since the meeting. One of them contained the address of his shop.

She finished off the bottle, noting that a whole bottle still made her feel very drunk. Getting out to the street was more difficult than she'd anticipated. It was all she could do to keep herself from trying to fly just to prevent stumbling.

§

When she got to Tureq's shop, the man he'd been talking with was walking away. The sign on the door said the shop was open from nine am to nine pm or by appointment. Shauna decided she had an appointment. Rather than knock or ring the doorbell, she tried the door. It was not locked. A bell hanging above rang as the door brushed against it and again as the door closed behind her.

The salesroom floor was mostly empty except for half a dozen erratically, perhaps artistically, placed displays, each with a single painting mounted on an easel. The walls, however, were lined in framed paintings. Shauna didn't know enough about art to identify it, but she was sure it was all recent.

"Did we have an appointment?" A man's voice came from behind a door near a framed piece in black and red that looked more like graphic art than fine art.

"Yes," Shauna said. "I was interested to learn more about your workshop."

Tureq came out through the door and stared at Shauna for several seconds before saying, "I suppose telling you I am a reseller of art and not a creator isn't going to work with you. You should know that a person sitting alone in a restaurant with just a bottle of wine is most conspicuous to those of us who keep an eye out for others of our kind."

Shauna shrugged. "I just overheard you mention the workshop at dinner and it piqued my curiosity."

"Whose child are you?" Tureq asked. "You're new, aren't you?"

"That's not so important," Shauna said. "If you could just wait until after the tour of the basement, I might be able to clarify why I'm here."

"Portia, right? She only had to ask," Tureq said. "She is a Medici like me. We have no secrets."

He led her to an old freight elevator—the kind with walls that were more like fences. It wasn't even electric, just a thick rope and a series of pulleys. Tureq worked the rope, lowering the elevator to the basement.

Once off the elevator, they passed through a curtain of clear plastic flaps into a small room with shelves full of supplies. Another curtain led to a room that took up the rest of his basement. The walls were lined with paintings without frames, some Shauna recognized as great works of famous masters.

When her eyes fell on the Mona Lisa, she realized what was going on. "You deal in fake art!" she said.

"That's not entirely accurate," Tureq said. He pointed to an easel holding a half finished painting that might have been a Picasso or some other cubist. A full sized photograph stood on another easel right next to the first. A huge steel toolbox sat with one drawer open revealing dozens of neatly arranged brushes. "I copy art."

"You're a forger?" Shauna asked. "I think Portia might have problems with one of us risking getting caught for such a huge crime." When she realized she might have antagonized a vampire that might be far stronger and was certainly far older, she resisted the urge to cower.

"It's only a crime to profit from passing off the copy as the original," Tureq said. "I merely provide the service of generating the copy. It's a perfectly legitimate way to earn money when sales in the shop are slow. More importantly, it keeps me painting."

"Your customers are always the owners of the original?" Shauna asked. Her knowledge of forgery laws was non-existent, but she felt she had to at least pretend to be keeping up with the conversation.

"That's the only way I work," Tureq said. "You're next question is going to be what do they do with the copies. My answer is that it's not my problem or my business to ask. Some want a copy they can hang on a wall while keeping the original locked in a safe. Perhaps some keep the copy and sell the original and I can't promise that none of them try to pass off the copy as the original. Unfortunately I use a classic formula in my paints that won't show up under those lights art appraisers use, so it might work."

"So that Mona Lisa is a legit copy?" Once Shauna voiced the question she realized she had assumed it was recent, but it could be centuries old.

Tureq looked at the painting and in a wistful voice, he said, "I made that in the mid sixteenth century while staying at a home in Florence where the original hung on the wall. I've never had a strong muse, but I love to paint, so I am happy to earn some coin painting for others."

"So you're staying off the radar of the cops, then?" Shauna asked, wandering along the wall looking at the art.

"No, I am very much on their radar. I don't keep my work a secret. I'm even in the phone book under custom art reproduction," Tureq said. "The works you are looking at now are either still drying or waiting for their customer to pick them up."

Shauna stopped in front of a nightscape with the moon illuminating the clouds over a misty valley. She'd seen the exact painting in James' bedroom. Portia hadn't been kidding when she said he seemed to have ties to several vampires.

"That's a copy of a John Atkinson Grimshaw," Tureq said. "It's taken me over a year to learn to duplicate the way he managed to make the moonlight almost luminescent."

"Who commissioned this?" Shauna asked.

"A local wine dealer, James Alden," Tureq said. "He has a shop just down the block."

"He does?" Shauna asked. She scrunched her eyes closed, wincing when she realized she'd admitted that she was familiar with James.

"You know him?" Tureq asked.

"He is a customer of my bookstore," Shauna said, hoping to save herself from another reveal. "Well, my former bookstore. It's still there, but I'm not. He is a regular, buying several books a week. He did always seem the wealthy type. I think he even rides around in a Limo."

"That's the guy," Tureq said. "He's the most polite person I've ever met. I particularly like that he's the type to pay in advance. I'm in no rush to let this piece go, but if you see him, tell him his copy is complete. I believe he wanted this to hang in his shop."

"Like I said, I don't work in the bookstore any longer." She hadn't really thought about her lack of a job since becoming a vampire. As long as Elsa and James were providing clothes and a home for her, she didn't need much, but she would need some income. She was still out of cash and vampire hours and bankers hours didn't overlap. She asked Tureq, "How do we bank?"

"We're big on ATMs these days," Tureq said. "In the past we had to rely on pets to handle our banking, most still do. Most of us learn to adapt quickly to new technologies, but not all. I know a few that still complain about the horseless carriages. Me, I'm happy to live in a world where people don't empty their chamber pots in the street gutters."

"Thanks," Shauna said. "I guess we're done here. If everything is on the up and up, I guess Portia will be more at ease now. You weren't being secretive; you just have a very limited potential client base. I doubt there are many masterpieces floating around in private collections in this city."

Since nothing in Tureq's demeanor had indicated anything but a familial outlook towards Portia, Shauna decided it was time to express her true reasons for the visit. "You should be aware; someone is taking out older vamps. Portia says its hunters and at least one vampire working together."

"Or a vampire taking on the role of hunter as well," Tureq added. "I've heard of the deaths. You're here to see if I'm making a move on Portia's crown. Maybe you're here to dissuade me or even to take me out of the picture."

"I'm not the one killing vampires," Shauna said. That she'd killed Charlie didn't matter to the conversation at hand, so she decided not to note that she had, in fact, been killing.

"I am still curious as to who your sire is," Tureq said. "We're being friendly; there is no need for secrets."

"Elisabet Davlos," Shauna said.

"I don't believe you," Tureq said. "Elizabeth Bathory hasn't successfully made a vampire, ever. She keeps the same pets she's had since the early eighteenth century because she is afraid to try to turn them."

That he referred to her by her real name set Shauna's mind tumbling. She hadn't prepared for him to actually know her. She didn't know what secrets she had to keep if she didn't have to keep them all. "I'm just lucky, I guess." Shauna shrugged. "It was a situation where I was going to die, so it didn't risk anything for her to give it a try."

"Dracul can walk through walls," Tureq said. "It's a trait unique to the descendents of Vlad. You're new, so I'll make it easy. Just pass through the curtain to my supply room without moving it."

"I haven't learned that yet," Shauna said.

"Then it's about time you did," Tureq said. "Give your maker a call. I'm sure she can explain it."

Shauna sighed and pulled out her phone and called Elsa. "I'm being tested by an older Medici," Shauna said. "I need to know how to phase through walls."

Elsa replied, "You know that aura you see when you touch another vamp?"

"Yeah," Shauna replied. She hadn't told Elsa that she could see the aura by merely blinking.

"You need to move closer into the direction that aura comes from," Elsa said. "Just a little. Do it as you walk towards a wall. And jump through the wall, don't step. You want to be back, anchored in the usual dimensions, when you're feet hit the floor of the next room, otherwise you'll fall. If that happens, you're going to have to learn to phase swim, which isn't hard, it's just exhausting. If you find yourself stuck in the ground, phase back just a little until the ground feels like water and swim up."

"This sounds dangerous," Shauna said.

Elsa asked, "Who is testing you? You do know that is only something a Dracul can do. It's a hereditary trait, passed down through our Venae."

"It's not important," Shauna said. "I'll catch up to you later." She hung up the phone and blinked several times, trying to find a bearing toward the aura. She found a direction she could feel more than see where she could will the aura brighter. When her feet began to sink into the floor, she pulled back, stumbling a little to regain her footing. She glanced at Tureq then jogged toward the curtain. She leapt into the air and willed herself to slide toward the aura. She passed through the curtain, it felt like diving into a pool of water, only to find herself in air once she passed through the surface. As soon as she'd completely passed through, she willed herself back into the solid world. She landed on her feet and turned and bowed. She noticed the curtain swinging slightly. She hadn't managed to keep it from moving, but she had passed through it.

"I'm sorry I doubted your integrity," Tureq said. He didn't seem to adhere strictly to the requirement that she not move the curtain. She decided he was likable enough because of it.

"And I yours." Shauna said. "If you're not behind the killings, you're a likely target. The theory is that someone is vying for Portia's crown and doesn't want there to be any competition when the position opens up."

"I see," Tureq said. "It sounds like a good time to revisit the old country."

"Yeah," Shauna said. "Where is that for you? You don't look terribly Italian."

"I was born in Spain," Tureq said. "I know I don't look Spanish, either, but I am. I was born with the name Carlos, son of Carlos. From the house where I was born, we had an exquisite view of the Alhambra. There were always artists around, drawing and painting pictures of that palace. I followed one of them back to Florence and that's how I got caught up with the Medici family."

"In five hundred years, I wonder if my birthplace will be significant," Shauna said.

"Last I checked," Tureq said, "Philadelphia is very significant to American history."

Of course it was. It just didn't seem special to her because she'd lived there her whole life.

CHAPTER 9

After leaving Tureq's, Shauna had a chance to look around the street. Half of the remaining stores were antique shops. She'd been down the street a hundred times, but had only noticed that most of the stores were beyond her means. Before her change, it had just been a place to window shop. Who was she kidding? She was still too poor to shop there.

She'd intended to visit James' store since Tureq had mentioned it was so close. But, then she noticed the shop across the street: "Serath's Eastern Imports". She was about to cross the street when her phone buzzed. It was a text from her sister that read, "Come to The Mists, a.s.a.p."

She was in the neighborhood, so the walk only took a couple minutes. Inside, she didn't see her sister. She headed to take a stool at the bar and wait when Peter intercepted her. He was sitting alone in a round booth and waved her over. He was dressed in jeans and a black t-shirt and wasn't wearing any eyeliner or lipstick. It didn't look like any of the other vamp wannabes were around. Since her sister wasn't there, whatever she wanted couldn't have been urgent, so she went to sit beside Peter.

"I hoped you'd be here," he said. His smile was cute and it was a pleasant change to be talking to someone who wasn't hiding something or trying to kill her. Elsa was too friendly and Shauna wasn't sure there were any boundaries in that vampire's life. It was just a matter of time before Elsa would manage to succeed in seducing her. It might be years or even centuries, but the day was probably inevitable. The more she thought about Elsa, the more she wanted to think about Peter.

"I might be becoming a regular," Shauna replied.

Peter scooted closer to her, almost hip to hip with her and asked, "Are you drinking wine again tonight?"

Shauna saw no harm in playing along with the boy. Normally, so close to a boy, in such an intimate situation, her body would react, but she didn't feel anything. Elsa had been right and the subconscious reactions were gone. When she intentionally began to imagine the possibilities with Peter, her body reacted. She scooted closer to him so their hips touched and put her hand on his thigh.

She felt his heartbeat accelerate and with that came the smell of blood. Confused, she looked for the source of the odor and pinpointed a leather bracer Peter was wearing which was doing a poor job of hiding gauze wrapping underneath.

"You're hurt," she said.

Peter held up his arm and rubbed it, saying, "Sometimes the girls in the club take the role-playing too far."

Shauna's desire had changed, grown far stronger, but what she wanted was no longer intimacy, but blood. She pushed her way out of the booth then said, "I'm sorry, I want to, but I have things I must do tonight." She leaned over the table and kissed Peter on the mouth and when she was sure he was kissing her back, she wrapped a hand around his head and held him to the kiss for several seconds. When she released him, she instinctively took a deep breath.

"Another time," she promised then walked toward the bar.

She couldn't see her sister anywhere when she sat at one of several empty stools. "Where's Laura?" She called to the bartender.

The bartender came over and leaned across the bar toward her. "Hey, are you her sister?" he asked.

"Yes, is she okay?" she asked.

The man replied, "I'm Mort, I run The Mists. I noticed Laura acting high and confronted her and she denied it. We got into a pretty heated argument about how it's not my business if she's using. I'm no saint and it pushes my buttons to see someone fall back into addiction. I might have fired her, but when you find her, tell her I was just mad and her job's safe. She and her friend stormed out without her purse. I used her phone to text you. That was a few minutes ago. I just hope she's okay."

Laura using again surprised Shauna. When her sister was using, she dropped contact with Shauna and everyone else in her normal life. She wouldn't have shown up for work during those times. It meant one of her old boyfriends had tracked her down. Shauna mentally ran through the list of Laura's exes, but couldn't think of one that wasn't in jail or another state. She asked Mort, "What did this friend of Laura's look like?"

"I'd seen her before, but she wasn't a regular," Mort said. "She acted like a friend of Laura's. She sat at the bar and talked her into doing a couple shots together. I never even saw her shoot up or snort anything, but I did take a break."

"I don't care about when she got high," Shauna said. Once she was using again, it was too late for any easy fix. Laura tended to drop straight into physical addiction. She'd gotten clean before and would do it again and it would be painful for both of them. "I care who she was with," Shauna said. She had some new tricks she could use to keep unsavory types away from her sister. Some were admittedly more violent than others, but she tried to not think of those. She pulled out her phone and showed some pictures of Laura with friends. While Mort looked at the pictures, Shauna noticed the low battery indicator flashing on her phone. Hopefully, her old charger would work for it, if she could find it when she got home.

After the third picture he pushed the phone away. His hand brushed Shauna's and his aura flashed. Mort's eyes widened, but he immediately relaxed, perhaps more so than he'd been when Shauna arrived. "The girl was pretty, but she had scars on her cheeks." His fingers drew imaginary lines down his face to demonstrate.

"Teresa," Shauna said.

"Okay," Mort said. "Ricardo's Teresa? I'd heard of her, but don't remember anyone talking about scars."

"They're new," Shauna said.

Mort shrugged. His indifference reassured Shauna that her sister's well being had his attention. "So you know who her friend is. You think they went to Grue's?"

"I hope not. I'm not fond of that place." Shauna replied. She hadn't planned on ever returning to Grue's Home.

"I hear that," Mort said. "Back when I was married my wife used to always say the last place she wanted to find me was my dealer's house and yet, she too often did."

"Rick is a dealer?" Shauna asked.

"I don't know that," Mort said. "You're new around here. I don't know where you're from but, around here, it would be unusual for one of us to be into the drug trade."

"Thanks, Mort," Shauna said then turned and jogged toward the door. It was all she could do to jog at a human speed and not run as fast as she could. Teresa's interest in Laura would not be a coincidence. Once outside she ran to an alley and lifted herself into the sky.

Finding Rick's building from a thousand feet up wasn't hard. She landed on the roof and found the access door unlocked. Taking the stairs down as far as they went, she stepped out into Grue's Home through the hidden door by the rear exit. There wasn't a band playing that night and the music playing wasn't loud enough to drown out a conversation. When she stepped out into the main area, she saw only a couple tables with customers. She didn't see Rick anywhere, but Grigor and Rhiannon were at the bar. Their pets were all sitting together in one of the booths by the pool table.

Rhiannon pulled her sunglasses down to the point of her nose and looked over them at Shauna. "Trouble," she said. "Get Rick."

The bartender, Grigor, pulled out a cell phone and dialed. Shauna considered rushing the bar, but opted to respect the laws and not expose her vampness to the customers up in the booths. She heard Grigor's phone reach Rick's voicemail. "That Shauna girl is in the bar," Grigor said then hung up the phone. He leaned to Rhiannon and whispered, "What do we do?"

Rhiannon shrugged.

"Give me the shotgun," Grigor said.

Rhiannon didn't react so Grigor stepped over by her and pulled a short double barreled shotgun out just as Shauna reached the bar. Shauna had seen the gun in Rick's hands before. Grigor kept the gun low, behind the bar.

Amber had mentioned two ways to kill a vampire and neither would be easy to accomplish with a shotgun. Though she had no desire to experience the pain of being shot, Shauna needed to find Laura. She said, "I'm not here to cause any problems. I just want to find my sister."

"No one here has seen Laura," Grigor said. "She's not a regular here."

Shauna didn't remember her sister's name ever coming up in conversation with the vamps. She leaned close to Grigor, placing her hand over his on the barrels of the shotgun. When his aura flashed for her, she assumed he saw hers as well. "Yet you have a gun in your hands and you somehow know my sister's name. Any pretense of ignorance is long gone. How messy do you want this to be?"

"Put the gun away, Grigor," Rhiannon said, her voice as monotonous as it had been the night Shauna had been attacked. "We can't shoot her with humans in the bar." She turned to Shauna and said. "I'm not saying any of us know anything or that Teresa had even been here tonight. If you are looking for your sister, maybe check the home of the person she'd go to for help. I'd hurry. Death is in the air tonight." Rhiannon pushed her glasses up her nose and turned back to the bar, drinking from a glass of wine as if Shauna wasn't standing behind her.

Shauna stared at Rhiannon for a moment then looked at Grigor, who was also staring at Rhiannon.

"Has anyone told you that you give away too many secrets?" Grigor asked.

"Call it a hobby," Rhiannon said, uncaring. Then with a little sardonic lilt to her voice she quipped, "Secrets are inherently boring. It's only in their reveal that the fun happens."

Shauna raced to the back door, moving as fast as she dared while trying to remain in the realm of human capability. Once out the back door, she flew to her apartment, landing hard on the balcony. She tore the sliding glass door open, shattering the glass with such force that it sprayed out, pelting Shauna's exposed skin. It felt like street dust on a windy day.

CHAPTER 10

Shauna found Laura on her couch, convulsing with a blank stare on her face. Shauna grabbed her sister and pulled her into a hug. "Don't worry, sis, you'll be okay."

"You got a shot of adrenaline?" Elsa's voice said from the doorway to her back porch.

"What the hell!" Shauna screamed. "Is everybody following me?"

"Sweetie," Elsa said, "I've been following you for a while. Ever since you started posting on the A. A. Aaronson fan boards about your theories of how vamps could be real. But, do we want to talk about my stalking habits or do you want to save your sister?"

"Call 911," Shauna said. She reached for her phone and was going to make the call herself when Elsa snatched her phone away.

"It's too late for that," Elsa said. "If you don't have a shot of adrenaline, you're going to have to give her your blood and make her a pet."

"Will it save her from a heroin overdose?" Shauna asked. Finding her sister dead from a drug overdose had been one of her fears since she'd first learned of Laura's addiction. Finding her dying wasn't something she was prepared for.

"If it doesn't kill her, it will save her," Elsa said. "Vamp blood is poison unless it bonds just right with a person. But, she's dying as we speak. A second ago her heart was racing. Right now, I don't hear a heartbeat. Bite your arm, I'll do chest compressions to keep her blood flowing." Elsa pulled Laura off the couch and laid her on the floor. She then straddled her and started pushing down on her chest. "Do you know CPR? How often do I do this?"

"I don't know," Shauna said. "I just bite my arm and stick in her mouth? What if she dies?"

"If the blood kills her, we hide the body," Elsa said. "If she dies of a heart attack, she might come back as a vamp. If she doesn't die, she'll be your pet. As either a pet or a vampire, her body will recover. The healing is the first thing to kick in as part of the physical change. Now, just bite your arm and feed her."

None of the options were good but it seemed only one had a possibility not to leave her sister dead. Shauna bit her forearm just below the wrist and shoved it up against Laura's mouth. Her twin began choking and for a moment her spasms got worse, almost throwing Elsa off of her. Laura then swallowed several times and Shauna could hear her sister's heart beating again at a very rapid rate. Shauna took a deep breath and sighed in relief. "She's breathing," she said to Elsa. "I think you can get up."

"I think not," Elsa said. "Remember how harsh it was to turn into a vamp? Turning into a pet isn't quite so horrible, but it's still bad and this furniture wasn't easy to find."

Shauna, realizing her sister was actively sucking at her arm, asked "When do I stop?" Keeping her new life a secret from Laura wouldn't be possible any longer. They were stuck together, which Shauna didn't mind. It would give her a reason to keep closer tabs on her sister if her sister still needed the guidance.

"You're good," Elsa said. "Now, grab a bottle of wine, something from the top right."

"I don't have wine," Shauna said, then, remembering Elsa had redone her apartment, asked, "Do I?"

"Your hall closet," Elsa said.

Shauna ran to her hall and opened what had been her linen closet to discover it had been converted to a floor to ceiling wine rack with two regions of temperature control. She grabbed the bottle from the top right and went back to Elsa. She handed the bottle to the elder vamp then went to the kitchen for a corkscrew.

Elsa took the bottle, gripping it around the neck with one hand she placed her thumbnail under the glass rim and flicked, throwing a ring of glass with a still imbedded cork flying across the room. "Vamp strength, gotta love it." She then started to drink from the bottle.

"I thought that was for Laura," Shauna said.

"Not this," Elsa said. "This is three-hundred-dollar-a-bottle Bordeaux. Your sister can recover on the boxed stuff. Want some?" She offered Shauna the bottle.

Shauna tried a sip and she came to believe that she was experiencing for the first time what wine should be. It was far more flavorful than any wine she'd ever tasted.

"I love the lingering flavor of chocolate and blackberries," Elsa said. "It's a little past its prime, but even so, this was a great year."

Shauna handed back the bottle and looked down at Laura. Her spasms had lessened into tossing and turning as if she were having a bad dream. "She'll be okay?"

"I think so," Elsa said. "You're stuck with her, though. You only get one pet at a time."

"So either I turn her into a vamp at some point or she dies and takes me with her?" Shauna asked.

Elsa shrugged. "In most cases, that's how it works. You can wean a pet. It takes months or longer, but it will break the bond without killing either of you."

"If I only get one, how do you have two?" Shauna asked. "Is it something to do with them being twins?"

Elsa took the bottle and drank quite a bit before answering. "There's a safer way to make a pet. It takes a long time of introducing larger and larger quantities of blood to avoid poisoning the person. They adapt better that way. I didn't even know I was dealing with twins. I thought it was just a pretty little magician's assistant. I learned the secret of the trick when I discovered I had two pets. I don't know why it worked, but I assume their being twins had something to do with it. You and your sister also being twins probably gave her better than even odds of survival."

"Jackie and Jonnie seem like a great pair of pets," Shauna said.

"That's not even their real names," Elsa said. "They're Russian, and I don't speak their language. I suppose that had something to do with my not knowing there were two of them. It took months for them to learn Magyar so we could talk."

"At least that won't be a problem with Laura," Shauna said. "When will she be better? It took me two days to transform into a vampire."

"Pets don't transform anything noticeable," Elsa said. "She could come to any minute or it could take a few hours." With Laura no longer moving other than her chest lifting and falling with slow breaths, Elsa stood up and took her bottle to the counter. She pulled a wine goblet from a cupboard and poured what remained in the bottle into the glass.

"Third row down, second in from the right is a pinot that's a little fruitier than this, but not quite as silky," Elsa said. "I suspect you're a little edgy from the sister scare. I promise to let you have half this time."

Shauna went to fetch the bottle, but called back, "You are a little too used to having servants, Blood Countess."

"Not so," Elsa called back. As Shauna came back into the room, Elsa said, "I just like to see what I can get people to do for me. It's the simple pleasures that make immortality worth living."

"So," Shauna said as she placed a goblet on the counter. "Tell me more about your stalking me for months on end." She took the bottle as Elsa had and flicked at the glass lip on the bottle. The top of the bottle flipped off, as had Elsa's. She'd seen a bottle opened with a sword at a restaurant once; she assumed it was the same principle. After filling the glass nearly to the rim, she slid the bottle across the counter to Elsa.

"It wasn't hard to track you down," Elsa said as she filled her own glass. "Your concept of how many vampires a city could sustain was frighteningly accurate. Since you used your work email, shaunam@stusbooknook, I had no problems finding you. The first time I saw you, you were talking to James, which gave me the impression that there was something special about you, so I kept tabs on you."

The realization that Elsa had been following her for months along with what she had learned of the elder vamp's personality made Shauna wonder if Elsa had orchestrated her becoming a vamp. She asked, "You didn't arrange all of this, did you?"

"How Machiavellian would that be?" Elsa asked. "I wish I could pull such a complex manipulation off, but I did not."

"Who are you?" Laura's voice was weak, but startled both Shauna and Elsa. "What are you talking about?"

"Um," Shauna said, not sure where to start.

Elsa didn't waste any time jumping in. "We were talking about vampires and how your sister is now one of us."

"Um," Shauna said again both nodding and shrugging at the same time.

"I don't know what drugs I was on, but you are both weirding me out a little," Laura said. "What do they do in those goth clubs these days?"

"The question is what did you do at The Mists to piss Mort off?" Shauna asked.

"I didn't do anything," Laura said. "Well, I did a couple shots of some fancy liquor with a chick with scars on her face. Teresa was her name, I think. It had a strong flavor, almost like black licorice."

"Mort said you were on heroin," Shauna said.

Laura climbed to her feet then flopped onto the couch. "Yeah, that's what he accused me of, but I didn't snort or shoot anything."

"Just the anisette," Elsa said.

"Yeah, that was the liquor," Laura said.

"Was there a bitter taste to it?" Elsa asked.

"A little in the after taste," Laura said. "Mostly it was just very strongly sweet."

"The sweet is the anisette," Elsa said. "The bitter was probably laudanum. I think your drink was spiked."

"Is that some kind of roofie?" Laura asked.

"No, it's some kind of heroin," Elsa said. "It was a popular drug in the late nineteenth century, usually taken in drops. I bet you drank an ounce or so."

"Are you saying Teresa was trying to kill me?" Laura asked.

"She came damned close to succeeding," Shauna said. "Which brings us back to what Elsa was telling you."

"This is Elsa?" Laura asked.

"Yes," Shauna said. "You can think of her as my mother of sorts. She made me into a vampire." If James ever came back, she'd tell her sister the truth, but, until then it would be best if she believed the story of Shauna being Elsa's child. Shauna lifted her lips to show her fangs.

Laura scrambled over the back of the couch and ran into the hall. She peered back around the corner and asked, "Are those real or are you just pranking me?"

Elsa flashed her fangs as well and said, "It seems your sister was right about us being real, and there are really just two ways we deal with people who find out about us. We kill them or invite them into the family."

"I don't want to be a vampire," Laura said. "I don't want to drink people's blood. More so, though, I don't want to die." Laura then stuck a finger into her mouth and felt at her teeth. "I worried for a minute you'd already changed me into one. Now I'm worried you're going to eat me."

"We saved you," Shauna said. "We're not going to kill you. We didn't make you into a vampire, but we did make into something a little different than human."

Laura started patting her hands over her body. "I feel human."

"You're my pet," Shauna said. "I had to feed you my blood, which creates a bond between us. It also makes you heal faster, which is what saved you."

"I'm a what?" Laura asked.

Calling her sister a pet bothered Shauna. Though Shauna was only an hour older, she'd always thought of Laura as her baby sister. Pet had distinct subservient connotations Shauna had difficulty stomaching. "Elsa," Shauna asked, "could you explain this?"

"A pet is what we call a human we are bonded with." Elsa said, stepping up to Laura. "Pets have many of the advantages of being a vampire, without most of the downsides. You're stronger and faster than you were and harder to hurt and quicker to heal. You don't need to fear sunlight like we do and you can continue to live in all ways like a human with one minor exception. The title may seem denigrating, but most pets are more like partners than slaves, though there are exceptions."

"You'll need to drink some of my blood from time to time," Shauna said.

"Just once a week or so," Elsa said. "If you don't you might die and if you die, Shauna dies too."

"That's a pretty nasty addiction there," Laura said. "It's ironic since my sister has been trying to break my addictions for so long that she gives me one that could be fatal."

"You were dying of heroin or something like it. Being my pet is what saved you. You won't age," Shauna said. "And you won't get sick. If I understand this stuff correctly, you won't be addicted to heroin anymore."

"The physical addiction is certainly gone," Elsa said. "Habits might be harder to break, but the drug may not affect you the same. You will metabolize it and everything else quicker. You'll also have to eat more and you can't get pregnant."

"I can't have kids?" Laura said. "I'm not sure I like the price of this life."

Shauna couldn't sympathize, but she knew her sister had always planned on a houseful of rug rats once she grew up. She never got the impression, however, that Laura ever had any intentions of growing up.

"The other option was death," Elsa said. "I'm sure whatever cost you think is too high, it's worth avoiding that particular alternative."

Laura looked at Elsa a moment then turned and walked down the hall. A moment later she walked back into the room, glared at Shauna and Elsa then turned and walked down the hall again. She repeated the pacing for several minutes before walking over to Shauna and looking very closely at her face. "This is real, isn't it?"

"Very," Shauna said.

"You're still my sister?" Laura asked. "You're not just some monster wearing her skin?"

"Sis," Shauna said, "it's still just me in here."

Laura walked to the end of the hall and back one more time before stopping at the counter. She took the bottle of wine and warily eyed the cut glass at the top of the neck before putting it to her lips. After she drank several gulps, she said, "I guess any life is better than death." Laura raised an eyebrow and tilted her head, watching her sister. "Now the question I have is: Why would that Teresa chick want to hurt me?"

"You saw the scars," Elsa said. "That was Shauna's revenge for Teresa's role in almost killing her."

"Yes," Shauna said. "We're not friends."

"But, you know her?" Laura asked.

"I do," Shauna said.

"You know where to find her?" Laura asked.

Shauna didn't like where the conversation was going but she nodded.

"Then it's my turn for revenge," Laura said.

"We can't kill her," Shauna said. "We have rules in our society, but the ones you need to know right now are not to tell anyone about us directly or indirectly and not to kill any vampire or their pet."

"But, I can hurt her?" Laura asked. "You didn't say I couldn't break her legs."

"No," Elsa said. "She didn't say that. It's considered bad manners but not a violation of our laws."

"I'm driving," Laura said, "Shauna drives like a puss."

Her sister hadn't been in a car with her going a hundred miles per hour yet. As tempting as it was to show Laura how little of a puss she'd become as a driver, she had a better plan. "We're not driving," Shauna said. "We'll fly."

"Are you freakin' kidding me?" Laura asked.

"Just a sec," Elsa said. She pulled out her phone and dialed.

"Who are you calling?" Shauna asked.

Rather than respond, Elsa spoke to whoever answered the phone. "Hey, Rick. This is Elsa. I just thought I should warn you that Shauna is on her way there and she seems a bit angry about what you did to her sister." She then hung up.

"Why did you just warn him we were coming?" Shauna asked.

Elsa smirked. "To make sure he stayed there and waited. He wants blood and if he thinks you're going alone, he'll wait for you so he can get some. He'll think he can use self defense as a reason to hurt you."

"I'm not going alone," Shauna said. "You're coming to help, right?"

"I wouldn't miss it," Elsa said. "Don't count on me in a fight. I'll help, but I'm not the type to throw punches. At the least, I'll cheer you on."

"Rick's been a vamp far longer than me, sis," Shauna said. "I'm not sure this is a great idea."

"He can't kill us either," Laura said. "Besides, I plan to cold cock the girl, I don't care about her vampire friend. After that, my plan mostly involves running away."

§

Laura gripped Shauna's waist tightly for several seconds after they landed.

"That was wrong on so many levels," Laura said. "It's just terribly unnerving flying without the wings and flight attendants and having to trust in your own grip to not fall to your death."

"You're plenty strong enough to hold your own weight," Elsa said. "If you'd fallen, I'm sure Shauna or I would catch you. It would probably be me since I haven't explained how to fly down faster than gravity will pull."

Closing time had passed an hour earlier so the doormen were not out front at the top of the stairs. The whole place was ominously quiet. Shauna still hadn't come up with a plan to do anything but yell at Rick and she hoped having someone as old as Elsa around would keep it from becoming violent. She hadn't figured out a way to keep Laura in check and she didn't want to coerce her own sister.

She led Elsa and Laura down the stairs. The front door was not locked. Inside, Rick stood alone behind the bar with Teresa sitting on a stool leaning over a tall cocktail, drinking it through the stirrer. Rick's pet glanced back toward the door when it closed behind Elsa.

"You said she'd come alone," Rick said, shouting to Elsa.

"I did not," Elsa said. "I said she was coming. I just didn't mention me or Shauna's new pet."

"The girl didn't die," Rick said with a bit of a growl, directing the comment to his own pet. Turning to Shauna he added with even more ire in his voice, "That's for the best; no need to waste life. Have you come to declare a truce?"

"I suppose I have," Shauna said. It hadn't been her plan at all, but once presented with the option it seemed better than waiting for her sister to punch Teresa.

"The countess did find Shauna's actions to be in the best interest of our community, and not only within our laws but actively defending them," Elsa said. "Still, if you two wanted to go a few rounds, I wouldn't mind pulling out a bottle and watching. Was James able to find more of that Bordeaux? I just drank my last bottle."

Laura walked slowly to stand behind Teresa, who then turned around and said, "For what it's worth, I didn't like the idea of drugging you. You shouldn't have been brought into this. But, I'm just a pet and a slave to my master's biddings." Teresa's scars had faded since the last time Shauna had seen them, but they were still clear.

Shauna had expected Laura to tear into Teresa physically, but instead her sister turned and asked. "Is this how it's going to be for me? Am I your slave now?"

"It won't be like that," Shauna said. "You're my sister."

"Portia made me promise not to hurt you," Rick said to Shauna. "Elsa will just have to be disappointed."

Shauna turned to look at Elsa who gestured for Shauna to turn back around, but when she did she heard the blast. "I didn't make any promises about your pet," Rick said to Shauna. Rick had fired his shotgun at Laura, tearing through the knees of her pants. Shauna started to run towards her sister, but her sister was just standing there, staring at Rick.

"Was that supposed to hurt?" Laura asked. She had no blood on the shredded cloth around her knee.

"Grab him!" Elsa screamed. She ran over and pulled Teresa from her chair and held her tight, pinning the pet's arms behind her back.

Rick stared at her, mouth agape. His eyes darted toward the back door and he started to run. Before he took his second step, Shauna was sitting on his chest as he laid flat on the floor. "Now do I get to kill him?" she asked. She didn't mean it, but had no idea what Elsa had in mind.

"Give him some of your blood," Elsa said then bit her own finger and jammed it between Teresa's lips. "You'll remember we came here and made peace. Rick fired his shotgun but only as a warning shot. He didn't hit anyone with it."

Shauna repeated Elsa's actions and words with Rick. Elsa then ushered Shauna and her sister out the back door.

"Will that work on another vamp?" Shauna asked once the back door closed.

"I can only do it with the vampires of the least purity of Venae," Elsa said. "Vlad spoke of the wars against his elders. Some of the eldest were difficult to kill because they could only be harmed with weapons engraved with gold. Those vampires could coerce other vamps, even those of Vlad's purity."

"Are you saying I'm that pure?" Shauna asked.

"I'm saying your pet is that pure," Elsa said. "That shotgun blast didn't even scratch her. You'd be much purer."

"What are you talking about?" Laura asked. "For the record, I got shot and it did actually hurt." She paused a moment before saying. "Well, a little anyway."

While the knee on Laura's pants had been torn up, there hadn't been any blood. It wasn't that Laura had healed instantly—the shot never broke her skin. "So I can't be killed?" Shauna asked. She'd understood that vampires didn't age, but being unable to die was a level of immortality beyond her comprehension.

Elsa shook her head. "We'd be having a completely different conversation if that shotgun had been loaded with gold shot. It's a bit harder, but not impossible, to kill a vamp of such pure Venae. There is always the sun, though. Amber is not going to be happy to hear about this."

"That we provoked Rick enough to get my sister shot or that we learned a little more about how pure of Venae I am?" Shauna asked. Knowing Amber, it was the latter.

As if on cue, a familiar red convertible pulled into the end of the alley they were walking down. Amber sat behind the wheel and called out, "Shauna, get in!"

Shauna looked at the two-seater sports car and realized Amber only meant for her to go. She looked over at her sister who was walking along just staring at where her pants had been shredded. "I guess I'm going with her," Shauna said to Elsa. "Can you take care of Laura?"

"Your sis will be fine," Elsa said. "I'll take her shopping." She turned to Laura, who was still wearing her bartender uniform, and asked, "You're more rock-star-wannabe than goth, right?"

Laura scrunched her lips and looked at Elsa with a raised eyebrow. "What kind of question is that? I just got shot. You guys are talking about Venae, whatever that is, and then you suddenly want to go shopping at this time of night? Now, your blonde friend shows up in a fricken Ferrari and offers you a ride. Who are you people?"

In the little bit of time Shauna had spent with Elsa, she'd come to know her well enough to not question the tangents of Elsa's thoughts. "Jeans and leather would make her happiest," Shauna said. If she'd had time, she'd have asked where Elsa shopped at three in the morning. When Amber honked the horn, Shauna looked apologetically at her sister then jogged over and hopped into the car, this time jumping over the door.

"Nice form," Amber said. "Portia called and asked how we were doing in our investigations. She says you weren't answering your phone or responding to her messages."

Shauna pulled her phone out and noticed it was completely dead. She hadn't charged it since Amber gave it to her. It had been part of her nightly before-bed habits, but none of her routines seemed to apply to her new life.

"So we go to Serath's?" Shauna asked.

"Sure," Amber said. "Zahaira lives too far out of the city to get there and back before sunrise. There's a charger in the glove box."

CHAPTER 11

Amber parked in front of the wine store over The Mists. The sign over the door read, 'The Wine Store of Philadelphia'. "This is James' shop," she said. "He only handles the imports and a few special orders. Otherwise you'll never find him here."

"I haven't found him anywhere," Shauna said. Down the street she could see Tureq's art shop and Serath's Asian Imports shop. Both looked closed, as any shop should be at four in the morning. "How many of the stores on this street are run by Vampires?"

"Well," Amber said, pointing to the various shops while tallying numbers on her other hand. "All of them except that camera store. James owns The Wine Store, that dance studio, the antique collectibles store and the book store. The other dozen shops are owned by ten or so different vamps, I think. I haven't been inside most of them."

"And other vamps don't suspect James is one of them?" Shauna asked as Amber led her up to the door of The Wine Store. She then realized one of the stores Amber mentioned was her old bookstore. "James owns Stu's Book Nook?"

"I just said that," Amber said. She unlocked the door and walked in.

"Stuart doesn't own Stu's?" Shauna asked

"He's a minority partner," Amber said. "I doubt he's ever met James other than as a customer. He just knows the Alden Investment Group owns a majority stake in his store. We don't really converse with the vampires on the street, so if they suspect anything, we haven't heard."

"And James had nothing to do with me losing my job?" Shauna asked. Inside the store was just three rows of wooden wine racks with a cooler along one wall also containing a wine rack. The only parts of each bottle Shauna could see were the corked ends. There weren't labels or prices on the racks either.

Amber sighed then said, "It seems it's a bad week for keeping secrets so I won't bother lying." The pet didn't say anything else. She rifled through some papers by the cash register and walked into the back room.

Shauna called back to her, "So by not saying anything about it, you aren't lying. Why would James have me fired?"

"I think he likes you," Amber said, walking back to stand by the register. She picked up the shop phone and hit some buttons before setting the handset back down. "Every decade or so he tries to have a relationship with a mortal woman, and it lasts until the subject of marriage comes up. Mostly they break up at that point. Once or twice he's tried to turn them into vamps, but that hasn't gone well, ever."

Shauna recalled Elsa talking about how rare it was for a person to survive the change, so she just nodded sympathetically.

"I'm going to make a call," Amber said. "I'll be right back." Again the pet went to the back room.

After a moment, Shauna could hear the pet whispering frantically. She couldn't pick out much of what Amber was saying but she got the gist. Clearly the pet had reached James' voicemail and the message she left seemed to both be worried for James and distraught over not knowing how to deal properly with his new kid.

When Amber came back out, she looked at Shauna and said, "I'm sure you heard that. Don't take it personally. This isn't like him."

Shauna thought she understood, but the pet's uncertainty about James wasn't reassuring. They didn't speak again as they left the shop and walked down the street.

Trying the door at Serath's, Shauna was a little surprised to find it locked.

"Ring the bell," Amber said. "It's not like anyone is sleeping in there."

Shauna pressed a brass button beside the door. A series of chimes went off inside the shop. A moment later the lights in the store came on and a man dressed in gilt Indian style clothing opened the door.

"Come in," the man said. "Sorry for the lights being off. I wasn't expecting you for another few minutes."

"We didn't make an appointment," Shauna said. "How would you know when we were coming?"

"You're not my four-thirty?" the man said. "Well, don't let me be one to turn away a customer. I am Serath. Welcome to Serath's imports. What can we interest you in today? A Ming Vase, perhaps?"

Shauna looked around. There were only a few dozen items for sale, each on its own pedestal. On the left side of the room, a dragon mask and two rice paper paintings were displayed on the wall. The other side of the room was mirrored from floor to ceiling along the whole length of the store.

"Portia sent us," Shauna said. The direct approach seemed better than trying to make small talk when she had a bad habit of letting secrets slip. "Someone's out to take her job and killing off the competition. The main suspects are, of course, the competition, of which you are one."

"Not even a pretense to commerce?" Serath said as if Shauna's words were discussing the weather.

"Excuse me?" Shauna said. "Someone could be trying to kill you."

Serath said, "Yes, Tureq mentioned you'd visited him. I have plans to go into hiding until the storm passes, but I wouldn't mind making a sale or two while you are here. We haven't formally met." Serath offered his hand to Shauna. "I've seen your pet before, window shopping, but I have not met you."

Amber hopped in front of Shauna and shook Serath's hand. "I'm sure Tureq mentioned Shauna and she's not my mistress." She then picked a jade bowl off of a pedestal and examined it a moment before asking, "How much?"

"Two hundred," Serath said. "That includes the family discount."

"It's a fake," Amber said. "This is manmade material."

"Of course it's fake," Serath said. "These are all first quality fakes. These things would be impossible to export from China if they were real."

"I have no interest in reproductions," Amber said. "If this were original, then we might have been able to help you out with getting some travel funds for your impending journey."

"If that were real it would be hundreds of thousands of dollars," Serath said.

"Tens," Amber corrected, "Not hundreds. Several tens, but tens."

"And you would buy it if it were original?" Serath asked.

"Absolutely," Amber said. "I love Jin Dynasty Jade. I remember the first time I saw it among the treasures Marco brought back. It was love at first sight."

"You're older than I if you recall the days of Marco Polo," Serath said. "Not many of us are that old."

"Or she saw the exhibit in the Louvre in the 1930's," Shauna said, covering Amber's slip. She had no idea if there had been such an exhibit, but hoped Serath didn't know there hadn't.

"You want to talk about exhibition," Serath said. He pulled a tiny fob from his pocket and aimed it toward the back of his store then pressed a button on it. For a moment, Shauna thought nothing had changed, and then she noticed her reflection no longer showed in the mirror, but neither did Serath's or Amber's. All of the pieces were in the reflection, but not the people.

"Neat trick," Amber said. "How'd you do that?"

"You assume you are looking into a mirror," Serath said.

Then Shauna saw what else wasn't reflected. The front door and shop windows were a plain brick wall in the reflection. It wasn't a mirror; it was a window to a room that was a mirror image of the showroom. Serath stepped up to the glass and walked along for a few steps before turning and pressing on the glass. The pane swung open as a door into the adjoining room.

He nodded to the bowl, "I can't take less than six figures, but if you want to pay it, it's yours."

Amber walked past the proprietor and over to the mirrored room's jade bowl. "I can't lose a haggle," she said. "But I do want this. I'll counter with a penny under six figures."

"Done," Serath said. "I only deal in direct bank transfers. I assume if you can buy things in this price range, you can arrange such a thing."

Amber pulled out her phone and hit a number she had on speed dial. Shauna heard the ringing on the other line for almost a minute before someone picked up. Amber apologized for waking whoever it was and went on to complete the transaction with Serath.

As Serath and Amber worked on paperwork, Shauna noticed someone walk in the front door. It was the vamp-wannabe, Peter. He was wearing a black turtleneck, black jeans and a matching knit cap, looking more hipster than goth.

She walked out to the main room to meet him.

For a moment he seemed surprised, but he smiled at her.

"Hi, Peter," she said. "I wouldn't normally think to see you in a place like this."

"Me?" Peter asked. He looked around, clearly a little puzzled by Amber and Serath being in the reflection of the room. He then looked Shauna in the eye and said, "I just saw you here and wanted to see if you'd like to go get some coffee."

"I'm with a friend," Shauna nodded towards Amber. "I could probably ditch her though. She'd forgive me."

A trill rang from Peter's jean's pocket. He looked apologetically at Shauna as he answered it. "Sorry Hank, something came up." After a pause he said, "Yes tomorrow is still a go, for sure." Another break then, "See you then." He hung up the phone and pocketed it. "Sorry about that."

"Don't worry about it," Shauna said. "How about that coffee?"

"Nah," Peter said. "I don't want to start anything on the bad side of your friends. I'm sure I'll see you again at Grue's or The Mists."

Though disappointed by Peter forcing her to use Amber as an excuse, she was relieved to not have to ditch the pet. She said, "I probably won't be going back to Grue's for a while. Since my sister works at The Mists, I'm sure I'll be there again."

"See you there," Peter said. He bowed his head then walked out of the store.

"Was that the boy from the other night?" Amber asked as Serath locked up the reflection room behind her.

"Yeah," Shauna said.

"He's an odd one," Amber said. "You two just had a whole conversation and never got within ten feet of each other."

That was true. Peter had stopped just a few steps in the door and Shauna hadn't gotten close before his phone rang.

"You didn't just scare off my appointment, did you?" Serath asked. "I mean, I appreciate the business, but I'd like the opportunity to sell one more thing before I head out of town."

"He wasn't your customer," Shauna said. "He's a friend of mine." He was barely an acquaintance, but she didn't feel the need to go into details.

"I see," Serath said. "Well, I should be prepared to give my next customer my full attention. Thank you for the business."

Shauna understood. She and Amber headed for the door. As they were leaving, he reached for Shauna's hand, as if to shake it, but pulled back when she snapped a glare his way. She'd had enough people touching her and seeing her aura for one day.

Serath said, "There's only one reason vamps avoid touch, but I'll respect your privacy if you'll respect mine."

"Oh?" Shauna asked.

"Don't tell the countess that I have a room of true artifacts, please." Serath begged, even bending his knees a little. "It took me ninety years to build my infrastructure."

"It's a dangerous trade," Amber said. "You are risking gaining the attention of international police forces if you are smuggling."

"Of course I'm smuggling. It's a perfect operation. I find artifacts in China and purchase them then take them to my workshop in Hong Kong where I make a hundred copies as cheaply as possible. Customs doesn't check every one of a hundred identical items. But, this secret, you will keep it?" Serath asked, actually falling to one knee.

"I don't see why not," Shauna said. She couldn't find anything inherently vampirish to being an artifact smuggler. If he hadn't been caught, he probably knew how not to be. She'd been asked to find a killer, not a smuggler.

As they walked back to Amber's car, the pet cradling the bowl like a newborn, Shauna asked, "Should we have questioned him more? We never really asked if he was behind the schemes against Portia."

"He's too meek," Amber said. "You saw him. Ambitious men wouldn't be operating retail stores, alone. Both he and Tureq are not the types to seek leadership roles."

"So that leaves Zahaira?" Shauna asked.

"Tomorrow we'll see," Amber said. "She's been my primary suspect all along. She owns the majority of stock in the three companies that do the most contract work at the Navy Yard. She has similar holdings as far south as Charleston. She has the means to successfully pull off a coup." She looked at the eastern sky where the sky was beginning to lighten. "I wish we had time today. Tomorrow, Zahaira will be ready for us and if she is behind this, it won't be a friendly conversation."

"If Serath knew we were coming, so will Zahaira," Shauna said. "Will we be ready for her being ready for us?"

"You are thinking too much," Amber said,."We go in, we deal with what we find and we report to Portia. It's simple, really."

It sounded simple, but Shauna was left wondering just how many shotguns would it take to hurt her and didn't ever want to know the answer.

Amber drove Shauna back to her apartment then left. When Shauna peered into her apartment, Laura was asleep on her couch and Elsa was sitting on the settee cuddling with her sleeping pets who were partially sprawled onto the carpet. Shauna crept to her bedroom and went to sleep for the day.

CHAPTER 12

Shauna woke to find Jackie cuddled up to her back and Elsa and Jonnie behind her. All three of her bedmates were completely naked. Shauna wore an oversized t-shirt, as she usually did when she slept. Elsa was already awake and watching Shauna.

Having someone just staring at her while she slept unnerved her for a moment. It being Elsa, Shauna relaxed a little. Expecting odd behavior from the elder vamp allowed Shauna to accept a weird situation involving Elsa as at least normal in her world view. "This is not what I expected to wake to," Shauna said. "I didn't notice you come in." She lifted Jackie's arm and climbed out of bed.

"You wouldn't have," Elsa said. "Vamps sleep the sleep of the dead. Nothing would wake you once you were out. It's why we have pets. They guard us so we don't wake up staked to the mattress."

"So I need to get Laura a gun or some karate lessons," Shauna said.

"I'm still partial to swords," Elsa said. She kissed the twins on the forehead as she climbed out of bed. After taking a red silk robe off the back of the closet door and slipping her arms in without tying up the front, she added, "Guns are less useful against vampires. They are easier to conceal, though."

"I own neither," Shauna said.

"Just don't go buying anything without me or Amber," Elsa said. "No sense in getting anything inferior. Don't buy anything you'd find in the back of some of those little stores on Market St."

"I thought you didn't get into fights," Shauna said.

"I don't," Elsa said, pausing a moment before smirking and adding, "...anymore. New vamps are tested as they try to fit into our society. You don't have a reputation yet for being dangerous or for not being a pushover in the face of violence. There will be vamps who want to make sure you know your place is beneath theirs."

"Zahaira?" Shauna asked.

"She'll try to unnerve you," Elsa said. "She will have two armed guards standing at her side with big guns and even bigger swords. Guns can hurt us, but it takes a lot of bullets to truly disable us and they won't kill us. And the swords they use are far too big for the low ceilings in Zahaira's grotto."

"Are you coming with me?" Shauna said.

"Zahaira and I haven't really gotten along since the Revolutionary War," Elsa said.

"You were on opposite sides?" Shauna ventured.

"Hell no," Elsa said. "Vamps don't usually take sides in human conflict. It draws too much attention if you get shot and don't die or if you won't take part in daylight battles. Zahaira and I both wanted to make a pet of the same guy."

"Anyone famous?" Shauna asked.

"No, just a very cute cooper's boy," Elsa said with a deep sigh. "But Zahaira won that one. I'd have fought a little harder if I knew she only kept pets for thirty years at a time. Poor guy might still be alive or undead, today. What a waste."

Not sure what to say, Shauna just nodded sympathetically.

Elsa looked at the bed and smiled then said. "It was my feud with her that drove me back to Eastern Europe, which was a good thing, since that's where I met my twins." She went to the closet and started shuffling clothes aside. "Well, if you're going to see Zahaira, you should dress a little less club-goth and a little more leather. I have just the thing." She pulled out a long black leather jumpsuit and a pair of combat boots.

"You're kidding," Shauna said. She'd seen such outfits only in movies and never imagined they even existed in reality.

"I know the combat boots are a bit clunky," Elsa said. "But the stilettos that would normally go with this only work on the club scene and would be useless in a fight."

"I meant the leather jumpsuit itself," Shauna said.

"Sweetie, you will look hot," Elsa said. "You have the body for it and the best part is you always will. You may as well get used to flaunting it on occasion. If things do get violent, the two layers of Spanish glove leather will keep your skin a little safer and save you a bit of pain."

"Nothing's going to turn violent," Shauna said. "I could wear a blouse with a jacket to look serious."

"Would you wear it for me?" Elsa asked. "Pretty please."

"Are you really that into me?" Shauna said. "It's a little…" The word wasn't right, so she changed it, "…no, it's a lot weird and I'm not gay."

"At four hundred years old, I've learned to appreciate beauty and you, Shauna, are beautiful," Elsa said.

Laura had always been the beautiful sister. She was the sometimes model while Shauna had been the girl who worked in the library during study hall. Being called beautiful was all she needed to bend to Elsa's wishes. "Fine, I'll wear the leather."

It took a while to get into the leather. Despite numerous zippers to help mold the outfit to her arms and legs, the material had to be stretched just a little around her thighs. There were several straps that seemed superfluous as if they served no purpose other than decoration.

"That doesn't mean you're fat," Elsa assured her. "You're perfect. You have these made small because they will stretch to ideally contour your body. It's made to flex in the right places to keep you limber. Wear it around for a bit before you do anything too strenuous, though. If you burst a seam, what little this hides will cease to be hidden."

Before Shauna had finished tying up one boot, Elsa said, "Go barefoot. Those boots are not going to work. They're way too bulky."

"Barefoot into a potential fight?" Shauna asked, though, a skirmish was the last thing she wanted. Even if a bullet wouldn't hurt her, which she wasn't certain of and didn't want to become certain of, she was pretty sure she'd be useless if violence broke out.

"If there is a fight," Elsa said. "Amber will be handling most of it."

"True," Amber said, walking into the room. "I like the outfit. I have the same one, but in red. Today I opted for business attire." She was wearing a grey suit like James always wore with a knee length skirt with black pumps.

Shauna threw Elsa a glare.

"Hey," Elsa said. "You look way better than miss-flashback-to-Working-Girl here."

"You're just dressing Shauna up like your personal toy," Amber said. "She needs to establish her own identity and not just be the embodiment of one of your fantasies."

Shauna nodded, agreeing with Amber, though she was actually enjoying experimenting with the various styles Elsa was exposing her to. "Should I change?"

"We should go," Amber said. "And as hot as tight leather can make you look, it doesn't come off quickly."

"True," Elsa said. "I designed this particular piece myself. It gets around some of those limitations should the right situations arise. I don't see that happening at Zahaira's so I'll forego demonstrating for now. Amber is right, you should go. It's a long drive to the Poconos."

"Couldn't we fly?" Shauna asked.

"I have issues with heights," Amber said. "And anytime you're in the sky, it risks discovery, especially with modern advances in radar."

"The risk is low," Elsa said. "You just look like an eagle on radar. Still, Amber has a point; it should be reserved for occasions where time is critical."

Amber tugged at Shauna's arm. "If we don't get going, time will be critical."

Amber had left her sports car parked in the street by the apartment building's back door. Several cars were lined up behind her car, honking. They couldn't pull around due to several pieces of construction equipment lining the streets.

"New Jersey is almost as bad as Pennsylvania when it comes to road construction," Shauna said. "It seems as soon as they finish resurfacing, they start again."

"That's true anywhere," Amber said. "No one builds roads like the Romans did."

"I didn't think you were that old," Shauna said.

"I'm not, but the roads were still around and still used for most of my life," Amber said. "Heck, I think they're still in use today."

The drive up into the mountains took well over an hour and even with her accelerated senses, Shauna had a hard time with the speed Amber was taking the turns through the mountains. Anytime the wheels started to lose traction, the pet would squeak with glee. Twice, Shauna clenched her hands so tight as to draw blood from her palms, but the wounds healed in seconds. It was her first injury since becoming a vampire. She felt much more vulnerable realizing her skin could be cut.

A couple miles past Stroudsburg, Amber pulled into a long driveway which ended at a house that seemed more suited to a southern plantation than surrounded by the dense forests of Pennsylvania's mountains.

"She doesn't do much to hide her wealth," Shauna said.

"She does," Amber said. "The owner of her house is the descendant of one of her pets. Every generation she weans her old pet and takes on their son as a pet once they have procreated. Nothing seems unusual, even to the neighbors who've had vacation homes next door for just as many generations. They just assume the men of the family age well."

Once they rang the bell, a little girl answered. She was small, maybe only five or six. Nothing about her looked any different than any girl on the playground of any school.

"Who's there?" A woman's voice called from a distant room.

"Who's there?" The girl asked Shauna.

"We are here to see Auntie Zahaira," Amber said. "Is she here?"

"Silly," the girl said. "Auntie Zahaira can't go anywhere. Of course she's here."

"Can we see her?" Amber asked.

"Do you have candy?" the girl asked.

"I'm sorry, no," Amber said.

The girl's shoulders fell and she looked down at her feet. "Auntie is downstairs." She then ran off.

Amber nodded to Shauna to follow her as she stepped into the house. They walked around a staircase upward to an iron clad wooden door, which Amber opened. The walls beyond the door were stone blocks and a stairway led farther down than a single story. At the bottom of the stairs two men with machine guns strapped across their chests stepped up to block them.

"We have business with Zahaira," Amber said.

"She has no appointments tonight," one of the men said. "You can try to set up a video call with her secretary." He handed Amber a business card.

"We're here on business from Countess Portia," Shauna said. She wasn't sure how aware the guards would be of the vampire society, but if they hadn't heard of her, the name would mean nothing more than a random noble.

One of the guards jerked his head slightly and the other went down a dark hallway only to return a minute later. "She says to admit them."

"Relinquish your arms," the one that had been talking to them said.

Amber produced two handguns and a long knife from under her jacket and handed them to the guard. Shauna gestured to the curves of the leather catsuit showing there was nowhere to hide even a small knife.

"Go on," the guard gestured with his rifle to the hall. As they proceeded in, the guard followed them.

They passed by two heavy steel doors on the way through the dimly lit hall. They then came into a room with low vaulted ceilings and a stone walkway over a steaming pool of water. Televisions were mounted on pillars and showed several financial shows. Sitting in a recliner at the end of the walkway, an elderly woman was watching the screens and talking, seemingly to no one.

"Drop my holdings in Apex Energy and switch it to the railroad," the woman said. "Call me back in ten minutes."

When Shauna got closer, she realized the woman wasn't elderly at all. It was a combination of the style of chair and the way she sat wrapped in a shawl that had misled her.

"James' pet and the baby vampire come to pay their respects?" the woman, whom Shauna assumed to be Zahaira, asked.

"Zahaira," Amber said. "Are you killing off Portia's competition?"

"Right to the point," Zahaira said. "I've always liked that about you. I guess it's not respect you hold for me."

"I do," Amber said. "I am just out of suspects. The list of people who could challenge Portia is small and you're the last one on the list."

"Countess Bathory and my child Serath are the only two from this county who could make a claim on the crown," Zahaira said.

"And Tureq," Shauna added.

"I suppose," Zahaira said. "It wouldn't be Serath, he still loves me and I am his blood mother. Are you sure it's not Countess Bathory? She could want to return to power after so many centuries under someone else's rule."

"Elsa doesn't seem the type to want responsibility," Shauna said.

"So the new vamp defends her mother," Zahaira said. "I've heard so much about you. I'm glad to see she hasn't left another pretty corpse in her attempts make offspring."

The more people talked about Elsa, the more she doubted the tales of her early years were as exaggerated as Elsa claimed. She wouldn't be holding it against her mentor. It was so long in the past and she'd accepted that morality among vamps was not the same as among mortals. Elsa was someone who would be a good friend and she did have her back at Ricks, but in the end, she could really only be truly trusted to amuse herself.

Zahaira stood from her chair, dropping her shawl and revealing her nude body. She appeared to be in her mid twenties. She stepped up to Shauna and said, "I'm almost tempted to take you for a spin. Elsa and I have a bit of a rivalry and I like to keep the upper hand on her. But, I have never desired to be with a woman and I don't now." She jumped into the water and swam around a pillar. She came back over and leaned her elbows up on the walkway by Shauna's feet. "As Elsa's daughter, you are still purer of Venae than I. She's a direct descendent of one of the council. I am three generations removed. To me this makes you as much of a suspect as anyone. But, the killings started before you were made, so that removes you from the suspect list."

"Then we're out of suspects," Shauna said.

"I may have something for you," Zahaira said. "One of my businesses is a delivery service specializing in international commerce. Two weeks ago one of my trucks was hijacked. We recovered it this morning and the on-board video surveillance was intact. The camera watched the back of the truck, what goes in and what comes out." Zahaira gestured to one of her guards who then went to her chair and pulled out a computer tablet from a pocket behind the seat. He set it on the floor in front of Zahaira. She navigated to a video and played it.

Two men, both vampires by the way they moved, were unloading crates into an alley door. Both wore hoodies with baseball caps and sunglasses under the hoods.

"The truck was hijacked after it left customs," Zahaira said. "Those are supposed to be crates of wine intended for James' shop. But, those aren't the right shape for wine crates and that's not James' back door." The boxes were twice as long as wine crates but had labels marking them as wine. "I'm a trusted importer with customs. I can usually pull stuff straight through without waiting for inspections. I think someone was taking advantage of that."

"Are you accusing James?" Amber asked.

"The order came from his shop," Zahaira said. "I don't know if he intentionally ordered the contents of those crates or if someone swapped the crates out at the origin of the shipment. But this kind of smuggling is usually reserved for the types of crimes that would be investigated deeply enough to expose us."

"Do you know what's in the crates?" Shauna asked.

Zahaira moved the video forward a few minutes. "They check the contents right here."

One of the vampires popped the top of a crate and pulled out a rifle. Shauna knew nothing about guns, but the only place she'd seen guns like that one had been in movies.

"Those are Belgian," Amber said. "And they're the military issue variant, full automatics."

"I don't know what that means," Shauna said.

"Vampires don't usually amass machine guns," Amber said. "This is certainly associated with whoever is planning a coup."

An alarm sounded down the hall and all the screens changed to show images from inside the house. A woman ran into the room, cradling the little girl who had answered the front door. The girl looked scared and clung tight to the woman's neck the way a child would cling to their mother.

On the screens, several men in black clothes and armed with rifles were running across the yard, firing toward the house. Men were emerging from the house as well, returning fire. The fire fight seemed to be resolving in a very lopsided manner favoring the attackers.

"Whoever they are, they have top-notch Kevlar," Amber said, watching the screen. "Now I'm wishing I hadn't left my Kalashnikov in my trunk."

Zahaira pointed down the hall. "If you're that kind of suicidal, the door on the right is my armory."

"Come." Amber pulled Shauna along as she ran down the hall without throttling back to human speeds. They had to dodge around three men kneeling by the walls of the hall with machine guns aimed toward the stairs. They came to the two steel doors and both were wide open. The door on the left led to a room with several sets of bunk beds. The door on the right led to a room filled with weapon racks.

"Should we be moving this fast?" Shauna asked.

"Everyone here is brainwashed to ignore obvious signs of vampires," Amber said.

Shauna looked around the room at all the weapons. There were machine guns as well as pistols alongside rifles that looked like they were from the Revolutionary War. A rack of swords lined one wall. What stood out the most was a short sword in a glass case in the center of the room. The weapon and hilt shined of polished steel, but the blade also glittered with gold lines.

"I've heard of this sword, but never seen it," Amber said. "It was created in the days of the Roman Empire for killing elder vamps. I have no idea how they managed to fold gold into steel, but that weapon is dangerous." She took two swords off the wall. They were heavy like the swords on display by the suits of armor in the art museum. Rather than hand one of them to Shauna, she said, "Grab a sword. Bulletproof and sharp-edge proof are not the same thing."

Shauna picked a sword then followed Amber into the hall and up the stairs. Repetitive crashes came from the front of the house as if someone were having difficulty breaking down the front door. Amber kept running down a hall and up another flight of stairs. Shauna stayed close behind as the pet went into a bedroom and opened a window at the back of the house.

The sword felt awkward in Shauna's hand as she moved. She wasn't sure where to keep the point. Did she aim it down or keep it in front of her? She asked Amber, "You aren't actually expecting me to fight are you?"

"Actually, yes," Amber said. "You'll do fine. I assume you know how swords work."

Shauna tentatively swung the blade back and forth and made a thrusting motion. "I guess so, but they have guns and I'm still not comfortable being shot at and less comfortable with the idea of being shot."

"It's not as bad as you'd think," Amber said. "Follow me and take cover as soon as you land." The pet then dove out the window. Shauna followed, flying to the ground rather than jumping.

Gunfire reported off to their left and clods of dirt sprayed into the air near their feet. Shauna jumped behind a tree and Amber rolled to the ground behind a rock.

"I'm running out," Amber whispered. "When I do, rush the gunman. Swing for the arms or face. They have less armor there." She then leapt to her feet and ran into the woods, a hail of bullets trailed behind her.

Without time to consider her options, Shauna did as she'd been told to do and ran at the gunman using all of her preternatural speed. She swung at the man's arm and cut clear through and deep into the man's chest. He fell, his oozing blood distracting Shauna. She wouldn't look at the man's face, covered as it was with an armored mask, for fear she'd see his eyes.

Amber came up in front of her. "Dead blood is dead," she said. "You'll gain nothing from it. Come on, there's more of them. Maybe don't swing quite so hard and you might be able to fill up while we're out here."

"It's not the blood," Shauna said.

"Don't think of it as killing," Amber said. "Think of it as fighting."

"How is that better?"

"If you're fighting, killing is an unfortunate side effect of trying to save something," Amber said.

"What are we saving?" Shauna asked. "These guys can't hurt me and they don't seem to be able to hurt you."

"I don't know about you," Amber said. "For me, I'm thinking of that little girl inside. I don't think she's bullet proof."

Shauna nodded. "Right." She wasn't the only one in the fight. There were other lives at stake, even if hers wasn't. She could do this. She could fight to save people.

"Listen, Shauna," Amber said. "If you need more time to learn to kill, could you go stand out in the middle of the yard and at least let some of these guys point their guns your way?"

Finding the resolve, Shauna was ready to go on and find more of the attackers. Before Shauna could tell Amber, two more attackers came around the corner and shot at them. Amber threw one of her swords. It bounced harmlessly off the chest of one of the men, but both men made the mistake of watching it fall to the ground. By the time they looked back up, Shauna and Amber had closed with them. Trying to restrain herself, Shauna cut again at the man's arm. He tried to duck away and the blade cut across his throat, nearly severing his head.

"Not exactly in control of that thing, are we?" Amber asked. "Here, I saved this one for you. You'll learn sooner or later that when presented with a guilt-free meal, you take it." She held one of the men with an arm pinned behind is back. His helmet had been ripped off, leaving a bloody wound on his chin. "The neck's fine in this case."

"I don't need to feed," Shauna said, though the blood on his neck was causing her saliva to flow. She couldn't take her eyes off the wound.

"I think you shouldn't turn away a free meal," Amber said.

Shauna couldn't argue and didn't want to spend more time debating. She bit into the man's neck and drank. The pulsing blood became too strong a reminder that he was alive and she pulled away. "He's out of the fight," Shauna said. "I don't need to kill him."

Blood flowed from where she'd bitten him and the man had already fallen unconscious.

"He'll bleed out whether you ingest the blood or it's wasted," Amber said. "You can't stop it now."

"I can try," Shauna said. Remembering her saliva could heal a bite, she licked her hand and held it over the man's wound. The blood continued to pulse out but she could feel the rate slowing. She hoped it was because the wound was closing and not because the man was running out of blood.

"This is taking longer than killing him," Amber said. "We have to go."

"I'm not killing someone I don't have to," Shauna said. The blood was barely seeping onto her hand. Whatever his fate, she'd done something to try to save him. She pulled her hand away and licked his neck. When she pulled away, Amber dropped him and grabbed Shauna's arm, dragging her along as she ran around the house.

"You did what you could," Amber said. "If I'd have thought you wouldn't kill him, I'd have snapped his neck."

"I'm not the soldier you are," Shauna said. At that time, she wasn't sure where the line existed between soldier and monster. She would have put it directly between killing the men who were shooting at her and killing the man that was already subdued, which might put Amber on the far side. Amber hadn't actually killed the man either, though, so the line hadn't been crossed.

The front yard was empty and the door had been smashed in, off of its hinges. "They're inside," Amber said, though Shauna had already come to the same conclusion. They climbed over the fallen door and looked around.

Sounds of gunfire came from the basement and a light flittered through the second floor atop the stairs. Someone was up there with a flashlight.

"I'll help out below," Amber said. "Go get that guy upstairs."

The pet ran off into the house and Shauna ran up the stairs. As soon as she reached the landing, she became aware of three separate lights flittering through the rooms. Three of the attackers were searching for something. One stepped into the hallway and shined his light in Shauna's face. He squeezed his trigger but didn't manage to get a shot off before she sliced through his elbow with her sword. The gun hit the ground spraying bullets into a wall.

Shauna pushed the man aside and ran to a room where another man sat, crouched behind a bed with his gun aimed at the door. Before Shauna could leap at him, he pulled his trigger, releasing a burst of bullets into Shauna's chest and abdomen. It felt like hailstones hitting her. She pushed ahead and flipped the bed onto the man. He still fired his weapon, shooting through the mattress, but missing Shauna completely. She chopped at his leg, which stuck out from under the overturned bed, hitting his inner thigh. She caught a lot of floor with the tip of her sword, so her blade didn't cut very deep. Still, the wound bled heavily. The gunfire stopped. Shauna didn't feel any hunger for the blood, having just fed on the other attacker outside. She left the room. The man in the hall had disappeared, but she heard a voice coming from two rooms at once. One of them was where she'd left the man bleeding under the bed.

"Objective complete," the voice said. "Return to transport."

The men must have had radios in their helmets. She went to the room where the other voice had come from. As soon as she entered she found herself staring right down the barrel of a machine gun, the flashlight under the barrel nearly blinding her.

"Return to transport," the voice said again, coming from inside the gunman's helmet.

Shauna swatted the weapon away from her face. She swung at the man's neck but he blocked with his gun, allowing her blade to cut into the barrel. She slapped his hand with the flat of her sword. She'd heard bones snap. He dropped the gun and drew a knife with his other hand.

"Shauna!" Amber's voice came over the radio in the man's helmet. "If you can hear this, I need you down here, stat."

Nodding at the door, she said, "Run." The man dropped his knife and ran, holding his broken hand in the other.

Rather than try to run down, Shauna pulled herself out of phase with the world and fell through the floor. Once on the first floor, she stepped back into the physical world and ran down the stairs. Dead bodies, both the security guards and the attackers were strewn around the hall.

"Here!" Amber called from Zahaira's room.

Responding to the urgency in Amber's voice, Shauna ran faster than she had before. Reaching the room she saw the bloodshed had more than spilled into this room. Six of the attackers lay dead and Amber, the girl and her mother were kneeling on the floor. As she got closer she saw Zahaira's body had shriveled and she had a stake through her heart. Her head had been severed and the woman was cradling it in her arms, sobbing.

The girl was clasping to Zahaira's shriveled body, shaking and choking on tears.

"I don't think I can save her," Shauna said. "Can I?"

"Zahaira is dead," Amber said. "Very dead. Nothing can be done for her. The girl and her mother, however, can forget they saw this. Take them upstairs and alter their memories."

Shauna took Zahaira's head, which was dry and starting to crumble, and handed it to Amber. She then picked up the girl and carried her upstairs with the mother following listlessly behind her.

"Relax," Shauna said once they were in the garage. She bit her finger and gave each of them a drop of her blood. She then gave them a story about how they felt the need to get away for their own little vacation after Zahaira went to stay with a cousin in Europe. She told the mother to go into the house just to get her purse and keys and that she would see nothing out of the ordinary as nothing extraordinary had happened that night. They would then go off to pick up the husband and take him with them. Above all else, they were not going to return to the house for at least a week.

The father, wherever he was, likely died when Zahaira died. She wouldn't be able to create a cover for that. As Shauna watched the girl and her mother drive off, she wondered if there was anything she could have done to lessen that loss.

She then pulled out her phone and called Portia. Portia sounded more distressed to learn that none of the local vampires were behind the attacks and that humans were so involved.

"What of Zahaira's family?" Shauna asked.

"They're rich," Portia said. "They'll be separated from the vamp community once Edmund has cleared the house of evidence and cleaned up the place. I don't think we need to worry about them. You should come see me at the museum as soon as you can get here. I'll send Edmund to Zahaira's. Tell Amber to hold down the fort until we get there."

"I'll head that way," Shauna said. She hung up and went inside to find Amber.

The pet stood alone in Zahaira's armory staring at an empty pedestal surrounded by shattered glass. "This explains a lot," Amber said.

"So we have something?" Shauna asked. "There are a lot of dead people here. We're going to need a lot of explanation."

"The sword is one of only a very few weapons that can harm me," Amber said. "Like you and Laura, I'm rife with Venae. I'm not used to having to worry about actually getting hurt. Someone wanted to make sure they could take down any vampire."

"Gold is bad?" Shauna asked. Elsa had mentioned it after Rick had shot Laura. There hadn't been time for Elsa to explain.

"Gold is a pure substance," Amber said. "It doesn't naturally bond with other elements. A wound that has contact with gold will not regenerate quickly, sometimes taking weeks to heal. In the ages when vampires were purer of Venae, which means they were impure of the stuff of this world, before the Council purged the oldest vampires, it required a weapon inlaid with gold to even harm vampires of significant Venae. Such a weapon is very dangerous."

Shauna looked at the rack of machine guns on the wall. They were not the same as the ones on the video. Those, however, had been the same as the ones the attackers used. She pointed out her realization to Amber.

"Yeah," Amber said. "I think they wanted the guns to get to this sword and kill Zahaira. Their next step is probably to go after Portia."

"I'm heading there now," Shauna said. "Edmund is on the way to clean up here. Is there anyone else I need to coerce before I leave?"

"No one here is alive but me," Amber said. "It's been a long time since I've seen so much blood. All twenty of Zahaira's guards are dead and I think we got eight of the attackers. Go and guard Portia or whatever she needs you for. Don't forget the computer."

"Looks like you got the fight you wanted," Shauna said somberly. "And then some."

"Be careful what you wish for, eh?" Amber said with a sigh. "When I long for a fight, it seems I don't recall the consequences."

Shauna went to the pool room and took the tablet computer. Zahaira was nothing but ash on the floor. Shauna was careful to step around her remains as she left.

During the flight to Portia's museum, Shauna thought about the battle. Killing had been something she'd accepted long ago when she'd first decided to find a way to become a vampire, but that had all been just her theorizing, before she'd encountered death firsthand, before she'd killed. With Allison there had been no guilt, no remorse in the act of revenge. The attackers, she didn't know anything about.

For all she knew, she'd orphaned a dozen children. She wanted to believe it was a battle for her life, but, after having a machine gun emptied at her chest, she knew they couldn't have hurt her. Amber called it guilt-free and Shauna tried to see it that way. She had been fighting for someone other than herself. Thinking that the girl and her mother survived staved off much of the guilt.

And someone out there, someone on the other side of the conflict, had a sword designed to kill vampires like Shauna. She didn't know how to process that. She'd just become aware of how immortal she really was in the face of gunfire only to learn there were still weapons and people out there that would be able to kill her.

§

She arrived at the museum and Natalia escorted her into Portia's chambers. The room was covered in white sheets and a column of scaffolding climbed all the way to the ceiling.

"I'm up here," Portia's voice carried from the top of the scaffolding.

Shauna flew up, finding Portia lying on her back, painting the face of a pilgrim in a scene of the Mayflower landing at Plymouth Rock. Portia wore only a pair of denim overalls which were covered in paint splotches.

"How Michelangelo of you," Shauna said, bringing herself to lie at Portia's side. She was careful not to touch the ceiling.

"It needed touching up," Portia said. "They always do. I remember working on the Sistine Chapel in the early sixteenth century. It seemed every five years we had to go back and repaint or wash soot off, which usually led to repainting."

"So you worked with Michelangelo?" Shauna asked.

"Of course," Portia said. "He was my father."

"He was a vampire?" Shauna asked.

"No, he was my mortal father," Portia said.

"I thought Michelangelo was gay," Shauna said. "I didn't know he had children."

Portia laid her brush on a palette and set it aside. "Neither did he until I lost my mortal mother and my blood father and tracked him down. In sixteenth century Italy, fear of the plague drove people to drastic actions. I was made, along with my mother, in 1508 when the plague was threatening Florence. Just over two decades later we were living at a country estate when two cows died. The local villagers burned every building to the ground. My blood father and mortal mother died. My blood brother, Francesco Medici, and Rick were there and the three of us and our pets escaped into a root cellar."

"Amber told me that only the sun and losing our head would kill us." Shauna said. James' pet hadn't mentioned fire.

"Anything that separates your brain from your heart will kill you. Burning is not a quick death," Portia said. "In the time it takes for fire to kill us, we can usually do something to stop it. But, if we panic in the pain and run into the sunlight, as my mother and blood father did... Well, you get the idea. They then sent me to live with my father. But, he couldn't have a girl as an apprentice and couldn't admit to having a child out of wedlock, so I lived as a boy for decades as one of his students. My name was Tommasso dei Cavalieri. I suppose it was because we were so close that the rumors of his being gay got started. He certainly loved both men and women. Someone would become his muse and he would dote over them for years until another caught his eye."

"Which makes Rick, Michelangelo's brother?" Shauna asked, piecing together what she'd learned of Portia and Rick's relationship when she'd first met the countess.

"Ricardo Buonoratti." Portia rolled off the scaffolding and floated to the floor. Shauna followed, certain that she hadn't looked as graceful as the countess. "Uncle Rick stuck to the family tradition as a banker. I still let him balance the county's books now and then. He's very shrewd with money, or he was until that last recession. He invested too heavily in the real estate boom and now owns only a handful of the scores of buildings that used to be his."

"That's interesting," Shauna said. Truly she loved hearing anything about vampire history, but the timing was not right. "Should we talk about Zahaira's video?"

"You didn't mention a video," Portia said. "What will we see?"

"Vampires unloading machine guns from crates that were supposed to be shipped to James' wine shop," Shauna said. She showed the clip to the countess.

After the clip ended, Portia said, "So, you're going down to James' shop to find some hint of where these were ordered from? If you find something incriminating James, would you tell me?"

The question left Shauna dumbstruck. She could not entertain the possibility that James was anything but an upstanding gentleman. "I don't know," Shauna said.

"I wouldn't expect you to," Portia said. "But, it may weigh heavy on your conscience should you learn something and, by not telling me, allow vampires and people to die."

"This isn't the bloodsucker life I signed up for," Shauna said. "It's supposed to be a life of dark parties, hedonism and opulence and I'm supposed to find some doomed but passionate love affair."

"And A. A. Aaronson is still getting to you," Portia said. "Mostly our lives are the same as human lives, only at night and there's quite a bit more of it. Opulence comes with wealth and wealth comes with time. I can assure you that even the most reclusive among us have passionate love affairs at least once or twice each century. You just have to watch for the opportunities and seize them."

"But, right now I need to investigate my maker," Shauna said. She realized she didn't know James well enough to be certain that he wasn't the one behind the killings. All she had was hope that he wasn't.

"I'd appreciate it," Portia said. "I'll come with you, if you'd like."

"I suppose that way I won't be tempted to hide anything that might point to James," Shauna said.

CHAPTER 13

Portia's pet, Rachel, drove them to James' shop above The Mists. It was barely past midnight when they arrived and a light was still on inside the store. The door was unlocked although the sign on the door said 'closed'. Inside, a middle aged man was yelling on a phone in German.

The man paused his ranting and put a hand over the receiver. He then said, "We closed at eleven."

"James sent us," Shauna said. It was a lie, but she doubted James was in contact with the shop if he wasn't in contact with Amber.

"You're not his secretary. Are you Shauna?" the man asked.

"Yes," Shauna said tentatively. Why, of all people, James' shop manager would know about her, perplexed her.

"I was expecting someone wearing shoes," the man said.

Shauna hadn't had time to change. "I left them at the club, I guess. Dancing in heels takes its toll on the feet." She hoped the explanation would also cover the catsuit. Maybe he'd think the many spots of skin showing were intentional and not think they were bullet holes.

"Well, at least you're finally here," the man said. He then yelled something into the phone and hung up. "When we last spoke, James said he'd hired a new accounts manager and that you might stop by. Since then, I haven't been able to reach him and his secretary keeps brushing me off. We've been getting orders in all week, but so much of it is crap I can't put on our shelves without souring our fine reputation. I am so frustrated that I stopped even opening the boxes. Are you going to at least handle the special deliveries?"

"There aren't guns in the crates, are there?" Shauna asked.

"No, this is a wine store," the man said slowly and deliberately as if Shauna had some gross misunderstanding of where she was.

"Let's see the crates," Shauna said, ignoring the man's tone.

Rachel added, "And the invoices."

"Of course," the man said then started rummaging through a file box he'd pulled from under the counter. "The crates are stacked by the back door. Go on back."

The back room was dark with only a couple of red lights illuminating a row of wine racks. Six crates were stacked by the back door. All of them looked like they were holding a dozen wine bottles. Shauna and Portia went through them. They were all imports.

The wines inside all but one box were of the previous year's vintage, at least the ones that had a date on them. Several did not. Three of the boxes had Italian labels, two had French and one was in a language Shauna didn't recognize.

"What's this writing?" Shauna asked, holding up a bottle in the strange language.

"Flemish," Rachel said.

"Okay," Shauna said. "I've never heard of a country with that name."

"Flanders, it's a part of Belgium," Rachel said.

"The guns were from Belgium," Shauna said. "Could it be a coincidence?"

The manager came in with the invoices and handed them to Rachel. "I've got some stocking to do. Let me know if you need anything else," he said before selecting several bottles from the racks and going back to the front of the store.

Portia took Zahaira's tablet computer from her purse and walked over to the back door. Rachel handed Shauna an invoice. "This one is three crates," she said. "It's the Belgian order, but there's only one crate here. Five of these were charged to the same account. But one is different."

"The Flemish box?" Shauna asked.

"No, the box of Italian reds from 2007," Rachel said. "Maybe it was a good year for Chianti."

"Anything else about the other five boxes in common?" Shauna said.

"Not that I can tell. Give me a sec." Rachel flipped to one of the French invoices and pulled out her phone and dialed.

"You're calling the exporter?" Shauna asked.

Rachel nodded.

"Shouldn't we be calling the Flemish one?" Shauna asked.

"I only speak English and French," Rachel said. At that moment someone answered the phone. After a moment of complaints from the other end of the phone and Rachel speaking in soothing French, the conversation seemed to be productive or, at least, cordial.

"James didn't bring the guns here," Portia said, showing a paused frame of the video. "The back door in the video is not the same one here. They're not the same color and James doesn't have a 'Beware of Dog' sign on his door. So the guns didn't come here."

Rachel hung up the phone. "Anyone know a Stanislav?"

"No," Shauna said.

"As in Grigor Stanislav?" Portia asked.

"Grigor?" Shauna asked, thinking of one of Rick's cronies. "Let me see that image." Portia handed her the computer. She'd seen the sign before. "This is Grue's Home's back door," she said.

"Yes," Portia said. "Tomorrow night we visit with my uncle."

"Why not now?" Shauna asked, though she was not particularly eager to go back to the Grue's Home.

Portia nodded at Rachel. "This isn't exactly a tactical team. I'd want Edmund and Natalia there and I'm sure you would like Amber with you."

"And Elsa," Shauna said before realizing the folly.

"Getting Elsa to engage would be a miracle, but not the first from her," Portia said. "Go, talk to her and Amber. We'll see you after nightfall."

§

As she stepped out of the alley by the Wine Shop, Shauna saw Peter head down the stairs to The Mists. It was an odd time to be heading into a bar, being very close to last call, but she needed something of her own life after spending the day working on the problems of the County and she'd found Peter to be at least interesting.

The Mists was more crowded than usual. Shauna was surprised to see Laura back at work, but noticing that, she wasn't surprised to see Elsa and her twins sitting at the bar. Peter was talking to the crowd from the vamp wannabe club. She bumped against him and smiled as she walked by on the way to the bar. He looked at her, but it took a moment for him to smile and it seemed a little forced. Unsure what that meant, she stopped and turned to talk to him.

"Hey," she said. "Fancy seeing you here again."

"Yeah," Peter replied. "Who knew I came here, ever?"

Another man from Peter's table stood up and offered Shauna a hand. "Didn't I see you in Grue's Home?"

Shauna went to shake his hand, but he pulled her hand up to his lips and kissed it. His lips lingered on her knuckles a little too long for her liking and she pulled away. "Maybe," she said.

"Buzz off, Kurt," Peter said. "She's not your type."

While Shauna agreed, she couldn't help but look at Peter differently. He was short, almost mean in his tone. But, previously, she'd only spoken with him when he was probably trying to seduce her, when he'd be at his best.

"Is this why you told us all to leave and never come back to this place?" Kurt asked. "Are you trying to keep this pretty lady to yourself?"

"Yes," Peter said and cracked a tight grin. "I was afraid you'd meet her and sweep her off her feet."

"Get a life," Kurt said. "The girl will do what she wants to do and she just might like me better."

Shauna looked at Kurt and shook her head.

"I get it," Kurt said. "If you change your mind, I'm usually at Grue's Home on Thursdays and Saturdays. Despite Peter's wishes, I'll probably be back here next Wednesday." He then went back to take his seat at the table.

"Can I get you a drink?" Peter asked.

"Why not," Shauna said. "If they're still serving, I'm still drinking. Red wine."

Peter put down a glass of wine he'd been holding and picked up a bottle from the table and poured some into a clean glass that had been sitting next to it. He then set down the wine bottle and passed her the glass. He'd done it all with just one hand, which Shauna found odd. Then she noticed the cast on his right hand.

"You broke your hand?" Shauna asked.

Peter looked at her a moment in the same way he had when she'd first bumped into him then answered. "Not intentionally," he said. "The door on the train closed with a little too much force. Glitchy mechanism or something, so they tell me."

He was lying. Something in the way he staggered his words put Shauna off. She was about to ask what had really happened when Elsa stepped up behind her and wrapped her arms around Shauna's waist. "Who's your boyfriend?" Elsa asked.

"This is Peter," Shauna said. "He's um..." She couldn't think of how to describe him. She couldn't call him a vamp wannabe with him standing right there. He hadn't actually ever told her much about himself.

"Afraid," Elsa whispered. "How strongly are you coming on to the poor boy, Shauna?"

When Elsa mentioned fear, Shauna knew she was right. That had been the look he'd given her. He knew something.

"You smell like blood," Elsa said so quietly, Shauna barely heard her.

Shauna hadn't washed since the fight at Zahaira's. She looked down and saw she did have droplets on one thigh and a sleeve, but they were barely noticeable on the black leather. Surely Peter couldn't see them or smell them. The dozens of tiny tears where bullets had hit her were less subtle, but they weren't as obvious as she would have expected. Peter should have noticed them, but he didn't look at her arms or chest or even her bare feet. He watched her face. She took that as more evidence he was afraid of her. His gaze never lowered to admire how tightly the leather fit her curves.

"He smells of blood, too," Elsa whispered with her lips brushing her ear. "He smells of the same blood. You shouldn't take a non-petted human hunting with you."

"Now I'm thinking I'm the one intruding," Peter said.

Shauna looked at Peter. She didn't see any blood. He looked clean and smelled mostly like shampoo as if he'd just showered. Then she noticed the hand holding the wine glass. There was definitely blood under several of his fingernails. Realizing how he had blood on his hands and the fact that he had a broken hand were connected to why he looked upon her with fear, Shauna said, "I guess maybe you are. My friend here is feeling affectionate tonight and who am I to rebuff such a beauty." She took Elsa by the hand and walked back to the bar.

"You're shaking," Elsa said as they walked. "What's going on with both of you being bloody and afraid?"

"He's a hunter," Shauna said. "We bumped into each other at Zahaira's tonight, only I didn't recognize him then because he had an armored mask on. I was not masked, so he would have recognized me when I broke his hand in the fight. The blood would be from one of his friends, probably the one I left armless."

Elsa tugged at Shauna's hand and pulled her to the bar.

"Mort, pull the fire alarm," Elsa said. "Do you have a panic room?"

"Just an escape tunnel, under the bar," Mort said. "This place started as a speakeasy. The tunnel leads to a train line maintenance stairwell. You can't get lost."

"You're coming with us," Elsa said. "There are hunters here. Pull the damned alarm."

The bartender reached back and pulled the red switch on the wall. Lights flashed and alarms whooped throughout the bar. The people started rushing toward the exit. Shauna looked to see Peter swept into the wave of patrons rushing to leave.

Mort opened a floor panel under the bar and led the way down a steep stairwell beneath it. Elsa ushered her pets through and followed with Laura behind her. Shauna brought up the rear and pulled the panel down. The stairway had been steel surrounded by concrete walls. The tunnel at the bottom of the stairwell was just dirt with wooden beams holding the tunnel up. In several places the dirt had fallen from the ceiling creating large piles they had to climb over.

"Now I'm thinking we should have just killed Peter," Elsa said. "Witnesses or not. Maybe Shauna could use her uber suggestion skills to brainwash a mob."

"Now I'm wishing I'd opted for the clunky boots," Shauna said. "Barefoot in the dirt stopped being fun when I turned thirteen."

Elsa said, "If I'd known you were going to get in a fight, I'd have made you wear the boots, clunky or not. What happened at Zahaira's?"

"About two dozen hunters showed up and wiped out Zahaira's guards, killed Zahaira and died by Amber's and my hands. Only a handful escaped." Shauna then went into details about the gold laced sword and the evidence against Grigor.

"Grigor is Mort's blood father," Elsa said.

"We're not close," Mort said. "I never liked the way he went behind Rick's back when I worked at Grue's Home.

When James offered me this job a few years back, I jumped at it."

"I thought Grigor was Rick's child," Shauna said.

"No, they're blood brothers," Mort said. "Only Rick is half a millennia older than Grigor. When I was made, Grigor and I lived in New York. We came here at his blood father's request."

"Francesco Medici," Elsa said. "He's an exile. None of the Kingdoms want him. He's never done anything to warrant a death sentence, but he pushes the limits. Some say he was behind the high turnover in organized crime bosses in the nineteen-seventies."

"I don't know anything about that," Mort said. "Sure, Grigor and I ran some heroin together once or twice, but most of the time we just ran a mundane life as bar owner and bartender."

Eventually they emerged up to the street a couple blocks away.

"Where do we go now?" Laura asked. "Is life among vampires always this dramatic?"

"Usually only if you want it to be," Elsa said. "We can't go to my place. I'm squarely in the demographic of vampires these hunters are targeting." She stepped close to Shauna, tilted her head towards Mort and said, "There was a small alcohol fire on the bar and Mort panicked and pulled the alarm. The fire was contained before it even scorched the bar and we all left with the crowd. We, as a group, never spoke. Send him back to explain to the firefighters that arrived."

"Wait," Mort said as Shauna pricked her finger on her fang. "You can't coerce another vampire."

Shauna moved quickly, grabbing him by the neck and jabbing a pricked finger into his mouth. "I can't coerce another vampire," she said. She then went on to repeat Elsa's tale word for word before sending Mort off to talk to the firemen.

Elsa hailed a cab and they all squeezed into the back seat with Jackie climbing into Shauna's lap. "We're going to your place," Elsa said to Shauna. "I've been making a few changes. I hope you don't mind." She gave Shauna's address to the cabbie.

§

Amber was standing on the sidewalk in front of Shauna's apartment building when they arrived. The whole building was encased in scaffolding and plywood. The parking lot was empty except for Shauna's old car and Amber's convertible.

"I can't get in," Amber said.

"I don't remember giving you keys," Shauna said. "I will if you'd like them, though."

"I have keys," Amber said. She held up a ring with three keys on it. "The problem is the door man. He's particularly stubborn and doesn't respond to threats."

"The building doesn't have a doorman," Shauna said. Her words dwindled as she looked at Elsa, expecting some kind of explanation.

"Voivod Security only hires combat weathered former military police," Elsa said. "He's doing his job." She opened the door and ushered everyone into an atrium that had previously only housed a set of mailboxes. It now had a desk and a security guard.

The guard stood as they entered and said. "Good evening Miss McAllister. Is the blonde woman with you?"

"She is," Shauna said skeptically.

"Add her to the allowed to enter list," Elsa said. "Her name is Amber."

"Sorry Ma'am," the guard said. "Only the owner can add or remove people from the list." He looked to Shauna expectantly.

"Do it," Shauna said.

"Last name?" The guard asked.

"Alden," Amber said.

"A.A?" Shauna asked, suddenly adding another suspect to her A. A. Aaronson list. She glanced at Amber with a raised eyebrow.

"Coincidence," Amber said.

Shauna was fairly certain it was just that. Nothing she'd learned of James' pet would indicate she had the patience to write a novel.

The guard called out, "Door, open," and the door leading further into the building opened.

"Voice commands," Elsa said. "That way, no one can steal a key or kill the guard to gain entry. In a pinch, your voice will work. So will Laura's."

"And yours?" Shauna asked.

"Of course," Elsa replied.

"And the other people who live here?" Shauna asked.

"Yes, Jonnie and Jackie can do it, too," Elsa said. "Careful, sweetie, the paint is still wet."

Shauna stopped at the foot of the stairs. To her right, where the manager's apartment had been, there were now elevator doors, braced open with a sign that said 'out of order'. Beyond the doors was a dark shaft.

"There's only so much even two dozen workers can get done in one day," Elsa said. "I'd have hired more, but at some point it becomes diminishing returns; they just get in each other's way."

"What did my neighbors think?" Shauna said as she started to walk up the stairs. The vinyl stair coverings had been torn up and the first three steps had been replaced with rough surfaced marble slabs.

"You don't really have neighbors anymore," Elsa said.

"Tell me you didn't eat them," Shauna said.

Elsa laughed. "Please, Mr. Nichols must weigh four hundred pounds. Cholesterol is not my favorite flavor. I just shot them all. They're under concrete slabs in the basement."

"Oh," Shauna said. She stopped climbing the stairs. She tried to be indifferent to the killing of humans, but she still couldn't avoid thinking about what would become of the people that cared about the newly deceased.

"Relax, cookie," Elsa said. "I bought them out. Well, you bought them out. It seems someone has an eight figure bank account and hasn't been putting it to good use, so I took the responsibility unto myself."

"James gave me money?" Shauna asked Amber.

"No," Amber said. "He wouldn't do anything behind your back. He's too straightforward to give a surprise gift. He also doesn't give money. He might give you a job or even a company, but he doesn't give money."

As they reached Shauna's floor, Elsa said, "Did you know that your great-grandfather, Andrew McAllister, left all his belongings to you in a trust when he died?"

"My McAllister Great-Grandfather was Shaun. I was named after him. He died two years ago and left more medical bills than money," Shauna said.

"I have a trail of authenticated birth certificates that proves otherwise," Elsa said. "Poor Andrew lost contact with his son during World War I and left his trust to be distributed among all his living heirs who kept the family name, which would be you."

"My father is still alive," Shauna said.

"John Edward McAllister?" Elsa asked.

"John Martin McAllister," Shauna answered. She stopped where her door had been. There weren't any doors in the hall. What had been Mrs. Holland's apartment was now an open, empty space with just a large sectional couch surrounding a sculpted gas firepit.

"And I'm a twin," Shauna said.

"My apologies, Laura," Elsa said. "My forger was hesitant enough to create three birth certificates on the same day. I'm sure your sister will share the family fortune."

"It's not mine," Shauna said.

Elsa said, "Legally, well officially, you're wrong." She walked to the kitchen counter and pulled out a binder. "This is your ledger."

Shauna took it and opened it. The account had been opened in her name over a year earlier. "You're really creepy, Elsa."

"Hey, a great plan takes time," Elsa said.

"And yet, you have my entire building renovated in twelve hours," Shauna said.

"Because of great planning," Elsa affirmed. "But, this is going to take a couple weeks to get finished. The extra eight inches of reinforced concrete will be done tomorrow. The elevator will take a week. The interior design, the furniture and all will take even more time to do right."

"I'm not taking this man's money," Shauna said.

"Are you going to stop me from taking this man's money and spending it on you?" Elsa asked.

Shauna glared at Elsa. "How can I trust you to mentor me as a vampire and totally distrust your morality?"

"Are you saying you don't trust me?" Elsa asked.

"That's just it," Shauna said. "I totally trust you but it makes no sense. Did you coerce me?"

"I would that I could," Elsa said. "It would be easier. If you trust me, it's your instincts telling you that I only have your best interests at heart."

"There's no way she could coerce you," Amber said. "I think she's in love with you."

"Um," Shauna said. Everyone in the room was now staring at her. She looked at Elsa and tried to think of a way to say that she appreciated the sentiment and the attention, but she wasn't interested in romance. The words wouldn't come to her when she met Elsa's eyes. Love was out of the question, but she didn't hate Elsa enough to break her heart. "I have to shower," Shauna said. "Please tell me I have hot water."

"Today, yes," Elsa said. "The hot water will be off most of the day Saturday. We can stay at my place then."

"You haven't moved in here, have you?" Shauna asked.

"No, I like my view," Elsa said. "For when I visit you, I've laid claim to the second floor guest suite, when it's finished."

Shauna figured Elsa would claim territory. She went to her bedroom and tried for several minutes to get out of the leather. She discovered how to unstrap a panel that had covered most of her buttocks all the way under to a few inches below her navel. It would help if she needed to use a toilet, but not if she wanted to shower.

Amber had told her she didn't sweat but, judging by how sticky the slight stickiness of the leather, it wasn't entirely true. The leather also seemed to have shrunk. She started to peel it down her arm when a pair of hands showed up to help her.

Jackie said, "The trick is not to rush it. You don't want to over-stretch the leather." She pulled the sleeves down a little at a time until Shauna's arm slipped out.

Jackie continued pulling the leather off of her. Shauna headed to the bathroom, but not before noticing Elsa's pet had sat on the bed and started unlacing her boots.

Convincing the girl not to sleep in her bed would be a battle for after the shower. Shauna hadn't learned how to use her sense of smell as well as Elsa could, but she could smell the traces of blood on her hands.

Her shower was running when she got there and already hot. There might be perks to having a pet to serve her. Helping her undress and starting her shower were not likely things Laura would do for her on a daily basis, or ever. Shauna stepped under the water and turned her back to it and let it run down her scalp, through her hair and down her back for several minutes.

She heard Jackie come into the bathroom and said, "I don't need help in the shower."

"It's not about what you need," Jackie said, emphasizing both 'you' and 'need' in such a way that Shauna wasn't sure of Jackie's motivations.

"I'm not in a place to want what you have to offer," Shauna said.

"Everyone in a shower wants someone to wash their back," Jackie said as she stepped into the shower and stood before Shauna. "I can wash your hair as well."

"And I suppose you'd do anything I asked of you," Shauna said.

"I do have limits," Jackie said. "I don't foresee any possibility of you breaching any of them, but they exist."

"Would you be doing this if Elsa didn't tell you to?" Shauna asked.

"You assume I am under instructions," Jackie said. She reached down and picked up a bar of soap then reached it behind Shauna to wet it. She then rolled it through her hands, creating foamy soap bubbles.

"You would lie to me to protect her," Shauna said.

"I would," Jackie said. "You could coerce me to speak the truth. It's rude to do so to another vamp's pet, and Elsa has been most kind to you." She set the soap down and reached over to Shauna's shoulders and began massaging the soap into the skin of her neck and upper back.

Shauna surprised herself that she didn't flinch away. "It's impossible to trust you," Shauna said.

"Then coerce me," Jackie said. "You have my permission, which someone like you would value more than Elsa's opinion on the subject of what I want." She picked up the soap again and this time rubbed the bar against Shauna's skin, scrubbing down the length of Shauna's arm.

"Fine," Shauna said. She pricked a finger on the arm Jackie wasn't rubbing and held it up to Jackie. Elsa's pet leaned forward and sucked Shauna's finger into her mouth, suckling at the blood. Shauna watched, curious at how much pleasure Jackie got from her blood. The pet's mouth lingered on her finger until the wound healed after several seconds.

"My instructions to you are simple," Shauna said. "Never lie to me."

Jackie stopped rubbing her arm, but didn't let go. The pet stared her in the eye as she said, "I'm not entirely sure you didn't just cross one of my boundaries. I guess we'll find out by what you ask next." She set Shauna's arm down and went to work on the other, taking extra time to scrub where there was blood.

"Are you here by your own choice?" Shauna asked.

"Yes," Jackie said.

"A choice to do what would please your mistress?" Shauna asked.

"I do like to please Elsa, but that has never been due to any coercion over my sister or me," Jackie said. "I am here because I desire to please you." The pet knelt and began soaping Shauna's foot and working her way up her calf.

"What?" Shauna asked. She'd expected to break through Elsa's control over the pet.

"Do you really think Elsa spends her night scouring the internet?" Jackie said. "Who do you think pointed your posts out to her? You do know we've been social media friends for almost two years, you and me?"

At that moment, Shauna knew. "Jack E.? I thought you were a man."

"I don't know why you would," Jackie said. When she got to Shauna's thigh, she dropped and started up again from the other foot. "All my profiles label me as a thirty-three year old woman. I was eighteen on my profile when I started it. I realized five years later that my not aging in my pictures might hint at things I shouldn't hint at online, so there aren't pictures anymore."

"You always make me laugh," Shauna said. Jack E. and she had had long back and forth's on so many topics online, almost never about vampires.

"Tonight, 'laugh' is not what I hope to make you do," Jackie said, looking straight up into her eyes. Her hands were lingering, rubbing her thigh. Shauna stared back as Jackie dared to go higher. The girl was succeeding and it didn't bother Shauna, which surprised her. But it was a step Shauna wasn't ready to take. She reached down and pulled Jackie up so they were standing face to face. She turned so her back was to Jackie and said, "You said you'd wash my hair."

"I did," Jackie replied. Seconds later her hands were entwined in Shauna's hair.

Shauna closed her eyes and let the girl play with her locks as she mentally merged the person she'd enjoyed talking with online into the girl who was so affectionately caressing her.

"Rinse," Jackie said. When Shauna turned and leaned her hair back under the shower, Jackie embraced her and kissed her exposed neck. Shauna returned the embrace. When Jackie's lips moved up toward hers, Shauna panicked and gently pushed Jackie back.

"What of Elsa?" Shauna said breathlessly.

"She likes you," Jackie said. "I think she had plans to see if she could replicate making twins pets, but I'm glad it didn't come to that. She hasn't had a great track record in making vampires and such is my sister and I's fate when she decides to get new pets. She'll likely seduce you someday and keep you for a while as a playmate. But she's not possessive. The best part is that I get to keep you before, during and after the whole affair."

"I don't think I've committed to anything with you either," Shauna said. "I may come to my senses when I step out of the shower."

"I do hope so," Jackie said. "Your body tells me it's your mind that needs to catch up."

Shauna stepped from the shower and grabbed a towel. "Maybe it's my body that needs to be reigned in," she said.

Jackie shut the water off and stepped out to join Shauna. She said, "Maybe," then pounced forward and grabbed Shauna's cheeks, planting a long kiss on her lips. When she backed away, she said, "God, I hope not."

Still dripping, Jackie skipped from room singing, "She kissed me back!"

Shauna had, but she cringed having the act broadcast to everyone in the apartment, especially her sister. She finished drying and slipped into a black silk robe that had been left on her bed. Deciding to face the music at that moment rather than wait for her sister to have time to come up with snappy jibes, she went out to the sitting room.

Jackie wasn't out there, neither was Jonnie.

Laura grinned up from the kitchen bar where she sat with Amber and Elsa. "Don't look at me to be judgy, sis. I've had all flavors of fun at one time or another. Similar things may have happened when I was high."

"You're still too young for me," Amber said.

Elsa stood and walked slowly over to her. She leaned to her ear and whispered. "You're a bit more my type now." After a quick kiss on the cheek, Elsa walked out into the hall. "See you tonight," she said, waving.

"You need to rest as well," Amber said. "Tonight will be another fight if we're lucky."

"Are you that bloodthirsty?" Shauna asked. "Why is it lucky if we have another fight?"

Amber shook her head saying, "Fights are never lucky, but yes, I do love a good battle. We'll be lucky if we make it to tonight without the fight coming to us. Peter knows who you are."

"So we need to take shifts watching the doors?" Shauna asked.

"No," Amber said. "I only sleep a couple nights a week and never during the day. I'll be fine."

"I'm going to sleep," Laura said. "Elsa says my room is on the first floor. I've decided I'm staying in the guest suite up here."

Shauna shrugged and headed back to her bedroom.

§

When Shauna awoke, Jackie was again naked and cuddled against Shauna's back. Shauna pondered foregoing the oversized t-shirt she was wearing when she slept next. For a while she just lay there, letting Jackie hold her. She couldn't bring her thoughts and emotions to a consensus on how to deal with Jackie. For the moment, she would just let the white haired girl adore her and would treat her like the friend she thought of her as.

The floor shook and the sound of thunder rumbled outside.

"What was that?" Jackie asked.

"Thunder?" Shauna ventured.

"The sky is clear," Jackie said.

Shauna stood from the bed and walked over and opened her curtains. She briefly saw a blue sky and felt a moment of warmth on her skin where the sunlight hit it before Jackie threw the curtains closed. "They haven't changed the windows," Jackie said.

"I noticed," Shauna said. "I also noticed the very blue, cloudless sky. I also hear sirens; that can't be good."

Jackie popped her head through the curtains and said, "It's getting hazy."

"Shauna!" Amber called from down the hall then ran into the room. "You should come out here." She then turned and ran back.

Noting the urgency of Amber's tone, Shauna rushed after her. Jackie followed.

Laura, Elsa and Jonnie were standing in front of a large screen that seemed to have come out of her ceiling. A projector above her couch threw images of Philadelphia from above on the screen. Captions under the images said, "Bomb threat on Cherry Street!" A large cloud of dust covered the city.

"That's…" Elsa said, but tears choked anything else she would say. Jonnie was holding Elsa tight. Tears ran down her face as well. Jackie went and held her mistress as well.

"Her home," Amber said. "That was the rumble and the thunder."

An announcer was talking but only saying that they were still trying to figure out what happened, what casualties there were. The caption changed to, "What Happened on Cherry Street?"

"Someone burned down her apartment?" Shauna asked.

"Her building," Laura said. "And it wasn't a fire, just an explosion and a collapse."

The caption at the bottom of the screen changed to, "Terror in Philly." The announcer said, "We have confirmed reports that, minutes before the explosion, the building received a bomb threat. Most of the residents evacuated safely."

"How many lived there?" Shauna asked.

"Seven hundred or so," Elsa said. "There's no way forty of them made it out."

"Too high up to evacuate?" Shauna asked.

"Too much sun in the sky," Elsa said. "I wasn't the only vamp in the house and most of them had pets. Maybe a few of them made it to the tunnels, but it was daytime, minutes isn't always enough to rouse a vamp. And the tunnels don't work if the building falls on them."

"Someone was out to kill all of you," Amber said. "These hunters are well informed."

"Someone was out to kill me," Elsa said. "The other vamps, their pets and any humans who couldn't move fast enough, they're all just collateral damage. I'm the one they want dead. Maybe it's time Elisabet Davlos passed on." She turned to Jackie and asked, "Who is my next identity?"

"Isobel Garcia Rodriguez," Jackie said. "I'm Carolina and she's Consuelo."

"I'm not a fan," Elsa said. "I might just accept that I wasn't home." She turned to Shauna and said, "I wasn't planning on being there tonight, but now, I'm coming and I'm going to kill someone. I'd like it to be someone at least partially responsible for this."

They watched the news for the rest of the afternoon. By the time the sunset, it was officially a terrorist attack accomplished by bombs placed all around the perimeter of the building.

CHAPTER 14

Twenty minutes after sunset, Portia arrived with Edmund.

"Just the two of you?" Shauna asked.

"Natalia lived in that building," Portia said, her voice sharp and not at her usual seductive lilt. "We need to find out who's behind this and kill them, tonight. When we find Grigor, we will make him tell us everything."

"I can do that," Elsa said. When Shauna looked at her, she wished she hadn't when Elsa said, "Not everything they wrote about the Blood Countess was false. I did have a very um, interesting, collection of devices in my dungeon. Of course, that's where Vlad lived and they were his toys, but I did learn how to use them."

"And I think you're a little less my type," Shauna said.

"Don't be a prude," Elsa said. "In four hundred years, you'll have skeletons in your closet too."

"Not so literally as yesterday," Jackie said. Elsa's glare provoked Jackie to say, "Too soon, I guess."

"Come on," Portia said. "Elsa is out for blood and I'm out of patience."

"The streets are closed," Laura said. "There's a curfew on the whole city."

"I don't know you," Portia said, "Let's pretend I'm the queen around here and that I'm smart enough to deal with such insignificant problems."

"She is the queen," Jonnie said.

Laura nodded then said, "Of course she is. Do I bow?"

"Let's just fix this mess," Portia said. "We'll go over the pleasantries when I'm in a more pleasant mood. I have a way into the city."

Shauna wasn't going to question the countess's capabilities, but wasn't sure how she planned to move all of them. Flying was certainly not a possibility with all the helicopters flying around with cameras. She followed Portia downstairs and found her answer at the front door. A Sheriff's van sat in the parking lot and it looked like an actual sheriff sat at the wheel.

The driver rolled down the window. It was Edmund wearing a sheriff's uniform. "I am the Sheriff of the County," he said. "Ok, so in the mortal world I'm just a deputy."

"I'm getting my armor from my trunk," Amber said. She went to the convertible and pulled a large duffel bag from the trunk as well as a sheathed sword.

As they all rode to the bar, Amber changed into a suit of plate armor made of steel with brass accents in the shapes of eagles' wings and heads.

"Football fan?" Edmund asked.

"This armor is older than that," Amber said. "It predates southern Europeans coming to America."

"And it still works?" Edmund asked.

"Maintaining steel across centuries is tricky but not impossible," Amber said.

By the time they parked, Amber was covered from ankle to neck in plates of armor. She'd drawn the sword to reveal an entirely golden blade. Plated, she noted. She also said it wasn't as cool as Zahaira's sword but would work just as well. Amber was the first to jump from the van when they stopped on Lombard Street. With the pet wearing armor, Shauna felt underdressed in jeans and a biker-style jacket she had to dig out of her storage locker in the basement.

She had never seen the streets the way they were that night. The whole city seemed abandoned. At the far end of the alley, a handful of policemen were sitting at a coffee shop, but they were the only customers. For a moment, Shauna expected to be confronted for violating the curfew, or at least for Amber walking around with armor and a sword, but the cops barely glanced their way as they approached Rick's bar.

"You think it's odd they are just sitting there?" Amber said.

"Yeah, it's like they're going out of their way to ignore us." Shauna replied. "You think it's a trap?"

"Trap?" Amber said. "No, but we're not surprising anyone down there." She nodded towards Rick's bar. "I'd bet they've been coerced to ignore whatever is about to happen."

Grue's Home was dark from the outside. A chain ran across the top of the staircase with a sign that said 'Closed'. Shauna bent her head down and peered in through the darkened windows. She saw the lights above the bar were on and at least two people were sitting talking to someone behind the bar. She relayed what she saw.

Edmund unhooked the chain and they all descended into Grue's Home.

"Hey, nipote, what's this?" Rick asked from behind the bar. He gestured to the four chairs around a table in the center of the room. "I was expecting a smaller party." The two people sitting at the bar were Teresa and Rhiannon. Rick's pet turned to watch them. Rhiannon sat staring, through her red lensed glasses, into a glass of wine on the bar, shaking her head.

"I'm sure you weren't expecting me," Elsa said, storming past Shauna and the Countess toward Rick.

He raised a shotgun from his side and said, "Gold Shot. It's blessed too, just in case that helps."

Elsa stopped in her tracks. "That won't help you with all of us," she said.

"Two shots are all I need for the revenge I've been planning," Rick said. "Neither is for you, Elsa."

"Are you still holding Charlie against me?" Shauna asked.

"We came to an agreement," Rick said. "I was sincere. You're not even the folks I was expecting."

"There's someone else you want to shoot badly enough to use gold shot?" Portia asked.

"I left New York to get away from my blood father," Rick said. "I've always been good with money and content with moderate returns from safe investments. Frank insisted on finding ways to double his money every year, whatever the price, and I'm not talking monetary cost."

"You knew Frank was here?" Portia asked.

Rick shook his head. "I didn't know until today where he'd gone. The King of New Amsterdam expelled him from New York because he gets too involved in organized crime," Rick said. "Now, I come to find he's been building a network of crime in Philly. Not just that, but my closest friend, my baby brother, Grigor has been helping him. Nipote, tonight you'll either thank me or send me to the roof, but nothing you do can change what I will do to them." He walked around the end of the bar. Shauna then noticed he had an axe with a wide straight blade strapped to his back. It made sense. Gold bullets wouldn't kill a vampire, but could bring them down long enough to get to them with a clean cut from an axe.

The front door of the bar flew open and the sounds of gunfire erupted. A handful of men dressed like the attackers at Zahaira's ran into the room shooting. Shauna felt the sting of several bullets hit her and her sister screamed and covered her face.

"I'm fine," Laura grunted. "It just surprised me."

Elsa turned to the door and Shauna could see she'd phased out just a little. The twins fell to the floor and scrambled to knock tables over and hide behind them.

Edmund swore and dove for the end of the bar. He rolled into a crouch and started to return fire with his sidearm. He had a couple wounds in his side. The bullets from his pistol weren't even deterring the men with their military body armor.

Portia didn't move. She stood serenely in the middle of the chaos, but no one shot her. Everyone else in the bar had taken cover other than Shauna, her sister, the countess, Amber and Elsa.

One of the gunmen rose into the air. Shauna noticed Elsa staring at that one. When he reached the ceiling he fell to the floor. The fall had been less than thirty feet and thudding to the floor brought a grunt from the man. As he tried to climb to his feet, Elsa lifted him into the air again.

Amber rushed headlong into the black-clad attackers. Most didn't have a chance to retrain their guns on James' pet before her sword cut through them. Two in the rear did, but their bullets didn't have any effect.

"Don't bother shooting that one," a man entering the bar said. He, like Amber, wore medieval armor, though his was of a far simpler design and adorned in brass crosses. He held Zahaira's sword. "She's mine." He charged Amber, swinging. To Shauna's surprise, he forced Amber to backpedal.

"Henry the Inquisitor," Portia said to Shauna. "All I can do for you is wish you luck. She then walked off toward a corner of the room.

Shauna didn't have much time to wonder just who was there to help her. She noticed the familiar man following Henry. "Peter," she mumbled his name, just a little surprised at how much it came out as a growl. He had a crossbow braced over his casted hand. "Laura, get behind the bar."

"Bullets don't scare me," Laura said. "Amber has the man with the gold sword. I think she'll win."

The same thoughts are what kept Shauna from seeking cover. Rick's gold bullets weren't meant for her or he'd have shot her. She was certain he meant to take down Frank.

"Shauna," Amber called. "Kill the men with the guns, please!"

The two remaining men in black body armor looked her way and sprayed her with bullets. The stings were annoying and she allowed them to fuel her anger. She ran over and grabbed one and threw him against the wall. She hadn't realized the wall had been concrete until a portion of it crumbled around the man's body. The other man was frantically trying to reload his gun. In his panic, he dropped the magazine he was trying to insert into the rifle. He looked at Shauna and turned to run.

Shauna jumped ahead of him and backhanded his face. She felt his skull crush under the blow and he fell. She then stood face to face with Peter.

"I'm betting you won't kill me," he said. He pulled the trigger of his crossbow, but he hadn't been aiming at her. The quarrel flew past her, catching Rick in the chest. The bar owner fell, dropping his shotgun.

"You lose," Shauna said. She grabbed Peter, cradling his head in her hands. "I don't like being played." Thinking of how he must've known what she was, and he'd led her on romantically, she twisted his neck far beyond the snap of his spine.

"That was damned cold," Laura said. Shauna hadn't realized her sister followed her into the fray. "I wasn't imagining so much violence when you talked about vampires. This isn't exactly blood and roses. Blood, yes…"

Shauna looked at the crumpled bodies of Peter and his cohorts. For a moment she just stared, wondering when she'd become such a monster as to be able to kill without thinking twice.

Two men came into the room from the back hall. Shauna recognized Grigor. The other man gestured to Rick and Grigor headed over to the fallen bar owner.

"Francesco," Portia said, walking out of her corner to confront the other man. "You go too far inviting a hunter in your pathetic attempt to usurp my territory."

"And you underestimate my ambition," Frank said. "The hunters and I have a deal. I help them reduce the number of potent vampires and they let me rule those who remain."

"You're a fool," Portia said. "And you can't take my county by force."

"And that's why I brought a hunter," Frank said. "He claims to be immune to vampire wiles. Your gift of appearing too sweet to harm won't save you from someone who doesn't care."

Shauna heard Amber scream and turned to see her fall to the ground. She started to run towards James' pet when Grigor yelled behind her.

"This is for Charlie," he said. She heard a blast and turned just in time to see he held Rick's shotgun and had it aimed at her. He turned it to her and pulled the trigger again. The shot felt just like the machine guns except all the stings happened at the same time.

"I guess gold doesn't hurt me," Shauna said stepping toward Grigor.

"Doesn't matter, bitch," Grigor said. "Your pet wasn't so lucky."

Looking behind her she saw Laura sitting on the floor looking at her. Her hands were over her chest and red blood was pouring down her shirt. "I'm sorry, sis," Laura said, coughing blood.

"Behind you!" Elsa yelled.

Shauna didn't turn in time. Something hard hit Shauna in the back of the neck, knocking her to the ground beside her sister. Henry had struck her with Zahaira's sword. When she looked back at him, his eyes were wide. He turned and ran toward the back door, the metal plates of his armor clamoring.

"I hired you to kill her," Frank yelled, pointing to where Portia stood in the corner.

"Not with that one here," Henry said.

"You get paid to kill vampires," Frank said.

"If you insist," Henry said as he passed Frank, he swung Zahaira's sword, removing Frank's head. "I'll be back for the rest of you demons. You haven't seen the last of me." He then ran out the back door.

Shauna couldn't bring herself to chase him. She cradled Laura in her arms "You'll be okay," Shauna said.

"I don't think so," Elsa said, kneeling by her. "That's heart blood. If she were a mere human, she'd be dead already. Even as a pet, she has minutes, maybe only seconds."

"Which means I have minutes or seconds," Shauna said. She wondered what would become of her after she died. She suspected she'd learn fairly soon if there really was a hell.

"Feed her," Elsa said.

"What?" Shauna asked.

"Your blood can save her and save you," Elsa said.

"You mean turn her into a vamp?" Shauna asked. She bit into her wrist and placed it against Laura's lips. "You know what to do," she said gently to Laura. She then looked back at Elsa and said, "This could kill her."

"One in a million odds are better than she had a second ago," Elsa said. "You survived the change without any time as a pet. She's genetically identical to you and she's had a few days for her body to adjust to the blood. She'll live."

"If you're wrong, I'll haunt you," Shauna said.

"And you'd join a cast of thousands," Elsa said. "Without guilt we are monsters."

"I killed them without guilt," Shauna nodded to the men by the door.

"Did you?" Elsa said. "I thought you killed them because they were trying to kill us."

"That was my motivation," Shauna said. As long as she considered it a matter of choosing a life for a life, she could deal with the killing, until she just considered that she'd ended lives. When her thoughts went that direction, she forced herself to think of other things, which was easy as long as she had her sister demanding immediate attention.

"Your voice betrays your sorrow from killing them," Elsa said. "You are still human inside. It's not something you want to lose. Trust me when I say it's something you'd regret. Alcohol and sex only go so far in burying centuries of guilt. It's the guilt we don't face head on that haunts us. You are lucky in that the people you killed were malicious towards us and killing them prevented death." She reached over and pulled Shauna's hand from Laura's mouth. "That's enough blood. We need to get her to a tomb."

Laura had fallen into unconsciousness, but her chest had stopped bleeding. Shauna couldn't hear a heartbeat. "She's dead?" Shauna asked.

"That's part of the process," Elsa said. "But she'll be back. If she were gone, you'd be gone too. As a nigh unkillable vamp, she'll be less death prone."

"There's a tomb in the subbasement," Rick said. He sat, propped against the bar with Allison holding him. The bloody arrow was still in her hand. "Rhiannon can show you."

Rhiannon and Grigor were at the end of the bar, kneeling at Portia's feet. Edmund stood behind Portia with the shotgun broken open under his arm.

Amber lay sprawled on the floor. The chest plate of her armor had a sharp dent. "Is she dead?" Shauna asked, pointing to the pet.

"Hardly a scratch on her," Elsa said. "She's breathing. Henry conked her in the head pretty good with the cross guard of his sword. Henry then tried really hard to hack into her chest when she fell but then you killed the kid with the crossbow and got shot with gold so he came after you before he could get through that armor of hers."

Rhiannon came over and helped Shauna to her feet while she still cradled her sister. She took her glasses off and looked Shauna in the eye. "I am sorry, but I did not know Allison was the copycat killer."

Shauna nodded. She couldn't remember Rhiannon doing anything but sitting by, watching through her red-tinted glasses. When Shauna looked at the glasses hanging from Rhiannon's fingers, she realized why they looked familiar. She'd seen them before she'd met Rhiannon, only they hadn't been in color and they hadn't been on a face. "You're A. A. Aaronson," Shauna said. "You signed my book that night when I was killed."

"I was A. A. Aaronson," Rhiannon said. "It seems I may have been revealing secrets and Portia has forbidden me from ever again writing about vampires. Come, the crypt is this way." She walked by the bar and pushed a section of the wall. It folded back, revealing a tunnel.

"That's your punishment?" Shauna asked. "Apologize to me and no more writing?"

"No more writing about vampires," Rhiannon clarified. "And the apology was all me. It was not required."

Rhiannon, though present when Rick had been hostile, hadn't ever taken an active role to antagonize her. Not being an enemy was enough, Shauna decided. That Rhiannon was her favorite author might have made her easy to forgive. "And Grigor?" Shauna asked.

"Will be spending tomorrow on Portia's roof," Rhiannon said. "Which means he'll see the sun for a few seconds—his last few seconds. It's not for his part in what he did to you, but he brought a hunter among us and had an active role in the killings of several vampires. There's no avoiding that sentence for him."

She led Shauna into a wine cellar where she grabbed two bottles of wine. Using a corkscrew mounted on one of the racks, she loosened the corks. She then led Shauna through a heavy steel door and down a ramp to an empty room with black marble walls.

"I can take this from here," Shauna said. She sat her sister on the floor and leaned her against the wall and waited. Rhiannon set the bottles on the floor and stepped away.

When her sister groggily opened her eyes, Shauna crouched by her and said, "I hope your first week as a vamp is less exciting than mine."

She went on to explain the wine and promised to be up in the bar when Laura was done changing.

"You can't stay," Rhiannon said. "She'll tear you to pieces."

"I guessed as much," Shauna said. "James left me alone. I figured it was for a reason."

"Who's James?" Rhiannon asked.

Shauna sighed. She'd finally revealed the secret to someone who hadn't known. She looked Rhiannon in the eye and said, "Forget I said that." She wasn't sure coercion would work on another vampire without blood, but figured Rhiannon didn't know enough to make it worth the hassle of forcing blood into her mouth.

When she returned to the barroom, Amber was standing by Portia. Edmund and Grigor were gone. "What happens now?" Shauna asked. "Do we go after Henry?"

"He's augmented," Amber said. "I don't know how, but he's beyond human in strength and speed. I think he's a pet. I'm not sure I want to try to go toe to toe with him again."

"He won't be back anytime soon," Portia said. "He won't act alone and it will take time for him to train another team. As intimidated as you are by him, he's far more scared of Shauna. I've never heard of a vamp who couldn't be harmed by gold. I've already taken care of Edmund, but Shauna will have to coerce us all to forget we saw that sword bounce harmlessly off her neck."

"Excuse me?" Shauna asked. Using her coercion against Rick was one thing, but she couldn't fathom doing it to her friends. Perhaps it was best, but she felt it would be violating them in some way.

Elsa stepped up behind her and wrapped her arms around Shauna's waist. "She's right," the elder vampire said. "We can't know you're that powerful."

"How powerful am I," Shauna asked.

Portia said, "Let me put it this way. There is a secret temple in Paris where vampires wishing to claim a crown must go to be ordained. The vampire there is supposed to be the first and his name is Amenhetop. He is an old catatonic vampire who just wanders an underground temple there. There is a ritual new kings and queens must go through that involves drinking some of his blood. No other vampire's teeth can pierce his skin so a golden needle is used. If gold cannot penetrate your skin, you are more powerful than he, of purer Venae than he."

"I never believed Amenhetop was real. I thought it was just another of the origin rumors," Elsa said. "So he's not the first. Does that mean that the first vampire has been here in Philly for years and none of us suspected? Is James the first?"

"I am not she." James stood at the bottom of the stairs. Shauna hadn't noticed anyone enter the bar. In a bellowing voice that rattled the walls of the barroom, he said. "No one here need forget anything of tonight, but none of you will speak of it to anyone who is not here." Shauna suspected he'd just coerced everyone without even needing to make eye contact.

Amber ran over and hugged him, "Where were you?"

"Germany," James said. "My blood-grandson Dun lived there. Something killed him."

"So a vampire hunter like Henry is on a rampage in Europe?" Shauna asked.

"No," James said. "Dun was too pure to be harmed by anything a vampire hunter could wield. Whatever it is, it's worse than a hunter. I didn't find who did it, but I found their lair and I found this." He held up a little leather clad book. "It has my address, Elsa's address and the addresses of every vampire on the east coast pure enough to claim a crown."

"Henry was just a minion," Amber said. "A highly trained minion. Someone is very serious about culling vamps."

"I don't think you fully understand who that someone is," James said. "There are five beings other than myself that I know of with the ability to harm Dun and I've seen all of them in the past day. I am certain none of them are involved. This is why you will not forget what you know. I am going to need whatever help I can get."

"Those vampires who could kill Dun: Shauna is one of them, isn't she?" Elsa asked.

James said, "She is my blood-daughter, which makes her purer than my blood-grandson. She could harm him, but he died on the night she was made."

Shauna took a moment to gather her courage then said, "If that's how it works, you should probably know that there will soon be another vamp of that power. My sister is transitioning now. I'm sorry. I had no choice. If she'd died I would have died."

James nodded. "I wouldn't have wanted you to die. The bloodline stops at your sister. I will make that clear to her when she finishes the change. Tonight we clean up this mess. Tomorrow we plan a war against something even I can't imagine."

"So, James," Elsa said. "Since we're all forcibly sworn to secrecy anyway, can you tell me who the first vampire is?"

James said. "Her name is Reilla."

"That's all you're going to tell me, isn't it?" Elsa asked.

"Probably not," James said. "You seem to have a way to get to my secrets. I suspect someday you will get me to reveal everything I know. That day is not today."

THE BLOODDAUGHTER TRILOGY
BOOK II: BLOOD HUNTRESS

CHAPTER 1

"You need to feed."

The voice of Shauna's maker, James, resonated through her memory as she walked alone down the street. She'd been meandering between South and Market, waiting for someone to look appealing. He'd told her repeatedly that she showed amazing control over her thirst, the kind of control he'd rarely seen in vampires less than a century old, let alone in a vampire less than two months into her existence after her death.

Most of the people she'd encountered were in groups. She opted to ignore those, but she could deal with several people if she had to. Most of the people were too normal looking. She had standards, or so she decided. She would only feed on men she found attractive enough to date. Perhaps she was just making an excuse to avoid feeding. The guy who'd just parked his car in an alley would be a good opportunity. Shauna hesitated until the man walked out of the alley and up to an apartment building.

Following him inside wouldn't be hard, but she didn't feel right violating a person's home.

She'd fed four times since that night in November. It was enough to sate her need, but less than she could use. She'd be stronger if she kept herself full. James wasn't the only one to tell her that. Her other mentor and best friend, Elsa, had tried to get her to drink more than an ounce or two at a time. Two pints wouldn't kill a person, or so Elsa had assured her. It would fill her tanks, so to say. She'd have full access to all her strengths. Shauna wasn't sure what that meant. She was immeasurably stronger than she'd been as a mere human.

She couldn't put a finger on why she was hesitant. She'd fed before. She'd killed, as all vampires must on their first feed. She didn't have to kill again. She liked the taste. She enjoyed the palpable energy of blood.

Yet, Shauna felt immoral, feeding, even when it was from a willing subject like another vampire's pet. She could justify it when she needed it to survive, but she got what she needed from an ounce or two a week. Perhaps she needed to do more than just survive.

Maybe she was weaker than she'd been after she first fed until full. That had killed her prey, a murderous bitch named Allison. She tried to remember if she'd felt more powerful back then. She had, but it might have been a matter of perspective, having just been mortal a couple days before.

There was only one way Shauna would know if she were missing something by drinking just enough to sate her needs. Resolved to take the next person she found alone, Shauna kept walking.

Passing the old graveyard for the third time, Shauna noticed the girl walking along the gravestones, touching each one. She looked young, perhaps only twenty, but there was a child like glee in her eyes when her fingertips ran across the names on the markers. The dyed blue and black hair and heavy eyeliner put the girl squarely inside the goth subculture, though the plaid skirt and black pea-coat were less stereotypical. The girl had a fascination with the dead. She was the kind of girl who would wish vampires were real and relish the prospect of being fed on. Though she'd been hoping to find an attractive man, everything about the girl intrigued Shauna; she'd found her meal.

For a moment, she watched the girl in the graveyard, finding the courage within herself to act. She wasn't even sure what was stopping her. She had the ability and the power to do it. The morality of it was something she'd come to terms with well enough. What worried her, she realized, was her ability to stop if she let herself drink freely. The only time she'd fed alone, she'd killed. However, when she'd fed with Elsa at her side, she'd stopped herself long before Elsa would have. Shauna was confident, mostly, that she could stop before putting her prey in real danger.

With her own hair dyed blood red and wearing a black lace gown under a tattered bright red leather jacket, Shauna would fit right in with the goth girl. Looking around the streets and not seeing moving cars or other pedestrians, Shauna made sure her prey was looking the other way then flew up over the brick wall that surrounded the graveyard and landed gently a few paces behind the girl. The scent of lavender oil carried through the crisp winter air as Shauna stepped closer.

"Don't be afraid," Shauna said, imbuing her will into the words. The girl turned and looked at her a moment. Her eyes were open wide, shocked, but the tilt of the girls neck bespoke curiosity. It also allowed Shauna to see the pulse along the girl's carotid artery. Shauna asked, "Come here often?" Inwardly she winced at the cliché pickup line.

"Only on Thursdays," the girl said. "The church is closed so there's no one to tell me I shouldn't be here after dark."

Shauna tried to think of what to say next. She'd never picked anyone up before, for any reason. In the clubs, she let her prey come to her and moving from kissing to biting a man's shoulder was a natural progression. She wondered if maybe she'd gone about this encounter wrong. Perhaps she should have just attacked from behind, taking the girl's blood. It would have avoided the awkward moment Shauna currently experienced, though it might have made the girl scream.

Lacking any more ideas for small talk, Shauna decided to just move in. She stepped close to the girl and said, again using her coercion, "You're going to enjoy this." She gently cupped the back of the girls head and kissed her. Carefully she guided the girl to the ground and lay atop her. The girl returned the kisses fervently, even moaning. She'd taken the coercion wholeheartedly, taking immense pleasure from the kisses.

Shauna undid the buttons on the girl's pea coat and pulled it down one shoulder. She kissed her way down the girls neck, restraining herself from biting the artery. Though, as her passions grew, so did her hunger. The girl had a black t-shirt under the coat. Shauna tore it along the shoulder seam, nearly ripping it off completely. The act caused the girl to let out an anticipative whimper. When Shauna bit her, the girl cried out. Shauna quickly placed the side of her hand between the girl's lips, between her teeth. The cry had been one of pleasure, but would draw attention if anyone heard.

Shauna's fangs had penetrated the shoulder muscles and found a vein. She drank, forcing herself past the first two sips, allowing herself to enjoy the flavor of the thick, warm blood. She felt the rush of energy as the blood recharged her. As the blood flowed, the girl's muffled screams grew louder and by the way the girl writhed, they weren't from fear or pain.

Unsure how to gauge two pints, Shauna drank until she'd swallowed the equivalent of a couple glasses of wine. Feeling fuller than she had since her first feed, Shauna pulled away, careful to lick the wound as she did. The punctures healed instantly, but there had been quite a bit of blood Shauna hadn't caught. She'd torn away the shirt, hoping to avoid leaving evidence of blood loss, but both the shirt and coat had blood on them.

She returned her kisses to the girl's lips and slowed them until the girl's moans quieted.

"We had fun," Shauna said, then using her coercion, added, "I am not a vampire. I didn't bite you or drink your blood. We met and fooled around a little. We got a little carried away and we stumbled and you hit a stone with your shoulder, tearing your shirt and getting a minor cut." She reached out and scraped the girl's shoulder with her fingernail. She still needed to find a way to trim them; they were getting a little too long. The new cut bled, but not much. Shauna had to push herself away to avoid the desire to drink more.

"We had fun," the girl said. "I know I enjoyed myself. Stay, let me return the favor."

"I wish I could," Shauna said. "I have somewhere I need to be."

"Do you have a name?" the girl asked. "I at least want a name to go with the memory."

"I'm Shauna."

"My friends call me Azure," the girl said.

Shauna nodded and repeated the girl's name, "Azure." Standing, Shauna pulled the girl to her feet as gently as she could. "Maybe I'll find you here again some Thursday."

"Maybe," Azure said with a hopeful tease in her voice.

Shauna walked towards the gate by the church. There was no way she'd get away with flying with the girl's eyes locked on her, entranced. She wanted to fly. She had the energy to do anything, or she felt like she did. Perhaps Elsa and James were right. She was stronger and hadn't hurt anyone, at least not badly. Azure would walk away from the encounter happy. Shauna began to think she could embrace existence as a vampire without having to become a monster.

Checking the time on her phone, she realized she did have somewhere to be. Elsa was going to meet her at a boutique on Fourth Street ten minutes earlier and Elsa was never late for shopping.

§

Shauna hadn't taken two steps into the boutique before Elsa said, "Interesting scent, beautiful. Where did you find a girl wearing lavender?"

"I don't…" Shauna wasn't sure how much she should be talking openly in the shop, though the only people there were Elsa, her twin human pets, Jackie and Jonnie, and two salesgirls.

One of the salesgirls stood by Elsa, holding a black scarf against Elsa's hair. The other held a stack of dresses draped over her arm.

"That one matches my hair too well," Elsa said of the scarf. "It took years to get these tresses so long and lustrous.

I prefer to show them off. Let's see the purple ones." As the girl with the scarf walked away, Elsa took a dress from the other's hands, walked up to Shauna and held it against her. As an older vampire, Elsa had tricks Shauna hadn't learned yet. One of which was the ability to speak to her so that no one else would hear the words. She said, "It's nice to see you full of Venae; you glow like a fresh bride. I was worried about you." Elsa changed to a normally audible voice and said. "Now, I'm worried Jackie will be jealous."

"Of a kiss?" Jackie, one of the twins, stepped up by Shauna and bumped hips with her. Jackie had been twenty-some years old for almost two centuries, but Elsa dressed her twins to look a few years younger. Shauna had concluded the elder vampire's reasons were somewhere between shock value and perversion.

The thought stirred images from old books of Elizabeth Bathory bathing in the blood of teenage girls. Those tales were fiction, mostly, Elsa would say. Hapsburg lies. Shauna believed Elsa had been maligned by history. It was only by believing the horrors were greatly exaggerated that she could like herself for being friends with Elsa, who had once been the infamous Blood Countess.

Twirling a short, white blonde pigtail around her finger, Jackie asked, "It was just a kiss, right?"

"Unless she managed to shower off everything but the lavender," Elsa said, sniffing. "It wasn't more than that." She winked at Shauna and said, "So proud of you."

The other twin pet, Jonnie, stood on a pedestal modeling a formal blue evening gown. She gave Shauna a thumbs up.

"Thanks," Shauna said, feeling good. She wasn't sure if it was from the blood, from the compliment or perhaps, from the pride of taking another step into embracing her role in the world as a vampire. The dress Elsa held up to Shauna's chest was a simple ivory dress. It reminded Shauna of the kind of wedding dress someone would wear for a ceremony in their own living room. "Are you sure this is me?" she asked.

When Elsa dressed Shauna in goth styles, and she always did so, wedding gowns were not unusual. They were never new and always distressed either with age stains or tears. Looking around the store, Shauna was surprised to notice that everything in the boutique was new. Elsa normally took her to vintage clothing boutiques.

"White is a bit misleading for an evening gown," Elsa said. "Which designer sent us this?" she asked the salesgirl.

The salesgirl with the armful of dresses said, "I didn't like it either. I was bringing you this pile to show you what kind of junk we've been getting lately."

"Toss 'em," Elsa said. "Bring me something red and light."

The other salesgirl came back with several purple scarves draped over one arm; she had a disheveled stack of blouses and skirts over the other. "Your friend in the dressing room told me to stop bringing her anything you told me to bring her. She just wants to know what we have in denim."

Shauna laughed. She hadn't realized her sister, Laura, would be there. Like Elsa's pets. Shauna and her sister were identical twins. Due to a nearly tragic string of violent events in November, Laura was also Shauna's blooddaughter.

"Still trying to get two matched pairs?" Shauna asked Elsa.

"Never been a goal," Elsa said with a shrug. "I play her game. I send her the most obnoxiously opulent gowns and the most revealing casual wear and she wears more denim and more black. With her hair, getting the two of you to match is impossible and I would never wish you to cut your lovely locks." She ran her fingers through Shauna's hair down to the middle of her back. Laura's hair barely covered her ears on most days, and other than a few fading highlights, still held the natural brown color.

"Remember who signs your paychecks," Elsa said to the sales girl. "Take her that red and gold kimono looking dress and a patent leather skirt. If you have any denim in the store, take her something a size too small."

"Yes, Miss Davlos," the girl said, using Elsa's modern name.

The other salesgirl came back with what looked like little more than a sliver of red gauze and handed it to Elsa, who then handed it to Shauna and said, "Put this on."

Shauna took the dress and headed to one of the dressing rooms. As she walked away, she heard Elsa say, "Jonnie, step down, I think we'll go with plan 'Cowboy'."

§

Shauna stood on the pedestal by the mirrors as Elsa and her pets walked around and admired the red gauze dress. They definitely gave Shauna the impression they weren't so much looking at the dress as what it wasn't hiding beneath.

"Should she wear a black bra and panties underneath?" Jackie asked as she reached out and caressed Shauna's hip.

The touch caused Shauna to involuntarily inhale. She didn't need the air; she only needed air to talk. Jackie's touches were never innocent. That she was in love with Shauna wasn't a secret from anyone. Shauna felt a closeness for Jackie, but wasn't sure what she'd call it. Sexual orientation didn't come into play as a vampire, or so Elsa kept trying to convince Shauna. Vampires no longer had the hormones to drive attraction. However, vamps could still experience pleasure and get excited by the anticipation of that pleasure. That Shauna had chosen a woman to feed on that night, and seduced her, allowed her to believe Elsa was at least a little right.

Jackie's touch had excited her, which surprised Shauna. It had been Jackie's lips she'd kissed more than anyone's in the past month, but that had been just about the kissing. Perhaps her touch reminded Shauna that she would be more comfortable sitting on the settee by the wall, kissing the pet, than she was standing on a pedestal like an object of art to be admired.

"Go with the black panties," Elsa said. "I think the top is just a little more than a hint, a tease to make people want to look closer and that's always the purpose."

Elsa made no secret of her attraction to Shauna either, but was waiting for her to make the first move, while constantly inviting her to.

Laura was still somewhere in the boutique. One of the dressing room doors was closed. Laura wouldn't be out to seek the feedback of anyone else. The door might stay closed until they were ready to leave the boutique.

As kids, being twins, Shauna and Laura dressed alike and hung out in the same crowds until the last two years of high school. Then Laura cut her hair and started hanging with the crowds who were experimenting with recreational drugs. In the years since, Shauna had bailed her sister out of jail more than once and drove her to rehab a few times as well. They had grown apart, but despite their differences in lifestyles, Laura was the most important person in the world to Shauna.

"Do you need new panties?" Elsa asked, bringing back Shauna's attention from Laura's door.

"You buy me two new pairs nearly every day," Shauna said. "I have more lingerie than a strip club, thanks to you."

"Let's be going then," Elsa said. "James' party is tomorrow night and I know how picky you get when buying shoes."

Shauna guffawed at her friend. It wasn't Shauna who was picky. She went to the open dressing room and changed back to the black lace gown and tattered leather jacket Elsa had dressed her in before they'd gone out. When she emerged from the dressing room, Laura was standing at the cash register with Elsa, who looked at her sister, clearly disapproving of the clothing she'd chosen for herself.

Elsa slid Laura's pile across the counter along with Shauna's new dress and two pairs of black panties. "Put these on my account," Elsa said.

"Of course, Miss Davlos," the cashier said as she folded the items and placed them into a large bag.

"You were excellent tonight," Elsa said to the cashier. "Go ahead and close up early. Follow us out the door and lock up then take the rest of the night off and celebrate." She slid a hundred dollar bill across the counter. Her suggestion wasn't just words, Elsa had coerced the cashier. She'd do as Elsa said and not think twice about it.

"Did you tip the other salesgirl too?" Shauna asked. "I'm not sure she was as deserving. She disappeared about halfway through our shopping." The last Shauna had seen the girl, she was bringing Shauna and her sister dresses while they were in the dressing rooms.

"I haven't seen her for a while," Elsa said. "She may have left early when she realized I was the shop's owner and there was no commission in selling to me."

Older vampires seemed to invest in their hobbies, and fashion was Elsa's second favorite hobby. From what Shauna could tell, she was Elsa's first.

As they left the shop, Elsa said to Jonnie, "Call the carpet cleaners; I saw a stain in the back."

"Already did," Jonnie said.

"It was barely noticeable," Laura said.

"I didn't even notice a stain," Shauna said. She hadn't been looking at the carpet. She still felt star-struck shopping in boutiques where the only way to find the price of something was to ask. Just a couple months earlier, most of Shauna's clothing had come from discount department stores.

"See?" Laura said.

"Still," Elsa replied in an unusually stern voice while looking straight at Laura. "That kind of thing cannot be ignored for long."

"Whatever," Laura said then walked ahead of the group, out of conversation range.

The relationship between Elsa and Laura was one of mutual tolerance. Laura respected Elsa's experience as a vampire and accepted her as Shauna's friend, but refused to be manipulated and saw everything Elsa did as an attempt at manipulation. Elsa, on the other hand, usually treated Laura with strained kindness, often making it clear she was being nicer than she wanted to be. Each accepted the other because both were inseparable from Shauna and neither made any attempt to hide their reasons.

"Now, on to shoes," Elsa said. "Black stilettos or red?"

That Shauna had four or five pairs of each in her closet wouldn't matter to Elsa. Shauna actually enjoyed her friend's joy at dressing her up so Shauna answered, "Black, obviously. And we'll need a belt to match. I'm thinking something satin or suede. Patent would be too shiny and won't work with the gauze."

"You are learning," Elsa said. "Maybe someday you won't need me to pick out your clothes."

Even if Shauna didn't need air, she wasn't holding her breath.

CHAPTER 2

The party was livelier than Shauna had expected. If it were one of Elsa's parties, it would be louder, with more people and less clothing, but Shauna's bloodfather, James, had insisted on throwing the New Year's Eve party. With his staid demeanor, Shauna had been expecting nothing more than a dinner party with a handful of vampires sitting at a long table, sipping wine.

She had never actually been to one of Elsa's parties, but had heard the stories from Jackie. Had Elsa not lost her apartment to vampire hunters, she might have fought with James over who got to host for New Year's.

James had music playing. It wasn't current but it wasn't classical either. Someday, Shauna planned to ask why his music collection ended at 1982 and why he had so many disco records.

There were more than a handful of people spread through James' living room and dining room. Most of them were vampires, but a few were the pets of the vampires. Of all the people there, only Shauna and her sister were younger than the music. But of all the other vampires in the room, only one was from a time after Mozart; they were the local elders.

Shauna stood with Elsa and James by the door to the library. All three had wine glasses. The table by James' side had a few opened wine bottles, as did almost every surface in the room except the dining room table. Elsa's twins were on the table dancing to the disco music with Laura. Shauna was watching the twins. James couldn't be distracted from Elsa, though he probably wanted to be. He had his usual pleasant smile on his face as Elsa vocally surmised several things about him, his age, and his origin.

"Enough," James said. "If I answer three questions, will you stop asking and let us both enjoy the party?"

"Will the answers be whole and not coy or sly?" Elsa asked.

James nodded. "You have my word."

"Yay!" Elsa said. She stepped up close to James. He wasn't particularly tall, maybe six feet, maybe a tad more. Elsa, with her pale skin and straight raven black hair that hung to her thighs, looked like a doll beside him despite being less than a foot shorter. "How many New Year's Eves have you celebrated?"

James smiled then said, "I have celebrated every New Year on this night every year since Caesar changed the Roman calendar."

"Are you Roman or Egyptian?" Elsa asked.

"No," James said. "I was not born in either Rome or Egypt or in any land claimed by them at the time I was born."

Shauna had always assumed James was Egyptian. He had dark brown eyes and black hair and his skin was bronzed as if he had a tan. Because of his skin tone, she hadn't originally suspected he was a vampire despite talking to him regularly as a customer of the bookstore where she had worked. She only learned of his secret when he turned her. Shauna wasn't the only one oblivious to his being a vampire. Every other vampire in the room had known him, but, other than Elsa and Countess Portia, none knew he was a vampire until after Shauna had learned his secret.

"So, where were you born?" Elsa asked.

"The game is over," James said. He wasn't wry or sarcastic, he spoke matter-of-factly. "I have answered three questions."

"You counted my asking if you'd be coy?" Elsa asked.

"Again," James said, "I cannot answer as I have already answered the three questions I agreed to." That time, the corner of his lip lifted into a smile. Shauna couldn't help but to chuckle.

"You are so fucking frustrating," Elsa growled loudly enough to drown the music out for a moment.

"You could stop trying to get me to reveal my secrets," James suggested. "Or we could play another game. I'll tell you another secret about myself and then I'll tell Shauna a secret about you."

Elsa let out a frustrated growl and grabbed a bottle of wine from the table. She then flew over to dance on the table with her twins. Shauna had never seen her fly indoors. Elsa taught Shauna how to use her Venae to manipulate objects through apportation, and ultimately to push against the ground to fly, but Shauna wouldn't dare fly without open sky. She was sure she would crash through the chandelier if not the ceiling or a wall.

The other vampires in the room stared at James, waiting to see how he'd react to Elsa's outburst. They feared him because none knew how old or pure he was. They only knew he was purer of Venae than Shauna and she was purer than any of them. James' calm demeanor wasn't hiding a bound spring waiting to suddenly uncoil. He was as cool as they came and it wasn't an act. Shauna suspected that after a couple thousand years, a vampire would learn near infinite patience.

Elsa had patience, but rarely allowed it to get in the way of her fun. Elsa was, without question, Shauna's best friend. Elsa had been there for Shauna when James disappeared immediately after turning her. As close to Elsa as Shauna was, she had learned some of her secrets. Other than Countess Portia, James and Laura, Shauna was the only vampire in the room that knew Elsa was Elizabeth Bathory. Everyone else knew her as Elsabet Davlos, a real estate magnate.

Elsa had been made into a vampire sometime around the year sixteen hundred after spending a few years as a pet to her maker, Vlad Dracula the Impaler. Elsa pinned most of the murdered girls that weren't just Hapsburg lies on Vlad. She had met her pets in Eastern Europe in the weeks after Dracula was killed in the early nineteenth century. Jackie and Jonnie were magician's assistants from Russia at the time.

They specialized in a trick where one would go into one door and the other would come out another, seemingly one person moving through a magic doorway.

Elsa enjoyed her pets and treated them like treasured dolls and they liked to be spoiled by her. Many vampires treated their pets as servants working for them for the privilege of drinking small amounts of the vampires blood from time to time. The blood kept the pets young and altered their metabolism so they would heal faster. Too much vampire blood, more than an ounce, was poisonous to both vampires and humans. It wouldn't usually kill them unless they fought to keep it down. Small amounts could create a bond between a human and a vampire. No one understood how Elsa had two pets when every other vampire could only have one at a time. Shauna didn't have a pet. Laura had been her pet for a few days, just after Shauna was made, but she'd made her sister into a vampire when the healing of being a pet hadn't been fast enough to save her from a shotgun wound during a fight with Henry the Inquisitor, a vampire hunter.

While Elsa dressed goth, in stained white lace and leather, she dressed her pets in provocative outfits, most often like school girls, but that night they wore torn and tied t-shirts, jeans cut off above the legs, and stylized knee high cowboy boots. The accompanying hats hadn't lasted five minutes into their dancing.

Shauna wore the outfit they had bought the night before. Earlier that day she'd re-dyed her hair, covering the brown roots with her usual blood red. She checked it in the mirror and it was just a shade brighter than the dress. She'd started dying her hair in her last year as a mortal as a way to take control over something in her life and to help her otherwise boring self stand out in a crowd. She no longer needed the latter reason, but as potent as the Venae made Shauna, she still didn't feel in control of very much of her life.

Somewhere out there, hunters were still looking for her and the other vampires in the room. The last time, the hunters hadn't come prepared to deal with a vampire of Shauna's purity. It would just be a matter of time before they showed up again with better weapons.

"You don't appear to be having fun," James said. "It's been a while since I've thrown a party. Am I doing it wrong?"

"I'm having fun," Shauna said. "I just had a moment."

"This is why you wanted to be a vampire?" James asked. "You wanted to enjoy a more interesting night life and have more fun at parties."

Shauna had never thought of it that way. It was true that she'd wanted to be a vampire long before she believed they actually existed. She'd had many reasons, the main one had been to worry less about death, or so she'd told herself. The irony there was that she'd faced more life and death situations in the time since becoming a vampire than she'd ever faced as a human.

"Is that what you think?" Shauna asked. "Why do you say that?"

"Remember, you've had the attention of both me and Elsa for almost a year," James said. "You intrigued me by showing both intellect and, well, I found you attractive. While it was a rushed decision to make you, to save you, it was a likely outcome after a few years."

"And Elsa liked me because you liked me," Shauna said. "She saw me as a path to you." It was more complex than that, and Shauna knew it. Elsa had tracked down Shauna after Jackie had become infatuated with her on a vampire fiction fan website. When Elsa saw James talking to Shauna, it drew her in, cinching her interest.

"And that worked," James said. "She is very good at getting what she wants. And now, she has you."

"Are you jealous?" Shauna asked. James had always been a gentleman, never pushing for romance. He'd hinted at it before the change, but not since. Their relationship had become like father and daughter.

"Live a thousand years, and jealousy fades," James said. "I have eons to know you."

Shauna didn't know what to say. Had he just admitted he still had romantic interest in her? She wasn't sure, but it seemed that way. "I guess I can see that," Shauna said. She wasn't sure she could grasp how her perceptions would change with time, but she knew they would.

"So, how do you plan to spend your immortality?" James asked. "Are you a seeker of knowledge or a party-girl?"

"I'm not sure I want to define myself as either," Shauna said. "You might have been onto something when you said I wanted a more interesting night life, but there is more to each day than just the night."

"And that kind of answer is why you intrigued me," James said.

"Why did you become a vampire?" Shauna asked.

"It wasn't a choice for me," James said. "Not that it was a choice for you, but it was something you were prepared to do. For me, my maker never asked and never explained beforehand. She just did it to me."

"You're good at telling secrets without revealing anything," Shauna said. She was still curious to know more of where vampires came from, but not as much as Elsa. Most of what Shauna knew of vampire history, she'd learned from Elsa. All James had revealed in weeks of conversations, was that Elsa's version of history wasn't always correct.

"I've had a few years to practice," James said. He then nudged her shoulder, pointed at his table and said, "You're being summoned."

With a finger, Elsa beckoned for Shauna to join her on the table.

"I don't know if your table can handle much more," Shauna said to James.

"It's three hundred years old," James said. "Back then, they truly built furniture to last the ages. If it does break, then it's probably about time to get a new one anyway. Go. Dance. It's a party; people should enjoy themselves."

As Shauna walked to the table, she noticed that all the partygoers did seem to be enjoying themselves. Countess Portia, the local royal, was laughing at something Rhiannon, a local author, had said. The other vampires chatted over the various bottles of wine. The only person not having fun was James' pet Amber.

In the fight with the hunters at Grue's Home the previous November, Amber had been humiliated, knocked unconscious by Henry the Inquisitor and he'd escaped. She stood by the archway to the atrium with one hand resting on her hip above a holstered pistol and her other loosely gripping her sword with the gold-plated blade as it hung in its scabbard.

Shauna hopped onto the table and let her body fall into the melodic rhythm of the disco beat. The table didn't even creak under the weight of five women. Elsa came close and pressed her body to Shauna's as Jackie did the same from behind.

They danced through several songs, sometimes close, sometimes skipping around the tabletop. When Jackie put her arms around Shauna and brought her face cheek to cheek, Shauna found herself resisting the urge to kiss her. It just wasn't appropriate for the setting. Jackie didn't try, only brushing her lips against Shauna's cheek and neck as they danced.

The music stopped abruptly. Amber stood by the stereo console with her sword drawn. "Something's not right here," she said in a hissing whisper.

Shauna wasn't sure who Amber was trying to hide her voice from until she heard the voices outside on the lawn.

"Get the pets to the library," James shouted.

Elsa nodded and Jonnie and Jackie leapt from the table and ran past James. All of the other pets, besides Amber, also rushed into the library. James opened a panel in the wall and pressed some buttons. A steel door dropped from the ceiling, closing off the library.

"That's a two inch thick door of layered steel, Kevlar and asbestos," James said. "I treasure my books and couldn't bear the thought of a fire reaching that room."

The voices outside spoke in codes Shauna had heard before when the hunters assaulted one of the city's oldest vampires' home, killing Zahaira.

"What's going on?" Countess Portia asked.

"Two vans stopped on the street at the end of the driveway," Amber said.

"Shouldn't we also be in the safety of the library?" Portia asked.

The scream of glass shattering from all directions kept anyone from answering. Once the windows were out, the popping sound of gunfire carried into the room. Bullets flew around Shauna on all sides. They weren't aiming at anything, yet.

"How would we kick their ass from in there?" Amber asked.

Shauna wished the table legs were thinner as she searched the room for a viable weapon. She considered grabbing a wine bottle until the first men dove into the room through the windows. They were wearing blackened Kevlar armor from head to toe. A bottle, even with vampiric strength behind it, would shatter on first impact and do nothing to the man under the armor.

Amber rushed toward a group of the attackers. James' pet screamed when a bullet tore through her abdomen, but she kept up her charge. She had both her pistol and sword out, but her bullets weren't even giving the armored men pause. Two more bullets passed through Amber, one through the arm holding the pistol and another through her thigh, before she slammed into the closest gunman. Her sword pierced deep into his chest.

Though Amber had insisted Shauna learn how to use a gun and she'd taught her how to handle both revolvers and semi-automatic pistols, Shauna didn't carry a gun and there weren't any lying around. As bullets started stinging her skin, tearing into her new clothes, Shauna realized she couldn't just stand there. They couldn't really hurt her, but they were hurting her friends. Shauna leapt at a squatting gunman. Amber hadn't taught her any fancy karate, but she had shown Shauna how to punch without breaking her thumb and how to kick without hurting her toes. Shauna relied purely on vampiric strength when she kicked the closest man to into the wall. He crushed through the plaster, splintering whatever wood was behind it. Shauna felt his ribs crack. He might not have died, but he was done for the night.

Elsa had a trick Shauna thought was ingenious but a little unfair. However, fair should not really come into play when fighting to survive, Shauna thought. Elsa phased her body, fading as she did when she would walk through walls. She then grabbed a pair of men with her psychokinesis and slammed them into each other. She'd pull them apart and then repeat until she felt pleased, which was long after they fell unconscious or died. While Elsa was phased, bullets passed straight through her without hurting her.

Shauna had the abilities to do what Elsa did, but it seemed too distant from the fight. For some reason, if she had to fight, Shauna wanted the physical sensation of her opponents trying to hurt her. It gave her the justification she needed to hurt them back.

Laura seemed to have the same view as Shauna. She sat on a gunman's chest, pummeling and scratching at his face. That the man died early in Laura's onslaught didn't seem to reduce her fervor. Shauna understood. It was hard to deal with the idea that these people hated them so much that they would go to so much effort to try to kill them. And the bullets, though they couldn't break Shauna or Laura's skin or even bruise them, still hurt like hell.

James, as Shauna's bloodfather, was even more impervious. He had a much calmer approach. He walked up to a gunman and picked him up by the shoulders. Looking into the gunman's eyes, he said, "Go home. Move to Alaska. Vampires are a myth." He then set the man on his feet. The man walked away, behind his fellow attackers, and then left through the front door.

Shauna couldn't help but admire the simplicity of James' method. She looked around for a gunman to try the trick on, but couldn't see any that were actively fighting. The gunfire had stopped and the only sounds were the moaning of men and vampires who lay on the ground amid puddles of blood.

The smell of human blood made her hungry, but vampires only drank from living people. Licking blood off the floor would provide no nutritive value. She had other things to worry about besides eating, so she pushed her hunger away as best she could.

Amber was badly wounded, standing over a pile of bodies with blood dripping from her sword as well as several bullet holes on her body. As an ancient pet to a very pure vampire, she'd heal from anything that didn't kill her instantly.

"Are they all dead?" Amber asked.

"Working on it," Laura said. She'd been feeding on a gunman that had been moaning in pain. He was now silent.

The snap of a bowstring drew Shauna's attention to a window. An arrow flew past her and impacted James' back. The arrow passed into Shauna's bloodfather and he twisted around and fell to his knees with a puzzled expression.

Looking to the window, Shauna saw a face she'd seen once before. Henry the Inquisitor dropped a crossbow into the room and ran off. Shauna was sure Amber would go after him, so she rushed to James. Amber did the same.

James knelt with his hands on the floor, steadying himself. He tried to speak, but only coughed up dark blood.

"How the hell did they hurt him?" Shauna asked. "Every one of those bullets was made of gold and they couldn't hurt me. I saw them bouncing off James as well."

Amber reached for the arrow, but slumped over, leaning against James. She had several wounds and seemed to have trouble breathing.

"The hunters are gone," Portia said. "Are James and Amber okay?"

"I hope so," Elsa said. "Amber isn't dead, so she'll heal. The gold might make it go slower than usual. I have no idea what's going on with James. How about everyone else?"

"Rhiannon and Rick both took bullets." Portia, who showed no evidence of having been injured, waved to a couch where the two sat with their hands covering their wounds. "They still have their heads, so they'll live. James somehow seems the worst of us."

Elsa yanked the arrow out, causing only a twitch in James. Her brow furrowed as she examined the blood coated arrowhead. "I wouldn't have expected this, but it makes perfect sense."

James fell forward on the rug and his eyes closed. Blood continued to drip from his mouth and the wound on his back. Shauna put her ear to James chest and listened carefully. She waited, hopeful. She heard the thump of a heartbeat after almost a minute. "He's alive," she said. One heartbeat every minute or two was normal for a vampire. She then noticed the white glint of the arrowhead. "That's not gold."

"It's bone," Elsa said. "It's vampire bone."

"Vampires don't leave bones when they die," Shauna said, sitting up. They would turn to dust after a few hours. She'd seen it happen to Zahaira when the hunters killed her and to Charlie when Shauna killed his pet, which, due to the bond between a master and their pet, killed Charlie.

"That's what makes this so weird," Elsa said. "If my theories are right, this is from a vampire nearly as pure as James or more so. A vampire of sufficiently diluted Venae cannot harm a much purer vamp, but anyone can harm a vamp of similar purity. Give me your hand."

Shauna held her hand out to the elder vampire. Elsa took and lifted it to her lips and then bit, hard. Shauna yanked her hand away, more from surprise than pain. It was really just a pinch. There was blood on Shauna's hand, but it wasn't hers.

"Dammit," Elsa mumbled. She reached into her mouth and yanked. She then held up a cracked canine. It was broken in half, straight down the middle. "I broke a fang."

"That's bad, right?" Shauna asked.

Elsa shrugged. "Like every other part, this will grow back in an hour or so. The point is that I cannot harm you."

"I see," Shauna said, but she already had assumed as much. She felt there was a much bigger difference in their purity than anyone was admitting.

"Now, give me your hand again," Elsa said. When Shauna did, the elder vamp took it and brought it to James' hand. She then ran Shauna's fingernail over the back of James' hand. A small welt rose. Elsa said, "If you put any effort into it, you'd be able to cut him. Your body is one of the few things in the world that can harm a vampire as pure as you or your sire. This bone is also from a vampire that pure. And, like my fang, it won't crumble as long as the vampire it came from is alive."

"How do you know that is vampire bone?" Portia asked.

"Do you really want to ask that of her?" Shauna asked, careful not to say Elsa's real name. Portia knew she was Countess Bathory, but most of the vampires present did not.

"You don't," Elsa said. Her voice had an odd lisp due to the missing tooth. "This is a cross section of a shin bone. The marrow is still spongy. Even I shudder to think of how they got this out of a vampire."

"The man who can tell us just got away," Shauna said, wondering if it was too late to give chase.

"No, he didn't," Laura said from the doorway. She held Henry by the collar, his body dragging alongside her. "He's alive, but getting hit by a vamp flying down at a thousand miles per hour might have knocked him out for a few days." Laura exaggerated her speed. Shauna had never broken the sound barrier and, knowing what even a hundred miles an hour would do to her clothing, doubted she wanted to.

"Are the vans still there?" Shauna asked.

"One is," Laura said. "A guy walked right by me and got in the other and drove off. I'd have stopped him, but I figured Henry was more important."

Shauna remembered the one James had let walk out. "Henry is the most important one to have captured," she said.

Laura grinned then said, "But, other than that, we wiped out these assholes. What do I do with this guy?"

After considering waking him up, Shauna wondered how they'd do that, but then couldn't figure a way to keep him controlled when he was awake. Then she remembered James' basement. "Take that one down to the basement and strip-search him, Sis," Shauna said. "If that crypt could hold me when I changed, it'll hold a pet." They'd assumed Henry was someone's pet after he bested Amber in a one-on-one swordfight a month earlier. It wasn't something Shauna knew how to perceive.

"I'm not doing a cavity search," Laura said. "If he's got lock picks up there, he can keep them."

"There's not even a doorknob on the inside or access to the lock," Shauna said. "It can only be opened from the kitchen. Once he's locked in, phase through and keep an eye on him. Let us know when he wakes up."

"Okay, sis," Laura said then drug the unconscious Henry away. She wasn't particularly careful about not bumping him into walls and furniture as she left the room. Or, Shauna realized, she was being careful. Shauna couldn't say she wouldn't have done the same thing.

"We've removed the arrow; James should recover," Elsa said. "I don't know what else we can do for him. But, Amber is still alive. We can help her. I thought the gold would make her slow to heal, but it's slower that I hoped it'd be."

Shauna could hear weak, raspy breaths coming from Amber. "She's breathing," Shauna said.

Amber's body spasmed in a wracking fit of coughs. When the coughing subsided, her breaths were quicker, but weaker.

"Undress her," Elsa said. She knelt by Amber and, setting the arrow down, grabbed the pet's shirt and yanked. The heavy cotton tore like paper. "We need to know how many bullets went in and how many came out. It could be bad if she managed to heal with one inside her."

Kneeling beside Elsa, Shauna grabbed Amber's jeans and tore them along the seams. For the last month, she'd been forced to live life as if everything were made of eggshells. It felt good to use her strength, like letting out a breath she'd been holding for weeks. Once Amber was wearing nothing, Elsa ran her hands over the blood coated skin, wiping blood away from any bullet holes with the remnants from Amber's shirt.

"I thought she'd be softer," Elsa said, running a finger along the sharply defined musculature of Amber's shoulder. "I've known marathon runners with more body fat and Olympic wrestlers with smaller muscles. They were all men."

"We're counting bullets, not checking her cup size," Shauna said.

"I can multitask," Elsa said, her voice slow and even, without the hint of amused lilt. "Four entry wounds on her torso, one on the left leg, none on the right and two on each arm. Also, an exit wound on her chest and one on the left calf."

Shauna nodded. The total count matched what she'd come up with, but Shauna had no idea how to tell an entry wound from an exit wound.

"Flip her," Elsa said, lifting Amber by the shoulders. Shauna did the same with the pet's knees. They rolled Amber over so that she lay on her belly.

"The numbers don't match," Elsa said. "There were two more bullets in than came out. Flip her again." Once Amber was on her back, Elsa grabbed Shauna's hand and held her thumb up. "I noticed your long nails a moment ago. I guess you haven't found a way to trim them."

She hadn't. "Broke two pairs of clippers," Shauna said. One of the two had been an eighty dollar set that claimed it could cut steel cable without dulling. "I can't even bite them. With my fangs, my teeth line up differently than I'm used to."

"Lucky for Amber," Elsa said. "We need you to cut here," Elsa drew an imaginary line above a bullet hole under Amber's collarbone. "And here," she traced a line near a bullet hole to the side of Amber's navel.

Shauna's nails were a little sharp, but not like a scalpel or even a steak knife. "We could use her sword," she suggested. "We know gold will cut her."

"That would get inside her," Elsa said. "But, we're trying not to kill her. That means precision and avoiding much more blood loss. She'll heal, but only if she keeps most of her blood in her body."

Placing the nail of her forefinger between her fang and bottom teeth, Shauna tried to chip at the nail and managed to tear away a sliver from it. It made it sharper, but it now looked broken in addition to being long. Sharp had been her goal, so she was pleased. Cutting into Amber made Shauna nervous. She set a fingertip near the wound and took a deep breath.

"Don't hold that in," Elsa said. "Full lungs are stressful, especially to those of us that don't need them. Calm down, let most of that back out."

Shauna exhaled until she felt comfortable. "You've had medical training?" Shauna ventured.

"I wrote a book in the eighteenth century," Elsa said. "It was used by several schools of surgery in Eastern Europe until the early twentieth century."

"A book?" The Elsa Shauna knew didn't have that kind of patience. "You took the time to write a book?"

"And I drew pictures. Hundreds of pictures of what people look like under the skin. The book is 'Vivisection', by El Baath." Elsa said.

"I've heard that word," Shauna said. "Does that mean surgery?"

Elsa put a bloody finger over Shauna's lips, shushing her. "We don't have time to dawdle. With those cuts, you should be able to stick two fingers in and grab the bullets," Elsa said. "You may have to feel around a bit."

Shauna pressed her nail along the lines Elsa had suggested, cutting just deep enough to get through the pet's skin. She then pushed two fingers into the incision on Amber's shoulder. Feeling all the slimy, squishy bits inside Amber, Shauna had to focus to do as Elsa said. The first bullet was simple to find. It had lodged against a bone in Amber's shoulder. As Shauna dug carefully through Amber's abdomen, she needed to think of something other than intestines, so she asked. "What language is 'vivisection'?"

"English," Elsa said. "I translated for you. The original was written in Greek, but I did a Latin translation as well."

"Not Magyar?" Shauna asked, more to keep herself distracted by what soft parts of Amber she was groping inside her belly.

"No one wrote in Magyar," Elsa said. "If I wanted to be taken seriously I had to write in the classic languages. Still, the book was banned in every Christian nation. It didn't stop them from using it as a text book however. At the time, they had to hire grave robbers to learn anatomy. Owning a banned book carried a far lesser punishment than hanging."

"Vivisection is not synonymous with surgery," Portia said. "It's just the cutting into a living body. Surgery would imply putting things back together. Vivisection is just taking them apart."

"Without killing them," Elsa added.

"And that doesn't make it better," Portia said.

Shauna glared at Elsa. Knowing of her past didn't make it easy to accept her in the present. She was a different person than the woman who committed those atrocities centuries ago. The better Shauna knew her, the more she knew that wasn't true. Elsa was the same person with an evolved morality. She was still driven by curiosity as much as hedonism, but not at the expense of innocent life. No matter what else Elsa was, she was a loyal friend.

Finally, Shauna's fingers clasped around a pair of small metal objects. She pulled them out. As soon as her hands were clear of Amber's wounds, the skin mended. All of the pet's injuries closed, leaving nary a scar.

"As I suspected," Elsa said. "Now the gold is out, she'll be fine."

"I guess there's not much danger of infection," Shauna said, noticing her bare, blood covered, hands. Whatever microbes she had on them wouldn't stand a chance against Amber's regeneration.

CHAPTER 3

During the following days and nights Shauna, Elsa and Amber took shifts watching over James as he lay in his bed. It was all Shauna and Elsa could do to keep Amber from sitting there the whole time. James' pet didn't sleep more than a few hours twice a week under normal circumstances. The stress of James' condition made her look like she needed rest.

Amber would spend her time kneeling by James' bed holding his hand.

Shauna understood. She'd only been close to James for a little more than a month. But, since his injury, she spent half of each night and all day sitting in his room, hoping that, each time he stirred, he would wake and be better. Sometimes his eyes would open and stare at the ceiling for a minute or two and then close again. If Amber put her wrist to his lips, he'd drink from her. The blood loss wasn't doing Amber any favors.

On the third night, Shauna was alone in the room with James when he spoke. His voice was weak and raspy when he asked, "What happened to me?"

Shauna thought to call to Amber, but didn't want to startle James, so she knelt by the bed and told him, "It was Henry the Inquisitor. He shot you with this." She carefully picked up the crossbow bolt from the nightstand and handed it to him. The weapon scared Shauna. If it could bring down James, she was sure it would do worse to her if she cut herself on the razor sharp arrowhead.

Moving slowly, almost clumsily, James took the arrow. "This is…," he said, his voice stuttering and uneven. "…new to me. Living vampire tissue as a weapon: I've never considered it an option. For so many years we worked to eliminate all the threats that could harm us." As he spoke, his voice got stronger. He seemed like a person waking up from an interrupted dream. "Moving so many tons of Syrian obsidian in the days before the wheel and dropping them in the ocean was a tedious task. But, until now, the only weapons that would harm me were made of those obsidian remnants from the side effects of the spell that created Reilla."

He'd mentioned Reilla's name once before. When Elsa had asked him if he was the first vampire, he'd replied that he was not she, and told her that the first vampire was named Reilla. Elsa frequently spoke of how knowing the name was entirely unhelpful. It would be like knowing the first caveman called himself Ugg.

"I understand why you are so confused," Shauna said. Her mind was racing through the implications of the information he'd just slipped to her. She tried to stay focused on James, while he was coherent. "Elsa has Henry in your basement. She's brought in a few devices that I refused to look at too closely and certainly didn't want to see how they worked."

Shauna had made the mistake of visiting with Elsa in the basement the day before. She wasn't sure what she saw but there had been an awful lot of blood and she was pretty sure she saw parts of Henry's body that were never meant to be seen outside his skin. Normally, the smell of blood would make her hungry, but what she saw turned her stomach.

After setting the crossbow bolt on the nightstand, James pushed himself up so his back rested against the headboard. He then stared at his hands a moment before saying, "Henry won't talk."

"He hasn't yet," Shauna said. "I'm not sure it's upsetting Elsa though. Having a toy that can regenerate as a pet does is making her disturbingly giddy. She's convinced he's someone's pet and Amber agrees with that assessment. When he's left in a condition he can speak, he prays to Christ and God and someone named Bertellus."

"I've never met any of those three," James said. "I'm surprised you allow Elsa to do such things. I would have expected you to have a more modern view of torture, such as that it is inhumane."

Shauna didn't approve, she wanted to say, but wasn't sure that would be an honest response. James was her bloodfather and she didn't want to disappoint his expectations, but she didn't want to lie, either. "I've chosen to remove myself from decisions regarding Henry. I'm leaving his treatment to Elsa and Amber, and now that you're awake, you. Elsa is doing what she's doing at Amber's behest; your pet seems to think Elsa has some expertise in the art of interrogation."

"There's a difference between torture and interrogation using torture," James said. "And with torture, there are two kinds of victims. There are those who will break and those who will not. Interrogation isn't about pain, it's about fear. Henry won't be afraid of Elsa. He is resolute and will tolerate pain rather than fear it. If he's as pious as his reputation, he will see the ordeal as proving his devotion. And since he knows he will heal, that also alleviates the fear. The only thing Henry is doing in the basement is providing Elsa with a bit of guilty sadistic pleasure."

"It's a side of her I don't like so much," Shauna said. She thought about Elsa's origins as little as possible, but there always seemed to be someone or some situation that reminded her. Shauna just couldn't reconcile the Elsa she knew with a sadistic killer.

"Countess Bathory was born in a different era," James said. "Admittedly, even for her time, she was a dark soul. Torture was considered a morally acceptable method to get information in her day."

"Yeah," Shauna said. "I guess vamps tend to stick with the morality they learned in life."

"We adapt to the times," James said. "Most of us do, anyway. Still, we live in a harsher reality than humanity does. We do not have the luxury of maintaining their high morality. We each must kill at least once, and no matter how hard we try to see it otherwise, humans are our food source."

He slid his legs over the edge of the bed then stared at the floor a moment. "Elsa is going a bit far if she's been at this for days and gotten nothing."

"Should I tell Elsa to stop?" Shauna asked.

"No," James said. "I think I can walk." He held out his hand to Shauna. She took it and helped pull him to his feet. He moved like an elderly man, though he still looked like a man in his forties. "I can't use any of my blood-given abilities. I can't fly or even lift that arrow with my mind, and I can't phase. I can't even move my muscles at the speed I am accustomed to. For some reason, that weapon has debilitated me to the level of a mere human."

Shauna had seen his dark red aura when they touched; the aura told her he was a vampire and it's color indicated he was purer than she. "You still look like a vampire."

"My hunger confirms that I am." James started to chuckle but nearly fell over choking and coughing. Deep red blood dripped from his mouth.

Taking a tissue from the nightstand, Shauna handed it to James. "Shall I tell Amber?" she asked.

"I've fed on her too much since I was shot," James said after patting off the blood from his chin. "I don't think she can spare more blood. She is out, hunting for food."

Shauna thought Amber was resting, but being James' pet gave them a connection. He probably knew more about what she was doing. Shauna said, "I'm sure she's a good hunter." She couldn't think of how a pet could convince people to come to James' house to offer blood, but wasn't as old as Amber.

"I don't know," James said. "In over a thousand years, I've never been hungry enough to send her out to find someone for me. Come to think of it, I don't remember actually feeling hunger in over ten thousand years."

"James, are you okay?" Shauna asked, but felt stupid for asking. It was clear that he wasn't well. He'd just volunteered a huge secret about himself. She recalled that just moments earlier he'd said something about vampires originating in Syria.

He looked at her a moment. Shauna wasn't sure if he was studying her or having a moment of introspection. "Don't mind me," he said. "My mind, it's..." He trailed off, looking again at the arrow. "I'm all here," he said. "This is a good deal of information to process. It's been a long time since I've had my understanding of reality shaken. I say what I say to let you know the impact this is having on me. I trust you will not share, even with Elsa."

"Could you coerce me to forget?" Shauna asked. "I'm not sure I can trust myself against Elsa's wiles."

"I suppose Elsa learning is not the end of the world. She will keep the secret because she understands that knowledge has power, especially when she knows something others don't. I'd prefer she didn't know, but I cannot coerce you," James said. "Just as a vampire cannot coerce their own pet, they cannot coerce their bloodchildren either. I can coerce vampires of much more diluted Venae, but not you or your sister or Amber."

"Didn't you coerce Amber to not feel pain when you feed from her?" Shauna asked. She recalled that Jonnie and Jackie both experienced the bite as pleasurable. Elsa had said they'd been coerced to do so. Shauna had assumed it was Elsa doing the coercing.

"No," James said. "My mother could do that, but Amber has not met my mother. She still feels the pain, but she's tough and can handle it."

"I didn't realize that pets served their masters purely out of free will," Shauna said.

"More or less," James said. "Amber would go all hackles if I ever called myself her master. I am her vampire." Without pausing to put a robe over his nightshirt, James headed for the stairs.

"Do you need help down?" Shauna asked as she followed.

"I feel weak, but not that weak," James said. He took the first step down slowly but seemed to gain confidence as he went. By the bottom, he was going at a normal speed, if he were a human.

Shauna phased through the walls to get ahead of him. No matter how often she did it, it scared her a little. When she emerged on the other side of the wall, she felt a thrill that more than offset her trepidation.

She opened the door to James' crypt as he walked into the kitchen. As he descended into his concrete basement, moving with confidence, Shauna debated waiting for him in the kitchen. She didn't hear any screaming and the smell of blood was not as strong, so she decided to brave Elsa's activities and follow.

An electric whir filled the air along with a grinding sound as Shauna rounded the bottom of the stairs. Henry stood with his feet on the floor and his hands bound behind him, tied to a steel support. He was covered in sweat and didn't have any open wounds. The power washer sitting on the floor near Henry and the puddle of watered down blood running toward the drain led her to think it wasn't sweat, but he'd been freshly rinsed.

Elsa sat at an old grindstone sharpening some bladed implement that looked like the sickle on the old soviet flags.

"We're done, Elsa," James said. "There's nothing more to be gained from this."

"Good," Elsa said. "My creativity was running dry. I was almost out of ways to play with this boy without causing damage that a pet couldn't heal. What's the new plan?"

"He's a pet," James said. "He will need his master's blood or he'll die."

"So we starve him?" Elsa asked.

"We will feed him three meals a day," James said. "It's the humane thing to do. However, only his master's blood will keep him alive and we don't have any or know where to get it. If he tells us, we'll happily get some for him."

"You'll be dead before me," Henry's voice was weaker than James' but seethed with defiance. "I am not the only Supplicant of the Three. They will come for me and they will bring the weapon that killed the eldest vampire in the world."

James turned to Shauna and asked, "Would you mind if I leaned on you a little; my strength is fading."

She took James' arm over her shoulders and put her arm around his waist to steady him. She couldn't help but ask Henry, "Who are the Three?"

Elsa sighed then said, "He isn't going to..."

"The Angels of Purity," Henry interrupted. "They will end the taint of vampires on this world."

"We're done here," James said with a forceful growl. "Elsa, leave him and come upstairs."

"But, he's talking now," Elsa said. Still, she walked toward the stairs.

James stumbled as they followed Elsa. At the bottom of the stairs, James was leaning so heavily on Shauna that she didn't think he could make the climb. He made no motion to stop her when she cradled him into her arms and carried him upstairs.

Elsa scowled the whole way up. When Shauna set James on the bed, Elsa asked, "Can we talk about why the interrogations ended?"

"We know what we need to," James said, his voice barely more than a croaking whisper. His eyes closed and even lying on the bed, his body slumped.

"James, are you okay?" Shauna asked.

"What do you mean, James?" Elsa asked. She leaned over him and whispered, "No dying until you tell me why I had to stop."

"I'm not dying," James said. "I'm tired and weak, but I'm not getting worse."

"You're not getting better," Shauna said, unsure his self-diagnosis was accurate.

"Not quickly," James said. He opened his eyes and looked into Shauna's. "I need to ask more of you than you're ready for."

"I owe you everything," Shauna said. "I'll do anything for you."

"You need to go to Europe and find where these angels are," James said.

"I don't remember Henry mentioning Europe," Elsa said.

James pulled himself up to a sitting position. "When I disappeared after Shauna was made, I was in Germany, looking for a bloodgrandson, Dun. It was he that Henry spoke of killing."

"But that's not Dun's bone, is it?" Shauna asked.

"Dun is dead," James said. "Once I confirmed that, I came home. I don't have the connections I once had there and I never knew who I could trust."

"But, being a new, unknown vamp, people will trust me?" Shauna asked.

"Not there," James said. "You will have to avoid the other vampires of Europe, especially the council. Trust only…" he trailed off.

"He's asleep," Elsa said. "That's just like him, teasing with almost information." She pushed at James' shoulder. "Trust who?" Elsa asked. James didn't stir.

"We'll ask again the next time he's awake," Shauna said.

"If he wakes again," Elsa said. When Shauna glared at her, Elsa added, "I'm sure he'll be fine in time."

"So, we get Amber and go to Europe to find a cure?" Shauna asked Elsa. "You don't think they are actually angels do you?"

"They're vampires," Elsa said. "I don't doubt it for a bit. Henry may be deluding himself or simply be, well, simple. He's a pet to a vampire. He might be coerced to believe they're angels."

"A master cannot coerce his pet," Shauna said. "But, there are three; they could coerce each other's pets. Like you had done to Jackie and Jonnie." Elsa hadn't mentioned who had coerced her pets, merely that they had been coerced to enjoy a vampire's bite.

"Yes," Elsa said. "Henry will need his master's blood. It might be a week, it might be a month, but he'll need blood from the angels. I vote to let him die and hope he takes his angel with him."

"Henry said three," Shauna said. "Three angels or vampires. We need him to find all three angels."

Elsa sighed. "You're right."

"And they're in Europe." Shauna said.

"So, that's where we're going," Elsa said, though she seemed unenthusiastic at the prospect.. "I've been meaning to get back home for a few decades now. But it'll just be you and me and the twins. Amber needs to stay with James."

"So we follow him to Europe?" Shauna said. "What if he takes a daytime flight?"

"Which he will," Elsa said. "Only we won't be following him. We'll be waiting for him." Elsa went on to explain a plan where they would travel to Europe. When they got to Paris, Amber would arrange for Henry to escape and then follow him to the airport and see which flight he took. Paris was a short enough drive to the most used international airports that Shauna and Elsa or her twins could pick up Henry's trail when he landed.

"So how do we deal with the angels when we find them?" Shauna asked. She was pretty sure the answer included violence.

"Then it will be all Amber and you," Elsa said. "And Laura, I guess. She's pretty scrappy in a fight. You're the strongest vamps we've got since James is out of commission. If anyone has a chance to get the answer to how to help James, it's you three."

"I'm actually a little shocked that you're so interested in helping, especially knowing the danger." Shauna said. Elsa was incapable of seeing the world from other than an egocentric point of view.

"The potential for answers as to where we came from is huge here. And with James starting to open up to me, I don't want to lose him. Besides, I'm not in danger," Elsa said. "I can phase out."

"So could James," Shauna said. "They got him by surprise."

"Yes, but as long as you're with me, I'm not going to be the first target, so I won't be surprised," Elsa said. "If they shoot you, I phase out."

Shauna couldn't think of how to respond to that, but it was more in line with what she'd come to expect from Elsa.

"I'll call Amber and tell her the plan," Elsa said as she walked out of James' bedroom.

CHAPTER 4

Shauna had never been on a boat before the night they left for Calais. They'd boarded late, after sunset and just minutes before the ship set sail.

Once Shauna saw the suite, she was pleased with the prospects of a vacation enroute to whatever dangers awaited in Europe. It was small but more cozy than cramped. It had two bedrooms, a dining table and a sitting room. The bathrooms were cramped. Shauna wasn't sure how Jackie would manage to squeeze into the shower with her, but was sure she'd try. Jackie always insisted Shauna needed help washing her back, and Shauna's efforts to dissuade Elsa's pet weren't even convincing to Shauna.

She stowed her suitcases in the small closet in the bedroom, intending to unpack later, and went out to the sitting room.

Laura's luggage still sat at the door. Shauna's sister sat at the dining table, drinking the bottle of complimentary champagne. Shauna wasn't sure why Laura drank as much as she did; she couldn't have a physical addiction and, as often as she fed, she wouldn't need the wine to thin her blood. The alcohol wouldn't affect her as strongly as it did when she was human. Perhaps Laura was trying to drink enough to feel more than a slight sense of relaxation.

Shauna considered taking Laura's clothes into their room, but forced herself to relax and get into the spirit of a cruise. The huge cruise ship was an ideal method of travel for a vampire. There were activities going on day and night and no one would take particular notice of a passenger spending the day in their cabin. There were two bars, a casino, several restaurants and a theatre they could get to without stepping foot in sunlight.

Jackie sat on one of the couches, thumbing through a room service menu. "This is so much better than that mano-war we hitched a ride on to get to America. Shauna, would you like to share a hot fudge sundae?"

Vampires can't ingest anything other than blood and translucent liquids. When Jackie offered to share, she meant she would eat a spoonful and then kiss Shauna to share the flavors.

"Later," Shauna said. She wondered how she would make it through a week of sharing such a small space and manage to fend off Jackie's increasingly aggressive advances. She could handle kissing her; she enjoyed it, but wasn't fond of doing it with people around. "When we have less of an audience."

No one in the suite, certainly not Elsa and not even Laura, would be bothered if Jackie and Shauna started making out on the couch. It was only Shauna's moralities that were so delicate. Laura had been heavily into a party scene where people often did more than kiss in public and Elsa would appreciate the chance to enjoy the show.

"Which of the clubs will be the vamp club?" Jonnie asked, calling from the room she shared with her sister and Elsa.

"The Bilge," Elsa said as she walked naked into the doorway to the sitting room. She held a gown in each hand and alternated holding them over herself and checking the mirrors on the bedroom door. The suite wasn't so fancy as to feature antique silver backed mirrors, so her reflection shone just fine. "It's the only club without windows and I'm just not interested in a vamp that would sit in a bar without a dance floor."

"The Bilge is the theatre," Jonnie said. "It does have an open dance floor when there isn't a show, though."

"Exactly," Elsa said. "It's the vamp club, for sure."

"Vamp club?" Shauna asked.

"We're not going to be the only vampires crossing the ocean. It's a safe bet there will be others on board. I did tell you, this is the only way to go, didn't I?"

Shauna had wanted to go by airplane, but there weren't any that both took off and landed in a timeframe that guaranteed they could be indoors before sunrise. They could have travelled by cargo ship, but even with those, there is a chance for a random inspection by whatever navy or coast guard the ship encounters in coastal waters. Swimming or walking across the ocean floor would take longer than most vampires could go without feeding. A transatlantic cruise was the best option.

Settling on the a blue silk dress, Elsa tossed the other, a sea foam gown, to Shauna.

"I don't have the make up for green," Shauna said. "Or the shoes."

"Use the frosted acrylic heels in your big suitcase," Elsa said.

"I didn't pack acrylic heels," Shauna said.

"You packed?" Elsa asked incredulously. "You mean that stuff in your suitcase was there on purpose?"

Shauna smiled weakly at her friend. She wasn't surprised Elsa had packed for her. Shauna didn't know why she ever thought she should have tried to pack for herself.

"Change." Elsa said. "I want to go check out the competition in the food chain. Jackie," she said as she patted her pet on the shoulder, "help her with her makeup. Keep the playtime short. I want good seats."

"I could go hold a spot," Laura offered. She still wore the black jeans and heavy metal t-shirt she slipped into after waking up that night. Shauna would have suggested she also change, but wasn't ready to deal with the argument that would ensue once Laura opened her suitcase to find Elsa had packed for her as well. Surely Elsa took the opportunity to be in total control of Shauna's sister's wardrobe for a week and Laura wouldn't appreciate the fashions available in the cruise ship shops enough to do anything more than complain as she wore whatever fashions Elsa had selected for her.

"Do that," Elsa said. "I'll cover the bar tab. I want a well lit corner, away from the speakers but close to the dance floor."

"I know," Laura said. "You want the power seats—where you can be seen watching over everyone else."

"And get a bottle of reserve Bordeaux and two bottles of their most expensive champagne," Elsa said.

"And make sure the labels are facing out," Laura said. "I know. Opulence is meant to be flaunted." She rolled her eyes, but Elsa didn't notice as she slipped into her dress, watching herself in the mirror.

"You do know me," Elsa said.

Shauna went into her room to change. Jackie followed close behind, knocking Shauna onto the bed and then feigned it had been accidental. The pet then pounced on top of Shauna and put her lips up to Shauna's ear. "I'm going to hold you to that promise to share the sundae," Jackie whispered then gave Shauna a quick peck on the cheek before bouncing off and pulling out the smaller of Shauna's suitcases. Shauna wasn't sure if something was changing about her or if she'd just gotten so used to Jackie's attention that she had hopeful anticipation for time alone with Elsa's pet. She was disappointed Jackie hadn't kissed her lips.

Shauna slipped the sea foam gown over her head. Elsa and she were almost, but not quite the same size. Shauna had to tug it gently to fit it over her curves. Because she was a little taller than Elsa, the dress was almost scandalously slit up the thigh. Shauna would have never dressed herself in so little fabric. She let Elsa's audacity make up for her lack of bravery.

Jackie sat Shauna on the bed and knelt in front of her while she applied Shauna's makeup. It was actually a new experience for Shauna. Up until that night, Elsa had been satisfied to let her do her own. It was odd for Shauna to have Jackie so close, and so focused on a part of her that Shauna almost felt ignored. When she finally managed to catch Jackie's eyes, the pet smiled and Shauna smiled back.

"Hold still, beautiful," Jackie said.

When she finished and held up a mirror, Shauna understood why Elsa had Jackie apply the makeup. She didn't see herself in the mirror, just a beautiful woman whose perfectly shaded eyes should have their own close up in a magazine. Jackie had used so many subtle shades that, the more Shauna analyzed it, the more details she saw.

"It's going to be sad when I wash this off," Shauna said.

"I can do it again," Jackie said. "I've had decades of practice."

"I wouldn't call this practice," Shauna said. "You're an artist."

Jackie blushed and turned away as she stood. "Credit goes to the canvas, not the paint," she said.

"I look like a model," Shauna said.

"You do look good," Jackie said. "It's the style Elsa wants, kind of a sixties glam throwback. I prefer your more pristine, fresh out of the shower and dripping wet look, but that's difficult to maintain."

It was Shauna's turn to blush. Vampires don't change shades quickly when they blush. Their blood flows too slowly. But, sustained embarrassment, anger or excitement can make them flush.

Jackie leaned in as if to kiss Shauna then dodged her lips and landed a kiss on her neck. Jackie gave the briefest of nibbles before pulling away and heading out of the room. "Time for me to get changed," Jackie said. "No wine until we hit the club. I'll have a kit with me to touch you up, but I'll make you earn it."

After Jackie left her room, Shauna admired the work in the mirror. She'd never spent so much time on lipstick to worry about having to retouch it. Elsa had a way of drinking wine where she poured from the glass into her mouth, her lips never touching the glass. Shauna didn't have the dexterity to even risk everything that could go wrong if she tried that.

§

Other than a single spotlight shining on the center of the empty stage, the only lights in The Bilge were red, blue or green. Around the bar there weren't any green lights, giving the area a purple look. The lighting on the small dance floor shifted, changing the color of each corner periodically. Each table had all three colors, making the lighting almost normal.

Elsa paused at the entrance with her pets to either side of her. They were, as usual, dressed identically. That night, they wore skimpy pink gauze outfits with rows of brass colored coins strategically covering enough to almost keep the outfits from being obscene. Their hair, tied in a ponytail topknot, flopped into a mushroom shape. They looked like a teenage boys dream of genies or belly dancers. Shauna often thought the only difference between Elsa's and an adolescent boy's mind was that Elsa had the resources to make her imagination into reality.

Laura sat in a raised booth in the center of the club, overlooking the stage and dance floor. Three well dressed men in their thirties or early forties sat with her. Most of the people Shauna had passed on the way to the club were wearing beach wear or bathing suits. Two of the three men wore dark colored dress shirts and darker ties while the third wore a nearly black suit and a silvery white tie.

Shauna led the twins up to the booth while Elsa strolled up to the bar, weaving past as many tables as she could without making it obvious she was casing the other patrons. Shauna knew Elsa's methods. The elder vamp would assume she was the most important person in the club and make sure everyone else saw her that way. She would go to the bar, stand beside whomever she deemed almost as attention grabbing as her, and ask for a wine list. She would then ask if they had anything better that wasn't on the list. She'd then ask for something notable and walk away before the bartender could hand it to her, forcing him to deliver it to the table, giving the appearance of personal catering by the people in charge of the bar. That there were already three bottles on the table that bespoke her ability to spend was immaterial.

When the twins and Shauna got to the booth, the men were all sitting close to Laura. She giggled as the men tried to talk about the band on Laura's shirt. Shauna barely knew the band but could tell the men were floundering. A quick blink confirmed none of the men were vampires, but a man and woman sitting in a shadowed booth in the far corner showed a pale pink aura. Pale pink meant they weren't as pure of Venae as Shauna. The ability to see a vampire's aura without having to touch them was unique to Shauna. The aura was briefly visible after she blinked.

Shauna sat across from Laura with Jackie and Jonnie on each side. The men at the table looked at them and back at Laura, most likely trying to decide who to dedicate their seduction efforts. Somehow all three kept their attentions on Shauna's sister. She had mastered the art of getting men to fawn over her long before Shauna made her a vampire. Despite being twins, Shauna always thought Laura looked younger with her pixie cut hair and exuberance to match.

When Elsa did rejoin the others, she stood at the end of the table and leaned to Laura, "Who are you kidding Laura, none of these twerps are up to your standards." She craned her neck to gaze around the table, clearly examining the men below the belts.

Two of the men made clumsy excuses and left. The man in the suit stayed but slid around the u-shaped booth, closer to Laura. "I should make room for your friends," he said.

Laura trilled a fake giggle and nudged his shoulder with hers.

Elsa sat at Laura's side and said, "I guess we know what you're having for dinner, then."

"I was expecting music," Shauna said. There was an easy listening tune playing in the background but it was much quieter than the din of dozens of conversations among the bar's patrons.

Elsa looked at Shauna and whispered, using a voice that only Shauna would hear and hear clearly no matter how much background noise there was, "I wonder how many vamps are here."

Elsa's whisper was an ability the Venae gave her that Shauna either hadn't figured out how to use or simply didn't have. As she was about to reply to Elsa, a man stepped onto the stage. He was a vampire, as well, adding to Shauna's count. "Including the man on the stage," Shauna said. "There are thirteen acts I'd like to see here." Shauna had confidence Elsa would understand the simple code. Shauna couldn't talk about vampires with a stranger at the table. By vampire law, humans that knew of vampires' existence came in two kinds: pets and dead.

Elsa's eyes widened for a brief moment. It was the first time Shauna had seen her surprised by anything. Shauna glanced around the room at the other vampires. When Elsa's eyes didn't follow, Shauna realized it wasn't the number of vamps that surprised her friend. Shauna had never before divulged the ability to see vampires auras without touching them.

"Good evening, voyagers," the vampire on the stage said. "I am Vladimir the Confounding. If you'd please indulge me, I'd like to present you with a preview of a show I'll be putting on at midnight in the Moonlight Lounge."

He paused while the audience's burst of applause died down. "For this display of mystical prowess I will require two assistants from the audience and I see just the two." He gestured to Elsa and Shauna's table.

Elsa smiled mischievously and nodded her assent for Jackie and Jonnie to join the magician on the stage. Shauna understood why Elsa had dressed the twins exceptionally provocatively. She had anticipated that very scenario. She was up to something and had done her homework. Perhaps the vampire magician did the same act at the beginning of each voyage.

"What do you have planned?" Shauna whispered.

Elsa smirked, confirming she'd planned something. "You'll see," she said. "As beautiful as my twins are, keep your eye on the magician."

When Jackie and Jonnie stepped up to the stage, Vladimir spread open the curtains behind him. A display with two archery targets stood with an inflated balloon over the bullseye of each target. The man picked up a pair of small crossbows from the stage and then handed one to each of the twins. He then placed them at marks on the stage and said, "I assume you both understand the basics of these contraptions."

Jackie and Jonnie both nodded.

"I would like you to aim at the balloon farthest from you, but do not fire," Vladimir said. Once the twins had their weapons leveled at the balloons, Vladimir told them to hold their aim as he stepped to a point where both crossbow shots would cross on their way to the targets. He then held out his arms towards the pets and two more balloons inflated into his hands.

"On three, I want you to discharge your crossbows," Vladimir said. He then counted, "One. Two." After a dramatic pause he said, loudly, "Three."

The bows fired with simultaneous cracks followed quickly by the sounds of four balloons popping. Vladimir stood unscathed, though the arrows had visibly passed through him.

The audience broke into vibrant applause with several people standing at their tables.

"I have to go," the man sitting with Laura said. "Excuse me, if you would. I do hope we'll meet again."

Laura and Elsa slid out of the booth to allow the man in the suit to leave. He walked hastily from the club.

"Were you watching? He phased," Elsa whispered, nodding at Vladimir, as she and Laura sat back down.

Shauna'd seen it, too. That had been what Elsa wanted to see. Phasing was a particularly rare ability among vampires. Only those of James' bloodline and the descendants of Vlad

Dracul, such as Elsa, could do it. James' blood family consisted of five vampires that Shauna knew of and Elsa's wasn't much larger. The Dracul family was the smallest of the six surviving bloodlines represented by the Elder Council. James' family was not part of the council and other than the vampires who had been at his party, none even knew it existed who weren't of his blood.

"He's related to you?" Shauna asked. Shauna guessed it was no coincidence that he used the name 'Vladimir'.

"A descendant of Lucy, most likely," Elsa said. "She's been slightly more successful than I at procreating."

When the applause finally started to die down, Vladimir held up his hands to quiet the crowd and bowed. Once upright again, he said, "Thanks to Karina and Katina for their assistance." Elsa clenched the table tight enough that Shauna heard the wood crack.

"Let me guess," Shauna said. "Somehow he knows Jackie and Jonnie's real names." In the time she'd known them, Shauna had learned Jackie and Jonnie weren't their birth names. She hadn't actually ever asked or been told what their real names were.

Elsa looked at Shauna and opened her mouth as if to speak only to close it again and clench her jaw. Three or four times she did that until the twins came back to the table. Both seemed paler and had confused looks to their eyes.

"We'll figure this out," Shauna said, trying to reassure Elsa and her pets. That there was a descendant of Vlad Dracula that Elsa hadn't known about wasn't too much of a surprise. That he knew Elsa's pets by their original names was. Shauna looked back to the stage, intent to question the magician, but he was gone.

"We should talk about the boy," Laura said.

"The guy in the suit?" Shauna asked. "You have a crush?"

"He was packing," Laura said. "That's why he wore a suit, to hide the shoulder holster."

"A cop?" Elsa asked.

"Maybe," Laura said. "But he held my hand just for a moment, just long enough to notice I was a little colder than he was." A vampire's body temperature was naturally room temperature, but they could raise their temperature with activity, feeding or using their vampiric powers. Laura or Shauna could do it just by willing it, but it took time. Elsa maintained human body temperature by sexual activity, usually heavy petting with Jonnie and Jackie several times a night. The man in the suit might have touched Laura earlier than she'd anticipated.

Techno music started pumping through the club speakers, loud enough to easily overcome the sounds of all the conversations.

"Do we dance?" Shauna asked Elsa, hoping to distract her for a moment from the magician.

Elsa, who had been staring at a glass of wine, looked up at Shauna. She reached across the table and took Shauna's hand. "We dance." Four songs of writhing on the stage with Elsa and the twins passed. Shauna had lost track of her sister midway through the first song when one of the boys came back to Laura with the courage to ask for a dance. Elsa embraced Shauna, placing her lips to Shauna's ear. "Shall we find a snack?" Elsa whispered then nipped Shauna's earlobe playfully.

"Here?" Shauna asked. She wasn't hungry. Since feeding on Azure a few nights earlier, she hadn't felt her power wane.

"Your sister is going to town behind the amps," Elsa said. Shauna looked in the dark corner by the door that led backstage. Sure enough, Laura had some boy pressed against the wall and was sucking at his shoulder. The young man had an expression of bliss on his face and was groping feebly at Laura's jeans. She'd coerced him to believe the pain of her bite was pleasurable.

When it was clear the boy had succeeded in unbuttoning Laura's pants, Shauna couldn't watch any longer. She looked around to see if anyone else was looking at her sister's activities, but most of the patrons were focused on the people at their own table or the dance floor. Then, Shauna saw the three men at the bar; one of whom was the man in the suit that had left so abruptly earlier. The other two wore sport jackets over polo shirts. All three were staring at a table by the stage where a vampire couple were sitting and flirting with a young human couple.

The male vampire wore a modern tuxedo with a ruffled shirt and had a top hat perched on a black cane leaning on the seat beside him. His partner wore a dark green gown with rows of gold beads covering the mid section. Even if she couldn't see their aura, Shauna would have guessed the two were vampires.

"You're staring," Elsa whispered, her voice as clear as if her lips were pressed to Shauna's ear, though she was an arm's length away. "Are you looking to make new friends among our kind? Shall we introduce ourselves?"

Shauna pulled Elsa into an embrace so close their cheeks touched. "I was watching because the man with the gun under his suit jacket came back with friends," Shauna said. "They seem to have taken an interest in the two vampires by the stage."

"We might want to leave soon," Elsa said. "I wasn't planning on spilling blood on this part of our vacation. I didn't pack leather for the ship, at least not the kind you'd wear outside of the bedroom. Jackie and Jonnie might wear it out, but not you and your prudish sensitivities."

"Then let's find another bar," Shauna said. "Maybe one with a live band."

"Not just yet," Elsa said. "I'm actually enjoying watching that poor boy try to please your sister."

Shauna started to glance over, but closed her eyes before she could actually see what Laura was doing. She turned back to Elsa and glared. "I'm sitting down." She went back up to the table and sat with her back to the corner with her sister. She took some wine from the table and drank directly from the bottle.

Her efforts to ignore the three men at the bar were failing. Her interest rose when the human woman who'd been sitting with the vampire couple went up to the bar and said something to the man in the suit. The two were obviously avoiding eye contact, making them even more suspicious.

Jackie plopped into the seat beside Shauna, slipping an arm around her. "Elsa tells me I am to crawl under the table and help you relax if you can't manage it on your own."

Shauna glared at Jackie.

"That's not a very relaxed look," Jackie purred.

There was no way Shauna was going to let Jackie down there. Instead, she leaned towards Elsa's pet and kissed her. It was a pleasant distraction and it was a boundary Shauna knew she could maintain.

She lost track of time playfully fighting to keep Jackie's hands above the table. The ventures weren't serious, just a game. Shauna still trusted Jackie to progress the physical relationship only at the pace Shauna chose.

Laura slid into the seat across the table, bringing Shauna's participation to a dead stop. Jackie continued to cuddle close and kiss Shauna's neck. Shauna had to ask, "Sis, are you really so hungry to need to eat again?"

"I wouldn't say need," Laura said. "I wanted to. I like to. It makes the sex better."

"Are you…"Shauna started to ask, pacing her words carefully, tentatively.

"Addicted?" Laura finished with her usual impatience. "I might be. I can't be addicted to heroin or alcohol anymore, but who's to say I can't be addicted to blood. We're all dependant on it. We're all addicted, really. Maybe I just need it more or want it more or need to want it more. I don't know and don't care. I like it; let's leave it at that."

"Are you feeding every night?" Shauna asked.

"This isn't leaving it at that," Laura said. "I'm not talking about it."

"Fine," Shauna said. A moment of physical bliss reminded her to nudge Jackie's attention upward, back to her neck. Despite the distraction she managed to nod towards the bar, "Your friend is back."

Laura looked towards the bar. "Which friend?" she asked.

Shauna hadn't been keeping tabs. The men at the bar were leaving. Shauna checked the table by the stage. It was empty.

"They're gone," Shauna said. "Your friend is gone again and I think he's chasing a pair of vamps. I'd bet he's a hunter."

"We should go help," Laura said.

Shauna nodded. Elsa and Jonnie had a young man between them and were dancing close enough to kiss each other over his shoulder. There was no reason to involve them. "Let's go," Shauna said to her sister.

They climbed out of the booth and Jackie followed close behind. "You don't need to come," Shauna said to the pet.

"Oh, I do," Jackie said. "But, I'll follow your heroic butts anyway. Let's go save some vamps."

CHAPTER 5

When Shauna had fantasized about becoming a vampire, months before James turned her, she thought it would be a mostly quiet life of gathering knowledge and wealth and cycling through lovers, constantly trying to avoid eternal heartache. She even allowed for the occasional dark ball or gala in her visions. That was all before she even suspected they were more than a myth.

Within days of the change, she had been thrust into a violent battle, forced to defend the local vampires from a usurper who'd taken up with Henry the Inquisitor and his well organized, well equipped hunters. Shauna relied on her purity of Venae to keep her safe and it worked. Henry hadn't been prepared to deal with a vampire like her.

After the fighting ended, she fully intended to embrace Elsa's lifestyle of spending her days napping with an occasional delve into research and spending her nights drinking and dancing. She had been doing well until the New Years' party.

When she set out on the cruise, Shauna was still angry about James. She wasn't looking for a fight, she was looking for answers. But when she saw there were hunters on the boat, her anger found a target. Shauna wasn't out to save anyone, she wasn't looking for answers. She wanted blood and wasn't looking for a meal.

Vampire hunters had no place in Shauna's long term plans, which meant, in the present, they had to go.

As a vampire, all of Shauna's senses were heightened compared to when she was human. She could hear better, see more, and smell more clearly. But, she hadn't enough experience to use her senses like Elsa could. When they reached the first intersection in the passageways, they stopped. Shauna couldn't tell which way the hunters and their quarry had gone. If Elsa were with them, she'd know how to use the scents in the air to track them, but Shauna did not. She could smell lingering perfume and even gun oil, but her sense was not directional.

"They didn't go straight," Jackie said.

"How can you be sure?" Laura asked.

"I'm hoping; I'm not sure," Jackie said. "We would still be able to see them, unless they went into a cabin." Jackie pointed down the passageway. There wasn't another intersection for more than a hundred feet. "Let's assume they didn't go into a room since that scenario would make it particularly difficult to get to the vampires in time to save them."

It was crass logic, Shauna thought. But, the pets were as smart as they were pretty and had two centuries to hone their minds. Shauna knew any advice they offered was well thought through. There was no reason to waste energy on the scenario they wouldn't win anyway. Instead, Shauna hoped and acted on the winnable options. "So we're thinking the vampires took the human couple that sat at their table with them. Where would a pair of vampires take a pair of humans to feed?" Shauna asked. "That is, if they don't have an exhibitionist streak." Shauna cast a disapproving glance toward her sister. Laura ignored it.

"It's still early in the night," Jackie said. "They wouldn't have an excuse to drag strangers back to their cabin from a bar. They may have decided to leave because the music got too loud to chat."

"They'll be on deck," Laura said. "Wanting to see the stars over the ocean is the excuse to leave the bar. After a while of small talk over the rails, they'll suggest a quiet drink, somewhere they can talk and mention they have a suite and a couple bottles of complimentary champagne."

"Sounds plausible," Shauna said. "Unless anyone has a better idea, we head up to the deck." Shauna led the way down the passageway which had an arrow pointing to the elevators.

Rounding the corner to the elevators, Shauna saw one of the sport coat wearing men from the bar leaning against the wall across from a stairwell door. The man said, louder than he needed to for the three women to hear, "These elevators are broke and the stairwell is locked. There's another set on the starboard side."

"I'd bet they've got them in the stairway," Jackie whispered. She then turned and walked back, stopping to peer at Shauna around the corner. "I'll just watch from back here."

"You deaf?" the man said. "You need to go to the other side of the ship."

"I'm not looking for the elevator, fucktard," Laura said. "I'm looking for your friend: the one with the better tailor. Sport coats are so twentieth century."

Shauna stepped toward the man and he stepped back. He reached into his coat, under his shoulder, and drew a gun with a silencer.

"Smile for me," he said. "Show me your pearly whites."

Shauna obliged, smiling wide, making sure to show her teeth. Her elongated canines would be clearly visible from a few steps away, though they weren't more than a quarter inch longer than her other teeth. The hunter clearly knew vampires couldn't hide their fangs other than behind their upper lip.

"Please tell me you don't have wooden bullets," Shauna said. It was one of Amber's favorite things to mock. Amateur hunters often tried various ways to change bullets, but only the softest metals wouldn't shatter under the pressures inside a gun.

"Silver, bitch," he said. He pulled the trigger three times. Twice, fragments of silver bounced off of Shauna's chest and face, stinging her and making her angry. She wanted to be angry. The hunter's third shot jammed the gun.

Laura burst into such raucous laughter she had to brace herself against the passageway wall. The only place silver had any effect on vampires was in old mirrors. For some reason no one had been able to explain to Shauna, vampires didn't reflect in silver. Only the most unprepared and uneducated hunter would use it for bullets.

He ran across the hall, tearing open the door and yelled, "There's more out here!" as he ran into the stairwell.

"Shoot em," a voice in the stairwell yelled back. "Delay them somehow. We need a minute for the ceremony to finish these off. Then we'll help you."

Shauna didn't wait to see if the man would try to clear the jam in his gun and waste more silver. She rushed into the stairwell, grabbed the first man's head and slammed it into the hand-rail. He fell to the floor. She'd learned to control her strength. Even with her wrath, she hadn't killed the man, but it might be days before he woke up.

The two vampires Shauna had seen sitting by the stage were lying on the floor with wooden stakes in their hearts. Each also had a large, plain, wooden cross sitting on their chests. Both vampires were unconscious.

The man in the suit was kneeling by one with a large knife in one hand. He looked up at Shauna and threw the knife. Instinctively, Shauna ducked. She berated herself briefly when she realized the knife had been nothing more than a distraction while the man in the suit, and another man on the next platform up the stairs, drew guns.

"Should we tell them the silver bullets are stupid or let them find out the hard way?" Laura asked.

Shauna assumed the question was rhetorical and used her telekinetic hand to grab the hunter in the suit by his gun hand and lift him into the air. His pistol fell, bouncing harmlessly down the stairs.

Laura started climbing the stairs slowly, which allowed her hunter to fire his weapon at her until it jammed. Unlike the hunter in the hall, this one didn't stop pulling the trigger and the gun shattered in his hand, causing him to cry in pain.

As the sound of his cries echoed through the stairwell, Laura leapt at him and tore out his throat.

"If you can speak quietly," Shauna said to the man in the suit, "you'll live."

"You're lying," the man in the suit said, his voice strained as he struggled, dangling, trying to free his hand from Shauna's mental grip. "You're going to eat me, whatever I do."

She'd fed on enemies before. They weren't as satisfying as a seduced feed. She felt blood should be given, not taken. Shauna lowered the man so that his toes could reach the floor. He could support his weight but still wouldn't be comfortable. "You have my word; neither my sister nor I will harm you if you cooperate."

"And I should believe a Satan worshipping abomination of the night?" the man asked.

"So, you're new at this." Shauna stated. "Clearly you have more faith and motivation than knowledge. Even so, I need to know what you know." She caught his eye and commanded, "I am not a vampire, just an experienced vampire hunter you want to impress. Laura is my apprentice. We just arrived and killed the vampire that tore your friend's throat out. That vampire just desiccated and we were discussing what to do with your quarry here." She let the man down and knelt by one of the vampires on the ground.

"I think we should kill them," the man in the suit said. "That's what we came here to do."

"We will," Shauna said. "I'm going to interrogate them first. They might know which vampires on board are the most influential, which, when destroyed, would have the biggest impact on society."

"Can we control them if we wake them?" the man asked.

"I have a plan," Shauna said. The plan she was putting together in her head was how to get the two vampires safely awake without having to kill the man in the suit. There was already one body to deal with and she wasn't sure the one she'd knocked out with the railing would live much longer. When she'd left the bar, she'd envisioned killing the hunters, but faced with ones she'd already subdued, she'd lost the will. For the moment, she wanted answers from the man in the suit. "Who taught you how to make a silver bullet?"

"My friends and I are self-taught," the man said. "Barry saw a vampire drinking blood from a man in an alley in Boston. We threw together a kit of stakes, garlic and holy water. Rob repacked some cartridges with silver bullets."

"So you've been prowling the alleys of Boston?" Shauna asked.

"We never did find that vampire again," the man said. "I tried finding out more online, digging as deep as I could into so many websites and forums filled with crazy people who made up stories, hoping to find a glimmer of the truth."

"And you did…" Shauna prodded.

"They found me," The man said. "Someone saying they represented the Supplicants of the Three invited us to come to Paris. They told us about this cruise and how we'd have ample opportunity to prove our mettle and that they'd be watching us."

"And we were," Shauna said. She jumped on the opportunity to claim to be the hunters he was expecting to meet, hoping he hadn't already met them. She said, "I'm going to need a flare gun. Check up by the lifeboats. Bring me a couple extra flares as well."

The man started up the stairs then paused and looked back. "What are you going to do with a flare gun?"

Shauna didn't have any plans for the flares. She just wanted to get the man out of her hair. "You'll see," Shauna said. It was enough for the man in the suit. He continued up the stairs. When he was a couple levels up, Shauna leaned out the door and whispered, "Jackie, tell Elsa to meet him by the lifeboats and delay his return." The pet, also having Venae in her system, had heightened senses and would have heard the conversation, just as she would hear the whisper from several yards away.

Laura was kneeling by the staked vampires. "Room 259," Laura said, holding up a key card. "That's down a deck. Do we try to wake them here or carry them home?"

"Wake them here," Shauna said. "I don't want to carry around a guy with a stake in his chest. At least here, we can control some of the access points."

"Um," Laura said and then asked, "Will the crosses hurt us?"

Shauna's sister hadn't spent any time since changing in learning the history of vampires. All she cared about was partying all night, every night. Elsa could go on for hours with stories of vampires through history when the mood struck. Laura wouldn't stay in the room when that happened. Being immune to disease and drug addiction gave her an excuse to not care about partying to excess.

"No," Shauna said. "Vampires have nothing to do with religion, good or bad."

"We're not damned souls?" Laura asked.

Elsa hadn't been able to explain whether vampires had souls at all when Shauna had asked. Shauna assumed, as vampire literature had told her, that vampires relinquished their souls when they turned. To her, it was a price she wouldn't have to worry about until she truly died and, as far as she knew, she was nearly immortal, though less so than she believed last week.

"You can touch the cross," Shauna said. "If it wouldn't kill you as a human, it won't kill you as a vamp."

Laura nudged the crosses off of the vampires' chests with the tip of her finger, making sure they slid down the stairs, far away from her. She then yanked both stakes out and jumped back to stand alongside Shauna.

It took a moment before the vampires' hearts beat again. As soon as they did, the vampires leapt to their feet, their hands groping at their chests where the stakes had been. The woman snarled at Shauna and Laura before the man tugged at her shoulder.

"I don't think they are hunters, dear," the man said. He turned to Shauna and Laura and asked, "You are vampires?"

"Yes," Shauna said. "We're not friends with these guys." She nudged the side of the hunter lying on the floor by her.

Looking up the stairs at the blood soaked landing where the hunter with the torn throat lay, the woman said, "I guess not." She knelt by the man whose head Shauna had bashed against the railing. "This one lives, do you mind?" She bared her fangs.

"I imagine you are hungry," Shauna said. Healing would make a vampire hungry, especially healing something as serious as a heart wound. She hadn't planned on killing the man, but, short of more violence, couldn't see a way to prevent the other vampires from exacting a revenge they'd feel was justified.

Both of the well dressed vampires bent down to bite into the man's neck, one on each side. They drank for nearly a minute until the man died. Shauna didn't know how she could sense it, but there was a chill that ran through her body when someone died within a few feet of her.

The door opened to the stairwell. Shauna rushed to the door, ready to grab whoever walked in and coerce them to walk away. Jackie and Jonnie stood outside the door, pushing a maid's cart.

"We'll clean up," Jonnie said. "Elsa said to meet her in the cabin. She said to bring the babies if they lived."

"Babies?" the male vampire they saved said. "I am Lord Ruthven and this is Lady Eunice Aubrey. We are centuries old."

Shauna offered her hand to Ruthven. "Apologies for my friends' terms," she said. When Ruthven took her hand, she saw the faint pinkish aura of a vampire less pure of Venae. His eyes widened. Perhaps he was surprised to see a purer vampire.

Laura said, "When Jonnie mentioned Elsa, she was talking of Elizabeth Bathory. I'm sure you've heard of her."

Shauna gave Laura a quick glare, trying to scold her for revealing Elsa's identity to a stranger.

"She's the daughter of the first vampire," Ruthven said. "A progeny of Dracula himself. Of course we've heard of her."

"Are all the vampires on the boat of the Dracul line?" Shauna asked.

"All vampires are," Ruthven said.

"Right," Shauna said, trying not to sound patronizing. "Shall we meet Countess Bathory?"

Ruthven looked at Lady Aubrey a moment before nodding. "We wouldn't turn down an offer to meet one of the first vampires."

Ruthven and Aubrey followed in silence down to the suite. As they rounded the last corner, they saw two ship's security police standing by the cabin door.

"Is there a problem?" Shauna asked the police, showing them her room key.

"We're just here to escort the captain ma'am," One of the guards said. "Go on in."

Opening the door, Shauna immediately saw a man in a white uniform lounging on one of the couches; a white walking cane rested across his lap. Another man, who'd been speaking but stopped when the door opened, was pacing the room while Elsa sat in a plush chair drinking from a bottle of wine.

"It's about time," Elsa said. "I was beginning to doubt I could drink enough to make this bore tolerable."

Shauna then recognized the pacing man as Vladimir, the magician from the club. "I'm sorry to be such a bother, but we don't condone killing on our boat."

"It hasn't been ten minutes since I asked you to delay that hunter on deck," Shauna said.

"It didn't take me that long," Elsa said. "I just sent him for a little swim."

"You threw him off the deck," Vladimir said. "The captain and I both saw it."

"I hadn't planned on witnesses," Elsa said. "There were fireworks off the aft of the ship. I thought it would be a distraction."

"Luckily, the captain had just finished his appearance at the voyages inaugural ceremony and was walking with me,"

Vladimir said. "So we were able to see the poor man be flung out into the darkness."

"A man could survive that fall," Shauna said, thinking the deck was, at most, fifty feet above the water.

"She threw him," Vladimir said. "She didn't drop him."

"How far?" Shauna asked.

"As far as I could," Elsa said then drank again from her bottle. She had a huge grin splayed from each side of the bottle's ring.

Shauna wasn't going to mourn a dead hunter. She wasn't sure she wouldn't have had to kill him herself if Elsa hadn't. "He was just a hunter," Shauna said. "He tried to kill Lord Ruthven and Lady Aubrey here."

"Ruthven and Aubrey?" Elsa asked then laughed vigorously. "As in Polidori's 'The Vampyre'?"

"That's us," Ruthven said.

"Really?" Elsa's tone was not just incredulous but she was clearly having difficulty containing her laughter.

"You claim to be Countess Elizabeth Bathory," Ruthven said. "I claim to be Lord Ruthven. Can either of us challenge the other with any authority?" Elsa raised her hand and pointed at Ruthven but Vladimir interrupted her before she spoke.

"I can challenge both of you," he said. "I am the King of the Sea and you have violated my rules."

Turning from Ruthven, Elsa leaned over the arm of her chair towards Vladimir. "I didn't get the pamphlet," she said dryly. "Could you clarify how your rules differ from the five laws?"

"Vampires don't kill on my boat," Vladimir said. "I prefer showing up in port without any dead bodies in my morgue."

"We didn't leave bodies," Elsa said. "My pets know how to clean up without leaving any trace evidence."

"The law is no killing," Vladimir said. "Without exceptions."

Shauna connected the dots and was confused by Vladimir's priorities. "Not even self-defense? Are you saying you care more for human lives than vampire lives?"

"I'm saying you may not kill on my boat." Vladimir said. "One of the five laws states you must obey the royalty. I am the King here, you will obey me."

"I didn't kill anyone on the boat," Elsa said.

"No throwing people off the boat," Vladimir replied. "Do I really need to get method specific or am I clear?"

The captain stood from his couch and walked to the cabin entrance, using his cane for support alongside his left foot, and closed the door. He then hobbled over to stand by Ruthven and Aubrey.

"I think you're about as clear as milk," Elsa said.

Vladimir nodded and, in a single smooth motion, the captain drew a sword blade from his cane and cut through both Ruthven and Aubrey's necks. The heads fell with a pair of thuds, their dead faces still calm and concerned with the conversation.

Before the bodies hit the ground, Laura had a small pistol in her hand aimed at the captain.

"Now am I clear?" Vladimir asked.

Shauna grabbed an unopened champagne bottle and held it threateningly. "What crime did they commit?" She asked. Her frustration turned to anger quickly and she felt the bottle cracking in her hand. She squeezed, shattering the bottle to small fragments and spilling the champagne at her feet. Breaking the bottle was less satisfying than she'd anticipated. The champagne that had splashed on her legs didn't help. She didn't need a weapon to hurt anyone, but she'd hoped it would help her look threatening.

"People were killed," Vladimir said in a forced even voice. "So I had to carry out the sentence. You know our laws; there is only one punishment."

"They were the victims," Shauna said, barely keeping her voice under a scream. "I killed the hunters." In truth, Laura had killed one, Elsa had killed one and the two vampires desiccating on the floor had killed one, but Shauna didn't care to get into the details.

"I am King of the Sea," Vladimir said, stepping so close to Shauna, she had to fight the urge to back away. "I choose how to enforce my laws. Today, I chose not to kill another of my great-great-grandfather's bloodline or her offspring. I did this out of respect for my family. Do not test the limits of that respect. Ruthven and Miss Aubrey…" Vladimir winced with a smile after he said the names, "They are the price we pay for this luxurious ride across the ocean."

"Could someone tell me why it was funny that they were Ruthven and Aubrey?" Laura asked.

The king stepped away from Shauna, giving her a last glare as he turned away. "You're new to our culture, obviously. Weak vampires often assume names of famous people of ages past. If they choose fictional names, no one can contest their identities," Vladimir said. "They think age and infamy will give them the status their lack of purity cannot."

"And, I knew John Polidori," Elsa said, "We were all part of the same crowd back in the day. The Ruthven he wrote about was my bloodfather, only John had the decency to change the name. Miss Aubrey was entirely fictional. I should know, I told the story by the fireplace and then John adapted it to the written word."

"Are you saying you knew Lord Byron and Mary Shelly?" Shauna asked. She recalled that 'The Vampyre' had been written at the same gathering as 'Frankenstein', a vacation organized by Lord Byron.

"Of course," Elsa said. "Though not for long. As unbelievable as it may seem, that group was a little too…"she pursed her lips and stared at the table for a moment. "They were too libertine for my tastes at the time."

"As much as I'd like to stay for the history lesson," Vladimir said, "my pet has a ship to run and I have a show in twenty minutes that I need to prepare for."

"It was good to meet you, nephew," Elsa said, too cheerfully. "I do hope we see smooth sailing for the remainder of the voyage."

"As do I," Vladimir said. The captain exited the cabin first with the magician close behind. "I'll send a cleaning crew with a vacuum in a couple of hours when these two are done drying up," he said before closing the door behind him.

Once the door closed, Shauna said, "Did he rub you wrong too?"

"You have to ask? He rubbed me wrong the minute he started using Vlad's name," Elsa said. "Now I have who-knows-how-many years of pent up bad rubs. As long as we can avoid him for the rest of the trip, I think I'll be fine."

"And Laura," Shauna said, turning to her sister. "Do I want to know where you got a gun?"

"The derringer?" Laura patted her pocket. "It was part of a set of garters Elsa packed for me, part of what I can only describe as a wild-west burlesque get-up. I think it's the only thing in my suitcase I can use. I kind of wish Mister King of the Sea dude had killed some vamps with better taste. I don't see myself hitting an old-fashioned dress kick anytime soon."

Shauna tried to glare at Elsa, but the elder vamp smiled back and then said, "She's taken Amber's 'Intro to Shooting Assholes' class." Despite Amber's best efforts, Shauna refused to carry a gun. She didn't like them when she was mortal and saw no need for them as a vampire who couldn't be shot.

Shauna turned her glare to her sister. Laura pointed the gun at Shauna and said, "Bang, bang, sis. Lighten up; it's just a little gun."

CHAPTER 6

During the next four nights, Shauna enjoyed the cruise. She danced; she drank; she even swam in the pools. The ship took a southerly route across the Atlantic, and the temperatures wouldn't be warm enough to swim in summer, but, for people coming from freezing temperatures, mid-seventies was bathing suit weather. Though Elsa playfully berated her for staying underwater longer than a human would, Shauna enjoyed the quiet solitude of sitting on the bottom of the pool where all the sounds were muffled even to her enhanced hearing.

Shauna was walking along the deck alone, on her way to meet up with Elsa and the twins at a midnight pool party. She noticed the two women and the man leaning on the rail, watching the sea. The man wore only a pair of shorts, but had a gym bag slung over some impressively muscled shoulders.

The numerous shirtless men onboard were getting to Shauna. It had been months since she'd last had a man's arms wrapped around her in an affectionate embrace and longer since that affection had led to intimacy. Jackie's advances stopped pushing Shauna's limits. When they had time alone, Jackie would kiss her lips, kiss her neck and rest her head on Shauna's chest, but she'd stopped teasingly running her hands to the places where Shauna would push them away. It was out of respect, and not a lack of desire, Shauna was sure. Jackie wanted Shauna to make the next move. All the visible flesh on the ships decks brought Shauna to think she wouldn't make it the rest of the voyage before she gave Jackie what she wanted. When Shauna realized it wasn't only men she'd been admiring, she was sure.

The distraction of the man's body kept Shauna from noticing the other man hiding around the corner until he rushed out, slamming into her and throwing her to the deck at the feet of the other three. The man with the gym bag pulled out a gold tipped wooden stake and a heavy wooden mallet while the two women tried to kneel on her shoulders, attempting to pin her to the deck.

"Finally got her alone," the man who slammed into her said in a violent whisper. "I thought that black haired elder would never leave her side."

"Shut up and grab her legs," the man with the stake and mallet said. "If Vladimir was right about this one, we can't afford to miss."

Shauna struggled, and the women couldn't keep her shoulders down and the man grabbing her legs could only hold on to one at a time.

"Hold her still," the man with the bag said.

"The bitch is strong," one of the women said. "Vladimir said she'd be a little stronger than him, but this vamp is insane strong."

"You have no idea," Shauna said. She kicked hard and threw the man who'd been trying to hold her legs over the rail.

"Mark!" one of the girls yelled as she jumped up and leaned over the rail.

Shauna pushed the last woman off her shoulders then stood and growled. She hoped to scare the other three away. Killing them would be too easy and she couldn't justify it as self defense if they couldn't hurt her and there were no weaker vampires or pets to protect.

The girls fled, sprinting down the deck. The man lunged at her, jamming the stake at her ribs. As Shauna expected the point hurt but didn't penetrate her skin. Shauna batted the stake away, knocking it into the ocean. The man didn't give up, he swung the mallet at Shauna's head. She ducked and grabbed him by the throat. She crossed the deck and held him up against the ship's bulkhead.

"Vladimir the magician sent you?" Shauna asked.

The man didn't reply.

Realizing he wouldn't be able to with her hand holding his throat, Shauna commanded, "You'll not flee from me. You'll stay and answer my every question." She set the man on the deck. His eyes darted up and down the deck as if he were looking to run, but he didn't move. Shauna said, "Tell me about Vladimir."

"He pays us bonuses to keep his ship clear of vampires," the man said. His voice dripped with loathing. "He gives us names, sometimes cabin numbers, and we cull your kind."

"So you guys are staff on the boat?" Shauna asked. The answer was obvious, so she asked, "What's your name?"

"Tom," he said with even more growl to his tone. "Yeah, we're staff. We're fun-spreaders. It's our job to help vacationers enjoy the journey by involving them in the ships activities while pretending to be fellow vacationers. It's less pushy and less insulting than having a staff member suggest a customer isn't having enough fun. At night we clear out the vampires."

"You've killed a lot of vampires?" Shauna asked.

"One a night, usually," Tom said. "Sometimes, if we get a good drop on them, we'd take on two. With Mark gone, I doubt that will happen again. None of it will likely happen again. Stop coercing me to answer you and just kill me."

"Who's your new boy-toy?" Laura asked, coming down the deck from the pool area. "Elsa told me to tell you they're having a wet-whitey-tighties contest. It was her idea."

"Of course it was," Shauna said. "This is Tom, he's a vamp hunter who recently watched his teammate take a midnight dive. He doesn't like me, but he'll answer whatever I ask."

"He's too cute to kill," Laura said. "If you're not going to keep him, can I?"

"He's not a stray puppy," Shauna said. "He's a killer."

Laura stepped close to Tom, so close she could kiss him. She didn't. Instead she just looked him in the eye a moment then said, "I'm a vampire. He's human; that makes him a puppy if I want him to be a puppy." She glanced at Shauna and gave her a twisted smile then turned back to Tom. "You're going to enjoy this. You're going to obey my every command, serve my every whim, and be happy about it."

"What would you ask of me?" Tom asked, his voice demure. He'd completely lost his defiant attitude.

After sinking her teeth into her palm, she held it up to Tom's mouth. "I want you to drink."

The hunter suckled at Laura's hand for a while, until the wound healed and he could no longer drink. He then grunted and fell to the deck, clutching his chest.

"What's going on?" Laura asked.

"You know our blood is poison," Shauna said. "This will probably kill him. If it doesn't, he'll be bound to you." She'd thought her sister would have learned something of the way vampire blood affected humans in the weeks since the change. Typical of Laura, she'd been so blasé about it, focusing instead on her ability to party endlessly, that she didn't know how to make a pet. "Sit on him, so he doesn't roll overboard."

Laura climbed on top of Tom straddling his chest and holding his wrists against the deck. "I didn't realize I could kill him. I suppose it's not an entirely bad thing, his being a hunter and all."

Tom's body continued to spasm for several minutes. In that time, two couples walked by, but Shauna handled them by suggesting they saw nothing on their walk along the deck except the lovely stars reflecting on the waves of the ocean.

After a moment of calm, he looked at Laura and said, "What did you do to me? Get off of me, bitch."

"I thought he was supposed to love me," Laura said. "I coerced him. He was so compliant a moment ago."

"You can't coerce your pet," Shauna said. "And he's apparently now yours."

"You mean I'm stuck with a hunter who will hate me?" Laura asked. "I can't even kill him or I'd die, too."

"So you do know something," Shauna said. "You can't coerce him; I can." She knelt by her sister and grabbed

Tom's chin, turning his face and forcing him to meet her gaze. "Look at me," she commanded. "Laura is your goddess and you adore her. You will respect vampires and never harm one again. Any touch of Laura's, especially her bite, will bring you pleasure. Serving her whims will make you happy."

"I'm not sure that's a kinder sentence than death," Laura said. "I feel a little dirty taking so much of his free will, so much of his self, away."

"Don't feel bad, goddess," Tom said. "I am overjoyed at the opportunities this bond will give me to please you."

Laura stepped off of her pet, "Stand up, come with me."

"We need to find Elsa," Shauna said. "She's waiting for us."

"Yep," Laura said. "I just hope the contest hasn't started yet. I'd like to see what my new boy-toy is packing." She turned to Tom and said, "Please be wearing tighty-whities."

"I'm happy to say, I am," her pet replied.

"This is going to be the start of a great relationship," Laura said.

The contest hadn't started when they arrived. Shauna didn't know what to expect. She'd never heard of a tighty whities contest. Elsa stood by the pool with several men who were in the process of disrobing. Laura had time to get Tom stripped to his underwear and join the other men. After a lap across the pool they lined up on the far side of the pool and posed. Some flexed their arms and chests and others wiggled their hips as they waited to be judged. A small crowd gathered to watch Elsa's event.

"I thought you couldn't coerce a whole crowd," Shauna said, noticing the enthusiasm of the gathered party-goers.

"I barely had to coerce the assistant cruise director." Elsa nodded to the woman holding a microphone and walking behind the line of men. "It's amazing what inhibitions normal people leave behind when they go on vacation."

"I could see that," Shauna said, remembering her own epiphany. With the crowd around her whistling and some women calling for the men to dance, it wasn't the time to relay her desires to Elsa. She had intended to show Jackie before she told anyone. Telling Elsa about the hunters would have to wait as well.

Elsa waved the girl with the microphone over then said to her, "This isn't as exciting as I'd hoped. I think the pool water must be too cold."

"You could judge on what's above the waistline," Shauna suggested. She was still inhibited enough to be unable to sustain any gaze below the men's waistbands. Most of the men were in better than decent shape. Her eyes were on the body of a boy who couldn't be more than twenty, probably an employee of the ship. A swimmer, perhaps the lifeguard, she guessed by his trim, defined muscles.

"I think we raise the bar here, and a few other things, I'd hope," Elsa said. She stepped between her pets, who were wearing matching red bikinis, and put her hands on their shoulders. "Jackie, Jonnie, why don't you give the boys a little show." When the twins stepped forward, towards the pool, Elsa was holding a bikini top dangling from each of her hands.

Jonnie and Jackie took a deck chair and moved it to across the pool from the underwear-clad men. They set it so it was flat like a bed.

Then their show started. The twins began mimicking a sexual encounter. Somehow, they did this in such perfect choreography that their bodies never touched one another. They responded to each other as if stimulated, writhing and undulating, with moaning and culminating in simultaneous screams as they mimicked rubbing their bodies together.

"This is more exciting," Elsa said, nodding to the men.

All were having difficulty maintaining containment. Between their aroused state and the saturated fabric, there was no need for imagination.

The cruise director went from man to man, asking the crowd to applaud. At the end, she came to Elsa and asked, "Which man won?"

"Which do you like," Elsa asked Shauna.

"I'm partial to the young one," Shauna said of the man with the swimmer's body.

"A modest choice," Elsa said. "I'm not drawn to overly endowed men either, but the man at the end," Elsa pointed to an older man, who, though still in shape, looked a little like his skin was stretched over his muscles. "He has a good set of equipment and he looks like he has the wisdom to know how to use it. Bring them here."

Elsa could charm anyone from a few yards away, causing them to be drawn to her. Shauna could do it with anyone who could see her. It only took catching their eyes for a split second and both men headed over towards her.

"I was talking to Denise," Elsa said, placing a hand on the cruise director's shoulder. "But, nevermind. They seem to be heading this way on their own. Thank you, Denise. I'll put in a good word with the Captain. Give all the participants a few drink coupons, would you?"

Denise said, into the microphone, "Thanks to all the great sports we had participate. Come see me for some drink coupons."

"Have we won?" the younger man asked as he stopped in front of Shauna.

"You have." Elsa took the older man's hand. "The prize is down in our cabin, if you would like to accompany us. Are either of you here with a wife or girlfriend?"

Both men shook their heads, though the older one turned and gave a thumbs up to someone in the crowd. Shauna gave Elsa a questioning look but the elder vamp just smiled and nodded at her.

"Let's head down, then," Shauna said. She looked around for Laura. Her sister was sitting at a bar, talking with her new pet, so she let them be. Elsa hooked both men by the elbow, one on each side, and headed to the cabin. As Shauna followed behind, the twins caught up, putting their arms around her as they walked. Neither the men nor the twins bothered to put their clothing back on.

CHAPTER 7

Shauna woke to someone knocking on the door. She found herself in a pile of limbs. Jackie, instead of cuddling her from behind had her in an embrace from the front, the twin's face nuzzled up against Shauna's breast. A man groaned and Shauna peered over her shoulder to see the older man from the contest sprawled on the bed with Jonnie lying on top of him. The younger man was curled up by the pillows. It took a moment to find Elsa, but she soon located her wedged between Shauna and Jackie, intertwined with both of their legs.

"The maid will come back later," Elsa moaned. "I'm up for round four," she paused to kiss Shauna's thigh. "Or is it five?"

Every memory of the previous night came to Shauna at once. Her first full sexual experience since becoming a vampire had been a blur of bodies. The night had started with Shauna taking the younger man, alone, to her bed, while Elsa stayed with the twins and the older man in the sitting room, making creative use of the couches.

In the heated moments, Jackie's lips came as a surprise to Shauna, but a welcome one. From there to six people crowding her bed, might have been minutes or hours. Shauna had lost herself to the passions. The intensity of the pleasure at times overwhelmed her making her scream, which had never happened when she was human, with human lovers. It wasn't just that Elsa and the twins knew what to do, and they did, even the young man's clumsy attempts brought waves of bliss unlike Shauna ever imagined possible.

The energy of the experience was palpable, almost as nourishing as feeding. The men had lost the ability to participate hours before Elsa and the twins finally let Shauna fall asleep.

"What time is it, anyway?" Elsa asked.

Shauna picked up the nearest phone and checked. "Seven," Shauna read. "In the morning," she added. It was not yet dawn, in January in the North Atlantic.

The knocking at the door came harder and more rapid, rattling the cabin walls.

"I'm coming," Shauna called.

"Not anymore, you're not," Elsa said. "But, if you stay in bed, I'll be sure to change that."

Shauna smiled and petted Elsa's hair. "Don't worry, baby," Shauna said, surprised at feeling brazen enough to use an endearment with Elsa. "I'm sure this wasn't a onetime thing."

Elsa responded by nipping Shauna's thigh. Shauna extracted herself as gracefully as she could and grabbed a bathrobe from the floor as she crawled out of bed.

She closed her bedroom door and made sure her bathrobe was tied closed before answering the door. When Shauna turned the doorknob, it flew open, slamming against the wall of the cabin. Several men wearing ship's security uniforms rushed through.

"Another visit from the captain?" Shauna asked.

"No, ma'am," a security officer with more stripes on his uniforms than the others said as he walked into the room. "This time you'll be visiting him. The captain has requested all the women in this suite join him for brunch in his private dining room."

Shauna leaned out the door, counting eight security guards in the hall to add to the handful already in the room. "By the dozen men you've sent to escort us, I imagine you were using the word 'request' very liberally."

"I was instructed to not take 'no' for an answer," the officer said.

"What's going on?" Laura asked, walking naked out of Elsa's bedroom. "Don't mind me, I'm getting dressed." She crossed the suite to the door to the room she and Shauna were supposed to be sharing.

"Wait," Shauna said, too late.

Laura had opened the door and glanced at Shauna with a raised eyebrow and gave Shauna an impish smile. "So this is why the cops are here. You're having too much fun for the cruise!"

"Yeah, well," Shauna replied trying to keep her embarrassment in check. It became more difficult when she realized at some point her sister had come in and discovered her room too occupied and opted to use Elsa's instead. Shauna focused instead on the immediate presence of the ship's security team. "We're going to meet Vladimir again," Shauna said.

"All of us?" Laura asked.

"All the women," Shauna said, repeating the officer's earlier invitation.

"And," the officer added. "If there is a man named Tom here, he is to come as well." He'd turned and was facing the suite's galley which was the only direction to look without seeing naked flesh.

"My puppy?" Laura asked.

Shauna glared at her sister but nodded. "You can't call him that."

"You underestimate me, sis," Laura said. "I am capable of many things. Calling my puppy a puppy is just one of those things."

The lead security guard seemed neither amused or interested in Laura, although everyone on the security team was watching the naked sister.

"Are you capable of getting dressed, sis?" Shauna asked.

"Oh," Laura said, looking down at herself then winking at the officer. "Silly me. I'll be a minute." She returned to her room, but left the door open as she dug through her suitcases.

It took Shauna and her suite mates a while to get dressed and shuffle out the overnight guests. Elsa seemed particularly determined to take her time in getting outfits picked out for the twins and Shauna. The guards were patient, only twice asking if they would hasten.

It was almost noon when they walked into the captain's dining room. The magician, Vladimir, sat at the head of the table with the captain at his right. Two girls stood behind the King of the Sea. The hunters who'd run away from the previous night's fight stared at Shauna with loathing in their eyes.

"Please, sit." Vladimir said. He had a smug look, watching each of them enter the room, until Tom entered. Shauna noticed a brief narrowing of the magician's eyes but he was quick to regain his composure. Elsa sat with a pet on each side at the other end of the table from Vladimir. Shauna sat between the captain and Jackie, leaving Laura and her new pet to sit on the other side with Laura closest to the captain.

Shauna had expected the officers to leave, but instead they took up positions around the wall of the room.

"This is unexpected," Elsa said. "I had hoped to enjoy the remainder of my cruise without such unseemly distractions."

"You killed a human when you knew that had a price on my boat," Vladimir said. "Disobeying a king has consequences."

"You can't hurt us," Elsa said. "You're of my bloodline. You know we can phase out of danger." As far as Vladimir knew, Shauna and Laura were blood descendants of Elsa. They could both phase, so the ruse would hold if tested.

"I have no intention of harming you, Countess Bathory," Vladimir said. "I have decided to give you a choice. You will pay a fine of ten million dollars or I will have your pets executed." He turned to Tom and said, "You knew you were expendable. Now that you've betrayed me, you're exceptionally so."

The men around the room drew pistols and each aimed at the nearest pet.

Vladimir then said, "This has been a costly cruise for me in terms of lives. You killed two people, who you say were hunters, and threw another two overboard."

"Just one," Elsa corrected.

"And another one," Shauna admitted. The two girls behind Vladimir had clearly already told him of the events from the night before.

"You didn't tell me?" Elsa asked.

"We were busy, remember?" Shauna said. "Or was I that forgettable."

"No, love, nothing about you is forgettable," Elsa said.

"We're not here to wed the two of you," Vladimir said, "As I was saying, there have been an unusual number of deaths on this trip. Six other humans have disappeared and I've had to drop two others off mid-sea who couldn't be convinced their loved ones hadn't come along for the journey. I can't prove you had anything to do with the six, but who says I have to? My ship, my rules. Right now, my rule is that ten million dollars will buy my forgiveness." he motioned to the captain who then produced a laptop from a satchel at his side. He slid the laptop down the table to Elsa. "Men, please cock your guns," Vlad said. "If there is any non-compliance here, microseconds will count."

The ships security officers all clicked back the hammers on their pistols.

"Elsa!" Jackie whimpered, "I don't like this."

"Don't panic," Elsa said. She leaned over the table, locked eyes with Vladimir, and said, "In case you haven't heard, I'm broke. My holdings were all in my building which was destroyed by hunters. I'm sure it made the news."

"I don't believe you," Vladimir said. "I think you had the wisdom to squirrel funds away across the globe. I'm not in this purely for profit. I had to set my captain's launch afloat to explain the disappearances. It seems a group of passengers got drunk and stole it. That will be the story, anyway. It's believable since most of the people who disappeared were men in their twenties. I will, however, need a new captain's launch. You have one minute to log into a viable account."

Shauna didn't know anything about Elsa's finances, but her own accounts had more than Vladimir was asking. She didn't consider it her money, it had been an inheritance Elsa had arranged, and Shauna hadn't willingly spent any of it. However, she allowed Elsa to manage the account and Elsa spent freely on Shauna, renovating her home and buying new clothes faster than Shauna could wear them. Still, Shauna shared Vladimir's opinion that Elsa had money somewhere. As much as Elsa liked to act carefree, most of her life was planned in detail.

"You can use my money," Shauna suggested quietly.

"That's sweet, beautiful," Elsa said, "But I have a better idea. Why don't you explain to Vlad the Imposter how things work."

Understanding that Elsa wasn't asking for a rundown of finances, Shauna nodded. "No one is going to shoot anyone," she commanded, confident she shared James' ability to coerce without eye contact. "Engage the safeties on your guns and holster them." Shauna silently thanked Amber. Her class had produced some useful knowledge. To make sure, she looked straight at Vladimir, who was starting to squirm and had an expression of pure wrath. Confirming her abilities, the guards all secured and holstered their weapons.

"You can't..." Vladimir started to say, but Shauna didn't give him the chance to continue.

"You like us," Shauna said. "You have the utmost respect for an Elder of the Dracul blood. In fact, all of these guards are here as a show of that respect. Such a large escort would only be given to the most deserving of passengers." Shauna was pleased that she had settled the Vlad problem without violence. With Jackie and Jonnie, and, through Tom, her sister, in danger, Shauna was sure she'd have killed too many people if it had come to violence.

"Why were you giving me money?" Vladimir asked, his ire turned to obvious confusion.

"Elsa was just discussing methods for passing money to ourselves as we change names," Shauna said. "You were just about to send the captain to check on our lunch. I believe it was lobster for the pets and an assortment of your most beautiful crew for my sister, myself and Elsa."

"Ron," Vladimir said, nodding to the captain, "see what's taking the staff so long." The captain nodded then stood from his chair and hobbled through the door behind Vlad.

"Vladimir," Elsa said, "while we're waiting, I'd like to know more about your heritage. I am the blooddaughter of Vlad Dracula, the Impaler. From where do you derive the right to use his name?"

"I have this." He reached into his coat and pulled out an obsidian spearhead. "It's said this was Vlad's favorite, used to impale the most notable officers in the armies he defeated. It was a gift from my bloodmother, which she received from her bloodfather and he got it from Vlad the Impaler."

"I never saw that," Elsa said. "Vlad and I lived together for fifty years and I never heard of such an object."

"Maybe it was from before your time. My ancestor was made half a century before you were born. She made my grandfather in the first few years of her life as one of us," Vladimir said.

"Are you claiming to be older than me?" Elsa said.

"No. I am telling you my lineage, my birthright. I am the bloodson of Mirela who is blooddaughter to Ivan, who was the blood son of Nadya." Vladimir said. "Nadya was a gypsy princess, one of Vlad Dracula's three brides."

"I didn't know the brides had blood children." Elsa said.

"Clearly, Nadya did," Vladimir said.

"Your mother was killed by the hunter who killed Dracula," Elsa said.

Vladimir nodded.

"Van Helsing?" Shauna asked.

"Please, Shauna," Elsa said. "So much of that book was fiction, so many names were changed. The hunter that killed Vlad was named Michael or something like that; I killed him just minutes after he cut off my bloodfather's head."

"You weren't mentioned in the book," Shauna said.

"I was," Elsa replied. "But so many details were changed with my name, you wouldn't recognize me. Somehow they made me the victim, but I was the driving force in the actual events that inspired the story."

"You're saying you were Wilhelmina Harker?" Shauna asked, making sure she understood.

"She was," Jackie said. "It was around that time she made us her pets. The name is pure fiction, but Elsa married a young British socialite, planning to move herself and her bloodfather to England. Things didn't go as planned, so we went to Philly after Dracula died. Both Jonnie and I are named after Jonathan 'Jack' Gainer, who was renamed Harker in the book. She liked him right up until he helped to kill Drac."

"The spear of Dracula," Elsa said. "I guess that does prove your right to rule the seas."

The captain came back into the room. He said to Vladimir, "The crew was confused, they didn't have any order for brunch. Shall I ask them to quickly prepare a meal? I don't think it would be up to our standards if we rush it."

"It's not necessary," Elsa said. "We'll be leaving now." She whispered to Shauna. "See to it that we aren't bothered again, please."

"Vladimir, you won't bother us, or any other vampires, again." Shauna said.

"And send the lobster to our room when it's ready," Jonnie said. "Don't rush it."

"Yes," Shauna said. "Do that."

As they were standing, Elsa said, "One last thing. Vlad, what is your actual name. Certainly you aren't actually a Vladimir."

"I am Allesandro," Vlad said. "I was made in Florence during The Great War."

Shauna held back a snort. He was barely a century old. She thought it was ridiculous that someone so young would claim a station as austere as king.

§

As they left the captain's dining room, Shauna felt suddenly tired. "Did he poison us?" Shauna asked.

"It's just the crest of last night's fun falling away," Elsa said. "It feels like feeding, but it's not. I told you to feed during the fun."

"It just seemed out of place," Shauna said. "I was never one for eating in bed. Crumbs in my sheets make my skin crawl."

"If you feed, you drink their blood while their blood is enriched with the experience," Elsa said. "It's better quality. You need less and it lasts longer. Any primal urge will do, but the reproductive urges are my personal favorite. Some vamps like adrenaline, some like fear. I like lust."

"I tried to tell her," Laura said to Elsa, rolling her eyes at Shauna.

§

The remainder of the voyage was spent dancing, without fear of hunters. Each evening, Shauna woke with only Jackie in her bed. When the ship docked it was mid-day, so they waited until dusk before disembarking.

On the way off the ship, as they reached the elevators, Elsa stopped and looked back. "I left something in the room; go on without me," she said.

Shauna didn't see her again until they reached the bottom of the gangplank. Elsa was waiting, sitting on their luggage and whistling, which was not something Shauna had seen her do before. It was as if she were being too obviously nonchalant.

Shauna bit. "What did you do?"

"Wait for it," Elsa said, she looked off in the distance, down the road where service trucks were driving too and from the ship. Within seconds, Shauna heard sirens.

"Do we need to run?" Shauna asked.

"Why would we need to run from an ambulance?" Elsa said. Sure enough, the vehicle coming down the street was a blue and white vehicle with a medical insignia on the hood. "If I had to guess, the captain had a heart attack after the ships doctors had departed for the day." She reached into her handbag and pulled out an obsidian spearhead and tossed it to Shauna. "You'll want to put that somewhere safe."

"You ki…" Shauna's words were cut off by Elsa rushing over and kissing her.

When Elsa broke off a moment later, she said, "Let's just not talk about it. You know what happened; I know what happened. Let's leave it at that."

CHAPTER 8

"This is not the town I remember," Elsa said as she walked along the canal with Shauna. "This is all new."

"It's been two hundred years," Shauna said. "If I'm tracking your timeline correctly, that is."

"Close enough," Elsa said. "Still, in most cities, there are still a few landmark buildings that stand through the ages. Everything here is new—within the past half century."

"You've heard of World War II?" Shauna said. "That's the English Channel over there. I'd bet, like most coastal cities on both sides of the water, this city was leveled in the nineteen-forties."

"That's going to be a problem," Elsa said. "I don't know where to go. There used to be a wool brokerage right here. At least, I think it was right here. The King of the Northern Roman Empire kept their court on the brokerage's auction floor."

"Where would he keep it now?" Shauna asked. "And, is it important for us to know?"

"We're going to be staying in his territory for a while," Elsa said. "We might want to avoid having him surprise us. It's not my goal to leave a trail of crowns laying on the ground during this quest of yours."

"Mine?" Shauna asked. "I thought we were in this together."

"Sweety," Elsa said. "We're in everything together, or did you forget the other night? We may have slightly different reasons and goals, but the path we're on leads to all of them."

"And what happens when it doesn't?" Shauna asked.

"Again, remember the other night." Elsa winked. "We take turns."

"So, now that you've gotten what you wanted of me, you're not going to go away?" Shauna asked.

Elsa stopped and turned to face Shauna. She stepped up and embraced her, kissing her cheek. "First," Elsa said, "What I want from you is not what we had the other night. That is just a bonus. Second, I'm in this to the end, just hopefully not my end." After stepping away and starting to walk again, Elsa stopped and said. "Or yours."

"Or James'," Shauna added.

"He's the great source of all secrets in the world I've lived in for four centuries," Elsa said. "If I have an addiction, it's information, and James is the only one who can sate that need. He's at least a millennium older than any other vampire I have ever met, and I've stood before the Council. There is no way I would willingly let him die."

"Beth!" A woman's voice called from the other side of the canal. Shauna turned to see a woman flying across the water towards them. She wore a gauzy gown of white and pale blue layers and had flowing silvery gray hair that hung below her feet when she flew. Her skin was pale, and she had a pair of mirrored glasses hiding her eyes.

"What is she?" Shauna whispered.

"That's Zylpha. I wasn't expecting to see her in Calais or anywhere west of Constantinople," Elsa said.

"You mean Istanbul?" Shauna asked. "It's been Istanbul since before you were born."

"I do mean what you said." Elsa nodded. "But spend fifty years around my bloodfather and you wouldn't say that word ever again either. It was a bit of a sore spot." She stepped to the edge of the canal and knelt with her head bowed as the pale woman landed.

Shauna mimicked Elsa.

"Queen Zylpha," Elsa said. "I am honored to be in your presence."

Shauna knew the name. Zylpha was one of the founding members of the Elders Council. The head of her bloodline.

The silvery haired woman held out her hands, saying "Stand, please."

Shauna took the hand, cringing as she saw the pale aura. Someday she'd remember to not allow courtesy to give away the secret of her Venae.

"Oh my lord," Zylpha said, stepping back, dropping Shauna and Elsa's hands. "How in God's name…?"

"Um," Elsa said. "She's a little purer than most of us."

"I wasn't looking at her," Zylpha said. "I was looking at your aura. Are you telling me this woman is purer than you are?"

Elsa looked confused and stepped up to Zylpha and touched the pale white skin of her arm. "I wasn't looking," Elsa said. "You are less pure than I. I thought you were of the same purity as my bloodfather."

"I was," Zylpha said. "We spent centuries together. During the wars with the elders before us, Vlad was always trying to find a way to purify his blood. It seems he found it. I thought it was impossible. Is it something she did that increased your purity?" Zylpha nodded to Shauna

"Unless sex can purify us," Elsa said, "It wasn't Shauna."

"This is Shauna?" Zylpha asked. "Who…"

"She's my partner," Elsa said, interrupting Zylpha.

"If sex purified vampires, we'd all be your purity," Zylpha said. "No, I don't think we've ever had contact before; you could have been made this way."

"Things were more formal back in the day," Elsa said. "I haven't seen you in person since you coerced my pets for me. You and the council sat at your marble bench looking down on any that dared come before you."

"We haven't met like that since the telegram was perfected. Nowadays, we use webcams," Zylpha said.

"Is that why you're here?" Elsa asked. "Because I didn't call you when we landed?"

"I tried to reach you online," Zylpha said. "One of your lovely pets answered and told me you'd be out here."

"You were expecting us?" Shauna asked.

"Elsa was running an errand for me," Zylpha said. "One I'd asked her to do a few decades ago."

"Well," Elsa said. "I had to wait until I had the right equipment for the job." She nodded to Shauna.

"Wait," Shauna said. "You mean all this time, you've been using me for something?"

Elsa purred, "Lover, everyone uses everyone. It's all about giving enough back so they are happy to be used. But, no, what we did was more from opportunity than planning. I promise you, everything I've told you about why I like you is true."

"What, exactly, did you use me for?" Shauna asked.

"Killing Vladimir, I'd guess," Zylpha answered.

"I didn't," Shauna said. "Are you saying you asked Elsa to kill that jerk?"

"I asked Elsa to find out why some vampires that make that voyage disappear." Zylpa stepped close to Elsa. "Killing another vampire is against our laws and being a jerk isn't enough excuse to violate them. I do hope Vladimir's demise indicates he was involved."

"He was," Elsa said.

"He worked with hunters," Shauna said. "He arranged for them to use his boat to train and practice. How would he get away with that for so long?"

"She's young for being so pure," Zylpha said to Elsa.

"Yes," Elsa said.

Zylpha said to Shauna, "Vampires often 'disappear' their identities and create new ones without telling anyone. If we don't hear from a friend for a few weeks, years or even decades, we don't always assume the worst. The ocean liner was still the safest way to cross an ocean." Zylpha turned to include Elsa and continued, "Knowing he was only a few generations removed from Vlad, I am sure Vladimir was not a weak vampire. There are very few vampires of the potency needed to deal with him."

"Like Elsa," Shauna said.

"I didn't know she was as pure as she is, but even if she were slightly less pure than I, she would be one of two or three dozen in the world. As she is, she is one of three that

I've met since the Purge who are purer than I. Amenhetop in the Blood Temple is purer as well. You, Shauna, would be another. Since Elsa didn't make you, that means there is yet at least one more out there as well. This tells me that Vlad's plan failed. We didn't succeed in eradicating the purer vampires of the world."

"I didn't know I was among those," Elsa said. "Should I be worried that you will try to purge me?"

"As I said," Zylpha explained, "we didn't start the purge and we have seen enough warfare. You are safe from me."

"I have to admit, it was my love for continued existence that prevented me from investigating sooner," Elsa said to Zylpha. "I don't know how much purer than you I am, but knowing three generations separated Vladimir and Vlad, there's a good chance he was purer than you as well. If I'd known that, I would have sent Shauna alone." She turned to Shauna and said, "Sorry, my love, but they can't hurt you. It would be the prudent course of action."

"These days we have to take every precaution for our safety," Zylpha said. "I wouldn't be here if I didn't need to speak to you, Elsa."

"It was that important that I kill Vladimir?" Elsa asked.

Zylpha shrugged. "Vladimir doesn't matter one way or another. The council never approved his claim to a crown. He never sought the Blood Temple's confirmation."

"How could the council let him make such a claim?" Elsa asked.

"That's a long story," Zylpha said. "Let's get to that from another angle. Your pet told me you were seeking King Wolfram to introduce yourselves and seek permission to feed in his territory."

"Yes" Elsa said. "It's proper etiquette to at least visit with King Wolfram."

"That won't happen," Zylpha said. "You missed him by almost two weeks."

"Will he be back?" Elsa asked, but it must've been the dour look on Zylpha's face that answered the question. Elsa then asked, "How?"

"Europe is having a hunter problem," Zylpha said. "Someone is tracking down vampires and eliminating them, starting with the purest. I'm here to warn you."

"We saw that in Philadelphia," Shauna said. "Henry the Inquisitor."

"He's been here," Zylpha said. "He has lackeys and, if rumors are correct, angels. Ten years ago there were five hundred vampires in France alone. Today there are half that many in all of the Northern Roman Empire. King Wolfram is dead and the new king is on his way to Paris to gain the approval of Amenhetop. "

"Countess Portia mentioned Amenhetop," Shauna said. "What's the deal with him?"

"The Blood Temple," Zylpha said. "It's actually the council that approves new kings. Amenhetop oversees the temple, or so tradition tells it. He's an odd vamp. He just stands there, oblivious or catatonic. Each time I've been there, he's been standing in a different place, so I think he's still in there. He's just so old that he doesn't care. But he's the father of us all, older than the bible. After four or five thousand years, I'd probably be bored to death, too."

Shauna stopped herself from contradicting Zylpha's history. Maybe James still held a secret or two from most vampires.

"You are four or five thousand years old," Elsa said. "Or so I thought. You are the oldest of the Elders, aren't you?"

Zylpha nodded. "I'm the oldest but, I'm not even three. My bloodline propogated quickly, but I'm young enough that, when I was alive, Moses was already history. Amenhetop was already in his temple under the river in Gallia. I never met him until after the Purge, when the old elders were gone and I was one of the nine new elders. Now there are only six of us."

"Vampires have been hunted since people suspected we existed," Elsa said.

"If truth be told, it's been mostly by other vampires," Zylpha said. "Your bloodfather personally eradicated the families of two of the three lost Elders. Perhaps the expedition to kill him was funded by others among the council."

"Or it was just Lucy," Elsa said. "I always assumed it was her ambition that ended Vlad."

"It wasn't your sister," Zylpha said. "I wasn't really guessing when I said 'perhaps'. He was the war monger among us and the rest of us were done with fighting; at least, we hoped to be."

"I see," Elsa said. She turned away from Zylpha. "I think you should go. I'm sure you did the right thing, but I loved my bloodfather. He was every bit the monster history makes him out to be, but he was family. Go, Queen Zylpha." Elsa stepped close to Shauna and took her hand. Elsa squeezed tight enough that it was uncomfortable. She turned back to the queen and said in a slow, even voice, "When we meet again, this will be behind us, but today, revenge seems to be tempting me."

"As you wish, Beth," Zylpha said. "It was time you knew the truth. I should warn you: avoid the new royal, King Napoleon. You would do better to hope he doesn't notice you in his kingdom. He's already abusing his power. Once he gets the Council's blessing, he will be intolerable. We will have to approve him if his blood is pure enough. There are too few left of any purity, so we cannot be picky. I fear that if you meet him, you will kill him and the council cannot condone the killing of a king."

Zylpha then flew away, much faster than she'd arrived. In a blink she was gone from sight, lost among the stars.

"Napoleon?" Shauna asked. "*The* Napoleon?"

"There was more than one," Elsa said. "A first and third, if I recall. I've not met either. I have no fondness for military types."

"So which is this Napoleon?" Shauna asked.

"My bet is neither," Elsa said. "Vampires change their names every few decades by necessity. Every so often, one chooses to assume the persona of a historical figure, as we saw with Ruthven."

"And if someone as famous as Napoleon became a vampire you'd have heard?" Shauna asked.

"Not necessarily," Elsa said. "As I mentioned, if a historical figure was made into a vampire, they probably changed their name. Political figures have enemies, even in death. It's possible one of the Emperors faked their passing and has now decided they missed having a crown. But, I wouldn't put money on it, not even a single Franc."

"Euro," Shauna said. "Francs are worthless now."

"Exactly," Elsa said. "The last piece of evidence is that the current claimant calls himself 'King Napoleon.' Royals choose their titles. No emperor would reduce himself to a king."

"So much for meeting another great figure from history," Shauna said.

"You won't meet many," Elsa said. "Vampires don't thrive in the public spotlight. People notice when someone is never seen in daylight. It's best to be a person the public has no interest in."

"I see," Shauna said. "I believe this is the part of the plan where we call Amber and have her let Henry escape."

"Jonnie called already." Elsa held up her phone and showed Shauna a text message from Amber. It read: We're returning the wolf to the wild at noon.

Shauna checked her phone and she had the same message. She did the math in her head, figuring out the difference between Paris time and Philly time. "Tomorrow at sunset?"

Elsa nodded.

CHAPTER 9

The four digit number Amber had sent was a flight number to Paris. After checking the schedules and realizing the flight wouldn't arrive in Paris until after dawn, Elsa announced they would be spending the night enjoying the tastes of the City of Lights.

Their train arrived in Paris just before midnight. Elsa insisted on starting from a familiar place so they went straight to the Notre Dame Cathedral. From there, she seemed to know where to go.

"Is it luck that Henry is coming to Paris or did Elsa buy all the other open tickets?" Laura asked as they walked north along Rue Pierre Fontaine.

"You guys always seem to come up with these great manipulations that make me feel like I'm losing my touch," Elsa said. "It's luck, but I wish I'd thought to do that."

"You have to admit, you give Machiavelli a run for his money when it comes to scheming," Shauna said. "I wouldn't be surprised if he learned from you."

"He was before my time," Elsa said. "My sister, Lucy, knew him."

"That's the Moulin Rouge ahead?" Laura asked.

Shauna had seen it, and recognized it. "Yes," Shauna said.

"What's it like there, Elsa?" Laura asked.

"I've never been," Elsa said. "It is new to me. I've been meaning to check it out."

"Is that where we're going?" Shauna asked.

"Tonight?" Elsa replied, "No, it's too late. We're looking for the Sacred Heart. Portia said the temple is under that."

"What if we run into the king there?" Shauna said. "Zylpha said to avoid him and we know he's going there too."

"Piffle," Elsa said. "Tomorrow, we may be chasing Henry all the way to Moscow. I've got to see this place.

Imagine learning that the Garden of Eden was real. Could you pass by it without stopping to peek in?"

"I guess not," Shauna said. Elsa had mentioned she'd never believed in the temple until Portia mentioned that it was a real place. Shauna was curious about the ancient catatonic vampire, Amenhetop, as well.

Laura's new pet, Tom, asked, "The Blood Temple? It's under a hotel, two blocks west of the windmill. The Sacred Heart is the Basilica northeast of here, but the Blood Temple isn't there. The entrance is through a bank across the street. The hunters haven't made it past that point yet."

"I know," Elsa said. "Well, not so much about the hunters, but I know where I'm going."

When they reached the Boulevarde de Clichy, Jackie handed her phone to Jonnie and grabbed Shauna. "Let's get a picture!" she said.

Once Jonnie snapped their picture with the lights of the Moulin Rouge behind them, everyone else insisted on getting their picture taken as well. Even after midnight, they weren't the only ones doing it. They were the only vampires Shauna could see. For some reason she expected to see more in Paris at such a notorious nightspot. She hadn't seen any since they arrived in the city.

After getting another tourist to take a full group picture, Elsa dragged them away. "Tom, did you carry your wallet in your back pocket?" Elsa asked.

"What do you mean by, 'Did you?'" Tom replied as he patted his pants. "Dammit!"

"So the pickpockets aren't just a rumor?" Shauna ventured.

"Apparently not," Elsa said. "It was that guy in the red knit cap." She pointed down a side street to a man walking hastily away.

"Wait for us at the bank," Laura said and took Tom's hand and headed after the man in the red cap.

"We will," Elsa called after them. After a few minutes, as they continued down the Boulevard de Clichy, Elsa said casually, "You do know Laura's going to kill that man, right?"

"For taking her pet's wallet?" Shauna asked. She hardly thought Laura would be so vengeful over money.

"For being alone on that dark street," Elsa said. "The wallet will just be an excuse."

"She wouldn't," Shauna said, but as she thought about it, she wondered if maybe Elsa was seeing something she wasn't. She stopped and started walking back toward the road her sister had gone down.

"Not now," Elsa said. "We don't have time for that argument."

"I could save a man's life," Shauna said, but as she spoke the words she knew they weren't true. The few minutes it had been were more than enough time for her sister to have drained that man beyond the point of recovery.

She started to lift herself into the air. Perhaps she could make it if she flew. Elsa pulled at her. "Not in the city," she said. "Not in a city with so many cameras. You can't act like a superhero; you'll be noticed."

Shauna dropped and looked at Elsa, not sure what she should do or ask.

"Your sister has an addiction," Elsa said. "People who have problems with addictions don't always lose them when they become vampires. Sometimes the only thing that changes is what they're addicted to. I think Laura is addicted to her victims' deaths. I began to suspect when she killed my shop girl the night before James' party."

"She did what?" Shauna asked, trying to remember how she'd missed her sister killing someone while she was in the same shop.

"Kelli went into Laura's dressing room to help with a zipper and never came out," Elsa said. "I'm pretty pissed about it, actually. I liked Kelli."

Shauna looked back at the dark street. She wondered how she could confront her sister and how she'd break an addiction so connected with something Laura, as a vampire, needed to survive. Could Laura learn to only feed as she needed?

"Come on," Elsa said. "Soon enough we'll be trekking across Europe. There will be plenty of time for an intervention. I want enough time in the temple to learn as much as I can."

"But," Shauna said as she started walking toward the bank. Elsa had a point. Shauna couldn't save the pickpocket and Laura wouldn't feed again until the next night. There would be time to confront her while the sun was up.

Elsa walked alongside Shauna and threw an arm around her shoulders. "I know you value human life. Believe it or not, so do I. You know it wasn't always so true about me. Even with your speed and strength, you can't be a superhero."

"I know," Shauna said.

"Do you?" Elsa asked. "On the boat, you took it onto yourself to save other vampires. I know you're new at this, but vampires don't do that. We are a live and let die species. You can't take it upon yourself to save everyone. You'll go mad when you discover no matter how much effort you put into it, there will always be people you can't save. I try to think how I should have kept Kelli out of Laura's dressing room, but at the time, I didn't know she was a killer. I thought she was like you."

"Are you saying Laura is beyond saving?" Shauna asked.

"We can save Laura," Elsa said. "We may not succeed in a day. She'll likely kill again. And when she does, you need to accept that it won't be your fault. You're already starting to think you made the mistake in changing her and taking the blame for her murders."

Shauna nodded. Those were exactly the thoughts running through her mind. She was also wondering how far she'd go to stop the killing. Would she kill her sister?

"You couldn't foresee what kind of vamp she would be," Elsa continued. "She is not your responsibility. Her actions are her own. There will be a price she will pay. Karma always wins. I spent three centuries ostracized by my own kind for my reputation."

"Everyone I've met has only respect for you," Shauna said.

"They may respect me," Elsa said. "But, most young vampires don't know I am Elizabeth Bathory and those few who do know, like Portia, keep me at arm's length. I don't make friends because when I do, and vamps learn who I am, they look at me differently and start to back away from me socially. That's the price I paid for the indifference to life I had in my youth."

"I don't want people to die," Shauna said. "I don't want vampires to die either."

Elsa petted Shauna's hair and said, "Your naiveté isn't actually one of your most attractive features, beautiful. We're predators of man and we are hunted. Death rules our moonlit world."

"Just because I don't like it doesn't mean I don't accept it," Shauna said. "I'm not out to change the world."

"Then why are you here?" Elsa asked.

Shauna stopped and looked at Elsa. She'd almost forgotten why they were there. "James," Shauna said. "I owe him my life. And because I wanted to be a vampire to live forever, or at least for centuries. I want the time to learn and experience the world. I fear the possibilities of that dwindle with these hunters around. I just want to end that threat so I can feel more secure in this life. Is that why you're here?"

Elsa squeezed Shauna into a hug and whispered, "Lover, I'm here for you. I like James. He has information and I do love what he tells me, when he tells me anything, but I'm here because you're here and I enjoy your company. Besides, you need me to navigate this continent."

"Right, you love me for my mind," Shauna joked, poking Elsa's side. "You've said that."

"That, and you accept me for me," Elsa said. "I've not had a best friend in all my life until I met you."

"Don't get sappy on me, Blood Countess," Shauna said. "Besties with benefits, that's us."

"Ahem," Jackie said.

"You're my…," Shauna started to reply to Jackie, but shocked herself by the word that followed. She considered Elsa her best friend, but she felt closer to Jackie, emotionally.

"If you say, 'best friend too'," Jackie threatened but didn't finish.

"We're here," Elsa said, pointing to the door of the building they'd been standing in front of. 'Banque' was etched into the glass of an ATM vestibule. Another door on the other side of the vestibule read 'Platine Membres Seulement.' The door was made of heavy looking iron with thick reinforcing metal bands. It looked out of date with the rest of the vestibule.

They filed through the first door and stood in front of the metal door. It didn't have a handle or a knob, just a camera set in the middle of the door. A woman's voice over a speaker asked, "Please show proof of membership."

"Proof of membership?" Elsa asked. "Portia said nothing about membership cards."

"Smile," Shauna said. She bared her teeth at the camera. Elsa did the same.

The door opened back. Shauna saw the door was almost a foot thick. After passing through the door, they stood in a room with a woman, a vampire, sitting at a desk. She looked up from her laptop and said, "The safe deposit boxes are through here." She pressed a sequence of buttons on her desk phone. A wall panel opened revealing an elevator.

Elsa, Shauna and the twins got into the elevator. It had a pair of levers instead of a panel of buttons. "I don't know what to do with this," Shauna said.

"Let me," Jackie said as she shifted one lever, closing the elevator doors. When she shifted the other lever, the elevator began to descend.

"How far down do we go?" Shauna asked.

"Portia's directions ended at the bank door," Elsa said. "I'm hoping things from here out will be straightforward."

The elevator didn't have any indicators to say how far down they'd gone or how much further they had to go. Shauna kept expecting the elevator to slow at any moment, but it kept descending. The passengers didn't speak much except to occasionally notice how long the trip was taking and to postulate that they must surely be nearing the end of the journey.

"If this thing isn't equipped with automatic slowing as it nears the bottom, this is going to hurt," Jackie said, a few minutes into the ride.

Over fifteen minutes later, a bell rang. Jackie shifted a lever and the elevator began to slow. When the elevator came to a halt, Jackie opened the door, revealing a small square room with carved stone walls. Sconces with dried, burned down torches lined the walls. A single white globe sitting atop a pole in the center of the room illuminated the area. Shauna thought the style of the frescos looked more Greek or Roman than Egyptian. It didn't appear to be writing, but an elaborate scene of some kind of Dionysian orgy with hundreds of figures drinking and taking pleasures with one another. The ceiling had carvings of a moon surrounded by stars arranged in constellations.

"My kind of party," Elsa said.

"How far down are we?" Jonnie asked.

"Not as far as you'd think," Jackie said. "That's an old elevator and wasn't moving very fast. It's warm here but not hot. If we were half a mile down, it would be over a hundred degrees down here. So, we're less than that."

"You spend too much time online," Shauna said, nudging Jackie. Like many older pets, Jackie didn't sleep much. She spent much of the time while Elsa was away or asleep, surfing the internet. Shauna had seen a documentary on gold mines in Africa, so she knew what Jackie was talking about. Deeper meant hotter and it wasn't terribly hot.

"Is there another door here or do we get back in the elevator?" Jonnie asked.

"I don't think the elevator goes any further down," Jackie said.

"There's a door," Elsa said as she stepped up to the wall across from the elevator. "The panels here do not have any mortar between them." She leaned close, peering at the carvings. "Perhaps there is a loose figure, a switch of some kind."

"Or we could just see if they push open," Shauna said. She stepped past Elsa and pressed one of the panels lightly, not wanting to break anything. When her hands touched the carved stone, the stone started to glow red.

The glow got brighter and spread across two panels of images before a creaking noise echoed through the room. The panels slowly slid apart revealing another, larger, chamber. Tiers of stone stairs led up to a large wooden door across the room. A pair of torches burned by the door, providing flickering light throughout the room. Other than the stairs and the doorway, the room was rough hewn stone. Shauna hadn't noticed that the outer room was so well kept until she saw the thick dust covering the floor of the stone room. Above the doorway, written in the language of vampires, were the words, "Royals and their guests may enter."

"We're here," Elsa said. "Now, who wants to be the royal and who wants to be the guest?"

"Zylpha said the only guy on the other side of the door won't really care," Shauna said. That was how she interpreted catatonic to mean. "Let's just go in and see. If it matters, I'll follow your lead."

Elsa walked up toward the door and it opened, swinging inward, before she could reach the handle. She passed through the doorway. Shauna followed her into a chamber that was distinctly Egyptian in style. The walls looked like they'd been torn from some ancient Egyptian temple and were covered from floor to ceiling in hieroglyphs. They'd also been painted gold, which shimmered in the light of an electric chandelier swaying twenty feet above the chamber floor.

A lone vampire, dressed in a gold and enameled headdress and a gold embroidered white skirt, stood under the chandelier, staring at one of four alcoves off of the room. Shauna then realized the room had five sides if the door they'd entered through counted as one. Each side had an inset area.

"What's so interesting in there?" Elsa asked the catatonic vampire, whom Shauna assumed was Amenhetop, before heading towards a pedestal in the alcove, at which the man was staring. A tiny bronze globe, the size of a grapefruit, sat atop the pedestal. The globe was inlaid with various semi-precious stones.

"Everything in here is interesting," Jonnie said, staring at a wall of hieroglyphs. "These all predate the great pyramids."

"Sis took an interest in all things Egypt back in the thirties," Jackie said. "Jonnie's great at two things, Mixology and Egyptology."

"Bartending?" Shauna asked.

Jonnie grunted, "Bartending is a trade; Mixology is an art. Too bad you're a vamp or I could show you a mean White Russian."

Shauna hadn't tried drinking milk since changing. She was pretty sure she'd hold it down for an hour or two before it, and whatever else she had in her digestive tract, spewed out the way it came in.

"It's a joke," Jackie said. "When you ask her to go ahead and show you a mean White Russian, she stabs you in the back of the hand with a toothpick. But, she does make the best cocktails I've ever had."

"Holy Fuck!" Elsa shouted.

Shauna looked over to see Elsa jumping away from the pedestal. A spot was glowing on the globe and several stones on the front of the pedestal were also glowing. Shauna went to get a closer look.

On the globe, mother of pearl represented land and turquoise represented sea. Lights shaped like small rubies were scattered around the land areas. One in the middle of Europe was blinking brightly. Five of seven larger lights, also faceted like gemstones, on the front of the pedestal glowed as well.

In another alcove, a series of video monitors arranged on the wall lit up. A man's voice echoed through the chamber. It said, "I, Mascare of House Mascare, approve."

"I, Gerard of Hasan, approve," another man's voice said.

Shauna saw the speakers above the apse with the monitors. A man's face appeared on one of the nine monitors. Three other monitors had the words 'No Video' sprawled across them. One of the other two had a blonde woman and the last, Zylpha.

"Of course, I, Lucrezia of House Dracul approve," the blonde woman said. "It will be nice to have her back in the neighborhood."

"I, Zylpha, approve," Zylpha said.

Another woman's voice said, "I, Thalia of House Artemis, approve."

"House Zhu abstains," a male voice said. "Did you all not see the lights?"

"She lit all five; we saw," the man whose face showed, spoke. His matched the first voice Shauna heard after Elsa touched the globe. "Elizabeth, Child of Vlad, you are pure enough and have been confirmed as Queen of the Northern Roman Empire."

"He knows you," Shauna said.

"I heard him," Elsa said. "I don't like what I heard. I'm not a queen." She walked over and grabbed Shauna's hand and pulled her to the globe. "Touch here."

Shauna tried to pull away, but too late. Elsa had pressed her finger to the glowing red stone. The lights on the front of the pedestal changed, only four were illuminated and of those four, three were among the five that had been lit and one was at the top of the line of sevens. Elsa had illuminated the five at the bottom of the column.

The male vampire spoke again, "Shauna, Son of James, the Northern Roman Empire is under the control of Elizabeth."

"Who's James?" Lucrezia asked.

"A myth," a different male voice responded. "From the tales of James and Una, the Adam and Eve of vampires."

"The stones don't lie," the man with the video feed answered. "I only repeat the names that the stones give me."

"We're taking this offline," Zylpha said.

Elsa strode over and pushed her finger against the monitor with the blonde woman. "Undo it, Lucy!" she growled and then repeated the words more slowly, "Undo it, now!"

"Stay close, my sister," the blonde woman said. "We'll be in touch."

"Try abdicating," Shauna suggested. "Remove yourself."

Elsa stood back from the monitors and said, "I, Elizabeth Bathory, Empress of the Northern Roman Empire, hereby abdicate that seat."

"Before that can happen, you must present a successor," the blonde woman, Lucy, said.

Elsa looked to Shauna and then at her pets and asked. "Can you imagine me as queen?"

"Empress," Jackie said. "You called yourself an empress."

"As you are now?" Shauna asked. "You'd be as good a royal as Portia."

"Please," Elsa said. "No one makes a better royal than Miss Barbie, Everyone-Loves-Me, Portia."

"You like her too," Shauna said.

"I do," Elsa said. "And that irritates me a little. I'm not sure I like her for being nice and honest, or because she has some charm power from her Venae. You've noticed how she's been in two battles with the hunters and no one has ever pointed a gun her way."

"I did," Shauna said. She hadn't thought anything of it until Elsa mentioned it. "How would that work?"

"Magic," Elsa said.

"Magic isn't a thing," Shauna said. "It's not real."

"Like vampires?" Elsa asked.

"But, Venae explains that," Shauna said, her voice meek when she realized she couldn't explain Venae.

Elsa asked, "If not magic, what would you call it when those stones glowed when you touched them on the way in here?"

"I assumed there were imbedded lights," Shauna said. "I have no reason to believe it isn't electrical or mechanical."

Elsa said, "I don't really believe in magic either. I believe in the scientific method and that science can explain everything. I just think we haven't figured out the science of some things yet, and that which we can't explain through science is, by very definition, magic."

Several aspects of Elsa's history and personality fell into place. Everything Elsa had been accused of doing, especially the things she'd admitted were true, could be explained by pursuing understanding the universe through science. Primitive science at times, but scientific curiosity was what drove Elsa when she wasn't pursuing simple hedonism. Or, perhaps it was the hedonism that filled the gaps when Elsa couldn't pursue her experiments.

"I think I understand you a little better," Shauna said. "You're just a terribly curious beast with the means to find some answers."

"I'm a curious monster," Elsa said. "In case you haven't been paying attention, I've pursued finding my answers at a very high cost, including several innocent lives."

"Reminding me isn't helping," Shauna said. "You know that I've already come to terms with who you were." Shauna hadn't asked specifics about when Elsa had lost her sociopathic tendencies, but she chose to believe it had been before she'd taken the twins as pets. The thought of Jackie being involved in Elsa's human experiments was something

Shauna kept out of her head. That Jackie and Jonnie hadn't visited Elsa in James' basement while she'd been interrogating Henry supported Shauna's theory.

"It's impolite to keep the council waiting," one of the faceless male voices said. "We are not discussing the reality of magic. We are begrudgingly accepting a new royal."

"Hush, Yoshi," Zylpha said. "We'll have time to talk after Beth comes to terms with her new responsibilities."

"We don't have to go back to Philly," Jonnie said. "Our home there is still gone."

"What are you saying?" Elsa asked.

"Jackie and me," Jonnie said. "We think you should keep the crown of Europe."

"Why would I want that?" Elsa asked. "Last I checked, someone was hunting the royals."

"You're already on their list," Jackie said. "I thought the whole point of this trip was to remove the threat."

"A royal is always a target," Elsa said.

"That changes nothing about you," Jackie said. "You've always been a target and you've never even been hurt by a hunter. You're old, wise and rich and you're honestly not terribly good at accepting other people having authority over you."

"The crown is yours," Jonnie said.

"But, Napoleon is on the way," Shauna said. "It's going to earn us a quick enemy if you do it."

Elsa looked at Shauna, eyes tight in contemplation. A smile crept onto her face. "I don't like him. From what Zylpha said, he sounds like an ass." As she walked over to the pedestal, she said. "My only caveat here is that no one here shares this with anyone until the threat from those angels is gone. Are you okay with this, Shauna?"

"Does my opinion matter?" Shauna asked.

"We're here for you," Elsa said. "This could have implications that hinder your quest. I won't do this without your support."

Shauna was taken aback. Elsa had done plenty to act in Shauna's interest, but always with selfish undertones. Giving Shauna veto power over her future made Shauna think that, perhaps, the selfish undertones were just her perception. "I think you'd be a good Empress," Shauna said. "A true queen of the night." Portia had been too proper for Shauna's vision of a vampire queen. Queen Lorna, a human member of a roleplaying society that pretended to be vampires, sitting on a throne with collared slaves and a fountain of fake blood, fit better to Shauna's ideal. She could see Elsa doing something like that, even including a fountain of wine, since blood was useless to a vampire once it was removed from a body.

"Can we assume the debate is over?" Zylpha asked.

"Yes," Elsa said. "If I can control the dissemination of the announcement of my coronation."

"We accept your caveat," the man on the video screen said.

"Mascare?" Yoshi asked, giving a name to the man on the video screen. "Since when do we allow caveats?"

"Do you object?" Mascare asked. "Did you not see the lights?" His voice mocked Yoshi's as he'd asked the same question earlier.

"I am not formally objecting," Yoshi said. "And I see no one else will either. Cut the feed to the temple, please. We have things to discuss."

"Goodbye sis, see you soon," Lucy said, leaning forward toward the screen. The monitors went black and the speakers fell silent after several clicking noises.

"We should go," Elsa said. "I don't want to be here when Napoleon shows up."

"Laura's not here yet and we haven't really seen all there is to see here," Shauna said. "There are books in that alcove over there I want to look at." She had barely noticed the books during the conversations with Elsa, but she did want to take more time to look around Amenhetop's temple.

"Bibles," Jonnie said. "Just various versions of the Torah, The Quran and other religion's bibles. Nothing I haven't read before. Nothing older than the Codex Sinaiticus."

Shauna hadn't realized Jonnie was a religious scholar, but the pet knew more about the books than she did, which only made Shauna want to read them.

"I really don't want to be here when Napoleon arrives," Elsa said. "I'd rather do my explaining once I can establish a throne room where he'd have to look up to argue with me. That alone will win the fight, although having the council confirm my right to power, should also be enough."

"If he annoys you, you could just kick his ass," Shauna suggested.

"That's why I brought you along, sweety," Elsa said then chuckled.

They left Amenhetop and his tomb and returned to the elevator. Shauna promised herself that she would have an opportunity to return when she had fewer constraints on her time.

The elevator ride up was much less boring. Knowing how much time they'd have, Elsa had some suggestions on the ways the twins could provide entertainment.

§

In the lobby, Laura and Tom were waiting. Laura said, "About time, either that elevator was slow or Elsa talked you into some more pillow time." After getting closer, Laura wrinkled her nose at Shauna. "Both?"

Shauna refused to answer. She did her best to keep her face unresponsive.

"Silence can only mean one thing," Laura said.

Changing the subject was the only way Shauna could avoid utter embarrassment. "Why didn't you come down?"

Laura shrugged. "The vamp at the desk says the only controls for the elevator are inside it and I'm just not dressed to climb or fly down a dark elevator shaft."

"You didn't miss much," Elsa said. "Just some catatonic vampire and some fancy gold paint. I must say that I was underwhelmed." Shauna saw that Elsa was just trying to make Laura feel like she didn't miss anything.

"Yeah," Laura said. "This vamp history stuff is interesting and all, if we're talking about it over a few bottles of wine, but I don't like digging in the dust for old crap. History is mostly boring bits. Just give me the good bits version, later." She looked straight at Shauna and added, "Over wine. Okay, so I care more about the wine than a musty vamp cellar."

Shauna rolled her eyes but said nothing about her sister's intentional ignorance. She asked Elsa, "Where are we going to stay for the day and shouldn't Jackie and Jonnie get some sleep if they're going to be tailing Henry?"

"We sent the luggage to a hotel Jackie found online," Elsa said. "It's not far, but farther than I want to walk. We'll catch a cab." She headed outside. Shauna and the others followed.

Jackie waved at a cab that looked big enough for the six of them. It pulled over and stopped by the bank. As they gathered by the door, two dark cars stopped on the road by the cab. Four people jumped out of each car and another five climbed out of the cab. Laura had her gun out, as the people surrounded Shauna and her group. Shauna was beginning to think carrying a gun wasn't such a bad idea. It might intimidate people out of confronting her. Then again, it could get her shot, which would lead to her trying to explain why bullets weren't working on her.

When she realized the people had no weapons, and were all dressed in styles she'd see at an upscale dance club, Shauna relaxed. They weren't hunters, which meant, at worst, they'd be an annoyance.

"What's this?" Elsa asked.

"King Napoleon sends his regards to the visiting royalty," a blonde woman in a tight white dress with circles of fabric strategically absent, said. "He bids you join him at the council meeting and perhaps for a tasting tour after."

"Which of us is he inviting?" Elsa asked.

"Whichever of you is the visiting royalty," the woman said. "No one else would dare enter the Temple of Blood."

"We hate to be so impolite as to turn down an invitation from the King," Elsa said. "But since we've already established our lack of couth by being tourists in the sacred temple, why change. Send the king our regrets."

"You'd turn down an opportunity to meet the council?" the blond woman asked.

"Wasn't that...," Shauna pointed back at the bank and started to ask if Zylpha and the others they'd spoken with were the council, as she'd assumed they were. Elsa's hand over Shauna's mouth stopped the question.

"Tonight?" Elsa said. "In a mouse's heartbeat. I'm just not in the mood and I fear I'd spoil the solemn mood of a council meeting." Without turning her head, Elsa whispered to Shauna in her voice no one else would hear, "Are they all vampires?"

"Yes," Shauna said in a normal voice. She still hadn't learned Elsa's trick and was beginning to doubt she ever could. When Elsa glanced at her, Shauna nodded, letting her know she was answering the question. "Yes," Shauna said again, thinking fast about what she could say next. "It's been a long trip for us and we should rest."

"If you are not royalty, the invitation is not optional," the woman in white said. "Shall we be polite or shall we tussle?"

Shauna looked to Elsa for a response. The elder vamp shrugged. "Fine. Take us to your leader," she said drolly.

The trip was awkward, forcing them all into the tiny cab along with the blonde woman and a driver. The other two cars followed close behind as they wound through the city's streets. When they came to a stop, Shauna wouldn't have guessed they were in Paris. The building they parked in front of was an old brick building, perhaps some kind of factory.

"I know this place," Elsa said. "They make the most wonderful perfumes."

"The factory never re-opened after The Great War," the blonde woman said. "It's a historically significant building, long owned by the government, but they do nothing with it but let it rot."

"The Council is inside?" Elsa asked, adding a very skeptical lilt to her words.

"They are," the woman said. "Well, most of us. I am still out here with you."

"You're not on the Council," Elsa said. "I know the Council and I don't know you."

Shauna agreed. The blonde woman was not Lucy or Zylpha and didn't sound like the woman of House Artemis.

"Things change," the woman said. "You may call me Madame deWinter."

"Or just Milady?" Elsa asked.

"Three Musketeers?" Laura asked.

"You read Dumas?" Shauna asked.

"I saw a movie," Laura said.

Shauna sighed. Of course it was the movie for Laura. She turned to Madame deWinter and asked, "You get this a lot?"

"Not really," deWinter said. "The general assumption is that I cannot be she. The woman Alex wrote about was fictional and surely there were hundreds of Lady deWinter's throughout the years."

Shauna was among those who believed the woman couldn't be the same woman from the works of Dumas. Rather than press the subject, she motioned for the door. "Do we knock or just walk in?" The sooner they went in, the sooner they'd be out and on their way.

"Marcus, open the door for our guests," deWinter said. A vampire dressed in a dark suit and black shirt without a tie opened the door and bowed as he gestured for the group to enter.

Madame deWinter led the way into a building that looked like it had briefly seen time as an underground night club.

The entryway was made of plywood that had been painted matte black. They passed through a tunnel by an area that might have been a coat room and into a large area that still, despite the neon painted walls, bore more resemblance to a factory floor than to a nightclub. Several people sat along one side of a table in the middle of the room, while several others milled around a bar, drinking beer or wine. A blink told Shauna all of the people at the table were vampires. The ones at the bar were not.

"Stand here," deWinter indicated a painted white spot on the floor before the table. She then went around and took a seat beside the man sitting at the center of the table.

As Shauna stepped up to the white spot, she studied the vampires at the table. Other than deWinter, they were all dressed in formal clothes from centuries past. The man in the middle wore a military uniform; he was undoubtedly Napoleon.

"Highness," Shauna said and bowed. Elsa and Laura did the same. The twins and Tom were escorted over to the bar by Marcus and another vampire.

"My liege, these vampires claim to be tourists," deWinter said.

"None but royals and the council are to know of the temple," the man in the uniform said. "Which are you?"

"I'm neither," Elsa said. "Nor are my daughter or granddaughter." She gestured to Shauna and Laura. "Who do I have the pleasure of speaking with? I assume you are Napoleon; who are these others?"

"King Napoleon," the man corrected sternly. "You've met Milady deWinter. The lady to my left is Marie Antionette, after her is Charles Maurice de Talleyrand, and my brother Louis. And on the other side of Milady deWinter is Voltaire and Alphonse de Lamartine. We are the Council of Elders."

"And Zylpha?" Elsa asked.

"You've heard, I'm sure, of the troubles we've been having with vampire hunters," Napoleon said. "Zylpha, the last of the old council, fell recently."

"I see," Elsa said. She then turned and looked around the room. "This is an interesting location. I believe this was a perfumery." As she was facing the door, she whispered to Shauna, "They are not who they claim to be."

"Oh?" Shauna asked. They were clearly not the true Elders Council. Elsa must have been talking about their names.

"I was here, once," Elsa said, turning back to face the table. "Back then, the chemistry was primitive and they kept a yard of pigs behind the building. Watching the process of making perfume from start to finish made me never want to wear it again. Instead, I took up bathing once a day. I think I smell fine without the pig piss. Shauna, do you agree."

Shauna understood what Elsa was doing. She leaned in across Elsa and sniffed at her neck.

Elsa whispered, "Marie has a smallpox vaccination mark on her shoulder and I know Voltaire and that's not him. He's with Lucy down in Florence."

"I do love the way you smell," Shauna said.

"Nothing more than crushed rose petals," Elsa said. "Some days I use lavender."

"You haven't given us your name, yet you claim to be centuries old."

"Four," Elsa said. "I am four hundred years old. You may call me Countess Bathory."

"So you wish to claim you are nobility and a legend among us," Napoleon said.

"You have your claims, I have mine," Elsa said.

"What are you implying, Countess?" The title was spat in pure disdain.

"I wouldn't imply anything against the most esteemed Council of Elders or one of its members." Elsa said, her emphasis making it clear she held them in very low esteem.

"Am I missing something?" Laura asked. She'd been quiet and Shauna realized she wouldn't have heard Elsa's whispers.

"No," Elsa said. "there's nothing here to miss."

"I'll explain later," Shauna promised her sister.

"Now that we have the pleasantries out of the way," Napoleon said. "there is the matter of taxes."

"Taxes?" Shauna asked. "You have a tax on vampires passing through?"

"Normally, the tax is a paltry hundred Euros," Napoleon said. "But, one of you killed a human in my domain. For that, the tax will be higher. I think a night with the twin pets should cover it."

Elsa started forward, teeth bared. Shauna reached out and held her back. Elsa started to phase and kept pushing but Shauna matched her, phasing at the same rate. This kept her hand on Elsa's chest.

The elder vamp turned and looked Shauna in the eye. Shauna had never seen Elsa so angry, not even when her apartment building had been destroyed. Elsa yelled to her pets, "Jackie, Jonnie we're leaving." She then said to Shauna, "Don't come with us."

"You will be hunted if you do not pay the tax," Napoleon said, but Elsa was already at the door and she didn't look back.

"I guess we're going as well," Shauna said. She bowed slightly and said to her sister, "Come on."

Laura called to Tom and they all started to the door when Napoleon screamed again. "I should tear you apart right here, right now for your disrespect."

Shauna turned to face the council, for a moment completely understanding Elsa's rage. She wanted to tell them to go ahead and try, but she just sneered at Napoleon and then left the building.

She looked down the streets but couldn't see Elsa anywhere.

"She'll forgive you," Laura said.

"I'm not so sure," Shauna said. She could barely speak. Between her anger at the hubris of Napoleon and the fear that she'd just lost her best friend and her... The thought didn't finish. "Jackie," she said.

"Huh?" Laura asked. "She's not even going to be mad at you. She won't have to forgive anything."

CHAPTER 10

Laura's phone buzzed on the nightstand between the beds. Shauna's had run out of battery power sometime that morning and she'd left her charger in her suitcase. Not that it would have helped. She'd forgotten that European outlets were not the same standard as American ones. She wasn't even sure where her suitcase was. Elsa hadn't shared the name of the hotel so Laura and Shauna had just picked the first one they came to that looked clean.

Laura carried a spare battery in her purse. It seemed no matter how irresponsible Shauna thought Laura was, her sister took her phone very seriously.

"Amber says Henry's plane will be landing soon," Laura said.

"We can't do anything," Shauna said. "We were going to rely on Jackie and Jonnie to track him from there."

"Now we have Tom," Laura said. "I have a picture of Henry here." She held up the phone. "I wanted something to remember him by after I kicked his ass. He probably won't look this beat up, but do you think you can recognize him?" She held the phone up to Tom.

"If you send me that pic, I'll be fine," Tom said. "But, I know where Henry will go."

"You do?" Laura asked. "Why didn't you say so?"

"Because, as much as I adore you," Tom said, "you scare the shit out of me. I was just waiting for a time I could tell you with not so many vamps around."

"Where will he go?" Laura asked.

"The hunters I was trying to get in with," Tom said. "They have a station in Paris. I'm pretty sure Henry is their leader."

"Where is this place?" Shauna asked.

"By the graveyard," Tom said. "Surprisingly close to the vamp bank."

"Go, make sure that's where he goes," Laura said. "Call me when the sun sets and tell us where to meet you."

Tom left, leaving Shauna and Laura sitting on the bed.

"This is the worst day in Paris, ever. Can't sleep," Laura said. "And couldn't play with my pet, cause you're here."

Shauna wanted to say she wouldn't have minded, but it wasn't true. She didn't want to see her sister doing anything like that. Her sister was resourceful. She had ways to do what she wanted to do. "You're saying that long shower was eventless?" Shauna asked. "And then later when he helped you brush your hair? I think the bathroom door's been locked more than not since we got here."

"Shut up," Laura said. "You and Jackie go at it all the time."

"That's just kissing," Shauna said. "And I can't help her appetite for me."

"Yeah, 'cause it's all her," Laura said. She walked over to the window and stood in front of the heavy, closed curtains. "I bet we have a great view of the Eiffel Tower and the Arc de Triumph."

"You saw the tower all lit up last night," Shauna said.

"And I want to see it and not just the lights," Laura said. She ran her hand under the curtain, where the light bled through. She pulled her hand back. "That gets warm fast," she said. "I don't want to find out how long it takes to burn."

Shauna had seen the sun once since turning into a vampire. It felt like a warm wind on her face. But that had been only for a split second before Jackie had saved her by closing the curtains.

"Should we try to call Elsa?" Laura asked.

They'd called her numerous times since she'd stormed off. Neither she nor her pets were answering their phones. "No," Shauna said. "They know our numbers."

"So we just sit and wait," Laura said.

Shauna wanted to confront her sister about killing people, but couldn't find the courage when all she could think about was Elsa and Jackie being gone. "Let's see what's on TV. I hear French Soap Operas are steamier than ours."

"My French is not conversational," Laura said. They'd been in the same French classes in high school, and they both got the same high grades.

"Your French was great," Shauna said.

"Years ago," Laura said. She grabbed the TV remote and started surfing channels.

By sunset, Shauna had enough of a refresher in French from the television. Laura was giddy, insisting they speak only French for more than an hour.

As soon as the sun set, Laura's phone rang. Laura answered and had a brief conversation before hanging up and reading a series of instant messages. "Tom's tracking Henry. He sent a map to the hunter lair. Do you think it's a trap? Can we really trust him?"

"Absolutely," Shauna said. "The coercion took with him and it lasts at least a few centuries if not forever. It's not a trap set by Tom, but Henry might have something up his sleeve."

A loud rapping came from the door. Expecting Elsa, Shauna rushed to the door and opened it. She slammed it again when she saw a man in a leather trench coat on the other side. She hadn't been careful enough and the door splintered through the threshold and tore from the hinges.

"Ouch!" the man called from the hall. The door had certainly hit him. Shauna leaned out the doorway and saw the man leaning against the wall, unscathed. She blinked, confirming he was a vampire.

"If the king sent you, this will not go well for you," Shauna said.

"Amber sent me," the man said. "My name is Gui. I've worked with her before, usually tracking down rare wines, but I'm good at finding people, too."

"You're a detective?" Shauna asked.

"I'm not police, but that would be a good description of what I do," Gui said. He was taller than Shauna by a few inches and had dark brown, not quite black, hair. He had a short haircut, just long enough on top to be swept back with gel. Shauna wasn't sure if his eyes were green or blue behind a thin pair of sunglasses that couldn't possibly do more than look fashionable.

"Amber says you lost some of your team and you need to track down Henry the Inquisitor," Gui said.

Given that he knew names and their situation, Shauna couldn't help but believe Gui was who he said he was. "Welcome to the team," Shauna said.

Gui held out his hand, as if he expected a handshake. Shauna wasn't falling for it. Letting other vampires see her purity was a dangerous practice. It created a need for too many lies.

"I'm a thin blood," Gui said. "They don't come less pure of Venae than I. I already know you're going to be purer than me."

"Still," Shauna said. "I have only your word at the moment. Perhaps later."

Gui pulled his hand back and said, "Fair enough."

"How did you get here?" Shauna asked. "It's daylight."

Gui smirked. "You're in my city now. I've lived here since the war. Paris is an old city. There are five sets of tunnels under the city. The storm drain system is not recommended during the day. The sewer tunnels aren't used for their original purpose any more. There's the Metro and the catacombs, as well. There are very few places I can't get to during the day."

"That was four," Laura said. "You said five."

"There are some tunnels built by the resistance during the war that are still accessible. They're not as clean as the others and I only use those in a real pinch." Gui dusted his shoulder, but there wasn't a speck of dust on it.

"I assume you are Laura," Gui again offered his hand.

"I am," Laura said as she took his hand and gave it a slight shake.

Shauna groaned.

"And you are Shauna," Gui said. "Amber said you'd be a bit stiff."

Not knowing how to respond to that, Shauna went back into the room and grabbed her handbag, a tiny thing barely big enough for her phone, passport, and credit cards. She returned to the door and said, "Can you get us to the vampire hunter's office?"

"No," Gui said. "I can get us to a bar down the street from it, but we'll be close when night comes."

"We won't have to go through any dirt tunnels?" Laura asked.

"No, we're taking the Metro most of the way and a sewer line for half a block," Gui said. "Keep a tight grip on your handbags, the pick pockets are not just a tourist myth."

"Laura found that out," Shauna said.

"I got payback," Laura said.

"Let's not talk about it," Shauna said. She intended to, but not when there was a stranger around. The next time she had her sister alone, she'd have the talk, she promised herself.

§

They emerged into the women's bathroom of a small bar through a manhole. It was still early afternoon, but the bar was below street level.

"Welcome to Le Obscurité Infinie," the bartender said as they stepped out of the bathroom. "Can I get you a couple bottles of wine while you wait for sunset?" The bar was otherwise empty.

"So, only vampires come in that way?" Laura asked.

Shauna wouldn't have been so brazen about their being vamps, but it was clear the bartender, though not a vampire, was nonplussed by their presence. It wasn't the only assumption the bartender made that bothered Shauna. "Why do you assume we don't speak French?" Shauna asked.

"You're with Gui," the bartender said. "The local vamps wouldn't be seen with him. So, if you're with him, it means you come from out of town, and with foreigners, English is always the best bet. With your dyed hair, I actually thought you'd be German, but I don't speak that language."

"Stephan is a pet," Gui said. "His master is usually back there." He gestured to a booth behind a bead curtain in the back of the bar.

"Are we here to meet him?" Shauna asked.

"Nope," Gui said. "We're just here because it's close to where we are going at sunset. Ali's not very social."

"The usual, Gui?" Stephan asked.

"None of that Vin de Table crap today, Stephan," Gui said. "Give me three bottles of your best."

"Not the most expensive," Shauna added. "The best."

"I have three hundred bottles of wine, and everyone's taste is different," Stephan said. "Best is very subjective."

"Missing Elsa now?" Laura asked.

"Shut up, sis," Shauna said. She turned back to the bartender and said. "Just give me something dark, red and a little fruity."

He set three glasses on the bar then pulled three bottles from a cabinet behind the bar. "These three are popular with the people who think they know wine. If you were a vintner, I'd have better suggestions. One hundred eighty Euros."

"I'm sure they're fine," Shauna said. She set her credit card on the bar.

"I could've gotten that," Gui said.

"You lie, Gui," Stephan said. "But, if you're suddenly wealthy how about you pay your tab today?"

"Maybe next week," Gui said. "How much do I owe?"

"The last three visits, three bottles of the usual," Stephan said. "Eight Euros."

"Toss that on my bill," Shauna said. She turned to Gui, "Am I paying you?"

"Of course," Gui said. "Amber said my rates wouldn't be an issue. She said you're quite wealthy."

"Don't get carried away," Laura said. "She's stingy."

She still had problems spending money she hadn't earned. But, she decided before crossing the ocean that she'd not worry about money while in Europe. Still, she cringed a little when she signed the bill for the wine.

They sat at the bar and drank their wine discussing the vampires in Paris. Gui felt most of them were too elitist. He, and a handful of Vamps of similar Venae, were social outcasts. But even the snooty vampires were wary of the new Council. They obeyed because the Council had enough muscle to enforce its will, but no one was happy about them.

There had been countless vampire disappearances in recent months. Gui was sure some were just relocating away from the Council. Two viable claimants disappeared just after King Wolfram was killed. He'd been at odds with the Council. They kept their distance from each other.

Two bottles later, a vampire stepped up to the bar. Shauna hadn't seen him enter but he hadn't come from the street or the women's bathroom.

"That's Ali," Gui said. "It's best to ignore him."

Laura leaned across the table and whispered, "That's the guy from the temple."

"Amenhetop?" Shauna asked, keeping her voice low to match her sister's.

"That's Ali," Gui said. "He's as old as the bar and probably should be King, but Napoleon bullied his way to the crown."

Shauna looked closely. Ali had similar skin complexion to James and a shaved head. When she first met James she had thought he was Egyptian. "Well, either way, I think we'll learn something if we talk to him."

She followed Ali as he walked back to his booth. When she parted the bead curtain, he said. "I drink alone." He turned the volume up on a television on the booth wall. It was showing a soccer game.

"I'm not drinking," Shauna said, sitting across from him in the booth. "I'm talking. Short of some form of insanity, that usually takes two people."

Ali's eyes were wide as he watched her. His irises were olive green, not black as she'd expected of an Egyptian. She hadn't looked closely enough at Amenhetop to notice eye color. Half of the temple vampire's face had been covered with a gold mask.

"You see too much for your own good," Ali said. She felt his foot touch her calf and his pale pink aura flashed. Suddenly he pulled back, sitting as close to the back of the booth as he could. "That's not possible. I am the first."

"So you are Amenhetop?" Shauna asked. She reached up and turned the television off.

"Obviously," Ali-slash-Amenhetop said.

"Why touch me if you knew I would be less pure?" Shauna asked.

"Because I can tell how many vampires separate us," Ali said. "Or I would be able to if you were less pure than me. I saw the lights on the stone. I don't know what they mean, but it caused a stir among the Council. Who are you?"

"I'm Shauna and you will never discuss my purity with anyone," she said, staring in his eyes. She broke the eye contact and said, "When I am not with you, you will think of yourself as the first vampire. Which Amenhetop are you, the first or the father of King Tut?"

"Tutankhamen's father was Akenhaten," Amenhetop said. "I was never a Pharaoh. You have my name confused with Amenhotep. It's a subtle difference but important. I was just what we'd call a doctor, and my time was a thousand years before any of the Pharaohs named Amenhotep."

"Why the act, Amenhetop?" Shauna asked.

"Call me Ali. I've used the name for a thousand years. I've never used the other in conversation."

"What do you think of Napoleon?" Shauna asked.

"I don't," Ali said. "I don't leave the bar except to tend to the temple. Politics mean nothing to me. And, until the council approves him, he's no king."

"And the stone won't approve him," Shauna said. "Elsa is the royal here, now."

"He's not even pure enough to open the temple doors," Ali said. "He's been to the doors three times and had to turn back. He wouldn't be approved by the stone."

"Tell me how the stone works," Shauna said. "Is it magic?"

"Yes," Ali said. "It's ancient, as old as me, as old as vampires."

"Or so you thought," Shauna said. "I'm of a line older than you." She knew he was less than five thousand years old and James had used the number ten thousand.

"So it appears," Ali said. "I'm not convinced you are not using some form of trickery."

"Tell me about the stone," Shauna said.

"It is a device in telepathic contact with the Council of Elders," Ali said. "They have bracelets that allow them to convene mentally and approve or disapprove an applicant's request."

"Milady deWinter and Napoleon or the other council?" Shauna asked, although the answer was obvious.

"I am one of the seven vampires connected through the stone, but I am not a voting member of the Council. I mean Lucrezia, Zylpha, Mascare, Thalia, Gerard, and Yoshi. The Council that orchestrated and survived the last purge six centuries ago." Ali said. "They left me alive to oversee the temple and protect it, but I've never had to do so.

A chirping sound came from under the table. Ali pulled a computer tablet out and opened an image. Shauna recognized the elevator that led to the tomb. A dozen people were crammed into the elevator and Shauna recognized Zylpha.

"What's going on?"

"I've not seen this in two centuries, not since Vlad died," Ali said. "They're having a council meeting in the temple."

"Did the sun set?" Shauna asked.

"Twenty minutes ago," Ali said. "That's when I usually come up here. It could draw attention if I arrived in daylight."

"Won't they be surprised to find the temple without you in it?" Shauna asked.

"I have time," Ali said. "The elevator is slow for a reason."

"And you have another way down, I suspect?" Shauna asked.

Ali nodded and said, "They don't call this place 'The Infinite Darkness' for no reason. Behind the wall panel over there is a room, with what looks like an old well, but it's just a hole that goes down for miles. A little ways down is a way into the temple. I'll have to excuse myself as soon as I finish this bottle." He took the bottle and drank from it. Pausing he said, "Excuse my manners, but my time is limited."

"I'm coming with you," Shauna said.

"And I'll have no say in that," Ali said as he stood from the booth.

"No," Shauna said, following him. "I'd just coerce you." She hollered for Laura to join her. Her sister and Gui came over.

"Ali's about to leave," Shauna said. "We're going down to the temple."

"I'd like to see that," Gui said.

"You cannot," Ali said. "You are a Thin Blood. It's very unlikely you have the ability to fly."

"No elevator on the back door?" Shauna asked.

"No," Ali said. He stepped up to Gui and grabbed the thin blood's face. "You left the bar before I arrived. You left these two ladies here. Go." Gui walked quickly out of the bar. Ali pushed on a wall panel and it swung open. Behind it was a small room with a stone circle extending a couple feet from the floor. He climbed in and fell away into a dark pit.

"This is not my idea of fun," Laura said. She finished typing something into her phone then climbed into the well.

Shauna followed her sister. They went far enough down that they were in total darkness. Shauna had to check where the walls were with her fingertips. For the last moments of the journey, it was only the walls that told her which way was up. It was disconcerting how quickly she lost her sense of direction in the complete darkness. They came to a lit cave off of the pit. Ali had already exited and was standing a few feet in the cave undressing. His Egyptian regalia sat on a wooden shelf next to him.

"The temple is just down a few yards. Just push on the wall at the end," Ali said.

His directions were accurate. They entered the temple into an alcove full of small wooden crates, each about the size of a carton of milk. The top crate was opened and Shauna peered in. It was filled with gold coins.

"Whoa," Laura said. "If all of these are filled with gold, this guy is richer than you."

"No," Shauna said. "He's not." There were only twelve crates and each held a couple dozen coins and almost half of the crates were already empty. Shauna didn't know the exact price of gold, but she knew it wasn't anywhere near what she had in the bank, and certainly not what she had in investments.

Laura had her phone out again and was looking at it with a sunken expression on her face.

"No signal?" Shauna asked.

"Duh," Laura said. "I was just checking to see if I missed anything from Elsa or the twins. I've been updating them on where we were all day."

"So, that's what you were typing at the top of the pit?" Shauna asked.

"Telling Elsa we were going back to the temple," Laura said.

"And no response?" Shauna asked.

"Nope," Laura said.

Shauna sighed in frustration. To distract herself she began looking around the temple, noticing things she hadn't before. Each of the alcoves had one of the five laws inscribed above it in the language of vampires, but everything else in the temple was carved in hieroglyphics. Murals in the backs of four of the alcoves depicted scenes from the various religions. Shauna couldn't find a common theme. They had a Hindu scene of creation, a version of The Last Supper, an image of Moses speaking to a Pharaoh and Aphrodite rising from the sea foam.

The pile of books Jonnie had been so interested in were sitting on a table that was, in fact, some kind of climate controlled display case. It held hundreds of scrolls of parchment, paper and animal skins. Shauna didn't risk touching those. The books had dates spread from the early fifth century to a few books published within the past year.

"I study religion," Ali said, stepping up behind Shauna, dressed in his full regalia. "It's what I do between football games."

"Why?" Laura asked. "Church was boring."

"Would you like to know which religion is the true one?" Ali-slash-Amenhetop asked.

"I guess I would," Shauna said.

"So would I," Amenhetop said. "But, I haven't found it, yet. There are paradoxes and inconsistencies in each of these books, but there are a lot of common ideas. Currently I'm leaning towards atheism, but I'm open to agnosticism."

"I had you pegged for a pagan, following Isis and Osiris," Shauna said.

"When I was mortal, yes," Amenhetop said. "And their religion has lasted longer than any other I've encountered, but I lost faith when I hadn't seen any true evidence of them for a thousand years."

The scraping sound of the stone doors by the elevator opening quieted them. Amenhetop put a finger to his lips and went to stand in the alcove with the gold. He stood perfectly still, not even breathing as he stared at the wall.

A moment later a man entered the room and stopped when his eyes fell on Shauna and Laura. The people who followed him in also paused when they noticed them.

"Shauna?" Zylpha said as she entered. "Are you here without Empress Elsa?"

"Just me and my sister," Shauna said. "Mortal sister and blooddaughter."

"It's you that brings us here," Zylpha said as she and five others stood in a semi-circle around Shauna and Laura. Four of the five had vampiric auras. The rest of the people in the room were all human. "You touched the Kingstone and a stone lit on my bracelet I have never seen lit before." She held up a thick gold bracelet with seven rubies set around it. I don't know what it means exactly, but the consensus is that it means you are the purest vampire in the world."

Zylpha must have been talking for the benefit of the other elders. She already knew Shauna was purer than Elsa.

"The seven stones that light up indicate the purity of our Venae?" Shauna asked.

"So we believe," Zylpha said. "No one has actually deciphered it. "

"It's binary," Laura said. "That's the only number system made of sequences of two values, one and zero or on and off."

Shauna looked at Laura, mouth agape.

"Please, sis," Laura said. "That's eighth grade math."

"We're not idiots," Zylpha said. "It's not binary. We've tested and the number sequence does not change by one when a Vampire and their progeny touch it. And the value change is not constant from one generation to the next. But, we think binary is close enough to tell us when a vampire is purer of Venae. Generally, we only care about the highest stone a vampire lights. We require the fifth stone to light for prospective royals, but those are getting rarer and rarer. Nine in ten vampires only light the third. And you, Shauna, are the only vampire we've seen light the seventh stone."

"Not true," a woman, dressed in a short white deerskin dress replied. "I light the seventh stone, but only the seventh stone."

"Who are you?" Shauna asked. "Who are all of you?"

The woman in the white deerskin said, "I am Artemis. I'm not part of this council, but the youngest of my line is. She couldn't make it here, so I came in her stead." She said she was a vampire, but Shauna didn't see an aura around her when she blinked.

"You said your name was Diana and that you were the blooddaughter of Thalia," one of the men said.

"I lied," Artemis said.

"If you are Artemis, the progenitor of your house, you cannot light the seventh stone. Even the statue over there doesn't light the seventh stone."

"And yet, you've seen the seventh stone lit," Artemis said as she walked to the pedestal. She touched it and the top stone, the seventh, lit.

"We thought Thalia was the eldest of your line." the man replied.

"And you'll think that again when we're done here," Artemis said. "We have this discussion everytime we meet, you know."

"We've never met," the man replied.

"To be precise, Mascare," Artemis said. "You mean to say you don't remember us meeting."

He clenched his fists a moment and closed his eyes then turned to Shauna and said, "Pardon my manners, I am Mascare." He wore a pair of blue jeans and a plaid shirt. His heavy leather boots had small clumps of mud on them. He offered his hand and Shauna took it, knowing her Venae was not a secret. He kissed it gently and let it go.

"Portia's family," Shauna said.

"Yes," Mascare said.

"I'm Lucrezia," a blonde woman in an elegant red silk dress and a golden choker said. "I am Elsa's blood sister, but her reading on the stone was also confusing. I light the fifth and the second. As do Gerard and Yoshi." She gestured to the other men. "As you've learned, they are the leaders of the Hasan and Zhu families, respectively."

The other two vampires bowed when their names were said.

"You didn't know I was going to be here," Shauna said. "What were you going to discuss?"

"How to kill you," Zylpha said. "You're outnumbered and we have weapons made of Syrian Obsidian. Five of the Elders, all but Artemis, drew knives with black blades.

"We are not killing them," Artemis said.

"We should kill you, too," Zylpha said. "The Council was formed to purge the world of vampires purer than us. It is what we're here to do."

"I think not," Shauna said. She pondered what to say to coerce them all to forget about killing purer vamps. Before she could formulate her sentence, an explosion echoed through the temple. A split second later, a pressure wave blew into the temple, knocking everyone except Shauna, Laura and Artemis from their feet.

"How did you..." Zylpha began to ask in a broken voice. Her words stopped when the sound of gunfire echoed into the room. Bullets were sinking into the stone walls, but some ricocheted. None hurt Shauna.

Laura stood and watched the door. "It's Henry," Laura said. "And he's got a dozen or so men with him."

Artemis put her back to the wall and waited by the door. Amenhetop crouched behind the stack of crates filled with gold.

The other vampires in the room were screaming or moaning in pain as were two pets who hadn't crawled to cover.

"Gold plated bullets," Artemis said. These men came unprepared for the three of us. But they'd need gold to harm Zylpha, Ali or Mascare."

Unlike previous encounters with Henry, the men with the guns didn't enter the room. Instead, only three men came into the room. Henry led; he and another man wore golden plate armor. The third wore white robes that reminded Shauna of classic European monk's habits.

Henry had his gold sword and the other man carried a weapon like a sword, but was made of two pieces of wood holding several pieces of obsidian in the form of a jagged blade. The man in white robes didn't carry a weapon. Shauna saw that he was a vampire, but still the pink of a weaker vampire.

Artemis grabbed Henry and threw him against the far wall. The other man in armor swung his jagged sword at her, cutting a gash across her throat. She fell back, holding her neck, which seeped dark blood. He stepped closer, ready to swing again, but Laura ran into him, bowling him into the door. As they fell, he managed to swing at Laura, catching her in the knee. The sword broke, sending chunks of obsidian skittering across the floor. It didn't leave a mark on her skin.

The vampire in white moved slowly toward Shauna, kicking any of the Elders on the floor as he passed.

Shauna stepped up and punched at him, hoping Amber's training had taught her something. He had a cocky smile as he made no attempt to get out of the way or block her punch. The smile disappeared when her punch shattered his nose. He fell back a step but regained his balance and swung at Shauna with an open hand. It was then Shauna noticed that his fingernails were exceptionally long and sharpened to thin points.

She jumped back, but his claws grazed her shoulder, drawing blood.

"You're the bitch Henry talked about," the vampire in white said. "I've been training to take on someone like you for years." He dropped and spun, kicking out to catch Shauna in the calf. She fell to the ground and before she could get up, the man was sitting on her chest swinging constantly at her face and throat.

She tried to grab a hold of him psychokinetically, but he was holding on to something with his mind as well and she couldn't budge him. All she could do was try to shield her throat and face, but his nails dug repeatedly into her forearm. He gave up on the swinging and grabbed her forearms. He was strong and managed to pin her arms above her head with one hand. He then pressed his other hand against her stomach. She screamed when his nails dug into her.

Despite her struggling, he dug his hand into her abdomen. Shauna had never been in so much pain. He started to reach up, under her ribcage when he went still and gasped, "No." He then collapsed.

Shauna couldn't see anyone nearby. Then she noticed Laura standing with her back to the wall. She released the man she'd been fighting, dropping his body to the ground. Blood ran down her chin.

"Sorry Sis," Laura said. "I drank as fast as I could."

Shauna was too weak to stand, but she looked around and couldn't see Henry any longer.

"He got away, again," Laura said. "I was too busy slurping down the guy with the weird sword."

"What made you think he was the vampire's pet?" Shauna asked as the pain in her abdomen subsided. "What if he wasn't. I'd be dead now." She put her hands over her stomach. She felt thick blood, her blood, but the wound from the other vampire's hand had already closed.

"Don't you see the silver lines?" Laura asked.

"Silver lines?" Shauna asked.

"Pets and their masters," Laura said. "There's always a silver line of light connecting them when they're close to each other. I can't always tell which one is the vampire, but it was pretty obvious in this case."

Zylpha stood and looked around then said, "I've never seen anything like this since the days of Vlad's wars."

"Is everyone okay?" Lucrezia asked, crawling to her hands and knees. Her red gown was shredded by bullet holes. She then fell back to the ground.

"She still has a bullet or two inside her," Zylpha said. "She fared better than Mascare and Amenhetop."

Shauna looked and saw the head of Amenhetop lying on the floor beside his body. Mascare was in a similar state by the door.

"I'll live," Gerard said as he pulled himself up to lean against a wall. "I've got a few bullets left in me though."

"I am the same." Yoshi lay on his back staring straight up. "The pets seem to have survived, except Mascare's"

"I'm going to need some licks," one of the pets said. "I might need stitches." While vampires' blood was poison, their saliva could heal small wounds, such as bites. Larger wounds would need medical attention if they were more severe than a pet could regenerate. A pet's regenerative ability was directly linked to the purity of their vampire.

The wound in Shauna's stomach healed. She'd wondered if it would linger like the arrowshot to James, but it felt fine. "Laura, get the obsidian weapons," Shauna said, stepping up to Zylpha. "I'm sure this is exactly why you want us all dead, but I am not the enemy." She took the obsidian knife from Zylpha's hand. She pressed her finger against the blade and was unable to draw blood. She held the knife out. "This is useless against me." To demonstrate, she thrust the knife at her chest, opposite her heart in case she was wrong. She wasn't. The blade shattered into millions of tiny shards without penetrating her skin.

"We need to go after Henry," Laura said.

"Go," Zylpha said. "Meet me later at the Hongre Rampante. It's an old style inn in the alley of the block north of here."

"Send Artemis," Shauna said. "I don't trust you at the moment." Though her deerskins were stained red, Artemis was standing by the kingstone, glaring at the surviving members of the council.

"I can't hurt you," Zylpha said. "It won't be a trap."

"Still," Shauna said. "Artemis, will you meet me there later?"

"I will," Artemis said. "But we need to make these idiots forget they know our purity."

Shauna bit her finger and said to Zylpha, "Open wide." Coercion took better if the subject ingested some of the vampire's blood. Shauna had never had one of her coercions not take and she'd never had one fade, but she wasn't taking chances with the Council.

Zylpha's head and shoulders fell, crestfallen. "Fine," she said and stuck out her tongue at Shauna.

CHAPTER 11

Henry had destroyed the elevator; he'd cut the roof away. Half a dozen black ropes hung down the shaft. Shauna and her sister flew to the top. Henry was already gone. At the top of each rope, they found motorized devices the hunters had used to ascend quickly. The vampire behind the desk was dead, her severed head already starting to flake into dust.

Shauna and Laura stepped out of the bank to find a crowd of people standing by the doorway. They weren't looking at the bank, however, but at a blood soaked girl laying on the pavement. The sounds of an ambulance screamed in the distance, getting nearer. Shauna rushed over, when she recognized Jonnie. Elsa knelt by her, holding Jonnie's stomach with blood soaked hands. Jackie lay on the pavement, sobbing, her head close to her sister's.

"She's alive," Shauna said.

"Yes," Elsa said, her voice cold and hard. "We got here just as Henry was leaving. He swung at me, I phased and he hit Jonnie behind me. Promise me we're going to kill him, soon."

"We will," Shauna said.

"And we'll make it slow?" Elsa said.

"Yes," Shauna replied.

EMTs nudged Shauna aside and laid a backboard on the ground beside Jonnie.

They asked Elsa to move her hands. As soon as she did, blood poured out. She put her hands back on the wound. The EMTs shouted at each other for a moment then slid Jonnie onto the board and lifted her onto a gurney. They then rushed her into the back of the ambulance, keeping Elsa with her to hold the wound.

Within a minute of its arrival, the ambulance was speeding off. Jackie climbed to her feet and wrapped her arms around Shauna and just held her tight. Shauna had no words. Jonnie was a pet and should be able to heal anything that didn't kill her, but Shauna had seen the wound and wasn't sure.

"Napoleon," Laura said.

"What?" Shauna asked.

"He's sitting in a parked car, half a block away, watching us with binoculars," Laura said. "I'd point him out, but I don't want him to know I see him."

"Leave him," Shauna said. She couldn't think of any good reason for him to be watching the bank, but she wasn't able to take her mind off of Jonnie long enough to contemplate. "We need to get to a hospital."

"Which one?" Laura asked.

"I really hope its whichever one is closest." Shauna looked for a cab, but most of the crowd was still there, staring at them. She looked out over the crowd and said, "Everyone close your eyes and count to twenty." She repeated the statement in French. As the crowd chanted their numbers, she flew up into the sky, holding Jackie as tight as she dared. Laura stayed close.

Looking over the city, she spotted a building with a white cross on the roof and the letter 'H' centered in the cross. She flew there, landing on the 'H'. She then cradled Jackie in her arms as she ran to the door, which led directly to an elevator.

It took them several minutes to find Elsa. She was standing by the window of a room with her forehead pressed to the glass and she was crying.

Shauna set Jackie down and went and hugged Elsa. The elder vampire turned and held Shauna, then whispered, "You love me. You won't leave me?"

"No one's leaving you," Shauna said. "I love you and Jonnie will be fine."

Elsa just hugged her tighter. Jackie and Laura came over and wrapped their arms around them.

They stood that way for hours. A doctor, covered with blood, came out of the operating room and approached Elsa.

"Is she okay?" Elsa asked, sobbing.

"She's alive," the doctor said. "She's in a coma from the blood loss. She should be dead."

"Thank god," Elsa said.

"Don't yet," the doctor said. "She was cut through her pancreas, liver, kidney and intestines. Her body still has a lot of toxic material to deal with and the blood loss will make that hard. We've given her four units of blood, but I can't promise she'll ever wake up."

"Can I see her?" Elsa asked.

"You can," the doctor said. "We've done everything we can do."

They entered the room. The doctor asked the staff members cleaning up from the surgery to give Elsa a moment with the patient, then he, too, left the room. For a moment, the only sounds in the room were a periodic whoosh from a breathing machine and, every second or two, a beep from the heart monitor.

"You have to do it," Shauna said.

Elsa nodded. "I know."

"She's been a pet for two centuries," Shauna said. "Your blood won't kill her."

"That, I'm not so sure of," Elsa said.

"You've killed pets before?" Shauna asked.

Elsa nodded.

"And you survived?" Shauna asked.

"I've lost dozens of pets trying to make them into vamps," Elsa said. "I seem to be immune to the death effect if they die this way. That's why I have to do this. If she dies from the wound, I die and Jackie dies."

"So you have to," Shauna said. "There's no time like the present."

Elsa nodded. "If we pull that out, an alarm will go off." Jonnie had a breathing tube in and it was connected to a machine.

"I'll handle the staff," Laura said. "I can coerce huge crowds, too."

"Ready?" Shauna asked after peeling the tape off that had been holding the mouthpiece in place.

Elsa nodded and bit into the palm of her hand. Shauna pulled the tube out and Elsa put her bleeding hand to Jonnie's mouth. "Drink, baby," Elsa said.

Alarms started blaring in the room and Laura stepped out of the door. The sounds of rushing footsteps stopped and the alarms quieted.

"She's swallowing," Jackie said.

"It's a reflex," Shauna said.

Jonnie's eye's popped open and she looked at Elsa with wide fearful eyes, but she kept drinking. Her eyes calmed and then rolled back into her head. The heartbeat monitor raced, counting twenty beats per second for a few seconds and then fell into silence.

"Now we wait," Elsa said, pulling her hand from Jonnie's mouth.

"Take her to a crypt," Shauna said.

"I don't know this city well enough," Elsa said.

"The catacombs," Laura said. "Sixty feet straight down, I'd imagine. There's a huge church across the street, surely they have an entrance."

Elsa tore the wires and tubes from Jonnie's body and cradled her in her arms. She then sank into the floor, taking Jonnie with her.

"She can take passengers?" Shauna asked. "We can do that while carrying someone?"

"It's not fun for the person being carried," Jackie said. "It scares me silly. Elsa had to stop doing that with my sister and I after we saw her take a street ruffian down and not bring him back." Jackie shivered. "I can't even think about it."

"This is out of our hands now," Laura said. "Can we go to whatever hotel has our luggage and change clothes? We're all covered in blood."

§

When they arrived in the hotel room, the first thing they did was take showers. Despite the three of them being crowded into the bathroom, no one spoke. Jackie washed Shauna, as she'd done most days, but this time it was just cleansing. Jackie did nothing to make it erotic.

There were two outfits laid out on the bed. Surprising Shauna, Laura grabbed the one meant for her, a black lace dress and black and red fishnet stocking with sparkling red shoes. Shauna had the same outfit with white instead of black.

Jackie sat on the bed and stared at the dresser.

"Are you going to be okay?" Shauna asked.

Jackie turned her head slowly and glared at Shauna, tears were streaming down her face.

"Okay," Shauna admitted, "That was a dumb question. How can I help?"

"I suppose holding me, forever, is out of the question?" Jackie asked with a weak voice and then gave a weaker smile.

Shauna sat on the bed beside Jackie and pulled her into a hug. "I'm sure Jonnie will pull through," she said, trying to sound more hopeful than she actually was. Elsa's history of killing her pets didn't bode well and Shauna couldn't ignore that no matter how hard she tried to remind herself that Jackie and Jonnie had been Elsa's pets for more than half her time as a vampire. Surely their bodies had adapted to the blood by now.

"I don't know what to wear," Jackie said, her voice quaking. She then broke down into a full-out cry.

Of course, Elsa had always dressed the twins and she'd always dressed them alike. Even if Shauna helped Jackie pick out clothing, it would be the first time she wasn't wearing the same thing as her sister in who knew how many decades. It would be a reminder of how she wasn't with her sister.

"We'll set out the clothes for Jonnie," Shauna said. "She can put them on when she gets back here."

Jackie nodded, accepting Shauna's lie. If Jonnie survived, she wouldn't be back for a couple days. By then, barring another catastrophe, Jackie would be wearing something else.

Shauna went to the dresser and selected a pair of outfits consisting of torn blue jeans and a tight, strategically torn black babydoll. She set both on the bed beside Jackie.

Tom called as they were changing. He'd tried to reach Laura several times to tell her Henry and a group of hunters were heading to the temple, but Laura's phone was too far below ground to get the call. He'd followed Henry and his troops after he left and they didn't return to the hunter's safehouse. They'd gone straight to the airport and boarded a flight, but Tom couldn't get past security to see where they went.

Laura told him to meet them at the Hongre Rampante. She then called Gui to tell him that the hunters wouldn't be returning to their base and to see what he could find there.

Shauna's phone had time to get a weak charge. She found a few texts from Elsa, telling them she was going to the temple because Zylpha had called her, but nothing since the hospital.

"She's in the catacombs," Laura said, reminding Shauna that she'd not have a signal.

"That's a good sign, I guess," Shauna said. "If she's still down there, it means Jonnie's alive or dead or…" She didn't know how to say it and growled in frustration. "She's not gone," she blurted.

Jackie smiled at her with eyes gleaming with actual hope.

§

The Hongre Rampante was something out of centuries past. The only drinks they served came from one of two kegs mounted behind the bar. The tables were made of thick, ancient, cracked wood. The place was packed despite it being well past midnight. A fiddle player sitting on the end of the bar could barely be heard over the din of dozens of conversations. Stairs led up to two tiers of doors, and by the lingerie clad women leaning over the railings, the doors led to rooms with hourly rates.

"I've been here," Jackie said. "It hasn't changed at all since eighteen-twenty."

Not only was the room packed, at least a dozen of the patrons, one of the bartenders and half of the courtesans were vampires, as was the fiddle player.

"Do you think Artemis has a table somewhere in here?" Laura yelled in Shauna's ear.

Shauna looked around again, blinking to catch the auras and then examining who'd had them. Then she remembered that Artemis wouldn't have an aura. That's when she noticed the courtesan on the top floor sitting on the railing, wearing a gold silk girdle and nothing else. That was Artemis. She pointed up to her for Laura and Jackie and then headed to the stairs.

"Not the virgin goddess I was expecting," Shauna said as they got to Artemis.

"I think you forget my myth," Artemis said. "This is just a trap used to attract prey. I have a room, it's quieter in there." She climbed off the rail and opened a door leading to a small room with a bed, a wash basin and a shower.

"The showers are new," Jackie said.

She was clearly being subjective. The galvanized steel pipes leading to the shower head had more rust than steel showing.

A man lay slumped on the bed.

"Pardon the mess," Artemis said.

"Is he sleeping it off or is he...?" Shauna asked.

"Dead." Artemis said. "He had issues with boundaries."

"You're not actually the goddess," Laura said.

"Am I a goddess?" Artemis asked. "Or are you asking if I am the deity worshipped by the Greeks?"

"Well," Laura said, "both."

"I am a vampire," Artemis said. "I was known to hunt at night and my prey was usually those who went alone into the woods under the moonlight. And I do have powers that could be seen as divine. So, yes, I was worshipped."

"Are all the greek gods vampires?" Shauna asked.

"Are we here to talk history or discuss the hunter problem?" Artemis asked. "But, to answer you: No. I am the only one of the gods I've met and I can't confirm or deny the others even existed."

"Henry got away," Laura said. "He nearly killed Jackie's sister."

"This is Jackie?" Artemis asked, nodding toward the lone twin. "She's a pet, but not one of yours."

"I am Elsa Bathory's," Jackie said. "And Henry did kill my sister. She should be in the process of changing now."

Laura's phone bleeped. "Tom's here," Laura said, thumbing the keyboard of her phone. "I gave him the room number."

"I should dress," Artemis said and she pulled a silk robe on. "I'd hate to have to kill this Tom, but I do have rules about what happens to men who see me naked." She had a particularly mischievous grin.

"A hundred men out there saw what wasn't covered by the corset," Shauna said. "And that corset covered nothing."

"I counted seventy-nine," Artemis smiled, but said nothing more.

"Old vampires are creepy," Laura said.

Shauna wondered if all vampires were monsters and she'd somehow managed to first encounter the only vampires that were not. Elsa had long since overcome her vile inclinations. Artemis, who'd set a trap for seventy-nine men whose only crime was noticing one of many naked women in a whorehouse, was thousands of years old and still killed humans for sport.

"We find our hobbies," Artemis said. "Mine for the next fifty years will be tracking down seventy-nine men. It actually seems like a challenge, and I haven't had one in centuries."

Shauna tried to ignore that the woman just said she was about to become a serial killer. She had more pressing matters to discuss. "What do we know about Henry?" she asked.

"He killed Mascare and Amenhetop, which puts a wrinkle in all of vamp society," Artemis said. "That fellow had been selected for the role because he was so dull and just the right purity it took obsidian to kill him. James will not be happy."

"You know James?" Shauna said.

"Oh," Artemis said. "I shouldn't have mentioned him, but you know him or you know Una. Which is your sire?"

"James," Shauna said.

"He built the temple," Artemis said. "It was a ruse, meant to keep people from looking for older vampires after he purged all the vampires who could harm him from the world. To be fair, it was the generation of my bloodfather, Mikos, that started that war."

"I thought the purge started a few hundred years ago," Shauna said.

"There were two," Artemis said. "The first, the one I'm talking about, was about three thousand years ago. I only survived the purge because I don't have the aura. The last one, Vlad's, was a thousand years of violence among our kind. Vlad didn't even start it, but he kept it going after those who had started it perished."

"So what will happen to the temple?" Shauna asked.

Artemis said, "We'll clean it up and I'll have my blood granddaughter, who is a little purer than Amenhetop was, assume the role. She'll have to dress as a man, but with a modified mask and garb, she should be okay. There will be a Medici to replace Mascare. Your friend Portia is the highest purity of that bloodline anyone on the council knows of, but she is not pure enough to sit on the council. Mascare probably had other children we don't know of. He was the most prolific of the council."

"How is it you are so much purer than the other members of the council?" Shauna asked.

Tom walked in the room before Artemis answered. He gave Laura a hug and looked at the man on the bed. "Is he…?"

Laura nodded and said, "Not mine, though."

"I didn't have the means to buy a ticket to stay on their trail," Tom said. "I'm sorry."

"You couldn't go that far from me anyway," Laura said. "You still need my blood almost every day."

"I guess it's better I didn't go," Tom said.

"Shauna, you asked why I am different from the others on the council. I'm not on the council," Artemis said. "My descendant, who is of the same purity as the other founding members of the council, Thalia, is the only member of the council from our bloodline."

"I thought every bloodline only had one person on the council," Shauna said.

"Depends on where you define a bloodline's start," Artemis said. "In theory we are all descended from either James or Una, and even they have a common ancestor. Eight of the original nine were descendants of Una. Thalia, like me, is descended from James. There are distinctions that would give away a bloodline if you know what to look for. My descendants can only sire one vampire and we don't have auras. James' descendants can shift between this world and the world of pure Venae, though they can never quite fully enter that world."

"Phasing," Shauna said.

"Yes," Artemis said.

"But, Vlad could phase," Shauna said. "So can Elsa. So can many of the Dracul line, or so I've heard."

"Vlad is an abomination," Artemis said with a heavy sigh. "Around four hundred years ago he discovered a way to absorb the Venae of a purer vampire, killing them and giving him their strength and whatever abilities they had. No one has figured out what he did, but it was one of my line, one who was much purer than the council, he killed. It took the council two centuries to exact revenge."

"So Elsa is purer than the council?" Shauna asked.

"If she was made after he consumed Millicent, yes, she would be," Artemis said. "His heir to the Dracul seat, Lucrezia, is not. Most of the Dracul were hunted after Vlad's monstrous acts. I believe Elisabet Bathory is the last of the Dracul who retains my Venae and James' Venae. The only other I knew of has disappeared, Allessandro. Zylpha says we have Elisabet to thank for that.."

"You keep track of the Draculs?" Shauna asked.

"His bloodline was very problematic for a thousand years," Artemis said. "They warred against other families. Because of Vlad there are six seats on the council instead of nine, as there were when they first won their war against the generations before them."

"Elsa, or Elisabet as you call her, was allowed to live because she fled to America?" Shauna asked.

"Elisabet and Lucrezia were allowed to live because they didn't take part in Vlad's wars," Artemis said. "The sun will rise soon and I don't plan to sleep here. I have a home near Versailles if you'd like to join me."

"We need to stay in town," Shauna said. "Elsa is going through a very tough patch right now and she'll need our support."

Artemis went over to a chair and pulled a card from a purse there. She returned and handed it to Shauna. "It's an open invitation. I usually stay on my ranch in Wyoming, though." The card read: 'Wild Springs Bow Hunting Tours' and had a phone number. Shauna tucked it into her wallet.

CHAPTER 12

Sleep came hard the next day. At any time, either Jackie or Shauna would be unable to sleep and kept the other awake. Physically, neither vampires of significant purity nor their pets needed sleep. Their bodies didn't need rest. Their minds, however, suffered when they went too long without sleep. Stress could take a toll on the fragile sanity of vampiric existence. Shauna still had difficulty thinking of it as a life rather than an undeath.

Laura had a separate room with Tom, but, by the sounds coming through the wall, their sleep was often interrupted as well.

In the late afternoon, the hotel room door opened and Elsa walked in along with Jonnie. Jackie pounced on her sister and both cried together continuously as they went into the bathroom to shower.

"She's okay?" Shauna asked.

"She's ecstatic," Elsa said. "Imagine wanting something for two centuries but being afraid to touch it."

"I can't even," Shauna said then asked, "She's fed?"

"Yes," Elsa said. "She's hesistant to kill, which is a good thing."

"No," Shauna said, anticipating a turn in the conversation. "We're not talking about Laura right now."

"Leaving a trail of bodies is a bad thing," Elsa said.

Shauna thought about Artemis' quest to hunt down all the men from the the Hongre Rampante, which reminded her of the other things they'd talked about. "Can Lucy phase?" Shauna asked.

"No," Elsa replied. "Not every ability is passed, and sometimes new ones develop in blood children. To my knowledge, your sister's ability to see the link between vampires and their pets is unique. Until I made Jonnie, my ability to whisper to a distant ear was unique."

"You know of Laura's ability?" Shauna asked. They hadn't really talked about what happened in the temple.

"She doesn't talk to you about her vampiric activities," Elsa said. "She's pretty sure you'd disapprove. She talks to me."

"And you don't discourage her from killing?" Shauna asked.

"I do tell her it's wrong. It's dangerous and she needs to cut back on her feeding and stop the killing," Elsa said. "But, she knows my past so she likely doesn't put much weight to such advice from me. Why are you so interested in Lucy? Didn't you meet her with the rest of the council?"

"I did and I liked her right up until she tried to kill Laura and I," Shauna said. She went on to tell the whole story of the encounter in the temple and the later meeting with Artemis. Shauna paid particular detail to the discussions about Vlad.

"So Lucy and I are not the same purity," Elsa said. "I suppose it's possible."

"How close are you and Lucy?" Shauna asked.

"We're sisters," Elsa said. "We love each other."

"And you've slept with her?" Shauna asked.

"I've never actually been in the same room with her," Elsa said. "When I took the twins to the council, to have them coerced to enjoy being fed on, my bloodfather had just died and the council hadn't decided whether or not to allow my bloodline to retain a seat on the council."

"I don't think there really was a choice," Shauna said. "They either had to invite Lucy or eradicate your bloodline."

"You mean our bloodline? Through Artemis, we're both descendants of James. We're related?" Elsa said cautiously.

"By Venae, yes," Shauna replied.

"How deliciously incestuous," Elsa said and then leaned in to kiss Shauna.

Shauna returned the kiss for only a moment before pulling back to say, "Henry got away. He went to the airport and Tom couldn't follow him past security."

"Until we can find more about Henry," Elsa said. "I have business left to take care of in Paris. I am going to hold you to your promise, though. We will find Henry and kill him."

"Slowly," Shauna said. Utter hate was a new emotion for her; it was the only way she could describe how she felt when thinking of the hunter. Until he'd nearly killed Jonnie, Shauna had seen him as a nuisance she had to get rid of. She now wanted to. The local wannabe king was a nuisance. "Your business is Napoleon, right?" Shauna asked.

"Why was he watching at the moment Henry and his cohort were at the Temple?" Elsa asked.

"He's had people watching the temple," Shauna said. "That's how they noticed us. Perhaps someone just alerted him and he came to see for himself."

"Perhaps," Elsa said. "Let's get dressed. We're going out at sunset."

"Goth or glam?" Shauna asked.

"I'm getting in a fight," Elsa said. She grinned in a way that was exceptionally impish, even for her, then announced, "It's catsuit time!"

"You are joking, right?" Shauna said.

"Always dress for the occasion," Elsa said, opening the closet. She pulled out a footlocker and tossed it on the bed. It looked awkward, a tiny woman throwing around a big box, but Elsa was much stronger than she looked. The footlocker had postage stickers on it. It had been shipped air-mail from somewhere in Delaware. Elsa flipped open the lid, revealing stacks of folded black leather.

"Knowing we were pursuing Henry, I anticipated a fight," Elsa said. She lifted up one of the leather jumpsuits and tapped the leather. It was stiffer than Shauna expected. "Ceramic polymer plates," Elsa said. "One of my investments is a chemical company specializing in polymers. These have high collars, for obvious reasons." She tossed a catsuit to Shauna.

Noting a few places that didn't have armor plates, Shauna said, "So, you insisted we still have our curves?"

"What's the point of a catsuit without the figure?" Elsa said.

"Armor?" Shauna ventured.

"Priorities, my dear," Elsa replied. "Fashion first, protection second."

"My priorities might be different," Shauna said.

"That, my love, is why I arrange your wardrobe," Elsa said.

Laura walked in the room as they were changing. "Did I hear Elsa? Where's Jonnie?"

"Cleaning up," Shauna said.

"Did I interrupt something?" Laura asked raising an eyebrow towards Shauna and Elsa's state of undress. "Should I come back? Or maybe I should join you?"

"Don't be gross," Shauna said. She'd long since come to terms with Jonnie and Jackie's incestuous relationship, but there was no way she'd bend her inhibitions to ever be with her sister that way.

"You should join us," Elsa said, tossing Laura a leather suit.

"You're kidding me." Laura said.

"I asked that," Shauna said. "It's actually armor and since we can't take revenge on Henry tonight, we're paying it forward to Napoleon."

"I'm all for that," Laura said. "He annoyed the fuck out me."

"Where's Tom?" Shauna asked.

"Gui texted and wanted help scouring the hunter base for clues," Laura said. "I was going to ask you if you wanted to go help, but cracking skulls in Napoleon's court sounds like more fun."

"Gui's there in daylight?" Shauna asked.

"The hunter base is sun-proofed," Laura said. "Tinfoil on the windows and a darkroom door in the entryway."

"We know they work with vampires," Shauna said. The white robed vampire in the temple proved their theory right.

Henry's angels were nothing more than very potent vampires.

"Do they know?" Elsa asked. "If there's a vampire out there potent enough to harm James, I can easily imagine them coercing an entire legion of men to believe they are on a crusade."

"Or they could just be paying mercenaries a ton of money," Laura said.

"That's possible too," Elsa said. She turned her back to Shauna. "Could you zip the legs?"

Shauna used her apportation to pull the zippers up on Elsa's calves.

"I was hoping for something more intimate," Elsa said with a sad chuckle. "I could have done it that way, myself."

"So you're saying I should have used my teeth?" Shauna asked.

"That's a good idea," Elsa said. "But let's save that for the thank-the-gods-we're-alive-after-battle-sex."

"Is that a thing?" Laura asked.

Elsa shrugged, "If it's not, it will be."

When Jonnie and Jackie came out of the bathroom, Elsa tossed them much smaller bundles of shiny black material.

"Vinyl?" Shauna asked.

"Latex," Jonnie said, unwrapping hers. "We're not dry enough to put this on yet."

"We have time," Elsa said. "You could air dry on the bed while we wait."

"That would be easier with a body temperature thirty degrees higher," Jonnie said as she flew over and settled on the bed.

"Sis has already been over the basics," Jackie noted. She then flopped on the bed and asked, "Why do we get the latex and you get armor?"

Elsa replied, "What's your job in a fight?"

"Hide." Jackie said. "Run away, works too."

"She changed that," Jonnie said. "The new rule is 'Fade out and look cute.'" She reached over and took her sister's hand and phased. Both she and Jackie became partially translucent. She and her sister started to sink into the mattress before they jerked upward to hover above the bed. "Almost forgot to fly a little to stay above ground."

"When you get more practice," Shauna said, "you'll be able to fade your body in gradients, keeping the soles of your feet solid."

"Yeah," Jonnie said. "Elsa said that, but I'm a newb and not there yet."

Laura's phone rang. She answered it and put it on speaker. "Tom," she said. "I have you on speaker, so no pillow talk. Everyone's here."

"Um, okay," Tom's voice said. "Gui didn't find much other than some old books and a wall map with a bunch of pins that he says mark vamp homes and hangouts. The most notable thing about that was the perfume factory is not marked on that map, but the temple and Le Obscurité Infinie are. I should say 'were'. We trashed the map. Its existence is a violation of vampire laws."

"Okay, so we knew that they had ways to find vampires," Elsa said. "Did you learn anything new, any hints about where they went?"

"Yes," Tom said. "Gui reverse dialed the last number that called the phone here. Napoleon answered."

"You're sure?" Elsa asked.

"Well, no," Tom said. "Gui says he is, though. I guess he can hear everything you're saying even if I don't put you on speaker. There's some stuff in the books you should see, though. It doesn't mean much to either of us, but we can't bring them all to you."

"We'll swing by," Laura said and hung up.

"After we talk to Napoleon," Elsa said.

"So, Napoleon dies?" Shauna asked.

"I am the royal here," Elsa said. "I do have the right to declare such a sentence. But, I am the Blood Countess and I think, tonight, I will be revisiting some hobbies from past centuries."

"Didn't you do that with Henry?" Shauna asked.

"That wasn't anything more than a harsh interrogation," Elsa said. "If Napoleon had anything to do with Jonnie's near death, I'll be playing the part of karma tonight."

"So he near dies?" Shauna tried to translate what Elsa had said.

"You do get me," Elsa said flippantly. "Let's get my babies dressed."

"I'm a vampire now," Jonnie said. "I'm not yours anymore."

Elsa purred, "We can debate that later during the thank-the-gods-we're-alive-after-battle-sex."

§

"I can't believe you losers just sit around at this table, even when you're not holding court," Elsa said and then laughed, sounding honestly amused. She walked up to stand before the table, glanced down to one end then the other and then walked over and sat on the table in front of Napoleon.

Getting into the factory had been easy. They just coerced the guards to leave and Shauna tore the door from the wall. Exerting her strength always gave her a pleasant sense of power since she had so few opportunities to use even a fraction of her strength without drawing attention. The perfume factory was just isolated enough that Shauna felt free to let loose.

As a bonus, the racket brought all of Napoleons security guards into sight of the door and made sure the council would be paying attention as they entered.

"I'll cover the pets at the bar," Laura said and flew over to stand by the group of humans. It was another display of power. Elsa had asked them to show off subtly. Weak vampires wouldn't be able to fly or throw steel doors through walls.

"You are impudent," Napoleon said. "You risk a day in the sun for disobeying your king."

"You're not my king," Elsa said.

Napoleon set a goblet of wine down on the table hard enough to shake the numerous bottles that sat before the council. "If you are in Paris, or anywhere north of the Alps, you are in our territory, which makes us your king."

"It's cute how you've adopted a royal 'we'. You are no more my king than these posers constitute an elder's council," Elsa said. "I bet not one of you is a hundred years old."

"Again, impudence," Napoleon said. "This will not be tolerated. Guards, seize her. Take her friends as well if they resist."

Elsa turned to the guards and said, "Run home to your mommies."

The four closest guards dropped their guns and ran for the door. The other guards, upon seeing their number cut so quickly, fled immediately after.

"I could coerce you as well," Elsa said. "I could make you do anything I wanted."

"You can change my memories, maybe make me walk away for a night, but I am who I am and you cannot change me. I am the king."

"You're a fool." Shauna said. "Countess Bathory can make you into a whole other person."

Elsa caught Shauna's eyes for a second and whispered, in the voice only Shauna would hear, "Coercion cannot change a person. We can alter a moment's memories, create an alternate perception like pain to pleasure, but we can't make an asshole into a tolerable person. Any attempt to do so would fade after a few days at best." She then turned her gaze back to the table and said, "I'm contemplating some particularly humiliating acts I've only seen on the internet. I don't imagine you'd hold an esteemed place in either mortal or vampire society if, say, I coerced you and your council to strip and run around the room acting like chickens. I'd get more x-rated, but I'd want wide distribution. Perhaps after."

All of the vampires sitting at the table turned their heads away as if breaking eye contact would prevent it. Napoleon stood from his chair and leaned forward, "To do so to a royal would bring the wrath of the Elder's Council upon you."

"Indeed, it would," Elsa said. "As I said, I could coerce you, but where's the fun in that?" She hopped down and walked along the front of the table, laughing as each member turned further away from her. "Any poser that tells me their real name and the year they were born, may leave now and they will not be harmed this night."

"I am Evangeline deWinter, born in 1716."

When the woman beside Napoleon answered Elsa, he threw her a nasty look and said, "Do not respond to her threats. She is not who she says she is, either."

"Laura," Elsa called out and pointed to the man who claimed to be Voltaire. "Kill this vampire's pet."

The pet barely managed to look shocked before Laura was grasping his heart in her hand and holding it high above her head. Blood from the disembodied organ poured over her hair and face. Laura turned her gaze upward, seeming to revel in the gore. When she licked her lips, Shauna had to look away. The vampire using Voltaire's name jumped up from the table and ran toward Laura, but collapsed after a few steps and died in the middle of the floor.

Most of the other members of the council were on their feet, running to the door, shouting names and years, none of which were over a century and a half earlier. Shauna watched Elsa for a signal to stop them, but got none, so she let them flee.

Shauna heard the crack of a gunshot. She saw one of the pets laying on the ground as the others ran around her toward the door. Laura spun her derringer around her finger and blew at the trail of smoke coming out of the barrel.

"Napoleon's pet," Laura said, shrugging at Shauna. "I figured we wanted to keep her around to influence her master. Don't worry, I barely winged her thigh."

The fallen pet was writhing on the floor holding her leg.

Shauna would have let the pets go, but this was Elsa's party, though the newly crowned Empress paid no attention to the pets or Laura as she pressed on with her display of power to Napoleon.

Elsa leaned close to him and said, "Look at me, not at your human girl. She'll heal. Not only am I the Blood Countess, Elizabeth Bathory, I am the true, Elder Council recognized, temple imbued, Empress of the Northern Roman Empire." She turned to deWinter and asked in a quieter tone, "Why are you still here?"

"I have no reason to fear you," deWinter said. "I am who I claim to be and I have done nothing to bring harm or even to disrespect you. I can't miss what you're about to do, whatever that is."

"And who's this clown?" Elsa nodded to Napoleon.

"His name is Jean," deWinter said. "He's old enough to be Napoleon, but he's not. I'm only here because he has enough money to pay mercenaries to bring us here at gun point if we don't comply with his delusions of grandeur."

"You are a fraud as much as any of us," Napoleon hissed to deWinter. "You even had the audacity to pick the name of a fictional character."

"Why would I intentionally choose to be a person depicted as a traitor to my country?" deWinter said. "I bear my name proudly because I am not as I am depicted in Alex's work. He was just mad that I wouldn't sleep with him again after learning he was married. He's lucky I didn't drain him, but I was repulsed by his lecherousness."

"So, you are the infamous Milady deWinter, but nothing about the character is true?" Shauna asked skeptically. She wasn't sure what part she didn't believe, or even if there was something, anything, she did.

"The only thing he took is my name and my likeness," deWinter said. "I wasn't even a noblewoman. I only started using the 'Milady' after seeing Faye Dunaway play the part after the war."

"And you know Jean, here?" Elsa said.

"He's a blood-cousin," deWinter said. "Our sires share the same maker."

"Do you like Jean?" Elsa asked.

"Not as much as I once did," de Winter said. "But, even then I liked my horse more, and she'd bucked me off on several occasions."

Napoleon sat back in his seat, cringing at each of deWinter's words and cowering from Elsa. "Your council means nothing," he said defiantly, but his voice wavered. "They are outdated and they won't interfere with me. I have powerful friends. Friends more powerful than the council."

"I am more powerful than the council," Elsa said. "And I have friends more powerful than me. Why don't you tell me about your friends."

"I think not," Napoleon said. "I've called my friends. They will be here soon."

"Just a second," Elsa said. She turned and shouted to Laura, "Call Tom and tell him to reverse dial that phone again."

Laura pulled out her phone and had a brief conversation before hanging up. A moment later, a vibration hummed from Napoleon's pocket.

"Answer it," Elsa said. "See if that's our friend, Tom."

Napoleon pushed the table forward then ran, heading back towards a fire exit.

Since her change, Shauna had learned to slow her perceptions to the speed of the normal, human world. To be able to interact with the people around her, she kept her sense of time at that agonizing slow rate. At that moment, she let her perceptions slip back to their natural state. Napoleon's running became a slow motion jog. She leapt into the air and swooped down to stand in front of him.

Bracing herself telekinetically, she let Napoleon slam into her. He collapsed to the floor and Shauna kicked him in the ribs. The cracks she heard gave her a sense of satisfaction. She pushed away the shame she felt for feeling sadistic pleasure. He deserved whatever she could do to him. She, having been a victim of his actions, remembered the pain of the white robed vampire's hands inside her chest. Napoleon had led that vampire to her. She felt justified when she kicked him again.

He didn't scream, but let out a grunt and a whimper.

"Kill him?" Shauna asked, though she knew how Elsa would answer.

"No," Elsa's answer came as expected.

Shauna wasn't sure letting him live was showing mercy. His ribs would mend in a few hours, after that, Shauna shuddered to think what Elsa planned to break on him.

"Have you ever been to the Sorbonne?" Elsa asked as she floated over to land with one foot on Napoleon's chest. Shauna didn't know what the Sorbonne was, but, by the way Elsa said it, she was sure she didn't want to go there.

CHAPTER 13

Shauna browsed through the books the hunters had left behind in the house they'd been using as a base. She started with a pile on the largest desk in the building. She'd discovered latin literature explaining that obsidian could harm the most potent demons and that the most potent obsidian came from the Syrian Desert, but was exceedingly rare. In his delirium, James had mentioned Syrian obsidian. Shuana had a good idea what kind of demons the text was speaking of.

Elsa and the twins had taken Milady deWinter and Jean-slash-Napoleon to the Sorbonne, a place she said she'd find the equipment she needed to properly question Jean. She'd mentioned something about Templars facing trials there, and forced confessions. Shauna wasn't sure Elsa insisted DeWinter go along. As far as Shauna knew, the new Empress held no grudge against Milady.

Laura and Tom were searching through the basement, which still had numerous lockers full of firearms. They came up periodically with a box of grenades or a satchel filled with paper Euros. Shauna couldn't see a point to what they brought up, other than to give them an excuse to go back down and spend time alone together. When she suggested they instead investigate the bedrooms upstairs, they agreed. She didn't hear from them again for several hours.

Three computers in the house had passwords and Shauna wasn't a hacker. Gui had tried for hours, but all he could do was guess passwords. A catalog Shauna found tucked under a computer keyboard came from the Louvre from nineteen thirty and listed a stone age dagger made of obsidian. It was circled in yellow highlighter. A document from the Louvre from September of 1945 listed it as among antiquities stolen by the Germans.

For a while, she found no other clues in the books. Then she noticed the maps on the desk didn't show residences, but were geological maps. They were stacked with an old piece of animal skin with a very carefully, very ornately drawn map on it with Latin notations. It was a map of a salt mine.

"Why would they be looking for a salt mine?" Shauna asked aloud, to no one in particular.

"We're talking about art?" Gui asked.

"I thought so, but this is a salt mine," Shauna said, holding out the map.

"Let me see that list again, the stuff that wasn't recovered," Gui said. "I remember that as the Germans approached, the French scattered the art from the museums, stashing it here and there, but all of those stashes were returned to the Louvre after the war. Not everything was removed and some fell into the German hands."

"Obviously," Shauna said. "This list says as much."

"This list is broken into four parts, four storage rooms in the Louvre that weren't stashed and fell into German hands," Gui said.

Shauna could read French, so she already knew what the list said.

"I'm going to run to an art history professor I know," Gui said. "He works in the Louvre and was alive during the war. I'm going to see what he knows of these lists. He's living as a Frenchman now, but in the war he was German."

"I still want to decipher this pile of maps," Shauna said.

"Can I go with Gui?" Laura asked, coming down the stairs. "I'd like to at least walk through the Louvre."

"Since when are you an art connoisseur?" Shauna asked.

"Um," Laura replied.

Then Shauna realized her sister just wanted to get out of the hunter base. "Go on," she said. "Call me if you find anything."

"Your phone isn't dead?" Laura asked.

Shauna pointed to the floor by an outlet where her phone lay, plugged in. "I found a charger," Shauna said.

She spent hours searching through the pile of maps, searching for a name that would be on both the Roman and geological maps. She finally realized that the geological maps were printed in varying scales. The hunters had been trying to locate the salt mines. Once she realized that, it didn't take her long to pair up a modern map with the Roman one.

When she noticed the sun had come up outside, Shauna started going through the books, looking for something to read until sunset. She chose the oldest book she could actually read. Several of the hand written ones were in dialects that she couldn't make sense of. The book she settled on was by an eighteenth century archeologist who was searching for Atlantis. Most of the book used bad logic to justify envisioning Plato's philosophical utopia as a real place. The rest postulated three locations around the Mediterranean. Sea. One saw Atlantis as an island north of Alexandria, Egypt. Another placed it in Syria and the last was under the dunes of the Sahara.

Remembering James mentioning Syria, Shauna went back and read that chapter again after finishing the whole book. The arguments for all three were particularly weak. The author, a Martin Francis, seemed to be basing the logic on the lack of evidence to disprove the ideas rather than any evidence at all in favor of the hypotheses.

Francis chose the Syrian location because of large round volcanic caldera that he estimated to be from an eruption a few thousand years before Plato's time. It all fit too well with James' ramblings from his sickbed.

Shauna used her phone to search the internet for more information. The volcano had only been inactive for a century and a half, but it was far older than Francis had guessed, but new geologically speaking, being only thirty thousand years old. Being active, periodically, through recorded history meant it still produced obsidian now and then. There was something she wasn't connecting. James had specifically been interested in Syrian obsidian and the Elders Council all had weapons made of it. Shauna wondered what made it so dangerous to so many vampires.

She thought back and remembered James mentioned a spell that created Reilla and the obsidian that was created by the spell. Perhaps the side effect was actually causing the volcano, which would produce obsidian. Had she just pieced together the origin of vampires, she wondered. Somehow, when Reilla was created, a volcano erupted in Syria, which put the origins of vampires at thirty thousand years ago. Seeking confirmation of her discovery brought her to call Amber, hoping James was coherent.

"He's not waking up," Amber said. "For the last three days, he's just slept."

"Is he waking to feed?" Shauna asked.

"No," Amber replied. "I fed him before that, and he had an hour of semi-aware rambling. He dug some post card out of his drawers for a sail-boarding company in the Florida keys. It just read, 'Come, take some lessons. – Reilla.' The card is decades old and I don't know who Reilla is."

Shauna nearly choked when she heard the name. "Reilla is the first vampire," Shauna said. "He mentioned her name back in Grue's Home after the first run-in with Henry."

"I don't remember that," Amber said. "But, I guess I wouldn't, would I?"

"You were awake," Shauna said. "Maybe you just weren't paying attention."

"Whatever. I need to call her," Amber said, then hung up.

Shauna jumped, startled, when the front door opened. She hadn't realized night had come again. Elsa and the twins walked in. Elsa was dressed in a conservative skirt and a shirt and jacket and was wearing glasses, making her look like some kind of stereotypical librarian. The twins wore short plaid skirts and white shirts that were two sizes too small and wouldn't button all the way up. The knee high socks and patent leather shoes completed the look. Clearly Elsa was trying to assert her control role in the changed relationship. Jackie hopped past the others and hugged Shauna. A pale pink aura surrounded Jackie.

"It's only been a day," Shauna said. "How did you make the change so fast?"

"Been reading again?" Elsa asked as she ran her hand over the pile of books on the desk. "It's been three days."

Shauna noticed, as Jackie continued to hold her, that she didn't feel as warm as usual. She planted her lips on Jackie's and kissed. When the tip of Shauna's tongue found fangs that weren't hers, Jackie pulled away and giggled.

Jackie said, "Since it worked for Jonnie, I wanted it too."

Shauna took a moment to take in Jackie's new self as a vampire. She didn't really look different. For a moment Shauna regretted she hadn't offered to make Jackie, but Jackie wasn't used to her blood. Her body had built a tolerance for Elsa's. Shauna's blood would most likely have killed her rather than change her.

"You could have called," Shauna said.

"You didn't answer your phone," Jackie said.

Shauna picked up her phone. It didn't have any missed calls.

"That's not your phone," Jackie said. "Your home screen is a picture of you, me, Elsa and Jonnie."

"But, I used this to call James' house and I didn't type in the number." Shauna brought up the contacts list on the phone. It wasn't hers. There were far more numbers listed than she had, but she knew all the names. "This phone has all the names, addresses and phone numbers of the vampires in Philadelphia."

"That's bad," Elsa said. She grabbed the phone and scrolled and then sighed. "At least it doesn't list me as Elizabeth Bathory, just as Elisabet Davlos."

"That's Henry's phone," Jackie said. "Or maybe it's just a mission phone. Does it have any European numbers in it?"

Shauna checked several numbers of names she didn't recognize. "Nope," she said. "All Philly or New Jersey area codes. If this isn't my phone, where is mine?"

Elsa moved a stack of books and pulled out a phone. "It's dead," she said. "There's a surprise."

Shauna grabbed the phone and took it over and put it on the charger. She tried to power it up repeatedly until it did. She'd missed fourteen calls and had nine text messages, mostly from Laura.

The gist was that Gui's friend told them that the Germans used salt mines to store things where moisture would cause problems. She and Gui were going to check out the ones from the map; he had an idea of where they might be. That message had come two nights earlier.

"Laura's in trouble," Shauna said. "She hasn't called in two days. The last message I have from her is: Can't wait for you, going in."

She showed Elsa the map of the salt mines. "Do you think there's any way we could find this place?" Shauna had paired the tomb with a geological map but hadn't paired the geological map with anything geographical.

"Jonnie?" Elsa asked.

"They're not mines," Jonnie said. "They're The Salt Crypts. To some circles of treasure hunter's they're a white stag or holy grail. If the legends are right, these are like the Egyptian tombs, but for Gaelic Princes rather than Pharoahs."

"And, if what these documents suggest is true, the Germans found them," Shauna said.

"Come on," Elsa said, heading to the basement. "Jonnie said crypts. That means catacombs, right?"

Jonnie nodded. "They'll be at the eastern end. Let me pull up a map." She pulled out her phone and brought up a web page with a map of the French Catacombs. "Here." Jonnie fingered a spot on the catacombs map beyond the edge of the tunnels. "There will be a collapsed tunnel or concealed doorway, I'm sure."

"And we can get into them from the basement?" Shauna asked as they descended the stairs.

Jonnie nodded. "We're just over this tunnel, which is one of the entrances they sealed off. I wouldn't be surprised to find a door leading straight down there from here."

"We searched," Shauna said. Looking around the walls, she saw a wooden bookcase against the wall. The floor had clear tracks in the dust where the case had been moved. "Of course, we weren't looking for hidden passages." She slid the bookcase aside. Someone had dug a hole through the basement wall behind the bookshelf. The hole led to a rough tunnel lit by a string of Christmas lights.

"What are you waiting for?" Elsa asked. "Let's see where this goes." She nudged Shauna forward, into the tunnel.

It didn't go far before they came through a hole in the wall of a tight, brick-lined tunnel. The string of lights continued to the left, so they followed. After the string of lights ended, enough light came from the far end of the tunnel to see by. They came to a rusty iron gate closed with a padlocked chain. The padlock itself was new with a shiny brass casing. "Anyone pick locks?" Shauna asked.

"We both can," Jackie said, stepping up to the gate. She knelt by the lock and examined it a moment. She then stood up and grabbed the chain on either side of the lock and pulled, shattering the links connecting to the padlock. "I don't, however, carry lockpicks on most days."

Through the gate, they entered the tunnels of the Paris Catacombs. Jonnie led them along, checking the map she'd saved on her phone each time they came to an intersection. The sheer number of bones they passed astounded Shauna. "How many are there?" she asked.

"Millions," Jonnie said. "I think it's like everyone who died in or around Paris before 1800 or so."

As they meandered through the tunnels, Shauna remembered where Elsa had been. "Did Napoleon tell you anything?"

"He was miraculously stubborn," Elsa said. "I did get a new necklace." She held up a string of vampire fangs she had hanging around her neck. "All Jean's. It took me a while to convince him to be more scared of me than of the angels. I learned that he does know Henry and he was the one who told the hunters, not only where, but when to attack the temple to ambush the Council. He'd been watching, hoping I would return, but when the council showed up, he saw an opportunity to deal with his competition."

"And where did Henry go?" Shauna asked. "Does Napo…, er, Jean, know?"

"I think he does," Elsa said. "But, as I said, he's stubborn. I set him up on one of the least pleasant, slowest devices they had down in the dungeon there. After seeing some of their toys, I am pretty sure I understand why they walled up and forgot about that room five centuries ago. I thought I was creative, but I am shamed by some of the tools there."

"Not my favorite part of you, remember?" Shauna said.

"Right," Elsa said. "I'll get to the point, but first, since you brought it up, which is your favorite part?"

"Your devotion," Shauna said. "Your friendship."

"That's sweet," Elsa said. "But, I know that. I was hoping for something fun like my tongue or my…"

"We're here," Jonnie announced, standing in front of a wall of femurs.

"Another hidden door?" Shauna asked.

"I was hoping," Jonnie said, "but I don't think so. The modern catacombs are less than three centuries old. The ones we're looking for are fifteen or so and might be two thousand years old. I think they just walled over a passageway that should be here. The builders of the Salt Crypt might have walled it over when they converted the Roman salt mines."

"So the Germans didn't get in?" Shauna asked. "This is a wild goose chase?"

"This would have been a back door. The main entrance to the mines would be much larger, big enough for a large horse drawn cart," Jonnie said.

"Are you sure the Salt Crypts are in front of us?" Elsa asked.

"No more then twenty feet to the main chamber," Jonnie said. "It could be less than three to a passageway."

"I'll be back," Elsa said. She phased and walked into the wall of bones, which wasn't as surreal to Shauna as when Elsa walked out. "Yep, four feet," Elsa said then turned and went back into the wall.

Shauna insisted Jackie and Jonnie follow next. She wasn't sure what she'd be able to do if they got lost. She couldn't see while inside a wall. When Shauna went through, she found all three of the others on the far side. The dusty white walls of the cave made it easy to see with the light coming from the end of the tunnel.

"I smell blood," Elsa said. "But it's not fresh."

Worried for her sister, Shauna ran through the tunnel into a brightly lit room.

Six men standing by the back end of an old military truck were unloading wooden boxes, but dropped them when Shauna came into the room. They swung machine guns that had been strapped across their chests up and aimed at her.

"I think they have reinforcements," one of the men called out.

"Shoot them," a voice from inside the truck answered.

The men shot at Shauna. The stings of their bullets was far less than she was used to, but she was still wearing the armored catsuit.

"Gold bullets," Shauna called back to Elsa and the twins. They were just emerging from the tunnel. They all phased. When some of the gunmen turned their fire on the three, the bullets passed straight through them.

"They're all vamps," one of the gunmen yelled.

"I'll deal with them," a vampire in familiar white robes emerged from the back of the truck. He held Henry's gold laced sword in one hand and a large obsidian dagger in the other. "I found the knife."

He tossed the sword to one of the gunmen and said, "Don't waste the bullets on these. Use your knives and take out those three." He pointed to Elsa and the twins. "I'll handle the girl in leather."

He strode toward Shauna. Though he wasn't the same vampire that had died in the temple, he still intimidated Shauna enough that she backed away.

The gunmen started flying across the room, crashing into each other. Elsa had adapted her tricks to deal with multiple foes. The twins were doing what they were supposed to do and posing, twirling their pigtails and puckering kisses towards the gunmen.

Shauna found her courage and, remembering Zylpha's knife hadn't hurt her, started walking towards the vampire, slipping into her natural vampiric perceptions and speed. The other vampire sped up as well. He swung at her shoulder. Shauna successfully fought the reflex to dodge and regretted it. The knife hurt, but didn't cut her flesh. It hadn't even penetrated her armor.

Shauna punched at the vampire's face, but he blocked and cut at Shauna face. She dodged back, avoiding the blade. But the vampire swung back at her. That time she didn't get out of the way. The knife cut across her forehead, drawing enough blood to spatter his robes.

Shocked, Shauna fell back with her hand covering her forehead. The wound had already closed. Instead of swinging at her again, the vampire ran towards a door in an iron wall that spanned one end of the cave. Shauna couldn't bring herself to chase him. She was just glad he'd fled rather than attack her again.

There were a dozen bodies spread through the room. Most were wearing the black bullet proof vests and combat armor of the hunters' assault teams. The cave was large enough that the two German army trucks parked nearby didn't take up half of the cave. What Shauna had originally thought was an iron wall was a pair of large rusted steel doors that blocked one end of the cave. Six white sarcophogai sat at the other. Around the room were several puddles of drying blood.

"Most of these died yesterday," Jackie said, walking among the bodies. "They're cold."

"Over there," Jonnie said, pointing to a body lying between two of the sarcophagi.

That one, wearing street clothes, was too familiar. "Tom!" Shauna ran to the body, but he'd been dead a while. His body was colder than hers, as cold as the cave floor. He'd been among those who'd died the day before.

"Laura," Shauna wimpered, falling over and holding her head in her hands. Tom's death meant Laura would have died as well. She looked around. Nowhere could she see her sister's body. Of course, she was a vampire, she wouldn't leave remains.

"She's gone," Shauna said.

"I don't think so," Elsa said. "I don't see any remains."

"She was a vampire," Shauna said.

"Unless she was naked, she would have left a pile of clothes," Elsa said, kicking at a leather trenchcoat that lay on the floor. A pair of dark pants and slip on loafers were under the coat."Like this poor guy."

"Gui," Shauna said, climbing to her feet, suddenly hopeful that her sister was still alive. But why hadn't she called. "Do you think Henry took her?"

"I doubt Henry was here," Jonnie said. "The real question is why is his sword here. He gave it to someone between the temple and the airport."

"Tom," Shauna said. "He knew Henry and was a hunter before I coerced him."

Elsa nodded. "You can't change a person so drastically and have it stick for long. If you'd used blood, I would have expected it to last longer than a few days. With your purity, I was thinking years."

"Could another vampire un-coerce him?" Jackie asked.

"They'd have to be almost as pure as Shauna," Elsa said.

"Like the dude in the white robes," Jackie said.

"So, Tom turned on Laura and she killed him," Shauna said. "She might be just impulsive enough to not think about the consequences." The thought that she'd never see her sister act so foolish again overwhelmed Shauna. She grabbed Elsa, because she was closest and hugged her. Sobbing, Shauna said, "She was an idiot, but I loved her."

"And she kicked ass," Elsa said.

Shauna pulled away from the hug to admire her sister's last fight. At least a dozen of the bodies lying on the floor were not a result of Elsa's fight. "I didn't know Laura could fight well enough to do all this," Shauna said.

"Doesn't take much when your enemies can't hurt you," Elsa said. "That vamp in white seemed like he'd just found the knife as we arrived. I doubt he was here yesterday."

"Tom died by being drained," Jonnie said. "Look at him, he's pale and dehydrated. I think Laura killed him."

"If she fed on him until he died, Laura is fine," Elsa said. "It's the one way a vampire can get rid of an unwanted pet without risking their own death."

"She fed on all of these," Jonnie said, kneeling between two bodies. "Any of these that didn't die right away from their wounds have been drained."

"She couldn't hold that much blood," Shauna said.

"She didn't," Elsa said. "That's what all these blood puddles are. Your sister was so hungry for their deaths, she went bulimic so she could keep feeding."

"I'm going to talk to her," Shauna said. "I promise. But, first we have to find her." In many vampire tales, feeding too much would drive a vampire into a blood frenzy. "You don't think she went mad from all the killing, do you?"

"Shauna, my love," Elsa said. "Don't get disturbed that I am speaking from experience, but think about what you just said. These men were dying from their wounds when Laura fed on them. Killing them was not part of the combat, but came after, in cold blood. Cold blooded murder doesn't cause insanity. I think it's the other way around."

"Addiction is not insanity," Shauna said.

"Isn't it?" Elsa asked.

Shauna slumped. Elsa was right. Her sister was mentally broken.

"Also speaking from experience," Elsa said, "she can be cured of her illness. The question is: How many lives will she take before she is cured?"

Shauna didn't want to think that way. It had been Elsa who told her that Laura's actions weren't her fault. She wasn't ready to take responsibility for what her sister hadn't done yet. "The question is: Where is she?" Shauna said, pulling out her phone. Noticing it was unresponsive, she asked Elsa, "Do you still track mine and Laura's phones?"

"If she was showing up on it, I would have told you," Elsa said. "Of course, I don't have a signal at the moment." She shook her phone and held it above her head. "Nope, no signal."

"You could go check outside," Shauna suggested, pointing to a man sized door set in the large steel doors. That door was hanging slightly open. "That should lead outside."

"I'll be right back," Elsa said and headed to the door.

"The hunters didn't disturb the sarcophagi," Jackie said. "I guess they just might be righteous enough to not disturb the dead."

"I'm curious," Jonnie said, walking toward the white stone boxes.

"You're not going to open them, are you?" Shauna asked.

"I'm just making sure they're all there," Jonnie said. "What if this is where the so called angels came from."

"Then the room would have been looted a long time ago," Shauna said, reasoning that anyone in a coffin that old would need to re-establish their wealth.

Jonnie pulled out her phone, activated the screen, and held it by her face as she leaned into a coffin, phasing through the stone. "Yup, this one's got bones, and lots of jewelry. Neither the hunters nor the Nazi's that knew about this cave were grave robbers." She went to each of the other sarcophagi and made similar discoveries.

Elsa popped back in the door, "Don't mess with those," she said.

"I'm not touching anything," Jonnie said. "I'm just looking."

Elsa walked over and leaned down. She pointed to the symbols on the ends of the sarcophagi. "You've seen these glyphs before, haven't you, Jonnie?"

Jonnie knelt and examined them. "I have," she said. "Tut's tomb. How weird since these crypts are two thousand years newer and just as many miles away."

"I said I don't believe in magic," Elsa said, "But whatever science is involved, these are protected. Venae isn't the only thing science, as we know it, can't explain."

"Did you find Laura?" Shauna asked.

"She's at the hotel," Elsa said. "She's packing our stuff and meeting us at the train. We're going back to Calais tonight."

"Oh?" Shauna asked. "Shouldn't we be after Henry?"

"We can find him again," Elsa said. "Amber said our presence is required in the Florida Keys and, by her tone, even I wasn't about to question why. But, this is your quest. If you want to pursue Henry the Inquisitor, I've got your back."

"No," Shauna said. "We need to go to Florida. You'll want to when you learn what's there."

"What's that?" Elsa asked.

"Reilla," Shauna said.

"The first vampire?" Elsa asked.

"So it seems," Shauna said. "She lives in Florida."

"And you were going to tell me, when?" Elsa asked.

"I was," Shauna said. She was going to try to talk to James before she did and at least ask if she could tell Elsa. "You're sure Laura's okay?"

"I spoke with her," Elsa said. "She got pretty beat up fighting the hunters that ambushed her, and none of those were Henry. She's been at Le Obscurité Infinie trying to drink her sorrows away."

"Do I even want to ask about the bar tab?" Shauna asked.

"What tab?" Elsa said. "Laura's claimed ownership of the place. She has experience as a bartender and speaks okay French. She was the old bartender's favorite niece. Since he died suddenly a few days ago, around the time of the fight at the temple, she's inherited the bar. I'll get my guys working on the paperwork while we travel."

"So we're off?" Shauna asked.

"Yes," Elsa said.

"Should we call someone about this trove of lost art?" Shauna asked, nodding to the trucks.

"I guess," Elsa said. "I'd hoped to look for a piece or two for my personal collection, but I don't have time. I think I'll have Jackie and Jonnie call it in. They're not my wards anymore and could probably use the reward money."

"I wasn't planning on leaving you," Jonnie said.

"And I...," Jackie started to say, then started again, "I'm planning on sticking around, too. As long as Shauna's around you, I will be as well."

"I know, sweetie," Elsa said with a sad drop to her voice. "It'll be different without the bond of mistress and pet."

"There is a bond as bloodmother and blooddaughter," Jackie said. "It is different, but we're still bound to you for all eternity."

"We can sort this out on the train," Elsa said. "Amber made the arrangements already and our boat is leaving Calais tonight. We're catching the train in ten-minutes. Laura will meet us at the station."

"We're not making that by running," Shauna said. "So you plan on flying to the train station?"

"Now that Jackie and Jonnie can, yes," Elsa said. An impish grin crossed her face when she said, "Ironic how Tom's no longer dead-weight."

"Too soon, Elsa," Shauna said.

"I know, lover," Elsa replied. "That doesn't make it less ironic."

.

CHAPTER 14

Laura had only brought a small suitcase from the hotel. She'd had the rest delivered to her new bar. Without an adequate selection to change clothes, Shauna allowed Elsa to introduce her to a new kind of shopping. It involved walking the aisles of the train and finding someone of a similar build and then convincing or coercing them to exchange clothes.

Shauna worried needlessly about how Elsa would dress the twins identically until she found them wearing transit police uniforms. They'd removed the badges and other insignia. Shauna wound up dressed in a business suit and Elsa found a punk girl to trade with.

They arrived at the docks and looked around for the Megalodon, a private boat Amber had arranged. It took Shauna several minutes of trying to see around a pair of huge container ships to realize that one of those was the Megalodon.

As they were walking toward the ramp, Shauna noticed a woman in a dark green suit and skirt standing at the bottom, talking with a man, who by his uniform, was the captain of the ship. As she got closer, she noticed the woman was Artemis.

"Miss McAllister," Artemis said. "I was just confirming our contract with Captain Mical. He says he runs a tight ship and doesn't need a team of ergonomics consultants, but I coerced him into a bet. If you can find two dozen processes to improve on his ship, he won't notice what happens to container JHRR 006686 when he gets to Miami. It'll be left in the wrong place, where an opportunistic person might drive off with the brand new Italian sports car inside."

"Can we count losing track of containers?" Shauna asked, playing along with the Council vamps game.

"Not that one," Captain Mical said. "It won't go missing until after you've won the bet. It's not unusual, however, to lose a container to rough seas. Happens once or twice a year."

"What do we owe if we don't find enough things wrong?" Shauna asked.

"Then our service will be without charge," Artemis said.

"Seems unfair," Shauna said. "When I'm driving away from Miami with the top down, I'll try not to be laughing too hard."

The captain snorted and started up the ramp. "We weigh anchor in forty minutes. You should be settled and ready to watch my well oiled machine by then. Liam, my Boatswain, will show you the mercenaries quarters. Since we're not running up the West African Coast, we don't need gunmen on this trip. You got lucky, otherwise you'd be riding in a container."

After the captain was out of hearing distance, Artemis said, "You're riding in a container."

"What?" Shauna asked. She looked to Elsa to see her reaction, but her friend was just staring at Artemis with a furrowed brow.

"The mercenary quarters have windows and don't have the kind of curtains you'd trust to keep your skin from bursting into flame," Artemis said. "That container in the corner up there has some coffins and a battery powered light. It's not perfect, but it's a good place to spend your days."

"How did you find us here?" Shauna asked.

"I didn't," Artemis replied. "I followed your trail back to a house in the Philadelphia suburbs. It took a few calls to convince her that I was trustable. Perhaps she needed confirmation from James or Reilla. But, she came around."

"Okay, you're good," Shauna admitted.

"I have a team of forensic hackers," Artemis said. "I can find anyone. Anyway, I'm here to give you this." She pulled a bracelet from her wrist and handed it to Shauna. It was just like the one Zylpha and the rest of the council wore.

"Does this mean you want me on the council?" Shauna asked. "Is this Mascare's?"

"You're on the council," Artemis said. "And no, we found a Medici suitable to lead the Mascare line. This is from one of the lines that Vlad wiped out."

"That's where I know you," Elsa said.

"Forgive me," Artemis said. "I haven't been introduced. I am Artemis."

"I guessed," Elsa said. "Only the last time I saw you, you were dressed as a man and put a sword through my bloodfather's neck. I thought I killed you."

"I had hoped you wouldn't recognize me," Artemis said. "I am sorry for what had to be done two centuries ago. As I said, Vlad had a hobby of wiping out whole lineages of vampires. He'd been harassing my line in particular once he discovered how to steal a purer vampires Venae. Three of my line were killed over the years, all of them were purer than the council, but my line is small and always purer than the council, except Thalia, who is on par with them, so she represents us."

"And how do I hide my purity?" Shauna asked. "I've already coerced the council once. Do I just keep doing so?"

"I've taken care of it." Artemis said. "They are coerced to perceive your aura as if you were a founding member of the council. But, they've met in person three times in six centuries. I suspect your secret is safe enough."

"Is Artemis coming with us?" Laura asked.

"No," Artemis said. "I have seventy-seven more names on my list, so I need to be on my way. Good journey to you." She flew up into the sky.

§

The ride Amber had arranged was a shipping container with five steel coffins and a low wattage shop light connected to a car battery. Shauna was disappointed that they wouldn't be able to take a luxury cruise without the harassment of Vladimir, the King of the Sea. Laura was even less pleased with the travel arrangements.

"This won't do," Laura said.

"We don't stay in the container the whole trip," Elsa said. "The captain believes that we're a team of ergonomics consultants looking for ways to improve comfort and efficiency on the ship. We have free reign here."

"But no food," Laura said then asked, "There are, what, eight, maybe ten men on board?"

"Twenty six," Elsa said. "If we're responsible," She paused to look hard at Laura, "we'll be fine. We're at sea for nine days before they make port in Miami."

"I don't kill everyone I feed on," Laura said.

"How many have you killed since the last one you let live?" Elsa asked.

"That's not a fair question," Laura said. "I fed on all of those hunters who hadn't died instantly from their wounds."

"Other than those?" Elsa asked.

Laura looked at her sister. Shauna could see shame on her sister's face.

"You've never let your prey live?" Shauna asked.

"I think there's some. Well, I let Tom live," Laura said. "When we, you know, I would drink from him. That counts, right?"

"Not so much," Shauna said. "You can't murder people for a little bit of pleasure."

"It's not a little bit," Laura said. "It's like an orgasm that takes hours to subside. And is it really wrong for a wolf to kill a rabbit?"

"This isn't a food chain," Shauna said. "We're more like remoras feeding on a shark."

"Except I'm a goddess among mortals," Laura said. "We have so much power, and we aren't the first vampires to see themselves as gods. Artemis was a goddess and she killed at her whim."

"I don't mean to interject," Jonnie said. "Artemis killed for revenge when men attempted to take her against her will."

Shauna opted not to counter Jonnie's argument and remind Laura of Artemis's planned murder spree. Laura threw Jonnie a sharp glance then turned back to Shauna. "I don't have to live under human morality anymore. Nowhere in the laws of vampires does it forbid me from killing people. They are my prey and I am just a predator."

"You're not a wolf chasing a rabbit," Shauna said. "You're a child suckling at your mother's teat and then thrusting a knife through her heart. No matter how much power you think you have, you're still murdering a person, ending a life and ruining the lives of their families."

"I..." Laura stared at Shauna a moment and then phased through the floor of the cargo container.

"You can't go to her right now," Jackie said.

"I don't know," Shauna said.

"She's rationalizing and she knows it," Jackie said. "She's been to rehab; she knows what addiction does to the mind. Right now she's going somewhere to think and that might be fruitful."

"Or she's going to look for a lone crewman," Shauna said.

"Then we continue the intervention the next time she comes back," Jackie said.

"I feel like I should be chasing her, keeping her from harming another person," Shauna said. "But, I'm not. I'm just sitting here, hoping. Does that make me any less of a monster?"

"It makes you her family," Jackie said. "She's family to all of us, and it's human to accept flaws, even horrible flaws, in our family that we wouldn't tolerate in a stranger or even a friend."

"So, letting my sister be a monster is human of me?" Shauna said.

"And stupid," Elsa said. "I normally would sit by and watch, and I don't stand on any moral high ground, but your sister will need to be dealt with soon. Ships like this don't carry spare crewmen. If she eats the wrong person the boat has a very good chance of not making it to the destination until they can fly in a replacement."

"And, Elsa doesn't kill unless she has to," Jackie said. "She won't admit it, but she's seen enough killing in her life."

"I don't kill innocents," Elsa said. "I'm okay with killing murderers like the hunters and the vampires who support them."

"Speaking of, do we know any more from that wannabe king?" Shauna asked.

"Jean-slash-Napoleon was working with Henry," Elsa said. "I got a text from Milady DeWinter earlier. He's confessed to an arrangement where they work together to identify the purer vampires and Napoleon would be allowed to take over Europe."

"Napoleon is a fool," Shauna said. "When the purer vamps are gone, Napoleon will be next on Henry's list."

"Napoleon was a fool," Elsa said, holding up the thread she'd been wearing around her neck. The teeth were gone.

"But we knew he'd been working for the hunters," Shauna said. "What benefit does a confession give us other than to ease the guilt of killing him?"

"I also learned where Henry went," Elsa said. "Bucharest."

"What's in Bucharest?" Shauna asked.

"Nothing," Elsa said. "But about two hours drive into the mountains to the north will bring them to my bloodfather's castle."

"Dracula's castle?" Shauna asked. "You think he went to Peonari Citadel?"

"It's too much of a coincidence to not," Elsa said.

"You don't think Vlad Dracula has anything to do with this?" Shauna asked.

"I saw him die," Elsa said. "I was there when the hunters cut off his head and I watched him turn to dust."

"Why didn't the hunters kill you?" Shauna asked.

"Because I killed them first, or so I thought until an hour ago." Elsa said. "Vlad was overconfident and wouldn't believe the hunters could actually harm him. I had never been struck by a weapon, so I didn't know if I could be hurt or not and didn't want to find out. Come to think of it, I still don't know."

Jackie held up Zahaira's sword. "We can find out."

Shauna said, "Vlad's obsidian spearhead is among the stuff Laura brought from the hotel."

Elsa looked at the single suitcase Laura had brought and said, "Let's start with the sword."

Jackie stepped up and held the sword in front of her as if offering it to her maker, but Elsa just ran her thumb along the blade. She then held her thumb up to Shauna. "It cuts me," Elsa said. "I guess I'm not in your purity class."

"Jonnie, do you remember the binary theory on the stone?" Shauna asked. Of the twins, Jonnie was the most studious. Perhaps she knew math as well as she knew history.

"No," Jonnie said. "There's a binary theory?"

"Artemis says the Council thought that stone in the Blood Temple read purity in binary, but when they tested the theory, a blood parent and their offspring would rate more than one apart." Shauna said. "Do you remember the lights?"

"Yes," Jackie said. "Elsa lit five, you lit four."

"Do you remember the pattern?" Shauna said. "Do you know binary well enough to translate it?"

Jonnie nodded. "Well, assuming the number read from the bottom up, Elsa would be," Jonnie paused for a moment. "Thirty-one."

"And me?" Shauna asked.

Jackie nodded. "Eighty-six."

"Yeah, binary doesn't make sense with those numbers," Shauna said. "I just don't think there are that many generations of vampires between us."

"It does work," Jonnie said. "You're thinking backwards. If it measured generation, the numbers would start low and go up. You'd be a lower number than Elsa. But if they measured purity, the numbers would increase from Elsa to Shauna, and who is to say the variance has to be linear?"

"The Council had surmised it was," Shauna said.

"They were wrong, which is why their theory failed. But, I think there's got to be some kind of constant involved," Jonnie said. She took out her phone and started tapping the screen.

"I can't believe we're trying to make a science out of vampirism," Shauna said.

"Magic is only science we haven't learned yet," Elsa said.

"Maybe magic is just magic," Shauna said. It was certainly easier to think of things like phasing through walls as magic, but she was curious, occasionally, how it worked. It went against everything she believed to consider magic a possibility, but she'd seen too much that was too far outside of the scientific world as she knew it.

"And it's that kind of thinking that's kept the elders from figuring out what the stone is telling us," Elsa said then asked, "Weren't you going after Laura?"

"I was?" Shauna asked.

"You were," Elsa said. "Remember, crewmen are a limited resource."

"Am I going alone?" Shauna asked.

"I'm with you," Jackie said.

"I'm not," Elsa said. "Your sister brought one suitcase stuffed with souvenirs and weapons. She was kind enough to have the rest shipped to the bar, but the bar is not on this boat. That means I need to find a container of designer clothing and figure out a way to sort through it. There is no way in hell I am wearing the thirty-years-out-of-style-punk outfit for nine days.

§

They found Laura on the bridge; she stood in the corner with a clipboard, drawing pictures of cats and kittens, when Shauna found her. "So far, so good," Laura said to her. "The captain is right. The processes here are already pretty efficient."

Jackie looked around the room and said, "I think you two have this. I'm going up to the deck to take notes."

That Laura was in the open, not in danger of harming someone, meant Shauna didn't need backup. Shauna nodded then turned back to Laura. "Have you had dinner?" she asked, trying and nearly succeeding, to not sound accusatory.

"The mess is on self-serve chips and sandwiches until breakfast," Laura said. "But, you'll be happy to know I'll be on a diet for the voyage. I get seasick from too much food."

"Good point," Shauna said, though she was unsure exactly what Laura was getting at. She hoped her sister was trying to say she wouldn't kill anyone on the ship.

"There's ginger in the mess," the captain said. "Brew it into a tea and it'll keep the motion sickness at bay."

"Good to know," Laura said. "I think I'll try to stick to my diet, though."

The captain shrugged and walked over to stand by the pilot.

After a few minutes, they were out at sea and the captain sent half of the crew off the bridge. "You see, we are already perfect," he said to Shauna.

"Nearly so," Shauna said. "I noticed a couple things I'll need to discuss with my colleagues. We'll have notes for you at the end of the trip." She hadn't actually been paying any attention to the crew, but she'd already decided they were going to lose the bet with the captain.

"I'm going to go type these up," Laura said, tapping her clipboard. "See if you can get a ship's schedule and maybe some of their existing process documentation."

"Sure thing," Shauna said as her sister left. She then turned to the Captain and said, "You heard her. What have you got for me?"

The captain stepped to a wall and gestured to a bulletin board. "Some of what you're looking for is here. The rest, you'll find in the mess."

Shauna took pictures of a few documents and thanked the captain. "I'll go check out the mess," Shauna said.

"Eat whatever you like," the captain said. "We don't skimp on food on my ship. A fed crew is a happy crew."

"I like that," Shauna said and pretended to type it into her phone as she walked off the bridge.

She wandered the passageways of the ship for a few minutes, looking for clues that would lead to the mess or the mercenary quarters when she heard a man moan from under the stairwell.

"Laura," she said, teeth clenched as she rounded the bottom of the stairs.

Her sister was straddling a man who was lying on the ground. She had her face buried against his neck as she moved her hips up and down.

"Stop, sis," Shauna said. "No feeding."

Laura sat up and turned, glaring at her sister. She licked a drop of blood off her lips and then said, "Just this last one, I promise. Now, go away."

"I can't do that," Shauna said. "I'm stopping you, here and now."

"I just need five seconds," Laura said. "I'm so close."

"I'll tear you off him if I have to," Shauna said.

"No, you won't, sis," Laura said. She then leaned back into the man's neck.

As Shauna reached to grab her sister's shoulder and pull her away, she felt the man's death like a chill through her body. Her sister clearly felt it differently. Laura barely contained a long squeal.

That her sister would continue to do that, right in front of her face disturbed Shauna so much that she couldn't contain her anger. She grabbed her sister and threw her against the wall. But her sister phased in mid-air and passed through the wall. Shauna followed. Laura stood on the other side, standing between two huge engines. Her stance said she was ready to fight.

"You can't take me, Shauna."

"You'd kill me, too?" Shauna asked.

"Just let me go my own way," Laura said. "We don't have to fight, but you know I'll kick your ass if we do."

Shauna reached out with her Venae and telekinetically grabbed her sister. Laura flicked her wrists and Shauna felt her mental grip fall away.

"I've just fed, sis," Laura said. "I may be less pure than you, but my tank is full. You're probably still running on a few drops from Jackie a week or two ago."

That sounded accurate. Shauna hadn't really fed since the girl in the graveyard. It still felt too intimate to her and certainly felt intimate to those she'd coerced to feel her bite as pleasure.

"I don't care," Shauna said. "I have to try." She leapt at her sister, at full vamp speed, bowling Laura along the metal gridiron floor.

Her sister grappled her when she hit, forcing the roll to end with Laura on top. She grabbed Shauna by the throat and squeezed. Shauna felt fingernails dig into her neck.

"I won't kill you, sis," Laura said. "But I'll make you bleed so much you won't be able to follow me."

Shauna tried to push her sister off, using both her physical strength and her telekinesis. Laura fought back and squeezed harder at Shauna's throat.

The pain of Laura's nails tearing into her skin scared her. She wasn't sure Laura had the control to stop before killing her. Shauna saw a fire axe on a wall and changed tactics. Rather than using her telekinesis on her sister, she grabbed the axe and struck her sister in the back of the head.

The axe didn't do more than surprise her sister, but that was all Shauna needed to phase out just a little. Rather than pull away from her sister, Shauna thrust her hand into her sisters chest and then phased back in while gripping Laura's heart.

"You bitch," Laura said. She started to phase, but Shauna matched her and squeezed Laura's heart just enough to stop it from beating.

"You win, sis," Laura said. "Kill me or let me go my way. I don't think you have the guts to kill me."

"Is that what you want, Laura?" Shauna used her telekinesis to stand them both up, but kept squeezing.

Laura bared her fangs at Shauna and growled.

"Stop it," Shauna said. "Just stop." She'd have to hold on for a while to prevent the next heartbeat. When that happened, her sister would start to lose consciousness. She hoped to break through to Laura before then.

Pressing her own hand against Shauna's chest, Laura's nails started to dig in. Shauna tightened her grip until her sister cried in pain. It was all she could do to not let go at that moment.

Her sister pulled her hand away. Laura's shoulders dropped. She bowed her head and said, calmly, "I don't want to kill, I don't have a choice. Do it. Kill me. I'm a monster."

"You're my sister," Shauna said, loosening her grip, but keeping her fingers wrapped around the heart. "We're going to the cabin. I'm going to help you. If you run, run forever. I can only help you if you stay and you don't want to be a monster."

"I don't," Laura said. "I just think I can't change who I am."

"Then let me change you," Shauna said. "Or at least let me change your mind so you can change yourself."

"Fine, sis," Laura said. "Can I have my heart back now?"

Shauna pulled her hand from her sister's chest. The hole closed as she pulled out. "I'm going to clean up your mess," Shauna said. "Don't go anywhere but the mercenary cabin."

Laura nodded and floated up, through the ceiling.

Shauna went back to the stairwell and grabbed the body. Being dead, there was nothing she could do to heal the fang marks. She had to give Laura credit; she had only made two holes and hadn't let any blood drip to the floor.

She phased and dropped through the floor, continuing to do so until she hit water. Thinking the body might float, she pressed a finger between the man's ribs on each side, puncturing his lungs. After squeezing the air out, she released the body. She said a prayer, invoking no god in particular; she wasn't sure the ones she'd heard of would listen to a vampire. She then returned to the ship.

§

Once in the mercenary quarters, Laura sat on one of the bunks and said, "I've thought about what you were saying. You're right, we all know it."

"But are you ready to fight your addiction?" Shauna asked.

"I'm really trying," Laura said. "But, when I start to feed, I can't stop."

"Why are you feeding at all?" Shauna asked. "I can count on one hand the number of times I've fed in the last two months. You can't need to as often as you do."

"I don't know how long I can go," Laura said. "I've never gone even just two days without feeding."

"Are you saying that you've killed more than forty people?" Shauna asked.

"If you count the hunters?" Laura asked, then said "Yeah."

"Laura, I'm going to have to try to stop you," Shauna said. "I don't know how I'm going to do it. I can't coerce you."

"Kill me," Laura said. "I should be dead anyway. Twice even. You saved me from death twice but I don't deserve to be alive or undead or whatever we are."

"We're alive," Shauna said. "We have a pulse; that makes us alive. And I'm not going to change that for you. I'm not even sure I could kill you. Hurt you, yeah, I probably could if you weren't the better fighter."

"You'll have to stay with me," Laura said. "I mean all the time. I need a baby-sitter. Someone to stop me if I lose control."

"I'm sure Elsa and the twins are game for that," Shauna said.

Elsa burst through the door, with Jonnie close behind. "Tell them what you did," Elsa said.

"What did Jonnie do?" Jackie asked, walking into the room. She looked at Shauna and said, "I couldn't help but overhear. We'll help."

"Right," Elsa said, excitedly. "We will, but this is more important. Tell them Jonnie."

"I found the constant," Jonnie said, holding up her phone, showing the screen to Shauna. It was just a spreadsheet with lists of numbers.

"Um, okay," Shauna said.

"It's seven," Jonnie said. She was gleaming with pride.

"Seven what?" Shauna asked, still not sure what Jonnie was trying to say.

"Percent," Jonnie said. "I used the assumption that Reilla is the first, James is her bloodson and you are James' blooddaughter. The trick was to find the pattern that hit all the numbers we know of. Only seven worked."

Shauna was starting to understand. "So the stones measured a percent of purity compared to Reilla?" she asked.

"Right!" Jonnie said. "Every vampire is seven percent less pure than their sire. That's what made it tricky. It's not multiples of seven, but a relative percent."

"How pure is Artemis?" Elsa asked.

"Not as pure as me," Shauna said. "But she says she lights up the top gemstone."

"Which makes her a sixty-four," Jonnie said. "If Reilla is the base and James is the first generation removed and

Shauna is the second. Following the trend we find Artemis at the sixth generation removed."

"What are we talking about?" Laura asked.

"Jonnie's trying to decipher the stone from the Blood Temple." Shauna said.

"I'm not trying," Jonnie said. "I did it."

"And I am?" Elsa asked.

"According to your Venae, you're sixteen generations removed from Reilla." Jonnie said. "The founders of the council are twenty-two generations removed. We talked to Lucy to find out her light pattern and extrapolated from there."

Elsa said, "I always thought I'd be the same as Lucy; she's twenty-three removed. I know there were nineteen gradations of vamps less pure than the council, so at forty-one removed, we get the thinbloods."

"Five percent of Reilla's Venae," Jonnie said. "It sounds pathetic when we put numbers to it. The difference between generations gets smaller with each passing, but there were a lot of generations, forty-two, counting Reilla."

"All this math is giving me a headache," Laura said. "I understand it all, but I wish I didn't. Could we do something else, like play poker for the rights to sleep with that first mate? He's hot."

"We're babysitting you," Shauna said. "I'm not about to have a threesome with you and any guy or any one, period."

"Then I guess I'll have to take Jonnie along," Laura said. "I think I saw a deck of cards on the shelves over there. What do you say, Jonnie."

"I'm up for it," Jonnie said. "But why me?"

"Because Elsa is selfish in bed and I'm not getting between Shauna and her girlfriend."

"She's not..." Shauna started, but, noticing Jackie watching her closely, couldn't finish. "Fine," Shauna said. "Jackie is my girlfriend."

Jackie leapt into a hug with Shauna.

"Aww," Elsa said. "But where does that leave me?" she asked coyly.

Shauna looked at Jackie and nodded. She knew they both knew how to answer that, so they both replied, in harmony, "Besties with benefits."

"Ditto," Jonnie said.

"Hey," Laura said. "I'm just a sister and a friend, and let's leave it at that. Now, do we need to play cards or can Jonnie and I go track down the first mate?"

"Not today," Shauna said. "You're still coming down from your last snack."

Laura looked at Shauna and sat on a bunk. "This is gonna suck. I'm so bored."

Jonnie asked, "So tomorrow night then?"

"Tomorrow morning?" Laura asked hopefully while looking at her sister.

"Don't push it," Shauna said, putting her fingers to her temple as if she had a headache. She'd welcome the pain to think about anything but her sister's monstrosity. "Please, sis." Remembering Jonnie had done so much work and research into Venae, she turned to the twin and said, "Jonnie, would you like to elaborate on your discovery?"

"You should have killed me," Laura said and flopped back onto the bunk as Jonnie started to go into the detailed math of her spreadsheet.

CHAPTER 15

The movement had stopped. Shauna lay alone in one of the coffins, as Amber had requested they do as they approached the docks in the late morning of the ninth day at sea. Elsa, the twins and her sister were in the other coffins. Since then, the container was moved several times and then the coffins carried out of the container.

Shauna heard a loud cracking sound and then Elsa screaming. Shauna lifted the lid of her coffin, but seeing blue sky, dropped it again. Elsa's scream had only been a brief yelp. She must've seen the sky and taken cover.

A second crack and Jonnie screamed, again a brief yelp. Concerned Jackie would be next, Shauna gathered her courage. She wondered how long she could tolerate sunlight and if it would be enough to stop whatever was happening to her companions.

She closed her eyes and put her hands against the lid. She took a deep breath, mostly just to delay the necessary inevitability. Mid-inhale, the top flew off her coffin with a loud crack. Standing over her was a man in Bermuda shorts and straw hat smiling at her. Behind him was the sun, beating down on her, basking her in warmth.

She sat up, hoping to grab the lid and pull it back over her. The coffins were lined up on a beach and three of the lids were dozens of yards away, down by the water. Shauna closed her eyes and shielded her face from the sun. It was then she noticed the pale pink aura around the man standing over her.

He wasn't burning from the sun. Neither was she. It just felt warm on her skin, not unlike it had when she was human.

"My name is Xander," he said. "Welcome to Casa de Reilla. Are you Shauna or Laura?"

"I'm Shauna," she said. "How'd you know?"

"Countess Bathory and her twins would need to hide from the sun," he said. "You and your sister wouldn't."

"What?" Shauna asked.

"You'll want sunscreen," Xander said. "You'll tan and sunburn faster than you did as a human, but that's the worst of it for you."

Shauna stood tentatively. The other two open coffins were empty. "Elsa?" Shauna asked.

"Hiding under the sand with the white haired vamp," Xander said. "I wasn't expecting you to all be vampires. Amber only mentioned Elsa and your sister in addition to you. The white haired girls were supposed to be pets. I'll let you open the other two."

When he said Amber's name, he gestured to three women and a man lying in lounge chairs under an umbrella that wasn't big enough to shade them all. The four wore bathing suits without tops. One woman and the man had vampiric auras of dark red. Another woman had a white aura Shauna had not seen before. The last woman, the one without an aura, was Amber. Not having seen her sire in a bathing suit, or even imagined him in one, it took her a moment to realize the man, who was raising a wine glass to her, was James.

THE BLOODDAUGHTER TRILOGY
BOOK III: BLOOD REPRISAL

CHAPTER 1

The moonlight reflecting on the waves beyond the silhouettes of the palm trees seemed more sublime than the last time she'd walked in the sand. That had been a different path along a different beach, but there was nothing that stood out as particularly different between the beach from her memories and the beach she walked along that night. Shauna wasn't sure if it was love or her recently acquired vampiric senses that made the beach so much more beautiful.

Jackie walked at Shauna's side, holding her head against Shauna's arm as if the whole point of the excursion had been to enjoy the view and the company. Shauna gave Jackie's hand a little squeeze. Through weeks filled with life and death situations, Jackie had stayed focused on making sure Shauna felt appreciated and loved. Neither of them was willing to broach the change in dynamic that would come now that both of them were vampires.

With a vampire and a human pet, there could be a symbiosis. The pet provided nutrition to the vampire and the vampire provided immortality to the pet. Though Shauna had been a vampire for two months, Jackie was just into her second week as a vampire after two centuries as Elsa's pet.

Walking to Shauna's left, Elsa, her best friend and mentor, seemed more focused on the night's mission. "No one has to know," Elsa said. "I don't even have to do anything to help. I could just be a distraction."

"Reilla said I have to go in alone," Shauna said. "A lone vampire seems like easy prey. Three of us would instigate their retreat. If the hunters wait to fight another day, we have to wait, too. I think she means this as a test. She thinks I rely too much on my companions to really be useful."

Reilla hadn't said as much. In five days since they'd arrived on the beach, Reilla had been a perfect host. She had a nice big house with plenty of rooms without windows and she had different guests each night to provide a few ounces of fresh blood each day. She'd chat on just about any subject, cheerfully. However, much to Elsa's frustration, Reilla would always defer discussions of vampire history to another time, even going so far as to interrupt Mala or Xander if Elsa got them to start talking.

When Reilla mentioned she wanted Shauna to deal with a minor hunter problem she was having, Shauna leapt at the chance. She wanted the opportunity to endear herself to Reilla because, not only was Reilla the first and most powerful vampire in the world, she was her sire's mother. Reilla had born James as a human and when she became a vampire, she'd made James one as well.

"You rely on us?" Elsa said. "That's funny."

Shauna did rely on Elsa's guidance, but in a fight, it was Shauna that saw the more intense action. As a much purer vampire, Shauna was immeasurably stronger and nearly impossible to hurt.

They passed a rocky hill and their destination came into view. Abutting right up to the hill, La Fontana was the local watering hole. Like the walk along the beach, it looked familiar.

Eight summers earlier, she and her sister had visited their parents somewhere in the Florida Keys. Their mom and dad had abruptly up and moved as soon as Laura and Shauna had graduated high school. She knew how to get to her parent's trailer park from the mainland, but Shauna didn't really know where Reilla's home was in the Keys. She'd thought about figuring out where she was in relation to her parents but the thought of them noticing something had changed about her scared her. She couldn't fathom a way to explain to her parents how vampires were real things and that she was one. Any scenario she tried to run through in her head didn't go well and a few ended with one or both of her parents just keeling over from heart attacks. Since her parents weren't even fifty, she doubted that would happen, but the idea kept her from finding a way to visit them.

The bar looked familiar, but it looked like any beach bar from any movie she'd seen as well. When she was nineteen, she hadn't visited any of the bars near her parent's RV park. She'd barely given any of them a second glance back then.

"This is Reilla's bar?" Elsa asked.

"La Fontana," Shauna said. "Yep, this is the one."

"And her pet is the bartender?" Elsa asked, though she'd heard Reilla explain it all earlier and she knew the bartenders included not only Reilla's pet, but Mala's and Xander's as well.

"You know that," Shauna said.

"She's not getting it," Jackie said and reached over and tickled Shauna's side. "That's the Fountain of Youth."

Shauna sighed. "I should have realized vampires weren't the only myths that weren't actually myths."

"I think the fountain Ponce was looking for is a myth," Elsa said. "But, if you find a water hole surrounded by people who don't age, how would it look to you?"

"Now I get it," Shauna said. "You really think she's been here that long? Wasn't Ponce deLeon before your time? Don't tell me you knew him."

"Only from history books," Elsa said. She put a hand on Shauna's shoulder and stopped walking. "This is as close as Jackie and I should get. We'll hear you if you call for help."

They were just a few yards from the edge of the bar's parking lot. Shauna nodded. She gave Jackie a kiss and said, "See you in a few."

"Where's my kiss?" Elsa asked. She puckered her lips and made kissy noises.

Shauna smiled and let out a little chuckle. "If there's thank-the-gods-we're-alive-after-battle-sex, we might invite you." She turned and walked to the bar.

"If I help with the fight, I don't need an invitation," Elsa called after her.

The bar was touristier than Shauna expected. She'd thought it was just a bar for locals, but the first counter she passed after coming through the front door sold souvenirs. Elsa had been right, or so the souvenirs led Shauna to believe. Most of them said, "I drank at the Fountain of Youth."

The tables were mostly full, so Shauna took a seat at the bar. The bartender, Reilla's pet Miguel, slid a large glass mug in front of her. It had a picture of the bar on it on one side and on the other it said, "I drank my fill from the Fountain of Youth. La Fontana, Florida."

"Twenty five bucks," Miguel said.

"For a cup?" Shauna asked.

"The fountain is in the cave," Miguel said, pointing to a stone archway at the end of the bar. "It's free refills as long as you're not driving anywhere."

"Fine," Shauna said and pulled her credit card from her phone case and plopped it on the bar.

"Like I'd actually charge you," Miguel said as he slid her card back across the bar. Shauna hadn't been sure if he would or not. He'd been nice enough around the house, always making sure she knew which guests hadn't been fed from yet, but he wasn't the type to engage in a conversation with her. "You're early, you know. They don't start until nine."

"They have a schedule?" Shauna asked.

Miguel looked at her, clearly puzzled. He asked, "Why did Reilla say you should come here?"

"She said you have a hunter problem," Shauna said. "It seems everyone has a hunter problem these days."

"Oh," Miguel said. "If you're looking for a hunter, that guy in the back corner has been drinking diet soda all night, no fun juice. He's gone through three plates of nachos, which wouldn't be odd at all if this were a sports bar, but we're not. He's also been examining anyone that doesn't order food or eat the peanuts and pretzels."

"Oh?" Shauna asked.

"We get hunters all the time," Miguel said. "I know where there's a cove frequented by a couple dozen tiger sharks. Most hunters end up going for a swim there. You should go fill your glass. Not eating is suspicious. Not drinking and not eating is a 'stake me' sign."

Since becoming a vampire, Shauna could only drink translucent, or nearly translucent, liquids. She didn't gain nourishment from them, but they would pass through. Alcohol would have a similar, if weaker, effect than it had on mortals and it also helped thin the blood in her system, helping her go longer between feeding.

"What's in the fountain?" Shauna asked.

"Orange wine," Miguel said. "Blood oranges, so it's redder than you'd expect. Fill the glass from the tap in the fountain, not from the wine running through the fountain. We used to just let people fill from the fountain, but the health inspectors made us stop."

"Got it," Shauna said. She tried not to look at the hunter as she walked to the cave. When she caught herself glancing his way, she shifted her gaze to a table with three men drinking from mugs and eating pretzels. One of those men winked at her. She winked back.

The fountain was a series of pools in the exposed rock of the hill. They were filled with bubbling dark red, sweet smelling wine. Shauna could barely hear the purr of a pump behind the rocks. Most humans would only hear the bubbling liquid flowing from one pool to the next. A single tap jutted from the stone. Shauna put her mug under it and pulled the lever. The wine that filled the glass did smell much fresher and more alcoholic.

She gave it a taste. It was tarter than she expected, and the flavor was unusual for wine, but she liked it. She went back out to the bar and sat on a stool. Miguel smiled at her, but didn't come back over to talk.

She took a sip of the wine, angling her glass so that the hunter and only the hunter could see her fangs as she drank.

Her eyes stayed away from the hunter, and she continued to flirt with the table of three men.

After several minutes of fleeting eye contact and smiles, one of the three men stood and started walking towards her. Shauna took a deep breath and concentrated on raising her body temperature. She didn't want to feel clammy if he touched her. Before he got close enough to exchange words, the hunter took the seat beside Shauna and leaned close and whispered in her ear, with a Russian accent, "You're the most beautiful vampire I've seen on this side of the ocean."

The man she'd been flirting with changed course and headed towards the restrooms.

Shauna pondered playing coy and acting like the guy was insane, but she figured she wouldn't be fooling him after he'd seen her fangs. But, then she realized not playing coy might show she knew what he was. "Vampires?" she said. "I think the blood orange wine is messing with your brain. I am flattered you think I'm beautiful." Elsa had dressed her in a black string bikini and a pale blue gauze tied-on skirt that night. Her hair was tied in low pigtails. Shauna tried not to look in the mirror. She assumed a bar run by vampires wouldn't be using real silver backed mirrors, so she'd have a reflection and she didn't want to see how far her brown roots had grown out. She hadn't had time to refresh the blood red dye she'd been using for most of the past year.

"Come, now," the hunter said. "I saw your teeth. You should try harder to keep your lips closed when you drink. I didn't realize you were a young vampire."

"And you're not afraid of me?" Shauna asked.

"It's a fetish of mine," the hunter said. "I like to be bitten."

For a moment, Shauna wondered if he was a hunter at all. Perhaps he was a normal human who'd somehow learned of the existence of vampires and sought them for pleasure. Then she took special note of the way he was dressed. Even in February, that night the temperature was somewhere in the mid seventies. He wore jeans and boots to a beach bar and had a leather vest over a plaid shirt. He'd fit in better in a country bar. She glanced at the mirror behind the bar, checking for a gun tucked into the small of the hunter's back. There wasn't a gun, but there was something hidden under the back of his vest.

"You've done this before?" Shauna asked. "Picking up vampires, offering your blood just so they'll bite you?"

"No," the hunter said. "I was a pet for a few years, but my mistress weaned me so she could choose another."

His story was plausible, almost. A vampire wouldn't leave a human knowing vampires exist. The laws of the vampires would have them coerce the human to forget or kill them.

Shauna pulled her phone out and checked the time. Still ten minutes to nine. She hadn't established what happened at nine that she was supposed to be there for if it wasn't the arrival of the hunter.

"I don't ask for anything other than a bite," the hunter said. "We can make it quick if you're waiting for someone. There's a poorly lit nook against the hill here. A short nip and you'll be back here in no time."

The hunter was trying too hard to rush the deal. Shauna had dealt with several truly amateur hunters who'd come woefully unprepared for the reality of vampires. She expected this one would be no different. He might have wooden stakes or a gun with silver bullets; either would be harmless to her. At least he didn't reek of garlic.

"I could use a top-off," Shauna said. She took the hunter's hand and led him out of the bar. Miguel watched her leave with a concerned wrinkle between his eyes, but he said nothing.

Outside, Shauna saw the dark recess in the hill and tugged the hunter along. In truth, she needed to top-off. Shauna hadn't fed more than a sip or two at a time since she'd met a young girl in a graveyard in Philly a few weeks earlier. That girl, Azure, had been looking for a vampire as well, though she didn't really believe in them. When she and

Shauna parted, despite the torn and bloody shirt, Azure still didn't believe in vampires.

Shauna would drink the hunter dry, she decided. If he wasn't a hunter, she'd let him live, but he'd forget anything he knew of vampires. The first thing she had to do was figure out what he was hiding under his vest.

A few steps before they reached the shadows, the hunter's grip on her hand tightened and she felt immense pain tear through her back and into her heart. She screamed and fell to the ground. The hunter stood over her with a bloodied white bladed knife with a golden hilt. The gold wouldn't matter, but the blade had to be made from the bone of a potent vampire. It was the only material Shauna knew of that could hurt her.

She tried to roll away but the man stabbed her again. This time the knife pierced her belly, feeling like fire. He twisted the blade and she screamed again.

A popping sound came from behind the man and he stopped, letting go of the knife and clutching his chest. He fell to the side. Elsa stood behind him, holding a small gun with a silencer on the barrel. She shot the fallen man several more times. Shauna felt a chill, which she knew was the man dying.

"It's just a 20 caliber," Elsa said. "It sometimes takes more than one bullet to be sure." She squeezed at least half a dozen more shots into the man's body before the gun just clicked.

"Shauna!" Jackie said, kneeling by her. She pulled the knife from Shauna's stomach and handed it to Elsa.

"Same stuff as the arrow that dropped James," Elsa said. "A bone dagger with exposed marrow. This isn't going to be fun for you, my love."

Much of the pain had subsided, but the world around her seemed to be spinning as if she'd had more than just one mug of wine.

"Shauna?" a man's voice called. It was a familiar voice. It was her father's voice, not her bloodfather, James, but her natural human father. Shauna couldn't comprehend how he was there. "Shauna! What happened here?" She saw her dad come and kneel beside her, but her vision was blurring.

Shauna tried to speak, but could only grunt in pain.

"Don't strain yourself," her dad said. "We'll get you to Reilla. You'll be fine." He started to reach under her, but Elsa pulled him back.

"Who are you?" Elsa asked.

The man stood and held a hand out to Elsa, "I'm Roger McAllister. I'm Shauna's dad."

"Is he?" Elsa asked Shauna. Shauna nodded.

Her dad knelt again and picked her up. "You still have your head, that's the only thing that matters." He knew she was a vampire.

Shauna's mind reeled. She'd never told him. Heck, other than a twenty second phone call on Christmas, she hadn't spoken to him since she'd changed. She couldn't imagine how he could know. She tried to look up at him and smile, but her vision was nearly gone. She could barely make out the shape of his head. She could see Elsa and Jackie only by the pale pink of their vampiric auras, but she could see the aura's even without blinking. Another vampire was coming up from the bar. Before they got close, Shauna fell unconscious.

CHAPTER 2

"Baby?" her mother's voice called.

Shauna opened her eyes to find Jackie embracing her. They were lying on her bed at Reilla's home. Kneeling by the bed, Shauna's mother smiled at her. "Hi, baby girl."

Shauna blinked, adjusting to the light. Her mother radiated a pale pink vampiric aura. "You're…" Shauna tried to speak but could only get the one word out before feeling completely exhausted.

"Yes, I'm Xander's blooddaughter," Shauna's mother said. "I have been since before you graduated high school."

Shauna tried to ask how, but didn't have the energy to inhale. She didn't need air to live, but she couldn't speak without it.

Her mother explained anyway. "It was late April, your senior year. Your father and I took a vacation while the rates were low, before summer break hit. We were walking on the beach one night and, out of nowhere, one of those four wheeled ATV things came over a dune and crashed right into me.

"Xander had been driving it. He'd broken several of my ribs, maybe all of them," Shauna's mom said. "I was going to die; it was obvious. So, he gave me a one-in-a-million shot to live and fed me his blood. Maybe it was luck, maybe there's something in our blood that makes us resilient to the poison of vampiric blood, but I was one of the lucky ones that survived the change.

Shauna couldn't believe her mother had been a vampire for so many years and never told her. But a vampire couldn't tell a mortal, so said the five laws.

"Your father is my pet," Shauna's mother said. "He didn't like getting older when I wasn't aging anymore. We were planning on coming up to visit you once we heard about you and Laura's change, but you've been busy."

"You knew?" Shauna squeaked. The exertion of speaking was too much for her. Darkness overcame her again.

§

She awoke again, lying on a lounge chair on the beach. The Sun was directly overhead.

"You're healing," James said. "Lucky you were here when you were infected with the marrow."

"Oh?" Shauna asked. She felt fine, mostly. She could breathe in and out and even sit up without feeling tired.

"My mother," James said, speaking of Reilla. "She is more of an expert on harming vampires than she ever let on, even to me. It seems she and my bloodsister spent years fighting each other. She knows the bone marrow weapon trick. The cure is sunlight."

Shauna looked up and down the beach. James' pet Amber was paddling a surf board around out on the small waves, but Shauna didn't recognize any of the other hundreds of people on the beach. She still wasn't used to the idea of sunbathing. Once she became a vampire, she figured she'd never again feel sunlight without burning. But, being so pure of Venae, the stuff that made vampires, she healed faster than sunlight burned. Even her sister, Laura, as Shauna's blooddaughter, could spend an hour or two in bright sunlight and only get a nasty sunburn. Shauna would get a tan, albeit one that would fade in a few days.

"As long as you heal faster than the marrow inside you, the sunlight will purify you," James said. "If the marrow inside you were more pure, the prognosis would be less sunny. You'd have to consume all of the blood of the vampire whose marrow it is and then kill them. Odds are that much vampire blood would kill you, too."

"How many vampires are there purer than me?" Shauna asked.

"Elsa's asked that a dozen times in half as many days," James said.

Shauna exasperated. "And every time you avoid the answer, just like you're doing now.

"Keeping our secrets is second nature to me," James said. "I shouldn't feel the need to keep secrets from my blooddaughter. There are three vampires in all the world purer than you: Reilla, myself and my bloodsister, Una. But Una might not still be alive. Mala can't see her anymore."

James' other blooddaughter, Mala, had the ability to sense the location of every other vampire in the world, with a very few exceptions. The current bloodline of Artemis didn't show up to Mala's sense. That there could be others wouldn't surprise Shauna.

"And there are two as pure as me?" Shauna asked. Mala would be the other.

"Yes," James said. "And two of Laura's purity that we know of. She and Xander, but we suspect the bones of the weapons come from a vampire of that purity as well. A vampire Mala cannot see. If that vampire exists, at least one more of your purity could exist." Vampire bones, like every other part of a vampire, would disintegrate if the vampire died, even if they were removed from their body beforehand. The vampire whose bone acted as the dagger's blade was still alive, or undead, somewhere.

"Right below Xander, there's only my mom," Shauna said, extrapolating James' vampire family tree. "I'm starting to doubt anything that's happened to me was by chance."

"No one planned on you becoming a vampire," James said.

"But, you weren't just bumping into me, either," Shauna said. "You were babysitting for my mom."

"A crude description, but essentially, yes," James said. "I met your mother for the first time two weeks ago. Before that, since I was already living near you, I took on a favor for Xander. When your mother moved here, I spent less time travelling and more time in the city keeping an eye on you and Laura. You were much easier to keep track of. Laura was determined to embrace her addictions. I removed at least a dozen heroin dealers from Philadelphia, and she somehow kept finding more. Addiction is so ingrained in Laura's personality; I couldn't even coerce her to remain clean. I almost turned your sister three times from her overdoses, but she never hit cardiac arrest."

"But, I wasn't long for the world without my throat," Shauna said, recalling the night Allison had slit her throat and left her for dead.

"You're still here, now," James said. "That's what is important."

"I can't help but feel lied to," Shauna said, "manipulated even. To think, I thought you were romantically drawn to me." Shauna laughed. "That's what's pathetic." She'd wondered why a man, clearly from a wealthier class than her, took such an interest in a lowly book store assistant manager.

"From the moment your mother became one of us, she was family to me. That makes you family, so romance was never a potential for us," James said.

"You were always my fairy godfather, and nothing more," Shauna summed up the conversation.

"You could see it that way, if it helps you," James said. "I just see you as family and I don't really have gradients. Either you're part of my family or you're not."

"I guess I can see that," Shauna said, accepting she would never truly understand the world the same as a vampire who was thousands of years old until she, herself, was a several-thousands-year-old vampire. "I'm just not sure which relationships in my life are real and which are an illusion."

"All of your relationships that I know of are real," James said. "Elsa, as far as I know, doesn't keep secrets from you. Her past is only shrouded because you won't ask her directly. You could, you know. And Jackie sees you like you're the sun of her universe."

"Neither would know I exist if I…you…" the train of thought couldn't finish. While James's interest in Shauna had heightened Elsa's awareness of Shauna, it was a connection

Shauna and Jackie had made online that initially drew Elsa to Shauna. That connection had nothing to do with James.

"Elsa's going to hate me for being able to sunbathe," Shauna said.

"Elsa gets motivated, she doesn't get jealous," James said. "I think she may find ways to use your ability to walk in daylight to fit her needs. She might even come up with new needs just to take advantage of your abilities."

"If she gets motivated, don't you worry she will follow Vlad's lead and try to eat an elder vampire? She might just eat you," Shauna said. "I don't think she'd eat me or my sister unless she had no other options." Vlad had discovered a way to steal a purer vampire's Venae; his method killed his victim. Though no one but Vlad knew exactly how the process worked.

"Assuming she learns of it, she wouldn't risk it," James said. "The process is just like the one to turn a human into a vampire except the purer vampire must be drained completely. The vampire stealing the potency will be poisoned and will die. If they wake again, they are as pure as the vampire they consumed. The odds are that they will stay dead."

Shauna stared at James, looking for empty wine bottles around him. He'd just revealed a secret she thought he wouldn't want shared. And he knew she had difficulties keeping secrets from Elsa. She wouldn't volunteer the information to Elsa, but if Elsa asked, Shauna wouldn't dodge answering.

"Dear girl, you look shocked," James said. "It doesn't take rocket science to put two and two together to figure out how it works. Vlad wasn't trying to figure out how; he was trying to figure out how to do it without risking permanent death."

Shauna ventured, "Wouldn't it be the same as making a pet more acclimated to vampire blood. Jackie and Jonnie could both be turned by Elsa because they spent two centuries sipping her blood. If I'd tried to turn them, they'd be dead. I got lucky with Laura."

James turned and stared at the ocean. "To answer your first question, yes, spending a year or so adapting your body to an elder vampire's blood will reduce or remove the risk of permanent death when you, as you said, eat them. It's unlikely an elder vampire would dole out daily doses knowing you intend to kill them in a year or so."

"Vlad kept them prisoner," Shauna said.

"So we assume," James said. "As to your sister's and your survival, it involved luck, but not as much as you'd think. I knew your mother survived the change, and your father survived being made into a pet. Some genetic make-ups are more resilient and you and your sister come from resilient parents."

"Tell me you haven't been controlling human breeding to make susceptible future vamps," Shauna said.

"That would assume our goal is to make more vampires of our purity," James said. "The truth is we spent a long time purging the world of vampires near our purity mostly because they sought to rid the world of vampires purer than they. Why would we want to make more?"

"You tell me," Shauna said. "I used to think it was because you had a crush on me, but now I think it was because you are family with my mother."

"You know the answer, why ask the question?" James said.

"Maybe I want to hear you say it," Shauna said.

"I made you one of us because I love you," James said. "For almost a decade, you've been a great-grand-daughter to me. Of course, it was because you are family."

"I'm a little heartbroken," Shauna said in jest. For the most part, it felt like a jest. She did feel a little sadness that her illusion of attraction had been popped.

"You have two lovers," James said. "Or is it three?"

"Technically, it's three, I guess," Shauna said. Though she shared a room with Jackie, Elsa joined them some nights and when Elsa came, she brought Jonnie, Jackie's twin. "Only Jackie is romantic," Shauna clarified. "Elsa is an opportunistic hedonist with our friendship and Jonnie is attached to both Elsa and Jackie."

"Is she well enough to walk?" Reilla called as she approached from the house. Like James, Reilla had black hair, dark brown eyes and skin that looked like a deep tan, and would even if she didn't spend her days sunbathing.

"I am," Shauna answered.

"You should both come inside," Reilla said. "We need to talk." She turned and went back to the house.

§

Reilla led them upstairs to a conservatory overlooking the ocean. The room was long with a wall of rose tinted windows and an arched ceiling of the same glass. Jackie, Jonnie and Elsa were lying on lounge chairs in bikinis, basking in the pale pink sunlight.

"How?" Shauna asked.

"Gold infused glass," Elsa said. "Ironic, isn't it? The stuff that's most deadly to us can render sunlight harmless. I'm using this trick when I build my new palace." Gold would make a weapon able to harm vampires of Elsa's purity, but wasn't enough to make a weapon effective against Shauna.

"We're here," James said. "Why?"

Reilla stepped to the end of the room and looked back at everyone who was there. Shauna's mother and Amber sat at a checkerboard at the other end of the room.

"Mala and Xander are not coming," Reilla said. "They've taken Laura to Miami to work on her feeding habits. Roger and the other pets are at La Fontana, tending the bar."

"Does this have something to do with the hunter that tried to kill me?" Shauna asked.

"I didn't send you to find a hunter," Reilla said. "You may have figured by now that it was just a ruse to get you to bump into your parents. They were being stubborn about coming to talk to you at the house, and I was tired of keeping someone else's secrets. The hunter surprised us all."

"Miguel said that hunters were not uncommon," Shauna said.

"We get two or three a year," Reilla said. "Always amateurs. We also get a few dozen who think they've found a fountain that will actually give them eternal youth. Both of these groups are little more than annoyances. This hunter had this." She held up the knife that had stabbed Shauna. "This is the first time I've seen a hunter so prepared in my bar."

"The same stuff that brought me down," James said.

"Yes," Reilla said. "I tried to stay out of this. I have done my share of battle in my time and thought I'd reached the end of my wars." She stepped over to the window and went silent a moment. After a deep breath, Reilla repeated, "I am determined to have reached the end of my wars. I will not be fighting again. However, they came to my bar and I can't have that. I need to know who they are."

"Bertellus," Shauna said. "We're pretty sure the vampire's name is Bertellus." It had been Henry's angel's name, and the only angel she'd met from Henry's group had been a vampire in white robes.

"I don't know who that is," Reilla said. "Mala cannot see him and she can see every vampire, everywhere."

"Except Artemis and Una," James said, "and their progeny."

"So Bertellus comes from Una, and recently," Reilla said.

"Could you clarify what you mean by 'recently'?" Elsa asked. "It's a bit subjective to someone who is ten thousand years old."

Reilla looked at Elsa a moment before answering. "Mala hasn't been able to track Una for two thousand years. That's when she learned the trick from Artemis to lose the aura. When that happened, Mala could no longer see her. Una's bloodchildren from after that time also do not have the aura, and thus Mala cannot see them, either."

"Do we even know Una is still alive?" James asked.

"No," Reilla said. "But this vampire must have come from her bloodline, unless Mala or Shauna made a child we don't know of."

"I only made Laura," Shauna said.

"Mala made no one other than Xander and Dun and we know for certain Dun died," Reilla said. "I can perceive the precise purity of Venae of the vampire this came from. They are of the same purity as Xander or Laura. This means it was the progeny of a child of Una."

"And the vampire whose bone that is may have killed Una," Shauna said.

"I tried for fifteen thousand years to kill Una," Reilla said. "The only thing that hurt her was my body, my teeth, my fingernails. Not even the obsidian that can cut my skin will harm her. I've never been determined enough to make a weapon from my own bones. Even if this dagger could have killed her, if I couldn't do it, I won't believe anyone else did."

"Una is opening old wounds?" James asked. "Perhaps her desire for revenge is boiling over again."

"After twenty millennia?" Reilla asked. "I can't see her going back to that."

"Wait!" Elsa said. "The two of you stopped a fifteen thousand year feud twenty thousand years ago?"

James covered his eyes with his hand and shook his head. "I hadn't told them so much of our history," he said.

"I know. I have been avoiding exposing our past to the daughter of Vlad." Reilla said, watching Elsa as if she were assessing something within her. She then turned to Shauna and gave her the same long look. "Either we trust them or we kill them. I know why you trust Shauna but I've never been sure why you trust Elsa. Still, if you do, I will."

James looked at Elsa for a moment; a gentle smile spread across his lips before he glanced at Shauna. He said, "I know them. We can trust them both."

"I don't think Emily and Roger would forgive me for killing their daughters," Reilla said. "I only killed one of Una's children and look how long she fought me."

"There's a story here," Elsa said.

"One we don't have time to tell," James said. "But, as my mother said, we've decided to trust you instead of kill you, so I will tell you the story later."

"Now, you need to find Una and Bertellus," Reilla said.

"You didn't say 'we need'," Shauna said. "You were serious about not fighting anymore."

"I was serious," Reilla said. "But, I will fight if my family is threatened by Una."

"Here, I'm hoping you see family the same way James does," Shauna said.

"My son and his children and their children and so forth," Reilla said.

"Bloodchildren?" Shauna asked.

"My mother doesn't differentiate," James said. "My mother's mortal descendants ended with me. I did not have any children as a human and my mother bore no other children."

"So, we're going to find Una and Bertellus and then call in Reilla to kick their asses?" Elsa asked.

"Exactly," Reilla said. "You and Shauna will return to Europe and find where Bertellus is hiding. James will be tracking down Una. I'll be honest with you now; if Una is not involved, I will not be aiding you. James should be sufficient to handle a handful of rogue young vampires of any purity."

"So, Shauna and Elsa, just find Bertellus," James said. "We already know Bertellus has the means to kill us. We want the upper hand when we fight him, so we'll have numbers and a plan and we'll all be there when we engage in battle."

"And Una?" Shauna asked.

"If Una has resumed her feud with my mother, we'll need more than a good plan and numbers," James said. "Right now, I'm debating which religion to take up so I can pray that isn't the case. We all inherit our powers differently. Una seems to have resilience beyond that of any other vampire."

"Reilla said the obsidian that would harm her wouldn't hurt Una," Elsa said.

"Syrian obsidian didn't hurt me," Shauna said, recalling shattering a Syrian obsidian weapon against her chest.

"You told me of the fight in the temple," James said. "I've had to think about that. Zylpha's weapon wasn't the right kind of obsidian. Perhaps it was newer than the weapons that will harm us."

"We never tried Vlad's spear," Elsa said. They'd taken a spearhead from one of Dracula's other descendants during their last trip to Europe. "I'll be right back." Her body faded a little and she fell through the floor of the conservatory. Elsa could phase through walls as naturally as most people could open doors. Shauna had gotten pretty quick with it, but she had to concentrate to do it.

"You brought the spear here?" Reilla asked, her voice uncharacteristically tense.

"You know it?" Shauna asked.

"If it's truly the spear of Vlad Dracula, I do," Reilla said. "James took great care to rid the world of all the obsidian that could harm us, but a few shards fell through his fingers. That spear was one of them."

Elsa glided up through the floor and phased back so that she was solid again. She handed a black spearhead to Reilla. Reilla took it, handing the bone dagger she'd been holding to James.

"Watching you phase is displeasing," Reilla said. "I'm always jealous to see James' descendants do that. I don't have that particular ability. It started with James. Watching you do that just reminds us that your bloodfather, who is not descended from James, learned to steal the Venae of other vampires."

"I am not responsible for my bloodfather's actions," Elsa said. "I gave you the spearhead; if you didn't already agree to trust me, that gift should ensure that you do."

Reilla pricked her finger with the spear, drawing a drop of dark blood. "I agree," she said. She picked up a beach towel and wiped the blade clean and held it towards Shauna. "Show me if you are resilient to this."

Shauna pressed her fingertip to the blade's end and it cut her.

"Now that you know," Reilla said, "You will be more careful when you see obsidian. Don't assume it's all newer than this shard." She handed the blade to Shauna. "I believe this was yours."

Elsa had given her the blade two weeks earlier. Shauna had kept it locked in her suitcase, though the lock clearly didn't keep Elsa out. She wasn't sure what she would do with it or why Reilla had entrusted her with a weapon that could hurt her. It seemed that once Reilla trusted someone, her trust was boundless.

James held out the bone dagger that the hunter had used to stab Shauna and said, "Tap this with the obsidian."

Shauna did, nicking the bone. Shauna held the blade gingerly and set it on a table by the door.

"Now we know the weapon will be useful if you find Bertellus," James said. "But, remember, you are just finding him. I will come when it is time to fight him."

"Please tell me we're taking the cruise ship back to Europe," Shauna said. "I don't want to sail on a container ship again, ever."

"James will be using the family jet," Reilla said. "There are just too many possibilities for where Una could be. That leaves you with the yacht, Shauna."

"I like yachts," Elsa said. "I keep meaning to get one."

"I'm surprised you don't have a private jet," Shauna said.

"I had one," Elsa said. "I didn't use it enough to make keeping it a sensible expense. Getting clearances and filing flight plans through all the airports is tedious and they don't make one that can cross the Atlantic with enough time to spare to guarantee avoiding sunlight getting on or off the plane."

"Maybe I should get one," Shauna pondered.

"Sweetie, you're rich," Elsa said. "You're not that rich."

Elsa had forged paperwork designating Shauna as the lone heir to a fortune worth something around ten million dollars. Shauna didn't like that the money was stolen, though, without her claim, the money would have just stayed in the trust and never gone to anyone. She spent the money, and only begrudgingly, because it was the only money she had.

"Are you that rich?" Shauna asked. Elsa had lost much of the holdings attributed to her current name, Elsabet Davlos, when hunters destroyed her apartment tower in November.

"No one is as rich as Elsa," James said. "I don't think she knows the exact amount of her holdings under her various aliases."

"I do," Jonnie said. She pulled up her phone and tapped the screen a few times and held it up. A cell from a spreadsheet was enlarged and highlighted. Shauna couldn't count the commas in the number at a glance.

"That's a joke," James said.

Jonnie shook her head.

"I didn't realize," Elsa said. "Why don't I have more stuff?"

"What don't you have that you ever wanted?" Jonnie asked.

"A yacht," Elsa said. "Right now, I want a yacht."

Jonnie nodded and rolled her eyes. "And if you still want one tomorrow, we'll make an appointment with a yacht builder. I assume you'll want it custom made."

"Of course," Elsa said.

CHAPTER 3

The windows of Reilla's yacht were made of the same rosy glass as Reilla's conservatory. Still, Shauna spent a couple hours each day sunning on the foredeck. She used the excuse that she still needed to purify from the dagger attack, but she'd healed from that before they'd left Reilla's island. She really just needed time to herself.

Since Jackie became a vampire, she'd gotten clingy. When she was Elsa's pet, Jackie came and went during the day and was content with the time they spent in bed. As a vampire, Jackie had developed insecurities about the relationship. The only time she wasn't at Shauna's side was in sunlight.

Shauna glanced in the window, expecting to see Jackie and Elsa staring back at her, but they were sitting on the couch with Jonnie. All three had crew members kneeling by them, rubbing their feet. Shauna considered joining them, but she was never relaxed in letting humans serve her like she was their master.

It was Reilla's boat, and there were two massage therapists on the crew. The girl rubbing Elsa's feet wasn't actually part of the crew but one of four models Reilla hired under the guise of a pan-European photo shoot. The photographer and the other models were probably on the aft deck.

Elsa finally glanced up at Shauna and raised a glass of wine to her. It wasn't helping the relationship with Jackie that Elsa was also always at Shauna's side. There was no question that Elsa was Shauna's best friend. The roles blurred since Elsa frequently shared their bed.

As a pet, Jackie had a clearer role as a lover. Shauna had learned to feed a little while their passions were aflame. Being charged with emotion made blood more potent. Without the feeding, Jackie had wondered aloud on more than one occasion, what made her special to Shauna.

Shauna had tried to explain that the differences were all in the emotions she felt. Sex with Elsa was hedonistic. Sex with Jackie was bonding. That Shauna rarely used the word 'love' probably wasn't helping. She loved both Jackie and Elsa. She even loved Jonnie, but she wasn't sure she was in love with any of them. When she thought too much on it, she couldn't help but wonder why she was sleeping with women at all. Until she'd met Elsa on the night she became a vampire, Shauna had never even considered taking anyone other than a man to bed.

Elsa and Jackie had taught her, convincingly, that Vampires didn't have the hormones to drive sexual attraction. As a vampire, sex was for pleasure and not a primal drive. Elsa's sex drive still seemed primal, judging solely by the amount of time she spent in a bed with the twins or Shauna or anyone she met.

Shauna realized she'd been so focused on her thoughts that she hadn't noticed Jackie standing at the window, pressing her lips against the glass. Sauna smiled and blew a kiss back. She wished she could define the relationship with Jackie better in a way that would make her lover happy and secure.

The photographer, Karlo, came up to the foredeck with two models. He leaned close and played with their hair a moment while talking to them about how beautiful they were and how they should catch the breeze with their hair. He had an accent Shauna couldn't place. It sounded almost Italian at times, but other times it sounded Greek and some of his words had a strong Russian flavor.

It didn't help that he referred to himself in third person as if he were an all important world-class photographer and not just a guy who'd answered an online ad looking for a photographer willing to travel on very short notice. Karlo wasn't a complete amateur; he did have several expensive looking cameras.

The models removed their bathing suits and crawled all the way to the prow of the yacht and began posing like cats in a sunbeam with one occasionally stalking the other. All Shauna could think about was how the models were amateurs compared to Jackie and Jonnie's shows. But the twin's shows were meant to be far more provocative.

Karlo was there to make the models feel they had a reason to be there beyond the real reason Reilla had hired them. She didn't want Shauna and her friends feeding on the crew.

The models stopped posing but Shauna still heard the camera clicks. She turned to see Karlo staring at her down his camera lens. She smiled and shook her hair into the wind, trying to look half as good as one of the models. Then she remembered she was also naked and she grabbed her towel off the deck and covered herself as she ran inside.

Sailing across the middle of the Atlantic Ocean meant she could sunbathe without risking other boats passing by. Reilla had told her the crew was used to such things, so she actually felt she'd draw more of their attention if she insisted on sunbathing in a bikini. She wasn't prepared to be immortalized on film.

"I can't believe that asshole," Shauna said, closing the door behind her.

Elsa and the twins peeked over from behind the couch. All three were glaring. Shauna had rushed so mindlessly into the sitting room, she hadn't thought to give the vampires inside enough time to hide from the sunlight that peeked through when Shauna opened the door. None of them looked even the slightest bit singed. Vampires could move extremely fast. Elsa and the twins could move two or three times as fast as a human and Shauna was more than twice as fast as Elsa. Still, she felt sheepish for not knocking first.

"Karlo is sweet," Jackie said. "He treats the models like they are works of art. When he touches them to help them pose it's like a harpist playing a lullaby."

"He's harmless," Elsa said.

"I'm pretty sure he's slept with all the models and half the crew in the three days since we left Reilla's." Shauna said.

"And me," Jonnie piped in, raising her hand.

"Yes, I was there, too," Elsa said, shrugging. "He seemed like a very giving lover."

Shauna looked to Jackie, but her girlfriend shook her head. "I was with you when they were playing with him. I thought we had an understanding: no other lovers without both of us present."

Shauna hadn't thought of it that way, but circumstances had not broken that rule since they'd met. She liked Jackie's understanding. They both would feed far more efficiently if they could drink from a sexual partner. If their prey were experiencing any emotion with a physiological effect, it added potency to their blood. "That's true," Shauna said, confirming Jackie's rule.

"Really?" Jackie asked. "I wasn't sure you felt the same. I was afraid to ask."

"You're my girlfriend," Shauna said. "We established that. Being a vampire won't change how I feel about you. We do both need to feed and we can't feed from each other. Why waste blood."

"So I can invite Karlo to our cabin tonight?" Jackie asked eagerly.

Shauna had to think about it a moment. She hadn't fed at all since they'd left Reilla's. "Sure," she said. It was still too intimate an act for Shauna to comfortably share with a stranger. In more than two months as a vampire, there had only been one stranger Shauna had been able to drink more than few drops from. She thought back to the blue haired girl in the old Philadelphia graveyard, Azure.

A smile swept across Shauna's face. Azure had been a perfect example of why Shauna didn't feed from strangers. It had been a very intimate moment for her and part of her longed to find Azure again. It was exactly the emotion Shauna wanted to avoid with her food. To be a proper vampire, she had to learn to feed without attachment.

§

Karlo leaned in for one last kiss as Shauna ushered him out the door. Shauna dodged the kiss. "Playtime is over, boy-toy," she said and closed the door behind him.

"I need a shower," Shauna said. As a vampire, she didn't sweat much, but Karlo did. Shauna also had blood on her chin and chest. However hard she tried, when she drank blood, it leaked past her lips. Jackie had blood on her as well, just not as much.

"You and me, too," Jackie said. She stood from the bed and wrapped a sheet around her and Shauna. "One of the showers better be open." The guests on the yacht shared two bathrooms and had to leave their cabins to get to them.

Together they slipped into the hall and into one of the bathrooms. Jackie started the shower while Shauna checked how bad she actually looked in the mirror. She was a mess. To make things worse, her hair had three solid inches of brown hair at the roots.

"When we get to Europe, remind me to get my hair colored again," Shauna said.

"I already set an alarm on your phone," Jackie said. "I love you, but I can't be seen hanging on the arm of a girl with such long roots showing." She kissed Shauna's nose, assuring her the words were only teasing.

They got into the shower and Jackie started her routine of washing Shauna.

"You know, I can wash myself," Shauna said. "You're not a pet anymore."

"As if you're the only one who gets anything from this," Jackie said. "I do what I do because I like to touch you. It's so much more fun now that I don't have the boundaries we used to. If you feel guilty, you could try returning the attention."

Shauna was fully aware of the imbalance in their relationship where showing affection was concerned. Jackie never brought it up until that moment. "Then I will," Shauna said. She took the soap from Jackie's hands and started soaping her lover up. Unlike how Jackie started at the hands and feet and teased her way in, Shauna started with Jackie's chest.

They wound up spending most of the rest of the night in the shower together and Shauna wasn't sure they ever managed to get completely clean. She had trouble admitting it, even to herself, but being with women seemed far simpler than being with men. When she was with Karlo, it reminded her she reacted more intensely to them, but there was something about women she found more relaxing, especially in the afterglow.

"We could keep him," Jackie said.

"What?" Shauna asked.

"We need pets," Jackie said. "We could do worse."

Anytime Shauna thought of taking a pet, she remembered watching a vampire, Charlie, die when she killed his pet. She hadn't harmed Charlie; it was only the bond between him and his pet that killed him when Shauna exacted her revenge on Charlie's pet, Allison. Shauna had Laura as a pet for a few days and still remembered the stress when Laura was dying and the fear she'd die too.

"I don't know," Shauna said. "I am still not convinced having a pet is worth the risk."

"Right, you had to deal with Laura and her train wreck of a life," Jackie said.

"She was a victim," Shauna said defensively. "They hurt her to hurt me. That's exactly why I don't want a pet."

"You don't feed from strangers," Jackie said. "You couldn't stand up to your sister on the last trip because you're nearly starving yourself."

"I drank from Karlo," Shauna said.

"Maybe half a cup," Jackie said. "Admittedly, he was already running low from the night with Elsa and Jonnie, but you need to drink more. You need a pet more than anyone."

"I don't want a pet," Shauna said.

"I do," Jackie said. "I want Karlo as a pet."

"You like him?" Shauna asked. "I mean he was good but he's a womanizer, a male slut."

"I detest him," Jackie said. "But, he's a perfect pet. He's doting and giving and avoids attachment. The attachment thing, he won't be able to avoid with the blood dependence, but I won't feel guilty making him serve me or making him serve us."

"I envisioned a pet relationship like the one you and Elsa had, one of mutual adoration," Shauna said. "I don't need a pet for that, I have you for that."

"You can't feed on me anymore," Jackie said. "While lovers make some of the best pets, and most pets are, at least occasionally, lovers, there is something to be said of having someone you can treat like a," she paused and smirked, "like a pet."

Shauna said, "Like I said, if I had a pet, I'd want the relationship you had with Elsa. I can't treat a human being like a house pet."

"Can I?" Jackie asked.

"You're asking my permission?" Shauna said. Since they were playing house together, it made sense that any decision that affected their shared space, literally or emotionally, should be made together.

"You'll have to trust me that I know how," Jackie said. "Elsa has kept toys around besides Jonnie and me. They weren't pets, but we, and they, had fun pretending."

Shauna considered Jackie's proposition. That she'd use Karlo as a lover was a given, but Shauna didn't question Jackie's devotion to her. And Jackie would not just share, but insist that Shauna partook of the pleasure and the blood. The downside was that Jackie could be killed by someone killing her pet.

They were already putting themselves in danger. She'd come to terms with the possibilities of her lovers dying over a week earlier. Her terms were that she'd likely go insane, but she accepted that. Pets were hard to kill. She'd seen how severe Jonnie had been wounded by Henry. He'd disemboweled her. Jonnie didn't technically survive, but she came very close. She's seen pets survive being shot several times and walk away after only a few minutes of recovery. Knowing there was danger ahead meant they could take precautions and keep the pet in a safe place.

"Well?" Jackie asked. "Am I asking too much, too soon?"

"No, love," Shauna said. "I agree with you."

"Can I make him stop talking funny?" Jackie asked. "Or do you like his pseudo accent?"

"You think it's fake?" Shauna asked. It made sense; she hadn't managed to place it yet.

"I've seen three dollar bills that were more real," Jackie said. "Okay, that's true. Back in the mid-nineteenth century, there really were three dollar bills. Most people forget they were real, well, almost real. Money was a bit fuzzier of a concept back then."

"Huh?" Shauna asked.

"Not all money was printed by the government back then. Some money was printed by banks and other big companies. For a while it was as useful as the government notes, but then something happened and they stopped using them. Jonnie would be able to tell you more."

"I don't know that I'm terribly curious about three dollar bills," Shauna said. "So, if Karlo's accent isn't real, where's he from?"

"Maybe the suburbs of Pittsburgh?" Jackie ventured. "He hasn't slipped out of it much, but there's no accent in the entire world with all the various inflections he uses. I heard him say 'worsh' instead of 'wash' once, though. That's not Russian. Remember, I am Russian. I think I'd know the accent, even one two centuries newer than mine."

"Feed him a good steak dinner, some beans and then find somewhere safe to do it," Shauna said, remembering how Laura's body strained and thrashed during the change.

Jackie said, "It's going to take most of the rest of the trip to get him used to my blood, but I don't want to go ashore without having done it. I know what he'll go through, and I know how to do it with a much lower risk."

"Of course you do," Shauna said. "I'm going to go find out what wine Elsa picked for breakfast."

"I'm right behind you," Jackie said.

§

Elsa sat alone by the front window, watching the waves and sipping from a glass of white wine. A half empty bottle of chardonnay sat on a table at her side. Shauna started across the room to join her when Jackie whispered to her, "Be careful, she only drinks white wine when she's just had an argument and I was with you. I better go find Jonnie." Jackie turned and went back downstairs.

Shauna sat in the empty chair across the table. "Are we sharing?" Shauna asked. There wasn't another glass.

"Sweetie," Elsa said, though her voice was less confident than usual, "We share everything."

"Jackie tells me you've probably just had a spat with Jonnie," Shauna said. "Wanna talk about it?"

"I do," Elsa said.

That surprised Shauna. Elsa didn't normally discuss herself on anything but the most superficial level. "Well, let's talk and drink. I assume someone will be coming with more wine." Reilla's crew had been efficient at making sure there was always a freshly opened bottle whenever one came in danger of being empty.

"Jonnie is feeling like a third wheel," Elsa said. "She won't listen to me when I assure her that she is welcome at my side, always."

"Did you say it like that?" Shauna asked.

"Almost exactly," Elsa said.

"I can see her problem," Shauna said. "You made her feel welcome when she needs to feel wanted. Right now, you're doting on me. Jackie is doting on me. Jonnie and I, we're opposite corners of a love square."

"But our square has bisecting lines," Elsa said. "Jackie and I still have our connection and you have a connection to Jonnie, don't you?"

Shauna did, but it wasn't something she had words for. "We talk, we play, but I'm your bestie and Jackie's girlfriend. To Jonnie, I'm her sister's girlfriend and a rival for your attention. To Jonnie, I'm like the new baby sister, the one who gets all of mom's attention. She loves me like family but realizes there's less love for her."

"That's so untrue," Elsa said. "You get me, right?"

Shauna nodded. She thought she did. To her, Elsa was a mentor. She also knew how to live a full life, enjoying so many aspects of the world around her. And, for the most part, Elsa never cared what other people thought enough to let it affect her actions. She seemed to actually care how her actions might make Shauna feel, sometimes.

"Well, Jonnie gets me better than you do. She and Jackie may be twins, but Jonnie and I are more synchronized and symbiotic. Jonnie understands my need for wealth and how I want to use it. She understands my physical desires, though Jackie's good at that too. Jackie trusts that I am not the person I once was, just like you do. Jonnie knows me well enough that she knows with absolute certainty which direction my moral compass points."

"That's a lot of words," Shauna said. "Jonnie's only looking for one."

"Love?" Elsa said. "Love is so small a word for the huge connection between Jonnie and me."

"Did you tell her that?" Shauna said. "And don't assume because you're so in sync with her that she already knows. Even if she knows; what you just said to me, you need to say to her."

"She knows I can't imagine life without her," Elsa said.

"She does," Shauna said. "But, that doesn't change her emotional need to hear you say it."

"I suppose," Elsa said. "Maybe Jonnie and I have a few slight differences. I don't need her to say it to me if I know."

"You're just that kind of special," Shauna said. "Especially now, when I'm here messing with her status quo."

"You're staying, too," Elsa said with complete confidence. "You know, with you and Jackie together, and me and Jonnie closer than ever, the bond between Jonnie and Jackie will keep the four of us as a foursome more often than not."

"I know," Shauna said. "I'm happy with that. But in the long run, whose happiness matters more to you, mine or Jonnie's?"

"Your happiness is not my concern," Elsa said. "I mean I'll help you if you're upset, but actually taking you from neutral to happy, that's up to the choices you make."

Elsa's words seemed right; she had never done anything for Shauna other than to alter Shauna's reality to fit with what Elsa wanted it to be. Some of it made Shauna happy but much of it was just things Shauna had simply accepted, sometimes begrudgingly, about Elsa.

"And Jonnie?" Shauna said.

"I do see her happiness as a motivation," Elsa said. "Definitely a priority."

"And it doesn't hurt that you've shaped her over two centuries so that the stuff that makes you happy makes her happy," Shauna said.

"You are making some pretty big assumptions there, bud," Elsa said. "I'm not sure I like where this is leading. Remember that my favorite thing about you is how you accept me without being judgy."

"You're telling me you had nothing to do with Jonnie and Jackie being incestuous?" Shauna asked.

"I'm actually insulted," Elsa said. By her tone, Shauna knew Elsa wasn't just jesting. Elsa set her glass down and leaned across the table. "You can blame me for a lot of things. I did a lot of evil things in my time. I did not do that."

"They're naturally that way?" Shauna asked.

"It's ingrained in who they are," Elsa said. "I am just kinky enough that I didn't try to change them when I found out, though. You can think less of me for that if you like, but you've already come to terms with that so what you're about to learn will only make you think more highly of me, even if it's just a little."

"Oh?" Shauna asked.

"You know how, when I met the twins, they were Karina and Katina, and were the assistants to a Russian illusionist?" Elsa asked. When Shauna nodded, Elsa continued. "What you don't know is that he'd bought them from their parents when they were ten. He didn't engage directly in carnal activities with them until they were older, I think around fifteen. He did use them to provide visual stimulation while he stimulated himself."

"He made them have sex while he watched?" Shauna sought clarification.

"That's what I said." Elsa grabbed the bottle of wine, held it over her head, and poured it into her mouth. Somehow, perhaps Elsa used her apportation, or perhaps she was just that graceful, not a single drop spilled anywhere other than into her open lips. After she swallowed the last of the wine, Elsa said. "By the time I made them my pets, it's just what they did together, even when no one was watching. I probably could have trained them out of it, over time. But, like I said, I'm naughty enough to not want to put that much effort into it."

"I haven't tried to change them," Shauna said. She'd accepted that after two hundred years, her opinion wouldn't affect much. She'd just learned to focus her attention away from anything Jonnie and Jackie did together in bed.

"So, you can't hold their odd relationship with each other against me," Elsa said.

"I guess not," Shauna said. That Elsa had rescued the twins had always been one of Elsa's more redeeming actions. Shauna's moral compass had become so warped the night she became a vampire, she was still trying to figure out where it pointed. Once she'd committed murder, no matter how justified, it was easy to do other questionable things just by thinking it wouldn't be the worst thing she'd done. She usually tried not to allow that flawed logic to sway her, but didn't always succeed.

"You assumed I changed them to fit to my expectation," Elsa said. "The truth is we all changed a little and met somewhere in the middle. Perhaps more skewed towards my desires, but every relationship is a compromise."

"True," Shauna said. "What will you be telling Jonnie when she comes up?"

"I love her?" Elsa ventured. With Shauna urging her to keep going, Elsa did. "That love isn't really a strong enough word. That she gets me better than anyone does and that I appreciate that more than I've told her?"

"I think you'll be fine," Shauna said.

CHAPTER 4

"Did you feel that?" Jackie asked as they sat inside, watching through the rose colored glass as Karlo continued to photograph the models. Nine days on the boat had finally managed to coax some real creativity out of the photographer. He draped the models only in white sheets and had them stand in the wind. At that precise moment, Karlo stopped shooting and looked into the sitting room at Jackie.

"Feel what?" Shauna asked. The only thing she'd felt was concern that the three bottles of wine they had left wouldn't last until they were scheduled to make port that afternoon.

"I think the bond just happened," Jackie said.

"There's a feeling?" Shauna said. The only feeling she'd had when Laura had been her pet was worry for her sister.

"It's pretty much the same as I felt for Elsa when I was her pet," Jackie said. "I can sense he's there and I get twangs of his emotions. Right now, he's very proud of the pictures he's taking."

"Remind me to coerce him for you," Shauna said. On the first night he shared their bed, Jackie had coerced him that he would feel the bite of a vampire as pleasurable. Now that he was her pet, her coercion would be broken; she couldn't coerce her own pet.

"Oh, I will." Jackie looked back at where Elsa and Jonnie slept, cuddled on one of the couches. "They're getting along well."

"They always have," Jackie said. "We always have. Elsa really is the best."

"She has her qualities," Shauna said. "She's the best friend I've had."

"Ahem," Jackie said.

"Don't play that game," Shauna said. "It's apples and oranges."

"I know," Jackie said. She didn't' sound convinced.

It was going to take time to work out exactly how the relationship between the four of them really worked. Shauna wasn't entirely sure what she wanted from each of the other three women. The status quo, however precarious, seemed to be working.

"Jonnie wants a pet now," Jackie said.

"They both do," Shauna said. "Elsa is used to the convenience of a pet. Jonnie might be jealous."

"She'll never admit it," Jackie said. "I bet she'll find some boy within a week."

"Why do you think she'll pick a guy?" Shauna asked.

"Because Elsa will pick a girl," Jackie said.

"You're sure?" Shauna asked.

"Elsa doesn't do men," Jackie said. "She won't say why. She'll talk like she does men and women, but she doesn't ever do men. She likes to watch my sister and me with men, but she won't touch a naked man and woe to the man who tries to touch her."

Shauna thought back, and couldn't remember Elsa actually coming into contact with a man in bed, though she'd been in beds with both Elsa and men at the same time.

"She's had kids," Shauna said. "So she wasn't always gay, right?"

"I'm pretty sure she was, at least when she was mortal," Jackie said. "We all know the hormonal attraction just doesn't exist for vamps, so we think of ourselves as hedonists, doing whatever gives us pleasure. But, from what Elsa's told me, she's never been into men at all."

"I can hear you," Elsa said.

"And?" Shauna asked.

"And I don't like men," Elsa said. "They're dirty and they smell. There's nothing appealing about their angles either. Women are just infinitely prettier. Speaking of…" Elsa stopped to point out the window. "Could you fetch me that blonde? I'm feeling a bit thirsty. Don't linger too long in the sun. It's taken three days for your tan to fade to believable vamp skin. When we meet with Zylpha later, she'll notice if you have a tan."

Shauna's skin wasn't nearly as pale as Elsa's. Shauna, as a mortal, hadn't been able to avoid all sunlight and her skin color would never be paler than it was when she made the change into a vampire. Elsa spent the last years of her mortal life in a windowless room.

§

They docked at a moderate sized city just past the border with Greece. The vampires had to wait several hours for the sun to set. Elsa didn't seem to care; she was kept busy sorting through several chests of clothing, trying to figure out a way to carry just one wheeled trunk ashore. The plan was to leave Karlo and the models on the boat and meet up with them in Venice in five days.

Periodically, Elsa would call someone in and change their outfit. Shauna hadn't realized how much shopping Elsa had gotten done in less than a week in Miami.

Elsa, Shauna and the twins left the boat as soon as the sun set. They passed Karlo and the models, who'd spent the afternoon touring the city, as they walked down the docks.

"Bon voyage," Elsa said.

"Oh, right," Jackie said. "They're setting sail soon. I have to go with Karlo. Shauna, are you coming?"

Shauna looked at Karlo and realized the new city had more appeal. As much as Elsa tried to convince her that hedonism was more fun than intimacy, Shauna couldn't truly separate sex from intimacy and she didn't desire a closeness to Karlo. She'd already coerced him to worship Jackie and feel vampire bites as pleasurable, so Jackie didn't need her there.

"You go it alone, my love," Shauna said. "You should be alone with him at least once and since he needs an ounce or two of your blood before they set sail, now's when to do it. Have fun. I'll be okay."

"See that minaret?" Elsa said to Jackie, pointing to a pinnacle rising above the city.

"Yeah," Jackie said.

"Meet there at nine," Elsa said. She looked at Shauna and said, "You and Jonnie, too. I have someone I need to see and he doesn't like strangers."

"Okay," Shauna said, stretching it out. She wanted to know more, but Elsa didn't keep secrets without her reasons. She'd talk about it later, and surely Elsa wouldn't be so clandestine once the meeting was in the past.

"This city hasn't changed much," Elsa said. "There's a night bazaar just past the warehouses east of us."

"Night Bazaar?" Shauna asked.

"Grey market," Elsa said. "The last time I was there, it was a collective of fences and very much a black market. The market square is still there, but according to the internet, it's mostly knock-offs and stuff that's fallen off trucks, wink-wink. Oh, and don't use your credit card with any of the merchants there, stick to cash. American dollars will work just fine there."

She walked away towards a taxi stand, waving as she went. The wheels of the trunk Elsa drug behind her weren't quite reaching the ground.

"See you later," Jackie said. She kissed Shauna on the cheek. "Oops, forgot PDAs aren't quite accepted this far east."

"It's legal," Jonnie said, "just expected to be kept private."

"Good to know," Jackie said as she headed back to the yacht.

"So it's just you and me," Jonnie said.

"Shopping?" Shauna asked.

"Knock offs aren't my thing," Jonnie said. "I don't know what Elsa was thinking. I was thinking more along the lines of a bar than a bazaar."

"Works for me," Shauna said. She had never been left alone with just Jonnie, Shauna realized. "Did you top off on a model or do you want to find someone to eat?"

"I'm okay," Jonnie said. "But, if someone particularly tasty walks by, I might change my mind."

They meandered toward the grey market, hoping to find a bar on the way. They found a block of bars, restaurants and crappy looking hotels. They stopped in the middle of the street and assessed the prospects.

"That one looks like the nicest," Shauna said, pointing to the only bar with all the lights working on the sign.

"Nah, we want that one," Jonnie said and pulled Shauna along by the hand to a passageway between two bars. "I've seen two well dressed men go down this passageway. There's something interesting back here."

"Interesting sounds less fun to me," Shauna said.

"You'll thank me," Jackie said. "That bar," she pointed to the one Shauna had liked, "will have three kinds of wine, eight kinds of beer and about twenty middle-age men watching soccer. This one will have lots of older men and a handful of men under forty. These guys will buy us drinks just to talk to someone as pretty as we are."

"We have money, we don't need men to buy them for us," Shauna said.

"You don't get out enough," Jonnie said. "Elsa should have taught you better by now. You may not know it yet, but, you need the flattery of having men buy you drinks."

She pulled Shauna deep into the passage. It led to a dark room. Two large men in suits stopped them at the door. One said something Shauna didn't understand and pointed to a hand painted sign on the wall. Several languages were represented by the sign, one of them English. 'Members only," it said.

She held up two American twenty dollar bills and said. "Give us a couple cards, then."

Jonnie had used her coercion. The guards each took a twenty dollar bill and one pulled two red plastic discs and handed one to Jonnie and one to Shauna. The disc was a circle and smaller than a credit card but larger than a poker chip.

Once past the guards, Shauna got a chance to look around. There was a bar, but most of the people were gathered around several tables at the far end of the room. Some of the patrons were lounging in hookah pits. By the smell, they weren't smoking tobacco.

"Is this what you were hoping for?" Shauna asked.

"This is better," Jonnie said. "Let's hit the blackjack table."

"I would never have taken you for a gambler," Shauna said.

"Card games are not gambling," Jonnie said.

"You count cards," Shauna accused Jonnie in a whisper.

"Of course," Jonnie said. "Come on."

There weren't any stools in the area. Everyone crowded around the tables. Jonnie handed Shauna a hundred dollar bill then squeezed in by the blackjack table between two men, obviously brushing against them in ways that would make them more than willing to make room for her.

They weren't the only women gambling, but there were six men for every woman present. Not being as forward as Jonnie, Shauna went to the roulette table.

After two hours, Shauna had discovered that roulette was not gambling if she could just nudge the ball a little with her Venae. She had to keep it gentle and wasn't graceful enough to pick exact numbers, but she could handle black or red choices easy enough. She was careful to only win two out of every three spins, betting about half her chips each time.

Jonnie tapped her on the shoulder. "Take your winnings," she said. "Tuck them in your bra and get ready for the fun."

"The gambling isn't the fun?" Shauna said. She really wasn't having that much fun.

"It takes a good spotter about an hour to confirm a gambler is counting cards," Jonnie said. "A little less if they're using a partner. The spotters here weren't very good, but judging by the four men heading my way, they finally figured it out."

Shauna had too much money to stuff in her bra comfortably. When she saw the four men, and blinked, she noticed one had the pink aura of a vampire. She gave up on comfort and just jammed the money into the pockets of her slacks. It had been so long since she'd worn anything with pockets she'd almost forgotten about them.

"You have pockets," Shauna told Jonnie, noting the handful of money the twin was trying to stuff through her collar.

Jonnie stuffed what she had left in her front pockets. "Ready?" Jonnie asked.

"Are we running?" Shauna asked. "Or coercing our way out of this?"

"Neither," Jonnie said. "Just remember your strength. Don't break anyone who won't heal."

"You haven't seen enough fighting?" Shauna asked.

"Fighting? Yes, I've seen enough," Jonnie said. "This is just going to be a brawl. If someone pulls a gun, coerce the place to remember us coming to terms and leaving."

"You've never gotten to fight as a vampire," Shauna said.

"Nope," Jonnie said. "But, I'm going to want to know what I can do if, I mean when, the situation comes up."

"Fine," Shauna said. "The vamp is yours."

"There's a vamp?" Jonnie asked.

"The one with the blue tie," Shauna said as the men approached.

"Babe, you can't keep our money," the vampire among the men said.

"I won it," Jonnie said. "It's mine."

"You were counting cards," blue-tie said. "Now, you can do this the nice way or you can do this the hard way. My boys are kind of hoping for the hard way."

"You're going to have to make me," Jonnie said. She backed into a fighting stance more reminiscent of a nineteenth century pugilist than a modern boxer.

"You know how to fight, right?" Shauna asked.

"Enough to handle a bar brawl," Jonnie said.

It was more than Shauna knew. James' pet Amber had tried to teach her some basics. Shauna spread her feet to a balanced stance and brought her fists up to guard her face.

"Let's keep this civilized," Shauna said. "Pull a knife and you risk me leaving it inside your gut."

The vamp in the blue tie must have seen something more threatening about Shauna. He nodded for the largest of his companions to go after her.

Shauna dodged several clumsy punches. She even let one of the men get behind her. She sidestepped when that man tried to grapple her.

Jonnie was toying with the blue-tied vamp. She easily dodged his punches. He might have been a vampire but he wasn't a very potent vampire. Even slow to Shauna's perceptions, Jonnie was making the blue-tie vamp look like a clumsy puppy chasing a squirrel.

It was Jonnie that landed the first punch, hitting the vampire in the lower back. Vampires, other than Shauna, only saw the aura with contact. His stumbling after being hit wasn't just because of the force of Jonnie's blow.

He muttered something that Shauna assumed was a swear word in Turkish. He then drew a gun and aimed it at Jonnie.

"Stop!" Shauna shouted. The entire bar went silent. Everyone ceased whatever action they had been doing. Most of them had been either trying to get away from the fight or trying to get a better view. Everyone was staring at Shauna, but no one moved a muscle.

"Jonnie, move freely," Shauna said.

Jonnie shook her head and looked around the bar. "Holy hell," she said. "There must be a hundred people here, all doing nothing because you told them to."

"And a vampire," Shauna said. "We know I'm uber."

"Yeah, it's still impressive," Jonnie said. "Can we make them all strip?"

"Probably," Shauna said. They were all a little decadent, being in a back alley casino. Stripping probably wouldn't be outside their nature. "We won't though."

"I guess it's time to go," Jonnie said. "We're supposed to meet at the minaret in three minutes."

"Everyone," Shauna said loudly with her will. "In two minutes you'll move around again. You'll remember there was a scuffle and two women, both with black hair, fled into the marketplace. Otherwise, it was a normal night here."

Jonnie and Shauna walked quickly out of the casino, trying to not look like they were running from something. They slowed their pace once they turned the corner.

"I'll let them know we're on the way." Shauna said. She pulled out her phone and sent a text that simply said they'd be a couple minutes late and that they were walking.

She got a text back with a picture of Jackie standing by the minaret pointing to a train station. An accompanying message said, "Fly. Train leaves in three minutes."

Shauna showed Jonnie the text and said, "Let's find a dark alley." There weren't any alleys on the block they were on, so they went to the next intersection and took the side street. Seeing an alley three buildings down, Shauna grabbed Jonnie's hand and ran to it. It wasn't dark, but it was empty.

"How's your flying?" Shauna asked.

"I'm okay," Jonnie said. "I'll follow you."

Shauna envisioned her imaginary hand, the same as she did when she used telekinesis. She pushed against the ground, lifting herself into the sky. She moved as fast as she dared. From above the buildings, finding the train station was easy. The only train in the station was already moving away. Jonnie was flying next to her but the wind moving around them made it impossible to talk while they were moving. She flew over and grabbed Jonnie around the waist and said to her ear, "Think you can set down on the landing by the rear door of the train?"

"I'll just let you carry me," Jonnie said.

Shauna followed the train until it left the lights of the city and then swooped in low. Instead of using the ground to guide her landing, she used her Venae to grab the railing on the back of the train. Even with telekinesis, she couldn't put more force on the train than her mass allowed, but she could use her grip on the rail to guide them slowly to a soft landing.

"Nice job," Jonnie said. She gave Shauna a quick kiss on the lips then opened the door of the train and stepped inside.

Shauna pulled out her phone again and called Jackie. She heard Jackie's phone ring in one of the private rooms on the train before she heard Jackie answer, "Hi love, you caught the train?"

Rather than answer, Shauna went in to the private cabin. Elsa had a young woman in her lap and was drinking from her shoulder. Jackie stood up and hugged Shauna. "You mussed your hair," Jackie said.

"I learned something new about Jonnie," Shauna said.

"You didn't let her take you to a dive bar and start a brawl, did you?" Jackie asked.

"It was an underground casino," Jonnie said in mock protest. She then produced the money from her pockets and threw it up into the room.

"Elsa doesn't let her do that," Jackie said. "At least not since everyone started carrying camera phones." Shauna hadn't seen anyone with a phone out during the fight at the casino. Vampires weren't the only people who wouldn't want to be recorded in that kind of place.

"She's not my pet anymore," Elsa said. She licked the wound on the girl's shoulder, closing it, and then said, "You met a nice man and he started to seduce you, but you realized he was married and fled. It was fun. Now go."

"The only real rule for starting bar brawls is to make sure someone has your back," Jonnie said. "Elsa and Jackie don't approve."

"I'm not sure I do either," Shauna said. "But, if you need to blow some steam off once in a while, I'll have your back."

"At least someone here loves me," Jonnie said, winking at Shauna. She then plopped into the seat beside Elsa and cuddled up to her.

"Where are we going?" Shauna asked.

"This train goes to Adrianople," Elsa said. "That's where we're staying for the day tomorrow."

"Are you going to tell us who you went to see?" Shauna asked.

"An old family friend," Elsa said. "He was killed in The Long War. I don't get a lot of opportunities to put flowers on his grave, so when I get the chance, I do."

CHAPTER 5

Once they got off the train in Edirne, which was the contemporary name of Adrianople and, like Istanbul instead of Constantinople, a name Elsa wouldn't use. Elsa led them to an old mosque behind high walls. Several police stood with submachine guns, guarding the gate.

"We're closed to the public," one of the guards said in heavily accented English.

"You can tell we're American?" Elsa asked.

"I can tell you're not Turkish," the guard said. "But everyone speaks English as long as you talk loud and slow enough, right?"

Shauna laughed and the guard smiled at her.

"It's actually true," Jackie said. "Well, in Europe it's mostly true."

"Does Zylpha have a password?" Elsa asked Jonnie.

"No," Jonnie said, pointing to her phone, which she held to her ear. "I'm calling her now." She held up her finger and spoke to the phone, "Queen Zylpha, this is Jonnie, calling on behalf of Countess Bathory. We're at your gate." She paused a moment while the voice on the other end said something about waiting. Jonnie replied. "We'll be here," then pocketed her phone. She looked at Elsa and said, "She's coming to get us."

"Next time, I'm Empress Bathory," Elsa said. She had explained she would be keeping her human name for her business and personal life. Among vampires, she wanted them to know she wasn't a novice under a crown.

"I knew that," Jonnie said. "We haven't really been doing much with your new role, so it hasn't settled into my brain yet." Elsa had taken the crown of the Northern Roman Empire, a vampire kingdom encompassing most of Europe north of the Alps. Her assuming the crown hadn't been entirely intentional and they'd made some quick enemies when she did. Of those enemies, the most important hadn't survived.

Shauna heard a voice in her head and she felt a warmth in the bracelet Artemis had given her. "You can use this to talk to me," Zylpha's voice said. "It's easy enough; you just think what you want to say and who you want to say it to. You can speak to any one member of the Council or all of us at once."

Shauna had mostly forgotten about the bracelet she wore on her left arm. It was a wide band of gold around her wrist with a lattice of gold chains that connected to a pair of rings, one on her middle finger and one on her pinky.

Shauna thought, "I didn't realize it did anything. I haven't heard anyone speak to me since I joined the council three weeks ago."

"We don't talk to each other often," Zylpha said. "The silence may last decades. Though, the hunter problems have been keeping some of us in daily discussions. If you're in Europe to deal with the hunters, we'll include you in these discussions."

"Did Elsa tell you we were here to deal with hunters?" Shauna asked through the bracelet.

Zylpha's answer came to Shauna's ears as Zylpha stood on the other side of the gate and waited while one of the guards unlocked it. "Elsa tells me she is merely visiting her neighbors before settling in. I am not sure I believe her since she is starting with the farthest of her neighbors. I would have expected a stop in London or Florence before coming here."

Zylpha wore a gown of silver threaded gossamer and she wore a coif of laced silver chains in her silvery blonde hair. The guards bowed as she walked past them to stand before Elsa. Zylpha extended a hand and Elsa took it and smiled. Zylpha didn't react to Elsa's touch as she had the last time, but since then, she'd been coerced to see Elsa and Shauna's auras as less pure than hers. Shauna was relieved to see the coercion still in effect.

"I wanted to sail past the Acropolis," Elsa said. "I merely used prioritizing visiting you as the excuse."

"I wouldn't have believed you if you'd said you came here first because you liked me the most," Zylpha said. "Come inside."

As Shauna, Elsa and the twins followed through the gate, Zylpha gestured to several more heavily armed police inside the courtyard. "Don't be alarmed by the security. They won't shoot anyone in my company."

"Seems tedious," Elsa said. "You have to personally escort anyone who comes to visit?"

"My business requires the utmost security," Zylpha said. "I have a back door for my customers. But, my customers are referral only and the security on that door is even deadlier."

"What is your business?" Shauna asked.

"People," Zylpha said. "Like every business, I deal with people."

Elsa looked at Shauna and shook her head quickly.

Inside the mosque, it looked more like a cathedral, laid out like a cross. The interior was pristine, though instead of pews, there were dozens of cushy chairs and what looked like cocktail tables. Where the altar would be, there was a stage. "They aren't actually fixing anything," Shauna said. "Are they?"

"The only work done to the building is day to day maintenance," Zylpha said. "The scaffolding outside is just to deter tourists. I have guest rooms that would suit royalty. You'll be staying the day, I assume?"

"Of course," Elsa said.

"Perhaps do some shopping while you're here," Zylpha said. They walked into an apse. At the center of the apse, a stone staircase spiraled down into the floor. Zylpha led the way down. The stairs spiraled down several times. Shauna guessed they'd gone down two or three stories. "Can I assume, since you arrived by yacht, that the rumors of your poverty are exaggerated?"

Shauna didn't recall mentioning they'd sailed in on a yacht, but as the local queen, Zylpha undoubtedly had eyes everywhere.

"I am not so foolish as to keep all my eggs in one basket," Elsa said. "I am still comfortable."

"Then I shall see that my finest wares are brought to your room for you to peruse," Zylpha said as they emerged into the lobby of what appeared to be a very fancy hotel.

Though she'd never been to Las Vegas, she imagined the best casino there would pale in comparison to the sheer amount of gold and silver that decorated the room.

"Yummy," Jonnie said.

Shauna saw why. Not only was the room gilt, several young men and women standing around the room wore heavy gold and silver jewelry, none of it covering the best parts. Those people weren't wearing any actual clothing.

"Is this a brothel?" Shauna asked.

Elsa gave her another quick shake of the head and Shauna realized she was way too far over her head in whatever depravity was going on around her.

"It's so much more than that," Zylpha said. "Though if anything you see pleases you, take it for the day. Everything here is complementary to our customers."

"We haven't agreed to buy anything yet," Elsa said.

"You will," Zylpha said. "Once you see the quality of what I offer, I am certain you won't walk away empty handed. If you do, you'll come back."

Shauna was about to ask what, exactly, Zylpha was selling since she was talking around it without naming it. Again, Elsa was shaking her head at Shauna. Her mind had arrived at the idea she was in a slave market, but she couldn't think of a politically correct way to ask. By Elsa's anticipatory shaking of the head, Shauna kept her mouth shut.

"I'm missing my pet a little right now," Jackie said.

"As I said," Zylpha gestured to one of the young men, a Nordic looking, well endowed young man. "Everything is complementary. Take two or three if you have that kind of stamina, and if you could keep up with Elsa, I'm sure you do."

Jackie looked at Shauna. "Will he do?" she asked.

Shauna shrugged, trying to act like she wasn't appalled by the wanton openness of Zylpha's flesh market. "Keep him with us, but we'll want another, a girl, I think."

Zylpha's voice passed into Shauna's mind. "I was worried someone so new to our lifestyle wouldn't understand how to enjoy my place. It pleases me to be able to please you."

Shauna smiled at her hostess.

"The nightly auction starts at four," Zylpha said aloud. "The brochures of the merchandise are in each room. Be sure to call the desk at least an hour ahead of time to request which of our inventory you'd like to see in the auction. There aren't usually more than three or four bidders, so don't worry too much about running the prices up. More often than not, we sell at the reserve price. Still, if you'd like to buy one outside of the auction setting, the price is significantly higher, but well within your means, I'm sure."

"I'm sure you offer only the best quality," Elsa said. "If so, it'll be worth the cost."

"Boy," Zylpha said to the Nordic man at Jackie's side. "Take these guests to suite five." She turned to Elsa and said, "All of my suites are suitable for royalty. They have to be since all of my customers are either princes, kings or wealthy enough to be one. I'll send up some snacks." She walked off to engage a man wearing a perfectly tailored suit.

As they walked away, once Shauna was sure they were far enough from Zylpha that a vampire wouldn't overhear, she said, "I'm not going to like this, am I?"

"I've never been here. I wasn't expecting her operation to be so extravagant," Elsa said. "I wasn't planning on exposing you to this much."

"It is what it is," Jonnie said. "We're here now and when in Rome…"

"We're supposed to have sex with prostitutes?" Shauna asked.

"Prostitutes get paid," Elsa said. "Zylpha was clear that these...," she paused to grab the hand of a nearly naked woman standing along the wall, "...are complimentary."

The Nordic man opened a door along the wall and Shauna followed Elsa in. Inside it was just one large room with several beds and lots of pillows strewn about. Even a bathtub sat out in the open. An open door led to a small room with a toilet and bidet and another led to a large closet.

"I am obligated to tell you Queen Zylpha's rules," the woman Elsa had pulled along said. "First, please limit yourself to one pint per item of merchandise. Second, the concierge will provide full kits for any fetish. The phone will connect to the concierge desk." She indicated a desk with a phone and a binder. "Third, if you break it, you buy it at ten times reserve price. Any mark that will not heal in seven days is considered a break."

Shauna had tried to disbelieve the possibility, but the woman's words hadn't left any other possibilities. "Zylpha is selling people?" she blurted.

"Yes," Elsa said. "She's been running the world's premiere pleasure slave market for almost two millennia, maybe more. She specializes in creating ideal vampire pets."

"Ooh," Jonnie said. "Can I get one?"

"You're not serious," Shauna said. "These are human beings."

"Which you kill and eat," Elsa said.

"You know that's not true of me," Shauna said. "It's not true of you, either. It's not true of any of you." She stepped up to the Nordic man and asked, "Don't you want to be free?"

"I wish to please," the man said. "It is my only desire."

Thinking Zylpha must have coerced him, Shauna focused and said, "Forget what Zylpha forced you to think. Be free."

The man looked confused a moment, then said, "Ultimate freedom is surrendering your will to please your master."

"You can't coerce a person to change their nature," Elsa said.

"No one's nature is to be a slave," Shauna said. "It's natural for human beings to want freedom."

"How modern of you," Elsa said. "I shouldn't have brought you here."

"I'd have found out about it," Shauna said. "I seem to be finding out all the secrets of our world."

"Yes," Elsa said. "Eventually, you'd learn of this place. What would you do with it?"

"We need to free these people," Shauna said.

"You can't," Elsa said.

"I can kill every guard in this place," Shauna said. "I can kill Zylpha."

"Didn't you just say you weren't a killer?" Elsa asked. She seemed annoyingly amused.

Jackie put her arms around Shauna's waist. "My love, you can't change the world all at once."

"I have to start somewhere," Shauna said. Jackie's arms were calming, but not enough to let Shauna drop the debate.

"This place is evil," Elsa said. "Perhaps more evil than anything I've done. If you want to know the truth, I had planned to bring you here someday so that you'd end what goes on here. But, today is not the day to do that."

"I'm sorry," Shauna said, asking for more explanation. "Why not tell James?"

"James undoubtedly knows; he comes from a time where slavery was a natural state," Elsa said. "Well, he comes from a time I know nothing about but he's lived through the Egyptian, Greek and Roman eras. Slavery was a normal thing there. Some people are just slaves, or so the thinking went at the time."

"No, they're not," Shauna said.

"Maybe not," Elsa said. "You and I both know slavery best from how it was practiced in the Americas, but that is not the historical norm. In the Americas, slaves were too often treated like beasts of burden. The perception was made easier by the different appearance of their slaves. Historically, slaves were a class of people, and they were people."

"What are they here?" Shauna asked.

"I've never been here," Elsa said. "I was curious to find the answer to that question, however. I'll admit it's not looking good for Zylpha."

"What do I do with these two?" Shauna said.

"I was planning on having sex with them," Elsa said. "I imagine they are well trained."

"We are," the woman said. "I've never failed to bring pleasure."

"You can't," Shauna said. "You..." Elsa probably could. She clearly didn't feel as passionate about freeing the slaves as Shauna did. "How can you?"

"I can because I know, in allowing these two to please us, we will bring them joy," Elsa said.

"It's not right," Shauna said.

"No," Elsa agreed. "It's not right. It is an odd juxtaposition of everyone being happy with the outcome and civil morality. The evil that has happened to these people is already done and nothing we do here will undo it, as you've seen with your attempt to coerce them. You may not be able to separate your feelings about the morality of it all from your ability to experience pleasure, but I can. I won't if you insist that I don't, though. I do assure you, in using these as they were trained to be used, they will experience emotional bliss."

"This is true," the man said. "Nothing pleases me more than bringing a man or woman to exquisite release."

"Do what you will," Shauna said, defeated. Elsa's arguments were flawless, though Shauna couldn't get past the wrongness of making human beings into servile creatures. "I'm going to find a drink."

"My blood is yours," the man said.

"Drink your fill," the woman said, holding her wrist out to Shauna.

Shauna closed her eyes and shook her head. She couldn't even look at the slaves. She left the room and walked down the hall towards the main area. Surely someone would bring her a bottle of wine if she asked.

Jackie caught up with her at the end of the hall and grabbed her arm, swinging her around and putting her back to a wall. She then kissed Shauna deeply. Breaking off, Jackie said, "You are so heroic."

"Too heroic," Shauna said. "I need to learn to adjust to our lifestyle."

"Says who?" Jackie asked.

"Elsa," Shauna said.

"You didn't hear her right," Jackie said. "She expects you to tear this place down. She wants you to be a hero."

"And she's back there fucking those slaves," Shauna said.

"In all likelihood, yes," Jackie said. "She is right, these people are already broken. We're not equipped to fix them and using them for what Zylpha has programmed them to be used for does cause them to feel happiness."

"It's immoral," Shauna said.

"It is," Jackie said, "which is why I'm out here with you. But, since when do you hold Elsa to any moral standard?"

Shauna didn't. She wasn't upset with Elsa at all. "I don't dislike Elsa even when I don't approve of what she does. She's the Blood Countess. As long as she's not bathing in their blood, nothing really seems evil in comparison."

"Wow," Jackie said. "That's more forgiving than I am of what she does. You have a pretty low bar set for her. I hope it's set higher for me. I don't want to simply exceed a rating of 'monster'."

"If you'd have stayed, I probably wouldn't have," Shauna said. "I guess I expect you to be up to my morality. Well, not my human morality, but where I think my morality should be." She still felt qualms when the morals she held as a human were tested, but she believed she had to concede to a certain level of monstrosity to allow for surviving as a vampire.

"And I have the same expectations of you," Jackie said. "To be honest, I expect you to be a super-hero."

"I'm just a vampire who doesn't drink enough blood to reach my full strength." Shauna said.

"You're a person willing to do whatever it takes to make the world a better place for people other than yourself," Jackie said. "Even if Elsa's definition of a better place isn't the same as ours, she still sees you as a hero, too."

"She's saved my life," Shauna said.

"And you're saving her soul," Jackie said. "She's been doing penance inside her mind for four centuries. With you, she finally sees a way to really make up for the evil she's done. You are not only saving the world from evil vampires, but you're giving her a yardstick, a measure, to live up to."

"And right now, she's not meeting the same measure as me," Shauna said.

"She's still Elsa," Jackie said. "There are situations where she will never see eye to eye with you. She'll never have the strong association between emotion and pleasure that you do. Elsa was broken by Vlad. She was taught to separate physical pleasure from emotional happiness."

"And you?" Shauna asked.

"I'm closer to Elsa than I am to you in that regard," Jackie said. "I can't deny that. Two centuries with her has taught us to be able to just feel the physical without emotional attachment. But, I feel emotional and pleasure together when I'm with you and that makes it infinitely better than with anyone else."

"Thank you," Shauna said. "But, if I don't do the same for Elsa, why does she want me so close all the time?"

"You're an idiot," Jackie said. "You're the only true emotional bond she has ever had. Jonnie and I do have an emotional bond to her, but it took years to form. We started as just physical. For almost a decade, we weren't much more than toys to her. That was still a better relationship than we had with the illusionist we'd been working for when we met Elsa."

"Is everyone in this vampiric existence broken?" Shauna asked.

"Um, duh," Jackie said.

"I don't know what to do with this," Shauna said, gesturing to her surroundings. "If this is normal for vampire life, I am starting to think I'm more like James than Elsa."

"You're like Shauna," Jackie said. "And this isn't normal for anyone. Elsa lived in vamp society for my whole life and I've never seen anything this depraved, but I've heard of it. It doesn't look as bad as the rumors."

"Rumors?" Shauna asked. "Do I want to know?"

"Probably not," Jackie said. "But you're going to ask anyway so I'll just get to the gist. Rumors say Zylpha sells people for any purpose from a lifetime of servitude to a single night with an ultimate end."

"Are you saying she sells people just to be killed?" Shauna asked.

"I'm saying the rumors say she does," Jackie said. "I don't see anything like that here."

"Where's Zylpha?" Shauna asked.

"I've been with you," Jackie said. "But, are you sure you want to confront her?"

"I'm not sure I don't want to kill her," Shauna said. "But, right now that's based solely on the rumors. I'd want to give her a chance to explain. It wouldn't be justice without offering her a chance to defend what she does." That Zylpha's rules specifically included a purely financial punishment for 'damaging the merchandise' told Shauna that the worst rumors weren't entirely just rumors.

"I've got your back," Jackie said, "and not just figuratively. I'm purer than her. I can take her down if you need me to." She made a fist and blew over her knuckles.

"She's on the Council." Shauna said. "I'm sure we could just waltz in and take her apart bone by bone, but we're trying to not revive the purge wars or whatever they were." Around twenty generations of vampires separated Shauna from the eldest of the Elder's Council because, over the centuries, the Council had found ways to kill off almost all of the vampires purer than they. Shauna and her ilk existed unmolested because they'd coerced the Council members to not perceive their actual purity. Shauna didn't want to do anything to bring on additional scrutiny.

"And she could warn the other council members with your magical walkie-talkie bracer thingy," Jackie said.

"And, the other elders know I'm here by now, I'm sure," Shauna said. "I could coerce Zylpha to change her ways, but if they changed too much, the other Elders might put two and two together and realize there is a vampire potent enough to coerce a council member. They'd probably assume it was Elsa, but…"

"For all intents a purposes, you and Elsa are connected at the hip," Jackie finished for Shauna.

"You won't think less of me if I do nothing?" Shauna asked.

"I won't believe you're Shauna McAllister if you do nothing," Jackie said. "I'm just waiting to see what it is that you do to Queen Zylpha. I'm just hoping whatever you do leaves us a way out of this underground palace."

"Palace," Shauna repeated. She looked around and that was exactly where they were. Zylpha enjoyed her riches. She made Elsa's opulent ways seem like a pauper playing rich. Only Elsa's was a precisely calculated persona, and nothing near as opulent as she could be. Zylpha's palace, on the other hand, held nothing back in its brash display of wealth. Zylpha cared more about the money than Elsa did, and Shauna might be able to use that. "I bet I could get to her with money," Shauna said.

"You're going to buy her out?" Jackie asked. "I know I'm not the financial expert twin, but I don't think you're that rich. Elsa, maybe, well certainly, but she would never spend money when manipulating someone would accomplish the same thing."

"I just need to get in the door," Shauna said. "I could use the promise of a big sale as a pretense to distract her."

"And then what?" Jackie asked. "Try to pickpocket the deed to her kingdom?"

"I'm still thinking," Shauna said. "But, it won't be more than coercion. I just need to figure out what wouldn't be anathema to her. I want whatever I do to stick."

"You won't be able to make her see people as, well, people," Jackie said. "She's ingrained to see vampires as superior, as dominant."

"I know," Shauna said. Perhaps she wouldn't have to change Zylpha's feelings about slaves, just her memories. Perceptions and memories could be changed with almost no risk of the coercion failing with time. Memories were the trickier of the two. A vampire couldn't coerce someone to remember something that didn't happen, but they can coerce someone to see what happened differently than it did. Shauna took a deep breath just so she could sigh. "Unfortunately, I don't know enough of how Zylpha lives day-to-day."

"We're thinking without drinking," Jackie said. "Maybe we should get some wine and ponder our options. Or we find a quiet corner and see if we can distract our minds and come at this from another angle later."

"Or both," Shauna said.

"I like both," Jackie agreed. "You find the wine, I'll find the corner."

§

After sunset the next night, Shauna and Jackie were sitting in a private booth, hidden from the rest of the bar by a curtain. The table had four bottles of varied wines, all opened and partially empty. The servants had taken away twice that many, fully empty, over the course of the day. Once or twice during that time, Shauna had drunk fast enough to actually feel drunk for a few minutes.

Jackie hadn't fully dressed since their last attempt at distraction, her shirt draped over one end of the table. She lay sprawled on the cushions with her head in Shauna's lap.

"I think it will work," Jackie said.

Shauna wasn't so sure. The plan she'd come up with involved making Zylpha remember that the best pets came from volunteers who wanted to be used. It wasn't the best plan and didn't resolve all the issues Shauna had with Zylpha's slave trade, but it was the only plan she could think of that would have a chance of working at all. She needed to know Zylpha or her organization better to create a fuller plan.

"There you are!" Elsa said as she threw back the curtain. "We're leaving."

"Leaving?" Shauna asked. "Right now?"

"Jonnie's in the car," Elsa said, then put a finger to her chin and pondered hastily, "Truck? Car? It's a military thing. It's very roomy."

"What?" Shauna asked, looking to Jackie, though she doubted her girlfriend could explain. She was hoping for an idea of how to implement her plan before she left.

Jackie was buttoning up her shirt and shrugged at Shauna.

"The thing is, we need to leave fast," Elsa said. Her words were so quick they were slightly higher in pitch than Elsa normally talked. "Zylpha's gone for the night and she left a vampire in charge that I could coerce."

"And?" Shauna asked.

"And we have to leave," Elsa said, bouncing on her toes and nodding behind her towards the main area, which Shauna presumed, led to an exit. "I want to make sure that when Zylpha realizes what we did, she'll have a long trip to catch up to us. Hopefully, long enough to let her rage drop to mere anger."

"So we're running for the door?" Shauna asked.

"Don't be ridiculous," Elsa said. "I said we need to leave right now. I didn't say we needed to look bad doing it." She pulled Shauna and Jackie out of the booth.

Jackie's hair was disheveled and her shirt was misbuttoned. Shauna assumed she looked just as bad, "You were saying something about not looking bad?"

Elsa looked them up and down. "You look exactly like two people should look who spent nine hours secluded behind a curtain together. That means you look respectable. Come, we're taking the back door."

She led them out of the bar and down a hall. They passed by several windows down a hallway. Behind each window, a guard stood with a machine gun. The barrels of the guns rested in a long, thin horizontal hole in the thick glass.

At the end of the hall a doorman opened a gilt door. Beyond the door was a parking garage and a large beige military car sat by the door with Jonnie at the wheel.

As she walked to the car, Shauna couldn't help but let her eyes run to the half dozen armed guards standing around the garage.

"Relax, sweetie," Elsa said. "As far as they know, we're just satisfied customers."

Shauna still wasn't sure why they were running as she opened the door and hopped in the back seat. Then she noticed the four mostly naked people in the third row of seats.

"You bought slaves?" Shauna asked.

"Yes," Jonnie said. "More or less."

"It's the less part that will have Zylpha on our tails, so get in the car," Elsa said as she climbed in the front seat.

Shauna closed her door and asked, "Now that we're all here, would you care to elaborate?"

Elsa looked back and explained as Jonnie drove the car out of the garage.

"Shauna, say hello to my new pet, Ma..." Elsa paused. "I haven't actually named her, yet. I'm leaning towards something that starts with an M."

"And my pet," Jonnie said, "Rudy."

An Italian looking man and an Asian girl said, almost in unison. "It's a pleasure to meet you."

"There are four back here," Shauna said. Her first guess was that there was one pet for each vampire in the car. Elsa and Jonnie wouldn't have tried to pick pets for Jackie and her, Shauna realized. "You weren't being presumptuous, Jackie already has a pet," Shauna said, pushing them to explain why they had four when they only needed two.

"We were being impulsive," Jonnie said. "Shauna-like impulsive."

"We had to save all of them," Elsa said. "So, yes, we were being Shauna-like impulsive."

"Do I get the full story?" Shauna asked.

It took a while. Back at Zylpha's, after Shauna had left the room, Elsa and Jonnie had concluded that they did, in fact, actually want to save at least a few slaves. They decided the best way to save slaves was to make them pets and then take the time to teach them how to be free human beings again.

Difficulties arose when the vampire handling the sale showed up to their room with three potential pets for each of them. Elsa and Jonnie had each selected their choices from the catalog, choosing second and third choices at the sales vampire's urging, just in case the first didn't meet their needs in person. The sales vampire assured them that the slaves had all built up a tolerance for vampire blood, but Zylpha's policy on pets meant they had to turn them before they left to ensure the pets weren't defective.

Elsa learned what that meant when her first choice died from her blood.

Jonnie's first choice had survived the change.

Elsa decided at that point that she didn't trust that the tolerance was strong enough for her blood and that, for the next one, she'd do it the safer way of starting with a drop a day and working up to a few ounces over time until the pet bond took hold. She coerced the sales vampire to recall her making the second choice into a pet.

As the sales vamp was leaving with the remaining three, Jonnie realized that the others would face a potential death the next time they were selected. She coerced the sales vamp to remember that all but two of the potential pets had died and to not notice as they left with five.

"Five?" Shauna asked. "I only see four." Other than Elsa's pet and Rudy, another man and woman sat in the seat.

"There's a girl behind the seat," Jonnie said. "She was small and young, maybe thirteen. Don't look at me like I'm a perv. They got one of my requests off by one number and brought her instead of a Ukrainian stud I'd been looking forward to."

If Shauna used her pre-vampire definition of 'perv', Jonnie more than qualified long before she started taking in sex slaves. Since being exposed to Elsa and the twins and all the things they did, Shauna was still in the process of redefining what constituted perverted behavior.

"You could have just bought them all," Jackie said.

Elsa turned and looked at Jackie then at Jonnie. "You should have thought of that," she said to the twin.

"Next time, we'll just buy all of her slaves and make her business seem exceptionally profitable," Jonnie said, sounding completely serious, almost angry.

"You're right," Elsa said. "My way was the better way."

CHAPTER 6

They reached the border to Bulgaria in less than an hour. As they approached the border station, Shauna asked Elsa, "Do we have passports for the slaves? You don't happen to carry spares, do you?"

"The ones we bought, yes, we have paperwork for," Elsa said. "The other three, no."

"So we're going to coerce the guards to not see the extra people?" Jonnie asked.

"Well, you will," Elsa said. "You're driving."

Four guards ran out and stood in front of their car, aiming sub machine guns at the windshield. They shouted something in Turkish. Elsa translated. "Get out, lay down."

"We're not fighting here, right?" Shauna asked.

"We?" Elsa responded, opening her door. She winked at Shauna and paused a moment before saying, in a flat voice. "No, no one is fighting here."

"Coerce them?" Shauna asked, stepping away from the car.

"Not them," Elsa said. "Their commander. Get on your knees." She kicked off her shoes and knelt on the road. She put her hands behind her head and said, "This better be enough for them. I'm not putting my face on the street."

Shauna did the same, as did the twins. The slaves, still naked, also complied. Having naked people in the street must have triggered something in the guards. They gestured for all of them to stand and then ushered them all into a building. Inside, they led them to a small area with four rows of uncomfortable looking plastic seats.

It wasn't a cell, as Shauna was expecting, but two of the guards stayed and watched over them with their hands on their machine guns.

One of the guards brought blankets and handed one to each of the slaves. Another guard asked something in

Turkish, to which Elsa responded with one word. Shauna assumed they'd asked if anyone spoke Turkish or who was in charge.

The guard took Elsa to another room. Elsa wasn't making a big deal of it, so Shauna didn't feel too anxious, just a bit confused.

"What's going on?" Shauna asked.

"I don't know," Jackie said. "Turkish isn't one of the languages I know. I didn't even know it was one Elsa knew. I hope Elsa is talking our way out of this mess."

The guards watched them when they talked but didn't speak or point their guns at anyone.

"I can't coerce anyone who doesn't understand me," Shauna said. "I thought everyone in Europe spoke English if we talked slow enough. Zylpha's guard, who was also Turkish, said so."

"Those two speak English, which is probably why they're the ones watching us." Jackie said. "Their expressions all change with every sentence."

Shauna looked at the closest guard. He looked back and gave a tiny shrug.

"Why are we being held?" Shauna asked the guard. She added her will to her words when she added, "Be nice."

"Your car," the guard said. "It's stolen."

"Oh," Shauna said. She didn't know what to say after that. She wondered, if Zylpha knew, why she hadn't been screaming at her through the bracer. Perhaps Zylpha didn't know and someone else at her palace picked up on the ruse. Deciding to get ahead of the argument, Shauna thought to Zylpha, "I can't be held responsible for Elsa's actions."

"I know what she did," Zylpha replied. "I will be bringing this crime to the council."

"There is no violation of our laws," Shauna said. "This is a mortal legal matter and we would just be wasting the council's time."

"If you're helping her, you cannot judge in this matter," Zylpha's mental voice said.

Unable to come up with a reason that could justify Elsa's actions without getting into a debate on the morality of Zylpha's business, Shauna simply conceded that Elsa was actually guilty of theft. She thought, "I will see to it you get paid. It is Elsa, and we both know her well. We have to let her have her fun for a little while."

"Two-million-three is not fun," Zylpha said.

Shauna gasped. She hadn't anticipated such a high price. For the briefest of moments she was relieved that Zylpha put such a high value on human life. Shauna then felt guilty for allowing there to be any monetary value to a person's freedom. Focusing her thoughts, she returned to the conversation with Zylpha. "Maybe you don't know Elsa as well as I do," Shauna said. "That sounds well within her range of fun."

"You have a week," Zylpha said.

"So you're going to clear up this mess at the border?" Shauna asked.

"No," Zylpha said. Shauna felt the mental connection fall away.

Elsa walked out of the other room, chatting in a friendly voice with a guard whose uniform had fancier epaulets than the others'. She giggled and touched his shoulder after he said something.

The man smiled and stepped over to one of the guards and spoke with him as Elsa came over to Shauna.

"I explained to the captain how my sister and I had a disagreement, the car is hers, but this is a family matter and not a legal one," Elsa said. "Proud of me?"

"For not eating everyone in the guard post?" Shauna asked.

"I wouldn't do that," Elsa said. "I was just thinking it was a particularly clever excuse. I barely had to coerce him."

"So, back to the car?" Shauna asked.

"Nope," Elsa said. "It's got a GPS thingy. The captain is giving us a tour bus he impounded yesterday. They take their title taxes seriously around here. It's registered in Turkey, so we shouldn't have any problems outside the country." She held up a key with a red tag and started walking deeper into the border station. "He said the impound lot is this way."

"He's just giving us a tour bus?" Jonnie asked. "You don't carry the checkbook, so I know you didn't buy it."

"He's promised to not notice that it's gone missing or that the security system inexplicably stopped functioning an hour ago," Elsa said, holding up a computer hard disk. "That's not to say the next shift won't notice, or the shift after that, but we should be good for a day or two. That's enough time to find a vehicle worth buying."

"Finding a car for four of us would be easier than for nine," Shauna said.

"Are you saying we shouldn't have freed five slaves?" Elsa asked.

"No," Shauna said. She didn't think that. Things were getting more complicated than a simple scouting mission. "You did the right thing."

"That tour bus?" Jackie asked as they exited the back of the building. She pointed to a solid black bus with something written in Turkish across the silhouette of a guitar.

"It's not a band bus," Elsa said. "It just says it's a V.I.P. bus. It's probably a rental."

"Elsabet Davlos using a rental?" Jackie asked sarcastically. "I think the world must be ending."

"That would be funny if we weren't off to battle angels," Elsa said.

"They're vampires," Shauna said. "Henry called them angels but we killed one in the Blood Temple. He was a vampire."

"You killed one," Elsa said. "You and your sister were there. I wasn't. I was on my way to find you when Henry came out and nearly killed my Jonnie. If we find Henry, can we just kill him or do we have to wait for James?"

Jonnie put her hand on Elsa's shoulder and stepped in front of her. "When Elsa says to just kill him, she means torture him slowly until he regrets every breath he ever took and then, when he begs for the thousandth time, let him die."

"Jonnie's right," Elsa said. "Only she's being too nice about it. I can imagine a few new things I'd like to try on Henry and you don't want to think about the things I didn't have to imagine getting to those new ideas."

"So, we all hate Henry," Shauna said. The thought of seeing Henry again scared Shauna silly. Henry may not have won every battle, but he'd always left vampires dead or dying in his wake. The last time they'd met up with him, he'd killed Amenhetop and Mascare and disemboweled Jonnie. "I promised I'd kill him slowly for you. I'll do my best to keep my word." She didn't have a plan on how to do that. She hoped when the opportunity arose, she'd figure something out.

"I know you will, sweetie," Elsa said. She tossed the key to Jackie. "Is your CDL still good?"

"Not since 1986," Jackie said.

"Still, that's better than any of us," Elsa said. "It's almost midnight; can you get us to Bucharest in four hours?"

"Not legally," Jackie said. "I assume you don't want me blowing through the border crossings. We've made it out of Turkey but not into Bulgaria, yet. In three hours we have to get out of Bulgaria and into Romania. Hopefully, we won't be stopped on both sides of that border."

"Where I want to go is up the mountains north of Bucharest," Elsa said. "I'd like to get there before dawn."

"Sunrise will be around 6:45," Jonnie said.

"Do you know everything?" Shauna asked.

"Just what's pertinent," Jonnie said. "I spent most of the boat ride collecting the information we'd need to navigate Eastern Europe."

"She's the nerd of the two of us," Jackie said. "I'm the geek." She pushed a panel by the door and it opened. She stood aside and ushered everyone on board.

Shauna followed last. As she watched the blanket clad slaves climb up the steps ahead of her, she said, "The slaves need clothes."

"If we pass any open boutiques, we'll stop and shop," Elsa said. "Even if we pass a closed one with a promising window display, we can pretend it's open. But this thing better have a bathroom on board because I don't want to stop for anything else. We're almost in Romania now. People take the idea of vampires more seriously there. We can't waltz into a hotel and ask for a room without windows or extra heavy curtains."

Shauna sat in the seat behind the driver's seat. Elsa and Jonnie were already cuddled together a couple rows behind them. The slaves were doing their best to stay close to their masters.

Jackie buckled into the driver's seat and started the engine. "Do you have a destination I can plug in the GPS or am I just driving north?"

"Cetatea Poienari," Elsa said.

"Vlad's castle?" Shauna asked.

"Not the castle itself," Elsa said. "That place was a mess when I left this part of the world two centuries ago. But the place we're going won't be on the map. The geography around there is pretty distinct so I should be able to give better directions when we get close."

§

Jackie pulled into a fueling station north of Bucharest. She got out and started fueling the bus.

"They've got a general store attached," Shauna said. It seemed like a decent sized truck stop. Shauna expected they'd sell heavy plaid shirts and jeans if it was anything like an American truck stop. "I bet we could get clothing for the slaves there."

Elsa gave her a blank look. Jonnie's face had the same expression.

"You're going to be picky about basic necessities?" Shauna asked.

"I think so," Elsa said.

"They do need to be clothed," Jonnie said. "It is cold out there."

"Fine," Elsa said. "But I get to burn whatever Shauna buys when we get real clothes."

"I buy?" Shauna asked. "You're not going to select their clothes?"

"You're funny," Elsa said. Her tone indicated she wasn't amused at all. "I won't set foot in such a place. They won't sell decent wine or halfway decent designers. Why would I subject myself to such a dingy hole?"

"Fine," Shauna said. "I'll get them something flammable. Let me see their feet, since I'll have to guess at their shoe sizes."

The women, even the girl, had gold strap heels. The men's feet were bare. Shauna did her best to guess at their sizes before hopping off the bus.

"If you're going in, we need flashlights," Elsa said.

"And a phone charger," Jonnie said.

"Make it a solar charger if they have one. And wine," Elsa said. "But only if it has a cork."

"Lowering your standards?" Shauna said.

"Don't go there," Elsa said. "I'm not happy about the situation."

Inside she found exactly what she expected to find. The clothing was pretty crappy. She bought two sets of workout sweats for each of the slaves and a bunch of work boots in various sizes. Just to annoy Elsa further, she picked up some baseball caps. She also got all six of the flashlights they had in stock, but the phone charger selection was small, so she settled for one that plugged into the bus.

When Shauna got back to the car, Elsa was appalled. She went so far as to throw the caps out of the window as they drove away. "As soon as the sun sets tonight, we're getting them real clothes," she said.

"Of course," Shauna said. "But you have to admit that we can't have them freeze."

Elsa said nothing. Even if her mentor agreed, Shauna assumed she'd never concede that anything was more important than fashion.

"We all need new clothes anyway," Shauna said. They'd packed light for the visit to Zylpha's but Elsa and Jonnie hadn't even bothered to grab their trunk during the escape.

"Jonnie, it's on you to have the shopping planned for tonight," Elsa said.

"Already working on it." Jonnie had her phone out and was scrolling across screens.

§

As they wound their way through the Carpathian Mountains, Elsa stood at the front of the bus, watching the landscape around them. She told Jackie to follow a small road, maybe a driveway off the main road. They went down a hill and parked overlooking a river.

"This is the closest we can get in the bus," Elsa said. "What time is it?"

"Five-Fifty," Jonnie said.

"Hmm," Elsa said. "I hope I can find this place. I haven't been here since they killed Vlad."

"The castle is up there." Shauna pointed to a stone wall at the top of the hill across the highway.

"Which makes where we're going across the river," Elsa said. "Even if the trees are different, the shape of the ground will be mostly the same. Don't worry about sunrise coming. I'm sure we'll get there in time."

"I wasn't worried about sunrise," Shauna said snarkily.

"Shut up," Elsa said.

CHAPTER 7

"This is a little scary," Jackie said as she followed Shauna into the dark cellar.

Elsa led them to an ancient steel bound wooden door that was thirty feet deep into an old mine tunnel. "It's older than me," she said, running her hands over the walls. Whoever had built the cellar had used large, cut stones. They were the kind Shauna would think a castle would be built from. "Vlad built it to hide from Charlemagne."

Shauna knew Vlad Dracula was older than the books claimed. History only knew him from one name he used. Elsa had talked about how he died, so similar to the Stoker novel, in the early nineteenth century. Even Elsa wasn't sure when he was born.

"Vlad was an Avar?" Jonnie asked.

"Not that I know of," Elsa said. "I assumed he was Cuman-Kipchak," she paused and wrinkled her lips, "which wouldn't jive with him being around here in the days of Charlemagne's attempts to wrest these lands from the Avar."

"This place is clean," Jackie said, running her flashlight along the corners between the floor and the walls. She stopped at a stack of plastic wrapped bottled water. "Someone's been here." She shined her light on a stone spiral staircase that descended into the floor. She whispered, "Do you think we're alone?"

"It's probably just Bela," Elsa said. She flipped a switch and bright lights along the top edges of the walls illuminated the room. "It seems Bela's modernized some."

"Bela?" Shauna asked.

"He's the caretaker," Elsa said. "He's supposed to keep this place stocked in the event someone needs to hide here for a while. There should be barrels of wine and some jerked meat downstairs. But, don't go down to the level below that. None of you are ready to see what's down there."

"Whose pet is Bela?" Shauna asked. "Will someone know we're here?"

"Bela is a servant to my family," Elsa said. "If a servant showed particular loyalty or skills, Vlad made them into a vampire, to keep them around. Bela is the last of those servants, but he's smart and loyal. I haven't spoken to him in two centuries, but we've exchanged letters up until email became posh. Since then, we haven't kept in touch."

"Bela keeps cashing his paychecks," Jonnie said. "At least there's activity on the account we deposit the money into. Last time we mailed him anything he was living in Germany. He may only come here once or twice a year."

"Wait," Shauna said. "There are other vampires of your purity?"

"Don't be ridiculous," Elsa said.

"Vlad made servants into vamps? How many?" Shauna asked.

"Don't worry. He didn't make them into potent vamps, he made them thinbloods," she said.

"Huh?" Shauna asked. Thinbloods were vampires whose Venae was so impure they couldn't create bloodchildren or pets. She didn't know anyway that a vampire could choose the purity of their bloodchildren.

"He didn't make them with his own blood," Elsa said. "He used the revenant's blood."

"Revenant?" Jackie asked. "That's a real thing?"

"What's a revenant?" Shauna asked.

Jackie's voice was shaky, showing her trepidation as she explained, "Most people die when they drink vamp blood. If they come back, they're vampires, physically. Not all of them maintain their sanity through the change. When they don't, they are pure monsters."

Shauna remembered her change; it was over a day and a half of unbearably painful seizures. She could see how it could drive someone mad.

"So a revenant is a vampire with the mind of a feral animal?" Shauna surmised.

"Normally, they don't survive long," Elsa said. "Vlad kept one just to make weaker vampires with." Her gaze fell on the stairs and she looked like she was going to say more, but her lips didn't open.

"It's downstairs," Shauna guessed. "That's what we're not ready to see."

"It's in dry-sleep," Elsa said. "Or it should be."

"Dry-sleep?" Shauna asked.

"It's what happens to vampires who go too long without blood," Elsa said. "They fall asleep and basically hibernate until they feed or are fed."

"I'm going to have to go see that," Jackie said.

"Me too," Shauna said. The idea of a feral vampire being kept in forced hibernation seemed abhorrent, but Shauna couldn't think of a better choice and wasn't positive that killing it was humane, though she leaned toward believing it was. At that moment, her curiosity overrode her sensibility.

She led the way down the stairs.

As she stepped off the bottom step of the next floor down, the room's light's came on. The room was larger than Shauna expected. Several couches were arranged around the room into conversation pits. The walls were finished and a dozen works of pop art hung around the room. They were actual paintings, not prints. The whole floor was covered in a deep burgundy shag rug.

A bar stood in one corner with beer taps and a floor to ceiling wine-rack. Not all the slots had bottles, but more than half did.

Open doors led out of the main room. Peering through a doorway, Shauna saw a bedroom with more mirrors than walls. Vampires seeking shelter here were living in comfort and doing more than just hiding.

"Bela hasn't updated the room since 1978," Shauna said as she looked for the next set of stairs down. An archway on one of the walls led to a stairwell that descended into darkness. She followed it down.

"Don't," Elsa called. "Trust me; you don't want to see what's down there."

After flipping a switch on the wall at the bottom of the stone stairs, Shauna knew Elsa was right. Shauna stared at the most horrific thing she'd ever seen. She recognized the iron maiden but cringed at the thick copper pipe that led from the bottom to end above a cage. Inside the cage was a table with several metal bands clearly meant to hold a person in place. Shauna breathed easier seeing the table was empty but had to look away from the contraption.

"Rufus is gone," Elsa said. "I can't say he won't be missed, but he's probably happier dead than he was here."

"You think?" Shauna said. Around the room were several cells behind closed gates made of thick steel bands. "I'm glad to find these empty, I guess." Shauna said then asked, "This is where Vlad kept his potential vamps as they changed?"

"Let's answer that with the truth," Elsa said. "Yes, he kept his potential vamps there while they changed. Now, can we go upstairs without talking about this room anymore?"

The floor had a few other places where steel bolts had been driven into the stone. There had been other tables, other devices, in the room at one time. "Did he keep other victims here?" Shauna asked.

"We're done talking about this room," Elsa said. "Being down here is bringing back memories I don't want to remember."

"Then upstairs we go," Shauna said. Once she got to the main room, she asked. "Do you think Bela has cable in here?"

"I don't see a TV," Jackie said.

"Or bookshelves," Jonnie said.

"So what shall we do all day?" Elsa said, eyeing the slaves. "Or who?"

§

Moana seemed uncomfortable in clothing. Elsa had given her a name the next evening and made a point of noting that her name had two 'a's. Elsa insisted her pet would accompany them back to Bucharest.

Shauna stood at the opening of the tunnel, looking out over the valley.

"That's Poienari," Elsa said, pointing to a handful of lights on the top of the hill opposite the river.

"It's barely walls," Shauna said. The castle, once the home of Vlad the Impaler, stood in ruins.

"There's no one there," Shauna said. "Vlad didn't come home."

"Vlad's dead," Elsa said quietly.

"Were you hoping he wasn't?" Shauna asked. They'd come to Romania looking for Henry the Inquisitor and his 'angel'. Because the trail led to Drac's old haunts, Elsa couldn't help but question whether she'd actually seen him die and turn to dust. She said often that she was certain she had.

"As much as I loved him and I miss him, the world is a better place without him," Elsa said. "I am a better woman without him. Vlad saw people much like Zylpha does; as a resource or commodity. If we hadn't parted ways, I can't say I'd have improved my perspective."

"Have you?" Shauna asked. "You have four slaves downstairs and one here."

"You know me well," Elsa said. "You were human less than a year ago. You still think of vampires and humans as two different types of people."

Shauna interjected, "Because they are."

Elsa nodded and said, "They are both 'people', but vampires are not humans. I am not human. You are not human. Our pets, they are barely human."

Shauna looked at Moana who stood behind Elsa, staring at the ground. "Because she's stronger or because she's a slave?"

"Moana is a pet," Elsa said. "She's my pet." She emphasized the 'my'. "I don't think of these people as lesser because they are human. I think everyone is lesser because they are not me."

"Even me? Even James?" Shauna asked.

"Sweetie, I love you," Elsa said and embraced her in a hug. "But I cannot help how I perceive the world. Or maybe I could but I won't. I embrace my egocentricity; that is who I am."

"So you're okay with being a selfish bitch?" Shauna asked.

"You can say it that way," Elsa said. "I wish you wouldn't. It's not particularly nice of you."

"So how would you be worse with Vlad around?"

"It's not a fine line between egocentricity and megalomania," Elsa said. "My world revolves around me. If I were still under Vlad's influence, I would make sure everyone else's world revolved around me too."

"You're the Empress of Europe," Shauna said.

"And I only took the crown because you said I'd be a good Empress," Elsa said.

"You took the crown by accident and couldn't convince the Council to let you give it up," Shauna corrected Elsa's recollection. "The twins and I do believe in your ability to rule a kingdom, though. You're not the evil countess you were as a mortal."

"I was evil for a century or so after I changed," Elsa said. "I broke away from Vlad because he was influencing me in ways I didn't like. I was trying to be good. I'd met John during my independent decades. And that's when Vlad decided I had to be close to him again. It was an odd confrontation, but, John's betrayal of my trust would have thrown me back in with Vlad if he'd survived. I think I would be queen, a megalomaniacal queen by right of conquest. Vampire society would be different. Zylpha has total control over humans because she can. She has the control over vampires the vampires let her have. She's strong but not strong enough to take power and enforce her control by might."

"And you are." Shauna said. "I see what you're saying. You are a good person because you could be so much worse, so being a selfish bitch is virtually righteous in comparison to what you could be."

"Exactly," Elsa said. "And could that be the last time you call me a selfish bitch?"

"Probably not," Shauna said, giving Elsa a teasing squeeze. "But, I'll refrain for a few weeks if I can."

"Now, what to do with the slaves," Elsa said.

"For starters, we could stop calling them 'slaves'," Shauna said. "Let's call them your staff. Do any others have names besides Moana and Rudy?"

"I'm waiting to see how they behave, to give them names that suit them," Elsa said.

"They're not kittens," Shauna said. "Just give them names." Ideally, they'd get the names they had before Zylpha kidnapped them. But the slaves had been so conditioned, they couldn't remember a time before they were slaves, even when Shauna coerced them to remember, and she'd tried again during the day.

"Fine, I'll call the girls Phoebe and Ursula and the boy, Ross." Elsa peered through the trees down at the road. "Do you think Jackie is back with a new car yet?"

Shauna shook her head. Jackie was supposed to drive to find a car dealer and trade the bus for something big. Since she'd left only an hour or so earlier, just after sunset, Shauna doubted she'd be back yet.

Thinking about the names Elsa used, Shauna recognized them from a television show she'd watched with her family while she was in grade school. "You're that obsessed with twins, that even though the two other girls are clearly not related, you'd name them after twins?" Shauna asked.

"I guess I shouldn't be surprised you got that reference," Elsa said.

"I am surprised you watched television," Shauna said.

"I binge watch sometimes," Elsa said. "Once or twice a month, I'll spend a few days doing nothing but watching TV until I realize I'm wasting my undeath. Jackie and Jonnie are worse than me. Jonnie would watch documentaries all day if I let her and Jackie likes those singing reality shows."

Shauna cringed at the thought of sitting with her lover, watching television. It wasn't something she'd envisioned before.

"American television is a plague on the world," a voice Shauna had heard before came from above her. Lucrezia, Elsa's bloodsister and member of the Elder's Council, flew down to stand next to them. She immediately joined Elsa and Shauna's embrace.

Seeing Lucrezia's pale pink aura as they touched threw Shauna into momentary panic. If Shauna saw a vampire's aura as pale pink, the vampire saw hers as dark red. Then she recalled that, like the other members of the Elder's Council, Artemis had coerced them all to perceive Shauna as the purity of a founding member and Elsa as the purity of Lucrezia.

"Lucy!" Elsa said. "Did Zylpha send you?"

"She said you were in the area," Lucy said. "She's mad at you for something. She says you owe her a few million dollars and an apology. I say you shouldn't pay her. I don't know why you owe her, but she's annoying me. She thinks, since she's the only founder left, she's in charge of the council."

"Shauna is her equal," Elsa said.

"Only in purity," Lucy said. "Thalia is also as pure, but wasn't on the council at the founding. She took over for her bloodsister, Artemis, a few centuries ago. I'm glad Thalia found your orphaned bloodline and brought you back in, though. With Mascare gone, we need more level-headed vamps to keep Zylpha in check."

"I'm back!" Jackie called as she climbed the hill to join them. "Lucy!" Jackie said, waving. "What a surprise." She looked at Shauna with questioning eyes. Shauna shook her head tightly. She didn't know how to answer covertly.

"Come here," Lucy said, stepping over to Jackie. "Let me welcome the newest vampire to our family." She embraced Jackie, but immediately pushed away and produced an obsidian knife. "What the hell?" she screamed.

"She's not coerced to see Jackie as less pure than she is," Elsa explained to Shauna. Jackie and Jonnie were made after Artemis had changed the council's perceptions.

"Don't even try that," Lucrezia said. "I didn't come alone. I have a sniper watching us with gold bullets and there's a cameraman filming this, to make sure I remember everything as it happened."

"So we have to kill you to make you forget?" Elsa asked.

Lucrezia raised her free hand and looked off across the valley. "He'll shoot you as soon as I drop my hand."

"Then I won't make you forget," Shauna said. "How about you," she paused to add her will to her next word, "remember."

Lucrezia eyes flew wide and she glanced at Elsa and Shauna and then back at Elsa. "Porca vacca!" she said and dropped the knife and her free hand. "I don't have a sniper or a cameraman," she said. "We let you coerce us before. You're going to have to do it again."

Jackie ran to Lucy and tore the bracer from her arm.

"Ouch," Lucy said.

"Had to," Jackie said. "Can't have you talking about us in your mind."

"You could have asked me to take it off," Lucy said, rubbing her arm. "I'm trying to be cooperative. I am not exactly in a situation where I have the upper hand. Three ultra-pure vamps versus lone Lucrezia? No, I'm not stupid."

"Just a moment ago, you were acting pretty stupid," Elsa said.

"I was surprised," Lucy said. "I reacted from reflex. Now that I've had time to soak in how my reality is not as I'd thought, I'm of the opinion, I'd rather have my delusions back. Please, coerce me to believe you are not so pure and not so different than the rest of us."

"As you wish," Shauna said. She was about to bite her finger, to enforce the coercion with her blood, when a black cylinder dropped at Jackie's feet.

"Dammit!" Elsa said. "Gren…"

The canister exploded. With her accelerated perceptions, Shauna saw the burst of light and the fragments of the canister fly outward. She saw Elsa reaching for Moana and Lucy jumping to the ground. Jackie was starting to phase out, but not quickly enough.

Shauna reached around the explosion with her telekinesis. About a foot from the center, the fragments stopped, forming a perfect sphere. Then, Shauna heard the explosion as a resonant deep boom. In her mind, Shauna felt the force push against her Venae powered mental hand. She released her telekinetic grip and tiny shards of metal and obsidian splashed harmlessly to the ground.

Lucrezia had dove for the ground. Elsa had jumped to Moana and phased them both.

"Nice," Jackie said after phasing back to normal. "I wouldn't have thought of that."

"Can we get into cover?" Lucrezia said. She flew to her feet and ran into the tunnel.

"I'll cover the rear," Shauna said.

"You can cover my rear anytime," Elsa said, though her voice was rushed as she pushed Moana ahead of her into the shelter.

As Shauna made her way down to the main room, she heard Lucy asking question after question about how Elsa could be purer than she.

"You're asking a lot of questions for someone who knows they're not going to remember any of the answers," Elsa said.

"So you have nothing to lose by telling me," Lucy said.

"I guess not," Elsa said.

"You realize we just entered an enclosed space when we're being chased by someone with grenades," Jackie said. "In case you didn't think it through, that's bad."

"We can all phase," Elsa said. "Take a human with you when you do."

"I can't phase," Lucy said.

"Right," Elsa said. "You were made before Drac figured out how to steal a purer vamp's Venae."

"There weren't any purer vamps when I was made," Lucy said. "The council was already in place and the purge was over." She looked at Shauna and Jackie and then added, "Or so we thought."

"You were coerced to believe," Elsa said.

"Until today, between the council and a handful of others, I knew of exactly thirteen vampires of my purity or purer," Lucy said. "Before you erase my mind, just tell me how many there really are and how pure are they?"

"If you were a mug of hot chocolate, Shauna would be a bar of Swiss dark chocolate," Elsa said. "And the cocoa beans are still out there."

"And you?" Lucy asked.

"I'm just you with half the milk," Elsa said. "Even I'm nothing compared to her." She nodded at Shauna. "The hunters that are harassing vamps across Europe, like the one that's out there now, they work for vamps like Shauna."

Lucy dropped to the carpet and sat against the wall. "Madonna! I knew I was screwed, I didn't realize how royally fucked."

Elsa sat beside her bloodsister and took her hand. "As soon as we take care of that hunter, we'll make you forget.'

"How about you don't," Lucy said. "I thought I was continuing my bloodfather's crusade to purge the purer vamps. Now that I know that's just not possible, I can put that idea behind me, forever. I will be free of trying to make a dead vamp happy."

"We can't trust you," Elsa said.

"Coerce me, just to ask if I'm being honest," Lucy said.

The door upstairs clanged against the wall. Shauna prepared to catch another grenade, but it never came. Instead she saw feet coming down the stairs, slowly. "You're just stringing out your inevitable demise," the man coming down the stairs said. Shauna recognized Henry the Inquisitor's voice.

Elsa stood, placing her hand on Lucy's shoulder as she did. "Stay down, sis. We've dealt with him before."

"Are you so sure, Henry?" Elsa said as he walked calmly down the stairs. He held a loaded crossbow with a bone arrowhead. "Didn't you recognize us? Don't you know who we are? Maybe you don't remember what I did to you last time."

Henry stood at the bottom of the stairs with a far too confident smirk. He said, "It's you who don't know what I am."

With a blink, Shauna saw his aura. "He's a vamp," Shauna said. "His master made him into one of us."

"And I do remember you," Henry said. He leveled the crossbow at Elsa and shot.

Elsa phased out instantly and the bolt passed through her faded body, imbedding itself into a painting hanging on the wall. Elsa fell to the ground, clutching at her chest where the quarrel had passed through.

Shauna ran at Henry. He dropped the crossbow and drew a long bone knife. It was almost long enough to be a sword. Shauna stopped out of weapons reach from Henry and tried to grab him with her mental hand. She couldn't get a grip on him. He was using the same ability to fight back.

Laughing, Henry walked towards Shauna, swishing his blade back and forth. "This is where you die, Shauna McAllister. I'm sending you to hell."

He swung at her and Shauna jumped back. She tried to use her Venae to grab the blade, but couldn't overpower Henry's grip. She looked around the room for anything she could fight with and saw the obsidian dagger in Lucy's hand.

Telekinetically, she yanked the knife into her hand. Henry swung at her and she put the knife between his blade and her body. The force of his blow threw her back into the wall. He was strong, fully fed, and she was still living on trickles of blood. She would be stronger than him if she were sated. She couldn't dwell on that while Henry was swinging at her. With her back to the wall, he wasn't throwing her back every time she blocked, but she was barely keeping up with his swings. It was almost a blur of white bone against black obsidian. Tiny white flecks were spraying into the air with every hit, making it look like there was a mist between them.

Realizing Lucy's knife was damaging the bone weapon, Shauna saw her one chance. On the next block she hit back at his weapon and grabbed the bone blade with her mind, flexing it forward, through the knife she held in her hand. Both weapons shattered.

Henry threw the handle of his knife at Shauna and ran. The handle hit her face and she flinched, though the weapon hadn't hit with any sharp parts and didn't penetrate her skin. When she looked to chase after him, he was gone.

"Elsa?" Shauna asked,

"I'm okay," her friend replied in a strained grunt. "It hurt like molten steel being poured through a wound, but the marrow didn't stick inside me. I'll be fine."

"You're chasing him, right?" Lucy asked.

"I can't beat him," Shauna said.

"You can," Elsa said. "Take a pint from Moana; you'll be stronger and faster than Henry."

"He's long gone by now," Shauna said.

"He ran down, not up," Elsa said. "He has something up his sleeve, I'm sure, but you're a smart girl, you can stop him. We don't want him coming back up after he's ready to fight again."

Moana had already stepped close to Shauna and held out her wrist. Pressed for time, Shauna pushed the wrist aside and went for the throat. Sinking her fangs into the jugular vein, her mouth filled with blood. Moana went instantly limp in her arms. Three gulps of blood were enough. Shauna pressed her tongue to the wounds and the bite holes closed.

"That was bold of you," Elsa said. "Most vampires can't heal a neck wound fast enough not to kill their prey."

"I've done it before," Shauna said. "And that bastard was far worse off than Moana. She'll be fine, right?"

Elsa nodded. "She fainted when her blood pressure dropped, I'm sure. But she still has a pulse; she'll come to."

"Here," Jackie said. She handed the crossbow to Shauna. She'd reloaded the bolt and it was ready to shoot. "Remember that asshole almost killed Jonnie," Jackie said. "You promised Elsa he'd die."

"Slowly," Elsa added. She struggled to stand up, still holding her shoulder. She pulled Vlad's spearhead from a hidden pocket that ran along the outside of her thigh. "You don't carry this with you and you should, so I do it for you. You'll want this." She gave the knife to Shauna.

Shauna tucked the obsidian knife into her belt then took the crossbow and looked at the bone arrowhead. It was exactly the weapon that could kill a vampire slowly. She imagined Henry cowering in the corner of the revenant's room and then wondered if she could pull the trigger and shoot an unarmed man. Then she wondered if she could hit him if he wasn't standing still. She only had the one shot.

She got to the bottom of the stairs and Henry stood at the far end of the room, holding a pair of much smaller bone knives, one in each hand.

"Hah," he said. "I may not have your phasing trick, but I can dodge an arrow and you've just got the one."

"That's true," Shauna said. She reached out with her mind's hand and grabbed Henry, pushing him back into the wall and lifting him off the ground. With her freshly fed strength, Henry's apportation offered only token resistance. She held him there as she walked forward.

He dropped his knives. "I surrender," he said. "Go on, take me back to James."

She considered the option, but that still required Henry to be incapacitated. She aimed at his heart and pulled the trigger. The shot went into Henry's chest an inch higher than Shauna had aimed, but was probably still in his heart. She released her mental grip on him and he fell to the ground and gripped the arrow with both hands. He pulled it out but collapsed to his hands and knees. "You've killed me," he said. "I'll not survive a trip across the ocean."

Shauna looked at the revenant cage and back at Henry. That would be exactly the kind of death Elsa wanted for him. The thought of a man, even Henry, slowly dying in the pains of the cage and from the poison of the arrow, made Shauna queasy. She felt Moana's blood well up in her throat so much that she could taste it.

She knelt by Henry and grabbed his hair, pulling his gaze up to meet hers. "I'm sorry," she said quietly.

"You're not," Henry said. "I can see the satisfaction in your eyes."

"I was apologizing to Elsa," Shauna said. She took the knife from her belt and removed Henry's head.

Setting the severed head by the body, Shauna stood and turned away. She shook as uncontrollable tremors ran through her body. She hadn't been ready to kill so coldly. Moana's blood shot from her mouth and she fell forward to her hands and knees. All she could think about was not looking back at Henry.

"Shauna?" Jackie called down.

Shauna opened her mouth to reply, but only blood came out.

"Shauna?" Jackie's voice was closer, but much quieter. A moment later she heard Jackie's shoes running across the stone floor. "Shauna!" Jackie screamed loud enough to rattle the steel cage.

Sitting back, Shauna looked up at Jackie and whispered, "I'm not hurt."

"You're crying," Jackie said. "And you're covered in blood." She leaned close and kissed Shauna's cheeks under her eyes.

"Thank you," Elsa said, her voice still strained. Shauna hadn't noticed her come down the stairs. Elsa walked past Shauna and tapped Henry's head with her foot.

"He died too fast," Shauna said, though the words were mumbled. She didn't feel in control of her own body yet. She still trembled and wasn't sure she'd gotten all of the blood she'd just drunk purged from her stomach.

"Dead is dead," Elsa said. "That's what was important to me. He's dead. More important to me is that you're not. Well, you're undead, not dead-dead."

Shauna smiled at Elsa's weak humor. Henry's body was starting to dry up and flake away. It wouldn't be long until nothing remained of Henry but his clothes and his weapons.

"That's all I needed to see," Lucy said. "After watching that, no one could convince me I could kill a vamp like you. Coerce me and I'll go back to secretly waiting to restart the purge if a purer vamp ever pops up. Leave me with my memories and I'll know better."

Shauna put her will to her words and asked, "Are you being sincere and honest?"

"I am," Lucy said. "You scare me bloodless."

Jackie handed Lucy the bracer back. "If the council can tell you had that off, tell them Henry took it off, but he's dead now."

"They can tell," Lucy said. "I'll be sure to use that."

When Lucy put the bracer back on, Shauna heard the voices in her head as Lucy explained and a few of the other council members expressed their concern for her. She wondered how different their thoughts sounded when they weren't speaking to the whole council.

CHAPTER 8

Henry's finding them within a day of their arrival told them they were close. At least they assumed they were. They spent the evenings searching the many castles and fortresses in the area or simply walking the streets of Bucharest looking for any signs of another vampire. There weren't any, which seemed to indicate that they were close to a group of hunters. They hoped the group would be Bertellus' group. Still, they kept searching for another vampire under the assumption that any vampire that survived this long would know how to find the hunters so they could avoid them.

"We should have interrogated Henry," Shauna said as she and Elsa wandered the club district on the third night.

"No," Elsa said. "You did the right thing. He's not the type that would have broken. We tried."

"You said you had other methods," Shauna said.

"I wasn't really thinking of getting him to talk," Elsa said. "Sometimes torture is just meant to cause suffering. I don't know if the person I am could have done the things I fantasized of doing to him. It was therapeutic to imagine it, but sometimes, fantasizing is as far as we really want to go with vengeance. At some point, taking it too far into reality can be scarring on the tormentor. I didn't change my ways by some epiphany while watching a sappy play or seeing children playing in the park."

"You didn't change your ways much," Shauna said. "I saw what you were doing to Henry back in James' basement and you tortured Napoleon to death."

"Trust me, we're not talking about the same thing," Elsa said. "Don't imagine. Don't ponder. What I did to Henry in James' basement and Napoleon at the Sorbonne was interrogation. Harsh interrogation, yes, but it wasn't anywhere near on the same level as what I dreamt of doing to Henry after he hurt Jonnie."

"Something you saw pushed your limits too far and you snapped back like a broken rubber band," Shauna guessed.

"And just like a broken rubber band, parts of me were forever removed," Elsa said. "If it matters to you, I wasn't the one doing the tormenting. I was merely an observer at that time."

"I'm very good at ignoring that you even had a past," Shauna said. "I really don't need any details to remind me why I ignore your past. It matters, but I'd still rather know as few details as possible."

The details had been getting harder and harder to avoid. Several of the places they stopped to check for hunters were the many places Vlad lived over his thousand years in the Carpathians. Every location seemed to have a room dedicated to causing suffering. Though all of the places were from before Elsa's time with Vlad, Shauna couldn't help but think how similar things must have been wherever Elsa had lived with Vlad. But that had been in Hungary, and they'd tracked Henry to Romania. If they hadn't found him there, Shauna would have suspected it was a wild goose chase. But they had found him. Shauna was sure Bertellus was close.

"Have you noticed anyone following us yet?" Shauna asked. If they couldn't find the hunters, they were hoping the hunters would find them.

"No one," Elsa said. "But we're not exactly leaving a trail of breadcrumbs. You vetoed the idea of leaving a trail of bodies."

"You were joking," Shauna said. "Please tell me you weren't serious."

Elsa reached around Shauna and squeezed her in a side hug. "Please tell me you know me better than to think I would be."

With all the reminders of who Elsa had been, Shauna's perception of who Elsa was now had blurred. Once she realized what was happening, Shauna apologized. "I know you," she said. "I'm just frustrated that we're not finding anything other than glimpses into a past we both want to forget."

"I think it's time we blow this town," Elsa said. "I am trying my hardest, but the fashion here is just not the same as Paris."

"We know Paris is a dead end," Shauna said.

"You're right," Elsa said. "The hunters are not there anymore. We wiped out their operations in that city. But…"

Shauna saw where Elsa was going and finished for her, "…you're the Empress of the Northern Roman Empire. If the hunters are looking for you, that's where they have the best chance of finding you."

"They're not looking for us here," Elsa said. "Since we can't find them, going back to Paris is the best way we can help them find us."

"Well we can't get to Paris before dawn," Shauna said.

"Nope," Elsa said. "We'll head west at sunset. Until then, there's only one thing we can do."

"And here's where you say 'Shop!'" Shauna said.

Elsa squeezed Shauna again. "And you doubted you knew me as well as you thought."

§

Around noon the next day, Shauna lounged on the couch, watching as Elsa's staff paraded across the room, modeling the clothing she'd bought that morning before dawn. Shauna didn't have Elsa's eye for couture and couldn't really see a significant difference between the skimpy dresses of that day with the ones from the day before. The suits on the men looked the same as well. Phoebe, the thirteen year old, seemed unhappy to wear long jeans and loose sweaters.

Shauna was sure Elsa was dressing the girl conservatively purely for Shauna's benefit. That Elsa could dress a young girl provocatively seemed well within Elsa's morality. Actually having sex with her, however, would not be something Elsa would do. That Phoebe was clearly frustrated by having her own bedroom further reminded Shauna that she would have to do something about Zylpha and she wouldn't just be sating her own need for morality.

Jackie lay on the couch with her head in Shauna's lap. Jonnie sat on another couch while Rudy rubbed her feet. Lucy, after two days of catching up with Elsa and failing in her attempts to milk Shauna for secrets, had returned to Italy.

"Have you decided on a pet yet?" Jackie asked. "I think Ursula is cute. Ross is a little too bulky for your tastes. You like muscles, but lean and mean muscles not the bulgy kind, right?"

"I like people," Shauna said. "For who they are, not what they look like. For a one night fling, sure, trim muscles are prettier. I can't see any of Elsa's staff as a pet. The reason for taking a pet is to have someone to handle our affairs in daylight. I know I need a pet to maintain the illusion of being harmed by the sun. These, however, are puppies and need to be cared for like puppies." Elsa hadn't been able to train one to run to the store and buy wine. They wouldn't leave the shelter without Elsa, though they would happily sleep on the floor by the foot of the bed and wait for her while she was out. They'd even clean if she asked them to.

"You're going to need to keep your Venae at full strength, which means a steady supply of blood," Jackie said. "The normal humans on Elsa's staff don't regenerate their blood fast enough to feed on once a month. A pet can be fed on a few ounces a night or a pint a week and be fine."

"You keep telling me," Shauna said. Jackie hadn't actually detailed the regeneration rate for a pet to that level before. She'd just said pets regenerate blood faster than normal humans.

"And you keep not taking a pet," Jackie said. "Henry wasn't our last battle. You need to be at full strength until whoever is leading these hunters, Bertellus or whatever leader there may be, is dead."

"We're just supposed to be gathering information," Shauna said. "If we're just spying, I don't need to overpower anyone."

Jackie sat up, "You do remember that pile of dust in the basement, right?"

There wasn't a pile of dust. After a couple days, even the dust disintegrated to nothing. Shauna said, "Henry was different. He had his vendetta against Elsa and Elsa was in full reciprocation."

"Fine," Jackie said. "Maybe Henry was a special worst case scenario. Is it a risk you want to take? It's not a risk I'm happy with you taking."

"It's sweet that you care so much for my well-being," Shauna said.

Jackie kissed Shauna's cheek. "It's not just that I love you, you're the biggest wall between me and vampire hunters from hell and I want you to be a wall and not a speed bump."

"Are you guys even watching?" Elsa asked.

"Watching, yes," Shauna said. Her eyes were facing the strutting staff. "Paying attention? Not really. Sorry. Jackie is insisting I find a pet."

"You didn't tell her?" Elsa asked Jackie. Jackie responded by glaring at Elsa. Whatever it was, Elsa had just rushed her timing.

"What didn't she tell me?" Shauna asked.

"Your sister is meeting us in Paris," Jackie said. "We leave at sunset."

"I guess if we can't find the party, we hope the party finds us," Shauna said. "Are we actually going to get involved in the politics or are we just passing through again? I'm sure they love us there since we mucked up the local politics and left."

"Right, Elsa killed the pretender," Jackie said. "And now she has to take care of her country."

"I don't know if you can say I killed him," Elsa said. "I was a thousand miles away when he died."

"He was strapped to some nefarious device that killed him slowly," Jackie said. "And you're the one that strapped him in."

"First, the death would have been instantaneous," Elsa said. "The impending doom took a few days but was, at times, painless."

"Are you even trying to not offend me?" Shauna asked.

"I didn't say that he suffered excruciating pain at all times unless the springs were resetting," Elsa said. "I was trying to be conscientious of your sensibilities. He'd be alive now if he'd told us about Bucharest sooner. From the time he blurted out this city's name as where to look for Henry, Milady didn't have time to undo the straps before the vorpal blade went snicker-snack. At least she said she didn't have time. I'm not convinced she wasn't lying. He did offend her as well."

Since they were going to Paris, Shauna had a way to get Elsa and Jackie to stop haranguing her about a pet. "What if I promised to take a pet before we left Paris?" Shauna spoke French. She could take a Frenchman or French woman as a pet, if Elsa and Jackie made her.

"I know you will," Jackie said.

Elsa blurted, "What she's saying is that she trusts you to try."

They were hiding something, but Shauna was tired of the games. "I'm napping until sunset. Come find me if you want to do something other than talk." She extricated herself from Jackie's embrace and went to the bedroom she and Jackie had laid claim to.

Elsa and Jackie did follow her and no one spoke a word until sunset.

CHAPTER 9

Le Obscurité Infinie was similar to how Shauna remembered it. Instead of a man behind the bar, the blonde vamp, Milady deWinter, sat on a stool watching movies on a tablet computer. The back booth, where Ali had been watching soccer, had a short haired woman watching soccer.

Milady had proven a loyal associate since they'd met her. She was not at all the conniving character Dumas had made her out to be in his novel. Then again, if Shauna looked at recent events from the pretend Napoleon's point of view, she wouldn't seem so unlike the character named for her. Still, Shauna believed deWinter's account that Dumas made her seem evil because she'd stopped being receptive to his advances once she learned he was a married man.

"Don't bother that dyke, she's scary as hell," deWinter said as Shauna was staring toward the back booth.

"I can hear you," the woman in the back booth called back. "I'm offended."

"Sorry for calling you a dyke," deWinter said.

"I don't mind that," the woman said as she walked to the bar. She wore an army green tank top and a plaid skirt with knee high army boots. Her hair wasn't just short; if it were just a little longer, Shauna could call it peach-fuzz. "I mean don't call me scary." She held out her hand to Shauna. "I'm Julia, Artemis' blooddaughter." Julia had a country twang to her voice, as if she were from Nashville or Texas.

Without taking the offered hand, Shauna introduced herself, the twins, Elsa and all of Elsa's staff.

Julia pulled her hand back, running it across her scalp and said, "I know you're a bad ass, Shauna. Artemis told me you're the blooddaughter of James. We vamps of purer blood than the council don't need to be so secretive around each other."

"You don't have the aura," Shauna said. It made sense. Artemis didn't have an aura either.

"Which council are you purer than?" Milady asked. "I know you're real council pure, not the fake one Jean controlled." Jean had been claiming the crown and the name 'Napoleon'. "But it sounds like Julia is talking about being more pure than the real council."

"She is," Elsa said. She then stared Milady in the eyes and said, "Things we discuss when I'm around you will only recall while I'm around. Ditto for Shauna here."

"Technically, as a member of the council, I am as pure as the council," Shauna said, holding up her bracer.

"Just like Julia's," Milady said. "Is she council too?"

"She's in contact with us, but not technically one of us," Shauna said. As the keeper of the Blood Temple, Julia would be connected to the council but wouldn't have any authority to speak. All she could do was listen.

"I'm Amenhetop," Julia said.

"You're a woman and Amenhetop is a myth," deWinter said.

"And that's how you'll think of me when talking to anyone but me," Julia said. Shauna had known Artemis had put one of her line in the Blood Temple to pretend to be Amenhetop, the keeper of the Temple and the alleged first vampire according to the Elder Council's knowledge. Henry had killed the real Amenhetop almost a month earlier. There was a well in the back of the bar that led down to the temple, which is why Amenhetop's alter-ego hung out at that bar. Shauna hadn't expected to find a vamp as pure as Artemis' blooddaughter.

"Laura's not here yet?" Shauna asked deWinter.

"She called to say she was on the way from the airport," deWinter said. "I told her I've been keeping her bar wet."

"And my kingdom?" Elsa asked. DeWinter had also been acting as Elsa's regent.

"Quiet," deWinter said. "Vamps whisper among themselves about the new Empress who truly is the Blood

Countess. No one wants to invoke the wrath of the woman who killed the pretender, and pretend, Napoleon."

"Do you mean me or you?" Elsa asked.

"Either," deWinter said. "Or Both. One vamp told me you just looked at Nap crossly and he exploded."

Shauna laughed along with Elsa and the twins. Only Milady had been present when the imposter Napoleon had died.

"Honey," Laura's voice rang from the bar's front door. "We're home."

Laura walked in with a tall woman Shauna had never seen before. Shauna didn't take the time to look closer at the tall woman when she recognized another human girl behind Laura. The blue hair stood out.

"Azure," Shauna said. "How?"

The Blue haired girl looked at the twins and said, "Whichever is Jackie, she told me to come here. She said you needed a pet, and told me what that entailed, and I'm here."

"You told a human about Vampires?" Shauna asked Jackie.

Jackie nodded and said. "I told her we're part of a very wealthy role-playing society."

"It sounds like a better job than working a call center and," Azure's voice took on a seductive lilt, "the benefits sounded better. So, is there some ritual or do I just get a leash and collar?"

"It's a bit more complex than that," Shauna said. "Let's get a bottle of wine and talk about it." She waved to Milady who had already set a bottle of wine on the bar with two glasses.

Laura waved her hand. When Shauna looked over, her sister said, "This is Brooke, she's Una's blooddaughter."

At the mention of Una's name, Shauna paused. Brooke was taller than Shauna, even wearing shorter heels. She had naturally red hair tied in a ponytail that hung over one shoulder and the kind of chest that made Shauna wonder if they were implants or real. She wore jeans and a varsity jacket.

Shauna introduced herself "I'm Shauna, but you've probably been told who we are."

"From your sister's stories, I know everyone but her," Brooke gestured to Julia.

Julia laughed. "Apparently, I'm just your average vamp in this crowd. I'm not used to that. This is my first time in almost two thousand years actually meeting a vampire more pure than me that wasn't Artemis, and there are three of you here. I'm humbled in these rare moments when I'm not the baddest bad ass in the room."

"I wouldn't think you're not," Shauna said. "You, as the bloodchild of Artemis, have probably been trained to fight, and certainly to hunt. That gives you an advantage over all of us."

"She's been trained." Julia pointed to Brooke. "From the look of her, she's trained twenty hours a day for at least a year. Her body language tells me she's dying to actually get into a fight and see how she does. She's a coiled spring, waiting for release."

"Two years," Brooke said. "Hunters attacked my bloodmother's home two years ago. Of her current brood, I am all there is."

Shauna found it interesting that Brooke so clearly separated the vampires descended from Una into two groups, the old brood and the current brood. Other than Artemis' line and Reilla's small family, all vampires were descended from Una. Shauna didn't consider herself any different than the rest of James's blood children. She wondered why Brooke so decisively declared herself the lone one of Una's current children.

"And she's all there will be until we kill John Bertellus," Laura said. "Her line has the Artemis curse. There can be only one per generation. It's the cost of not being visible to Mala and not having the aura."

Julia said, "It's not a curse. Magic has a price and the price of hiding from vampires who can see all the other vampires, and Mala wasn't always the only one, is that there can only be one bloodchild to each bloodparent of our lines."

"So Bertellus is Brooke's bloodson?" Shauna asked.

"No," Brooke said. "Bertellus consumed my love, my bloodson. He stole his Venae. A trick he learned from the journals of your father." She was looking at Elsa when she finished.

"Hey, don't look at me all accusingly," Elsa said. "I neither wrote nor read Drac's diaries. They disappeared when he died. And I don't know John Bertellus."

"He knows you," Brooke said. "He had pictures and paintings of you on his wall dating back four hundred years. He had pictures of many vampires, but only you got a whole wall."

"You guys have a script or something?" Azure asked. "This is pretty intense."

Shauna realized she would have to explain to Azure what was going on sooner rather than later. "You guys sort this out and figure out what we're going to do next. I need to chat with my pet."

"You're keeping her?" Jackie asked hopefully.

Shauna didn't answer; she didn't know a word for accusatory and thankful. She just gave Jackie a look, which she hoped could cover both. She took Azure by the arm to Julia's booth. She turned off the television and let Azure sit first. Shauna sat beside the blue haired girl.

"The first thing you need to know is that we're not playing at anything," Shauna said.

"Um, okay," Azure said. "I remember from the graveyard that night, you were a pretty intense chick, but that's okay. We all have our quirks."

"No, this isn't a game or a joke," Shauna said. "I am a vampire. The blood on your shirt was my being a sloppy eater and I'm sorry about that. You remember it differently because I can coerce you and alter your memories. In case you don't believe me…" Shauna interrupted herself to reach out with her Venae and carry the wine bottle and glasses from the bar to her table.

Sliding away from Shauna on the bench, Azure pulled her legs up and wrapped her arms around her knees. "So, how much of what I remember is real and how much is just something you made up for me?"

"The only thing I changed was how you were bloodied," Shauna said. "Everything else was real." It wasn't the whole truth. Shauna had coerced the entire encounter to go the way she wanted it to go.

"I'd never kissed a woman before that night," Azure said. "Are you sure you didn't coerce me to want to?"

Shauna paused before responding. Elsa had always assured her that she couldn't use coercion to change a person on a fundamental level. And she'd used the specific example that coercion could not change a person's sexuality. Shauna shook her head and said, "I didn't coerce you to make you gay or bisexual. Whatever you are, that's you."

"How can I trust you?" Azure asked.

"It's kind of an all or nothing thing," Shauna said. "You know I can manipulate your memories, but I can't change who you are. You have to accept that I will be trustworthy or that you don't care if I'm not."

"So you're really going to drink my blood?" Azure asked.

"That is part of the vampire-pet arrangement," Shauna said. "I drink some of your blood and you drink some of mine. In exchange, you won't age or get sick and you'll heal just about any wound that doesn't kill you outright and I'll do everything in my power to make sure that doesn't happen to you. If you died, it would kill me, and I'm not speaking figuratively there. That is the ultimate cost of the bond. We share life and we share death."

"I'm supposed to want to do this while you're in the middle of a war?" Azure asked.

"It sounds bad because it is bad," Shauna said. "But I do need a pet to have the strength I need to win this war, and Jackie seems to think you're my best choice for a pet. I have to agree with her. I picked you in the graveyard because you are so much like me."

"Do I get time to think on it?" Azure asked.

"Not really," Shauna said. "You'll have some time to change your mind if you say yes, but if you say no, it's final."

"Explain that," Azure said.

Shauna took a breath and thought. She liked Azure but couldn't think of a way to convince her, from free will, to stay as her pet. In the same situation, even when Shauna wanted to become a vampire, she'd have long since run out the door. Shauna wasn't convinced Azure only stayed because she was too afraid to try to run. "If you say no, we send you on a weeklong tour of Paris with a memory of meeting me, but me being too busy to spend time with you and then you go home. If you say yes, I start getting your body used to my blood by feeding you a drop on the first day and a little more on the second. At any time until the pet bond is made, you can stop and leave and take the tour of Paris and go home. Once that pet bond is final, and it could be a week or a month or longer, we're stuck together until we die or I make you into a vampire."

"I'd just be a pet, not a girlfriend?" Azure asked in such a way that she seemed disappointed at not being the girlfriend too.

"It's more complex than simple titles," Shauna said. "I'd want us to be lovers, but it wouldn't be exclusive. I have Jackie and sometimes Elsa and Jonnie. And Jackie has a pet, a man named Karlo, so…"

"So we're somewhere between Mormons and swingers?" Azure said. She wasn't sounding like she was questioning whether she'd do it, but looking for explanations for what she was going to do.

"Like I said, it's complicated." Shauna pricked her finger on her fang and held it out toward Azure. "And it all starts with this one drop of blood."

§

The perfume factory didn't look at all like it had when Napoleon had used it as his court. Previously it had looked like a makeshift night club with many walls and other surfaces being nothing more than black, spray-painted plywood. Elsa had remodeled, adding a heavy Victorian neo-classical look to it, but done in glossy black and metallic red. There were lots of mirrors and video screens as well. The lighting was black lights and dark red laser shows.

"How do you do this when you're not even on the continent?" Shauna asked Elsa. They'd been in Paris three days and this was the first time they visited Elsa's 'Throne Room'. She'd bought the factory from the government with the promise to clean up the façade and maintain it at its eighteenth century appearance. Inside, it had become 'Le Flueve de Sang'.

"I got the idea from Rick and his Grue's Home," Elsa explained as she gave Shauna and Azure a tour of the club. "Milady and Ursula will take turns being our 'Queen of Blood' and will hold court up in that VIP area. Zylpha trained her slaves to be able to play the dominant role in fetish play, so I'm sure Ursula will do fine." She pointed to a raised platform above and behind the main bar. "Milady will be managing the place when I'm gone and I intend to be gone a lot. And I'll have my personal VIP lounge downstairs and I'm not even going to pretend to have a blood fountain. My fountain will be wine. Artemis brought me an old tiered font that dispenses wine. It's supposed to be special and not allow the wine to become contaminated or evaporate while it's in the fountain."

"Rick's bar was fake," Shauna said. "Other than him and his cronies, the only vampire I saw at his bar was you, and you were only there for me. His VIP club was just a role-playing group. This looks like you're really trying to make a club for vamps."

"There will be a no-feeding rule outside of the throne room and the only people there will be vampires and their pets."

"Bold of you to put vampires right where people will look for them," Shauna said. "I'm surprised the other members of the council didn't object." They'd discussed it just that evening through the bracelets. All of them trusted Elsa to handle the situation with due discretion.

"Everyone's going to look like a vampire," Elsa said. "That's the beauty of it all. The cover charge includes a pair of the good fangs, the acrylic ones that glue onto the canines and everyone on the staff is going to have either more permanent glue or actual implants. This is France; when I hire someone, they'll expect to be employed for life. It's almost illegal to fire someone here, so I'm pushing for implants. The real coup is the fake mirrors. There are plenty of real mirrors, the kind both vampires and humans reflect in. But there are three that are just flipped video monitors running programs to edit people out of the images, leaving just their clothes."

"It'd be more fun to edit out the clothes," Azure said.

"It can do that, too." Elsa said. "Using infrared and ultraviolet light and special filters, the program doesn't even have to extrapolate much. But, I'm saving that one for special occasions. It has to be warmer, when men aren't wearing wool suits."

"You're hiding vampires by making everyone look like a vampire," Shauna said.

"I'll have enough human regulars to make finding a vampire here searching for a needle in a haystack," Elsa said. "It only really works because no one with any intelligence actually believes in us."

"I believed in us," Shauna said, then realized by Elsa's expression she'd been specifically needling her with the comment. "Are you sure you can guarantee this place will be a success?"

"I'm going to cheat," Elsa said. "As I meet and greet my guests, I'll coerce them to love the place."

Shauna tried to find a moral objection to that. It seemed wrong, but so harmless, Shauna couldn't make herself care. "Anyway, so are you going to have a wine list with three hundred dollar bottles?"

"Please," Elsa said. "We're in Europe, its all Euros here. But, no partier will pay that. For the champagne, three to four hundred a bottle is my price point, but the wine is all thirty a bottle and ten a glass. The selection is limited to eight varieties."

"Those are high prices," Shauna said.

"I'm not trying to be the bar on the corner," Elsa said. "I do want customers with standards. When someone tells their friends they spent the night at Le Flueve de Sang, I want their friends to be impressed. If I like someone, I'll tell them, 'Whenever you can afford to come to Le Flueve, you'll want to come.'"

It did seem a harmless coercion once Elsa spelled it out.

Several people wearing black pants and blood red shirts were working behind the bars, unpacking bottles and glasses.

"I thought your grand opening was still a month off," Shauna said.

"I'm open for private parties starting with my post coronation Friday night," Elsa said.

"Friday?" Shauna asked. Friday was only two days away. "I didn't get an invitation."

"Milady is handling the after-party invites, but for the coronation itself, I didn't send any," Elsa said. "I assumed you'd be with me, but I've let a few others know. All I need there are my friends and a council member to actually bestow the crown and title on me with the authority of the council."

"So me," Shauna said.

"Actually, Lucy," Elsa said. "I hope you're not insulted, but I wanted someone the vampires knew, rather than someone who was just a name and a mystery. Besides, I need you as my second, my de facto heir."

Shauna grabbed Elsa's shoulder. "I don't know how to do that," she said. "I don't know if I want to do that." Shauna had no desire to have power over other people or be responsible for them. She was still adjusting to having just one person dependant on her; she couldn't imagine hundreds.

"It's an honorary title, more tradition than rule," Elsa said. "Vampire royalty rarely leave their station in such a way that the heir matters in the succession. It's not like we die of illness or old age and the most likely person to kill me is someone with aspirations to the throne, which means they'll plan to kill you as well."

"That's comforting," Shauna said sarcastically. "And there are hunters who will still be after us."

"Not for long," Elsa said. "At least no serious hunters will be around for long. Or if they are, we won't be in a position to worry about them. I can deal with the run-of-the mill loon with a wooden stake and mallet. I have full faith that in the days to come you'll wipe the dangerous hunters off the globe. Specifically: Friday."

"What?" Shauna asked.

"The coronation: it's a trap," Elsa said. "Early Friday morning, when I officially become Empress Elisabet Bathory, I expect there will be party crashers."

"Maybe this would be a good day to start that tour of Paris we talked about," Azure said.

"It just might be," Shauna agreed dourly. She glared at Elsa and said, "You should have given me more time to prepare. We're supposed to have James here for the next big fight."

"Bertellus won't show himself," Elsa said. "He's demonstrated a resolve to send his minions to die at our feet. He replaced his last angel with Henry and I've no doubt that

Henry's replacement will show up at the coronation to die at our feet."

"I would have liked more time to come up with a plan," Shauna said.

"My love," Elsa said. "You're tough as nails but your tactics in a fight are scarcely more than raw pugilism. What kind of a plan do you need?"

Shauna looked around the room for ways to use the space to her advantage.

"Brooke is working on it," Elsa said. "And the coronation won't be here. I don't want my new place to get shot up. We booked Notre Dame. It's going to look like a wedding from a distance."

"Who's the groom?" Shauna asked, assuming Elsa would be playing the part of the bride.

"Two brides," Elsa said. "It took a hell of a donation to get the Catholic Church to agree to that in Notre Dame. They probably only agreed because it was in the wee hours of the morning. And don't be disappointed but Jonnie will be playing the part of Mrs. Elsa." She scrunched her lips and rolled her eyes and then added, "You know what I mean. Jackie is her Maid of Honor; you're mine. I got you a dress. It's a frosted pink. Jonnie's party will be in turquoise."

"You have all this planned and I didn't know?" Shauna asked.

"I've actually been too busy planning to talk about it," Elsa said. "By the way, could you tell Jonnie and Jackie? I don't think I've talked to them about it yet."

"Tell me Milady and Lucy know," Shauna said. She wasn't sure she knew how to ask Lucrezia to officiate a fake wedding and real coronation.

"They do," Elsa said.

CHAPTER 10

The white flowered garlands draping around the pillars of the cathedral brought back memories of when Shauna had a future planned that involved meeting a nice man and getting married. Marriage wasn't something she saw as impossible for her future; she just doubted it would be to a nice man. She looked across the altar to where Jackie was helping Jonnie arrange her veil. She doubted it would be to Jackie either. She could only imagine marrying a man. The part in question was how nice he would be, since he'd undoubtedly be a vampire. Or, maybe it would be Jackie. As much as her life had changed, not much would surprise her.

Elsa stood at Shauna's side, arguing with Lucy about how far to go with the charade wedding. Julia's voice came through an earpiece Shauna wore. "I found my position."

"Where?" Shauna asked. Julia was covering the outside as a sniper.

Julia said, "You wouldn't believe me if I told you."

"Oh?" Shauna said. "Try me."

"Well," Julia replied."It was tricky knowing the enemy could be doing the same thing over the same area and I didn't want to reveal we know we have an enemy. I had to think of where to be that could see where they'd put their snipers and not be somewhere their snipers would see. Once I found seven places they could be and have a shot through a window to the alter area, I only had one place in all of Paris that could see all seven."

"You're on the Eiffel Tower?" Shauna asked.

"It's a longer shot than I'm used to but, as long as the wind stays slow and constant, I can make this shot nine out of ten times. I will say, at three thirty in the morning, the City of Lights isn't really living up to its name."

Jackie answered her phone and talked to Laura a moment. Shauna could overhear most of the conversation.

Laura was at Le Obscurité Infinie with the pets. They were modifying some bullet proof tuxedos Elsa had shipped in to fit the pets and former slaves. Then Laura told Jackie to congratulate Shauna on making Azure her pet.

It surprised Shauna, but she didn't have any reason to doubt her sister. Every vampire had different strengths and weaknesses, some had abilities most vampires didn't and some lacked abilities most vampires had. Laura could perceive the link between a pet and their vampire as a silvery ropelike connection. Shauna lacked the ability to feel her pet's presence from any distance.

"I heard," Shauna said when Jackie got off the phone. "I guess it's too late for you to object."

"Why would I object?" Jackie asked. "I'm not jealous or stupid. You need blood and I can't give you that. The bed we sleep in is still our bed and the pets sleep in our bed, we don't sleep in theirs."

Shauna knew the relationship between pets and masters was never pure romantic love; the vampire controlled the relationship. The pet depended more on the vampire for immortality than the vampire depended on the pet. A vampire could get blood from anywhere; pets only got their immortality from their one vampire. However close a vamp got emotionally to their pet, that skew in their interdependence kept the relationship off balance.

The sound of shattering glass drew Shauna's attention away. Lucy, standing by the altar, let out a tiny yelp then collapsed to the ground. Elsa rushed to her side.

"Got him," Julia said. "The problem with being three miles away is that it took my bullet a couple seconds to hit him and he got a shot off. Was anyone hurt?"

"Lucy," Shauna said. Elsa had already dragged her behind the altar.

"You've got half a dozen guys running in," Julia said. "I dropped another one, but the others got past my kill zone. You try hitting a running man with a one point eight second lead time."

Shauna could see the men scattering at the other end of the Cathedral, trying to keep pillars between them and the vampires by the altar.

"We'll take it from here," Shauna said to Julia. She checked to make sure Jackie and Jonnie had taken cover. They had their backs pinned to pillars.

Elsa stood calmly in front of the altar, but she was half-transparent. She'd phased to the point she usually used to walk through walls. It might not be enough to keep a bone weapon from hurting her, but even gold bullets wouldn't touch her.

Bullets started flying, bouncing harmlessly off of Shauna. The sting, like sleet in a high wind, annoyed her, but she'd been shot so often in the past three months, she'd learned to ignore it.

A man wearing thick white robes walked down the center of the cathedral toward the altar. He had a shaved scalp and wore a thick gold band around his head like a coronet. If he was one of the vampires calling themselves an angel, the band was meant to look like a halo. He said, "Soldiers, return to base, you can't hurt these. No sense in getting you killed."

The bullets stopped and the men walked toward the entrance. They each paused before sprinting through the door. Clearly, they knew there was still a sniper out there, but they must have feared it less than they feared the vampires inside the cathedral.

The 'angel' drew a blade of gold flecked with shards of black glass or more likely, obsidian. "Shauna McAllister," he said, "You've been quite the headache and I wasn't expecting that of such newly dark blood." His aura was pink; he wasn't as pure as she.

"You're here to die," Shauna said. "I haven't met one of you yet that I haven't killed." Expecting the ambush, she had drunk a pint from Azure just before heading to the cathedral. Still, she didn't feel as ready as she acted.

"You haven't met me," the angel said. "This is my war; I'm more prepared to kill you than my disciples were."

"Who are you?" Shauna asked.

"Ask your lover," the man said as he walked slowly up the center of the Cathedral.

Shauna looked to Jackie, but realized the angel was watching Elsa.

Elsa was standing with her arms crossed over her chest and glaring at the angel. "His name is Jonathan Gainer. He was my husband until I killed him for killing my bloodfather."

"I am John Bertellus. Jonathan Gainer died," John said. "You made mockery of our vows. You betrayed me just as you betrayed Vlad. Somehow, in the midst of battle, convinced my ally, the most honorable man I've ever met, Michael, to turn on me. He tried to kill me, but I didn't die. I wasn't the only one left dying, though. One of Drac's brides was pinned to the stone wall with an arrow through her chest. I managed to drag myself to her and drink her blood before I succumbed to the sword in my chest. When I woke, I made sure I killed the bride, but you were gone, as was Michael, and Drac was little more than a fine dust being shuffled around the ruined chapel by the wind."

"And you stole Vlad's journals and learned to steal Venae," Elsa said. "Now you are killing all the vampires you can. Why?"

"As if revenge wouldn't be a good enough reason," John Bertellus said. "Perhaps I am an angel and ridding the world of a rotting blemish."

"I'd believe that of Jack Gainer," Elsa said. "He was a good man and a man I loved. But, you're not acting out of any kind of righteousness. You may have been, but you're not anymore. You've been coming after me and those I loved for months now."

"Mostly those you loved," Bertellus said. "We were good together as husband and wife. Vlad ruined what we had when you chose to return with him rather than stay with me."

"He would have killed you if I'd stayed," Elsa said. "I went with him to keep you alive."

"You could have killed him," Bertellus said. "It was always in your power to end his evil. And he trusted you; you could have gotten close enough to do it before he realized you were killing him."

"I would never forgive myself for that level of betrayal," Elsa said.

"Like you can't forgive me?" Bertellus said. "If you can't love me, no one may love you." He charged at Shauna, swinging his obsidian flecked gold sword.

Since they'd been planning to spring the trap on the hunters during the coronation, Shauna hadn't gotten the spearhead from Elsa yet. She reached out with her Venae and grabbed the closest metal object she could find, an iron rod with a simple cross at one end. She managed to block the angel's attacks, but he was cutting into the iron with each swing. She swung at him, but he was fast and tipped her rod away and riposted, cutting her shoulder.

The pain surprised her and she dropped the iron rod. He swung again and cut into her side. Shauna fell to her hands and knees and could barely keep herself up.

"Phase out," Elsa called.

Shauna tried, but couldn't focus through the pain. She looked up to see Bertellus moving to her side. He raised the sword and said, "You were almost a worthy challenge."

"Wait!" Elsa said.

"I don't think so," Bertellus replied. He started to swing.

"I still love you," Elsa said.

The sword stopped, but not until after it barely cut into the back of Shauna's neck.

"What?" Bertellus asked.

Shauna lost her strength and crumpled to the floor.

"I've always loved you, Jack," Elsa said. "I always will. End this, and I'll come with you. We can finally be husband and wife."

"Is this a ploy?" Bertellus asked. His sword now hung from his hands to rest the tip on the stone floor.

"It's a promise," Elsa said. "One we made to each other two hundred years ago." She stepped close to John and put one of her hands on his. From where Shauna lay, she could see Elsa pulling Vlad's black obsidian spearhead from its sheath.

"I'll do as you ask," Bertellus said. "I'll disband my army, declare victory and retire from the battlefield. Come with me, we can live in London or Romania. I don't care as long as I'm with you. That's all I ever really…" His words were cut short when he screamed in pain. Elsa jumped back. She had a hand on her thigh; she hadn't finished drawing Vlad's spearhead.

Bertellus spun around. Shauna saw Jonnie standing on the far side of him. A small bone knife stuck from the center of Bertellus' back.

"She's my love now, bastard," Jonnie said.

"I should have known," Bertellus said. He swung at Jonnie. He moved too fast for her to even get an arm up in the way of his blade.

Jackie screamed as her sister's head fell from her shoulders.

Shauna caught it before it hit the ground, but there was nothing she could do. Jonnie was dead.

Bertellus spun back, holding his sword at Elsa and waving it threateningly. Elsa had the obsidian knife out and ran at him. He tried to lift his sword but Elsa was too close and moving too quickly. She leapt onto his chest, grabbing a handful of robes with one hand and wrapping her legs around his waist. She cut his throat and stabbed his face with Vlad's obsidian blade.

"I lied," Elsa screamed. "I lied." She repeated the words over and over as she thrust the knife at Bertellus. The blade tangled in the robes more often than not, but she drew blood on several strikes. Bertellus couldn't untangle his sword from between them. He grunted and threw Elsa into the altar. A loud snap resonated through the hall as her back bent backward over the altar. "I lied," she whispered and closed her eyes.

"We're past killing now," Bertellus said. "Starting tonight, your friends all suffer and then die." He lifted the sword, but staggered. His actions were slow and unsteady. He backed away toward the door of the cathedral.

Shauna tried to stand up and chase him but couldn't move through her pain. She gave up and just lay there beside Jonnie's body. Shauna handed her head to Jackie and said, "I'm so sorry."

"She died a fool," Jackie said. "A stupid brave fool. She didn't know Elsa was bluffing. She should have known Elsa loved her and not him."

Shauna's phone rang. She couldn't get it out of her pocket to answer it. The rings fell silent and then Jackie's phone started to ring. Jackie pulled it out and answered it, "Laura, hi," Jackie said.

"Is Jonnie okay?" Laura asked. Shauna could hear the conversation on Jackie's phone. Her sister's voice was shaky and quiet. "Rudy just collapsed and died. There was nothing we could do for him."

"Bertellus killed Jonnie," Jackie sobbed. The words weren't really clear, but Shauna knew what she'd said.

Laura apparently knew, too. "I'm so sorry." After a moment of silence, Laura asked. "Is he dead? Did Shauna and Elsa get revenge for you?"

"He walked away," Jackie said. "We hurt him, he nearly killed us. He did kill us." She dropped the phone and climbed over Jonnie's body, hugging it.

Shauna crawled over and held Jackie. She couldn't think of words, so she remained silent.

"Jackie?" Laura's voice on the phone said. She repeated it twice before the phone fell silent.

Lucy helped Elsa as she climbed off the altar and both sat at Shauna's side. Elsa said, "I didn't see that outcome when I lied to John. Is it irony that she was killed by the man I named her after?"

No one answered her and she didn't say anything more. Other vampires came into the cathedral and sat beside them. Before long there was a circle of vampires. Laura, Brooke, Milady and Julia sat there and watched as Jonnie's body started to crumble.

"We always suspected this war would kill us," Jackie said, running her hands through the dust around Jonnie's body. "We wouldn't say it to anyone else. I would never have thought it would only be one of us. Elsa was so set on revenge for Henry almost killing Jonnie. I hoped the fighting ended with Henry's death. I suppose now, we're out to kill John Bertellus."

"I'll do it alone," Elsa said. "Well, me and Brooke and James." She ran her hand across Jackie's shoulder. "You and Shauna go find your happily ever after."

Shauna was about to protest, to promise not to let Elsa face such evil again alone. She wanted to comfort Jackie, and wasn't sure vowing revenge would be what Jackie wanted. "We can take time to think on this," Shauna said. "James and Una will come and they can take him out with all the effort of crushing an ant."

"They're enroute," Julia said. "Artemis is bringing our whole line to help. James and Una are with them on the cruise ship. They'll be here in six days."

"And we don't know where Bertellus is yet," Brooke said. "When they get here, Bertellus will die. But, they can't kill him if they can't find him."

"We'll find him," Jackie said. Her voice was quiet but crisp. "I want," she paused and clenched her jaw before continuing, "No, I need to see him dead."

"I kept my word with Henry," Shauna said. "I won't promise a slow death, but I do promise he won't survive another week." With James and Una due in six days, she just had to make sure to know where to find him. "Where do we start?"

"London or Romania," Elsa said. "His words. He has roots somewhere."

"Henry went to Romania," Shauna said, recalling where the hunter had run to after the fight at the Blood Temple.

"Is that the obvious answer?" Jackie said. "Don't you think he'd realize that?"

"No," Elsa said. "He won't be rational. I may have a broken heart, but I'm not crazy. He was not the least bit sane."

"He always seemed like a kook to me," Brooke said. "I really should have just walked away as soon as I saw his obsession wall. Anyone with a wall covered in pictures of Elizabeth Bathory and Lucrezia Borgia is probably someone to run far away from.

"I have a wall like that," Lucy said. "Does your rule hold true if one of those is a self-portrait?"

"Especially so," Brooke said.

Shauna tried to laugh but couldn't even get a smile up. Laura chuckled once and then the room fell back into silence. By sunrise they all stared at an empty spot on the floor. Jackie had already taken Jonnie's wedding gown and folded it neatly in front of her.

Laura kept the priests away and coerced them to ignore the circle of vampires sitting on the floor by the altar. She'd already talked to the police, convincing them that some tourists had set off fireworks near the cathedral.

"We need to get out of here," Lucy said. "Sunlight is already coming through the windows and it's getting uncomfortable, fast."

"I don't care," Jackie said.

"I do," Shauna said, taking Jackie by the hand. "Where do we go?"

"The catacombs?" Lucy ventured.

"You can't get there from here," Milady said. "Whatever we're going to do, we have about a minute or two before we conflagrate.

"There's a crypt here," Elsa said. "I saw a brochure."

"The archeological crypts are underground, but not under here. They're under the courtyard out front," Milady said, pointing to the door. "If we made a run for it, even as fast as we are, the sun is up so we're not fast enough. We'd fry in seconds."

That was enough information for Shauna. "Laura, take Julia. Elsa, Lucy's all yours. I'll take Milady. Jackie, if you can, bring Brooke, otherwise I'll come back for her."

"I can take her," Jackie said. "We're just going to drag these people through the mud to somewhere past the doors?"

"That's the plan," Shauna said. "I think we're out of time to come up with a better one."

No one did. Shauna grabbed Milady and shifted into the Venae, away from the mortal world. She did so until she started to sink, but the ground still felt like a heavy mist. With her free hand and her feet, she swam in the direction of the doors and kept going until she emerged in a dark open space. The crypts, which looked more like a museum, were dark; the exhibit was not open yet for the day.

Elsa and Lucy were there already and the others followed just behind Shauna.

Shauna asked, "Now do we brainstorm on where to find Bertellus?"

"We sleep," Elsa said. "Someone who isn't exhausted, go coerce someone to keep the museum closed for the day. Maybe one of the museum workers should come make some blood donations. Healing a broken spine seems to have drained my strength.

"Where is Jonnie's gown?" Shauna asked Jackie.

"I left it under the cathedral," Jackie replied. "It was all there was left to bury." She started to sob and fell forward into Shauna's arms.

Elsa said, "I imagine they'll be shocked in a thousand years to find twenty first century clothing buried under a twelfth century building." She found a corner and put her back against the wall and wrapped her arms around her legs and put her head down over them. Elsa's voice was muffled, either by her position or tears or both, when she said, "Shauna, be a sweetie and go find us some wine. Two cases should be enough."

Shauna, distraught by Jonnie's death, didn't think to call her pet. She came back to the crypts with two crates of whatever bottles of wine were on the top shelf of the first store she found. Like everywhere else in the city, it was closed. She hadn't been in the mood to go out of her way to do the right thing, though she vowed to return later and pay for the wine.

When she walked back into the room they were hiding in, Brooke said, "I think Elsa meant for you to call her pet. Vampires aren't supposed to be able to walk in sunlight."

"All I want right now is to drink," Shauna said. "I'm tired of coercing people to think what I want them to think. Today, I'm just going to drink until sunset. Until then, let them think what they will." She took a bottle of wine and pressed her thumbnail tight to the ring of the bottle and flicked the end of the bottle off. It was a handy trick when there weren't any corkscrews in the room.

"I'm not so cavalier about such things," Brooke said. "Milady, Lucy, Julia, Shauna had this wine delivered. She's been touring the museum and at no point did she enter sunlight." Shauna had no doubt the less pure vampires had been coerced.

CHAPTER 11

Lucy set a ruby encrusted platinum tiara on Elsa's head. "Serve your empire; don't make your empire serve you."

"Don't take all the fun out of this," Elsa said. "I can do both."

It was official. Elsa was the Empress of the Northern Roman Empire.

The hundreds of patrons at the party cheered with plastic champagne flutes. For most of them, it was a gaudy ceremony to mark the opening of Le Flueve de Sang. The DJ played a fanfare and then resumed the dance beats.

Lucy said, "You just had the most attended coronation in vampire history."

Elsa turned around and hugged Shauna and Jackie. "It's not the same without Jonnie," she said.

"She wanted this for you," Shauna said. "Do what you do with that in mind."

"You think I'm going to be a decadent queen?" Elsa asked.

"Decadent?" Shauna guffawed. "Certainly. Evil? Not at all."

Elsa went to Milady and said, "Now that I'm empress, I'm tasking you with letting all the vampires in my empire know. Tell them they are expected to come present themselves to me during the month of April, or else."

"Or else?" Milady asked.

"Or else they won't be invited to my parties," Elsa said. "And my parties are epic." She stepped past Lucy to sit on the throne of her V.I.P. area. They used the main club instead of the throne room because while her throne room was completed, her throne, a design of wrought iron and red velvet with some gold leaf and lots of rubies, was going to take a few months to finish. The V.I.P. throne, a gilt, high backed chair she'd liberated from the Museums

Department's storage warehouse, didn't look quite right for a vampire queen, which is what she was so obviously pretending to be. Less obviously, she wasn't pretending. "As a second order: all of Napoleon's false edicts are disavowed. I can't repeal them because he was never in the proper station to make them. For now, let's just stick to the five laws."

She stood from the throne and handed Milady her tiara. "Until I return, you are my regent, again. I'm off to make the world safe for all vampires."

"You make it sound like you're going on a crusade," Lucy said. "Shall we get the blessings of the Pope?"

"Do you think he'd do that?" Elsa asked.

"No," Lucy said. "Even when I was Pope, I wouldn't bless a vampire. Of course, I didn't know about them yet. Blessing demons is certainly against the Pope's nature. I doubt coercion would even work to make him give us a blessing."

"Darn," Elsa said. "That would be a picture worth framing and hanging on the wall."

"Speaking of pictures," Brooke said. "We can rule out London. You're consulting company had several hundred people reviewing all the camera footage since the fight. He's not in London. If he were there, we'd know. That's the most documented city on the planet. I doubt there's a shadow in the city that's not observed by three video cameras."

"So, back to Bucharest?" Elsa asked.

"I already bought tickets," Brooke said. "Train leaves in two hours. I booked the most expensive rooms in Vienna for tomorrow and in Bucharest for the next week. This is all on Elsa's account, but I was under the impression she could afford it."

"I hope so," Elsa said. "Jonnie was my accountant."

"She could keep it all in her head," Jackie said. "But, I know all six corporate accounting firms that handle your finances. They'll suffer a little without Jonnie's guidance, but if they were incompetent, they wouldn't be working for you."

"I know," Elsa said. "It won't be the same, though."

"We should have a memorial," Shauna said, "a ceremony for her. I know none of us are particularly religious, but we should do something to wish her well wherever she is."

Elsa pulled a pendant that hung around her neck from her shirt. It looked like a silver coin. The name Karina Jonnie Bathory was written above Jonnie's bust and the date of her death was under it. "I called a local jeweler today while we sat in the crypts. This is the prototype," Elsa said. "I'm having six made in platinum. I'm going to figure out a way to incorporate one into the architecture of Notre Dame. I couldn't put her birth on the coin, for obvious reasons."

"But a ceremony?" Shauna asked.

"When Bertellus is dead, we'll have time to mourn," Elsa said. "Until then, we need our sadness and our rage to fuel our revenge. I'm counting on you and Laura," she paused and looked around the room. "Where's Laura?"

"Tending her bar?" Shauna ventured.

"No, she was on her way here an hour ago," Elsa said. "Right, Jackie?"

"I thought Julia was watching the bar for her," Jackie said. "Laura was coming here. I was so focused on Elsa, I didn't notice she wasn't here."

"No," Milady said. "Julia is down there." She pointed to a handful of vampires. Julia was among them, dancing.

"Laura was supposed to be closing her bar," Shauna said. They'd clearly discussed the plans before leaving the crypt at dusk. She was supposed to come with Julia.

"She texted me, exactly sixty minutes ago," Jackie said. She read the text, "Hey, Shauna, I'm on my way now."

Shauna asked, "She sent you a text, calling you 'Shauna'?"

"You don't keep your phone charged reliably," Jackie said. "Did she text you first?"

Shauna pulled out her phone. The battery was charged and she had a good signal but she didn't have any unread text messages. The text to Jackie seemed wrong. "Did Laura spell out 'on my way'?" Shauna asked.

"Fuck," Jackie said. "This isn't from Laura. It's from her phone number, though."

"Then someone has her phone," Shauna said. She tried to figure out why they'd confuse Jackie for Shauna in Laura's phone, and Shauna remembered the picture her sister used for Jackie had both Jackie and Shauna in it. "We need to go!" She was already running for the door before she finished yelling. She didn't even try to keep her speed within human range. Brooke could coerce the crowd to keep vampires a secret, and she would.

Outside, Shauna took to the air, flying as fast as she could to Le Obscurité Infinie. The bar's front door was open but the lights were out inside. Shauna found the light switch and flipped it. The bar was empty. She went behind the bar to look for any hint of where her sister had gone.

Rounding the end of the bar, she saw a pile of clothing on the floor. Old jeans, a pair of beat up sneakers and a punk band T-shirt from an era before she was born lay spread out on the floor.

Shauna fell to her knees. Those were Laura's clothes and the only way they'd be lying on the floor like that was if Laura was dead.

The bar hadn't been on the hunter's radar as far as Shauna knew. There was no way they could have known the bar was in any way connected to them.

Shauna wanted to cry. She felt like she should be crying. She reached out and pulled the T-shirt close and held it. All she could think about was grabbing Bertellus by the throat and tearing his head off with her bare hands.

Jackie was hugging her. Shauna hadn't really been paying attention to notice how long she'd been sitting there or when Jackie had shown up. Acutely aware of the pain they both knew, Shauna returned her lover's embrace. Together they sobbed until their eyes went dry.

Shauna thought back as far as she could to when she and Laura were inseparable. From first grade until high school, they'd dressed identically and did their hair the same way as each other each day. They refused to go to school if they weren't in all the same classes.

When Laura discovered drugs, that ended. Shauna hated herself for not acting sooner to stop Laura. She protected her sister from their parents and helped hide her secrets. If she'd said something back then, Laura would have followed a completely different path. Shauna wouldn't have had to save her, twice. Perhaps they'd still be so close, Shauna would never have taken an interest in vampires.

And Shauna didn't know how she was going to tell her parents. Maybe they'd not take it so hard, knowing the dangers of vampire's existence. She was delusional, she decided. No parent, ever, would take their child's death well. Shauna decided then and there that she wouldn't say anything to her parents until she could declare vengeance had been accomplished.

Elsa dug Laura's phone out of a pocket in the jeans. She was touching it gingerly, holding it by the corners.

"Fingerprints," Elsa said. "Whoever used this would have left them."

"We can't just assume it was your husband?" Shauna said, trying not to sound like she was blaming Elsa. She didn't mean to, but she knew her words had come out as if she did. Shauna blamed John Bertellus. Even without proof, she did assume he was behind it. John Bertellus was going to die.

"Ex-husband," Elsa said. "Marriage is until death, and no one is a vampire without having died. Yes, this is ultimately my fault for not making sure he died when Vlad died. I stupidly assumed a sword through the middle of his chest would be instantly fatal. You're going to have to forgive me. What you're feeling right now, what we're all feeling, is not helping any of us think clearly."

Shauna shook her head. "I don't mean it that way," she said. "I know better than to blame you for Bertellus."

"Why send a text just an hour ago?" Jackie asked.

"Huh?" Shauna replied.

Jackie said. "Sure, vamps start to desiccate within minutes of dying, if not seconds, but it takes longer than an hour, usually several, until there's no dust left."

"They wanted to make sure we didn't come back and find a body?" Shauna ventured. "They waited until she was gone to send the text. For all we know, she's been dead since sunset. When we find John Bertellus, I may ask him why."

"Or we could just kill him," Elsa said. "I'm not really a fan of slow, torturous death for my enemies anymore. We made a mistake of letting Henry live once and it came back and bit us in the ass. From now on, any hunter we find, we kill. No questions, no mercy."

Shauna nodded. She'd already been on a mission of vengeance. But, now that it was so much more personal, she started to feel energized by thinking of tearing Bertellus limb from limb. Then the tears came again.

CHAPTER 12

Elsa had been neglecting her staff in the two days since the deaths of Jonnie and Laura. On the train, she'd completely ignored them once they were seated. Shauna understood. None of them were Jonnie. It was one thing to take a new pet when her old ones had graduated to vampires, but another when her old pet had been taken from her. With Jonnie still around, Moana wouldn't have been expected to fill her shoes. With Jonnie dead, Moana would never measure up.

Once they reached Bucharest, Elsa's female staff, including Moana, were given their own room at the hotel, unattached from the suite where Elsa, Jackie and Shauna stayed with Azure and Karlo, though the pets were each given their own room in the suite.

Brooke and Ross shared a different suite. Una's blooddaughter had commandeered Ross to use as her pet. She made it clear that she saw the arrangement as temporary, but necessary. Elsa didn't react to Brooke's insistence. She acquiesced with a shrug.

They didn't spend more than a nap in bed. Elsa kept herself distracted by having several local designers give her impromptu personal fashion shows. Whatever alias Elsa was using had as much influence as if she had met the designers in person and coerced them.

She still ordered several ensembles in pairs and didn't correct herself. It was as if she were stubbornly trying to force reality to bend to her desires. If she kept Jonnie's wardrobe full, she would come back.

Shauna spent the trip writing letters to her parents, apologizing, explaining and begging for understanding. Before reaching the end of any of them, she burned them. Nothing she could think to say would express her emotions. Without killing Bertellus first, Shauna couldn't face even writing her parents. Jackie did nothing but hold tight to Shauna, wherever they were. Shauna held her lover back, just as tightly.

"Who in Paris was betraying us?" Elsa asked, ignoring a model wearing the latest in translucent eveningwear.

"I don't know," Shauna said. "It must be someone we don't know or I just can't read people. I thought everyone we left there, that knew about the coronation and Laura's bar, was trustworthy."

"That list is short," Jackie said. "You've got us, our dead sisters, Julia and Milady, and our pets."

"Milady?" Shauna asked. "Maybe Dumas wasn't just getting revenge for her scorning his advances. What if she is truly duplicitous?"

"No," Elsa said. "I know loyal. Milady is totally loyal to me for all the reasons that keep someone loyal. She likes me as a person and I'm a better queen than the last royal."

"Julia?" Jackie asked. "We never actually saw her kill the hunters at Notre Dame. We only heard her claim to have killed two. No one went out to look for a body or blood."

"Artemis is old school," Shauna said. "She believes in honor. I can't see her having her only blooddaughter be anything but an honorable vampire."

"Artemis killed Vlad," Elsa said. "She did so while claiming to be Michael, a human and a vampire hunter."

Without the aura, Artemis could easily have hid her nature, even in close proximity to Elsa. To Shauna, the killing of Vlad, disguised as a human, didn't seem terribly honorable in retrospect.

"No," Jackie said. "We can trust Artemis. Though she killed Vlad, she let Elsa attack her without responding with violence. Elsa left Michael-slash-Artemis bleeding from the throat. A vampire would be hurt and annoyed but more than capable of fighting back. She let Elsa go because Elsa wasn't the great evil that Vlad was."

"That's how I remember that fight, but I am less sure of my memories than I was. Jack, in Notre Dame, gave a different accounting, and something in my mind tells me his version is closer to the truth than mine. Still, Artemis would be far more direct if she were our enemy. It wasn't her that betrayed us."

"I agree," Shauna said. Artemis, with her nonchalant attitude towards murder, made her uncomfortable. Elsa, was right, though. Artemis wasn't the kind to let someone else do her dirty work.

"Then who?" Elsa asked. "Surely not Laura?"

"What?" Shauna asked. "Tell me you didn't just go there." For a moment, she hoped her sister was complicit. At least, if she was, she'd be alive. But she couldn't fathom how her sister would betray her after everything they'd done for each other over the years.

"It doesn't jibe," Jackie said. "Laura would have sent her own text, and not to the wrong person if she intended to mislead us. And we all know her. She wouldn't. She just wouldn't."

"Brooke?" Shauna asked. "Maybe Una is behind all of this."

"I thought of that," Elsa said. "It seems to fit. Brooke was conspicuously exactly in the wrong place for the big fight. But, strategically, it doesn't make sense. We all know Brooke could take any one of us out in a heartbeat. She's as strong as Shauna and trained."

"Yeah," Shauna said. "How does that mean we can trust her?"

"We're not dead," Elsa said. "Well, you're not. I'm not sure Bertellus wanted me dead or even if he does now. But Brooke should have killed you all by now. She's had every opportunity to single you out and take you down. Tactically speaking, it would be stupid for her to be faking allegiance all this time to try to get us all in one place. Her odds are better one on one with you and Laura and she wouldn't have waited until now to start. It's not like she'd be waiting for us to expose our hand. She knows our plan. Even if she did want to take you and Laura out separately, she's had two days of easy access to you while you've been in no state to fight."

Shauna didn't feel she wasn't ready to fight. She hadn't slept since losing Laura and every muscle in her body felt taught and ready to wring the very Venae from Bertellus.

"I have a theory," Jackie said.

"Don't make us ask," Shauna said. "Just say it."

"We all have phones," Jackie said. "They're all smartphones and they all have GPS built in."

"You think he's tracking our phones?" Shauna asked.

"It's what I would be doing if I had that information," Jackie said. "All he'd need is one phone number to hack information on and get the rest of ours from contact lists. We know he's well funded. He might have access to a decent hacker."

"Are you a decent hacker?" Shauna asked.

"Please," Jackie said. "I'm okay, but I'm not a pro. I haven't replaced my laptop since we lost Elsa's tower. It would take me weeks to get another one set up with the tools I had on that thing."

"It doesn't take a pro," Elsa said. "Watch." She pulled out her phone and pressed two buttons. After a moment a customer service rep for the phone company answered. Elsa put the phone on speaker.

"Hi," Elsa said. "I've lost my phone. My friend lent me hers to call you. Could you tell me where mine is?"

"Sure," the rep responded. "I just need your name, phone number and security code."

"Laura McAllister," Elsa said. She then said Laura's phone number and, "I think my code was zero five zero nine."

"Just a sec," the rep responded. "Your phone is close to the phone you are using, probably in the same room. I show it as on. Shall I ring it for you?"

"No, thank you," Elsa said and hung up. "See?"

"How do you know her security code?" Shauna asked.

"I don't," Elsa said. "But, I know your birthday is May ninth."

"I'm a lot less of a fan of my phone right now," Shauna said. She didn't use her birthday as her security code, but she knew she could see well enough to watch someone unlock their phone from a block away, and read their code.

"So phones off?" Shauna asked.

"Until this is over, yeah." Elsa said. "We'll grab some pay-as-you go phones."

"And we trust Brooke?" Shauna asked. Una's blooddaughter hadn't been verbose in discussing her origins, but over the days since she'd joined them, Shauna had learned that Brooke was made after tagging along with a group of amateur vampire hunters as their documentary journalist. Though all of the hunters were college athletes, they were in far over their heads when they found Una. For whatever reason, Una spared Brooke, in a fashion. The hunters had been sponsored by John Bertellus, posing as a professor of film and literature.

"Her story checked out," Jackie said. "John Bertellus was a professor in Massachusetts and then somewhere in Nebraska until a couple years ago when he vanished over spring break along with half the football team's starters. One of whom was the campus station weathergirl's boyfriend."

"And Brooke was the weathergirl?" Shauna asked. Brooke had left out that detail, but she hadn't mentioned the hunter's specific sport either.

"She was," Jackie said.

"She looks like a weathergirl," Elsa said.

Shauna would agree if Brooke ever smiled. "So we trust her?" Shauna said.

"Yes," Elsa said. "If only because we're not dead, so she must not want us dead."

"I guess you don't see me as the biggest bad ass on the planet anymore," Shauna said.

"You'd stand a chance against her," Elsa said. "You can phase, and that trick where you reached a phased arm in and grabbed Laura's heart to subdue her is something Brooke can't do. You're smarter about being a vampire thanks to yours truly. But, in a toe-to-toe boxing match, you're not the biggest bad ass in the world anymore. You are still the biggest bad ass on my side of any fight. Brooke may fight on our side, but you'll always be on my side. That means more than any amount of muscle. For what it matters, I'd never bet against you."

Shauna rubbed the back of her neck. The wound from Bertellus' sword had healed in seconds, but she still felt the reminder that she didn't share Elsa's optimism.

§

When night came, they wandered the streets, trying to find someone who knew anything of John Bertellus. They again realized there were no other vampires in Bucharest. It made sense. If Bertellus' hunters were based nearby, the local vampire population would have been hunted to extinction. Shauna took that as a sign they were on the right track.

"Churches," Shauna said. "Bertellus fancies himself an angel. Perhaps he recruits his hunters from churches."

"There's a big cathedral by the hotel," Jackie said.

Brooke shook her head. "Think smaller," she said. "The big ones are more tourist based. We want a small one where the parishioners would have more zeal."

"So we ask any priest which local priest is the most radical?" Shauna asked.

"That's a good place to start," Brooke said.

Jackie brought up a map of the city on her phone and led them to a small basilica. The church itself was empty, but a nearby building was clearly the residence of someone who worked in the church. They assumed, correctly, that it was the priest.

The bearded man that opened the door for them had a friendly smile but said something in Romanian that sounded like a brush off. He was closing the door before even waiting for them to respond.

Elsa stopped him and asked, "Do you speak English?"

He shook his head and pushed against the door, but Elsa wasn't letting it budge.

"French?" Shauna asked.

Elsa said something that sounded Chinese.

"Russkij?" Jackie asked.

The man responded in what Shauna assumed was Russian. Shauna couldn't follow the conversation from there, but she was sure Jackie coerced him early into it. It was clear they had difficulties communicating, but after a few minutes, he closed the door with another friendly smile.

"It seems vampires aren't much of a secret with the local church," Jackie said as they walked down the street back towards the hotel. "They deal with a regular night culture tourism trade. Even since Bertellus' arrival almost two years ago, there are still young vampires coming to seek the origins of their history."

In the days after her change, Shauna had tried to ply the origin of vampires from everyone she met. Most vampires still believed Dracula was the first. Only a few knew of the Blood Temple and fewer still knew there was a history before that.

Jackie continued, "For some reason, ordained Romanian Orthodox priests are immune to coercion. But, our friend here doesn't have anything against vampires that don't kill. Bertellus isn't in Bucharest, but he has recruited here. About a month back, he came through and left with thirty or so young men and two or three women. They thought they were taking paying jobs in a radical branch of the church. Two of the men came back a week later. It was too military for them."

"And we know where these two men are?" Elsa asked.

"We do," Jackie said, leading them back down the street toward their hotel. "They've been drinking themselves stupid at a bar not far from where we're staying. It's not midnight yet, they might still be coherent."

"Might they speak English?" Elsa asked.

"Who knows?" Jackie said. "That priest barely spoke Russian, or maybe I barely speak Russian. It's changed a bit in two centuries. These kids are going to be too young to have been forced to learn Russian in school."

"What are their names?" Elsa asked.

"George and Constantin," Jackie said. She pointed to a blinking neon sign in a window. "That should be our bar."

The two weren't hard to find. They sat together with a pair of pitchers of beer on their table. Elsa and Jackie went to the table while Shauna and Brooke waited at the bar. The bartender didn't speak English either, but understood having a ten euro bill set on the bar and them pointing to the beer taps. It didn't look like the kind of bar to order wine from. Shauna hadn't drunk much beer since her change. She could, though it was less helpful than wine. Shauna found the variation from her normal drink to be surprisingly refreshing.

A few minutes later, Jackie and Elsa left the table and gestured for the others to follow them out of the bar. Once on the street they explained the results of the conversation.

"George spoke very little English, but we managed to get him to point to a map on the phone," Jackie said. "Bertellus is running his training camp in the forests outside Predulet."

Shauna didn't know Romania well enough to know where that was. "Should that mean something?"

"Predulet is less than a league from Bran," Elsa said.

"A league?" Shauna asked.

"A league is the distance a person walks in an hour," Jackie said. "Three miles."

"So we think Bertellus is at Bran Castle?" Shauna asked.

"That would be Drac's castle to Jack Gainer," Elsa said. "It's where he was living when I returned from London with Jack following me. It's where Jack and Artemis killed Vlad."

"The tourism sites say it's under reconstruction," Brooke said, tapping the screen of her phone. She held it up so

Shauna and Elsa could see a picture of the castle. "Notice anything odd?"

"No windows on the great hall," Elsa said. "Even Vlad had windows; he just never went into the great hall during daylight hours. He only rarely came up from the dungeons at all."

"So we call James and tell him we found him?" Shauna asked.

"Yes," Brooke said. "Then we go and get a layout so we can plan our strike."

"Alone?" Shauna asked.

"There are five of us," Brooke said.

"Can we wait for James?" Shauna asked.

"We can," Brooke said. "But, we're not engaging. We just go there tomorrow night and get a layout, figure out the best time and place to kill him."

"Isn't this classic vampire hunting rule one?" Jackie asked. "During the day, duh!"

"We want to set a trap for him," Brooke said. "If we go in daylight, he'll be there first, ready for us. We do our scouting at night, when he's out training his troops."

"Tomorrow night, then?" Shauna asked.

Brooke nodded. "We won't have time to travel there and back tonight. We will leave right after sunset tomorrow and it will take us a few hours to make the drive. I am assuming we don't want to spend the days any closer to Bertellus."

"Or any farther from the shopping," Elsa said.

"Everything is closed," Brooke said. "Money won't open stores this late."

"These will." Jackie pulled a small leather case from her purse. Shauna assumed the case contained lock picks. "I've been carrying them since we needed them in the catacombs and didn't have them with us."

"She can handle modern security systems, too," Elsa said.

"Oh the things we do when we have all the time in the world," Jackie said. Then she sulkily added, "Or when we think we do."

Shauna pulled Jackie under her arm and hugged her. "One thing no one will ever be able to say is that Jonnie lived a less than full life."

"Elsa certainly saw to that," Jackie said. "Jonnie lived more in each decade than a normal person lives in eighty years."

"Spend a few years locked in a room and you won't ever again let a moment pass you by without doing something with it," Elsa said.

"You don't look old enough to have not been a vampire by then," Shauna said.

"I was Vlad's pet," Elsa said. "It was by becoming a vampire that I finally got free of that accursed room."

"How old were you when Vlad made you a pet?" Shauna asked.

"He'd been like a god-father to me from the time I was born. But, he didn't make me a pet until I was thirteen," Elsa said.

Brooke piped in, "Didn't you have to be, um, not a virgin?"

It had been Elsa that explained to Shauna how virgin blood would not provide nutrition to a vampire and virgins could not become vampires or pets. Elsa's speculation was that something about the act of sexual awakening opened the channels to connect blood to Venae.

"I was about to go into labor," Elsa said. "It's fair to say I wasn't a virgin at the time. He did it to make sure I survived childbirth. It's helpful to know that becoming a pet induces labor. He let me wean off right after that so I would grow up but made me a pet again when I was eighteen. I weaned a few more times to become pregnant with my other children. I had to have kids, you know, otherwise my marriage would be annulled. My husband was never happy that my first daughter was not his. I suppose I aged about ten years from the time I was thirteen to when I became a vampire at fifty something."

"And looking twenty-three at fifty would certainly draw suspicions," Jackie said. "And jealousy."

"And I wasn't completely innocent," Elsa said. "But enough about me. If I'm to be traipsing about the Carpathian Mountains in February, at night, I need some sensible boots, and new boots means I'll need a new belt. My gloves should match as well. Of course it would be easier to just get a whole new ensemble than to figure out which of my current outfits I should match the new boots to."

"Please tell me, if we are breaking in, that we're using the back doors," Brooke said.

"I'm not stupid," Elsa said. "Admittedly, you won't catch me walking through the muck of an alleyway, but I'm not entirely against flying above muck when I need to."

Brooke laughed then said, "My mentor is close to forty thousand years old, but I think Shauna got a far better one for this day and age."

"Thank you," Elsa said. "I'm sure Una is a fine mentor."

"I'm not," Brooke said. "The world is not at all the same place to a person who fears nothing. All she wanted was to be left alone to raise her family."

"And Bertellus ruined that," Jackie said. "You've told me the details. Only Una, her daughter and her pet survived the attack on her home."

"You mean blooddaughter, as in Brooke, right?" Shauna asked.

"No," Brooke said. "Una has mortal children. For some reason she can bear children. The children are sterile girls, but they are human. Una loves them more than anything. There haven't been a lot of them, but because of Bertellus, she has only one left. Each of you lost a family member to Bertellus. Una lost nine."

"Done," Jackie said. Shauna hadn't realized she'd started anything. Jackie put her lock picks into her purse and opened the door on the side of a building. "As near as I can tell, this is the service door for this whole block of shops."

It was. They shopped until dawn.

CHAPTER 13

"It's bigger in my memories," Elsa said as they walked up to Bran Castle through the forest.

Shauna had seen only a few castles in the drives through the countryside, but it was dark and, even with her enhanced perceptions, she wasn't able to see them well as they drove past. Bran Castle didn't look small, by any measure. It also didn't look like it needed renovation. It looked like a tourist destination. She, Elsa and Azure went to scout the castle while Brooke went off to find the training grounds and make sure Bertellus was staying away from the castle. Jackie stayed, under protest, at the hotel to watch over her pet and Elsa's staff.

"I can't see the lord of all evil hunters running his organization from a tourist trap," Shauna said.

"Which is probably why he does," Elsa said. "There are dungeons around the castle that have been long since forgotten. Perhaps Bertellus is using them."

"There's still the suspicious act of removing the windows from the great hall," Shauna said.

"There weren't a lot of windows to begin with," Elsa said. "This is a fortress, not a palace."

"There's an underground stream here," Azure said. "It runs under the castle, but halfway between us and the castle, there's something slowing the water."

"How do you know that?" Shauna asked Azure.

"I just always know where the water is," the blue-haired pet said. "Like you can see vampires when you blink, I see water."

"And you could do this before I made you into a pet?" Shauna asked.

"Yes," Azure said. "It's not something I tell anyone, since, you know, it's weird. But I'm standing with a pair of freakin' vampires wondering if an angel has taken over

Dracula's castle. I think it's safe to say I'm not the weird one here. All I can do is see water and I do. It's odd because it's getting slowed down without a pool to spread out."

"A waterwheel," Elsa said. "That's the worst of Vlad's dungeons. I made him tear that thing apart when I moved back here from London. It shouldn't be operational."

"Yes," Azure said. "That would do it. If I were closer I'd probably be able to see the shape of the wheel cutting into the water."

"How do we get to that waterwheel?" Shauna asked. "I don't like the idea of phasing through the ground to an unknown depth. I'm not good enough to know how far I go."

"There's an entrance by that tree," Elsa pointed to a boulder by a huge stump outside the castle walls. "Well, there used to be a tree there. I doubt anyone found the entrance."

"What makes the entrance hard to find?" Azure asked.

"Because it's not there," Elsa said. "You will have to phase through the rock, but it's just a few inches thick and then it's a stairway going down—way down."

"I can see a problem with that," Azure said.

"We can bring you with us," Elsa said.

"Will it hurt?" Azure asked. "Or I guess you can make me think it doesn't. Why did I agree to this, again?"

"The bad news is that now that you're Shauna's pet, the only ones that can coerce you are vampires purer than Shauna." Elsa said. "So, if you're still here, either you want to live forever or you're just that in love with Shauna."

"No one wants to live forever," Azure said. "I wouldn't mind living a really long time, though. And I wouldn't say my feelings for my vamp are quite that strong. I think it sounded more about sex and less deadly when Jackie and I discussed it online."

"You can be weaned," Elsa said.

"Let's not get ahead of ourselves," Azure said. "I'm not there yet, though I can't guarantee I won't get there someday. Right now, I'm more curious than smart it appears. So let's go see what's behind rock number two."

As they crossed the field to the castle, Shauna heard a tour guide and about two dozen tourists walking through the courtyard beyond the wall. "Why'd they build a whole castle for a guy that wasn't real?" "Dracula was a real dude; he just wasn't a vampire, just a psychopathic megalomaniac." "Vampires are real. My sister used to date one. The guy slept in a coffin and ate or drank nothing but pig's blood from the butcher. He was a total loser and totally weird."

Shauna managed not to laugh, but Elsa was having trouble not chuckling. She sputtered out several guffaws and snorted.

"Stealthy we are not," Azure said, whispering.

"We just have to be quieter than the tourists," Shauna whispered.

"Through here," Elsa said. She stopped as she rounded the boulder. "This is different."

Shauna came around and saw the hole in the rock. It was large enough for a man to squeeze through and led to a stone staircase that descended down. A door of steel bars and steel mesh blocked entry and the door had a pair of modern deadbolt locks.

Elsa phased and stepped through the steel bars.

Shauna asked Azure, "Ready?" When Azure nodded slowly, Shauna picked her pet up and cradled her in her arms. She then stepped through. The stairs were dark. The only light came from Elsa's phone. She set Azure down and then dug out her own phone and started down the stairs behind Elsa.

"It doesn't look like anyone's been here," Shauna said, brushing aside a few cobwebs.

"We could phase through the webs," Elsa said. "But, you're right. No one's been on these stairs in a long time." Elsa hadn't phased, so Shauna didn't either. It was almost impossible to converse when her lungs and vocal cords were phased out and no longer interacting with the air.

"If he phases down, how would you be able to tell?" Shauna said.

"If he phased down, there would be more webs and less hole in the rock above," Elsa said. "Henry couldn't' phase. I doubt Bertellus can."

The stairs spun a slow circle and eventually emerged at the base of a huge underground chamber. The walls were made of cut stones and joined into a dome that had to be at least thirty feet up. Illumination came from industrial lighting that hung from wires that crisscrossed the dome about halfway up. The base of the dome seemed huge. Four volleyball courts would easily fit in the room with space to spare.

A stream ran along part of the wall, spinning a waterwheel, just as Azure has said. The wheel spun an axle that ran along the floor where it could be engaged to any number of other devices though a simple set of gears. Shauna couldn't bring herself to look at the devices, especially when she noticed three of them still had bodies in them. She hoped they were bodies. No one in that condition should still be alive.

"Tell me those are dead," Shauna begged Elsa.

"They're dead," Elsa said. "Within the past day."

"Your extensive knowledge of vivisection?" Shauna asked Elsa how she made that assessment. She'd written a whole textbook on the subject.

"I never did studies of decay," Elsa said. "These three can't have been dead more than a day because we spoke to them last night. That's Constantin and the priest we spoke too. That last one, though the face is barely recognizable, is George."

"So Bertellus knows we're here," Shauna said.

"We have to assume," Elsa replied. "Are any of us surprised?"

"So many cages," Azure said, noting the base of the outer wall was lined with cages not much larger than a big dog's travel carrier. They were built of thick black iron bands riveted together and smelled of rust and oil. Each of the several dozen cages had a fresh, shiny padlock with the key still in it.

"What's he doing with those?" Shauna asked.

"Whatever it is, he hasn't yet," Elsa said, probably noting, as Shauna did, that the keys were still in the locks.

"Why would he need so many cages ready to be used?" Azure asked. "He can't bring in that many vampires at one time."

Shauna realized how they could be used with vampires. "Unless what went into the cage wasn't a vampire until it came out."

"He's going to turn his soldiers to vampires," Elsa said, casually walking to a modern steel door on the far wall of the chamber.

"All of them," Shauna added. "I guess he didn't inherit Una's Artemis Curse."

"Did we know that?" Elsa asked. "Didn't he keep two disciple angels which would have been his bloodchildren?" She turned the doorknob on the door, but it didn't budge. She then phased a little and poked her head and her hand holding her phone through the door. After she pulled back and phased back in, she said. "This is odd."

"A locked door to a torture chamber is odd?" Shauna asked.

"This door and the passage on the other side were not here the last time I was," Elsa said. "Like you said, I don't think Bertellus can phase. Now that I've thought on it, I'm pretty sure."

"So, he didn't inherit phasing from Vlad's bride?" Shauna asked.

"I think the bride he drank from never had it," Elsa said. "All of his brides were older than me and two were made before Lucy. We know one of them could phase, but it would have been just one of them. I doubt that one would have been pinned to a wall with an arrow, like the one John said he drank from. I was there and can't remember which bride died in which way. I was a bit focused on staying alive myself and watching Vlad get killed, in that order of priority. The brides were not really important to me."

The sound of a door closing echoed from the passageway on the far side of the door near Elsa. "Someone is coming," Shauna said.

"And fast," Elsa said. She ran over to hide behind Shauna. "No, offense sweetie, but I want to know what I'm fighting before I choose how brave to be." She phased out as well.

Shauna didn't blame her. Henry had hurt her, though not badly, even while she'd been phased. Bravery in combat was not a virtue Shauna expected from Elsa.

The door unlocked. A man dressed in jeans and a wool coat stepped through with a crossbow in his hand. Shauna immediately noticed the bone tip on the arrowhead.

The man spat a word and levelled the crossbow at Shauna. She bared her teeth and started walking sideways, arcing away from Elsa and Azure.

"You've only got one shot, hunter," Shauna said. "And you need that for me." She couldn't risk him shooting Azure.

The hunter kept the bone arrowhead pointed directly at Shauna. "I'm not afraid of you, Shauna. You are Shauna, right?"

"I am," Shauna said. She blinked, he didn't have the aura of a vampire, but he moved like one. "You're a vampire, one of the angels?" she asked.

"I am Justin," the hunter said. "I am Bertellus' new first sword, since you killed Henry. At least we assume it was you since he died before that Nebraska girl got to Europe."

"Are you going to shoot me?" Shauna asked.

"I think I will, if I have to," Justin said. "I'm not a fool; I won't win if I do loose this arrow. Unless I save it until you're too close to dodge away, that is. So that's what I'm doing. This is my insurance that we stay at this impasse until you flee or help arrives for one of us, preferably me."

"Were you second sword before?" Elsa asked. She was phased back in, but walking in an arc much farther from Justin than Shauna. Azure had retreated to the stairwell.

"Johan has been the second sword for almost two years," Justin said. "You've now killed his first sword twice; I clearly can't let you do that again."

"So you do have Artemis' curse," Elsa said. "You can only have one vampire per generation."

"Artemis' curse?" Justin said. He was slowly stepping back towards the steel door.

"You know," Shauna explained. "No vamp aura, so only one vampire per generation."

"That's why?" Justin said. "Bertellus assumed it was just how Una's blood worked. You're saying that the first of the first swords, Walt, since he had an aura, might have been able to make more than Johan?"

"There's a link," Elsa said. "Does Johan have the aura?"

"No," Justin said. "Of all the chosen, only Walt had the aura. Bertellus saw it as a weakness. For an army of dozens of vampires of my purity, it's a weakness he'll have to tolerate."

"Shauna, make him shoot you," Elsa said. She used a trick only she and her offspring could do so that only Shauna would hear her words. "I have the dagger. Once he shoots, we'll kill him.

Shauna considered rushing him. She would survive the wound but she'd need a day or so in the sun to heal. She looked at the scores of cages around the room and stopped to ask one more question. "How are you going to make a hundred vampires at once if you can only make one per generation?"

Justin didn't respond. He turned halfway to unlock the door, keeping the crossbow aimed, wobbly, at Shauna with one hand while he fiddled with a key with the other.

Elsa rushed him. He turned his aim and shot at the Blood Countess, but missed. Shauna took the opportunity and beat Elsa to Justin. She grabbed him by the back of his neck and squeezed. He was weaker than Shauna expected, far weaker than Henry had been at the same purity. Perhaps Henry had fed and Justin still had qualms. Shauna crushed the bones in Justin's neck and he died. When Elsa got there, she made sure he was dead by severing the head.

"He was supposed to shoot at you, and I was supposed to be the one with the surprise attack," Elsa said. "Why'd you change the plan?"

"You're the one who charged him," Shauna said.

"You were taking too long," Elsa said. "You were about to let him unlock the door."

Shauna realized Elsa was right. She'd almost missed the opportunity to take down Justin. Something the man had said had started Shauna thinking and she'd spent too long waiting for the answer Justin didn't give.

"The math doesn't add up," Shauna said. "I know the odds of making a vamp aren't always great, but there are ways to improve the odds so he doesn't have to try a hundred simultaneously just to make one vampire."

"No, John wasn't that stupid," Elsa said. "Sure, I overestimated his intellect when I found him attractive. But, even as the fool he is, he wouldn't waste so much life at once. When he makes a new vamp, he's going to do it with someone accustomed to his blood, one person at a time."

"Maybe he thinks if it's simultaneous, he can get around the one per generation rule of the curse," Shauna ventured.

Azure came up to join them. She said, "Maybe these vampires weren't going to have the curse. He said they'd have his purity. Perhaps Bertellus has found a way around the curse. He'd have to be the sire of all vampires of Justin's purity."

"No," Elsa said. "It could be another."

"Xander?" Shauna asked, thinking of the only other vampire in the world left with Bertellus' purity.

"Laura," Elsa said.

"I told you," Shauna said, angrily, "she wouldn't be on anyone's side but mine. She wouldn't stab me or my parents in the back. She's not working with Bertellus."

"Not willingly," Elsa said. "Most of these devices are centuries old with a few new parts and new leather straps. The one over there is almost entirely new."

Shauna hadn't looked closely at any of the torture devices. When she looked at the one Elsa indicated, it looked familiar. It was a modern replica of the one in the safe house.

"How does that work?" Shauna asked, forcing the words out. She didn't want to know, but she had to.

"In the safe house, Vlad kept the revenant strapped to the table in the cage and put a human into the iron maiden. Blood poured out of the maiden into the revenant's mouth through the copper tube. The iron maiden is designed to cause blood loss without death. Blood loses Venae fast as it leaves the body, but those tubes are short. The revenant would still get some Venae in the blood if the person in the maiden still lived." Elsa started digging through a bag Justin had dropped just inside the door.

Shauna noticed the three sharpened steel pipes arranged to poke into anyone on the table in the cage. "That's how they get the revenant's blood out to make the other vampires."

"Only they weren't thinking they'd have an uber vamp to put in the cage," Elsa said. "They are now." She held up three obsidian rings and additional pipe fittings. She demonstrated how the fittings would attach to the rings to create a tube that would puncture a potent vampire. Shauna touched the obsidian rings and it scratched her finger enough to draw a few drops of blood.

"We killed him too soon," Shauna said, nodding to Justin's body.

Azure took the obsidian rings from Elsa and examined them. "These are bad, I take it?" Azure said. "At least we figured out the most important information Justin had."

"Laura is alive," Elsa said.

Shauna hadn't been willing to think it. Hearing someone else say it made it real. She hugged Elsa, unable to speak. The thoughts and realizations running through her mind were too conflicting. She was overjoyed that her sister was alive and not a willing participant on the side of the hunters. She was terrified trying to imagine what Laura was actually going through or where she was.

"He's getting desperate," Elsa said. "He came closer than he wanted to losing our last fight, and it wasn't our ultra pure vamp that hurt him. I think he's shaken up."

"James and Una will be here in three days," Shauna said. "And we don't have three days. Bertellus would have to start these vamps tomorrow to have them changed by Friday and most of them won't survive the process. We have to find Laura, now!" She went to the steel door and opened it.

"Wait!" Elsa grabbed Shauna's arm.

"I don't think so," Shauna said. "I need to find my sister. I need to save her."

"We all do," Elsa said. "We all love her, but they know we're coming now."

"How?" Shauna said. "He hasn't even started to dry up yet."

"If he had a pet, they'll know," Elsa said. "They will have an advantage in knowing the castle. Bertellus could be here from the training grounds by now. We need a better plan than rush up and see what's there."

"We can't wait for James," Shauna said.

"No," Elsa said. "We can't. We've forced their hand by killing Justin. They know we know their plan. They either have to scuttle it or rush it and my money, all of my money, is on their rushing it. Laura isn't someone they can hold for long. They have to keep her healthy enough to bleed the blood it would take to turn a hundred men. And they'd have to be keeping her in a gold lined box."

"Or they could be waiting to feed her when they're ready to turn the men," Shauna said. "Feed her two or three people all the way to death and a couple gallons of wine and she'd have all the blood they'd need."

"Yes," Elsa said. "That would be most likely, I suppose. Still, he's going to have to act fast. This is not an easy contraption to assemble. A skilled metalworker could probably make the bleeder in a week, with help. The hundred cages could take months to replicate."

"So we start by shattering these?" Azure held up the obsidian fittings for the bleeding tubes.

"No," Elsa said. "We leave them as if we never noticed them."

Shauna saw Elsa's point. The obvious thought would be to destroy the cages, but Elsa wasn't really driving towards that conclusion. "And we want him to rush because we don't want him to have to keep Laura so long that he might think it easier to kill her and capture another one of us."

"We know he has to rush," Elsa said. "He just thinks we know of his facility, so he thinks rushing his plan is better than starting over."

"So we wait here or come back later?" Azure said. "I think I'm more of a fan of coming back later since that probably doesn't include me."

"We come back," Elsa and Shauna said together.

"We're leaving." Shauna said, making sure they were all on the same page. She took one last look back and asked, "Is this all there is to see here?" She wasn't happy spending time in the room with tortured dead bodies and if Bertellus was coming, she didn't want to fight him without Brooke.

"There's the private dining room," Elsa said. "We should skip that. There's only room there for a dining table and five of the slowest, cruelest devices Vlad discovered or conceived. It's just below the kitchen pantries. Again, you can only get there if you can phase, or, you could. If Bertellus changed that, the world will think even less of Vlad, if that's possible."

"What use is that room?" Shauna said. That wasn't what she wanted to ask. She was trying to figure out where

Bertellus was storing the equipment for his army. "I mean, is there a place he would store large caches of weapons?"

"This is the only one that would have worked for that and not have been discovered," Elsa said. "More than likely, if they are modern weapons, they're kept near his army."

§

When they got back to the van, Azure asked, "Why cage them when they turn, do they go feral?"

"Briefly," Elsa said. "Most come back to sanity. Of course, we have to define sanity a little different than humans."

"As the body changes, it spasms like a continuous seizure for almost two days," Shauna explained. "And this is a body with vampire strength. I made the change in a concrete crypt and when I left, there wasn't a wall that wasn't cracked."

"You don't do a good job of making it sound worth it," Azure said.

"Most of the cases I've witnessed involved a death or undeath situation," Shauna said. Jackie had been the only healthy person she'd known to attempt the change. Shauna, her mother, Laura and Jonnie had all been dying when they made the change to become vampires.

"So we can go back to the car?" Shauna asked.

"Yes," Azure said. "I think we learned what we can here. Bertellus is an evil man with aspirations of warmongering."

"And his days are numbered," Elsa said.

They'd parked at a bus stop on the west side of the town of Bran and Brooke had walked one way while Shauna, Elsa and Azure went the other. When they returned to the van, Brooke was not there yet.

"I don't have the keys," Shauna said. "Brooke drove."

"So we wait," Elsa said. "There's a restaurant over there, maybe they have wine."

"Or food," Azure said. "Some of us still need to ingest solids now and then. We pets, with our super metabolism, appear to need lots of food, which is a perk no one mentioned."

"You don't drink as much as my pets used to," Elsa said. "You might want to think of starting a life of alcoholism. It's so much easier to drink your calories than eat them."

"Ignore her," Shauna said. "She means well, but the last time she ate solid food, refined sugar was rare, even for the rich. No one had learned to deep fat fry anything and there was no concept of a frozen dessert."

"Poor Elsa," Azure said. "How do you exist without intense jealousy for all the wondrous foods of today's world? You've never had a candy bar?"

"Don't be silly," Elsa said. "Vamps can taste food, we just can't swallow without having to regurgitate shortly thereafter. It's not pleasant, but it does mean I have tasted many modern delicacies. I still prefer blood and wine to anything that requires chewing."

CHAPTER 14

Once back at the hotel in Bucharest, Shauna went straight for the collection of wine bottles Elsa had amassed in the kitchenette. She didn't wait to see what Elsa chose. She just grabbed the first full bottle and popped the end from the bottle.

She kept telling herself the best chance she had for finding and saving Laura was to wait until they knew where she'd be. By then, they should have a fail proof plan, or so Brooke assured her.

Brooke spent her time sitting at a desk in the hotel drawing maps and annotating floor plans she'd downloaded, while Shauna tried to fathom all the details Brooke gathered. From her observations at the training camp, Brooke had discovered that Bertellus had one other 'angel', whom Shauna assumed to be Johan. That vampire was helping him train an army of over two hundred men. The men all looked exhausted but were hopeful of the promise of a celebratory night commemorating their completion of a training block.

"She's spending an awful lot of time planning an attack that's not going to be terribly complex," Elsa said.

"What makes you think that?" Shauna asked. "Good planning might be the only thing we have going for us."

"What we have going for us is two uber-vamps, both purer than Bertellus," Elsa said. "I'm pretty sure the strategy is going to be to pound down the front door and then pound anyone we find behind it. With superior firepower, strategy isn't so important. I believe it was some Prussian field marshal that said 'no plan survives contact with the enemy'."

"Hubris has cost many great generals throughout history," Shauna said. "Xerxes and Custer come to mind. I'm sure we will want more of a plan than 'Charge!' The plans have changed significantly since we decided not to wait for James and Una."

"My plans never involved waiting for James and Una," Brooke said. "We're going in at midnight tonight."

Shauna agreed, mostly. "We'd only have a couple days left to wait for James and Una, but I don't think we can wait. I'll go mad worrying about Laura."

"In two days he'll have a dozen or more new vampires with combat training," Brooke said. "And once he has his new vampires, he'll not have a use for Laura. I don't expect he'll set her free when he's done."

"That's all the convincing I needed," Shauna said. "You mentioned they trained hard and planned to party hard after."

Brooke nodded. "And once I put two and two together, hard drinking and a hundred or so cages, I realized we don't have two days. He was already planning on using the cages tonight."

"So our excursion won't really improve our odds in the fight," Shauna said.

"We killed Justin," Elsa said. "He won't be replaced by tonight."

"You think he's starting the change on his soldiers?" Shauna asked.

"I think he did," Brooke said. "When you changed, what did your maker give you?"

"Two bottles of wine," Shauna said, realizing Brooke's assessment wasn't off. "We're screwed."

"No," Brooke said. "Once we free Laura, we'll outnumber him and out-power him. Of you, me and Laura, the weakest of us is equal to Bertellus and he's the stronger of the two vamps they have. We also have two other vampires."

"They're not even in the same class of potency," Shauna said, and then added, to Jackie, "Sorry, love. You're centuries of being a pet, and Elsa's four as a vamp won't make up for the difference in purity."

"I don't care," Jackie said. "I am so out for blood over Jonnie. I'm ready to go as soon as the sun sets."

"Don't discount my wisdom, sweetie. I am not a big fan of a good fight," Elsa said, stepping up to Shauna and putting a hand on each shoulder. "I prefer to battle with a clear upper hand. I think we have that with Brooke and you."

"I'm scared," Shauna said, "But, I'll be at your side." She leaned close and looked over Brooke's plans and asked, "What advantages do we have?"

"Our strength and our wiles," Brooke said. "I have training, he has training. The rest of you are just going to have to be smarter."

That didn't seem a fair trade. Shauna considered herself to be intelligent, perhaps more intelligent than most, but couldn't see that helping in hand to hand combat against someone with decades of training. "You've had two years of training, he's had two hundred."

"He's had two," Brooke said. "Before then, he was training from an entirely different reality. He and I have had our strengths and our abilities for exactly the same length of time. At best, he's only had a sparring partner just a little weaker and slower than him. I trained against someone who was both stronger and faster than me."

Shauna nodded, acknowledging that she couldn't find grounds to argue with Brooke's logic. She turned to Elsa and asked, "What are your advantages?"

"I'm evil and not pretending to be something I'm not," Elsa said. "I might be trying to be nicer, gooder, if that's even a word. But, I'm not going to be either with Jack, or John, or Bertellus, whatever that asshole is calling himself." She pulled Vlad's spearhead from her thigh sheath and gripped it tightly in front of her. "At this point in time I am pure rage and that's going to either kill him or get me killed and I'm damned sure going to try to make it him, but the price would be worth it if it were both."

"That's not a healthy state of mind to be going into battle with," Shauna said. "I'm doing this to save our lives. All of our lives."

"You have our backs," Brooke said. "There's no one better for that job."

"Maybe James," Shauna said.

"There's no one better here, now," Brooke said.

"And Jackie?" Shauna asked.

"I'm with Elsa," Jackie said. "Bertellus needs to die tonight, whatever the cost."

Shauna sighed, but agreed. She would do everything she could to make sure the cost didn't include Elsa or Jackie's life. "Brooke, what other weapons do we have?" Shauna asked.

"That folded steel and gold sword Laura brought with her won't do any good against Bertellus or his offspring. Leave it here. I have these." Brooke held up her hand and showed Shauna her fingernails. They'd been sharpened to points. "Harder than any steel," Brooke said. "You should do the same."

Shauna had been keeping her nails short since she'd found a broken obsidian arrowhead that could cut her nails. Sharpening what was left wasn't possible. She showed Brooke her short manicure.

"Punching works," Brooke said. "It's not too hard to remove his head if he's unconscious."

"We have Henry's crossbow," Elsa said. "In hindsight, we should have grabbed Justin's, too."

"One is enough; give it to Jackie," Shauna said. The only reason she'd been able to use it against Henry was that he was so close. "Be careful with that. The only cure of vamp marrow in the system is to sun it out and the only way you'd survive that is to drink Bertellus dry and steal his Venae."

"What?" Elsa asked.

"Perhaps that isn't something she should have known," Brooke said.

"I don't keep secrets from her," Shauna said. "I hadn't realized she didn't know it." She shouldn't have mentioned it, Shauna realized too late. But it wasn't something she could take back.

"That much Vamp blood would kill me," Elsa said.

"Just like it would a human," Shauna said. "And just like a human, it could also bring you back. Being drained until dry by another vampire is one more way to kill one of us."

"And the draining vamp has to ingest the blood, not just extract it," Brooke said. "Vlad and Bertellus were willing to risk everything for their enhanced purity."

"So, burning by fire or sun, decapitation, poisoning by vamp blood or having another vamp drink us dry," Jackie said. "That's the full list?"

Elsa shook her head. "There are more, but most of those are just creative ways to accomplish one of those four. You can pretty much just go your whole undeath avoiding the sun and shaving too close and you'll be fine."

"Are the pets coming?" Jackie asked.

"I am weaning Moana," Elsa said. "I'm not ready for a new pet yet."

Azure said, "As much as I hate leaving my fate in your hands, and I do hate it, I wouldn't be an asset."

"Are you sure?" Elsa asked. "You're dowsing ability seems nifty. It makes me think you could do some other tricks as well."

"What are you saying about my pet?" Shauna asked.

"I'm saying there's more to her than she's telling us," Elsa said. "I think she's something we're not supposed to believe in."

"Like vampires?" Azure asked.

"Like witches," Elsa said. "Reilla was made with a spell. It's not too great a leap to think there are still people who can use magic around."

"You yourself said that magic was just science we didn't understand yet," Shauna said. "There is no such thing as magic."

"Semantics," Elsa said. "Azure is something more than human. I'm just curious what that is. You haven't dyed your hair in two months, and it's really starting to show. Look at her. She's been with us ten days and she hasn't dyed her hair in that time. How long have her roots gotten?"

When she looked at Azure and noticed her hair was blue all the way to the scalp, and that Azure was looking away, almost shamefully, Shauna realized this wasn't something they could talk about in just a moment or two. "This isn't the time for this," Shauna said. She agreed with Elsa, though. There was more to Azure than met the eye.

"No one calls us witches," Azure said. "And we're not so different than you. I'm an elementalist."

"So that's why you see water?" Shauna asked.

"Exactly," Azure said. "But that's not going to help your fight. If we could find a fire elementalist, they might help."

"So let's do that," Jackie said.

"There aren't any," Azure said. "They tend to explode before they can control the element within them. There aren't a whole lot of elementalists at all. There are six elements and earth elementalists are the most common, usually one in a million people or so. Combined there are half as many Air and Water elementalists. Necromancers, the elementalists of death, are so few that I can name all five and I know how to avoid them. And fire are pretty much extinct."

"You said six," Shauna said. "There should be life elementalists, too."

"In ancient times, it was a life elementalist that designed a spell to save her queen by taking just a tiny bit of each living thing's life and giving it to the queen. It was a dangerous spell that the elementalist tested first and accidentally created the vampire. The vampire has a far more direct link to Venae, shutting the elementalists out."

"We're not creatures of death?" Elsa asked.

"You're creatures of life," Azure said. "You epitomize the defiance of death."

"Does your blood taste better than human blood?" Elsa asked. "Shauna hasn't really shared you."

"She has," Jackie said. "She doesn't taste different or give more kick per pint."

"How boring," Elsa said. "I mean it's interesting to know they're out there, but it seems like trivial knowledge. It's mostly useless stuff."

"So you don't dye all the hair on your body?" Shauna asked. "That's all natural?"

"Yes," Azure said. "I am naturally blue-haired."

"That's less boring," Elsa said. "Can I see?"

"You've seen," Shauna said. Shauna hadn't kept track of who did what with who in bed when there were three vampires and their pets crammed onto a king-sized mattress, but she was sure everyone was there and naked at least twice in the past week or so.

"But, I didn't know what I was looking for," Elsa said.

"Then you'll have to survive the fight tonight," Shauna said.

"There's one incentive," Elsa said. "I'm holding you to it. If I live, can I let her be one of the naked servants tied to my throne in Paris?"

"No," Shauna and Azure said together.

"Fine," Elsa said. "But if I die, you'll have to live your whole life knowing you didn't offer me enough reason to live."

"Let's just none of us die," Sauna said. "We all live tonight, for Jonnie." Knowing in her heart that her sister lived, she didn't include Laura in the cheer.

"For Jonnie," Jackie said, raising a fist.

"For Jonnie." Elsa raised a glass of wine. "And Laura, we'll get her back."

"For Jonnie and Laura," Brooke said, also raising a fist.

§

As they drove north, the impending fight made Shauna wish James would hurry up and then she wondered how much easier the fight would be if James just brought all the vamps from Reilla's home. Surely, even Mala would know how to fight.

Thinking of Mala, Shauna smacked herself in the forehead. "Mala will know where Laura is," she said. "And she must be alive or Mala would have told my parents and my parents would have called me."

"If you call her, she'll know you lost your sister," Elsa said. "She'll tell your mother."

"We need to know where she is," Shauna said. "We don't want to be rushing into a massive fight in the wrong place."

"It's your ass," Elsa said. "It's less fun to think of your parents spanking it. It's counterproductive to the way I like to think of it."

"Shut up, Elsa," Shauna said, slightly surprised to hear her words simultaneously coming from Jackie's lips. She brought out the pay-as-you-go phone she'd gotten earlier that day and called Mala.

"Who's this?" Mala answered.

"It's Shauna. Where's my sister?"

"I assumed you knew since you're heading right toward her. Let me check a map." The phone was quiet a moment and then Mala came back. "Forty-five degrees, thirty minutes, fifty-two point sixty-two seconds north; twenty-five degrees, twenty-two minutes, two point three five seconds east."

"Got that," Jackie said. "We totally nailed it."

"Is she alone?" Shauna asked Mala.

"As far as I can see, yes," Mala said. "Anything else?"

"Thanks, Sis," Shauna said, hoping to offset the huge favor they'd asked of Mala by treating her like the bloodsister she was to Shauna. That Mala didn't see another vampire near Laura didn't really mean much. She wouldn't see Bertellus and probably wouldn't see his progeny either.

They parked in the same place they had the night before. Brooke adjusted herself under the tight leather as they got out of the van. "How did I let you talk me into a catsuit again?"

"It's Elsa's thing," Shauna said. "I think she aches for an excuse to put us all in them."

"It's armored," Elsa said. "Bulletproof might not mean much to you, but it won't part like butter for a sword either. It would fit better if you let the zipper down some. You're supposed to show some cleavage."

"How is that armor?" Brooke asked. She pulled her zipper down to her sternum and said, "That fits better. When did you measure me? I don't sleep that deeply."

"It's a gift," Elsa said. "I can measure anyone by sight. The real trick is overnight shipping from New York and getting through EU customs with body armor. People used to be so much easier to bribe. I swear three people hung up on me before I could get my numbers up to where they'd listen. Everyone has a price, though, so I got all the outfits here on time."

"I'm pretty sure Bertellus is strong enough to cut through the armor," Shauna said.

"He may be," Elsa said. "The steel isn't. The sword would break if he used all his strength."

"That's true," Brooke said. "Gold isn't potent against vampires because it's strong, because it's not. Something about gold nullifies the resistance Venae gives vampires. Some of us are just potent enough to overpower that nullification."

"And the obsidian that can hurt us is imbued with the fallout from the spell that created Reilla," Shauna said.

"The obsidian that can hurt you and I comes from the initial eruption," Brooke said. "Obsidian from later eruptions can hurt most vampires, but not you, me or Laura."

"His sword hurts me just fine," Shauna said.

"Does he have snipers or scouts watching for us?" Elsa asked.

"There are men posted on the ramparts," Brooke said. "They haven't taken any special note of us. They might once we start walking that way.

"Those weren't there last night," Shauna said. "We really don't have time to wait for James and Una."

"They could just fly off the boat," Elsa said. "Have we talked to them to tell them we're going in prematurely?"

"Yes," Jackie said. "James told us not to. Una said she has faith in Brooke to do what needs to be done. I get the impression Una is the reason things are taking so long. James won't leave her alone and she won't fly."

"She can't," Brooke said. "The only vamp abilities Una has are the coercion, regeneration, the speed and the strength. She won't let someone carry her, either. That puts her life in their hands and she won't do that. She also burns instantly in sunlight; I mean she actually catches fire. She heals as fast as she burns, but it's painful for her. Moonlight from more than a half-moon causes her pain."

Shauna saw the splinter of the crescent moon over the castle walls. The beauty of the scene inspired her to reach around Jackie's waist and hug her.

Brooke kept talking about her bloodline's abilities. "I can't sunbathe like Shauna. I'm like Laura. I can handle it for a few minutes, maybe an hour, but then it starts to hurt like sitting too close to a fire."

"So Bertellus won't be out in daylight either," Shauna said.

"Which is why we didn't scout here during daylight," Brooke said.

"And why didn't we attack earlier?" Shauna asked.

Brooke nodded to Elsa and Jackie.

"Right," Shauna said.

"And, if he is making more vamps, most of his army will be in cages by now," Elsa said.

"If he's not?" Shauna asked. "We still stay until we find and rescue Laura, right?"

"Exactly," Brooke said. "Now, who wants to go peek in and see if he's in the underground dome?"

"I'll do that," Elsa said. "I'm the best at phasing. I don't have to use the stairwell so he won't be watching for me where I peek in."

"Shauna, Jackie, you and I will get the guards on the walls," Brooke said. "One of you will have to get two. No shooting."

"So we phase to near translucent, fly up there and coerce them to go home?" Shauna asked.

"I like the phase trick," Brooke said. "I wasn't thinking of that, but it's a good idea. I was also just thinking to kill them by snapping their necks."

"Their walking out might be too obviously the work of a vampire," Jackie said.

"Right." Brooke nodded. "We have to go in there with complete disregard for the body count. This is war. If we win, it ends here. If we lose, it won't be our fight anymore."

Shauna didn't like indiscriminate killing. It was Jackie that voiced her concerns. "I don't think we should kill just anyone. Could we limit it to those who pose a threat?"

"Of course," Brooke said. "Right now, that starts with the four men on the ramparts."

"I'll get two," Shauna said. She was fairly certain she could handle two at once using her apportation. She didn't think she could coordinate four simultaneously. "How do we time this?"

"I'm going to count to sixty," Brooke said. "When I get to thirty, kill. At sixty we meet just outside the main gate." She started counting slowly and deliberately marking the even timing with her hand as she spoke the numbers.

Nodding to the beat of the counts, Shauna echoed the words in her head as she phased and flew up above the castle. Imagining the single invisible hand of Venae to manipulate things with her apportation was simple. When she concentrated, she could handle two things at once and that was her plan. She was going to simply grab two guards while she was flying high above and yank them into the sky and then drop them into the forest. Once she was holding herself aloft, she remembered how she flew; she was using an imaginary hand to push against the ground. In order for her plan to work she'd have to concentrate on three things at once.

Still counting in her head, she passed twenty and tried to focus her thoughts into three invisible hands. The most important, the one holding her aloft, stayed strong but she felt the other two wavering back and forth in strength. It wasn't terribly different than trying to draw two different pictures at once, one with each hand. Only in her situation, she was trying to draw three with only two hands. When she counted twenty-nine, she realized three was too many. She had to let one go and only one wasn't necessary for the timing. She let go of the ground.

At thirty she grabbed the two men and yanked them up as hard as she could. She expected their bodies to fly up to the sky. Apparently she yanked harder than she thought; she tore the men apart at the torso. The gore made her close her eyes.

When the sensation of falling made her look again she was only a few yards above the ground. She reached out, panicked and pushed hard against the ground. The sudden stop jarred her. She could see a large imprint of a palm and fingers in the lawn below her where she'd reached out with her imaginary hand. The effects were more literal than she'd guessed they'd be.

She'd lost her count and rushed to meet Brooke and the others just outside the gate. She phased back to solid as she landed beside Elsa. Two of Bertellus' soldiers slumped in the corner, against the wall, their necks clearly broken.

"Messy but effective, my dear," Elsa said.

"Shut up," Shauna said. "You have to know I didn't expect that."

"You drank a pint from Azure before we came out," Elsa said. "You're not used to being so full, so potent."

They'd all fed before heading out. Those that had pets fed from their pets. Brooke hadn't converted Ross to a pet yet, so she went out for a quick hunt before they'd set out. Shauna made a point of not asking how the hunt went. Brooke seemed the type who would justify drinking to a kill for the boost in strength before a fight.

"I only hope I'm strong enough when I need to be," Shauna said. "So, Elsa, do I need to be?"

"The cages were full, just like we thought they'd be," Elsa said. "Most of them have dead bodies. More than half of the remaining soldiers are dying fast. Of greatest importance, Laura is there, and it was all I could do to refrain from being heroic and trying to free her myself." Elsa smirked at Shauna. "I know, right? Me thinking heroically; who'd have ever thought? I didn't really have the guts it turns out, to none of our surprise. Bertellus is not down there. His remaining angel is there and every cage has a soldier guarding it with an obsidian pointed spear."

"Reilla said a few shards of obsidian slipped through James fingers; is a hundred the same as a few if you're forty thousand years old?" Shauna asked.

"No," Elsa said. "Perception of numbers only changes with age if we're talking about years to an old vamp. I don't believe for a second that Bertellus found a hundred spearhead sized pieces of obsidian from the original eruption."

"Then let's go," Shauna said. She started jogging towards the stairwell in the stone.

"Wait," Brooke called after her then gave chase. "I haven't told you the modified plan."

As much as Shauna wanted to just tear her way through two hundred men to rescue Laura, she slowed and let Brooke, and eventually, Elsa and Jackie catch up.

"Ok, General Brooke, tell us the plan," Shauna said.

"I'm going to take down the angel," Brooke said. "You coerce the humans to leave."

"That won't work," Elsa said. "The humans have likely been coerced by Bertellus to stay."

"Shauna's purer than Bertellus," Brooke said. "Her coercion will take precedence."

"Unless Bertellus enforced his coercion with a drop of his blood," Elsa said. "If he did, Shauna would have to do the same to be able to supersede whatever he coerced of them, which might just have been as simple as to ignore whatever we tell them."

"I don't speak their language anyway," Shauna said. "We haven't found a lot of these local guys that speak English."

"Then we have a slightly bloodier plan," Brooke said. "I'm still on the angel vamp, Elsa and Jackie will free Laura and Shauna will tear apart the humans until their self-preservation instincts get them to run."

"Remember, the goal is Laura," Shauna said.

"Right," Brooke said. "Laura is our mission here. If Bertellus shows up, we will have to kill him first, all of us. We can then get back to saving Laura."

"Okay," Shauna said after thinking about it. They would have to gang up on him. Shauna knew she couldn't take him out alone and wasn't convinced Brooke could either.

Brooke asked Elsa, "We're right above the chamber here, right?"

"Yes," Elsa said.

"Jackie," Brooke said. "Take me down and drop me on the angel. We go now."

Jackie wrapped her arms around Brooke and both sank through the ground. Shauna phased and let herself fall through the earth as well. When she passed into the dome, she phased back and fell to the floor. She landed the same time as Brooke.

The room was noisy with the screams of a dozen men.

The first thing Shauna noticed was Laura lying strapped to a table inside a gold trimmed iron cage. She was unconscious. A copper tube ran into Laura's mouth from above where it split off into two different iron maidens. Three steel tubes pierced her side and drained blood into three glass vials. One of the soldiers had been walking with another vial to a cage, but when Shauna showed up, he dropped the vial and ran for the steel door.

The rest of the scene was exactly as Elsa had described with a man in every cage and another guarding each cage with a black tipped spear. Some of the cages, those whose occupants were not moving, were unguarded and some cages had two guards. The process had begun and was already killing more soldiers than were surviving.

A lone figure stood in the center of the room. The word 'angel' immediately sprang to Shauna's mind. He had large white feathered wings sprouting from his back and a glowing halo over his head. The wings occasionally stretched out or shifted a little like a bored hand. Shauna blinked, but the man didn't emanate the aura of a vampire. It didn't surprise her; neither had Bertellus.

Shauna couldn't help but wonder if, in fact, the being was an angel. It wouldn't change what she was about to do. If he was an angel, he was still overseeing Laura's torture, which meant there was nothing righteous about him. The angel wore gold trimmed steel armor like a medieval knight and he held a steel shield in one hand and a long bone knife in the other.

"You're mine," Brooke yelled and charged at the vamp in the armor.

A pair of soldiers moved away from the cages toward Brooke. Shauna sprinted towards them. As she ran, she tore their weapons from their hands with her apportation. She threw the spears into the stream running along the wall.

Without weapons, the men paused. One drew a gun while the other ran for the door. This time Shauna chased the one going for the door. This was Bertellus' army. Anyone they didn't kill would survive to fight another day. She figured the man smart enough to run was more of a threat in the long run than the man dumb enough to reach for a gun to shoot a vampire. Bravery without wisdom was just foolishness.

However, when Shauna got to the door first, the smarter soldier cowered. He started to beg, though Shauna couldn't understand the words. She couldn't find it in herself to kill him. She stepped aside and let him run out the door.

Brooke had torn the shield away and was swiping quick punches at the angel, but she wasn't really committing to the hits since he managed to keep his knife between them. He wasn't trying to cut or stab her; he was just trying to keep her at bay. The outcome of that fight was inevitable. The angel's seconds were numbered.

Again, Shauna focused on the men moving in to try to get behind Brooke. She stuck to what worked, tearing the weapons away and letting the unarmed men flee. She did her best to ignore the soldiers shooting her. One soldier boldly turned his gun to Brooke, and Shauna couldn't have her get distracted from her battle. Shauna raced over and tore that man's arm off at the elbow. She'd only meant to swat the gun from his hand.

The sight of the gore must have been too much for the rest of the men. Most of them dropped their spears and their guns and ran for the door. Only a handful stayed, and only long enough to realize how few matched their valor. In less than a minute, the only fight in the room was between Brooke and the vamp in the armor.

Shauna walked over and stood behind the angel. For the first time, she got a good close look at his wings. His halo lay on the ground a few steps away, still glowing. The wings were clearly a mechanical construct attached to his armor. As they fought, the wings continued their random movements which were completely out of sync with the way the angel moved in the fight. "Brooke, can I do anything to help?"

"Sure," Brooke said.

The angel looked back at Shauna and then at Brooke and knelt, tossing the bone knife away so that it skittered across the floor to stop at the wall. "I surrender," the angel said. "Please, grant me the mercy you've given my men."

Shauna nodded to Brooke.

Brooke nodded back and walked slowly up to the angel. She gently put her hand on his shoulder. "Let this be a lesson," Brooke said. She quickly closed her hand on the angel's neck. Shauna heard the vertebrae shatter. Brooke tore her hand away. When Shauna saw the bones still in the other vamp's grip, she turned away.

"But," Shauna said. "What lesson?"

"I don't know," Brooke said. "It seemed like the time to say something, but that's all I could think of. You nodded for me to kill him."

"I nodded for you to grant mercy," Shauna said.

"Well, I wasn't going to do that," Brooke said. "We're here to win the war, not extend an olive branch. This isn't a border dispute. This is a war where both sides are seeking revenge. Historically speaking those tend to end with both sides losing and the remnants of society left behind making peace from losing the will to fight. We've just tilted the balance to make sure we can win without sacrificing ourselves to do it."

"She's right," Laura said. Elsa and Jackie were carrying her over, each with an arm under her shoulder. She was walking, but only barely. "The only threat left is Bertellus himself. We've bought a few days at least. He will want to make another first sword, and maybe another second, before he continues the war. We should be able to take him down before that with James and Una here in what, two or three days?"

"Yeah," Jackie said.

"What do we do with these?" Shauna asked, pointing to the men in the cages."

"Leave them to me," Brooke said. "I know you don't have the stomach for it."

"No," Shauna said. "We can't kill them all."

"Not the ones who haven't gotten vamp blood," Brooke said. "I will coerce them and use a drop of my blood to ensure Bertellus cannot override my command. I'll implant some memory of how Bertellus was really a delusional cannibal planning to consume all of them. And then I plan to let them go."

"Except two," Laura said.

"Huh?" Shauna asked.

"I'm sorry," Laura said. "I am weak from the blood in, blood out routine. Half the blood they were forcing into me was already dead. I don't think they were checking on the people in the maidens, but one died ten minutes ago."

"The other died one minute ago," Elsa said. "Trust me, it was merciful."

Shauna knew it had to be.

"I am going to kill two of these," Laura said. "Don't hate me, sis. I wouldn't if I didn't need it."

Shauna took a deep breath. She wanted to protest, to assure her sister there would be ample opportunity to feed safely. But she wasn't sure that was the case. Bertellus could arrive at any moment. They'd never reconnoitered the passageway beyond the steel door. It might lead directly to the castle's main hall. Rather than argue, she walked away. "I'm going to go gather spears," Shauna said. "I'll do my best to ignore whatever it is you and Brooke will be doing."

"I'll help with the spears," Jackie said.

"I'm going to set the humans free," Elsa said. "All but two. Do you have a particular two in mind?"

"Captain Galca and Sergeant Shadrova," Laura pointed to two men in cages. "Let's not ask why."

Shauna took the breastplate from the angel's armor and used her apportation to float it behind her. She went from spear to spear, tearing off the obsidian spearhead and dropping it onto the breastplate. She tested each one to see if it would prick her finger. She didn't find any that could.

When she started doing the same to the pile Jackie had gathered, she found two that would cut her. She tucked those two spearheads inside her catsuit. Elsa had designed the catsuit with only two pockets; one sized to hold a drivers license and a credit card or two and another to hold a few keys. Elsa's and only Elsa's had been modified to sheath a dagger along her thigh.

When Shauna became cognizant that the screams of the men transforming were being silenced one by one, she had to leave. Taking the breastplate full of obsidian, she flew out of the dome. As she phased through the soil, she released the armor, leaving the weapons several yards under the ground. When she returned to the van, Jackie and Elsa were right behind her.

"Is it too early to start the thank-the-gods-we're-alive-after-battle-sex?" Elsa asked.

Shauna couldn't help but laugh. It took several minutes before she could stop.

CHAPTER 15

The knock on the door roused Shauna. She extricated herself from the knot of grasping limbs and kisses, pushing Jackie and Elsa back.

"Nothing good ever comes of leaving our bed for a knock on the door," Elsa said.

"That's true," Shauna admitted, pausing and waiting for the next knock. When it came, it was a series of taps, less insistent than the first two flurries that had awakened Shauna. She slipped a bathrobe on as she stepped out of the bedroom. She looked back at the bed. Jackie had already slipped back to sleep.

Elsa watched Shauna with concern. The Blood Countess had separated herself from Jackie and sat at the edge of the bed.

On the far side of the bed, Azure hadn't even stirred. Shauna didn't see Karlo, but the shower was running.

Movement by the door caught Shauna's attention. A folded paper popped through the gap under the door. Shauna heard someone in the hall walk away.

Shauna picked up the paper and opened it. It was a piece of hotel stationary with a handwritten note. The handwriting was almost calligraphy. It was addressed to Elsa, so Shauna read it aloud as she walked back to the bedroom.

"Dearest Elizabeth, we clearly are no longer compatible in the ways a husband and wife should be. Your actions have left me without my army and I cannot see a way to press my cause. I fear I will continue to find one if I cannot resolve the conflict that most drives me. So, as much as it grieves me to accept this, one of us must die.

"Come to the chapel where my mortal eyes last saw you, where our story was meant to end. Come after sunset tonight and we will sort this out as nobility, on the field of honor. Understanding your weakness, I accept that you may appoint a champion. My remaining followers will respect my will and will not interfere. I hope you will treat this duel with such honor. With one of us dead, the war ends.

"Eternally Yours, Jack Gainer." The word 'eternally' was struck through.

"He's mad," Shauna said. "You know we can't do this."

"I know it would be foolish," Elsa said, her voice distant. She stood from the bed and went to the closet and started pushing garments aside.

"Isn't it early for you to dress?" Shauna asked. It wasn't even noon. If Elsa was awake at that time of day, she wasn't doing anything clothing wouldn't impede.

"It's an important event," Elsa said. "It's important that we're dressed well."

"You're not considering his offer," Shauna said. "We know where he'll be. We can all go, with a plan, and take him out." In her mind, Shauna knew that would be the outcome. Tonight, they would all go, and they would kill Bertellus and the remnants of his army. He'd long since made himself undeserving of honor.

"Since learning that he survived," Elsa started and then stared into the closet a moment before she tried again. "Since I learned Jack was still around, I've run through an encounter in my mind. What would I do if I had the chance to get close enough to him? I hate him for so many reasons and more deeply than I imagined emotions could run, but that's only because I love him as much as I do, as much as I can."

"So, this is where you tell me what the plan is while you distract him?" Shauna asked.

"Shauna, my love," Elsa said. "This has to be, and it has to be me, not a champion." She slammed the closet door closed and turned to Jackie, "Summon me every wedding dress maker in town. I need a white dress with trim the color of my blood. If I lose, I don't want to clash." Her voice was melancholy and flat, everything Elsa normally was not.

"Every dressmaker?" Jackie asked, already reaching for the phone.

"I'll need a dress for me with a long train, four or five yards at least," Elsa said. "And my bridesmaids will need dresses. I think I want alternating red and black, with the red also matching my blood. Let see: You'll be my maid of honor and then we have Shauna, Azure, Laura and Moana." She glanced sideways and said, "And let's include Brooke; she's not really my type but she's one of us. So, we need six bridesmaid dresses."

Karlo stepped out of the bathroom, still dripping, wearing only a towel around his head. "Karlo wasn't sure he could do it, but Karlo is ready for round four."

"And a tux for Karlo," Elsa said, then grabbed a sheet from the floor and left the bedroom.

"Karlo, get dressed," Jackie said. "There are plans to be made. I need you to go find a florist. We'll need flowers."

"Roses?" Karlo asked. "For the wedding?"

"Lillies," Jackie said. "This isn't going to be a wedding."

§

It took only two hours for Elsa to have designs drawn and two dozen seamstresses working together to create the dresses and Karlo's tux.

Shauna tried several times to get Elsa to talk about her plans to handle Bertellus, but Elsa shrugged off that discussion, promising to revisit it in the van on the way to the meeting.

By three, the entire top floor of the hotel was a factory putting everything together for Elsa's vision. Hairdressers were brought in and Shauna's hair had finally been re-dyed to hide her roots. She hadn't realized how badly her hair had faded until she saw it freshly colored.

Azure found Shauna while a beautician was working on her make-up. "Can you promise me that I'll be safe?" Azure asked timidly.

They both knew the real answer, but Shauna patronized her pet, "I'm sure Bertellus will be a man of honor and keep his word. The only one in danger tonight is Elsa."

"And Bertellus," Azure said, actually sounding hopeful. It wasn't an emotion Shauna could mirror.

Unless she could convince Elsa to let them spring a trap on Bertellus, Shauna's only hope was that Bertellus would try to spring a trap on all of them and fail. Elsa had already made it clear she wouldn't be choosing a champion to fight for her. Somehow Elsa was treating the fight like even odds and if Bertellus beat Elsa's champion, Elsa would still die. So Elsa wouldn't take a champion. She didn't see the sense in risking another life.

Brooke came in. She'd done her own make-up and did a professional level job. Shauna had forgotten that Brooke had been a television weather girl for a university station. She would have had to learn make-up techniques.

"So, what's the plan?" Brooke asked. "We're not going along with Elsa's insanity, right?"

Shauna shook her head. "I don't want to follow Elsa's plan. I don't know if she has something up her sleeve or not, but I can't fathom what it would be. My desire to end this is not enough to let Elsa die to do it."

"It's her choice," Jackie said as she walked in. "I overheard the question. We won't convince Elsa to allow us to use our superior numbers and just take John Bertellus out."

"He'll be anticipating we will try something," Brooke said. "This means, as a tactician, he'll have a plan to try something against us first."

Shauna asked, "So we need to plan to do something to him before his plans to do something to us before we do something to him preemptively?"

"Exactly," Brooke said. "I'm glad someone understands and we're not all living in Elsa's dream world of heroic sacrifice."

"Don't cheer just yet," Shauna said. "Elsa's not stupid. She knows we'll plan something. She may not be happy with us, however, if we act."

"She'll live," Jackie said. "Is anything important compared to that?"

"I like Elsa," Azure said. "I've learned quite a bit from her in the last week, but I'm not heroic enough to die for Elsa. There are a lot of things I'd do for her, but I draw the line just shy of pain."

"I don't have time to wean you," Shauna said. "I can't guarantee any of this will end with you alive."

"Death by proxy," Azure said and twisted her lips in annoyance. "I can't change that, but let's try to make this an 'everyone lives' scenario. And by everyone, I don't mean Bertellus. Then we can all come back and have Elsa's infamous thank-the-gods-we're-alive-after-battle-sex."

"If there's anything that's part of Elsa's plan with certainty, it's the after-battle-sex," Jackie said. "Even if there's not a battle, that's going to happen." She put her arm around Brooke, "When we win, will you be joining us this time?"

"No," Brooke said. "Can we focus on the plan?"

"Is there any way we could postpone the fight until James and Una arrive tomorrow night?" Azure asked. "They'd be useful if we have to kill all of Bertellus' army."

"Una would be useful, for sure," Jackie said. "I don't know if James is really a fighter or a killer."

Brooke nearly choked laughing. "James? Not a killer?" Shauna's face must have shown her confusion. Brooke asked, "You really don't know?"

"Know what?" Shauna asked.

"Maybe it's the whole feud thing, but Una seems to think James is the most monstrous being that ever lived," Brooke said.

"Perhaps you've not read about Vlad the Impaler, Hitler or Stalin." Jackie said.

"I know them," Brooke said. "But James really makes them all amateurs."

"What have you heard?" Shauna asked, although she was afraid to hear what might come next.

"Notice all the Neanderthals walking around Europe?" Brooke asked.

"Are you insulting someone or actually asking about the extinct species of humans?" Shauna asked.

"The extinct species," Brooke clarified. "You can thank James. It seems Neanderthals don't have the connection to Venae. Vampires couldn't feed on them and they were slowly edging Homo Sapiens out of Europe. Neanderthals were bigger, stronger and smarter than Homo Sapiens."

"And James killed off all the Neanderthals?" Shauna asked.

"Every last one," Brooke said. "His numbers might not equal Stalin's, but that's only because James ran out of Neanderthals to kill."

"Una is a Neanderthal?" Shauna asked, trying to piece multiple puzzles together.

"No," Jackie said. "Una is from the Mediterranean coast, where Israel is today. She looks a lot like Reilla, just a little taller. Neanderthals were mostly around here and west."

"Neanderthals lacked the connection to Venae," Brooke said. "They were like human virgins. Vampires couldn't feed from them which means they couldn't be turned either."

"So, James killed them all to make sure his food supply could flourish?" Shauna asked.

"So Una tells me," Brooke said.

"I'm sure Una, in thirty-some thousand years, has had a dark moment or two," Shauna said. The words came out snippy. She hadn't meant to be so defensive of James. It was the natural reaction to having a family member disparaged.

"Probably," Brooke said. "Una doesn't talk much about herself and she doesn't trust Reilla or James. She doesn't really think much of any other vampires descended from her first broods, either."

"It's amazing how revenge can bring us all together," Jackie offered cheerfully. "Sorry, Shauna, your sister lived. We're going to have to vote to see if you get to stay in the vengeance club."

Though Jackie had been speaking in jest, her words reminded Shauna that not everyone was thinking clearly when it came to Bertellus. "You're right," she said. "I am no longer driven by madness with him. I still hate him to his very bones, be they in his skin or mounted on the end of an arrow. But, I am not driven by any irrational need such as revenge. I, therefore, get veto power over any plan we come up with."

"I like that idea," Azure said.

Brooke snapped a glare at the blue haired girl. "I can't argue," Brooke said. "Don't abuse your power."

CHAPTER 16

"Back to Castle Bran?" Shauna asked as Jackie drove them through the Carpathians away from Bucharest.

"Not exactly," Elsa said from the front seat. "Vlad died in an old chapel on the top of a mountain near the castle, but not in the castle itself."

"The book said he died on the road to his castle," Shauna said.

"The book also said he wanted to marry me," Elsa said. "For everything the book got right, it got fifty things wrong."

"Why was he in a chapel?" Shauna asked. "I mean, if it wasn't to marry someone?"

"Vlad hated John Gainer because I loved him," Elsa said with the wistfulness of remembrance. "He made me leave John under threat of killing him if I didn't. But when I returned to him, I had no affection for him. Vlad realized his error. By denying me my love, he fostered my hatred for him. He wasn't an idiot. He agreed to give my husband his blessing, if and only if, we wed in the true church, the Orthodox Church. So we were at the chapel for a wedding, or so we thought. John and Michael-slash-Artemis had set a trap for Vlad."

"And the rest is history," Shauna said.

"History often repeats itself," Brooke said.

"You all think this is a trap, again," Elsa said. "Your plan, and don't tell me you don't have one, assumes I am being played a fool."

"Are you?" Shauna asked.

"I don't know," Elsa said. "But, Jack won't see what I have planned coming."

"You mean he won't expect you to have not chosen someone else to fight for you?" Shauna asked.

"Exactly," Elsa said. "Whatever he has planned, that fact will force him to rethink his tactics."

"His pause is our opportunity," Brooke said.

"No," Elsa said. "We must honor the spirit of the agreement. You may put your plan in motion only once he exposes his treachery."

"That's not prudent," Brooke said.

"You think you are protecting my life," Elsa said. "That's not something you can do. You can keep me from dying, but if I don't die, I will have a life left to live and I want to be able to live if I don't die."

"You're being redundant," Brooke said. "Are you sure you're thinking clearly through what must be a shit-pile of emotions?"

"Are any of us?" Elsa asked.

Shauna didn't look back, but caught Azure's hand raised in the back row of the van.

Elsa turned fully in her chair and looked back into the van. "You are all babies. None of you really understand how immortality will takes its toll on your psyches. No matter how long you live, the things that will stick with you the most are your loves and your lies. Just like memories of love can help you relive the bliss, the guilt of every betrayal you ever perpetrated will haunt you forever. If you happened to betray one of your loves, you will never again have that bliss.

"I hate Bertellus more than any of you. He betrayed my trust. But he hates me more than I hate him because he cannot remember loving me without the guilt of betraying me, so every time he thinks of me, however fondly, he has to hate himself. That kind of pestilence can only fester.

"I have never been an angel. I have tortured and killed six hundred and sixty-six girls in my life. The guilt I have from that isn't the violence, it's that at some point for many of those girls, I told them I wasn't going to hurt them and they believed me."

"You said the stories were exaggerated," Shauna said. "Were you lying to me?"

"Don't do this, sweetie," Elsa said. "We're talking about betrayal, not white lies. No I didn't lie, there were exaggerations. Yes, I misled you, but nothing of what I did or said to you could be construed as a betrayal of trust. For that to be true, you would have had to trust me, and honestly, did you ever trust me when the subject of my past has come up?"

Shauna shook her head. Her trust in Elsa was absolute, but only because she knew the borders of that trust.

"My point is," Elsa continued, "I don't want to live knowing I betrayed one of the great loves of my life. I have enough demons to deal with when the world gets too quiet or boring. I don't need to betray someone's love."

"And he still loves you," Jackie said. "As we learned the night he killed Jonnie."

"Love and hate are not two ends of one emotion," Elsa said. "They are separate like fire and water. When combined they can either cancel each other or explode."

"Your feelings for him cancelled," Shauna ventured. "His feelings exploded."

"Exactly," Elsa said.

"He has to die," Brooke said. "We can't let him spring his trap on us."

"You can," Elsa said. "He cannot be part of his trap; he has to play the bait. That means you are all stronger and faster than whoever is involved in his trap. Even if he has a pet, which is the strongest person he could have fighting for him, Azure is stronger and faster."

"What of Karlo?" Karlo asked.

Elsa ignored him and kept talking, "He won't see my plan coming. He won't be ready for that contingency. He might not even be able to put any part of his trap in motion."

"Are you going to share your genius or just make us wait and watch?" Jackie asked.

Elsa grinned proudly then said, "I'm going to mislead without lying. I'm going to be me and let his distrust and assumptions lead to his own downfall."

"So when you look back on the night we killed Bertellus, you will be righteous in your memories," Shauna said.

"So I won't have to look back," Elsa said. "Without guilt, there won't be haunting. I'll be able to just let it go."

§

They stood gathered at the top of the footpath that led up to the little church. The doors were closed and the windows were all draped over from the inside.

Elsa walked along and arranged them in a semi-circle facing the door. Shauna, in her red dress, then Azure in black, Jackie in red and then Karlo in black, Brooke in red and Moana in black and Laura, the last of them, in red. Elsa then went to stand by Laura. "Once we get inside, this is our formation," Elsa said. "Again, I am the only one to fight him. Whatever you think I'm doing, I'm not setting up any of you to fight, so don't fight him and don't let him fight you."

"Is he here?" Brooke asked Elsa. "Do you see anything to say it could be a trap?"

"Listen," Elsa said and placed a finger on her lips.

Shauna followed Elsa's gaze to the chapel on the hill. From inside she heard the chanting of dozens of voices. She didn't recognize the words, they weren't speaking English, but the rhythm was very similar to the Lord's Prayer.

"Bertellus isn't alone in there," Shauna said.

"Is he in there?" Elsa asked.

"I don't know," Shauna said. "I don't know his voice well enough to pick it from a crowd."

"Sadly," Elsa said. "I don't either anymore. Go look inside and tell us what's there."

Shauna nodded and walked to the doors to the main hall of the castle. Her companions followed close behind, keeping their semi-circle formation. She phased out slightly and leaned through the door just enough to see what was on the other side. Dozens of men in black robes sat on the floor, chanting. Bertellus stood at the head of the hall, wearing gold and silver armor. Huge white feathered wings splayed out from his back and there was a bright glowing circlet hovering over his head. He was using the same toys as his vamp in the dome.

Shauna pulled back and whispered her findings.

"You're absolutely sure we're not killing angels?" Laura said. "I believe you, but I wouldn't want to fuck up my chances of making it into heaven."

Shauna looked at Laura and wasn't sure if she should cry for her sister or laugh. After killing as many people as Laura had, an angel wasn't going to tip her odds of making it past the pearly gates. If heaven was real, Laura's only hope was either universal forgiveness or that her soul went to heaven before she became a vampire.

"How many of the people will we kill?" Shauna asked.

"As many as it takes to make the rest flee," Brooke said. "My bet is; all of them. We're doing this, now." After a glance around the group, Brooke added, "On three, phase me through the wall. Let's end this here, now."

"Veto," Shauna said. "We're doing Elsa's plan, at least until it falls apart."

"My plan won't fail," Elsa said.

"You won't tell us your whole plan," Shauna said.

"Nope," Elsa said. "But you know what you need to and you trust me. Unfortunately I don't trust your acting abilities so I can't tell you what lies to tell. You'll just have to play it as you see it and trust that's how I anticipated it to go when I came up with my perfect plan. Your role is the same it's always been."

"Get myself nearly killed?" Shauna asked.

"Hopefully not," Elsa said. "But, you could let him swing at you once or twice, if Plan A fails. Plan B is just 'Kill 'em all!'"

"For the record," Brooke said, "I am not happy with Plan A. Plan B sounds much better."

"Let me get my stenograph," Laura said. She mimicked typing on a tight keyboard and then said, "Noted, for the record."

"It's time to make our entrance," Elsa said. "Shauna, open the door."

Shauna tugged at the door handles, tearing both doors and their hinges from the stone walls of the chapel.

"It was locked?" Elsa asked.

Shauna hadn't really checked. For some reason she assumed it would be. Realizing they were expected, the doors, in all likelihood hadn't been latched shut.

Inside the doors, they lined up just as Elsa had arranged them. Elsa stood by Laura and bowed to Bertellus. "We have come to finish what was once started here."

Elsa walked to Moana and took a black bag from the girl. She unzipped it and pulled out Henry the Inquisitor's gold and steel sword and the long bone knife from the vampire guarding the dome the night before. She walked along and gave the sword to Laura, placing it in her hands so she held it before her like a large cross. She then went to Shauna and handed Shauna the knife, handle first.

She then turned and walked back to stand by Laura. She then said, "Shauna, return that to Bertellus. It is his and it should be again."

Shauna walked up the left side of the room, keeping the weapon exactly as Elsa had handed it to her. She looked at the knife, wondering what she was supposed to do with it. Elsa had said to return it. Twisting Elsa's words, Shauna could see the instruction as meaning to stab him with it. But Elsa had been clear; only she was to engage Bertellus. Shauna looked over and Elsa was also walking up toward Bertellus, along the far wall.

Looking back at Bertellus, Shauna noticed he was focused on her. As Shauna stepped up to the raised floor, Bertellus drew his obsidian flecked gold sword and strode towards her.

"I expected Elsa to choose the weathergirl," he said, meaning Brooke. "Tonight, you die, Shauna McAllister."

As he got close, he swung the blade in her direction, but he was still too far to reach. Shauna dodged back from reflex.

"You betrayed your words!" Elsa yelled. She stood the far end of the platform. "I came here to fight you myself. As a token of good faith, I was merely having Shauna return your body parts. She was never going to attack you. She doesn't even know how to hold a knife, let alone fight with one."

"I…" Bertellus stammered, but before he could make a meaningful sound, Elsa shouted. "It's a trap! Kill them all!"

Shauna watched Brooke tear into the men like a tornado through a trailer park. Bodies and blood flew against the walls. Some of the men drew swords, some fled and some tried to surrender. Brooke didn't stop, no matter what she encountered. Fleeing or fighting back, the men who got close to her died.

Elsa drew her pistol and shot into a group of men who'd pulled swords. She hit several. Those that didn't fall looked at her as if she were cheating by bringing a gun to a sword fight. It didn't stop her from shooting them again.

Shauna tried to grab Bertellus but there were invisible hands fighting against hers.

"I've got the one on the right," Laura said. Shauna watched as Laura reached out with her hand, as if to guide her own apportation. A robed man, standing back against the wall, cowering, flew up to the ceiling with such force that he cracked the plaster and left a large bloodstain when he fell away.

Bertellus pointed to Laura and gestured for the a group of men from the front row to get her while he strode toward Brooke. Shauna started grabbing robed men and throwing them out the doorway. She was hurried and didn't always get the squirming men through without crushing part of them against the stones. It was a small price to pay to give some of them a chance to survive, she told herself.

One of the men going after Laura dropped his dark robe, revealing a suit of gold armor. He then ran toward her, his armor clanging like a dull bell. Laura pulled out her derringer and shot at the man in the gold armor charging at her. The bullets dented the breastplate but didn't penetrate. The man laughed.

"You do know I'm a super pure vamp, right?" Laura asked loudly as she raised her sword to her shoulder.

"The purity of your blood is nothing to my righteousness," the armored man said, bringing his own golden sword up to a guard position between himself and Laura. He lunged forward, sword outstretched, and fell flat onto the stone floor. Shauna noticed Jackie had dove in front of the vampire's feet.

Elsa pulled her obsidian knife out and shoved it into the back of the man's skull. He went limp.

Brooke's screams drew everyone's attention back to Bertellus. Brooke's sharp nails hadn't been a match for the obsidian and gold sword. Brooke was bleeding from several wounds to her chest and a gash across one eye. Her left arm hung limp and she was backing away, barely staying out of the reach of Bertellus' sword. Shauna rushed to help.

With a quick turn, and a flick of his wrist, Bertellus intercepted Shauna with his sword, pushing it straight through the center of her chest. She collapsed, berating herself for acting so rashly. Brooke, at least, had made it back behind Laura and Elsa.

Bertellus lifted a boot and kicked Shauna off of his sword, sending her to the ground. She could barely crawl to her feet. His thrust had cut into her heart.

"I won't make the mistake of letting you live twice," he said. He threw his sword at her. It spun through the air. Shauna tried to reach out with her mind and push it, but she found Bertellus's mental hand controlling it, holding it on course. She brought her arms up to protect her neck, though she knew it would be futile against his power.

She closed her eyes as the spinning blade neared. With all the strength she could muster, she held the bone knife up, hoping to deflect the flying sword. She felt the bone knife shatter in her hand and then heard Laura scream. Shauna looked up to see her sister kneeling before her, Bertellus' sword protruding through the right side of her chest. It had cut through her collarbone and Laura was bleeding badly. The sword started to pull out, but Laura grabbed it.

"This is mine now," she said, sputtering blood with her words.

"I don't need my sword to kill Elsa," he said. He reached out and the dead armored man's golden sword flew into his hand.

"If you want Elsa, you're going to have to go through me," Jackie screamed. She held Henry's sword and she looked like she knew how to use it.

Bertellus laughed. "Silly Katina," he said. "You cannot hurt m…"

His words stopped and his face contorted in pain. Then Shauna saw Elsa, holding on to Bertellus from behind with one arm while her other disappeared into the side of his ribcage, reaching deep into his chest.

"I once had your heart," Elsa said. "Now I do again. Only, now it's less romantic, more literal."

Shauna saw Bertellus draw a bone dagger and she screamed, "Elsa, knife!"

The words didn't cover the space fast enough. Bertellus had already struck. He left the dagger in Elsa's stomach.

Elsa growled. "I will kill you," she said.

Bertellus fell to his knees and Elsa fell behind him. Her arm still imbedded in his chest. He went to grab his dagger again, but his movements were slow. Jackie got there first and pulled the knife out of Elsa and then ran to Shauna.

"Take this," Jackie said. "Finish him."

"My own marrow won't kill me," Bertellus croaked. "But it will kill her. Take her. With her dead, my war ends."

Shauna took the knife and crawled over to kneel by Bertellus and Elsa. Elsa was breathing heavy and shallow.

"I'm fading," Elsa said.

Shauna grabbed Bertellus's face and said, "The marrow won't kill you, but your own bone will cut you." She drew the blade across his carotid artery then forced his neck to Elsa's mouth. "You have one chance, bestie."

Elsa closed her lips over Bertellus' throat.

EPILOGUE

"This is not where I ever expected to be," Elsa said, rolling over. "Even if I only get to do it a few minutes each day, I don't think I'll ever go a day without it. Moana, lotion!"

Elsa's pet sat up and started rubbing lotion onto Elsa's chest. Her tan was coming along and almost looked appropriately Mediterranean.

Shauna sat up. Her own tan was coming along slower. Azure, on the other hand, had the deepest tan of all of them. Her blue hair faded after weeks in the sunlight to a paler, near white, shade. "This isn't the eternity of night you were expecting," Shauna said to her pet.

"My parents would never let me get tan," Azure said. "It would destroy my cover as an emo kid."

"And when they find out you're a vampire's pet?" James asked. "My experience with Elementalists tells me they're not particularly tolerant of vampires."

"I wasn't planning on sharing," Azure said. "I figure I'll tell them I got a scholarship to…" Azure looked around. "Which universities are near the French Riviera?"

"No idea," James said. "Mom? Do you know?"

"All I care about it is my lambic," Reilla said. "Where is that slave?"

"They're not slaves, Reilla," Shauna said. "We're rehabilitating them. They went to get fresh ice for the cooler."

"There's no slavery in my kingdom," Elsa said. "I think we're in my kingdom. This might be Lucy's area."

"So how is being empress treating you?" Shauna asked. "Jackie seems to think you are leaving all the hard work to her."

"She just says that because I spend the days on the beach down here and leave her in Paris to manage my kingdom. But being a queen is fun; you should try it."

"Oh, I intend to," Shauna said. "I think I'll be taking over the empty throne in Edirne."

"Empty?" Elsa asked. "What do you mean. Zylpha's not dead."

"Yet," said Shauna. In truth, she planned on setting Laura up as Queen of the Near Eastern Kingdom. Her sister needed something less self-centered to do with her time. Perhaps with a kingdom to be responsible for, she could think about something other than her next kill. Shauna planned on asking her parents to live with Laura for a few years or decades, whatever it took to straighten her out.

"So, James," Elsa said.

"Yes?" he responded.

Elsa sat up and looked across Shauna to James. "Becoming as pure as I am, now, it seems I am remembering things from my past. Things I'd forgotten or more accurately, been coerced to forget."

"Uh-oh," James said then laughed.

"I always thought it odd that I knew so much about wine, but never remembered learning about it," Elsa's story started. "I believe the year was 1771 when you appeared in my bedroom…"

BLOOD ATONEMENT: THE TRUE TALES OF ELIZABETH BATHORY, VAMPIRE.

Elsabet or Elizabeth Bathory's life is notorious and, for the most part, known to history. What she's done since is another story altogether. Haunted by the crimes of her life and by her bloodfather, Vlad Dracula, Elsa seeks a life of her own in the New World. But her past will always catch up to her and she must face her demon. Herein are the stories that led to Elizabeth Bathory's atonement, at least, with herself. She can never undo what she's done, but she can balance it. Some of these stories have been told, but without the truth of the tales as Elsa knows them. These are those dark truths.

NINE PRINCES OF BLOOD

The last of the vampire hunters, Nate Silver seeks a legend to aid him in his mission to cleanse the world of the bloodsuckers.

The trail has taken him to Los Angeles, but before he even settles in, the world of the night overwhelms him. Vampire society in southern California is especially chaotic and lacking leadership. A cohort of powerful vampires are maintaining anarchy in the city for their own deadly amusement.

Nate's morality is tested and twisted as he tried to find footing in a world where he cannot even comprehend the mortal society. When he finds himself forced to ally with one vampire faction against another, he wonders if he'll ever be the man he thought he was meant to be. He'll face the ultimate test when the cost of his integrity will be murder.

ABOUT THE AUTHOR

Wil Ogden was destined to be a wastrel but thwarted fate. During his second junior year in high school he discovered he had a muse and a talent for writing. Despite taking almost a decade to complete a bachelor's degree by changing majors eleven times, he managed to grow up. Along the way he worked as a blacksmith, a record store manager, a candy store manager, too many years in food service, a four year stint in the USAF, and finally settled down into Information Technology, which he uses to pay the bills and support his family of himself, his wife, two sons, a daughter, a dog, four cats, five chickens, a snake and two parakeets.

On Facebook: www.facebook.com/wilsbooks

Printed in Great Britain
by Amazon